Praise for *Wanderers*

"Engaging and entertaining . . . a timely novel that demands a place in the spotlight. [Chuck] Wendig takes science, politics, horror, and science fiction and blends them into an outstanding story about the human spirit in times of turmoil, claiming a spot on the list of must-read apocalyptic novels."

—NPR

"It's nearly impossible not to mention *The Stand* when describing the maddeningly prolific author's newest novel, and for good reason. [Wendig is] a keen student of how to fashion a ripping yarn, and here he does."

—*WIRED*

"This is a story about the end of the world but it's really about us, about the things we do to each other when we think we can get away with it and what we do to the world when we think we have no other choice. . . . In the great Chuck Wendig tradition, *Wanderers* doesn't just settle for a plot twist or two. He plot twists the plot twist then plot twists the plot twist's plot twist. . . . Wendig is a master at turning the screw and twisting the knife past what most authors would dare."

—*Tor.com*

"Makes the apocalypse beautiful . . . [an] epic new novel of a dark future that weaves everything from social media to climate change to artificial intelligence into its complex, multi-viewpoint narrative."

—*SyFyWire*

"Approach *Wanderers* like it's a primetime television series, along the lines of *The Passage* [or] *Lost.* . . . Make *Wanderers* a summer reading priority; you won't regret it."

—*Book Riot*

"[*Wanderers*] brings truth into the light. . . . *Wanderers* is a few things: a tense mystery; an *Outbreak*-style medical thriller; a sprawling, Stephen King-esque epic. But mostly it's a book about America *right now*—and much like America right now, it's a potent blend of fear, confusion, and guarded, fragile hope. It's also a book that has a lot to say, so it's a good thing Wendig is sharp and funny, with a live-wire imagination that sparks with his singular voice."

—*Portland Mercury*

"[Chuck Wendig] is set to make a significant literary statement in 2019 with this *Station 11*–esque panorama of a post-apocalyptic America."

—*Entertainment Weekly*

"Riveting . . . Chuck Wendig's *Wanderers* is a unique look at a potential Armageddon. . . . Wendig's greatest strength might be his character work, so I'm excited to fall in love (or love-to-hate) with the characters inhabiting this America. . . . Count me in for the novel and any adaptations that might come forth from it."

—*The Mary Sue*

"Brilliantly take[s] the scenic route along dystopian roads . . . Wendig builds plausible outcomes inspired by real world political events. Wendig's treatment of his characters is warm and moving, but the world they exist in is brutal [and] uncomfortably close to reality."

—*The Washington Post*

"A magnum opus . . . a story about survival that's not just about you and me, but all of us, together."

—*Kirkus Reviews* (starred review)

"This career-defining epic deserves its inevitable comparisons to Stephen King's *The Stand*."

"It's not easy to write the end of the world. . . . Very few authors can pull it off, and even fewer can master it. With *Wanderers,* Chuck Wendig has mastered it."

"Wendig shatters the boundaries of speculative and literary fiction in a saga that will touch every reader."

"A suspenseful, twisty, satisfying, surprising, thought-provoking epic."

"A true tour de force."

"A masterpiece with prose as sharp and heartbreaking as *Station Eleven*."

"A magnum opus . . . It reminded me of Stephen King's *The Stand*—but dare I say, this story is even better."

"An inventive, fierce, uncompromising, stay-up-way-past-bedtime master-work."

"An American epic for these times."

—CHARLES SOULE,
author of *The Oracle Year*

"*Wanderers* is amazing—huge, current, both broad and intensely personal, blending the contemplative apocalypse of *Station Eleven* with the compulsive readability of the best thrillers."

—DJANGO WEXLER,
author of the Shadow Campaigns series

"A riveting examination of America."

—SCOTT SIGLER,
#1 *New York Times* bestselling author of The Generations Trilogy

"If you ever wanted to know what America's soul might look like, here's its biography."

—RIN CHUPECO,
author of *The Bone Witch*

"A tsunami of a novel."

—MEG GARDINER,
Edgar Award–winning author of *Into the Black Nowhere*

"A defining moment in speculative fiction."

—ADAM CHRISTOPHER,
author of *Empire State* and *Made to Kill*

"Trust me: You're not ready for this book."

—DELILAH S. DAWSON,
New York Times bestselling author of *Star Wars: Phasma*

"An astounding adventure."

—FRAN WILDE,
Hugo, Nebula, and World Fantasy finalist and award-winning author of the Bone Universe trilogy

BY CHUCK WENDIG

Wanderers

FUTURE PROOF

Zer0es

Invasive

THE HEARTLAND TRILOGY

Under the Empyrean Sky

Blightborn

The Harvest

MIRIAM BLACK

Blackbirds

Mockingbird

The Cormorant

Thunderbird

The Raptor & the Wren

Vultures

ATLANTA BURNS

Atlanta Burns

Atlanta Burns: The Hunt

NONFICTION

The Kick-Ass Writer

Damn Fine Story

STAR WARS

Star Wars: Aftermath

Star Wars: Aftermath: Life Debt

Star Wars: Aftermath: Empire's End

WANDERERS

 NEW YORK

WANDERERS

A NOVEL

CHUCK WENDIG

2020 Del Rey Trade Paperback Edition

Copyright © 2019 by Terribleminds LLC

Published in the United States by Del Rey, an imprint of Random House, a division of Penguin Random House LLC, New York.

DEL REY is a registered trademark and the CIRCLE colophon is a trademark of Penguin Random House LLC.

Originally published in hardcover in the United States by Del Rey, an imprint of Random House, a division of Penguin Random House LLC, in 2019.

LIBRARY OF CONGRESS CATALOGING-IN-PUBLICATION DATA
Names: Wendig, Chuck, author.
Title: Wanderers / Chuck Wendig.
Description: New York: Del Rey, [2019]
Identifiers: LCCN 2019003080 | ISBN 9780399182129 (trade paperback) |
ISBN 9780399182112 (ebook)
Subjects: | GSAFD: Science fiction. | Fantasy fiction.
Classification: LCC PS3623.E534 W36 2019 | DDC 813/.6—dc23
LC record available at https://lccn.loc.gov/2019003080

Printed in the United States of America on acid-free paper

randomhousebooks.com

2 4 6 8 9 7 5 3 1

Book design by Susan Turner

For Kevin Hearne, who is kindness and coolness personified

A wilderness, in contrast with those areas where man and his works dominate the landscape, is hereby recognized as an area where the earth and its community of life are untrammeled by man, where man himself is a visitor who does not remain.

—The Wilderness Act of 1964

CONTENTS

CONTENTS

WANDERERS

THE COMET

THE WOMAN WHO DISCOVERED THE COMET, YUMIKO SAKAMOTO, AGE TWENTY-eight, was an amateur astronomer in Okayama Prefecture, in the town of Kurashiki. She found it on a lark, looking instead for an entirely different comet—a comet that was expected to strike Jupiter.

Yumiko Sakamoto said that the discovery changed her life. In an interview with the *Asahi Shimbun* newspaper, she said: "Up until now I have been focused too much on material things—getting a good job, finding a good husband—but I am relinquishing such shallow pursuits as romance and career. I will go back to school and learn more about our world and the cosmos beyond it. Not for financial gain, but because the pursuit of knowledge is itself noble."

She also said she was joining the growing asexual and aromantic community in Japan. She felt that the world was "overpopulated" already and did not need her to add to its "burden."

The comet—named Comet Sakamoto after her—passed within 0.1 AU (astronomical unit) of the earth on June 2. Not close enough to be a danger, but close enough that one could see it with the naked eye—and close enough to earn it the Great Comet moniker, joining other famous comets such as Halley's Comet and Hale-Bopp.

Yumiko Sakamoto was going to begin her new academic study the following October, but did not live long enough to see the chance. She died of a brain aneurysm the night the comet passed overhead.

PART ONE

THE BROOD

1

THE FIRST SLEEPWALKER

Last night's amateur astronomers got a treat in the form of clear skies, a new moon, and Comet Sakamoto. The last three Great Comets were Lovejoy in 2011, McNaught in 2007, and the famous—or infamous?—Hale-Bopp in 1997, which of course spawned the Heaven's Gate cult, whose members committed mass suicide in the belief it would allow them to hitch a ride with an extraterrestrial spaceship following that comet. You're listening to Tom Stonekettle of Stonekettle Radio, 970 BRG.
                        —*Stonekettle Radio Show,* 970AM WBRG, Pittsburgh

JUNE 3
Maker's Bell, Pennsylvania

SHANA STOOD THERE LOOKING AT HER LITTLE SISTER'S EMPTY BED, AND HER first thought was: *Nessie ran away again.*

She called to her a few times. Honestly, after Nessie had stayed up late last night to watch the comet through Dad's shitty telescope, Shana figured the younger girl would still be in bed, snoring up little earthquakes. She wasn't sure where the hell else Nessie could be—Shana had been up for an hour already, making their lunches, finishing the laundry, putting the trash and recycling together so she could haul it up the long driveway for tomorrow's pickup. So she knew Nessie wasn't in the kitchen. Maybe she was in the upstairs bathroom.

"Nessie?" She paused. Listened. "*Nessie,* c'mon."

But nothing.

Again the thought: *Nessie ran away again.*

It didn't make much sense. First time Nessie ran away, *that* made sense.

They'd just lost their mother—lost her in a very literal way. The four of them went to the grocery store, and only three of them came back. They feared Mom had been taken and hurt, but eventually security cameras from the Giant Eagle showed that nobody kidnapped her; she strolled out the automatic doors like nothing was wrong and then walked out of their lives for good. Mom became a big question mark stuck in their cheeks like a fish-hook.

But it was clear that their mother didn't want to be a part of their lives anymore. That, Shana knew even then, had been a long time coming, but the realization did not hit Nessie—and still had not reached her, even now. Nessie believed then that it was Dad's fault. And maybe Shana's, too. So two years ago almost to the day, after school was done for the year, Nessie packed a backpack full of canned goods and bottled water (plus a couple of candy bars), and ran away.

They found Nessie four hours later at the wooden bus shelter on Granger, hiding from a sudden rain squall. Shivering like a stray puppy. When Dad picked her up she kicked and thrashed, and it was like watching a wrestler try to pin a tornado. But then he gave up, said to her, "You want to run away, you run away, but if you're thinking of going after your mother, I don't think she wants to be found."

It was like watching a glass of water tip in slow motion. Nessie collapsed in his arms and wept so hard she could only catch her breath in these keening, air-sucking hitches. Her shoulders shook and she pressed both hands under her armpits as if hugging herself. They got her home. She slept for two days and then, slowly but surely, came back to life.

That was two years ago.

Today, though, Shana could not figure out why Nessie would want to run away again. Girl was fifteen now and hadn't hit the wall like Shana had at that age—as Dad put it, Shana "went full teenager." Mopey and mad and hormones like a kicking horse. Shana was almost eighteen, now. She was better these days. Mostly.

Nessie was still all right, hadn't turned into a werewolf. Still happy. Still optimistic. Eyes bright like new nickels. She had a little notebook, in which she wrote all the things she wanted to do (scuba dive with sharks, study bats, knit her own slippers like Mom-Mom used to do), all the places she wanted to go (Edinburgh, Tibet, San Diego), all the people she wanted to meet (the president, an astronaut, her future husband). She said to Shana one day, "I heard that if you complain it reprograms your brain like a computer virus and it just makes you more and more unhappy, so I'm going to stay positive because I bet the opposite is true, too."

That notebook sat there on her empty bed. Next to the bed was an open box—Nessie had gotten some package in the mail, some science thing she must've ordered. (Shana borrowed a part of it, a little test tube, to hold weed.) Her daffodil-yellow sheets looked rumpled and slept-in. Her pink pillow still showed her head-dent.

Shana peeked at the notebook. Nessie had started a new list: JOBS I MIGHT LIKE?? Included: zookeeper, beekeeper, alpaca farmer, photographer. *Photographer?* Shana thought. *That's my bag.* A weird flare of anger lanced through her. Nessie was good at everything. If she decided to do the thing that Shana wanted to do, she'd do it better and that would suck and they'd hate each other forever. (Well, no. Shana would hate Nessie. Nessie would love her unconditionally because that was Nessie.)

Shana called out for her again. "Ness? Nessie?" Her voice echoed and nothing but the echo answered. Shit.

Dad was probably already in the so-called milking parlor (he said if they're going to be part of the artisanal cheese movement here in Pennsylvania they needed to start talking like it, damnit), and he would be expecting Ness and Shana to staff the little shop up by the road. Then eventually he'd come get one of them to head into the cheese barn to check the curds on that Gouda or get the blues draining—then mix the silage and feed the cows and ah, hell, the vet was coming today to look at poor Belinda's red, crusty udders and—

Maybe *that's* why Nessie ran away. School was out already and summer vacation wasn't much of one: Everything was work, work, work. (Shana wondered if Nessie had the right idea. She could run away, too. Even for the day. Call up her buddy Zig in his Honda, smoke some weed, read comic books, talk shit about the seniors who just graduated . . .)

(God, she had to get out of here.)

(If she didn't get out of here soon, she'd stay here forever. This place felt like quicksand.)

Of course, Nessie was too good a girl to have run away again, so maybe she got the jump on Shana and was already out in the shop. Little worker bee, that one. What was the song on Dad's old REM album? "Shiny Happy People"? That was Nessie.

Shana'd already eaten, so she went in search of the little clip-on macro lens she used over her phone's camera to let her take photos of things real close-up, magnified. Little worlds revealed, the micro made macro. She didn't have a proper camera, but she was saving up to get a DSLR one day. In the meantime, that meant using the phone. Maybe she'd find something in the stable or in the cheesemaking room that would look cool up close: flaking rust, the red needle in the thermometer, the bubbles or crystals in the cheese itself.

It hit her where she'd left the lens last time—she was taking pictures of a house spider hanging in her window, and she left the lens on the sill. So she went there to grab it—

Something outside caught her eye. Movement up the driveway. *One of the cows loose* was her first thought.

Shana headed to the window.

Someone was out there, walking.

No. Not someone.

Little dum-dum was halfway up the driveway in her PJ pants and pink T-shirt. Barefoot, too, by the look of it. *Oh, what the hell, Nessie?*

Shana ran to the kitchen, forgetting her lens. She hurriedly popped on her sneakers and ran out the door to the back porch, nearly tripping on the one sneaker that wasn't all the way on yet, but she quick smashed her heel down into the shoe and kept on running.

She thought to yell to her little sister, but decided against it. No need to draw Dad's attention. He'd see they weren't out in the shop yet and give them a ration of hot shit about it, and Shana didn't want to hear it. This was not a morning for nonsense, and already the nonsense was mounting.

Instead she ran up along the driveway, the red gravel crunching underneath her sneaks. The Holsteins on the left bleated and mooed. A young calf—she thought it was Moo Radley—stood there on knock-knees watching her hurry to catch up to her tweedledum sister. "Nessie," she hissed. "*Nessie, hey!*"

But Nessie didn't turn around. She just kept on walking.

What a little asshole.

Shana jogged up ahead of her and planted her feet like roots.

"God, Nessie, what the hell are you—"

It was then she saw the girl's eyes. They were open. Her sister's gaze stood fixed at nothing, like she was looking through Shana or staring *around* her.

Dead eyes, dead like the flat tops of fat nails. Gone was the luster of wonder, that spark.

Barefoot, Nessie continued on. Shana didn't know what to do—move out of her way? Stand planted like a telephone pole? Her indecision forced her to do a little of both—she shifted left just a little, but still in her sister's inevitable path.

The girl's shoulder clipped her hard. Shana staggered left, taking the hit. The laugh that came up out of her was one of surprise. It was a pissed-off laugh, a bark of incredulity.

"That hurt, dummy," she said, and then grabbed for the girl's shoulder and shook her.

Nothing. Nessie just pulled away and kept going.

"Nessie. *Nessie.*"

Shana waved her hand in front of Nessie's eyes. Wave, wave, wave. She had the thought then, a stray thought she pretended could be true even though she knew deep down it couldn't be, *She's just playing a joke on me.* Even though Shana was the prankster and Nessie's only real joke was a cabinet of knock-knock jokes so bad it made their bad-joke-loving father wince. Still, just in case, she took her finger and poked Nessie's nose as if it were a button.

"Boop," she said. "Power down, little robot."

Nessie registered nothing. Didn't even blink.

Had she blinked the whole time? Shana didn't think so.

Then she saw, ahead, a big rain puddle. She warned her sister: "Nessie, watch out, there's a—"

Too late. Nessie plodded right through it. Splish. Splash. Feet in the water almost up to the ankles. Still going and going. Like a windup toy set to beeline in one direction.

Still staring ahead.

Still moving forward.

Arms stiff by her sides. Her gait sure and steady.

Something's wrong.

The thought hit Shana in the heart like a fist. Her guts went cold, her blood to slush. She couldn't hold back the chills. But she tried anyway and said to herself, *Maybe she's just sleepwalking. That's probably what this is.* Okay, no, Nessie had never done that before, but maybe this was how her brain chose to handle those hormones running through her like a pack of racehorses right now.

The question was: Go get Dad?

Ahead, the end of their driveway stretched out. There, the cheese and dairy shop made to look like a little red barn. There, the mailbox made to *also* look like a little barn, this one blue (and with a cow silhouette cut out of tin and stuck on top). And there, too, the road.

The road.

God, if Nessie walked to the road and a car came by . . .

She yelled for her dad. Screamed for him. "Dad! *Dad!*" But nothing. No response. He might've been out in the pasture or in the barn. Going to get him meant leaving Nessie alone . . .

In her head she could hear the make-believe sound of a truck grille hitting her sister, knocking her forward. The crunch of bones under tires. The thought made her queasy.

I can't get Dad. I'll stay with her.

This can't go on for long.

Sleepwalkers eventually wake up.

Don't they?

Ten minutes. *Ten minutes* had gone by. Nessie reached the top of the driveway and pivoted as if on an invisible track and then—

Kept walking. Like, no big deal.

Down Cassel, down Orchard, toward Herkimer Covered Bridge—the old one over the Scheiner's Crick, the one with the Amish hex on it. Nessie kept trucking. Mouth open just a little as if in small awe of something only she could see.

All the while, Shana talked. Faster and faster, like a jabbering idiot. "Nessie, you're freaking me the fuck out. Quit it, please quit it. Are you having some kind of breakdown? Are you having a stroke?" Their grandmother Mom-Mom had had one stroke, then a bunch more, and it turned her weird. She lay in the bed talking sometimes in English, sometimes in Lithuanian, but most of the time in gibberish. Sometimes she spoke to them, sometimes to people who weren't there. It left Shana with the understanding that a stroke broke your head like a stepped-on cookie. "Please stop walking. I'm going to have to go get Dad soon. He's probably already wondering where we are, Jesus. He's gonna kick our asses. Probably *my* ass because you're his favorite, you know. Oh, don't pretend like you didn't know that. You look like

Mom. I look like—well, him." *And nobody really likes themselves,* she thought. "Just quit this shit now. *Now. Now?*"

Ahead, the bridge loomed.

Probably shouldn't walk on that thing barefoot. She'll get a splinter. And then she might get an infection and now they said antibiotics didn't really work like they were supposed to anymore and Mister Schultz the bio-sci teacher at school said, "We're entering the post-antibiotic age."

That decided it.

Shana jogged ahead of Nessie and turned toward her, walking backward so that she faced her sister, holding up her hand and gesturing like it was a game-show prize. "Nessie, listen up, dummy. If you don't quit this right now, I'm going to haul back and smack the crap out of you. Okay? I'm just gonna— *boom,* whale on you. Last chance."

Her threat failed to land. Nessie did not register it at all.

Shana blinked back tears. *Don't show her you're crying.* A stupid thought but still, she was the big sister, and Nessie shouldn't see that.

I don't want to hit my baby sister.

I mean, she *did* want to hit her, kinda. But in a fantasy way. In the theater of her mind it sounded good, but now, for real? It scared the shit out of her. "I'm gonna do it," she warned.

Nessie did not care. She did not hear. She did not see.

Shana lifted her arm. Palm ready to smack.

She winced. She gritted her teeth. She swung her hand.

And then, she pulled the slap at the last second, crying out in frustration. "Goddamnit, Nessie!"

A shadow fell over them. Shana turned suddenly as the blacktop of Orchard Road gave way to the creaking boards of Herkimer Covered Bridge. Above, the beams hung like bones. Grass and sticks dangled—nests of birds whose babies had gone. Everything else was the kingdom of the spiders— webs draped between webs, flies mummified.

Spears of light poked through holes in the wood. And ahead, Shana spied a new danger in that light: the glittering glass of a broken bottle. Kids came here to drink sometimes. *Shana* came here to drink sometimes. Quick, Shana hurried ahead, tried to kick away some of the glass. But there was just too much of it, and Nessie walked ineluctably forward . . .

Okay, new plan.

Kill her with kindness.

Not literally, of course. But instead of smacking the taste out of her mouth, Shana decided to hug her. Grab her. *Stop* her.

Easy enough. Nessie was a little slip of a thing, but Shana was bigger, broader, more the tomboy. (Though that was an image she'd been trying to shake now for the better part of a year. It wasn't because she wanted to get a boy or anything but *okay* whatever, it's exactly because she wanted to get a boy. Cal Polette, as a matter of fact. Cal, who liked photography, too, whose dad owned a bank, who had a *very lickable* jawline. Cal who thought her name was Shawna.)

Shana said, "All right, little dingleberry. I'm coming in."

A stray thought landed in her head like a rock through a window: *When was the last time we hugged each other?*

She opened her arms and grabbed her sister.

The girl had surprising strength. She kept going, pushing Shana back— hard enough, in fact, that Shana's sneakers slid on the wood. Not willing to be denied so easily, Shana planted her feet hard—

And with that, Nessie stopped. She didn't stop *struggling*, though: She kept on wriggling like a mouse in a snake's crushing coils.

She began thrashing and Shana's mind went to that memory: the girl fighting their father in that old bus stop shelter.

A sound rose up out of her. A low whine, an animal sound. A new fear buried itself under Shana's skin like a burrowing tick. It was the sound of something in pain, alarmed, even full of rage.

"Nessie, settle down, it's okay," she whispered to her. Louder she said it so that she could be heard: "It's *okay*, I said."

The girl started to feel hot. Like a fever starting up. Shana kept her grip but pulled away just enough to look at her sister's face: Nessie's cheeks had grown flushed, and angry red streaks stretched across her forehead. The whites of her eyes suddenly erupted red, like grapes crushed. "Nessie, stop, please stop, please, oh shit, stop—"

Nessie's teeth chattered. Blood trickled from her nose as her body began to spasm and rise in temperature—it was hot, *too* hot, and Nessie's skin felt like the hood of a black car that had been sitting too long in the summer sun, and Shana thought to double down, to hold on *tighter*, bucking-bronco-style, but a panicked certainty screamed through her mind:

Let her go, let her go now.

Shana let go, backpedaling suddenly.

Nessie blinked for the first time this morning. Relief flooded through Shana. *I did it. She's okay.*

But then the girl's eyes clouded over once more. Her eyeballs rotated in her head like lottery balls and then pinned her gaze again on the horizon. Nessie walked forward anew, the shakes gone, her nose and upper lip still bloody.

Shana collapsed and wept as her sister kept on walking. Right across the broken glass, seeming not to feel it.

AND THEN THERE WERE TWO

I know I know I know I'm only a teenager, Dad reminds me like, every day, and my sister reminds me that I'm still young, and I don't care. I have so many things I want to do, so many boys to kiss and so many places to go and so many ways to change the world, I'm ready to get started. Because everything and everyone has to start somewhere, right? I'm starting now. Mom, if you're out there, and if you ever read this, I'm sorry you won't get to see what I do. Maybe you'll come back to us again. Maybe I'll find you, who knows? Maybe that's what this is all about. Me finding you.

—from the journal of Nessie Stewart, age 15

JUNE 3
Maker's Bell, Pennsylvania

SHANA'S LEGS PUMPED SO HARD, HER MUSCLES AND TENDONS FELT LIKE GUI-tar strings strung too tight, ready to snap. In gym class she always hated running the mile, often making an excuse to the teacher ("Sorry, Mister Orbach, it's my moon times, *if you know what I mean*"). But now running *had* to be her thing—she didn't want to leave Nessie alone out there for long, but she needed her father.

As she reached the bottom of their long driveway, a stitch hit her side like a steak knife stuck between her ribs, sawing back and forth. Her foot skidded on loose scree and she went down hard, twisting her body, her elbow driving into the ground. But she didn't stay down. She clambered to stand, launching herself down the driveway, gasping for air as she did.

One small blessing: Her father stood halfway down the driveway, looking around—probably for her and for Nessie—and when he saw her, he waved and ran to meet her.

Breathless, she cried out for him. Two minutes later, they were in his rat-trap pickup—an old Chevy Silverado fringed with rust—and barreling down Orchard Road, juddering over the groaning boards of the covered bridge.

Along the way, she tried, stammering, to tell her father what had happened. But Dad, he was only half listening. His eyes scanned the road ahead, the way an owl might look for fledglings that had prematurely fled the nest. He interrupted Shana—

"I don't see her. I don't see her!"

"She has to be out here." Tears pushed at the inside of her eyes, and she had to blink them away.

"You're sure she went this way?"

"Yes, Dad, I'm sure."

"Think, damnit. Because if you're wrong—"

"I'm sure, I'm sure," she said, but suddenly she *wasn't* sure. They did come this way? Right? It was all a blur. Shana felt crazy. Maybe Nessie was back at the house somewhere. Maybe Shana was dreaming.

Or worse, what if Nessie did come this way, but then she changed direction? What if she walked down to the stream? Could she have slipped and fallen in? Could she have *drowned*? Or what if she wandered into the woods, or what if someone came by and picked her up and put her in a van and drove far away—they always warned about that kind of thing in school. Shana always figured it was mostly just parents trying to control their kids more, trying to spook them into keeping close, but what if it was true? Nessie wouldn't have the presence of mind not to get taken away. They might hurt her. Touch her. Kill her.

Didn't they say that if you didn't find a missing person in the first forty-eight hours, you'd never find them? This was the first hour, and Shana had already lost her little sister. *If only I wouldn't have left her. I could've stayed with her. Shit, I'm so sorry . . .*

Dad pumped the brakes and Shana lurched forward. Orchard Road ended here at the intersection of Mine Hill Road. It went east and it went west. Dead ahead lurked tall oaks and maples giving shelter to darkness and the deep damp. "There!" her father called out. He pointed past Shana. She turned her head to look but by the time she did, Dad was already pounding the accelerator and cutting the wheel—stones screamed under the assault of spinning tires. And now, *now* Shana saw Nessie.

The girl walked ahead, up toward the bend that hooked around the old

Pemberton farm, the one that had gone to hell since the barn fire a few years back. Dad raced up alongside her, pulling ahead and cutting the engine.

They both flew out of the car and raced up to her. Shana hoped to see that her sister had regained some glimmer of who she was . . .

But it was not to be. Her eyes stared forward, watching nothing. They had cleared a little, going from full-blooded, ripe red fruits to merely blood-shot.

And still, Nessie kept walking.

Dad tried. He waved his hands in front of her.

He whistled. Clapped his hands. Snapped his fingers. Worry tightened his cheeks, dented his brow. No—not worry. Something else, something bigger. Fear. That's what Shana saw there—bold, bald-faced fear. Seeing her father scared only made her *more* scared.

Dad stepped aside. Nessie walked ahead.

Their eyes met. "Shana, I'm going to try to restrain her."

"You can't. Don't. It hurts her—"

"It's the only way. Okay? I'll be gentle."

It's not about being gentle, Shana thought. This was something else. This wasn't sleepwalking. This wasn't anything anyone understood, not yet, maybe not ever. Even now she turned her eyes to her little sister's feet—were her feet cut up? Injured in any way? Not that Shana could see. That wasn't right, either. *This feels like some kind of nightmare.*

"Dad, be careful—"

"I'll be careful," he hissed back at her. Usually, he was calm as a bowl of cookies, but now she saw his hand shaking and sweat beaded on his brow even though it was an unusually cool morning for early June.

He again stepped in front of Nessie.

He opened his arms wide, as if to hug her.

She stepped into his embrace hard, almost knocking him down—but he rooted himself low and wrapped his arms around her tight.

For a moment, Shana thought, *It's okay, it'll be okay.*

Then Nessie started to shake again. The shaking turned to thrashing. Dad held fast even as she started keening and wailing, the sound rising out of her like the bleat of a truck-struck deer broken on the road—Dad yelled over, "Shana, you come hold her, too." But Shana wouldn't. *Can't.*

"Dad, let her go, please—"

He picked her up, then, grunting as he stood. Nessie's legs kicked out. Her skin flushed. As the girl's head rotated wildly on her shoulders, Shana once more saw her eyes go all the way red—they started to bulge like corks straining at the top of a Champagne bottle, ready to *pop*—

"Dad!" Shana cried, hurrying over to her father, grabbing him, struggling with him. He fought back even as the sound coming out of Nessie became something otherworldly: a whooping, screaming alarm, inhuman in its volume and composition—it grew from that to something animalistic, then the shriek of a wild, vengeful banshee.

Shana slugged her father in the ribs, and again under his arm, in the armpit. He yelped, and his arms opened—

Nessie dropped to the ground in a crouch.

And then, once more, she stood, shook it off, and kept walking.

"I'm . . . sorry," Shana said to her father, gently touching his arm.

It was like he didn't hear her. Or like he didn't even realize that she'd hit him in the first place. His mouth formed her sister's name, but only when he said it a second time did he make any sound: "Nessie." A small utterance, like a plea or a prayer. His own eyes cleared anew as he looked to Shana. "I don't know what's happening. The way she was shaking . . . she got hot, so hot, like she was about to burn up in my hands."

"I know. I know. I *told* you. We need help."

"Help. Right." He blinked back tears. "I'm gonna go get help." A small thought hit her: *I shouldn't be the one telling him what to do. Dads are supposed to know what to do to fix every problem, make it all okay again.*

"Don't you have your cell?"

"I left it back in the stable." Of course he did. One of his bad habits, that. *Damnit, Dad.*

"It'll be fastest to get it and call," she said.

"Yeah, okay. Yeah." He reached in his pocket for the keys, then hurried forward to Nessie. He said something to her, something Shana couldn't hear, and kissed the younger girl on the cheek.

Nessie, unfazed, continued her journey. Feet slapping on wet road.

Shana saw someone else, now: A man, tall and lean, stepped out of the mist and onto the road. Over a hawk's-beak nose rested a pair of round spectacles, and Shana realized: *I know him.*

"Dad, Dad, look." She waved her hand in the air. "Mister Blamire, hey, over here." Mister Blamire was her geometry teacher. Shana sucked at math, but Blamire had always been patient, even helped her eke out a B–. She waved her hands again as he walked closer. "Do you have a phone? A cellphone? We need help!"

He kept walking toward them, saying nothing. Her father called, too, then jogged forward as if to meet him.

As Nessie walked forward, Blamire adjusted his step. His trajectory changed. He wasn't walking toward *them*.

He was walking toward *Nessie*.

A strange fear formed like a pit between Shana's heart and her stomach. Already she could see that something about him wasn't right—he wore jeans and a white T-shirt, but no shoes, only slippers. *Why slippers?*

What happened next was a thing part of her expected, not because it made sense but precisely because it didn't—

Blamire reached Nessie and turned his body so that he could walk alongside her. Together the two of them continued forward. Not in lockstep, not precisely at the same speed, but always within a foot or two of each other. Her father jogged over, and Shana followed.

"Hey, buddy," her father said, grabbing at his sleeve.

"Mister Blamire," Shana said, her voice smaller than she meant it to be. "It's me. Shana Stewart." But already she could see his eyes were the same as Nessie's—just as empty, just as dead. Her eyes were flush with blood, and his were still white. Their pupils were big as dimes.

She watched her father step in front of the man, a flash of anger across his face. "Get away from her," he growled, then gave Blamire a hard shove.

Not hard enough, though. Blamire pushed on. Like he'd never been touched. Her father almost fell on his ass. His hand formed a fist—

Shana grabbed his arm. "Dad. Dad." That shook him out of the rage that seemed ready to overtake him. "That's Mister Blamire. He's a teacher at school. I think . . ." And this didn't make any sense to say, but she said it anyway, because what other conclusion was there? "I think he's like her."

"What?"

"I think he's like Nessie. Go. Get help. Please!"

Her father nodded. He ran to the truck, and Shana followed her sister.

BLACK SWAN

Mystery Shrouds Murder-Suicide of Cedar Fort Man and Family

. . . Utah County Sheriff Peter Niebouer said the victims were identified as Brandon Sharpe, 31; his mother, Johnette Sharpe, 63; and father, Daniel Sharpe, 64. The three bodies were discovered Tuesday morning in the living room of the house owned by Daniel Sharpe. All three had gunshot wounds and police recovered a handgun, owned by Brandon Sharpe, at the scene. What has puzzled investigators are the messages written on the wall in the mother's blood: "Get out of my computer" and "White Mask is coming." Investigators also discovered an external hard drive containing child pornography. The hard drive was owned by Brandon Sharpe . . .

JUNE 3
Decatur, Georgia

THE JET LAG WAS ALREADY UPON BENJI RAY, LIKE HEAVY WEIGHTS HUNG UPON his bones. He never had any luck sleeping on planes, and flying made him anxious, so the best he could manage was simply to stay awake with a good book or magazine and ride it out. This wasn't as bad as some of his trips—China was the worst—but just the same, flying from Kailua-Kona to Seattle to Atlanta was twelve hours in the air, and more on the ground in airports.

Wearily, he slammed the trunk of his sedan after hauling out his duffel, and made the short miserable trek to his townhouse. Visions of a nap danced softly, seductively in his head; he knew the best way to get ahead of the lag was to stay up and sleep at a normal time like a normal human, but he felt so unmoored from everything, he wondered if it really mattered.

As he dragged the bag toward his front door, someone, a woman, said his name: "Doctor Benjamin Ray?" she asked.

He turned, wincing against the bright afternoon sun, the Georgia heat already wicking away his patience.

A young black woman, skin lighter than his own, stood there. He guessed late twenties, early thirties. Her attire was casual: jeans and a short-sleeved shirt, button-down. Her hair framed her face in springy ringlets.

"That's me," he said, wary. "Listen, I don't know if you're friend or foe, fan or . . . whatever the opposite of a *fan* is." *God,* he thought, *maybe she's a lawyer.* As if he hadn't dealt with enough of those already. "I'm sorry, this isn't an ideal time—"

"My name is Sadie Emeka," she said, a smile on her face. Not American, he realized. British, he guessed, though something else, too—something African. Ethiopian, maybe Nigerian. "I work for Benex-Voyager, which is a—"

"I know who they are," he said crisply. *Too* crisply, he was sure, but again, his patience felt like a tooth worn down to the squirming nerve.

"I'd like to speak with you, if you'll allow me the time."

"Not today," he said, waving her off. "I've just come off a long, long trip, you'll understand. Perhaps later in the week. Or next week. Or never." With that said, he turned toward his house once more.

"Something's gone wrong," she said. He turned, eyebrow arched. Sadie Emeka still wore that implacable smile, and her voice still had that chipper, upbeat tone—but he detected a tremor of consequence there, too.

"'Something.'"

"An outbreak." She hesitated. "Maybe."

"*Maybe* an outbreak. Mm. Okay. Where? Africa? China?"

"Here. Well. America. Pennsylvania, specifically."

He chewed the inside of his cheek. Everything ached. His soul was ready to leave this lump of meat he called a body and go find the rest it so desperately desired. *Not yet,* he told his soul.

"Come in," he said. "I'll fix us some coffee."

WATER POURED GENTLY FROM THE gooseneck kettle as he moved it in slow spirals above the ground coffee. The hot water saturated the grounds, and steam rose from it like ghosts from grave-earth. The aroma was enough to give him new, if temporary, life.

"I have a Keurig," Sadie said, watching him make the pour-over coffee with a kind of clinical fascination. "Actually, I've two! One at home, one at the office."

"They're wasteful," he said. Again, perhaps too curtly.

"I use the eco-friendly pods. Reusable."

"Still wasteful. And overindulgent. This—" He flicked the glass carafe that held the coffee filter, *ting ting.* "—is simple. Glass carafe. Metal filter. Hot water. Ground beans. No electronics needed. Besides, the Keurig machines are subject to mold and bacterial growth—even algae."

"My. You must be quite fun at parties."

There, that unswerving smile. A flash in her eyes, too, a spark of mischief.

"I apologize," he said. "I shouldn't lecture you. I like to think I'm better than that, but as I noted: I'm a little bit tired from my trip."

"Hawaii, yes?"

"That's right. How did you know that?"

"It is my job to know things, Doctor Ray."

"Call me Benji, please." He eyed her up. "Do you know what I was doing there? In Hawaii?"

"I do. You were on the Big Island, upcountry. Visiting with Kolohe Farm—a breeder of heritage pig breeds, yes? One guesses you were teaching them about, or at least giving them a *lecture* about, sustainable, safe farming practices. Correct me if I'm wrong, but I imagine you're *quite* the folk hero to a small farm like them."

"You do know a lot." His gaze darkened. "But be sure of one thing: I'm no hero, Miss Emeka."

"If I can call you Benji, you can call me Sadie."

"Ah. Sadie. Well." As he spoke, he pulled the filter out of the carafe, dumping the grounds in an empty bowl he used for countertop compost. "More to the point, the CDC in particular certainly considers me no hero, and in fact decided I was quite the liability to them. And they were right to decide that. I was a liability and I cost them considerable respect and fidelity. Which means that despite your company's affiliation with them, I have to guess you're not here on their behalf—unless Loretta had a serious change of heart, which is less likely than pigs building jet packs."

The CDC's deputy director, Loretta Shustack, had earned the nickname "The Immovable Object" for that very reason: Once she set course, she did not diverge from it. She was brutally effective and never backed down from a fight.

"I am not here at the CDC's request," she said. "That is correct."

He poured the coffee, passed her a mug. "Cream, sugar?"

"Please. An itty-bitty dollop of both, if you will."

He did as she asked, then kept his own coffee black as the Devil's heart. She took a sip, made a favorable mouth-noise.

"This is really good."

"It's a Colombian, made with a honey process—which has nothing to do with honey just as I assume your visit with me has nothing to do with coffee, so let's cut to the quick. You said there's an outbreak."

"Maybe an outbreak."

"Of what?"

"I don't know."

"Then how do you know it's an outbreak?"

"*Maybe* an outbreak," she clarified again with a waggle of her finger. "We don't know what it is, exactly."

"'We' as in you and the CDC?"

"'We' as in me and Black Swan."

He froze, the mug to his lips. Silence stretching out between them like a widening chasm. "All right."

Black Swan . . .

"You're familiar, then."

"I am."

"And yet you seem a bit *dubious.*"

"I *am* dubious. More than a bit. I am wary of our growing fascination with replacing human work with artificial intelligence. If some computer wants to recommend products for me to buy at Amazon or a video to watch on YouTube, so be it. But this . . . this job requires a human touch."

"And it gets the human touch. Humans evaluate the predictions, Benji, surely you know that."

There.

On her face, that indefatigable smile wavered. Her face tightened visibly; she was suddenly, inexplicably, on the defense. Benji's distrust of Black Swan and its predictions was not something she merely disagreed with; it cut her.

He wondered why.

What was her investment here? Her involvement?

This was what he knew about Black Swan:

Black Swan was a PMI, or a predictive machine intelligence. The system was commissioned by the former administration, under President Nolan, who for a Republican was surprisingly science-friendly (he at least acknowledged the realities of climate change, space exploration, GMOs, and so forth)—though also very *surveillance*-friendly, which in the context of urging the creation of artificial intelligence tended to raise one's hackles. Problem was, Black Swan didn't have a budget line, so the money for it came in part out of the CDC, which had been given considerable funding after an Ebola scare in New York City (one that Benji had himself investigated). So Benex-Voyager created Black Swan specifically with the ability to detect upcoming outbreaks, pandemics, and even zoonotic jumps, where a disease leapt from animal to human.

They called it Black Swan after Nassim Nicholas Taleb's black swan theory, which suggested that some events were utterly unpredictable; only after the events happened did we rationalize their occurrence as something we should have expected. Further, such unexpected events disproportionately affected the outcome of history—far greater than those events we were able to predict or expect.

Black swan events were therefore viewed as outliers—named as such from a statement made by the Roman poet Juvenal:

"Rara avis in terris nigroque simillima cygno."

Or, roughly translated: "A rare bird, like a black swan."

His statement was understood throughout history as one meant to symbolize something that was impossible. Because black swans were believed not to exist.

Except they did. Just as humankind often believed certain events or outcomes to be impossible—until they happened.

Benex-Voyager saw this as a challenge, and named its machine Black Swan ironically. The machine intelligence gathered and swept large swaths of data, looking for improbabilities or even theoretical impossibilities, and could thus draw conclusions—predictions—from them. The events of 9/11, of course, were labeled a black swan—and yet, looking back, signs *did* exist that such an attack was coming, signs that were routinely ignored by those in power. Black Swan, it was promised, would not ignore such signs.

The trick, as it was explained to Benji, was going outside known decision theory. Most prediction attempts used a set model with clear parameters and margins—put differently, humans did not know what they did not know. You could not predict a snowstorm if you did not know what a snowstorm was or if snowstorms even existed. You had to know what you were looking for to look for it in the first damn place. It meant a new design for predicting disaster, one that required a deep penetration into every system that connected to the 'net.

Now, under current president Nora Hunt, Black Swan had been fast-tracked. Two years ago, Benji had been tasked with translating what he did as a member of EIS—Epidemic Intelligence Service—to the needs of Black Swan.

He told them in polite but certain terms to go to hell.

Just as he would tell this woman, right now.

"Whatever this is," he began, "I'm not serving a machine—"

It was her turn to interrupt. "Benji, I do not 'serve' the machine. It's not *God*. It's a tool. A smart tool. Black Swan has already helped us immensely. Black Swan is not public knowledge, but in the last year, do you know all the things we've accomplished? All of what has been thwarted?"

In the last year.

Translation: *In the time since you were fired.*

"I do not," he said somewhat dourly.

"It helped us predict a multistate measles outbreak that could've decimated the West Coast: It saw what we did not, which was that local vaccination rates had dipped—all thanks to parents falling prey to misinformation about vaccines."

He *hmm*ed some small approval at that: These days, misinformation—or really, *dis*information—seemed so ubiquitous, it suffused the air, as common as pollen in spring.

Sadie went on: "It's not just epidemics, either—not just viruses or bacteria. We stopped a bridge collapse in Philadelphia. An Iranian computer virus that would've ransomed bank records. We caught a domestic terror cell operating out of Oregon, and Islamic hackers trying to attack the power grid, *and* a Russian spy who had long integrated himself into Blackheart, the private military contractor."

Benji sipped at his coffee, and pondered aloud: "Six months ago, the CDC caught a potential listeria outbreak originating at a dairy in Colorado." He'd read about it, of course, and wondered exactly where they got the tip—generally, in this country, you didn't catch an outbreak like that until it was, well, already broken out. He'd thought to make a call or two, see if someone would explain to him how they figured it out—but he was afraid they'd not want to talk to him. (A fear that still lingered, even now.) "Was that the result of Black Swan?"

"It was."

Shit.

Perhaps we truly are replaceable.

"So what do you need me for?" He finished his coffee, waiting for the caffeine to exorcise the demons of fatigue. "You've got your program. It should tell you all you need to know."

"It's not some app on your iPhone, Benji. Machine intelligence is, like people, imperfect. It has to be *trained*. We spent one whole year just teaching it to examine information, find patterns, and not only repeat what it learned but offer new iterations as well. Song titles, paint colors, poetry—oh, you have not *lived* until you've heard the poetry of an artificial intelligence. Sheer bloody *lunacy,* though as it got better, some of it started to sound like bad *human* poetry, not bad machine poetry."

"It recites poetry. Wonderful."

"More to the point, not only are humans necessary to train it, but we're also necessary to interpret it. Black Swan is a tool, and *we* must wield it."

Benji stood up and put his mug in the dishwasher. As he did, he said:

"Let me rephrase the question. Why me? Anybody in the CDC would tell you I'm not trustworthy. I burned that bridge. I made a choice, and nobody in their right mind would point you in my direction."

"Black Swan did."

"Black Swan did what?"

"Pointed me toward you."

He narrowed his eyes. "I'm sorry, I don't understand."

"Black Swan wants *you,* Benji. And that's why I'm here."

POP GOES THE WEASEL

Populist Ed Creel Clinches Republican Nomination

Today industrialist Ed Creel reached the magic number of delegates, 1,237, to secure the GOP nomination in the presidential race, pitting him against the incumbent Democrat, Nora Hunt, whose poll numbers remain strong. Creel has long been viewed as a dark horse candidate, but one by one he ousted the establishment Republicans to emerge ultimately victorious despite—or because of—running a controversial campaign . . .

JUNE 3
Near Granger, Pennsylvania

SHANA SAT IN THE BACK OF THE AMBULANCE. ONE OF THE TWO PARAMEDICS sat with her—a broad-shouldered white woman with a crooked nose and kind eyes. The woman introduced herself as Heather Burns. The other paramedic was Brian McGinty: a soft-spoken string bean with a pale beard. Also Caucasian. He stood outside the ambulance, speaking to her father. Shana couldn't hear what they were saying.

"Your sister," Paramedic Heather said. "She was the first?"

"Yeah. Yes." Shana felt her hands shaking, though she didn't know why. Over the paramedic's shoulder she caught a glimpse of the rickety wooden bus shelter where they'd found her sister two years ago after their mother left.

"And the other two?"

"Mister Blamire, the math teacher, he showed up . . . um, I dunno, over an hour ago, down on Orchard—no! No, uh, Mine Hill. And that third person, I don't know who she is, I'm sorry."

"But she just showed up?"

"Just before you guys got here, yeah."

The third person looked young, but not as young as her sister. Maybe midtwenties. Looked Hispanic. Or was it Latina? Shit. There was a difference, she was sure of it, but she couldn't think of what it was. Long hair down over her shoulders to the middle of her back. Wide hips but narrow shoulders. The woman wasn't wearing shoes, but *was* wearing socks. Pink socks, already looking red on the bottom from being wet and muddy.

She came up right after they turned onto Granger Road off Mine Hill. Shana watched this young woman walk out the door of a little garage apartment and make a beeline for Nessie and Mister Blamire. The woman had those same dead-nail eyes.

The woman joined the other two.

And then there were three.

Sleepwalkers, Shana thought. Three sleepwalkers.

She couldn't repress the cold feeling that swept over her. *Nobody home in there,* she thought. A strange vacancy. A small, troubling voice inside warned her: *This is the start of something, we just don't know what, yet.*

"Are they sick?" Shana asked the paramedic.

"I don't know. I'm not a doctor."

"Oh. Right." She blinked. "They seem like they're sleepwalking."

"That's a good way to describe it." Heather nodded and smiled—it gave Shana some small comfort, that smile. "Okay, before those three—the sleepwalkers—get too far ahead, I'm going to explain real quick what we want to do. We're going to inject a sedative, one at a time, in each—"

"Don't you need like, a vein for that? They won't stay still long enough for you to tap a vein or whatever—"

"This is Haldol. Goes right in the buttock."

"Oh. Okay. And if they fall over?"

"It doesn't necessarily sedate to unconsciousness—it's good for calming down agitated, even violent patients. But just in case, I'll do the injection, and I'll be behind the patient in case they fall backward. Brian will stay at the front in case it goes the other way."

Shana nodded. "You're starting with Nessie first?"

"Brian is securing your father's permission right now."

"Okay."

"Vanessa, to your knowledge, doesn't use drugs?"

At that, Shana had to laugh. "Drugs, no, God. Nessie is straight-edge all the way." She remembered one time she tried to get her little sister to taste a beer—Nessie made a puckered face at her like a juiced lemon and wouldn't even take a *sip*. Shana tried to literally press the beer to her lips, and at the last minute Nessie blew out, spraying beer foam all over Shana's face.

God, was Shana pissed. It seemed so stupid now.

"All right." Heather looked out at the other paramedic, who gave her a gentle nod. "Looks like we're all clear."

"I'd like to be close by."

"Of course. It'll be quick and painless and then maybe we can calm your sister down and get her and the others to the emergency room. Just to see what else is going on—if anything. Which it's probably not. Probably just a . . . strange moon or something."

Heather helped Shana hop down out of the back of the ambulance. Ahead, the three walkers were already down the road by a quarter mile. They walked in a staggered pattern—first Nessie, then Blamire was a couple of steps ahead in the middle, and then the new walker was last in line, and lagging behind by a few steps.

The paramedics took point and had to affect a gentle jog to catch up. Shana looked to her father with worry hanging heavy on her brow.

"It'll be okay," he said.

"I don't know about this."

"They know what they're doing."

"I know." She thought but did not say: *But something else is wrong.* She could feel it, the way you could feel a storm coming sometimes. A buzz in the air, a tension between molecules. She kept that fear to herself, though.

The paramedics arranged themselves—Brian stepping ahead of the three walkers, keeping pace with them while walking backward. Heather had a needle, which she plunged into a little bottle of clear liquid. The needle drank from the glass and emerged, sated.

The noonday light gleamed in the needle's tip.

Heather gave Shana one last smile, then hurried up behind her sister—

And fast as lightning, she stabbed the needle in.

Or rather, tried to stab the needle.

Tried, and failed.

"It didn't go in," the paramedic said. She offered an awkward, maybe even embarrassed smile. "Let's try this again."

And again she caught up to Nessie, and again she thrust the needle toward the girl's butt cheek, and—

Once more, nothing. It was like the paramedic was poking a leather couch with a dull fork—it just wouldn't go in.

Shana tried to think of how one day this would make a hilarious story she'd tell her sister:

So while you were spacing out like a total fucking spaz, the paramedic tried again and again to prick your butt with the needle but she couldn't get it to work. Ha ha, get it? A prick in your butt? Oh shut up, don't make that face. Be proud. You've got glutes of steel, little sister. They should make a comic about you and your superpower—we'll call you Bulletproof Booty Girl.

Heather looked up, her cheeks flushed. "I swear," she joked, "I *am* a professional."

The other paramedic, Brian, looked over and said in a low, frustrated voice: "Want me to try or what?"

"Brian. I got this. Third time's a charm and all that. I want you to grab her, though, around the middle—real gentle, hold her still for me—"

"*No,*" Shana said, storming over. Her father reached for her but she twisted out of his grip. "Wait, just stop. No! No, I told you what happens when you hold them still. No, no, no—"

"Problem is, Shana, I think it's her moving that's the issue. Vanessa's getting away from me even as I'm going in with the needle, so."

"Please. *Don't.*"

Heather looked at Shana and in her calm way said: "You told me it was, what, five, six, maybe even seven seconds before you really became alarmed by the girl's seizure? This'll be for one second. Maybe *half* that. Isn't that right, Brian?"

"Absolutely. And like she said, I'll be gentle."

Shana felt her father behind her. "Honey," he said. "Let them try."

"But, Dad—"

"Shana." Gently, he pulled her back. "These are medical professionals. You know that."

"She'll shake. When she does, it'll be hard for them to stick her—"

"I won't miss," Heather said. "I promise."

Reluctantly, Shana nodded.

"Okay. *Okay.*"

Heather and Brian caught up once more to the girl. "You grab her on three," she said. "One . . ."

Please be okay, Nessie.

"Two . . ."

I don't know what this is but I need you to get better.

"Three!"

Brian grabbed her. Nessie shook. The girl cried out, that otherworldly wail rising up out of her throat and mouth.

Heather went in with the needle, jabbing hard—

Something fell against the asphalt. A *tick-tack* sound.

Whatever it was gleamed in the emerging sun.

Nessie's whole body shook harder and harder, heels juddering against the road, so hard that Shana was sure her feet would be cut up. That sound rose louder and louder, and Shana yelled at them to *let her go, please, God, fucking let her go*—even as the other two sleepwalkers walked onward.

"The needle broke," Heather said. "Let her go!"

Brian's arms sprang open. The girl squirmed free, then shouldered past him with urgency in her step allowing her to join the other two.

The two paramedics appeared shaken. Brian most of all. "That was bad."

"It was just a seizure," Heather said.

"That wasn't *just* a seizure."

"What's going on?" Shana's father asked.

"I couldn't . . ." Heather drew a deep breath. "I couldn't get the needle in. She doesn't have anything in her pockets . . . ? A wallet or . . . or something tough? The needle broke and needles don't usually break unless—"

"She's wearing *pajamas*," Shana snapped.

That drove them all to a stretch of awkward silence as they all looked to one another for answers and reassurance—none of which would come.

"I think we need to call somebody," Brian said.

"Who?" Dad asked.

"The police," Heather said. "They'll know what to do."

It took an hour. By then, they'd followed the three sleepwalkers into Granger proper, which wasn't much of a town, really: a single road, all stop signs and no stoplights, one bar, two gas stations, three antiques stores, and an old wig store that had closed down a few years back but still had all its signage. Their procession was a strange one: an ambulance creeping along behind three people walking, and Shana and her father in the pickup. Whenever cars backed up behind them, they waved them around. Whenever the cars came the other way, they slowly figured out to maneuver around the people and the two vehicles. The walkers never seemed to take notice. Nothing altered their path. Nothing drew their gaze.

They didn't twitch or flinch or change their gait, not once.

Shana drove. She and her father didn't say much to each other along the way. It was mostly just him trying hard, too hard, to reassure her: "It'll be fine. Your sister is fine. You just wait and see."

Shana knew in her blood that it was bullshit.

THE COP THAT SHOWED UP was a stocky sort: short, but looked like a real gym rat. Wasn't just arms and legs; his *neck* had muscles. The cop, bald as a lightbulb, pulled them over and got the lowdown from the two paramedics before turning to Shana and her father.

"My name's Officer Chris Kyle. Young girl is your daughter?" he asked, and her father confirmed. He took a few more details: Nessie's age, any health issues they knew about, any drug issues. The paramedics briefed him on the seizures. Heather explained: "Contact seems to be the cause of the seizures."

Shana thought: *It's not just contact, though. It's what happens when you try to stop them.*

By now the three walkers were already halfway through town. Some folks had gathered to see. A few faces poked out of upstairs apartment windows to goggle. A couple of day-drinkers stood in the doorway of the bar, Glinchey's. A woman at the Mobil station stopped filling her car and stood at the pump, looking back and forth between the walkers and the cop and the ambulance. The cop kept a wandering eye ahead, then called the paramedics over.

"Goal is what?" he asked them.

"Hospital," Heather answered.

"And are they dangerous?"

"No," Brian said. "Not that we can see."

"They're sleepwalking," Shana said, even though her diagnosis was nowhere near scientific. Still, nobody corrected her.

"All right. Let's get 'em to the hospital," the cop said.

The officer cracked his knuckles, rolled his head on his neck like he was about to deadlift a fallen log, then got back in his car. He pulled it up ahead of the three walkers, parked it off to the side about a hundred yards past the gas station. He popped one of the back doors, then made his approach. As he did, Shana couldn't help but notice how the cop had this walk, a cocky rooster strut that looked like he had shit his pants at some point but was too proud to admit it or change his drawers. He stopped twenty feet ahead of the walkers, held up a hand, told them in a clear, loud voice:

"Halt."

They continued walking.

The cop scowled. "I said, stop there. Wake up. Slow your roll."

Brian, the paramedic, yelled over: "They don't . . . they can't hear you."

The cop gave a curt, irritated nod.

What happened next, happened fast. Chris reached to his belt, and drew a pistol, pointing it at the center of the trio. At Blamire.

By the time they were all yelling and running toward him—

He aimed and pulled the trigger.

THE MEAL AFTER LUNCH, ACCOMPANIED BY DRINKS

A neural network invents new desserts:
Shady Tough Crust
Caramelized Pecan Boffins
Bottled Chocolate
Dreamberry Pie
Tartless Fish Prongs
Cakey Cake
Butterscotch Chiffonade Yard Muffin
Unicorn Poo Cake

—as seen on the US of AI blog, *US-of-AI.com*

JUNE 3
Decatur, Georgia

MAKER'S BELL WAS NOT MUCH OF A TOWN WORTH TALKING ABOUT.

Sadie told him that was the place—the one Black Swan identified as a point-of-outbreak. So Benji pulled his laptop out of his travel bag, spun it around on the counter, and with her looked up Maker's Bell.

As he was fond of saying when an investigation yielded nothing:

There's no there *there.*

Maker's Bell sat on the map northwest of Allentown by about fifty miles—used to be a coal town, but that ship had long sailed. Not just for Maker's Bell, but for most of the country. (Politicians were always keen to try to "bring back coal," but you might as well try to bring back the buggy whip. Talking about coal was never about coal, though: It was always code for making promises to blue-collar America about their blue-collar ways of life.)

These days, Maker's Bell was home to 4,925 people. Looked mostly like a white immigrant community—the mine barons exploited populations of Irish and Eastern Europeans in the anthracite mines. They seemed to love something called kielbasy, or kielbasa? Some kind of Polish sausage. And that was about as notable as it got. Not much in the way of news: high school football scores, a sale at the new Toyota dealership, the occasional shoplifter. He scrolled deeper, found that they'd had a string of racial incidents a couple of years back: The town had seen an influx of non-white immigrants from Guatemala, some white folks got pissed, beat a couple of them up, a few vigilantes—a teen girl, of all people, among them—responded, but that simmering pot never boiled over—at least not into the news.

Of course, Benji knew from his own experiences as a black man in America that racism like *that* never really went away. Racism reminded him of Lyme, a tick-borne disease. A deer tick would bite a person, passing along a little bugger named *Borrelia burgdorferi*—the nasty bacterium that caused the disease. When you contracted it, it might look like a case of the flu. Then it could go dormant for weeks, months, sometimes even *years*—and then when it came back, it manifested ten times worse than it began. And it looked a little different every time: attacking different organs, the heart, the brain, the spine; affecting different limbs; conjuring unique symptoms, like facial paralysis.

Racism was a little like that. Sometimes the initial symptoms were small: microaggressions here, simmering resentment there. If you dealt with it head-on, maybe you could keep it contained. If you didn't deal with it, though, it came back with a vengeance: just like that little bacterium. Came back worse. Entrenched. So entrenched, in fact, the longer you let it go, the harder it was to control, and soon everything started to break down.

Now Benji had his mind on those two axes: racism and disease. Could that be what Black Swan was trying to show them about Maker's Bell? He said as much to Sadie: "What if it's not identifying an outbreak of disease? Does Black Swan differentiate between that and, say, an outbreak of terrorism? A school shooting? Because if it's that, you shouldn't be talking to me. You can find far smarter minds than mine on those subjects."

"Black Swan asked for you. Sorry, burden's still on your shoulders, mate."

He scratched the space between his eyes, above his nose: a nervous tic for when he was deep in thought. Maybe his line of thinking was right. Could it be Lyme? Climate change meant a swelling tick population. "Maybe it's tick-borne. Or mosquito. Or . . ." He sighed as options unspooled. "They eat sausage there. Worth a look at butchers. Been a while since trichinosis made the papers."

"Trick-a-what?"

"Trichinosis. A parasitic roundworm infection in meat. Severe cases are fatal. Common in pork. Found in unclean pig farms and butchers."

He felt her eyes burning holes in him. *Wait for it,* he thought. *Waaaait for it.* And sure enough, she said suddenly:

"Was that the disease that you, erm, *found* at Longacre?"

The way she said that word, *found* . . .

"No," he said, brushing past it. He expected that she knew full well what happened there. Was she trying to get him to talk about it? Why? "All this requires more study. Someone on the ground. Someone with resources—which, you'll note, I don't have. I don't have anything, Sadie. This isn't just trying to find a needle in a haystack—I can't even find the damn haystack."

"Let's get dinner."

"Dinner."

"Yes, have you heard of it? It's the meal after lunch, sometimes accompanied by drinks. We're within walking distance of downtown Decatur. Some nice restaurants there. A Jeni's Ice Cream, too. Can I bribe you?"

"I don't know, Sadie."

Again, that smile of hers dropped. "Black Swan hasn't been wrong yet. It's seeing something, we just don't know what. I need your help." The smile came back, then, the gleeful phoenix, reborn from the ashes. "Besides, I've got a rather robust expense account, so at least let me ply you with treats."

"All right." He sighed. "You are ceaseless, you know that?"

"I am, and I do."

PHONE OUT, SADIE SNAPPED A photo of her dessert: a chocolate ice cream so dark, it seemed to consume the light. "Sorry," she said, lining up her shot and taking it. *Cli-click.* "It's very Instagrammable. Just like those cocktails to-night, my my my."

Together the two of them walked through Decatur Square. Families were out under the trees. College students passed Frisbees back and forth. He scraped at the last remnants of his ice cream—goat cheese and cherries—and licked his lips.

"That whole dinner menu was Instagrammable," he said. Benji felt himself sophisticated until he ended up at a restaurant like the one they'd just come from. His view of food was that it was nutritive and functional more than it was a thing to be savored and enjoyed. Half the things on this menu he didn't even understand. What was a gastrique? Or mizuna? Or soubise? What made a quail egg better than an egg from a regular chicken? Looking at the cocktail menu only confused him further. Genever and amaro and cinchona bark and velvet falernum. "I'm pretty sure they made half that menu up, by the way."

"We had Black Swan make up a food menu once, and I confess, it . . . did sound that way, like it came off a fancy Brooklyn farm-to-table restaurant. *Bruised henwater* and *evaporated bacon reduction* and . . . oh God, what was the one thing? I remember! *Melancholy duck petals with scap zest.*"

"What in God's name is *scap zest?*"

She started laughing, tears in her eyes. "I don't even know! The damn thing even generated recipes. Not recipes you could eat, mind you. Recipes that I wager would *actually* kill you. Or set your house on fire." She sighed.

"Black Swan is something personal for you," he said.

"You think so?"

"I do. You're not just some . . . company liaison."

She licked her ice cream and stared off at the middle distance. "No, I suppose I'm not. I'm a neural designer. *The* neural designer."

He stopped walking.

"You designed Black Swan." *Of course.* It's why she took any fear or criticism of it so personally. It was her creation. Not just a program, or a design, but something that existed interstitially between *artwork* and *entity.*

"Correct." She pivoted to meet his gaze. "Not alone, of course. I was only as good as my team, but I was the lead of that team, yes, and most of the code began with me."

"And you trust it."

"As much as I trust myself."

"And it, the machine, trusts me."

She gave a playful shrug. "Apparently. Means I trust you, too."

"I don't think I can help it much."

"I think you two should meet."

You two should meet. The way she said it, it was as if the thing were alive. Which, he supposed, in a way it was—not alive, but aware in some capacity. Intelligent, by some metric. But you would never say that about a computer, or your refrigerator, would you?

"We can put something on the calendar—"

"Is your calendar free tonight? Are you busy at this very moment?" She eyed him up. "You seem to be done with your ice cream."

"Yes, but I would very much like to sleep."

She grinned. "Sleep is overrated, Benjamin Ray. Let's go, right now. We can hop on MARTA." The station was only a block away. "I can introduce you properly to Black Swan."

"And then what?"

"Then we see where the night takes us."

HE HATED THE FEELING: THE anxiety curdling in his gut like milk cut with vinegar. The train took them from Decatur just north of the Emory University campus. The closer they got, the more his nerves nearly dropped him to his knees. They came off the train, walked the few blocks it took to end up at the CDC—his home for nearly two decades. Almost literally, given the nights he slept here, in his office.

And then you threw it all away, didn't you?

Disappointment and shame warred with the righteousness inside him.

It made him sick, and he wasn't sure why.

In part because of what he did.

In part because of what they did to him in return.

Some moments he felt like, *I did the right thing, and they punished me for it.* In the next moment, the opposite came to him with grave certainty: *You lied to suit your agenda, and you deserved worse than you got.*

As they approached the building, the evening light gone diffuse behind the Atlanta skyline, he hesitated. Literally slowed his walk until he came to a stop. He swallowed.

"You okay?" she asked.

"Fine," he lied. "But I don't know that I'm allowed in the building anymore."

"You figure there's a poster hanging up inside with your face on it? Outlaw Benji Ray, wanted for crimes against disease?" She waved him off. "I've got clearance. Besides, Black Swan is in the basement with the server farm. You won't run into anybody if that's what you're worried about."

"I'm not worried," he said, snapping at her. He bit more words—worse ones—back. "Sorry. I just—a lot of memories here, is all."

She shrugged and continued walking with a careless sway to her arms, as if his pain were just a speed bump to her. And maybe it was.

Reluctantly, he followed. And with every step, that feeling in his stomach thickened.

Into the building they went. Sadie authorized a guest pass at the front desk, and, to his shock, they let him right in without pause. What did he expect, exactly? Klaxons and alarms? Metal shutters slamming down behind him? A SWAT response? He had damaged the center's credibility, perhaps, but he wasn't the Devil.

To the elevators they went. *And down we go.*

Sadie smirked, eyeing him as the elevator took them deep into the building's sublevels. An energy clung to her—the electric enthusiasm of a child about to show off a favorite toy or a new drawing.

Doors opened, and she led him through the lowest, deepest sublevels of the building. This was part of the CDC's server farm: room after room, contained behind thick glass walls, of massive server-blade arrays. Humming in the half dark, lights flickering and twitching across it all like digital fireflies. It was cool down here, because it had to be. This much tech generated considerable heat.

Sadie took him down one hall, then the next—she gestured toward a door that had her name on it. SADIE EMEKA, NEURAL DESIGNER (BENEX-VOYAGER). Beyond that stood another door.

This one was matte black.

No sign hung upon it.

She went to the door and opened it. No lock, and he noted as much.

"The room is just a room," she explained. "Black Swan does not live within it. The intrusions we fear are from *out there*—" She gestured toward, well, the entire world. "—rather than from someone walking through this door. Black Swan will not interact with simply anyone."

The room ahead was dark and deep. A consumptive void.

"Shall we?" he asked.

"You'll go into the Lair alone. I'll monitor from my office and can communicate with you from there."

He made a face. "The Lair?"

"Just a little name. Ideally, we don't anthropomorphize it, but just the same I quite like it. There's a Beowulf-meets-Grendel vibe I appreciate." She cleared her throat. Was she nervous? Benji thought that she was. Her nervousness oddly undid some of his own. "Way it works is this: You go in, and you can talk to it, ask it questions. It won't answer in words, but rather, with green pulses or red pulses to indicate *yes* or *no,* respectively. It can also answer with images and data, but it won't communicate with you the same way you communicate with it."

"That does not seem like an exact science."

"Benji, even an exact science is not an exact science—surely you know that above others." He wondered again: Was that a dig at him? A reference to Longacre? No. Surely he was just being overly sensitive. Or paranoid.

"I thought you said it could recite poetry."

"It could. And I also said it was very, very bad. Vogon poetry bad. We've instead chosen to simplify its communication. Speaking is complex. Language is another pattern, and one that ostensibly gets in the way of what we want it to achieve. This isn't Siri or Alexa or any of those other . . . nonsense digital assistants. Those entities, if you can call them that, have a very simple programmatic script—a recitation of certain patterns. But they're not thinking. Black Swan *is* thinking. And what it's thinking about—well, we don't want it to have to parse that through our messy language. It's far more useful to let it speak—um, so to speak—in images, sounds, raw data. And of course the binary *yes/no* system we've given it."

He took a deep breath. His heart was pounding in his chest. It *did* feel a bit like he was meant to go in there and fight a monster.

Or at least meet one.

THE DOOR CLOSED BEHIND HIM, and when it did, that darkness became absolute. The dull thrum of the server farm could not be heard in here, leaving this space feeling not unlike a sensory-deprivation chamber. How long would it be before it felt like he was floating, distant and unmoored from this world? Benji stood in the dark room and waited.

Suddenly, Sadie's voice punctuated the silence:

"Black Swan, coming online."

And with that, the room began to gently throb with soft white light. It pulsed in a way that suggested the gentle rise and fall of breath.

It wasn't alive, he knew. This glow-and-fade of light was a programmatic trick. It was done not because it needed to be done but rather, because they wanted you to feel like you were talking to a living thing.

Something you could trust.

Something just like you.

Ideally, we don't anthropomorphize it . . .

And yet.

"You can speak to it," Sadie said over the comm. Her voice came not from a single speaker but rather, from everywhere: omnidirectional sound that so perfectly filled the room, it felt like it came from within him.

He cleared his throat again and said, "Hello, ahh, Black Swan."

The room pulsed green once.

A yes? An affirmative? What did that mean, exactly? That it was acknowledging his presence? What a special day this was, acknowledged by a machine as existing. (Though given how many times technology—from facial-recognition software to automatic towel dispensers—seemed somehow not to realize that black people existed, failing to trigger when they approached, he guessed he should take it as a win and move on.)

"You called me here, is that correct?"

A green pulse.

And then a second green pulse.

What was that, exactly? Sadie must be reading his mind, because she came over the intercom. "Sorry, to explain: Black Swan may pulse an answer up to three times to invoke a degree of strength and certainty in the answer. Two green pulses means yes, a strong yes. An excited yes."

"It gets excited?" he asked her.

But it was Black Swan that answered with one green pulse.

When the pulse came, it brought a subtle sound: a gentle, womb-throb *vwomm*.

"Why me?" he asked.

He knew it wasn't a yes-or-no question.

How, then, would it answer?

Images began resolving on the wall ahead of him: First, snapshots of his résumé. Glimpses of papers he'd worked on at EIS—those flipping past him, from the wall ahead of him, to the walls at his sides, then discarded behind him and flung back into the data void once more. Images of himself—some taken from the AP, some from internal CDC communications. The photos showed him here in the US but also around the world: at an illegal meat market in Guangdong Province, standing by rows of chickens, ducks, and civet cats; in a Jeep riding the jungle roads of the CAR, on the hunt for monkeypox; he and his team members, like Cassie Tran and Martin Vargas, staring at a wall of maps in Sierra Leone tracing an Ebola outbreak.

And then, the kicker:

A photo of him at Longacre Farm in North Carolina.

There he stood between stalls of pigs, stalls that seemed to go on for infinity. The stall hogs crammed in so tight they hadn't an inch between them. Even in this photo—black and white—he could see the sores worn into their sides. It made him flinch.

Did Black Swan know what that moment represented?

Or was it just another in a line of photos taken from his time as a member of the Epidemic Intelligence Service here in the CDC?

Was there a reason Black Swan would show that to him?

Or could it just be Sadie? Could she just be the puppet master putting words into this digital creature so it could regurgitate them again?

"Why Maker's Bell?" he asked. "I don't see anything exceptional there. What is it that you see?"

Moments passed. And then . . .

On the wall ahead, the white glow of the room dissolved into a series of fat, blocky pixels—and those pixels then refined swiftly, breaking down and sharpening into an image. A map. Pennsylvania. It dissolved to pixels once more and reconstituted itself, zoomed in further, showing a town on the map. *The* town in question: Maker's Bell.

"Yes, yes," he said, frustrated. "I know where it is. What's going to happen there? Show me something."

You motherfucker, he added in his head.

Then, a video. Projected there on the wall.

It began simply enough: a cameraphone video looking down the street of a small town past a set of gas pumps. A cop car sat nearby, and presumably the car's driver—a bald, barrel-chested Caucasian police officer—stood in front of three people walking toward him. He asked them to stop, and they wouldn't.

Something wasn't right with the three walkers. They stared ahead. The video's clarity wasn't pristine, but even here it was easy to see those vacant eyes. The three comprised what looked like a young white girl, an older (maybe middle-aged) man of indeterminate race given the video quality, and a woman, maybe Latina.

The cop pulled a gun—

From behind the three walkers, people shouted and ran forward. Two paramedics, by the look of it—and as the phone moved, shaky, Benji could see the ambulance in the background. Following the two paramedics were a man in a baseball cap and overalls and another young girl—his daughter, maybe.

The gun in the cop's hand wasn't a gun, though, was it?

A *Taser*, Benji realized.

The cop fired it into the middle of the walkers—into the man's chest.

The probes went in through the shirt and ticked with electricity—but the man kept coming. And that's when the cop, apparently having had enough ("the fuck," he said), stormed up and grabbed the man.

The man—the walker the cop grabbed, the one the Taser failed to affect—stiffened, caught in some kind of seizure.

His eyes went dark. So dark it was easy to see even on the crummy phone video.

(The darkness, Benji guessed, was the result of the eyes going bloodshot from a subconjunctival hemorrhage. Benji knew it didn't necessarily mean damage to the eye, but came as a result of intense straining or trauma.)

As the man shook, the tremors worsening, the police officer continued to drag him toward the cruiser—despite the pleas of the paramedics.

The person taking the video must've stretched to zoom, because the image grew, closing in on the car as the cop forced the man inside it. The image was grainier, now, a little harder to parse—

Then:

The car shuddered. Something dark sprayed up across all the windows. Something *red*. The glass broke. Inside the car, the cop screamed. Others outside the vehicle began yelling, too, in panic—some running toward it, others fleeing in the opposite direction. The cop staggered out, covered in . . . something wet. Red and black. Clutching at himself. *It's gore,* Benji thought. *Someone's. Maybe his.*

Before the video ended, the person moved the camera one last time.

And pointed it at the two other walkers.

One was a girl, the other a young woman.

They continued walking forward as if none of this had happened or was happening around them. Their gait remained purposeful. Their eyes, dead as nails. Mouths formed into flat lines.

Then the video went black.

Benji stumbled through the darkness of Black Swan's Lair, seeking egress—he couldn't find the door here in the dark, and his hand hit the cold wall, and only when the slow steady throb of white light rose anew did he see the outline of the exit.

6

THE DAY'S END

fam check out this video my GF took holy SHIT does that dude fucking explode?! 😱 😩 😫 💥

@steviemifflin
147 replies 1298 RTs 3788 likes

JUNE 3
Minersville, Pennsylvania

IT WAS COMING UP ON MIDNIGHT, AND THEIR OLD PICKUP SAT PARKED ON A bridge crossing the West Branch of the Schuylkill River. Her father walked toward it, head held low, chin to his chest. Shana trailed behind, moving slow—slower than him, so that even at his easy walk he was outpacing her. The river murmured and gushed, and a few crickets sang along the banks in the moonless black of the night. The sound of her father's boots echoed on the bridge.

They were going the opposite direction of the sleepwalkers.

She felt it keenly—it was like a magnetic force trying to drag her back toward her sister and the others. *The others.* Jesus. It wasn't just Nessie and the other woman, a woman they now knew was named Rosie. Though Blamire was gone (and Shana purposefully did *not* let her mind wander to *how* he died), the sleepwalkers didn't stop there. Their numbers had grown—four more had joined. Two men, two women. Shana didn't know much about them because the cops wouldn't let them get close—but at least one of the four looked younger, a boy her age, maybe older. Two came out of their houses. One out of a restaurant. The last crossed a meadow. All merged with the herd in lockstep.

The herd. That's how they seemed. Dull-witted as livestock, but led by no shepherd.

"Dad," Shana yelled out. "Stop."

Her father stopped and turned. "Come on, Shana. Time to go home."

She ratcheted up as much courage as she could muster.

"I'm not coming."

He stood, silent for a span of seconds. "Don't mess around."

"I'm not messing around."

Her father stormed toward her. "Shana, this isn't the time."

"It's exactly the damn time."

"Your sister's in good hands. We have a farm to run. The dairy doesn't operate itself. I was able to wrangle Will and Essie from across the street to make sure the cows were fed today, but they won't come every day, and I can't afford to pay them much. We need to go home." He hesitated. "Nessie will be okay. They have the cops there, they've called doctors—"

"I'm going to stay with her."

"Shana, please, it's too late for this horseshit."

"I'm staying."

He reached out, caught her wrist, but she twisted out of his grip.

"*Someone* needs to protect her," Shana spat. Implicit in that comment: *It won't be you, it'll be me.*

"Like I said, Shana, they have *cops* there—we can trust the police."

The laugh that came out of her was a bitter recrimination. "You're fucking kidding me with this, right? Mister Blamire is dead *because* of that cop. That poor man, he just—" And here she fought to blink away tears and bite back a gasping, gaping sob. "He, he, he fucking *burst* from the inside like an over-full stomach—like something out of a horror movie. What if they did that to Nessie, huh? What if today, that dumb redneck gym-rat cop decided to grab *her* instead of my math teacher? If he did that—"

"Shana, don't—"

"If he did that, *she'd* be the one in the back of that car, all that blood and all that bone." One part of that horror revisited her every time she closed her eyes—when it happened, a little splinter of red bone had popped through the back window of the cop's cruiser. And it just stuck there. Dripping red. It belonged to Blamire. When he . . . erupted.

"It wasn't Nessie, though."

The next words came out of her through gritted teeth. They were angry, drenched in venom reserved for her father—the rage she felt toward him suddenly was probably wrong, surely misplaced, and she knew that in the back of her mind somewhere, but it didn't matter. It was there, and she let it all out.

"You always want to work, work, work. Since Mom left you've been head down in the job, and it's like you don't even see us there. You just think we should get up and work same as you—God, maybe that's why Mom left you. You ever think of that? Maybe she didn't want some future with a . . . a fucking cheesemaker and his hick daughters!" By now, she was yelling: She had to yell because it helped her not to cry. "And you don't need me because you love me, you need me because . . . I keep things running when you can't. Just like I pack Nessie's lunch, just like I make sure she takes her dumb allergy medications, just like . . ."

But her words shriveled up.

Her father grew quiet, then. Even in the dark she could see his eyes were wide as he stared not at her, but off the bridge, at an unfixed point.

"You're being this way because you're trying to push me away," he said. "I get that. You want me hurt or pissed off so I just leave."

"I . . . I don't know, Dad."

"Thing is, maybe you're right. Maybe that's why your mother left, I don't know. It's not like she ever told me. She seemed a little strange in the weeks leading up, but . . . she never said anything. I figured it was just a mood, she'd grow out of it, life would move on." He brought both hands to his face and wearily dragged the palms across the expanse of his cheeks. "It killed me when she left. Killed the both of you, too. And now . . . Nessie's walking away. Not like she means to, but . . ."

"Dad, she's not Mom—"

"But I can't have you leave, too. Don't leave me, Shana. Please."

"It's Nessie I can't leave, Dad. She's alone."

He sighed. "I know."

"And you can't go because you have a farm to run . . ."

"Shana—"

"But I can. I can go with her." *Wherever it is she's going.*

"There's nothing you can do."

"I can be there when she comes out of this. I can stop them from . . . from trying to throw her in the back of a cop car. Who's going to be there for her? We don't even know what's happening."

Just then, headlights. Two cop cars—one cruiser, one SUV—went past. No sirens or strobing lights, and they didn't seem in a rush. Just the same, it made Shana's guts tighten. *I'm wasting time. What if something new has gone wrong? What if it's Nessie?*

"Dad, Nessie is special."

"You're both special."

Another harsh, humorless laugh. "Don't."

"Honey," he said, reaching for her arm. "I mean it."

"I'm special to you because I'm your daughter, but . . . most kids at my school are going to college next year. I'm not."

"I know and—"

"You remember what you said when I told you?"

"I said okay, I said I respect your choices and—"

"*Exactly.* You said okay. Like, oh well, sure. You didn't fight me on it, not one bit. You didn't fight me like you're fighting me now."

"Shana . . ."

"And what if Nessie told you the same thing? What if she told you *she* wasn't going to college? Huh?" Her father didn't answer. He just stood there silent and guilty because they both knew the answer. "You'd be livid. You'd probably write the damn application for her because one day she's going to be whatever she wants to be and that means shipping her off to college. Me, though, I don't have anything. No plans, no . . . real skills."

"Your photography is beautiful."

"Like I said, no real skills. You figured me for working the dairy. Helping you out. For the rest of my life or until you marry me off."

"Shana, it's not like that. You can be whatever you want to be, but I know that college isn't for everybody—hell, I didn't do what anyone would consider proper college, I just did two years of ag school. That doesn't mean you're not special. It doesn't mean you can't do what you want."

"I'm eighteen in a month. And what I want is to go with her. You can't really stop me. I'd rather you help me."

It was like watching something high up on a shelf that you knew was going to fall but you were powerless to stop it—it was gonna tumble and it was probably gonna shatter. Her father fell to his knees. His hands went out and clasped hers. Dad wept. He wept like something broke inside him and spilled out.

He cried like Nessie cried that day in the Granger bus stop.

Shana had never seen him cry, not like this. When one of their animals died—one of the cows or the goats or those kittens he found in the barn—his eyes glazed over with the threat of tears, but not once did she see them spill over. He didn't cry when their mother left. But this was him wracked with hitching, shuddering sobs.

It made her feel like an asshole, because she stood there, and him crying so bad only made her tears dry up. She felt bad for him. And bad in a pity way, bad in a judgy way. Like part of her didn't want to see her father like this. She just wanted him to be strong and stoic.

That made her the worse person, not him. She knew that.

"Dad, I should get going."

"You can't walk with them forever."

"Maybe. I dunno. We'll see. I . . . need some things if you'd be willing to get them for me."

He stood up, nodding. Wiping his cheeks with the backs of his hands. "Tell me what you need and I'll bring it."

She told him. He left. Shana walked through the dark toward the walkers, listening to the crickets and the wind. A helicopter roared overhead, the rotors chopping the air.

Eventually, headlights bathed her anew. It was her father in his pickup as he caught back up with her, bringing the things she'd asked for: her iPhone, some food, some money, a few bottles of water, a couple changes of clothes. All in her old ratty-ass blue school backpack, which attached neatly to the roll-up sleeping bag he also brought. She asked him for one last thing:

A ride to get her closer to Nessie.

He obliged.

7

OBLIGATIONS

That's some al-Qaeda ISIS shit right there
We are straight-up under attack
                    @freedomfries11 replying to @steviemifflin

JUNE 3
The CDC, Atlanta, Georgia

THEY SAT IN SADIE'S OFFICE AND REWATCHED THE VIDEO.

Then, forwarding through it, Benji paused it as the cop was just starting to drag the man toward the car—the camera found and focused on a storefront sign:

MAKER'S BELL ANTIQUES EMPORIUM.

"Whatever this is," Benji said, "it's already happening."

"Black Swan knew."

"It knew something. But what this is . . ." The words turned to ash in his mouth. He struggled to make sense of it. "I have no idea."

"You want some tea?"

"I want something much harder than tea."

"Ah." Sadie hopped up and went around to her side of the desk. She slid open a drawer and returned with two little mini bottles of *blanco* tequila. Don Julio. "I don't have limes or salt or any of that, I'm afraid."

"Little bottles of tequila? You have a whole mini bar over there?"

She nodded "I do. Want something different? Whenever I'm on a company-funded trip, I tend to *pluck* them from the hotel room like a thief stealing apples from the king's orchard. I've got gin, vodka, brandy—no whiskey, though." She lowered her voice as if someone might be listening: "I drank all of that already."

"You have stressful days, too, eh?"

"Of course. This is the CDC."

"We have to tell Loretta."

"Now?"

"She'll still be here. She rarely goes home early." Loretta Shustack dug herself in like a fox in a hole when there was work to be done—and here, there was always work to be done. "She won't want to see me. But this . . . I have no way to explain this. She needs to know."

"Then we are off to see the wizard, aren't we?"

THE WOMAN WAS SMALL, BUT as stoic and stalwart as any: The Immovable Object earned her nickname with both her stubborn, unyielding ethics *and* the fact that she was a red belt in judo. Shustack came out of EIS, same as Benji did, then did time with the Emerging Infections Program, with a strong concentration in helping prevent and cure newborn infections. As deputy director, she was far more hands-on than the current director, Sarah Monroe.

He and Sadie entered her office. Deputy Director Shustack was in the midst of stapling forms to other forms—and when she saw him step in through her door, her hand curled tighter around the office implement.

"Deputy Director," he said. "Loretta. Hello."

"Doctor Ray." Her eyes met his and did not swerve. Nor did she let go of the stapler. Her knuckles grew bloodless. "This is a surprise."

The thought crossed his mind: *She's going to kill me with that stapler.*

"I imagine it must be. Do you know—"

"Sadie Emeka," Loretta said. "Of course."

Benji stammered: "You must be wondering—"

"Is this about Maker's Bell?" Loretta asked.

Sadie and Benji shared a look.

"It . . . is."

"We are aware of the situation, and an investigation is in process."

In her voice, a message clear as the tolling of a church bell: *Thank you, it's under control, you may go.*

Benji gave a short nod, then turned to leave—

But then, he spun back around. "I'd like to go. To be a part of the investigation." Whatever was going on there was maybe nothing, maybe it wasn't a disease at all—God, he hoped it wasn't—but whatever it was chewed at him, like an itch he couldn't reach to scratch.. "I can be a valuable asset to EIS—"

"Sadie," Loretta said, her voice as firm as her grip on that stapler. "Would you excuse us for a moment?"

She nodded. "Of course."

On the way out, she gave Benji the smallest touch—a gentle brush of a hand against his shoulder. It afforded him sudden and surprising comfort.

With Sadie gone, Loretta let loose.

"You're not EIS anymore. You're not CDC. You were let go for reasons of which I assume you remain wholly aware." Loretta leaned forward, softening her voice. She eased the stapler down on a stack of papers and made a visible effort to compose herself. "Benji, I understand your interest here. I do. I admire your curiosity and your tenacity, and whatever it is that brought you to my office today, I appreciate it. But I want you to understand that after Longacre, you would compromise the integrity of any investigation. After the lawsuits, the media, the endless accountability meetings . . . I can't do it. I like you. You were one of our best and I have little doubt you'd give this case the best of your mind. But I don't trust you."

He felt gutted. A doll slashed with scissors, its stuffing pulled inside out. The loss of trust from someone so trustworthy . . .

But he understood, too. So he forced a stiff smile and said, "Of course, Loretta. Do you mind if I ask who you have there?"

"We have Robbie Taylor there with ORT, and Martin is heading up the EIS investigation."

He nodded. ORT and EIS worked best when they were hand in hand. ORT was Outbreak Response Team. That meant Robbie and his team went onsite. Their mission was to control, contain, and ideally eliminate the disease. Benji, though, had been EIS: Epidemic Intelligence Service. He led a team—once upon a time, at least—of so-called disease detectives who looked not just for diseases before they ran through the population like wildfire, but also for new disease vectors: zoonotic jumps, undiscovered fungal activity, new bacteria, new viruses, prion diseases, and so forth.

Martin Vargas was a protégé of his, and Robbie was an old friend.

They were good people. Benji took it as a sign that things were well and truly in hand. They did not need him.

That gutted him most of all.

He thanked Loretta for her time. Apologized for interrupting. And with that, Benji left her office.

•   •   •

OUTSIDE, EVENING HAD CREPT IN. The air was finally cooling down as a breeze blew in from the north. The city lights were coming on as the blue-black bruise-dark sky settled in.

Sadie stood next to him. "I'm sorry," she said. "You know. For dragging you into all this. Into all of *that*." She gesticulated toward the CDC building and made a sour face.

"Yeah. Yes. Same." He rubbed his eyes with the heels of his hands. "Thank you. I just have to let it go. This isn't my job here anymore. Whatever's happening in Maker's Bell is . . . not my responsibility."

"And yet you want to know."

He laughed, though it was a bitter sound. "Of course I do! It's maddening. I don't know if it's that I feel I could really make a difference or . . . just that I blew the chance to." Benji made a guttural, frustrated sound: the bleat of a weary beast. "God, I'm tired."

"Do you have any luck sleeping on planes?"

"Sadly, not so much—"

He looked down, saw that she was waggling something in front of him. Two pieces of paper. Airline tickets.

ATL to ABE.

Atlanta to Allentown-Bethlehem airport.

"Sadie, what have you done?"

"I hereby christen you an employee of Benex-Voyager. Let's make up a job title here, mmm, let's see—machine intelligence and neural network beta-tester, mmm, level three. No! Level four, sounds better, but not as ego-tistical as level *five*. Good thing your bags weren't unpacked, because our flight is in . . ." She reeled the tickets back and gave them a look. "Three hours. Better get a move on, then."

He narrowed his gaze. "When did you buy these? And print these?"

"Oh, I didn't. Black Swan did. An hour before I came to your house."

"And Black Swan knew I'd come along?"

She smirked. "What can I say? I'm good at my job. I designed a very effective prediction engine." She linked her arm in his. "Now we'd better get a move on, don't you think? The mystery of Maker's Bell awaits."

8

DAWN BREAKS

Look at this photo of these 11 zombies—four of them are identifiable Antifa crisis actors. This isn't some foreign attack or some kind of outbreak. This is a leftie conspiracy in action. Stay frosty, spread the word.

Two words: fake. news.

—user KobraKommandr at r/conspiracy, answering the question, "What's the weirdest thing you've seen while alone?"

JUNE 4
Pine Grove, Pennsylvania

"SO LIKE, WHAT THE FUCK IS GOING ON HERE?" ZIG ASKED.

"I dunno," Shana said, her fingers drumming on the filthy dash of his little Honda Civic.

She'd called her friend Zig, woken him up out of a dead sleep, demanded he come hang with her. She'd told him what was happening. Said it might be the last time they hung for a while, she didn't know.

He leapt at the chance.

Because Zig liked her.

Like-liked her.

Definitely wanted to fuck her.

Maybe even *loved* her, ugh.

He didn't know she knew, but oh, *she knew.* The dude couldn't hide it. He gawked and gaped and did everything she asked (which, okay, maybe she took advantage of now and again, *sorry universe, jeez*). They DMed back and forth on Twitter, they texted, they sent funny pictures. He was always there when she wanted to bitch about someone or something. He was her best friend. So he loved her, maybe. She didn't love him back.

This was never spoken.

Zig hunched over his steering wheel—he had the long, ropy limbs of slumped-over Slenderman, a long Adrien Brody nose, and a Green Goblin chin. One day, he'd probably grow into all of it and would end up tall and dark and handsome, but right now he was a conglomeration of awkward parts put together awkwardly.

He handed over his weed pen: a vaporizer he called the Wand.

"A little magic?" he asked.

She'd asked him to bring the weed, and he did, but now when faced with it she wasn't sure. "I should stay clear."

"Shit, really? I'd think you'd wanna do the opposite."

"I dunno. Just gimme a sec." The car sat off on the shoulder of Old Route 443. Behind them, pine trees stood vigil, like the bayonets of dead soldiers stuck up out of mossy earth to mark their passing. Ahead, the hood of the car sat pointed toward the presently empty road. The sleepwalkers weren't here yet. But they were coming this way—unless they deviated, they'd arrive in ten, maybe fifteen minutes. First up, though, would be the police: They had a cop car at the front of the flock, and a cop car at the back. By now, she wondered how many there were of the walkers. Yesterday, after Mister Blamire . . . met his end, the walkers numbered only two. By midnight, another six had joined. By this morning, another three.

Possibly that number had grown. It wasn't like clockwork, not exactly. But it seemed like one arrived every couple of hours. Same nowhere stare. Same steady but urgent step.

Shana reached down, massaged her calves through her jeans. Walking all night had left her exhausted. She asked Zig: "You bring me breakfast?"

"Oh yeah," he said, spacing out. He reached into the back and grabbed a small plastic Wawa bag. She rescued three items from within it: an egg-and-cheese bagel sandwich, a greasy shingle of hash browns, and a Diet Dr Pepper.

Shana greedily ate and drank.

"Thanks," she said around a mouthful of sandwich.

"Sure." He watched her eat. "Sorry about Nessie."

"I don't want to talk about it."

"Okay."

When she finished, she found a ratty napkin in the bottom of the bag and used it to wipe the grease off her fingertips.

"Did you bring me the other thing?" she asked.

"I . . ."

"Zig. Did you?"

"Shana, I dunno."

"You dunno if you brought it?"

"I don't think it's a good idea."

She stiffened. "I need it."

"You know, I dunno what this is, Shana, but you've done enough for your family. You've already had to play mom when yours went away. Maybe it's time to just like, walk away from this. Let the cops handle it."

"I don't want the cops to handle it."

He looked down at his lap. "Dude, if my dad finds out, he'll literally kill me. He will *literally* kick my butt so hard I'll be tasting my own asshole for weeks."

"So you didn't bring it."

He sighed.

"I brought it."

"Okay. Good." She made an impatient gesture with her hands, like restive moths stirred from grass by stumbling feet. "Come on, before the cops."

Zig reached again into the backseat. He pulled out another package. This one: a brown paper bag. It tinkled as he handed it over, like the sound of dull wind chimes. Shana opened the bag.

The revolver's barrel was short, like a pig's nose. Six bullets clinked and clattered against the blued steel. Shana rolled the bag top tight, then chucked it into her backpack. "Thanks."

"Be careful."

"I'm not going to use it. It's just in case."

"Just in case of what?"

"I . . . don't know." *Just in case they try to do to my sister what they did to Mister Blamire.* "Blamire's dead, you know."

"I know."

"What's the news saying?"

"Not much yet. Just some kind of accident in Granger." He paused. "But like, social media is on it. I saw some shit on Twitter . . ."

She couldn't worry about that. People wouldn't understand this. Because none of it made any sense at all. Not to her, not to anyone. Soon, someone would come to help. Someone would come who understood.

For now, though, she was on her own.

As if on cue, she spotted the flashing lights of the police SUV down a ways. It crept slowly along. Not far behind, she knew, the sleepers walked.

"They let you get close?" Zig asked.

"Close like, near Nessie? No. Mostly I walk behind."

"How are you gonna like, sleep and go to the bathroom?"

"I dunno," she said. "I have a sleeping bag. I have a little money."

"But if you sleep, they'll keep going. How will you catch up?"

Sudden anger flared within her. "I don't know, okay? They can't walk forever. They'll have to . . . stop, or collapse in exhaustion." He opened his mouth to ask another question—one of Zig's more annoying habits was exactly that, question after question after question like he was doing a fucking BuzzFeed quiz on your behalf—but she cut him off. "It's my sister out there. Okay? I need to do this. I don't think it'll keep going. Somehow, it'll end soon." That, she said with almost zero confidence. She made that prediction only out of hope, and hope she knew had like, zero basis in reality.

"And if it doesn't?"

"Then I'll keep walking till my feet fall off."

9

THE FLY IN THE OINTMENT

President Hunt released a statement that she is quote-unquote "Aware of the situation in Maker's Bell, Pennsylvania, and is monitoring events closely." Doesn't exactly inspire confidence, does it, folks? Believe you me, she knows what this is. Maybe it's an attack by North Korea. Maybe it's something internal—we all know that both the CDC and FEMA are known rogue agencies, right? The truth will come out as long as we demand it. And this is your reminder: In November, we can pack Hunt's suitcase with a whole bunch of votes for Ed Creel.
—Hiram Golden, *The Golden Hour* podcast

JUNE 4
Pine Grove, Pennsylvania

PINE GROVE DIDN'T LOOK LIKE MUCH—JUST A SCATTERING OF OLD HOUSES, broken businesses, and trailer parks. True to its name, pine trees stood everywhere like tall, brooding sentinels. The morning had a chill to it; a dampness clung to the air.

Ahead stood the Pine Grove Diner—a little lemon-yellow building with a black-and-white-checkered band around the outside.

Sadie stood, rubbing her arms. "Your friend is late."

"He's usually late," Benji said, yawning. "He's great at what he does, but . . . less good at everything else in life. That's the trade-off."

Robbie Taylor was not a man who took good care of himself. Of course, having said that, here stood Benji, who had barely slept over the last . . . what was it now? Twenty-four hours? He'd managed some fits and starts in the rental car, and grabbed a quick hour in the motel. But he still felt like a man standing on his tiptoes at the edge of a cliff. *I'm not supposed to be here.*

There—a car came pulling in, stones popping under its tires. A white Dodge Crossover. It wheeled up fast, skidding hard on the brakes as it pulled in right next to Benji.

Robbie Taylor stepped out, looking no different than Benji remembered him: The man had a lazy, comfortable lean to him, frizzy hair pulled back with a scrunchie and sideburns like a pair of fuzzy pork chops. He was infinitely, endlessly rumpled. Like at the end of every day, he wadded himself up and piled himself on the floor.

The two men clasped hands, then pulled each other into a hug.

"My brother from another mother," Robbie said, then pulled back with one eyebrow askew. "Wait, is that racist?"

"What?"

"Calling you brother? That's racist, isn't it."

"I think technically the term is *cultural appropriation,* but don't worry, I'll give you an official Black American excuse card."

"Is that like a Monopoly *Get Out of Jail Free* card?"

"See, now you're being racist."

"Hey, whoa, I didn't mean it like that." Robbie held up both hands in surrender. He turned to Sadie and said with his hand out, "Sadie Emeka, right? I don't think we've met but—Robbie Taylor, senior ORT."

She shook it. "A pleasure. Thank you for entertaining our presence here. And"—she lowered her voice, sotto voce—"not telling Loretta."

"Yeah, when she finds out, she's gonna chew me up like Hubba Bubba bubble gum," Robbie said, "but fuck it, I'm happy to see you."

Benji laughed. The two of them had come up together in the CDC. Started the same year, eventually walked different paths—paths that converged under the umbrella of the NCEZID: the National Center for Emerging and Zoonotic Infectious Diseases. So just *seeing* Robbie again—and finding that the man didn't seem to hate him—helped ease the tension. A little.

"I'm glad Loretta put you on this," Benji said. "I expected you'd be busy, off somewhere halfway around the globe."

"I was. Kak City, this go-round." Kakata, in Liberia. "Ebola. World Health had us come in and confirm."

"False alarm?" Benji hadn't heard anything on the news.

"Fuckin' thankfully. All's quiet on the Ebola front, my friend. And with the new vaccine they're deploying, maybe we got this thing licked. You miss it?"

"Miss what?"

"This. The life. The job. Being in the shit."

"I was never like you."

"What's that mean?"

"A hot-zone worker. I was never really *in the shit.*"

"You were *literally* in the shit, don't give me that."

Benji laughed. Robbie wasn't wrong. How many times had he had to crawl through a slick cave chute of bat guano, or stomp around through pig-shit, chickenshit, monkeyshit, *human* shit?

"Fine, but nobody ever shot at me."

"Fair enough." Robbie looked at his watch. "All right, meeting starts in an hour. Let's get inside, pump black coffee straight into our fucking hearts, and get everyone up to speed."

THE INSIDE OF THE DINER was a garish mix of polished chrome and wood paneling. The fake red leather of the booths was cracked and patched with bits of tape. They sat at a big table to accommodate the upcoming meeting, and each ended up with a cup of coffee.

Benji needed it.

Robbie slapped down a report. Just a few slips of stapled paper tucked sloppily in a folder. A thin folder meant that so far, the CDC didn't know much, if anything, about what was going on here.

Together they went over the details.

At a certain point, Benji had to stop Robbie and ask: "Wait, the paramedic couldn't administer the sedative?"

"Said the needle wouldn't break the skin."

A symptom. But of what?

"Scleroderma, maybe."

Scleroderma hardened the skin—and inevitably, the internal organs—and without treatment, the autoimmune disorder could cause life-threatening complications.

"Ennh, maybe, but no visible signs. No calcinosis, no sclerodactyly, none of the capillary dilation on the skin."

Sadie jumped in and said: "Maybe the paramedic just . . . fucked up?"

"Yeah." Robbie nodded. "That's what I'm thinking. We're not exactly in a bustling metropolis here. Never know what you're going to find."

Benji leaned in over his coffee, keeping his voice low—though they didn't have anyone else sitting around them eating breakfast, he was cautious about causing any kind of panic. "What are we dealing with here, Robbie? This report . . . it started with one person, they walk, others catch the bug and join in? If this is communicable, we've never seen its like."

"I dunno, Benj, that used to be your job. I'm just here to contain it. It's your job—well, sorry, it's the job of EIS—to figure out the sheer what-the-fuckery of it. You said this . . . Black Swan predicted it?"

"That's right," Sadie said.

"And *that* means," Benji said, "there was something to presage this. Some clue that we're not seeing." Frustration mounted. He leaned back, arms crossed. His brain went over it again and again. "This can't be infectious. The symptoms—the sleepwalking, the violent seizures—that doesn't track with something communicable. And why would it only infect one person out of all those they pass? Sleep disorders, if that's what this is, don't have underlying infectious causes. You don't *catch* sleepwalking."

"Sleepwalkers also don't tend to erupt like Mount Vesuvius when you stop them from sleepwalking, Benji."

"Yes, there is that. But! Sleepwalking can have underlying *chemical* causes. Certain medications, for instance, cause somnambulism or other sleep disorders. Imagine if the walkers were all, say, drinking from the same source of water, or eating a similar food—something tainted with an anti-psychotic pharmaceutical, or maybe some new pesticide or herbicide—regulations have been watered down so much and so often, who knows what's out there?"

Robbie *tsk-tsk-tsk*ed him. "You're doing your old job, Benji. I thought you were just here to confirm the machine's prediction and then move along. Tiger can't change his stripes, huh?"

"I can't help being curious." Benji cautioned a glance toward Sadie. "And my job description here is . . . still under some negotiation. But I promise, I'll stay out of the way. I'm not here to intrude or corrupt the investigation or its reputation—"

"Nah, fuck all that. If you figure something out, I want to hear it. Your input isn't corrupt, not to me." Robbie stared off. "Because honestly, I think EIS is good, but it's not as good as it was when you were there. You always had an angle, a way of looking at things nobody else did. Like Yemen."

"Yemen?" Sadie asked.

"It was nothing," Benji said.

"Yeah, the kind of nothing that leads a guy to get a commendation from the top brass at the CDC. Benji figured out MERS-CoV."

Nearly a decade before, it was the first time they'd seen MERS-CoV, a SARS-like respiratory illness. It popped up out of nowhere in the city of Ataq. Had a 40 percent death rate. It wasn't the worst death—Ebola and other hemorrhagic fevers took that crown—but struggling for breath as your organs failed wasn't any picnic. Robbie was there as part of containment, but Benji and his team joined a WHO group to help figure out where the hell it was coming from in the first place. The SARS coronavirus was believed to come from bats, which in turn infected civet cats, from which in turn it jumped to humans in Guangdong Province in China, 2002. That led Benji to believe that MERS was similarly zoonotic. His instincts were right. It came from camels.

Specifically, camel piss.

Seeing the look of bewilderment on Sadie's face, Benji tried to explain all this, but already Robbie was laughing about it so hard he was wheezing and his eyes were shining. Benji chuckled, too, but waved his hands in the air as a caution.

"Hey, hey, it's not funny—"

"We had to tell them not to drink *camel piss,* Benji."

"Okay, but let's remember, it was a Bedouin and Yemeni folk cure with some real truth behind it. Those researchers out of Jeddah found that camel urine contained PMF701—camel milk, too. Nanobots have pulled out those particles and found that they help to fight both cancer and some skin conditions."

Turned out, that was where MERS came from.

"I'm not—" Robbie coughed, clearing his throat and still laughing. He wiped his eyes. "I'm not making fun of them drinking urine—I mean, okay, I am a little bit, because holy shit can you imagine? Jesus, fuck, the taste. But no, I'm thinking about the, the goddamn—" And the laughs started up again, uncontrollable guffaws like from someone trying not to laugh in church or at a funeral. "I'm thinking about the posters. The fucking posters!"

The posters.

Oh shit, *the posters.*

The World Health Organization had started an educational campaign that plastered the Arabian Peninsula with posters that told people why it was a bad idea to drink camel piss. Robbie said, still wheezing, "The little cartoon cutout camel with the—the little pee-pee bullets coming down into a glass. Like, 'Oh, excuse me, I'm just going to put this empty glass under this camel dick and serve me up a nice frothy pint.' Oh God, Jesus. What a fucking life."

Benji nodded, smiling. "What a life."

But the smile felt hollow. The posters *were* funny; Robbie wasn't wrong. Just the same, cultural practices around the world were tricky—you wanted to be respectful, you wanted to help preserve and protect ways of life, but when they became vectors for emerging diseases, you had to deal with it.

Bushmeat, for instance, in Africa. Poachers and hunters killed Old World primates, elephants, pygmy hippos—and three-quarters of emergent diseases were zoonotic. A clumsy hunter or inelegant butcher found himself covered in an animal's blood, spinal fluid, spit, shit, semen, and once in a while an infection in the animal found the *biological gumption* to leapfrog to the person. Then the hope became that the person couldn't infect others.

So you tried, best as you could, to stop any of that from happening in the first place.

And yet what could you do? Culture was culture, and money was money. Ways of life were hard to change. Benji remembered being on a hunt with a Congolese man who killed so many macaques in a day, he looked like he had a whole extended family of them on his back. That hunter, Mateso, said, "If it moves, we eat it. We learned that in the war. You eat grubs, you eat rats, you eat anything that crawls in the grass or climbs in the trees." He said he could sell one monkey carcass at the market for seven thousand Congolese francs—around five bucks, American.

It was part of their culture, and people needed to eat. So you did what you could do. You helped to educate. You taught hunters how to be clean. You helped them learn to test the blood of their kills. You tried to steer them away from endangered species or certain primary vectors—and then you hoped that the rest of the system held true: that the economy improved, that farming practices took hold, some fire-eyed dictator or warlord wasn't in place a year later. You did what you could and held faith that it would get better. Sometimes it did. A lot of times, it didn't.

And a lot of times, Benji thought, *systems stay in place to help make sure that nothing changes, even when it needs to.*

His mind drifted momentarily again to Longacre.

Those pigs.

Their stalls.

Sores all over . . .

No. That was not a productive line of thinking.

"Maybe there's something to Yemen," Benji said. "Something cultural that can help us here. Maybe it's something zoonotic. Do they eat something here? Something they shouldn't? A local culture of . . . I don't know, hunting and killing raccoons, or possum? Could be a niche vector we're not seeing."

"Well, you can ask our friends yourself. Because here we go." Robbie juggled a thumb toward the window. Outside in the line, they saw two cars pull into the diner lot: one white SUV, a Tahoe. The other, a black Town Car.

FROM THE SUV, A MAN stepped out in state trooper grays—an old white guy with too-tight skin stretched across his skull and a little white mustache like a line of salt on his lip. From the Town Car emerged a woman: tall, lean, heels, red hair in a humid, hurried tangle.

The two walked across the ragged gravel parking lot toward the diner. They came in and the woman introduced herself as Harriet French from the Office of Public Liaison, here at the behest of Governor Randazzo. The older gentleman was Doug Pett, deputy commissioner of operations for the Pennsylvania State Troopers.

With minimal pleasantries, they got right into it.

"We're pushing for quarantine and isolation," French said.

"Under what authority?" Benji asked, and realized immediately he was stepping outside the bounds. He winced.

"Disease Prevention and Control Law of 1955, recently re-ratified in 2011 under then-governor Lincoln. Governor Randazzo has the utmost safety of the citizens of Pennsylvania at the top of his mind—"

"Bullshit," Robbie said. "Excuse my French, Miss French, but Randazzo has politics at the top of his mind, not people--"

"Excuse him, really, apologies," Benji said, forcing a wan smile. He shot Robbie a look, then turned back to Harriet French. "Harriet, I think what Robbie is trying to say is that he doesn't quite see your justification as yet—we have not confirmed what this is, and quarantine requires a legal obligation to understand what it is before enacted—"

"I'm sorry, who are you again?" Harriet asked. "You didn't say you're with the CDC."

"I'm with, ahhh—"

Sadie jumped in: "He's with Benex-Voyager. We're a technology company whose function is to predict these kinds of outbreaks—"

"Outbreaks? Is that what we're calling it?" French's brow darkened. "Doctor Ray, it seems you're stepping outside your field of knowledge. Trust me when I say, our lawyers interpret the law fairly: If patients are suspected to have a communicable disease like tuberculosis, we can opt them into quarantine—"

"Not without their consent," Robbie objected.

"We can opt them into quarantine," she said, her words barging forward, "and in the *event* that the patient refuses to consent to testing for any of those illnesses, that quarantine can be enforced—"

"They *can't* consent," Benji interjected forcefully. "They're sleepwalking—"

"Precisely. That gives us legal justification."

"We're just trying to get ahead of this thing, boys," Doug Pett said, staring them down with those deep socket eyes. "Isn't that what you . . . doctor-types promote? Preventive medicine? You wouldn't let Ebola run wild up in here. You'd be on that like maggots on roadkill."

"This is not Ebola," Benji said.

"Yeah," Robbie said. "You know how we know it's not Ebola? *Because nobody is shitting blood out their eyeballs.* I've been up close and personal with it, and it's a mess. Bloody gums, loose bowels, rash everywhere. By day ten of that disease, the bleeding inside is so massive it comes out of every part of you. This ain't that."

Pett leaned forward. "And yet, sounds like what happened to that teacher, Blamire."

"That's not—no, that's not what happened to him. We don't *know* what happened to him."

"That instills us with little confidence," French snapped.

Benji offered both hands in a placating gesture. "That is how science and medicine are practiced best, though—we are best when we admit our ignorance up front, and then attempt to fill the darkness of not-knowing with the light of information and knowledge."

"That was very poetic," Robbie said.

"It's also not how *politics* works," French bit back. "Politics doesn't like big question marks. *Voters* like answers up front, out of the gate."

"See?" Robbie said, sneering. "Reelection campaign."

"We are accountable to the people of this state."

"And those people walking *are* the people of your state," Benji said. He felt his frustration rising. His *anger,* too. He knew he should shut his mouth but he kept on opening it and words kept on coming out of it: "The difficulty in containing them in a proper quarantine is the same difficulty Officer Kyle had containing Mark Blamire."

"Kyle was one of mine," Pett said, scowling. "A statie."

"And I'd like to speak to him when he's able," Benji added. *This is not your job,* he thought, repeating it like a mantra. *This is not your job.*

"Can't." Benji shot him a confused look, and then Pett said: "Kyle died two hours ago in the hospital."

Benji and Robbie looked to each other. Benji shook his head. "I'm . . . so sorry. I didn't know." His clinical mind quickly pushed past any sense of sorrow or dread and thought: *That will make it easier to test him for any infectious agents.* But then, following that, a sudden feeling of crushing pressure: There was so much to do, and Benji had little to no authority to do it.

That would be fine if this were something known.

But whatever they were dealing with had no analog he could see.

It was rare to come upon something *truly new* in the epidemiological world: Even the manifestation of a "new" disease was something that piggybacked *off* or mutated *from* a preexisting one. Flu was flu. A hemorrhagic fever was a hemorrhagic fever. They had no idea what this was, where it began, or what it could do. And thus the true danger of a brand-new pandemic became overwhelmingly clear: Act too slow, it could take over. By the time they figured out what it was, it could have raced through the population. Alternatively, act too fast, too rashly, and there were legal consequences: They did not have broad, sweeping powers, and for good reason. Had to be a balance between measured investigation and swift action, or else they'd be either in a full-blown pandemic or locking people up in camps.

Good news, at least: This disease, if it even was one, seemed to operate slowly, though without sensible, easy-to-discern logistics. Again he thought a chemical origin was likely. Or a parasite.

He kept that one in the back of his mind: *parasite.* Hm. Something to that. The way parasites hijacked hosts and commanded them to actions that served those parasites more than the hosts . . . that deserved deeper thought . . .

Robbie said what Benji was thinking: "We don't know what's causing this, so that's priority one for EIS. My team's priority—"

"Could be terrorists," Pett interjected.

"What?"

"Terrorists. Don't wanna rule them out. I got a buddy in Homeland Security. Once HomeSec catches wind of this—"

"It's not—it's not fucking terrorists, with all due respect."

Pett snarled, "Funny how people always say *with all due respect* just after they disrespected the hell out of you."

"It's not terrorists," Benji said, trying to keep everyone calm.

Harriet French, now, was on her smartphone, her fingers working to type something in. The phone vibrated now and again. A look of consternation and disgust drew lines on her face.

"Better hope not. We find out it is, then the solution isn't quarantine. The solution is a bullet for each of those walkers." Said like they were zombies in zombie films. Said like they weren't humans, but targets. Benji could not stomach that kind of talk.

"You sonofabitch. These are *people*," Benji began, but Robbie interrupted him—suddenly, Robbie was the calm one. A strange, if necessary, reversal.

"Hey, hey, whoa, listen, my team's priority, like I said, is to control and contain this thing on the ground while EIS plays disease detective. So what I propose is a loose, roving isolation—not too different from what you've got set up now. We keep new people from coming close. We keep the sleepwalkers together—and anyone who has been in close proximity to them should submit to hospital isolation. It means I'll need to work with you and your troopers in close coordination, Commissioner Pett. That sound good? Doug? Harriet? Anybody?"

Harriet set her phone down and looked up from it. Her stare pinned Benji to his seat. "*You*. I thought I remembered your name. Longacre. North Carolina. You're the one who conjured that whole witch hunt and based on what? Nothing." Torchlight flickered in her eyes as she said, "I had stock in that company. I lost money. A lot of people did."

"I'm sorry," Benji started to say—

French stood up suddenly, and Pett joined her. To Robbie she said, "I'll pass your plan to the governor and on through to the Department of Health. It's a start, but I warn you: If we decide that a forced stationary isolation is necessary, we will overrule you on this." And they could, Benji knew. The CDC had jurisdiction only when it became a federal matter—and that meant getting the secretary of Health and Human Services involved. They were not there yet, but if they had to rope in Secretary Flores, they would in order to do this right. To Benji she said: "As for you? You're a disgrace, and I intend to file a complaint. Your presence here is trouble."

And with that, they got up and stormed out.

"So, that went well," Robbie said.

The two of them stood out in front of the diner. Sadie was still inside, paying the bill.

"I shouldn't have come," Benji said. "It was a mistake. It just felt like . . . like old times, like settling into an old chair. Far too comfortable. I've compromised everything and I only just got here. Longacre. Damnit."

"Real-talk? What you did with Longacre was fucking stupid. And it was wrong. But I get it, too. You weren't *right,* but also . . . nnyeah, you were kinda right. I don't blame you. Others might; I'm not them. But I won't crucify you for that lapse in judgment."

"It wasn't just a lapse in judgment."

It was, Benji knew, premeditated. It was nothing short of a conspiracy. A small conspiracy, really, shared by one man and with no other. But what he saw there at Longacre that day . . .

He could pinpoint the moment, even now, that it had happened. Standing there, smelling the smell of piss and shit and sickness, the urine brining the hay under his feet, the animals crammed together in stalls too small for one or two pigs much less the dozen they held. Then there were the gestation crates where the sows were held, and the farrowing crates where piglets fed at the mothers—before being taken away and thrown in with their brothers and sisters. It wasn't just that the animals weren't treated well—Benji recognized that though one could bring some humaneness to killing an animal, killing was still killing, and doing so to feed the hungers of a massive, meat-eating civilization meant it became a tireless, never-ending slaughter. Mechanized and soulless. That was bad enough.

Worse was the potential for disease.

Already the pigs there were overfed using food supplemented with antibiotics, and still their sores and abscesses remained. Already there were strong causal links between antibiotic-resistant MRSA and factory pig farms. *Already* there were signs of evolving leptospirosis infections . . .

And this was the biggest factory farm in the nation.

It was a cauldron of disease waiting to spill over.

Something would emerge from this slurry of malnutrition and ill treatment, he knew. A superbug without bounds. An unstoppable flu. A pandemic would rise.

It was one line between two dots: This was a prediction a *child* could make.

Only problem: He had nothing actionable. Benji could make some recommendations, and Longacre would follow them or they wouldn't, and it would take years to follow up—and they would get their lobbyists to curry protection from the politicians, and the system would defend them while they were quietly, unwittingly, brewing the next pandemic.

Benji made a choice.

He submitted a report. He leaked it to the public.

And that report contained made-up numbers.

It contained evidence of MRSA in far larger quantities, using data stolen from a WHO report on Canadian hog farms ten years ago.

This act was, he told himself at the time, for the greater good. Forcing the pig farm to be accountable meant potentially heading off a major disaster. It was the only way anyone would listen. And they did listen, to his surprise. Longacre's stock prices plummeted. People stopped buying their pork from stores—and pork from other brands. Pork stopped being *the other white meat* and became *the way we all die.*

And then the industry hired investigators. And lawyers. And together they found out what Benji had done. They found the cribbed numbers, the data, the replicated samples.

He was lucky, in a way, that the worst that happened was his firing. The CDC took the brunt of it. He still got a severance package.

But his name became synonymous with a special kind of governmental overreach—a sense that the government would twist the numbers and force the data to tell a different story than the truth in order to fulfill some hazy agenda. The blame went up from him to the CDC to President Hunt herself (already a magnet attracting responsibility for problems that were not her fault). It gave the government less agency, not more. He did more harm to the mission than to anything else.

"Whatever with that shit," Robbie said. "You're here. We'll figure it out. Just, uhh. Stay more in the background, would you?"

With that, Sadie came out of the restaurant. She was wearing her best smile, like none of what had happened in there fazed her one little bit.

"Any sense of the reception I'm going to get from the rest of EIS?" Benji asked his old friend.

Robbie shrugged. "Can't say, Benj. That is a bandage you're just gonna have to rip off to see how badly it bleeds. Speaking of which: You wanna get a first look at the sleepwalkers?"

"Let's," Sadie said, jingling her keys.

SOME SECRET PURPOSE

Sleepwalking—also known as somnambulism—is a sleep disorder that of-
ten arises during deep sleep and results in a display of motor skills, which
can include walking, but may also involve other behaviors, from the simple
(sitting up in bed and looking around) to the complex (going to the bath-
room, and using a dry razor to shave one's face). Use of certain drugs can
increase the likelihood of somnambulism (Ambien is a known cause). Most
sleepwalkers remember nothing about the events during their actions, as
they are in deep sleep. This also makes them difficult to wake, but contrary
to popular myth, sleepwalkers should be woken during any somnambulist
activity to prevent potential injury or embarrassment.

—from an NSDC (National Sleep Disorder Center) pamphlet

JUNE 4
Pine Grove, Pennsylvania

ROUTE 443 WAS A RICKETY, CRATER-MARKED TWO-LANE ROAD WITH A FADED
line down the center. Across the street was an open, fallow field and a long
gravel parking lot for a nursery and greenhouse, which had been closed up
since the CDC took over. Behind Benji a tent and a mobile laboratory orbited
a flurry of activity: police officers, Robbie's ORT team, some lab techs. But
that wasn't what Benji was watching.

No, he kept his eye down the highway.

Because *they* were coming.

Sadie stood next to him, watching him as much as she watched the road,
like she was trying to gauge reality through his reaction to it.

Fine, let her look.

There, down the road, around the bend of the highway, came the first sign: a cop car driving ahead at a slow crawl. He knew these sleepwalkers were framed by police escorts, both to keep the walkers contained and to keep people or traffic from getting close.

Behind the car, the sleepwalkers followed.

Benji wasn't much for movies or TV, but he had a soft spot for zombie films—especially the ones that treated the zombie apocalypse as something more biological than supernatural. Biology had at its core a keen and singular horror that made all the bogeyman stuff as scary as a preschool playroom. Infectious diseases alone offered a host of terrors for one's fear to endlessly feast upon.

Rabies, for instance, delivered unto Benji a perfect example of that horror: An infected patient who failed to get the proper shots endured a bad, slow death. You went mad. You became afraid of water. You hallucinated wildly. After a week or two, a coma took you as the rabies *Lyssavirus* swarmed the brain. Benji knew of a case where a hunter shot a raccoon, not knowing it was rabid. He dispatched it with a head shot, then discarded the body—problem was, the hunter didn't know that a *little bit of brain matter* ended up on his hands. How it got in his mouth, who knows? Maybe he wiped his face or his nose. Maybe he grabbed a piece of jerky from his backpack but didn't wash his hand. Either way, he ate a bit of the brain, and with it a bit of the virus. The virus went dormant for a couple of months—and then it rose in him, wild like a winged demon, the shadow cast over his mind long and black.

He was dead in seven days.

Before he went into the coma, he screamed about the faces he saw in the walls, faces of people he knew who'd died and "gone to hell."

Rabies was a horror movie, but in real life.

It changed your behavior, ruined your mind, and you could catch it by eating brains—well, there was the seed of both the werewolf myth *and* the zombie myth.

Seeing the sleepwalkers was like that, at least a little. Benji did a quick count—they numbered a lucky thirteen. This was his first time looking upon them, and seeing their eyes—he shuddered at their flat, flinty stares. Gazing off at nothing. Or if they were looking at something (or *for* something), Benji couldn't see what it was. That was left only to them to see, or to seek.

But they weren't like the undead in ways that mattered. They walked forward with a steady step: This was no foot-dragging shamble, no scrape-and-stumble. They stood up straight. Their jaws were set tight in grim determination. A whiff of *Village of the Damned* crawled in: Those creepy kids had the same piercing glare, didn't they?

I'm a doctor. I am a man of science. I shouldn't be comparing these people to movie monsters. And that was the key, wasn't it? These were *people*. At the fore of the flock, a teenage girl, then a young woman, and farther down the line: a farmer in overalls, a middle-aged woman in a business suit, a teenage boy, a paunchy man in a pink bathrobe, an older woman down to her bra and panties, a young man in headphones with the wire dragging behind him and the plug juddering on the asphalt like a hopping cricket, on and on they came, different ages, a roughly equal split between men and women, a surprising mix of skin colors for a rural part of Pennsylvania. Benji didn't know what any of it meant.

Again he returned to the idea:

They're walking with purpose.

But what purpose? Why? Was this a disease?

Or was it something bigger, something far stranger?

He didn't know.

But the uncertainty punched a hole clean through him.

"You still think this is a disease?" he asked Sadie.

"I don't think anything. I write programs, remember?"

"Black Swan seems to think it is."

"Black Swan asked for you, but beyond that, I don't know what it's thinking. But it's seen something here. And it wants to find out what it is."

TOGETHER HE AND SADIE WALKED through the chaos to the tent. Off to the side, Robbie prepped his ORT team, getting them into their protective suits.

He recognized those faces: six people, all of whom traveled with Taylor and were instinctively loyal to him. They had been in some of the world's most dire conflict zones together. They'd literally taken fire. Avigail Danziger, an ex–Israeli ER doctor, took a bullet in Liberia *and kept on working.* Remy Cordova, a former army minister (of all things), fell down a ravine in Sierra Leone, broke both ankles, and impaled himself on the branch of some brittle, dead savanna tree. He was alone. He pulled himself up off the branch (which had gone in through his side, damaging a kidney), then tried to find his way out of the ravine while, according to him, a *leopard* hunted him for food. He was gone for three days.

He did not die.

The others in Robbie's team had all gone through various gauntlets: broken bones, rare diseases, animal bites, parasitic infections.

Robbie's team: ever the lunatics and badasses. Not necessarily typical for ORT, either: Most ORT members were domestic and investigated foodborne and flu.

But Robbie's team was both legacy and legend.

EIS, when Benji headed a team, was different. Eggheads, disease detectives, more Sherlock Holmes than Lethal Weapon.

Even now, as he stood outside the powder-blue tent, he heard the familiar voice of his protégé, Martin Vargas, prepping the team.

Benji's team.

Once upon a time, anyway.

Quietly, he and Sadie slipped in through the back of the tent, underneath a flap. Half a dozen lab techs and CDC workers were here, standing, listening to Vargas talk.

Vargas, late thirties, had a square-jawed chin and smoldering, campfire eyes. He looked older, wiser than he was—handsomeness radiated from him in a timeless George Clooney way. When Benji left the CDC, Vargas was an eternal bachelor, going from relationship to relationship like a bee pollinating a whole meadow of flowers. Benji wondered if the promotion had changed his perspective. Would Vargas ever settle down? Or would he remain everfickle?

Martin was saying: ". . . get me information I didn't even know that I needed. Health records, water quality, air quality, demographics, something, anything. What don't I know about this area? Is there a factory poisoning the water table with its runoff? Any new invasive species in the area? A wildlife survey has some value, so let's talk to local game wardens and wildlife rehabilitators, see if there's anything there—"

"We don't have enough people," Cassie said, in a singsongy voice.

"We *never* have enough people," Martin answered, also in song.

Cassie Tran: another EIS detective from his old team. Clad in a ratty Beastie Boys shirt, she had a rangy, long-limbed, coyote vibe. Half scavenger, half trickster, all punk. Her hair was a mermaid ombre in a waterfall down her back. Cassie had an expressive, almost elastic face. Her eye rolls were so vigorous they could knock satellites out of orbit. Her smile was sure to melt glaciers.

Martin continued: "While we're at it, I wanna see instances of tick-borne disease in this area. Lyme and Rocky Mountain spotted fever in particular.

Maybe call some exterminators, see what they have to say about mice populations. Or call some local tree people or botanists—ask about last year, see
if there was an acorn mast."

Benji nodded to himself. Smart. Ecologists and epidemiologists had recently come to realize that the number of acorns on the ground was an indicator of how severe Lyme would be in the region the following season.
Some years trees produced few acorns, other years bumper crops. Big acorn
deposits—a "mast year"—meant an increase in mice, and contrary to their
name, deer ticks *loved* mice. A single mouse could have dozens of ticks on its
face and body, and the mouse could transmit Lyme to those ticks. A surge in
acorns meant a surge in mice. And a surge in mice meant the Lyme numbers
went up, up, up.

"I'm picking up what you're laying down," Cassie said. "Rocky Mountain
can inflict certain sleep disorders. At acute stages in dogs, we start to see
strange behaviors, too: stupor, restlessness, seizures. Some edema." Benji
suddenly wondered if fluid accumulation could lead to the . . . rupture, as
with Blamire. Seemed like an overreach, but not enough to rule it out. Should
he go to them and mention it? *I'd better not . . .*

A young man Benji didn't know—maybe in his midtwenties—eagerly
stepped up. His slicked-back raven-black hair was so shiny and so perfect it
might as well have been a plastic wig like you'd snap onto a Lego figure. He
was as buttoned-up as his tartan-patterned shirt. "I can check with botanists," the young man said.

"No, Arav," Martin answered. "I'll need you as a liaison to Robbie Taylor's
ORT team."

"I want to do a good job, so point me where you want me to go and I'll
go," the young man—Arav—said. "But to remind you, I'm . . . not certified
yet for Level A PPE suits and—"

"Shit," Martin said. He briefly massaged his temples with his thumbs,
then moved the massage down his jawline. "That's fine. You won't go in the
field with them, then, but you will work with them here. Help them set up
the mobile lab and make sure we are informed of their discoveries and they're
informed of ours. But next opportunity: *Get certified*. Oh, and I need you to
start a list. I need to know who these sleepwalkers are. I need . . . everything
and anything you can get, that includes names, addresses, Social Security
numbers. It won't be easy because they obviously do not speak, but see what
you can do. Perhaps some of them have identification on them. Work with
Robbie's team on that one."

Arav nodded. "You got it, but maybe I could borrow a few techs—"

"We can help with data collection."

That voice came from someone unexpected.

It came from Sadie.

Benji shot her a look. She didn't return it.

All eyes in the room turned toward them. All the gathered lab techs turned to see who was talking. Martin, Cassie, and Arav looked, too.

Then they saw Benji.

Cassie, for her part, looked delighted. A big Pac-Man smile cut her face in half, and she threw up a pair of devil's horns. She mouthed his name—*Benji!*—and winked.

Martin did not share in her delight.

"Doctor Ray," Martin said. "And . . . whoever you are."

"Sadie Emeka," she said. "We're here on behalf of Benex-Voyager, ready to assist with data collection and analysis. The Black Swan module—"

"Get out," Martin said.

"Come on," Benji said quietly to Sadie. "We should go."

"No," she protested. Raising her voice louder, she said: "We can help you. You need help. This is something you don't understand. Something *new*. You need all the help you can get and—"

"I said, get out."

"Right." She stiffened. "Okay, then."

She and Benji left the tent.

BY NOW THE SLEEPWALKERS HAD already passed—though Benji could still see them, and the police cruiser that followed them, a quarter mile or more down Route 443, disappearing between a gauntlet of dead or dying ash trees. *Ash borer,* Benji thought idly. An invasive bug. Killing wide swaths of ash trees here in the Northeast.

"That fucking prick," Sadie seethed.

"It's all right, Sadie." He'd expected anger, or shame, or some caustic mix of the two. But suddenly, those were gone. He felt eerily alone, yes, but also at peace with it. "What I did, I did. I'm just not welcome."

"You bloody well should be. You're an expert. Probably more of an expert than any of *them*. They don't want our help, we'll commit to our own investigation, we'll use Black Swan and—"

The tent flap ruffled behind them. In a flash of movement, Cassie stormed out and made a bullet's line toward Benji. She swept upon him and wrapped her long arms around him in the manner of a face-hugger Xeno-morph baby from *Alien*. "Dude, it is fucking *awesome* to see you again," she said, still squeezing him. Finally releasing him from the hug, she asked: "The hell are you doing here? Did Loretta the Unswerving, the Unyielding, the Ever-Stubborn actually . . . ask for your help?"

"Ennnh," he said, waving the flat of his hand back and forth. "Not . . . so much, no. We're here on our own."

Mischievous madness flashed in Cassie's eyes. "Gone rogue. Couldn't stay away. I like it. *I like it.* C'mon." She hooked her hand around his elbow, and started dragging him toward a car.

"I'm sorry, where are we going?" he asked.

"I've got to interview the Exploding Man's wife and you're coming with me. *You,* though—" Cassie spun, pointing her index and pinkie fingers in a pair of bull horns at Sadie. "—can stay here. I'll bring him back, don't worry, lady."

Sadie started to protest, but Benji held out a surrendering hand. "Sadie, it's all right. Cassie is a bit . . . territorial."

"Like a fucking wolverine," the tall woman said, baring her teeth.

"I'll . . . work on some data collection," Sadie said, not without some re-sentment and suspicion.

He mouthed *thank you* to her, and then was again swept up in Cassie's tornado as they crossed the parking lot. "Did Martin tell you to bring me?"

"Nope," she said.

"Gone rogue." He grinned. "I like it."

11

THE EXPLODED MAN'S WIFE

Top 5 Items at Nu-Rish Lifestyle Products, from celebrity actress and entrepreneur Lanie Davies:

> 1. *Lapis Lazuli Vaginal Yoni Moon-Egg*
>
> 2. *Luxe Cashew Water Colonic Kit*
>
> 3. *Ayurvedic Moringa Smoothie Powder*
>
> 4. *Kambo Frog Venom Supercleanse Antibiotic Salve*
>
> 5. *Cordyceps Cloud Powder (Sex Power Flavor)*

JUNE 4
Maker's Bell, Pennsylvania

SAYING THAT CASSIE TRAN HAD A COFFEE HABIT WAS LIKE SAYING FISH HAD A water habit. Here in the rental car, Benji saw the artifacts of half a dozen coffees lying about: Dunkin' cups, La Colombe draft lattes, an Aeropress, a bag of beans, and a little hand-crank grinder. And the way she spoke reflected it, too, her conversation coming so fast that words at the *back* of each sentence struggled to get ahead of the words at the *front*.

"I'm thinking it's not infectious. I mean—" She made a Vanna White prize-reveal gesture toward the windshield and, by proxy, the world. "Better safe than sorry, obviously. But looking at the reports, these people are . . . 'catching' the disease in their own homes. Pretty erratic transmission pattern and nothing on the books looks like this. Nothing! It's too measured, too pretty, and as you well know, disease is *not* pretty. It's just chaos. Chaos with rules, but chaos just the same." She gunned the Hyundai Sonata down the back roads like scissors slicing ribbon.

"I agree. It's environmental, I'd guess. In the water table, maybe, or some . . . shared product use between houses."

"That's what we'll find out when you interview Blamire's wife."

"When *I* interview her?"

"Uh-huh."

"Cassie, I'll observe, nothing more."

"Pssh, you know me. I'm just Missy Mouthfart over here. This lady's husband just died. He died because he fucking *exploded* like an egg in the microwave. I come out of veterinary, man. I have the bedside manner of a weed-whacker." Benji had to admit her point. Though Martin Vargas came out of diagnostic medicine at U Penn, Cassie was an Atlanta-area veterinary specialist and virologist who before joining EIS did a stint with Merck as part of their animal health division. She was damn good at her job, as long as her job didn't include talking to other humans. She was as ungentle as a castration band.

"Don't tell Martin," he said.

"I promise not to tell Martin."

BENJI AND CASSIE SAT ACROSS the table from Mark Blamire's wife, Nancy. *Nance,* she said, doing that thing grieving people do sometimes: She laughed a little, a reflex reaction that felt hollow because it was her mind trying to force her to be normal, to pretend that her husband was *not* dead in bizarre, uncertain circumstances. Benji saw it at funerals: a grieving spouse washing the dishes, a child playing on the swing set outside, a brother pausing to turn on the TV to get the score for a game. Some thought it rude, and in some cases, that's what it was: shitty people being shitty. But a lot of the time, it was a defense mechanism. The act of holding on tight to the staircase railing as a tornado ripped your house apart.

Nancy—Nance—was barely holding it together.

She was also, to Benji's shock, pregnant.

About six months, by the look of her. One hand rested atop her belly as she sat across from him at their breakfast nook. Wraiths of steam rose from a cup of tea curled in the curve of her other hand, though she hadn't yet taken a sip. Benji had a cup of his own. Chamomile.

"I need you to tell me what happened," Benji said. "How it began."

"I . . ." Nance started, her mouth working soundlessly to summon the memory and to find the words that would explain it. Her gaze was not unlike that of the sleepwalkers: She looked through them, through the wall, through all of space and time and corporeal matter, to a place beyond it all.

"Did he just get up and walk out?" Benji asked, trying to—gently!—jump-start the conversation and her memory of yesterday's events.

"He, ahh. We'd been up for a few hours. We're both teachers and . . . and school is out now, out for the summer as of last week. Normally we might still be in school at this point in the year but the winter was warm and we, uh, we didn't have any snow days. Global warming, I guess. We were already awake but mostly just . . . you know, puttering around. He put on his jeans but hadn't changed the T-shirt he was wearing and we both headed downstairs. I started breakfast while he checked his phone, read the news—election stuff, we're pretty liberal even though the area really isn't. And . . ." Her eyes shone with the threat of tears. "I heard a sound, a thump. He'd dropped his phone. It fell out of his hand to the floor. And I said, sweetheart, your phone—and I remember he just, he just turned to me with this strange look on his face like he . . ." And now the river broke the dam as tears ran down her cheeks in twin rivulets. "Like he didn't recognize me at all. Then he stood up and there was this lift to his chin, like he was smelling for something, the way a dog does when he's caught a scent."

"Did he leave the house then?" Cassie asked.

"I . . . no, I don't know. My phone rang, but it was upstairs. I asked Mark if he was all right, and he was still standing there. I rolled my eyes thinking he was messing with me, because sometimes he did that. I told him to stop being weird and then I ran upstairs to get my phone. It was another teacher, Pauline Strahovsky, nothing important, she was just telling us that they moved the CFPO seminar—the Collaboration for Positive Outcomes class—from the Pensky building to the Troxell building on campus. We talked for a few minutes and when I went downstairs . . ."

Nancy Blamire shuddered.

"Mark was gone. And I didn't know where. His phone was still on the floor." She put the tea back onto the table without having taken a sip. "I ran outside looking for him but I didn't have my shoes on, like I said, it was early . . . so . . ."

"Did you put on shoes, go look for him?"

"Not at first. I thought maybe he was taking the compost out. By the time I did, I didn't know where to look. Our house is the corner property and

he could've gone . . . anywhere, including into the wetlands behind the back-
yard. I waited awhile and then I took a drive down Maple and didn't see
him—so I came back, and that's when I called the police. But they didn't
want to do anything, not yet—"

"Missing persons cases don't trigger until they're gone twenty-four hours."
Unless the missing person is a child, Benji thought. And Mark Blamire was
not.

"Yeah."

Cassie leaned in. "Did Mark eat any weird shit? Any funky trendy diet
things, any strange foods?"

Nancy seemed to flinch at Cassie's brusqueness. "No. Like I said, I was
making breakfast but he hadn't even eaten any yet. Eggs and sausage, by the
way. The breakfast. I would've made toast at the end but . . ." She visibly
swallowed, then wiped her eyes, blew her nose.

"How's your water?"

"My water?" She looked down at her belly.

"Sorry, your drinking water."

"Oh. It's fine. We have it tested, if that's what you mean. I don't understand—"

"Comes from a well?"

"Yes."

"It's filtered, the water?"

"We have a UV filter, a whole-house filter, and a fridge filter."

Filtered three times, Benji thought. *Should be good enough.* Just the same,
he reminded himself to have their water tested. Soil, too. And the contents
of their refrigerator and an air sample and . . .

"You're with the CDC, so are you saying Mark was sick?"

He tried to offer a consolatory smile. "I can't say, Mrs. Blamire, that's
why we're here. Has your husband been bitten by a tick recently? To your
knowledge, at least."

"I . . . what? No. Not that I know of. We get ticks here, though. The little
ones, the deer ticks, and the bigger ones, whatever they are?"

"Dog ticks, probably."

"Was this Lyme? I heard it was bad but not like this—"

"Again, I don't know. What I'm trying to do is establish a baseline of information, something that lets us find an avenue of investigation and exhaust
it." The task ahead loomed suddenly overwhelming, like they were given a
knife and fork and told to go eat that elephant over there. He steadied him-

self. *One bite at a time,* he thought. "Mrs. Blamire, on the off-chance that Mark's peculiar behavior and unfortunate demise were in some way related to an illness, that leaves open the possibility that it was an infectious disease. And that means—"

"It means you could be sick, too," Cassie said.

Nancy tightened up. She looked as if she'd just been kicked off her chair. "Sick? I'm pregnant. I have a baby inside me, a little girl, I . . ."

"We can call an ambulance for you," Benji said. "They will, with your permission, take you to a hospital to run some tests. Nothing invasive, you're in no danger. Hopefully you will be back in your bed by tonight, but in the meantime, we need you in relative isolation just in case. Would you like to go pack a bag? We have time. Alternatively, if you would rather call a relative to do that—?"

"I . . . I can pack a bag. Now?"

He nodded. "If you don't mind."

Nancy had lost her struggle for normalcy. She stood, no smile, not much of anything, and moved past him to head upstairs.

Benji breathed a sigh of relief. She wasn't going to fight them. He wondered if others would be so conciliatory. This would soon have to happen elsewhere—until they could rule out this being infectious, it meant that those who had been in contact with the sleepwalkers would need to submit to temporary isolation and testing. He feared suddenly that the quarantine plan of Harriet French and Doug Pett would yet need to be implemented— but to do that, they'd need federal intervention, and oh, that's right, *he didn't even work there anymore.* None of this was his business, or his job, and Vargas had made that eminently clear.

But ego suddenly arose in him—the same ego that had drawn up big and blustery that day at Longacre. They *needed* him. Or was it that *he* needed *this*? Just the same, the threat of whatever this was loomed large, and he desperately wanted to rise to meet it. They didn't have identifications for most of the walkers, yet. Didn't know where they came from, or who they talked to. It was easy for a disease, once out into the world, to spread like fire through fields of dead grass. A little voice inside Benji told him: *If you don't chase this fire with the extinguisher, if you don't find out how it started, it'll be too late.*

Cassie's phone rang as Benji heard drawers opening and closing upstairs. She tilted the phone toward him—the caller ID read, MARTIN VARGAS. She answered it, popped it on speakerphone with a playful shrug.

Cassie, damnit, no—

"It's Cass," she announced. "What's up?"

"Cassie," Martin said. "We've got problems."

"Yeah, no shit, we've got problems here, too. We still can't rule out infectious, so we're going to need boots on the ground—local law if it's all we can get—to start getting people in for testing."

Silence drew out from the phone like black thread. "Did you say 'we'? Who's 'we'? Cassie, tell me you don't have Benji there—"

"No," she said, fake-laughing. "I do not have Benji here, calm down. I meant the *royal* we, like, yeah, we all have problems, blah-blah-blah."

The man on the other end exhaled a sigh of relief. "Good. Because . . . we don't need him. You know that, right? We can handle this."

"Obviously, yes." As Benji winced, Cassie held up her hand like it was a sock puppet without the sock, and she made it yap, yap, yap. "You said you have problems there?"

"Like you wouldn't believe. First, Robbie's team can't get a blood sample from the walkers."

Benji silently mouthed: *Why not?*

She asked: "Why not?"

"The needles won't go in."

"I don't follow you."

Martin reiterated: "The needles would not pierce the skin."

A moment of dizziness overtook Benji. This lined up with what the paramedics had said—their report said they had tried to dose one of the sleep-walkers, the girl, with a sedative. He had assumed their failure was down to a lack of skill—but then when the trooper fired the Taser at Mark Blamire, that didn't work, either. He could not chalk this up to ineptitude. Robbie's people were aces, not first-year residents or backwoods paramedics.

This didn't make any sense.

"That's fucked up," Cassie said. "Scleroderma?"

"Doesn't look like it but . . . I don't know. I recommended they try through the mouth—"

"Soft tissue might allow for easier needle punctures," Cassie said. "Good idea, plus they can get a DNA scrape that way."

Benji leaned forward and tapped MUTE on the phone. Hastily, he said: "Have him check for alternatives to drawing blood. A device like the Pronto is a clip, goes over the finger, uses wavelengths of light to scan the blood through the fingernail—detects anomalies like anemia. I forget the name, but there's also a start-up out of Ventura that made a device that used a laser to pierce the skin at a microscopic level—"

"Hello?" Martin asked. "Cassie, did I lose you?"

She unmuted the call. "Nope. We're fine." *Shit.* "I'm fine." Cassie rattled off to Martin what Benji had just told her about the alternative ways to draw blood.

"Good idea," Martin said.

"I know," she said, grinning, her eyes sparkling.

"Maybe you can help me solve this next problem."

"I'm all ears."

"The hospital lost the bodies."

The two of them stared at each other. "What . . . bodies?" she asked.

Martin said: "Mark Blamire's body—or what was left of it—and the cop. Chris Kyle. Both gone. I was going to go down there to schedule an autopsy but . . . they don't have the bodies. They don't have *records* of the bodies. I swear to Christ, it's like dealing with a third-world country here."

"Martin, the Schuylkill County health system is well regarded—"

"Whatever. Point is, if you're headed down there with Mrs. Blamire, please go and check the morgue. See if you can discover whose head is up whose ass and have them find our two missing bodies. Check the morgue. Check security footage. Remind them that this is a screwup of *monumental* proportions—and do not, *do not* tell Nancy Blamire that her husband's body is missing." Pause. "I'm not on speakerphone, am I?"

"Nope," Cassie lied, quickly taking him off speakerphone.

Outside, Benji saw a flash of white movement on the road—

The ambulance.

Finally. Something going right, at least. As Cassie finished up her call, Nancy Blamire came down with a bag in her hand, her face plagued still by that faraway stare—the disconnection that suggested she believed this was all happening to someone else. Together they ushered her to the door and stepped outside. As he was contemplating the question of where exactly the remains of the two dead people could have gone . . . and, equally as bizarre, why the sleepwalkers were somehow *immune* to needles as if experiencing a psychosomatic case of high-intensity trypanophobia—

Another vehicle pulled up behind the ambulance.

This one, a van. A *news* van. WFMZ out of Allentown. *Shit.* He was not prepared to deal with the media. He wasn't even supposed to *be* here. He knew they'd be incoming eventually, but here? Now? How? A reporter was already out of the van—a woman, auburn hair, too much makeup, suit the color of a fresh peach. The camera guy—schlubby, jowly—adjusted the camera on his shoulder and they came hurrying up the driveway, leaving the two paramedics in the dust.

"This isn't good," Benji said.

"Well, fuck," Cassie muttered.

"Hello," the reporter was saying as she hurried up to them. "I'm Elena McClintock, WFMZ News. We're here seeking information about the mysterious death of a local math teacher, Mark Blamire—"

Cassie waved her hands. "No. Nope. No comment, I'm sorry."

Benji wasn't ready for this. This was spiraling. *He* was spiraling. Everything felt like sand slipping through his fingers. Chin to his chest, he ducked his head and held up his hand as they moved toward the ambulance.

The reporter kept on them:

"We have reports of an altercation between Mark Blamire and a state trooper, Officer Christopher Kyle—"

"No, that's not true."

That, said by Nancy Blamire.

Like a shark smelling the delicious tang of fresh chum, the camera operator immediately turned to Nancy as the reporter thrust the microphone toward her. Benji tried to interject himself, but it didn't matter.

"Mark *didn't* hurt that officer," Nancy said.

"Nancy, don't talk to these—" Benji started.

The reporter talked over him, asking for clarification.

"These people are from the CDC," Nancy stammered, and that was that. Benji knew they'd find that connection eventually—and it wasn't like they were hiding their presence, nor would they want to. Just the same, that changed the story for them. This had just become something bigger, stranger, scarier. And the news *loved* bigger, stranger, scarier. Ebola in this country was never really a serious threat—but the news media treated it like half a billion Americans were going to shit themselves to death (all while ignoring the very real peril for Africans in Liberia or Sierra Leone).

"Please," Benji begged Nancy, and that word and the look on his face must've gotten through to her. Perhaps she saw the panic flashing in his eyes or heard it in his voice—she went with him, then, his arm gently around the small of her back as he ushered her toward the ambulance.

The reporter followed, questions chasing at his back. "Why is the CDC involved? Is this some kind of epidemic?" And then, the kicker, the corker, the game ball: "Is this an Ebola outbreak?"

Benji turned, waving his hands. "It's not—*not!*—Ebola."

He helped Cassie and the paramedics get Nancy into the back of the ambulance, and then, with the reporter still hounding them, they hurried to Cassie's rental and hopped in.

Shit shit shit.

Shit.

12

ROAD RASH

Mystery of Saiga Die-Off Answered?

Scientists have determined that the sudden death of over 200,000 saiga antelope in Central Asia was caused by fatal blood poisoning—hemorrhagic septicemia—resulting from the Pasteurella multocida *bacteria that live inside the animals' large noses. The bacteria, present even at birth, coexist harmlessly inside the saiga, but only recently have helped to cause MMEs (mass mortality events) among the saiga over the last decade. Researchers now speculate that climate change is the cause, given the sharp rise in both temperature and humidity in the saiga's natural range.*

JUNE 4
Pine Grove, Pennsylvania

SHANA PACED.

A couple of deerflies buzzed around her head, looking for a landing spot of fresh skin to grab a drink. They were persistent but eventually found their way to the man walking next to her: a state trooper named Travis. She wasn't sure if Travis was his first name or last name. Officer Travis was how he introduced himself and she didn't care to ask for more details.

Officer Travis was her enemy.

Like, not her nemesis. Or if he was, he was only her *nemesis-of-the-moment*. Because he was stopping her from getting close to her sister. And right now, her sister was in danger.

Shana was sure of it.

Ahead, the sleepwalkers walked. And among them strode the men and women in lime-green hazmat suits. They called to mind astronauts wandering a new world: Each took slow, measured steps, as if not used to the gravity here. They wound their way through the walkers, examining them, taking notes, pointing digital thermometers at them, even going through pockets when they had a chance. They were mostly silent as they did so, except for the *vvvvip vvvvip vvviiiiip* of their suits.

Anytime they got near Nessie, Shana clenched her teeth.

Like, say, right now.

One of the CDC people—they were practically faceless, what with the way the light reflected off their windowed masks—came up to her sister, wrapping a blood pressure cuff around her arm.

Shana yelled: "Don't you hurt her!"

She started forward—right now, she was kept about a hundred feet from the back of the flock—but Travis put a hand out to block her.

"Nuh-uh," he said. "Stand back." She started to protest, but Travis scowled at her from underneath his horseshoe mustache. "Let them do their jobs, willya?" He took off his broad-brimmed state trooper hat and swung it uselessly at the pair of flies dueling above his head. "Goddamn flies."

"They bite."

"I know, they bit me a few times already. Little assholes."

You're a little asshole, she thought. It wasn't a good comeback, so she kept it to the confines of her own brain.

"Just let me go up to see my sister."

"They told me to keep you and the others back, so that's what I'm doing."

The others. It wasn't just her, now. The walkers weren't alone—they did not arise from nothing. Some had family members, though none were keeping pace the way she was. Mostly they drove up or drove ahead and checked in. There was a young black kid wearing Beats by Dre headphones, and his mother hung back—when he first got here, she was screaming and crying for him to listen to her, to stop walking away. She was half mad, half sad, all crazy. They got her calm. Shana was pretty sure the dude's mom was now up in the lead cruiser. Others, too, stayed nearby: the wife of the guy in the bathrobe, the son and husband of the woman in the business suit, the wife of the old lady sleepwalker who showed up in her skivvies—they all, far as Shana knew, were gathering about five miles down the road at Abram's Dutch Diner. They had a trooper with them, and someone from the CDC—a tall Asian lady in a Beastie Boys T-shirt, of all things—was there with them asking questions and whatever. They tried to get Shana to come with them, but she said no, hell no, she'd stay right here.

Shana had to watch over her sister.

It was her job. Her only job.

Too bad it doesn't pay dick, she thought.

She kept a hawk-eye on the CDC goon taking her sister's BP. "If they hurt her . . ." she started.

"Yeah, yeah," Officer Travis said.

"Don't *yeah, yeah* me. This is serious."

"Seriously fucked up is what you mean."

He wasn't wrong.

She pulled out her phone and tried to call her dad. *Again.* Still no answer. Shana had tried earlier this morning: went to voicemail. Tried again an hour ago, and *again* it went to voicemail. Just now: same deal.

Worry clawed at her insides. Maybe he'd just left the damn phone in the stable or out in the pasture again. Would be just like him. Since Mom was gone, Shana had to step up in many ways because as it turned out, Dad wouldn't be able to find his own butt with a map and a fully charged Ass Detector.

About half an hour ago, those goons in the suits tried taking blood samples—none from her sister, thank God—but like the paramedics before, they couldn't get a blood draw. The needles wouldn't go in. One broke.

Shana didn't know anything about medical stuff, but she was pretty sure that didn't make a whole lot of sense. It scared her. What *was* this? Her mind raced with crazy ideas: *Maybe it's the government.* Dad had a brother, Jeff. They didn't call him Uncle Jeff because he was never there for them and Dad didn't like him anyway, so he told Shana and Nessie that they didn't need to pretend Jeff was real family. Few times Jeff came over he got drunk and ranted about conspiracy shit—chemtrails and 9/11-was-an-inside-job and something about a place called Germ Island, whatever that was. Seemed bugfuck nuts at the time but maybe he was onto something.

Or maybe it was aliens.

Like that meme, the one with the crazy-haired guy in the History Channel screencap:

I'M NOT SAYING IT WAS ALIENS

BUT IT WAS ALIENS

She also heard one of the cops say something about terrorism. Could it be that? What did that even mean? Terrorists controlling people's bodies and minds? Why? *How?*

Up ahead, near her sister, a second CDC goon joined the first.

The hairs on Shana's neck prickled.

Why two? They stepped on each side of Nessie as she walked. They matched her stride. Something gleamed in the one's hand and they seemed to be . . . practicing something, miming some kind of action.

Around her sister.

They're doing something to her.

Or rather, they were about to.

With her pulse galloping in her neck and her wrists, Shana felt her mouth go dry, felt her skin shiver. It was now or never. If they tried to stop Nessie, if she started to shake—even if they didn't let her go kablooey like that cop did with Mister Blamire, who knew what was happening to her every time it started? Maybe it was cooking her brain, or damaging her heart, or—well, who knew? They didn't know. They saw her as a lab rat forever squirming outta their grip.

The one reached for Nessie's jaw.

No.

Shana pistoned an elbow into Officer Travis's breadbasket—he *oofed* and doubled over as she broke into a fast-if-clumsy run like one of their cows escaping a stable. She screamed, yelled, waved her hands at them. They stopped their ministrations on Nessie and turned toward her.

"Don't you touch her, you assholes!" She skidded her heels, slowing her run to a fast walk—both her hands were balled up in fists. The two CDC goons—one woman, one man—held up their hands. The woman had a small scalpel. The man had a needle. Shana growled: "I'm not gonna let you cut into my sis—"

Wham. Something slammed into her from behind, her backpack taking the brunt of it. Even still, Shana fell forward, arms out, her hands catching her and stopping her head from snapping against asphalt. Her palms stung and throbbed as they caught the rough road, but she had no time to worry about that—Officer Travis jammed his knee into the small of her back while wrenching her arms back behind her.

She heard the rattle of cuffs.

No, no, no. I need to be here for my sister. "Let me go! Get your stupid fuckin' hands offa me." She managed to yank one hand out of his grip—as she pawed at the ground to try to stand, she saw a smear of red there. Her palm was bleeding. An absurd thought did a fast lap around her head: *The gun. Reach into your bag. Get it out.* She didn't need to shoot anybody, she just needed to *show* it to them, show them she meant business—

Then, a new voice: "Hey! No! Stop, *stop,* let her go."

Shana craned her head, cheek against the road, to see who it was.

She recognized him—he was CDC, she thought. He looked young. Not teenager young, maybe college young—early twenties, or midtwenties with a boyish face. Slicked-back hair, brown skin, a button-down shirt and khaki pants.

He waved his hands. "Okay! Everyone stop. Please. Let's everyone just . . . just calm down, okay? Okay." Shana felt Travis let go of her hands, though he did not remove himself from pinning her, yet.

Now a new person showed up—a man, his CDC suit failing to hide his paunchiness, the windowed mask showing a face framed by fuzzy lamb-chop sideburns. "The fuck is going on here?"

Travis said: "This girl tried to rush the crowd—"

She objected, yelling over him: "Your fucking goons were going to cut into my sister—"

"None of you should be in the crowd without suits. And you, Avar—"

"Arav," the younger man said.

"*You* especially. Officer, please, get off the girl. She's just trying to protect her sister. This is hard for all of us."

Her now-very-much-fucking-nemesis-forever-and-ever Officer Travis hurried to climb off her back. "Wait, am I infected now?"

"I don't know," Sideburns said. "Just stay with the walkers."

Shana, meanwhile, stood up, braving a casual glance at her hands—each palm was road-burned just enough to draw beads of blood blowing up like little red balloons. Travis gave her a mean look, and she offered one of her bloody hands to him. "Sorry about that. Shake on it?"

His look went from mean to squicked out. It wasn't just the blood, she wagered—it was everything. The CDC, the suits, the chance he might be infected. Germs. Disease. Cooties and plague. Travis turned greasy with nausea, and it gave her considerable pleasure to see him scurry away. *Run, you dick, run.*

All the while, the walkers kept walking. Moving around them like they were just rocks in a stream. The two other CDC goons stood nearby in their suits, looking to the Sideburns dude for some kind of clue. He introduced himself to Shana, his voice loud through the suit: "I'm Robbie Taylor, head of the response team here."

"Tell your thugs to lay off my little sister."

"They're not—" The man sighed. "You know what, never mind. We're just trying to get a DNA scrape or a blood sample, but we can try it from someone else. Deal?"

"I guess."

"Great. Hey, Avar—" he said to the man, the one who'd run up yelling.

"Arav. Still Arav."

"I could just call you Guy Who Should Be Wearing a PPE Suit."

"I'm not trained—"

"Fine. Can you take—" To her again: "What's your name?"

"Shana Stewart."

"Can you take Miss Stewart here, maybe clean her injuries, get her some water? You could take her back to the tent—"

She protested: "No, hell no, the tent is like a mile back, I saw it. I saw it back there and I'm not going that way, because I'm staying with my sis."

"I have a small first-aid kit in my pack," Arav said. "And I have H_2O."

"Great. Go do that," Robbie said. He added impatiently: "Like now?"

Arav gave her a sympathetic look. "Can we?"

"*Fine.*"

Arav led the way, and she followed, but she kept a suspicious eye behind her. Just in case. *You leave Nessie alone, you pricks.*

"AM I GOING TO HAVE to go into quarantine?" Shana asked.

"I don't know. Protocol is still . . . uncertain."

"That doesn't sound good."

"It's not efficient. But we have to deal with local enforcement, federal enforcement, various agencies and hospitals. You may need tests—"

"I don't want to go anywhere for tests." Even now, she kept her eye on the walkers. On her sister. "I'm all Nessie has."

"I'm sorry."

"Yeah, well." Shana stepped off the road's shoulder and into the shade of a tulip tree. "You look young."

Arav shrugged. "I'm twenty-five."

"You're kinda baby-faced, though."

"Oh. I guess so."

She was about to say something else, but winced and sucked in a sharp intake of breath as he poured a little more water over her palms. The water washed away the blood. Arav wore blue latex gloves as he helped her apply a wide swaddling of gauze over each palm. His efforts were delicate and precise. She tried to look tough. She didn't know why.

"I bet you get carded," she said.

"I don't, actually."

"Oh. Cool."

He smiled. "I, ahh, I don't drink."

"Oh. Is that like, a Muslim thing?"

"I am not Muslim. My parents are Hindu, though I'm mostly . . . not anything, really?"

"So why don't you drink?"

He shrugged. Though the bandages were applied, and the work was done, he remained holding her hands. "I don't know? It never seemed my thing. I was too busy in college to do that whole . . . 'college experience,' the get-drunk-and-pee-in-a-potted-plant-at-the-frat-house deal."

"Why aren't you religious like your parents?"

Suddenly he let go of her hands and retreated from her now-bandaged palms. He was done, he had no cause to remain. Embarrassment passed over his face like a shadow from a cloud. "They're not that religious, either, really. For me, the religion has a lot of beauty but . . . I just had other things to worry about is all. I think you're done, by the way. Your hands."

"Thanks." She flexed her hands. The gauze was light and airy, didn't make it hard or uncomfortable to close her fists. "Shouldn't you be in one of those hazmat suits?"

"You ask a lot of questions."

"Sorry. I'm nervous. And tired."

"I totally get that. Anyway, yes, those are PPE suits. Personal protective equipment." Almost confessionally, he said: "I'm not trained."

"Shouldn't you be in one if you're near them?" *Or*, she realized, *near me?* Because if Nessie was infected with something, couldn't Shana be, too? She pushed that thought out to sea. "That Robbie guy seemed peeved."

"I mean, yeah, I should've been. I'm not supposed to get that close to the patients—I don't suspect it's respiratory, though, so mostly I'm trying to protect against blood and all that."

"Like, what about my blood?"

He held up his hands, still gloved. "It's not a PPE suit, but it's something." His fingers wiggled.

"Why did you get that close? Without a suit, I mean."

"You seemed in trouble."

"I was fine."

"You were most decidedly not fine."

She paused. "Okay, I wasn't fine."

"Your sister, she'll be okay."

"You can't know that."

He looked down at his feet as he said, "So, I'm not religious, like I said, but I do like the stories. And so there's this one story, right? There was this princess, Mirabai. I forget when, exactly? Like, four hundred years ago. She did not want to *be* a princess, though, so instead she became this wandering . . . poet, like a poet-saint, singing and speaking poems to the gods and for the gods. One of her poems always stayed with me, and it's this: *O my mind / Worship the lotus feet of the Indestructible One / Whatever you see between earth and sky / Will perish.*"

Shana blinked. "That's fucked up."

"What? Why?"

"You just told me we're all gonna die. I'm worried about my sister and you're trying to comfort me by telling me we will all . . . perish."

"No, I mean—" He cleared his throat, looking at this point like he was so embarrassed he might climb the tulip tree behind them and hide among its leaves until she was gone. "Okay, I guess that is pretty fucked up. I'm sorry. I just—it helps me to think that we're all in this together and we'll all be okay even as we're not okay. And though I'm not really religious, Hinduism accepts you whether or not you accept it, and part of that is the assumption that this isn't the end. We just keep going around and around, and we get to come back and do it over."

"It's still kinda fucked up."

"I'm sorry."

"I'm going to walk away now because I'm a little weirded out."

"That's probably fair."

"My sister's not going to be okay, is she?"

"I . . . I really don't know, Shana, I'm sorry."

"Then you shouldn't have said she was going to be."

And with that, Shana turned around and stormed away.

• • •

ONCE AGAIN, SHE WAS AT the back of the flock, feeling agitated like she had ants crawling all over her. Officer Travis gave her the stinkeye from about twenty feet away, and it took every ounce of self-control she could muster not to give him the middle finger. Instead she grabbed her phone, tried *once more* to call her father.

Ring, ring, ring.

Meanwhile, ahead, the CDC goons were near Headphones Kid. They had his mouth craned wide like he was one of those little coin purses you had to squeeze to open, and they were working in his mouth, juggling their own feet forward as he unstoppably walked.

Ring, ring, ring.

She turned her gaze to Nessie. Walking ahead. Bare feet padding on asphalt. Fingers of faint wind ruffling the girl's long hair. Memories flicked through Shana's mind like someone fast-tapping the button on a slide projector. Them as kids, chasing each other at the Jersey Shore. Shana teasing Nessie with a dead jellyfish. Nessie teasing Shana with little crab claws she found. That time Nessie fell in a big steaming pile of cow crap. That other time Shana got sprayed by a skunk and Nessie helped her wash off with a bath of tomato soup. The day their mother left.

Ring, ring, ring.

She looked down at her watch. Coming up on afternoon already. Where was Dad? Noon also meant that they might see another sleepwalker, soon. Another to join the flock. Another drop of rain to feed the river.

At least, if the pattern held.

Was this a pattern? A pattern of what? And why?

Officer Travis turned his head the way a spooked animal does—like he was on sudden alert. But his alarm turned fast to irritation, and when Shana followed his gaze, she saw why: because riding behind the flock was this obnoxious recreational vehicle, a boxy RV rocking side-to-side as it rolled on up. Already the trooper was marching out in front of it, waving his arms. Because this road was so narrow and the walkers numbered so many, the cops had set up a detour a few miles back and one a few miles ahead, rerouting traffic up around Sweet Arrow Lake.

"Turn around," he yelled. "Go back a couple miles, turn off on Salt Bridge—if you're local traffic, you'll have to wait."

The RV slowed but honked its horn a few times. The horn sounded about as obnoxious as it could, bleating a big, blustery *braaaamp braaaamp.* (*At least it doesn't play some dumb song,* Shana thought.) Officer Travis covered his ears as it beeped—and by now, lots of the CDC folks had looked up, too. The trooper started to yell again, but here came the horn as the RV slowed to a crawl:

Braaaaamp.

Braaaaaaaaamp.

Then something caught Shana's eye.

The person driving was waving his hands.

Waving his hands and looking right at *her.*

"D . . . Dad?" she said. Next thing she knew, the driver's-side window of the RV was down, and sure enough, her father hung his head out the window and called her name. A pink flush of teenage humiliation rose to her cheeks.

But at the same time, a surge of happiness rose, too.

Dad.

With the RV pulled off to the side, her father spread his arms wide as she stepped inside, like he was showing off a prize pig at the Grange fair.

"What do you think?" he asked.

It looked ancient. Had a smell to match: musty-dusty, moldy-oldy. It was all tan walls and plastic-covered furniture and cheapy-ass laminates. "Dad, I don't know what this is."

"It's an RV."

"I know *that,* I just . . ."

"I thought a lot about what you said on the bridge last night. I haven't been all there for you and Nessie since your mother left. She's gone, and I don't know where and I don't know why, but what I do know is that I can't leave the two of you. I don't know what . . . all this is, or what's happening, but we're a family, and we need to be together. I love you and I am sorry that I have not been—"

Shana did not let him finish.

She threw her arms around him, blinking back tears.

He returned the embrace.

"Thanks, Dad."

"Anything for my girls."

The hug lasted for a while and it felt nice. Even so, she pulled away and arched an eyebrow. "Hey, uh, where'd you get an RV?"

"I bought it."

Oh no.

"With . . . what money?"

"Don't worry about that."

"The farm—"

"Will be *fine*. Will and Essie's son, Jessie, is home from college for the summer—he's going to help out."

"He doesn't know how to make the cheese—"

"But Essie does, so."

"Dad, I—" And then, in that moment, she decided to stow it. It didn't matter. It was his farm, not hers. His life, not hers. His *money,* not hers. Further, she was glad he was here no matter what that meant in the long run. Sometimes what happened now was more important to her than what would happen later, so to hell with it. "Okay. I trust you."

She didn't, not really. But that had to be okay.

For now.

"I'm still not real clear why you bought an RV," she said.

"I always talked about getting one for family vacations and who knows how long you'll be at home before you strike out on your own. I figure in the meantime, we can use it as we . . . follow your sister to wherever it is she and the others are going. You can't walk forever with her. Your legs will give out. Maybe hers will, too. And when that happens, you'll need a bed. The RV has one bed and a pullout couch, so."

"I like it." She didn't, not really—it was ugly as a flabby butt, and it was in dire need of some air freshener. But she liked the *idea* of it, and that was enough. "I guess this is home for the next however many days."

"It'll be nice spending some time with you. Even under these . . . circumstances."

"Nessie will be all right," she said, repeating to her father Arav's lie.

But she and her father both needed the lie right now.

Later, when her father took her up to the cockpit (as he called it) and showed her how to start it up, they saw a ghostly shape walking alone out of the woods: a woman, pale and thin and almost diaphanous, in a sundress that rolled in the wind. Her stare was empty. Her face devoid of emotion. She fell in line behind the rest of the flock.

13

TEST OF FAITH

Gabchain Forum Post
Anon ID Bzwwxtypol June 5th No. 14098790 Replies: >>ID 19248
 > *fuck this shit, it's aliens*
 > *mark my words this is aliens coming down, and they're taking control, in our stories we always thought they'd invade themselves in their ships, but what if they're using *us* to invade?*
 > *those zombies are their puppets*
 > *they're going SOMEWHERE, I wanna know where*
 Dude, they're not aliens, they're not possessed by aliens. It's the Russians. They've hacked everything else: our elections, our power grid, our social media. Now they're hacking PEOPLE.

JUNE 5
Tall Cedars Motel, Three Corners, Pennsylvania

JUST PAST MIDNIGHT IN NOWHERESVILLE, PENNSYLVANIA.

His body was tired even as his mind raced, and Benji wanted nothing more than to go back to his room and sleep for eight, ten, maybe twelve hours.

But instead, he was here. Watching Martin Vargas pace.

The motel wasn't much to look at. Wood paneling, water stains, a carpet that was as much a sediment of dust mite husks as it was an aggregate of fibers and glue. The TV was an old CRT. The bed had a dip in the middle that looked like it once cradled a baby elephant.

He and Cassie had come here after trying—and failing—to procure security footage from the hospital. They had nothing. They said their systems had been hacked and the images erased. So for a time, he did what he always did: He relied on his faith in the numbers. Numbers did not lie. Oh, you could lie *using* numbers (to which Benji could personally attest), but the numbers themselves were inert, unbiased, and pure.

At the end of yesterday, the sleepwalkers numbered ten—though it would have been eleven with Blamire. And now at the end of the second day, the number stood at twenty-two.

The flock walked three miles an hour.

They had not yet stopped for sleep—it was as if they were already sleeping. That meant they traveled around sixty miles in a twenty-four-hour period. That couldn't last forever, of course—their minds, like his, might be racing, but eventually their bodies would give out. Wouldn't they?

If they traveled three miles in an hour, then they'd be walking past this motel in . . . just around five hours, prior to sunrise.

By then they'd likely have more of their own.

More sleepwalkers. One seemed to join every two hours.

How long did this go? How far would they—*could* they—walk?

While he worried at all of this, Cassie stood off to the side, arms crossed, also watching Vargas pace the worn carpet in this dank, musty room. Sadie was—well, Benji didn't know where. All he knew was what he got from her last text: **Found something out, omw.**

Watching Vargas pace was like watching a panther walk the margins of its cage. He fumed, fists at his sides. He wound his way past the artifacts of the investigation: papers spread out across the dresser, across the bed, pinned to a corkboard on an easel. Vargas had found out that Benji was still on the case thanks to the news, which got to Loretta, who ended up in a call to Martin, which led Martin to summon them. It was a good two minutes before he finally spoke.

"I can't fucking believe it" was what he said.

"I'm sorry, Martin—" Benji began.

"No, you don't get to be sorry. Sorry only counts when you back that shit up, Benjamin. When you learn from your mistakes. But here you are. Poisoning the well yet again. And *you*—" Martin halted his march and thrust an accusing finger toward Cassie. "You were an accomplice to this."

Cassie shrugged. "Maybe you want to relax a little, dude. Benji's good people. Benji's *our* people."

"Oh? Is he? Our people are scientists. We have no agenda but truth. Data. What we feel? What we want? It doesn't enter into the goddamn equation. What he did—" Martin turned to Benji. "What *you* did, it poisoned us.

Munchausen by proxy: You poisoned us just enough so you could make your point and get your glory. You hurt us to help yourself."

"No," Benji said with some firmness. "I saw something at Longacre and thought that if there was a way to get ahead of my prediction—"

"Your *prediction*. Listen to you. You and that fucking machine, Black Swan, a pair of Amazing Kreskins. We're scientists, not *psychics*."

"It was a onetime mistake, I own that. I'm not here to hamper this investigation, I'm here—"

"Why? You're here why? Just to piss in my Cheerios? Or maybe you want to do what you did with Longacre? Pick and choose some data from Column A, slap together with some samples from Column Z, and stick them together to see what damage you can do? What *lies* you can concoct—"

Cassie stepped forward, both hands out. "I think you're pushing it, Martin. Benji knows he fucked up, that's not why he's here."

But Martin pushed past her, getting right up in Benji's face. "If it's not that, then what? What is it?"

"I'm here to help."

"You're here to take over." He narrowed his gaze to arrow-slits. Suspicion came off him in hot waves. In a low, dark voice he said: "You don't think I can do this."

"Don't be paranoid, Martin. We're all tired, it's been a long day—"

"I want to know," Martin said, leaning in. "Do you think you're better than me? A better leader? A sharper mind?"

All it took was a little hesitation.

Benji should've answered quickly, he should've—

Well, he should've lied.

Whap.

It happened fast. Martin grunted and clubbed Benji in the mouth with an open hand, staggering him before slamming him up against the wall. Stars spangled the black flag behind Benji's eyes as the wind blasted from his lungs. The other man held him there, and Cassie intervened quickly, working to wrestle Martin off him—but Benji shook his head.

"It's fine, Cass," Benji said, wincing, tasting blood. His lip was split. It throbbed. It would be big as a night crawler soon enough. "We're okay."

She backed off.

He saw something now on Martin's face. Something that transcended anger. It was pain. Betrayal. Sadness, even.

"You could've told us what you were doing," Martin said. "With Longacre? You should've said what you had seen. We could've figured something out together. But you had to take that ego of yours and go off—you had to do this stupid thing. You don't betray the data." But Benji heard something else in there: *You don't betray your team.* "I lost faith in you. Because you lost faith in *us.*"

"No! No. That's not it, I swear, Martin." He shook his head as blood trickled from his lip to his chin and hung there. "I kept my faith in you. I kept my faith in God. I didn't lose faith in myself. I just . . . lost faith in the system. The prediction I made that day wasn't just about some superbug or a new flu pandemic—I predicted how the system would fail us right then and there. I'd make my warning. I'd show the data—the real data. And then what? The system would protect *itself*. It wouldn't protect *people*. It would protect money and the people who make it. Nothing would change. Nobody's out there making a universal flu vaccine because the money doesn't support it. Nobody's making new antibiotics because—again? No money in a cheap pill with a short prescription life. And here? The money was epic. It would protect itself. It would protect the system. And in that moment . . . I wanted to do something about that."

Martin let him go. The fight had gone out of him. Out of both of them.

"Christ, Benji. You really should've talked to us."

"I know. I should've. I just want you to know, it wasn't a picnic for me, either. After it happened, even before I got caught—I felt like I was losing my mind. Sometimes I couldn't sleep, other times I slept so hard I thought I was dying. I actually started to worry I had some kind of . . . strange sleep disorder or sickness and—"

There.

Between them passed a flare of recognition. Inspiration, even.

"Sleeping sickness," Martin said.

"*Trypanosoma,*" Benji said.

They talked it out.

It didn't make perfect sense.

But it made . . . some sense, didn't it?

A protozoan like that affected behavior in strange ways—no, this didn't look like Zika, or tularemia, or Lyme, or Rocky Mountain. Nothing looked like this except maybe, *maybe,* a parasitic infection. *Toxoplasma gondii,* the feline parasite, could alter a human host's brain chemistry and behaviors—some even felt it was one potential cause of schizophrenia. *Naegleria fowleri,* an amoeba, chowed down on actual brain tissue, driving a person into rampant incoherency and eventually, death.

Then there was *Trypanosoma*.

Those little unicellular monsters arrived in a human's bloodstream via an insect bite, like the tsetse fly. Then the protozoans hunkered down, breeding in the blood until it was time to pierce the blood–brain barrier. When *that* happened, the patient's behavior was altered in ways subtle enough that their friends and family might miss the shift: indolence and depression, neither of which was particularly strange.

Further, it often caused sleep disorders: Deep in the throes of the disease, the host might wake at night and sleep during the day. Then came confusion and anxiety. After that: aggressive behavior coupled with psychosis. And often, tremors or seizures. Untreated, the body fell into disrepair. Organs broke down. Bodily function ceased as neurological function dwindled. The host would enter a coma and soon die.

That was just from one of the dozens of *Trypanosoma* varieties.

And though the symptoms of African sleeping sickness did not precisely match what they were seeing with the sleepwalkers . . .

There remained troubling connections.

Sleep disorder? Seizures? Neurological changes?

What if this was similar? What if these people were all marching toward their deaths? Were their minds breaking down with every step they took? Would they soon begin falling to the ground even as others joined the herd? Their blood, brimming with little protozoans, their organs failing as their brains died? He shuddered at the thought. *Trypanosoma* was an adaptable sonofabitch. It evolved to find new life in new hosts.

Maybe it had done that, here.

The way you *tested* for *Trypanosoma,* of course, was a blood panel.

Which they could not get.

The inside-the-cheek idea that Martin had was a good one; it also didn't work. Tomorrow Benji hoped those start-ups he'd recommended would agree to send prototypes.

Their inability to pierce the skin and get a blood sample was just one head on this mysterious hydra. Other bizarre questions rose to taunt them: Why didn't the walkers need food or water? So far, none had stopped. And so far, none had urinated or defecated, either. Nothing in, nothing out. And yet *something* must have been in there already—several of the families reported that the patients ate meals at various periods before entering the sleepwalking phase. The inability to vacate one's bowels or bladder was, seeming silliness aside, another killer. The bowels could burst. The kidneys could go south, which would in turn poison the body.

Already the three of them had hunkered down in front of an iPad on a metal Compass stand, flicking through pages of data. Talking it out as they did. "Chagas disease," Cassie said. "No cases here in PA, but they have the kissing bug. They're a known vector for the parasite—a triatomine bug that drinks blood from mammals, including humans. Often the face, hence: *kissing*. After they feed, they shit, and the protozoan gets in the blood."

"Chagas doesn't match well," Martin said.

"So," Benji countered, "probably not *T. cruzi* but rather, *T. brucei*—sleeping sickness."

Cassie's mouth puckered and her lips popped as she thought. "I can see it. Though worth noting: It's never been seen here in North America."

"No, but there was an instance in London a few years ago. And diseases like SARS and West Nile have both shown a propensity to hop borders. *And* the protozoan has shown an inclination toward evolution."

"What's the vector?"

"I don't know."

"In Africa, it's the tsetse."

"Some species transmit, yes. They drink their bloodmeal and pass along the parasite. Others pick it up again and . . . well."

"Sharing is caring," Cassie said. "Still doesn't explain how we're going to get a blood panel test for this shit—"

Just then, a knock at the door. Benji's phone dinged:

A message from Sadie: It's me.

He said as much, then stood to answer the door. She stepped in, then did a double take as she saw the line of crusted blood down Benji's chin. "You're bleeding!"

"Martin punched me."

"I slapped you," Martin said, "and you deserved it."

Benji gave a smirk and a shrug. "He's not wrong. Come on in. We're looking at a new possibility for the disease—*Trypanosoma*. Parasitic protozoan. A real pain."

"I've got something, too."

With that, out came her phone.

Wait—Benji had seen her phone before. This wasn't that. This was something different: a smartphone still, by the look of it, but one that was all screen and beveled corners. As she palmed the device, turning it around, Benji saw that each edge had a small, barely noticeable lens.

No, not a lens—a projector.

His suspicion was immediately confirmed as, sure enough, a beam of light projected out from the top edge of the phone, bright enough that Sadie didn't even have to turn the lights down.

What played in the projection was a brief video.

The camera looked upon what seemed to be a hospital morgue. And now Benji realized what Sadie had brought them: security camera footage from the hospital. Where two bodies had gone missing.

In the room, he saw morgue drawers against the back wall. In the foreground were six tables, two occupied—one with a sheet covering an entire corpse, the second also with the sheets pulled up, except this time they did not cover anything necessarily human-shaped, but rather, hills and mounds of . . . *something.*

One minute, the bodies (or what was left of them) were present. And then the video fritzed out. The black-and-white footage turned into a glitchy rainbow, broken video artifacts that seemed to melt and resolve into one another. Then the screen went black for one, two, three seconds—

When it came back, the camera feed had returned.

But both tables were empty.

"Shit," Cassie said.

Sadie answered: "Wait for it. There's more."

That video ended and another began.

It overlooked a parking lot in what appeared to be the back of the hospital, near to where they discarded everything from sharps, to radioactive waste, to chemo drugs, to spent or harmful pharmaceutical remainders. Plus blood, infectious material, contaminated equipment. All of it sat separated out by dumpsters divided by color. The back doors to the hospital opened. Someone, a man by the look of it, tall and thin and in hospital blues—with a mask over his mouth—exited wheeling a single stretcher. The stretcher sat mounded with what looked like more than one body. Only problem was: The camera recording this was not as close in proximity as the one in the morgue. *It must sit higher up,* Benji thought. *On a pole or post—probably sitting under a streetlight.*

As the man wheeled the stretcher down the ramp toward the dumpsters, Benji found himself offering a small prayer to the heavens: *Please, let whoever this is dispose of the bodies in there. If they're in there, we can still recover some-thing. Please.*

That did not happen.

Instead an ambulance wheeled into the frame, reversing to the bottom of the ramp. Someone still inside the ambulance opened a door—all that could be seen of them was an arm, the hand in a latex glove.

The tall man wheeled the stretcher into the ambulance.

And then it was gone, driving out of view of the camera.

Someone stole two bodies, Benji thought.

They stole *evidence.*

Nausea swirled at the bottom of his stomach like foul water circling a drain. Someone knew what they were looking for. Someone stole those bod-ies, that evidence. They edited or hacked the hospital cameras. That indi-cated they knew more about all of this than Benji knew even now.

They're hiding something.

Who are they? And why?

The worst answer surfaced:

Because someone did this.

All of it.

Call it bioterror. Call it an attack. Call it whatever—it suggested that there was intentionality behind it at the worst. At the best, it meant someone created this problem accidentally—

And now was struggling to hide the evidence.

Martin said it first:

"The game just changed."

THE LIFE AND DEATH OF
JERRY GARLIN

Six months ago, in San Antonio, Texas:

THE CROWD DIDN'T KNOW WHAT WAS COMING.

Jerry Garlin did. Or at least, he thought he did. This was his moment. His time to *shine,* incandescent like the sun itself. No longer did he need to live in his father's shadow. Dirk Garlin, may he rest in peace, the so-called architect of dreams, the mastermind of the country's second-largest theme park wonderland—Garlin Gardens in Raleigh, North Carolina—cast a long shadow, indeed. Jerry had lived in that shadow for *fifty* goddamn years.

But now, Jerry would not merely step *out* of that shadow —

Why, he would obliterate it.

He stood out there on the makeshift stage, the late-day sky behind him big and blue, speakers nestled among the little scrubby pines. All around had gathered friends and family—and, of course, the media, who drooled like a dog at a T-bone steak when he dangled the choice tidbit in front of them that he might, *might* just be planning on expanding the Garlin Gardens legacy. Hundreds had gathered. Cameras sat pointed at the podium on the dais. *His* podium. *His* dais.

Jerry's right-hand man, his go-to guy, Vic McCaffrey, stood up there pumping the crowd, getting them *wet and juicy* for what was to come—then Vic invited up the mayor of San Antonio and *then* the governor of Texas, both of whom spoke at length (too great a length, Jerry thought with some impatience) about the vital American legacy of Dirk Garlin and the Garlin Gardens theme park—and TV channel and animation studio and toy manufacturer and restaurants and, and, and.

And then it was time for Jerry.

He rubbed his hands together. Buttoned the buttons on his blue suit. (*Need to lose a little weight,* he thought. But all his upcoming travel might afford him that chance—so much to do!) Then up he went, and the crowd applauded—a *mild* applause, he thought, but that was okay he told himself. Not like he was some kind of pop musician or A-list actor. But after today, he would secure his place amid that panoply of stars, maybe even be deserving of his own goddamn constellation, by God and by glory.

He began his pitch.

He wasn't like his father in this regard—Dirk Garlin was an old-school pitchman. In the early days of his career, that man sold everything from soap to sodas to hunting rifles, all on the road, hand to hand, word of mouth. The old man was like a carnival barker or circus ringleader in the Barnum way: *Step right up, folks, right this way to the great egress.* Except his circus was capitalism: the buying and selling of goods.

And later, the buying and selling of *fun.* And *dreams.* And, some might say, America its own-damn-self.

No, Jerry was not that, not exactly. His father could sell ice to an Eskimo (or as his father was wont to put it, *Boy, I could sell binoculars to a blind man*), but he could be persuasive when the need arose.

Jerry reminded himself to smile.

He tried very hard not to sweat.

And then he began.

He said, his voice big and loud and proud: "Garlin Gardens is a place of America—not just in it, but of it, a part of the American heart and the American spirit. Ask a sixty-five-year-old or a five-year-old if they know who Gary Gopher or Shirley Squirrel is—or Lady Beetle or Dimwit Dog or Princess Flutterby—and they'll not only tell you who they are, they'll tell you their favorite movie starring them, they'll tell you about a beloved stuffed animal or snow globe—hell, they'll even do the voices for you."

And here he affected his best Dimwit Dog stutter:

"Well buh-buh-buh-golly fuh-folks." The crowd didn't react too well, but that was just as Vic said it would be—and more important, *had* to be (even if it rankled Jerry just a little), because it let him sell the next joke. Under his breath he then said: "Guess I shouldn't quit my day job, should I?"

It was a mediocre joke, but it worked. They laughed. They applauded. Vic at the time of crafting the speech said, *Never underestimate the power of a bad joke, and better yet one that pokes fun at yourself.*

God bless Vic, that clever bastard. Knew people better than people knew themselves.

Jerry continued on: "Even more so, the elderly person or that young child would also go on to tell you about that summer their family took them down to Garlin Gardens. And maybe not just one summer, but three summers, or summer after summer—or maybe they saw the Christmas Whamboree, or the fireworks on Imagination Day. Garlin Gardens has long been imprinted into the minds of Americans, but there comes a time when a garden gets too big—it *strains* at its margins, trying to grow over the fences and around the gates like a dream that doesn't want to stay a dream anymore. And the only thing you can do is grow that garden."

There. Out there, in their eyes, a flash of something. Curiosity. Hope. Wonder. They knew something was coming. Not just because he'd promised an announcement, but it had been so long since the Garlin Company had revealed any new major initiatives. They all eased forward, almost imperceptibly, and Jerry almost imagined that he could *hear* it—the squeak of shoe soles, the creak of knees, the slight intake of breath through the nose.

"And so today, we grow that garden."

He held, like Vic told him to hold.

Waiting for gasps.

Waiting for all of *them* waiting to hear what he meant.

Vic said, *Sell the next line big, hoss.*

So sell it, he did. Big voice, big smile, two big thumbs-up.

"I'd like to announce that behind me is the site of the second official Garlin Gardens: Garlin Gardens, San Antonio!"

And *big* applause. Both the mayor and the governor led the way, standing up and applauding, shaking each other's hands, then turning to him and applauding in his general direction. (And boy did that feel good.)

Still, he wasn't done. Not by a long shot.

"And now I'm here to tell you that this is just the *first*. We will simultaneously open *five* new Garlin Gardens parks, with San Antonio being the flagship—" Not really true, but he wanted them to feel special. "And the others being Sacramento, California; Boston, Massachusetts; Berlin, Germany; and finally, Chengdu, China!"

Now it was rip-roaring applause. He shot a glance at Vic—his attaché stood there, a knowing smirk on his pretty-boy face, not clapping, no. Just nodding. Nodding because they did it. *They did it.*

And still, he wasn't done.

Vic told him, *Don't wait, don't let the applause ride out. Jump the gun. They don't know what's coming, and you don't want to give them the chance to anticipate anything.* So that's what Jerry did.

He started speaking over them, louder than their applause: "Folks, folks, the first thing you do on a garden, folks, before it's even a garden is—what?" He lifted his hands and gave them a comical shrug. "Why, that's right, you have to get your shovel and you gotta *break ground.*"

Jerry turned his shrug into two fists raised in the air—

And with that—

Boom.

Behind him, the pyrotechnics went off—the ground shook as gouts of smoke and stone erupted miles behind him. The audience took a collective gasp and a half step back—the looks of wonder on their faces registered shock and concern, now. But that was okay. A reaction was a reaction, his father always said. The best punctuation in the English language, according to Dirk, was the exclamation point followed by the question mark. "No periods," he would say, "and no commas. Question marks and exclamation points are the best tools in your toolbox—use 'em and get that reaction."

So Jerry just smiled and spread his arms wide. "That's us breaking ground on the new Garlin Gardens, folks, and I leave you now with a quote from my father, Dirk Garlin—he always said, *The best gift you can give somebody is a surprise, because they never—*"

The last words of that were *forget it.*

But Jerry did not get the chance to say them.

First, he saw the eyes of the audience disconnect from him all at once— their gaze turned away, looking not at him but rather, *behind* him.

Then he heard the sound. A susurrus, a rush, a flurry.

"What the—" he said into the mic, then turned around.

The blue sky was punctuated with black. Slashes and vees, rising together like little dark pen-marks etched across the expanse. They moved nearly as one, joining up into a single dark mass, and he thought, *Birds, they're birds, like something out of Hitchcock,* and he willed himself to think it was fine, just fine, nothing serious, because birds were birds and Hitchcock's movie was just that: a movie, a fiction, some made-up bogeyman bullshit.

Then he realized—once he heard the chittering and the screeching— *Those are not birds.*

They're bats.

They swept up across him en masse—a sky-darkening swarm skimming over the trees and straight across the stage. He cried out, swatting his arms as they brushed against his cheeks, his hair, as one got caught up in his clothing and tried to get out through the armpit. Jerry yelped like a kicked dog, pirouetting drunkenly as one of his feet left the stage without him meaning to—and then he fell, landing three feet down on the other ankle as bats swarmed him and the ankle bone broke like a broomstick—

Five months ago, in the sky above the Atlantic Ocean:

THE CAST ITCHED. THE TWO PINS ITCHED. JERRY GARLIN STRUGGLED IN HIS seat to get comfortable, grousing under his breath as he did.

Vic, sitting across from him, said: "Four more weeks." He meant until they got the pins out and the cast off.

"Four weeks too goddamn many."

His attaché leaned backward in the seat of the private jet, relaxed as he always was. If stress was a bullet, Vic McCaffrey was bulletproof glass.

"Don't focus on the leg. Don't focus on that day. Things are good."

"They ain't that good." There in the well of Jerry's voice rose the banjo twang of a Kentucky upbringing. He kept it down most days—nobody wanted a business run by someone who sounded like some hicky rube—but when he was pissed off or worried, it tended to creep out. "They *aren't* good. Not as good as I want 'em to be, Vic."

"Berlin went well."

"And Chengdu didn't."

"The Chinese market is a tough one. We're strangers in a strange land there—they'll come around. Tensions are strained right now between them and us, too." China said the US was a currency manipulator. The US said China was the manipulator. More talk of tariffs and trade wars. "It's a tiff, but it'll end."

"Yeah, I guess." He grunted again as he strained to find a position that didn't cause pain to shoot up from his broken ankle—the misery was like lightning striking from the heel of his foot all the way up to his hip. "I'm looking for a couple-few days at home. Peace and quiet." His daughter Mary and his son-in-law Kenneth were coming to their Florida house to stay with Jerry and his wife, Susan.

"Don't get too comfy, I got you an interview."

Jerry pouted. "Interview with who?"

"With whom," Vic corrected, and Jerry hated when Vic did that. The man knew a lot. Maybe knew everything. But it still rankled. Nobody liked being told they weren't speaking right. But he let it slide, because Vic was so essential, he'd saved Jerry's bacon from the fire again and again. "Interview's with *Newsweek*. They'll send a reporter—a good one, probably Dave Jacobs or Samantha Brower—on Saturday."

"*Newsweek*, c'mon. I don't need that."

"*Newsweek* is venerable."

"*Newsweek* had, what, a peak circulation of two, three million? They shut down print a few years ago because they dipped under 100k. I'm told that magazines are a dead format, Vic."

Vic leaned forward. "Dead in print, but not online. People click."

"Get me on Fox. They like me." And they should. Jerry was a big donor to the Republican party—and the Republicans basically ran Fox News these days. "You know what this *Newsweek* fiasco is gonna be? It's gonna be like that goddamn *Boston Globe* interview. Some . . . fuckin' *gotcha* interview. They'll ask me about San Antonio. They'll ask about the video."

The video. That still burned his ass like a bundle of kindling. Day after the San Antonio groundbreaking, a YouTube video surfaced of him being swarmed by bats—the news footage cut away and missed his fall, but some yahoo out there had his *phone* on and the camera rolling. It captured everything, his speech, the dramatic gesture, the big boom—

Then the bats.

And his squeals.

And his *fall*.

Jerry had watched that video more times than he could count, though he'd never tell Vic or even his own family that. Though his views on that video were a drop in the bucket compared with *how many* had watched it. Last he checked (two hours ago), the view count on that video was up over *three million*. The future wasn't *Newsweek*. It was fucking YouTube.

And that sucked. Because YouTube—the whole damn internet—was the antithesis of Garlin Gardens. It wasn't fun and whimsical. Dreams were not made on the internet; they were *killed* there. By mean, nasty little shits who were all looking to one-up each other.

Like crayfish in a bucket, all trying to climb over one another to get to the top.

"They won't ask about the video," Vic assured him. "I have their promise."

"That fella from *The Boston Globe* did. Then he asked about the remix videos. And the remixes of the remixes. They're calling me Batman, now, you know that? And not in a serious way. A funny, ha ha, laugh-at-the-man kinda way. It isn't right, Vic. Isn't. Right."

"They won't ask about the video." Vic shrugged. The next thing he said, he said it like it was no big deal, but to Jerry it was a helluva big deal. "They might ask about that day, though."

"No. *Hell* no."

"Jerry, you should talk about it. Like I said, being self-aware, being a little self-deprecating—laughing about this kind of thing—it has value. Makes you look confident, like everything will bounce off you."

"I'm not you."

"I know you're not me. You're a whole lot richer."

"Now, don't overstep, Vic. You sound sour."

"I'm not sour. Just truthful. You inherited a company, one of the biggest. Your father was immeasurably wealthy—you're one of the hundred richest people in the country. Your family has a legacy mine will never have."

"You ain't—you *aren't* exactly poor."

"Didn't say I was. I'm standing on a ladder, no doubt. But you're on top of a skyscraper like King Kong. Embrace it. Enjoy it."

Jerry crossed his arms and leered. He didn't like this kind of talk. Made it sound like he didn't deserve what he got, like he was just sitting here on his laurels—like he wasn't the one who came up with the new Garlin Gardens plan. Like he didn't work his ass off to get here. Okay, *no,* maybe up until now he wasn't exactly the Idea Man, but he did his time. He had to appease his father, for one thing—oh sure, Dirk could be all smiles. With everyone else, he felt like their best friend or funny uncle. But to Jerry, Dirk would be cold and mean. Always in his eyes was that dull finish of disappointment, looking down at his son like he was lesser, like, *Oh,* this *is who will inherit the earth after I'm gone? Well, shit.*

Vic pushed past that, started to say, "We have a lot of good stuff to talk about—hit the high points of the Garlin Gardens plan. Remind them that, unlike with Disney, we won't have duplicated rides. Each park will be its own unique entity, giving people a reason to visit not just one park, but each of them, and we'll have packages that—"

"I know the fuckin' talking points, Vic!" he snapped. "Here, let me ask you a question: Why didn't you tell me about the bats?"

"We did tell you."

"No, *no,* you told me it was a conservation area back there, and that's why we had to hire security to remove those protesters—"

"And I also gave you a legal document to sign that indicated very clearly that the conservation area bordered Bracken Cave, and Bracken Cave is one of the biggest bat colonies in the country. We're lucky we only disturbed the one type of bat—in the main part of the cave, the Mexican bats number in the *millions,* Jerry. The millions."

Mexican bats. That figured.

"Those bats were all over me. I got scratches. Bites."

"They weren't serious."

"The rabies shots sure as shit were serious. That shit hurts, Vic. Five doses of those meds—"

"Four. It was four shots."

"You shoulda told me about the damn bats."

"We told you."

"Not in a memo! To my face! *To my face.*"

"I told you, Jerry, you have to read the memos."

"You fuckin'—" Jerry stiffened. "Go sit somewhere else."

"All right, Jerry."

"But get me a—" He was about to say *gin and tonic,* but then he sneezed so hard, he thought his brain might come out of his head. Then again, achoo. Eyes watering. Nose running. "Get me some tissues, then get me a gin and tonic."

And then go sit somewhere else, you smug little know-it-all.

Three months ago, in Raleigh, North Carolina:

JERRY BLEW HIS NOSE. "THIS DAMN COLD."

Vic stood by his desk. "Go to the doctor."

"I'm not going to that doctor."

"You're not going because he's going to tell you that you need all the maintenance—the physical, the prostate exam, the colonoscopy."

He thought but did not say, *Like I'm going to let them stick things up my ass.* Not a finger, not a tube. Exit door only. "I'm fine. Just a cold."

"A cold that's hung on for a month. Might be allergies. He'll tell you to get on Claritin, end of story. Here, come on, stand up. You need to do your physical therapy." Vic reached for his hand. Jerry thought idly to swipe at it, but he grumbled and gave in.

With his attaché's help, Jerry stood up from his desk, gingerly putting pressure on his leg—the pins came out and the cast came off five days ago. It felt good to walk on it, but the muscles on that leg had gone to pudding. They told him he needed to exercise it—even just a lap around his desk a few times a day would be something.

"Tell me," he said, grunting and *oof*ing as he hobbled around the desk, "about Chengdu."

"The permits still aren't in."

"We need to break ground on that. Soon. *Now.*"

"You need to start seriously considering the possibility that Chengdu isn't going to happen, Jerry."

Upper lip curled back in a feral sneer, Jerry said, "That's not an option. China is a huge market. A *necessary* market. We score this, it gives us inroads with film—China's outpacing Hollywood as a global film market, and we're behind that eight ball, Vic. Get it done."

"I can't *get it done*. China's not a maître d' at a booked-up restaurant. I can't flash a palm of cash and get you a table. We have to be patient—we'll make inroads there. In the meantime, make them jealous—consider Tokyo again as an option to—"

"No!" he bellowed, stopping to lean against the desk. "Tokyo sets us back. All the Garlin Gardens need to open up in the *same year.* That's the deal. That's how we sell this. It's how the dream works, *Victor.* I'm not going to be thwarted by the . . . fucking *Yellow Curtain* of China. Hunt, that bitch president, it's her, isn't it? Her fault. She should be opening up trade instead of introducing new tariffs—it's looking like Creel is going to tidy up the GOP nomination, and *he* will sign off on the TAP—"

"Creel doesn't support the Trans-Asia Partnership." Vic gave him a look like, *What kind of an asshole are you?* Same look Dirk used to give him. "President Hunt signed the TAP. But getting in bed with China means a long dance first, and a slow seduction—"

Jerry sneezed again. His eyes felt thick in their sockets. His sinuses felt like concrete. "You can't get it done, I'll find someone who will."

"Jerry, I'm your go-to guy, but I'm not magic."

Cool as a cucumber, that Vic.

Well, fuck him.

"You're fired."

Vic laughed. "Let's get you some lunch—"

"Fuck lunch and fuck you, you're fucking fired."

The man paused. Like he was taking a moment to register the reality of this, that it wasn't just some joke. Vic had been with him for—well, Jerry couldn't remember how long now, whatever—but he just wasn't cutting it anymore. And Jerry didn't like the way Vic spoke down to him. What had Vic ever done? What had he ever accomplished? What had he *made*?

"Jerry. Think about this."

"I thought about it. I don't like you. Think you're so smart all the time. Correcting my words. Looking at me like you think I'm some entitled titty-baby."

"That cold is going to your head. Maybe take a day, go relax. Hit the links—the caddie will drive you around and it'll be good for your legs and it'll let you clear your head a little—"

Jerry got up in his face. "You're not my daddy. I'm *your* daddy and I'm kicking you out of the house, boy."

"Okay." Vic's face was a mask of restrained anger. "If you say so."

"Tell you what, you want your severance package, do something for me on the way out—call Kevin, get him in here."

Vic raised an eyebrow. "Kevin who? Mahoney?"

"No not—who the fuck is Kevin Mahoney?"

"Kevin Mahoney, of Lighthouse Pictures—"

"No, I don't—" Jerry was pissed now. Magma coursing through his veins. He wanted to grab Vic, choke him until his tongue turned blue and his eyes popped like grapes. "Kevin, send in *Kevin*."

"Who is Kevin?"

"My goddamn *son-in-law*."

Vic paused. Like he'd been slapped.

"What?" Jerry asked.

"Your son-in-law's name is *Kenneth*."

"Well." Jerry felt suddenly flustered. Was that right? That couldn't be right. Frothing, he roared: "Send him in! Kevin. Or Kenneth! Shit! And then get the fuck out!"

Two months ago, in Raleigh, North Carolina:

JERRY WAS AT HOME, SIPPING BOURBON ON THE BACK DECK OF HIS PLANTATION-style house, when Vic showed up. The sun was shining. A breeze blowing.

Down at the edges of the estate and around the pond, all the daffodils and hyacinths had sprung up, a panoply of color. When Vic came up behind him, Jerry wouldn't look his way.

"Who let you in?" he asked, droll and pretending not to care.

Vic said, "Susan did, Jerry."

Susan. Jerry's wife. "Bullshit. I told you to give me your key."

"I did give you my key."

"You made a copy, then."

"Jerry, your behavior has been erratic."

"*Viiiiic,*" Jerry said, affecting a whiny, mocking voice. "You were fired. You need to get your ass off my property before I call the police."

"You call the police a lot these days."

Jerry lowered his voice. "I've had . . . intruders."

"Have you? They didn't find anybody."

"Maybe it was *you,*" Jerry sneered.

"If you say so, Jerry. Listen, the BOD hired me—"

The board of directors saddled up with this cocky prick? *Figures,* Jerry thought. They were all a bunch of quislings. That was one of his father's words. *Quislings.* Meant traitor or some such. "Tell them not to worry. I've got this. Garlin Gardens is all moving ahead."

"It is, no thanks to you. You missed the planning meeting in Somerville. You showed up at Berlin, then wandered out halfway through, saying you were—what was it? 'Bored.' You don't answer calls, but call people in the middle of the night. You email all these wild political conspiracy theories—"

"Those aren't just theories. The Dems are hiding kid-touchers in plain sight, Vic, *in plain fucking sight.* You listen to that Hiram Golden show and, and—"

"You need a doctor. You might be experiencing early-onset dementia, Parkinson's, Alzheimer's—something's up."

Jerry lifted his chin and scowled.

"I'm doing fine. The company is doing fine. Get out."

"The board is letting you go."

On this, he spun around, glass held so tight in his hand he was surprised it didn't pop. "You listen to me, you little shit. I founded this company, they can't—"

"Your father founded it. You inherited it."

"They can't fire me."

"They can. With a vote."

"I am a majority shareholder."

"And they will graciously be buying you out."

He seethed. "That isn't their choice. It's mine, and I say no."

"It is their choice," Vic said. "You can thank your father for that. Part of the deal of you inheriting those shares was that, should the BOD find you lacking in some way, they would be able to wrest control painlessly."

Jerry stood, now. His chest heaved like a storm-tossed sea. "Oh, it won't be painlessly. I'll make it hurt. I'll make them bleed."

"Whatever you say. Jerry, I have to tell you: It has not been a pleasure. Your father, Dirk, was a man of ideas, but *you* were just a man who had *Dirk's* ideas, and even then you couldn't do much with them."

And with that, Vic turned to leave.

"Get out!" Jerry said.

"Go to a doctor," Vic called over his shoulder.

Jerry flung the bourbon glass at him. It missed, hitting the side of the house. The glass shattered, left a ding in the house's stone exterior. Bourbon drooled down the wall, and the ice landed in the flower beds.

Vic was gone.

One month ago, in Garlin Gardens Park, Raleigh, North Carolina:

PARK SECURITY CAUGHT HIM OUTSIDE THE TREASURE TOWN "HAUNTED" roller coaster in the Mysterious Island part of the park. Jerry, wearing a rumpled suit even in the growing heat, pounded and kicked on a hidden door in the fake mountain that supported the ride as the animatronic skeletons and pirates (and yes, skeleton-pirates) leered above him, swishing their mugs of grog and swiping at their bony parrots.

Jerry did not look good. His face was red and raw. Around his nose were rings of a crusty white rime. Half-moons of that same crusty-yet-somehow-moist muck hung at the bottoms of his swollen eyes, with little boulders of the stuff gathering at the corners. His lips were dry. His tongue was pale.

Park security knew him, of course. Not individually, for it had been over a decade now since Jerry had aped the actions of his father and come to visit all the staff at the park. But they were aware of him, and looked kindly on someone whom they felt had contributed to the legacy of this place.

As such, they let him go without calling the police.

They did, however, advise Jerry to go to the doctor.

Jerry told them to go to hell. And on the way out, he bellowed at them, "And you tell my father to go to hell, too! Next time I knock on his office door, you tell him to open right up." The security staff looked to one another with puzzled expressions, none of them aware that, thirty years ago, the park administration building was still onsite. It moved in later years to make way for more attractions—such as, of course, the Treasure Town roller coaster. Dirk Garlin's office was famously on the ground floor—so it was accessible to everyone, he said, so that he could hear their dreams if they cared to share them. The door leading into the operational bowels of the Treasure Town ride was roughly in the same spot.

Today, in the Everglades:

THE MAN WANDERED THE EVERGLADES.

Some memory eluded him—a fishing cabin, Chokoloskee, a bottle of bourbon. Another memory chased that one: a gun, a foot through the glass, a man in a bathtub, and then *bang.* All that blood.

Now, though, whoever he was, he had more pressing concerns.

He was chasing his father, who was in turn chasing a dog. The dog was sometimes a cartoon: big goofy paws, a comical red nose, a pink tongue that sometimes unrolled like a necktie. Sometimes the dog was a dog that he remembered, a real dog, a dog from when he was just a kid. Dimwit, they called the dog. His father would doodle that dog in the margins of his invoices, just a few circles and lines—swish-slash-swish.

The dog was lost, and now so was his father.

I'll come for you, Daddy. I'll save you.

Ahead, his father wound through the cypress and the mangrove, staggering through ruts of water and over clumps of mounding grass. The man pushed on after. His father looked over his shoulder, and now he was wearing a mask: the comical gray mask of Shirley Squirrel, what with her button nose and pink cheeks and those fuzzy, fuzzy ears. The mask looked real, until it didn't, and then it just looked like cheap rubber.

The man felt sick and had to stop. He pawed at his face. His hand came away smeared with greasy white. Everything itched. He wanted to lie down and sleep for a while and forget this nonsense, but his father kept running and running, and who would catch him? But when he looked up again, he found he didn't have to. Because there his father stood. Hands on hips. Disapproving stare on his face. "I was a man of ideas," Dirk said, if that was his name. "But you're just a man of *my* ideas."

"I'm sorry," the man, who could not remember his own name, said.

Then his father was gone.

And the name of his father was gone, too.

The man sat down on a tree. He looked in his hand and found a gun there—a boxy, engraved Colt Defender .45 with white ivory grips. It was flecked with rust. No, not rust. Blood. Same blood that sat on the back of the man's hands in dark-brown dots. A name floated through his mind: *Vic*. And then the gun was gone again, a phantom. Had it ever existed? And who, exactly, was Vic?

Then, like everything else, it was gone, too.

The man sneezed. What came out of his nose and mouth was not mucus, not really. It was just more of that greasy white powder, like oiled cornstarch. It almost seemed to glow with a faint white light. *I am incandescent,* he thought. *I shine, like the sun itself. Well, buh-buh-buh-golly, fuh-folks, I shuh-sure don't fuh-feel too guh-good.* His lips felt tacky, glued together. He sneezed again. More of the same came out of him.

The dog was gone. He couldn't see him anymore.

His father—gone, too.

He felt tired. *Just a minute, now. They will wait for me.* Then he'd sneak up on them when they got comfortable. He'd creep through the brush and find them there, and he'd jump out, *boo.*

"The best gift you can give somebody is a surprise . . ." he mumbled, cackling as he said it, strings of sticky saliva connecting his lower lip to his upper. He could barely get the rest out, he was laughing so hard now, his eyes watering, his nose running. The words came out a bubbling gush, a mushy hot mess of slur and slush: ". . . because they never forget it."

He collapsed, face forward.

He fell into a slumber, which gave way to a coma.

He did not wake.

Jerry Garlin's body wouldn't be discovered for two more weeks. And by then, it would be far too late for him—and for everyone else.

PART TWO

SHEPHERDS AND FLOCK

14

GOD'S LIGHT

The number is 232.

JUNE 19
God's Light Church, Burnsville, Indiana

THE CHURCH WASN'T MUCH TO LOOK AT. IF YOU DIDN'T LOOK AT THE LITTLE graveyard framed in by a chain-link fence or the cross hanging on the scant red brick by the door, or at the sign with the block letters that read IF YOU'RE ALMOST SAVED YOU'RE ALL THE WAY LOST, then you might've thought it was just a house. White clapboard siding. Dirt-and-gravel driveway up the side. Windows with patched screens. Gutters hanging low like the broken branches on a dying tree. In the back, the church proper stood with a low steeple looking out over a muddy grass field.

Matthew Bird, pastor of God's Light Church, didn't mind that it looked like a house. He wanted it to feel like home. In part because it *was* a home: It was his home, it was home to those practitioners who sometimes needed a place to stay (like the Geringers, who lost their house to a small tornado two years back), and of course, to Christ Himself.

God lives here, Matthew was wont to say. But then he also would tap his chest and the chest of whoever he was talking to. *But He's in here, too.*

Still, the church needed some attention. With summer about to start, he hoped he could count on some local students to help out.

Hope, though, didn't get the job done. And he quietly suspected that he would be the one out there, doing the work, the lone soldier. God may live here, and Jesus might've been the son of a carpenter, but neither was likely to show up with a hammer and some nails.

That work fell to men.

Today, though, the work was different. Matthew stood on the front porch and said goodbye to those who had come for the meeting of the Graceful Shift recovery program—a Christ-centered approach to conquering addiction, *any* addiction, from alcohol to drugs to sex to online gaming and gambling.

He shook hands and gave hugs to those who walked out. He said goodbye to Dave Mercer, who was addicted to opiate pills after a tractor accident. He gave a long and lingering hug to Colleen Hugh, who found herself in thrall to alcohol after working as a bar waitress for too many years. He whispered a few encouraging words into the ear of Fred Dinsdale, a nice fella coming up on sixty who, in the wake of his wife's passing from breast cancer last year, found himself unable to pull away from internet pornography and eventually, prostitutes. All good people. All people from the community he knew that he cared about, and that he had faith would eventually transcend the burdens put upon them.

Before he passed, Fred leaned in close with his droopy hound-dog face and asked: "Can we talk about it now?"

Matthew smiled when he answered: "If you'd like, Fred. I just didn't want the topic to get in the way of the meeting." Even though he could tell they were all straining to talk about it, like dogs pulling hard on the leash. Everyone was, these days. "We have greater concerns than what's on TV."

"What do you think they are?" Fred asked, almost conspiratorially.

"People," Matthew said. "They're just people."

"But something isn't right. They're taken over by something—the CDC is there with them, but so far they haven't found anything. I heard Homeland Security has been called in. There're *five hundred* of them now—"

Colleen hurried back up the porch, and as she did she said, "No, no, that isn't right, Fred, they're not even at half that—two hundred at most."

"I read an email said there's more than we see on TV."

"You ought not to read every piece of trash comes through your email." She leaned in, the crow's-feet around her eyes deepening as her eyes tapered to slits. "Honestly, you ask me, I think it's aliens," she said, fast putting an end to her moment as the voice of sanity.

Now of course here came roly-poly Dave Mercer, hobbling his way up the steps on his bum knee. "We talking about the sleepwalkers? I think we're looking at some kind of *invasion,* maybe extraterrestrial, but maybe *ultra-*terrestrials, like people or reptilians from another dimension—"

"That's not a thing," Matthew said, but they kept going.

"They're gonna be here tomorrow," Colleen said.

"Not here, but close," Dave said. "News said they might end up in Waldron—or if they go a different way, Milford or even Shelbyville."

Fred prickled. "I don't want to become one of them walkers. I want to keep my mind, my faculties—"

"Hey, c'mon, everybody relax." It was time to intervene. Matthew waved his hands and shook his head. "No one is ever served by jumping to conclusions before all the information is in. Here's a quote for you, and I think it's a good one: 'Your assumptions are your windows on the world. Scrub them off every once in a while, or the light won't come in.'"

Colleen's face scrunched up. "What Bible passage is that?"

"It's not the Bible, it's Isaac Asimov."

They gave him a puzzled look.

"What? You can read other books besides the Bible," Matthew said, laughing. "Pick up a novel once in a while. Now go on, go home."

They left the porch, talking as they went. The cork was out of the bottle, and all the spirits were pouring out. They were animated as anything. Worried. Excited. Confused. He felt it, too. A buzz in the air, like they were all antennae receiving strange signals from those walkers. But he didn't have time to ruminate on the subject of the sleepwalkers, because as the others left, one remained: Out walked DeCarlo James.

Young kid, African American, sixteen. Hair shorn close to the head. White T-shirt, baggy jeans. He had his chin lifted in perpetual disregard. The cross this one bore upon his shoulders and upon his soul was heroin addiction.

The dubious look on the boy's face only deepened as Matthew approached him for a handshake or a hug.

"Naw," DeCarlo said.

"Meeting didn't work for you?" Matthew asked.

"It did not, Pastor Matt."

"It was just your first. There's still time. Care to share why?"

"I dunno."

"I think you do."

It took a second, then DeCarlo sucked air between his teeth and let it fly: "Some of that shit you said is bullshit. The twelve steps."

"Why is it bull?"

"I'm not powerless."

"Oh." The first three steps were about being powerless, about putting yourself in God's hands and allowing yourself to be smaller than Him. "I think faith is very much about trusting in a higher power."

"I trust in *me*. I have faith in *me*."

"I have faith in you, too. But I have faith that you'll let God in. Because without God, that's how you got here. That's how you got . . . to this place, to this meeting, to your *addiction*."

DeCarlo made a face like someone just pressed a cat turd to his lips, tried to make him kiss it. "So, lemme get this straight. I fuck up, it's my fault. But if I do right, it's not really me, it's God."

"If you do right, it's because *you* made a choice to let God in. The point is that you made the choice to get help, and that it doesn't have to all be on your shoulders. Let God shoulder some of that weight."

"You know that the twelve steps are like, maybe eight percent effective, right? And that drug therapy plus psychiatric therapy is ten times more effective than the shit you're slinging in that meeting room?"

Matthew stepped back, faking like he'd just been punched. "DeCarlo, I don't agree with that statistic. It's hurtful. Tell that little fact of yours to Fred, Colleen, and Dave. Tell that to everyone else who's gone through the Graceful Shift program. Yes, some . . . falter, but God picks them up again when they reach for His hand." He narrowed his eyes. "Where did you get your numbers, anyway?"

"Where else? The internet, man. I go to the library."

"Everything you read on the internet isn't automatically true."

"And everything some nice preacher tells you isn't automatically true, either, Pastor Matt. Listen, when we were up in Indianapolis, my sister Tanesha went through therapy, real therapy, and she's been good for two years. Got a nice job, cashier at Aldi. Got a little apartment. Doing okay. Then we come out here to the boonies and only thing a court mandates is *this* place." DeCarlo scuffed his foot on the peeling paint of the porch wood beneath him. "I wanna kick this thing, but I dunno about your program, man."

"My program is what's keeping you out of juvie, DeCarlo. You have to go through it, *all* the way through it. But . . ." He looked over his shoulder to make sure the others had gone. "I know somebody. Drug treatment counselor in Bloomington. She's good."

"And expensive, I bet."

"I'll raise those stakes and bet that if I asked her, she'd come up, work with you on the side for nothing. Pro bono—that means free. How'd that be?"

"You for real?"

"I am. But you have to keep coming *here,* too. That's the deal." Matthew offered his hand to seal the bargain.

DeCarlo looked at the proffered handshake like Matthew might secretly be hiding a tarantula in the palm of his hand. But then he shook.

"Deal."

"See you, DeCarlo."

"Later, Pastor Matt. Oh, hey, you ask me, those sleepwalkers—I think it's like some X-Men shit. Maybe they're mutants."

Matthew laughed. "Go on, DeCarlo. Say hi to your mama for me."

"All right, all right. Thanks, Pastor Matt."

The kid strolled off the porch toward the road. He had a lift to his steps. Matthew hoped he hadn't just imagined that—the kid deserved a bit of happiness and hope.

Pastor Matt sighed.

With that meeting over, it was time for another, different meeting.

This one about addiction, too. Of a sort.

ADDICTION. IT WASN'T REALLY THAT, Matthew knew. He knew he wasn't being fair to her. Just the same, Matthew felt what he felt, which was this: Drugs were not the answer, not illegal drugs, not doctor-prescribed ones. Not for this. But helping his wife come to the same conclusion was . . . not easy.

It wasn't easy because people became addicted to ideas as easy as they became addicted to drugs. And his wife, well, she'd become addicted to the *idea* of her having some kind of *disorder,* some mental condition, that couldn't be solved the way it needed to be solved.

Autumn Bird sat on the corner of their bed, staring out the window. When Matthew came into the room, the floorboards creaking under the fraying, bubbled-up carpet, his wife did not look his way. All she said was, "Hi, baby."

"Autumn, hey."

He came and sat next to her. Took her hand in his.

"So, this isn't a good day," she said. Looked like she had been crying: Her eyes were puffy and raw. But for now, the storm had passed. He felt terrible, but he was glad to have missed it. When she was in the throes of one of those storms—that's what she called them, her storms—there was nothing he could do but batten down the hatches and wait it out.

"I know. That happens. We all have good and bad days."

The look she gave him was one of pity, a look that said, *It's a shame you just don't get it*. And that's more or less what she told him time and time again, and what she told him now.

"My bad days are not like your bad days," she said.

"I know. I'm sorry. I didn't mean . . ." But the words wilted. "We should talk about the thing you asked me last night. I—"

"You don't think I should go back on meds." That sentence, sick with disappointment. "Matthew, please."

"We don't have the money. Our health insurance plan is less than bare bones, it's . . . down to the marrow. The Zoloft is over fifty bucks a month, and that's with our insurance, *and* with us buying the generic brand. And it's not like the Zoloft didn't have its side effects, sometimes you seemed like a zombie on that stuff, and then the headaches, and the . . . the other parts of it." It made Autumn unreceptive to sex, for one. And two, sometimes she said she had really black, bleak urges. Not suicide, not exactly. But the urge for self-harm. That stuff, he decided, was poison.

Worse, she was mother to their son. Their son needed a mom who was present and stable. Not someone lost in a pharmaceutical forest.

She squeezed his hand.

"I know, but the doctor said there are other medications, we just need to find the one that works with my brain chemistry."

"The Zoloft made you damn near want to kill yourself, Autumn."

"No, the *depression* makes me want to kill myself, the Zoloft just . . . put an edge on that knife, okay? Other pills could tamp that down."

"And what will they cost? How many doctor visits will that take? We go up that roller coaster and down the roller coaster and . . ." He sighed, held her hand tight. "Honey, they've shown time and again that prayer and Christ-forward thinking can help conquer this—"

"No, they *haven't* shown that," she snapped, pulling her hand away from his. "Nobody's shown that. They've *said* it, but they haven't *shown* it. Do you think it's possible to pray away someone's gayness?"

"Of course not. *Pray away the gay* doesn't work, and worse, it's harmful. People are who people are."

She stood up. Arms crossed. Completely closed off, now. "And who I am is someone with depression, and that means you can't just pray it away. It's not a *mood*, Matt. I'm not just *sad*. It's like I've got a hole inside my mind and inside that hole is a . . . a voice. Sometimes it's loud, sometimes it's quiet, but it's always, *always* there. That voice tells me that I'm not good enough, and the world is going to hell, and nothing matters. I'll never be a famous artist. The coral reef is bleached and dead. I'll never have more kids than the one we have. I'll die without ever accomplishing anything and it doesn't matter anyway because global warming is going to boil us or bake us but that only happens if North Korea doesn't drop a bomb in our lap first, or maybe a plane will crash on my head, or maybe the ground will swallow me up, or maybe I'll get cancer and it'll eat me up. And then—*then* I turn on the TV and everybody's talking about those walkers and that sends me into a different spiral. What are they? Do they need our help? Do we need *their* help? Is it a disease, is it climate change, is it . . . some terrorist group in the Middle East? It repeats again and again, this cycle. I get sad, then I get worried, and then I get helpless. Lost in a . . . in a fog. I just need something to help clear away the fog. Okay?"

He nodded and reached for her hand again. She did not pull away.

"Okay," he said. If he had to follow her down this path—even if only to disprove its value—he would. "Call the doctor. Make the appointment. We'll try something else, a new prescription, see how that goes."

She watched him, wary.

"Are you sure?"

"I'm sure. We'll find the money." *Somehow.*

He wrapped her up in a hug. They did not kiss. They hadn't kissed in months. But the hug felt nice, and he hoped it felt nice for her, too.

HE KNELT OUTSIDE, PULLING WEEDS, thinking about Autumn. *Worrying* about Autumn. It nagged at him. What if he was wrong? What if her point was right? You couldn't pray away gayness. Maybe you couldn't just pray away her depression, if it really was that. But he'd known Christ-focused therapy programs that made good on that promise . . .

He heard a truck rumbling down the road. The diesel grumble vibrated up through his knees and his hands and, as it grew closer, into his teeth. Matthew wiped the dirt on his jeans and plucked the gardening gloves off as the black pickup pulled up. It was an older-model Chevy, lifted high on mammoth tires. The back was piled high with junk: bales of barbed wire, a couple of old dining room chairs, two different toolboxes, a rust-bellied pellet stove. On the side was a logo that read: STOVER JUNK AND SALVAGE.

The truck pulled up, tilting as it eased a front tire into the drainage ditch.

The passenger side opened up, and Bo got out of the truck, jumping over the ditch into the grass. The boy, Matthew's son, had a mop of greasy-messy hair on his head and cheeks riddled with a volcanic topography of pimples. At fifteen, he was having a rough go of things. It was a hard time, Matthew knew, in any kid's life. In both body and mind, Bo was halfway between a boy and a man. He had the desires and anger of a grown adult but didn't have the maturity to process it—plus, the poor kid's body was like a washing machine full of gasoline. All it took was one spark and then: *kaboom.*

He started to walk past. Matthew gave him a drive-by hair-mussing, which Bo grumpily retreated from. "Dad," Bo warned.

The truck's engine cut out.

The driver's-side door opened.

This is new.

Out stepped the big man: big in every direction, like an ox bristling with both fat and muscle. The fellow had a beard hanging from his chin that called to mind the root system of an overturned tree. Dark eyes stared out over a nose that had surely been broken many times over. Ship-cannon arms swung by his side as he loped around the front of the truck, a big smile on his face.

"Bo!" the man called, his voice a growling thrum, in many ways more impressive than the roar of the truck he drove. "Don't you walk past your father like that. You pay him respect."

No hesitation found, the boy turned heel-to-toe and marched dutifully back to Matthew. He looked up at his father and said, "Hi, Dad."

"Hey, kid. You good?"

"I'm good."

"Go on inside, get washed up for supper." As Bo trotted off, Matthew called after him: "Don't forget to tell Mom you're home."

"Uh-huh," the boy moped, and then was gone.

And now Matthew was left alone with the big man.

Ozark Stover.

The pastor was not a small man, exactly: At five-foot-ten he was of average height, with a slim build (a build his son inherited). But standing face-to-face with Stover made him feel like a little kid looking up at an angry parent.

Before today, Ozark never got out of his truck. He always dropped Bo off—Bo had been working at Stover's junkyard on weekends since January, and now with summer here he went there every day to help out—but the big man never got out of his truck. He just dropped the boy off every day, then drove away. Never waved, never said a word. It was what it was. Matthew was not always comfortable with the arrangement, knowing so little about the man, but Bo wanted it, and he felt it was time to give the boy some independence while also lending him a sense of responsibility.

"Preacher," Ozark said with a curt nod.

"Mister Stover, it's an honor and a pleasure to see you again—and please, no need to call me preacher. It's pastor, for one, but I'm good with Matt or Matthew."

"Hnh." The man crossed both tree-trunk arms and rested them upon his prodigious girth. "My friends call me Oz or Ozzy."

"Well, Oz, thanks for dropping Bo off today—"

"You're not a friend yet, Preacher. Ozark will be fine."

"Oh. Ah. Of course, apologies." He laughed in a self-effacing way. "Ozark, thanks for coming by, is there anything I can do for you?"

"There is." He sniffed. "You're a man of God."

"That is what they tell me."

Stover leaned off to the side, pressed one finger against his nostril, then blew a snot-dart out of his other nose-hole: the farmer's blow, they used to call it, though the kids today just called that a snot-rocket.

The man went on as if nothing had happened. "I want to get your feeling on the state of the world today, Preacher."

Blink, blink.

"Oh. You mean—politics? I know there's a presidential race going on but I try to keep my concerns to the spirit and soul of the country." People always wanted to know if Matthew was a Democrat or a Republican, did he vote with the evangelicals, was he a libertarian and if so, what flavor. Did he like sitting president Nora Hunt? Would he back the dark horse of the GOP, Ed Creel? Matthew preferred not to talk about any of that. What he told Stover was true: He preferred to worry about deeper, more moral matters. Politics, despite what some believed, was not morality, nor reflective of it.

Stover sighed. "Politics isn't the whole of it, though I can't in my right mind imagine why anyone would vote for Hunt the Cunt. Creel's right, that bitch'll chop this country up for parts, sell us to Wall Street who will sell us to China. Time for a change in this country. Creel's one of us."

Matthew wasn't so sure that Ed Creel was "one of them." He came from one of the richest families in America. President Hunt got saddled with the label that she was some out-of-touch coastal elite, but truth was, her family came from South Carolina, while Creel was born in Boston with a gold skeleton key in his mouth. Not that Matthew cared for Hunt, either—she was pro-choice, which was to him the same thing as being anti-life. He couldn't in good conscience vote for that. But the hypocrisy even there was keenly felt: Creel mouthed off about how he was all pro-life, but was on the record as supporting the death penalty. *And* they'd proved that he'd paid for *at least* three abortions in his lifetime. Not that anyone cared. And not that Matthew would tell Ozark Stover any different. You didn't change anyone's mind about politics by hammering away at them—all that did was drive the nail deeper into the wall of their own certainty.

"No," Stover went on, and Matthew knew what he was going to ask before he asked it, "I want to hear your thinking on the walkers."

"Oh. Ozark, I don't know that I'm much of an expert. What's happening there—"

"What's happening *here,* soon enough. They'll be passing through Waldron tomorrow, it looks like."

"Maybe. Point is, I'm more concerned about the spiritual health of my parishioners. I just want them to make the right decisions for themselves and their families—and, of course, for God. If I can give them those tools, then whatever happens in the day-to-day is something they're prepared for. The old teach-a-man-to-fish situation, you might say."

Now Stover stepped in closer. Uncomfortably so. The man was already quite the presence, like a grizzly bear standing on its back legs, but now this, *this* felt somehow like a threat. Or perhaps, in some bizarre way, an expression of comfort and camaraderie. Matthew hoped it to be the latter.

"This situation with the walkers might *be* a spiritual matter." Stover's voice was low and deep. His breath was heavy with a rough, mineral stink—it smelled the way a bitten tongue tastes, of blood and meat.

"How so?" Matthew asked, clearing his throat. He tried to take a step back, but Stover just took another step forward.

"They walk like they're on a pilgrimage. But there's nothing godly or spiritual about them. I want you to imagine it, Preacher. I've read the accounts of families who are dealing with this, who have watched what happened to their loved ones. One day everything is normal, next thing you know, your wife, your son—or maybe you yourself—are gone. Your body stolen out from under you like *that.*" Ozark snapped his fingers. It sounded like a branch snapping off a tree in a storm. "Think about that, Preacher. One minute you're you, the next—you're one of *them.*"

Matthew had to agree: That sounded horrific.

"And what do you think they are?" the pastor asked.

"I don't know. That's why I'm asking you. The boys at the yard are saying it's terrorism—some Islamic shit, some drug they put in the water or sprayed over people. But I don't buy that. Those animals in the Middle East aren't that sophisticated. They live in caves. They don't attack with fancy weapons— they drive cars and trucks into people. It's guns and knives and maybe a crude explosive now and again. This is a whole other level. China, could be. They got weapons we wouldn't believe. But I dunno."

"It is quite the puzzle," he agreed, though to what he was agreeing precisely, he did not know. He nodded, though, and said, "You are right, I should take this up with my parishioners."

"Maybe it was the comet," Ozark said, like he was barely listening.

"Comet?"

"Night before they appeared, that comet went past."

Matthew remembered hearing about the comet. Named after a Japanese astronomer? "I apologize, but I don't follow."

Stover seemed irritated at that.

"It's a *comet.* Like in Revelation."

"You mean Wormwood."

"Wormwood. That's right."

Matthew wondered aloud: "In the book they called it a falling star, and some translations don't even name it—you have to understand, Ozark, Revelation is likely more a historical document than one about prophesying the end. John of Patmos was exiled and imprisoned as part of Roman persecution of Christians, and he wrote these coded letters to the churches in order to empower them and . . ." He struggled to contextualize it; it had been a long time since he'd had to go over this. Since college. "And paint a picture of their enduring cosmic reward under the aegis of Heaven."

"You're saying it's fake."

"I'm not saying it's fake. I'm saying it's metaphor."

"A metaphor isn't something real, Preacher."

"It is real in its way. Like Obi-Wan said in *Star Wars,* 'from a certain point of view.'"

"You're saying the Bible isn't real."

"No, I'm saying it's metaphor—"

"The whole Bible is metaphor?"

"No! No. I just mean—" His words stumbled over one another. "I just mean that one book."

"The Bible *is* one book, least it was last time I held one."

"The Bible comprises many books."

"Uh-huh." Stover went quiet, stared cigarette burns into him. "Here's what I know, Preacher. I'm not much of a good Christian, I confess. But something's gone wrong. Gone *sour*. Maybe it was that comet, maybe I'm reaching, but I know that the word for Wormwood in ancient Greek— *apsinthos*—means 'bitterness, from a bitter herb.'" He must've seen Matthew's face, as he smiled, then, the great cleft of his mouth stretching wide in the center of that dark beard. "You didn't think I knew that, did you? Too high-minded for my kind. No, I'm not a good Christian, but I can read. And maybe something did poison those waters, turn these people into those . . . things, those sleepwalking strangers. Maybe it was the comet. Maybe the Devil himself. Maybe this is a sign of something worse to come. Those walkers don't serve God. God wouldn't do that to Americans."

"I . . . will take that all into consideration, Ozark."

Then Stover softened a little. He took a step back, the smile on his face lingering longer. "I apologize, Pastor. Here you are, going about your day, and I've rolled up on you, pinning you down like a fly under a swatter. You don't owe me your free time, and I admit . . ." He looked momentarily embarrassed. "I come on a little strong. I'm just concerned, is all."

"I can understand that."

"Your free time is your time, and I look forward to what you have to say about it tomorrow during church."

"Tomorrow," he repeated, almost like he didn't understand the word.

"Tomorrow is Sunday, isn't it?"

"It . . . is. I'm just not used to seeing you in attendance."

Now Ozark's smile grew big and broad, like a billboard made of teeth. "Preacher, count on me. I'll bring a few of my boys, too, as I think we could all use a little spiritual instruction in this strange and tumultuous time."

"So be it," Matthew said, offering a wan smile. He didn't know how to feel—on the one hand, he was happy that his church would see an increased attendance, and that Stover and his men might be inclined to seek out God when before they had not. On the other hand, Stover scared Matthew. He didn't know why. Perhaps it was his size. Or his intensity. Maybe, to Matthew's own shame, it was a class issue: Matthew grew up roundly middle-class, his father a banker, his mother a caterer, whereas Stover lived out on the fringes. He was backwoods in the truest sense: Though he wasn't poor now, Bo said Stover grew up poor, once. If that was the problem, Matthew saw fit to conquer that prejudice in himself posthaste. "I look forward to seeing you in the morning, then, Ozark."

"I'll see you, Preacher. Oh, word of caution—storm is coming tonight. Sounds like a big one, too. Maybe it'll wash all those walkers away and come tomorrow we won't have much to talk about."

With that, as he sauntered back to his truck, thunder rumbled far off in the distance, making Matthew jump just a little.

15

THE STORM

Local Indiana Residents Protest Repeal of Healthcare Law

. . . local resident Clade Berman, 45, stepped up to the microphone and gave state senator Olly Turell a piece of his mind on Tuesday. Berman, a local contractor, said to Turell, "Ten years ago I couldn't get health insurance because I had a bum knee, and preexisting clauses kept me from keeping myself healthy. Those clauses being struck down helped me to get insurance again, but now you're telling me you want me to get sick again? No safety net? We're all living hand to mouth out here, Senator, and it seems you want us to suffer for it. To hell with that." Those gathered showed their support in a rally of applause for Berman . . .

JUNE 19
Ten miles outside Waldron, Indiana

IT WAS 7 P.M., A FEW DAYS FROM SUMMER SOLSTICE, THE LONGEST DAY OF THE year, but way out over the cornfield the sky had gone so dark with the coming storm it looked like clouds of blackflies gathering over the horizon.

Shana stood there, looking at it through her iPhone. She snapped a few pics of the brooding sky, then slid a few Instagram filters over them to make them look grimmer, nastier. A quick tap of the button and they were posted to IG.

Lately, her IG following had doubled. In part because she'd been taking snaps of the walkers, the RV, things like that. Yesterday she took a quick shot of a couple of old white people on the side of the road holding up signs that said, WALKERS ARE TERRORISTS, except of course it was misspelled TER-

RARISTS, and she made up a hashtag for it: #WalkersAreTerrariums. That went kinda viral, got attached to anybody holding a stupid-ass, misspelled protest sign. Any other day that might've made her feel awesome but now mostly it just bummed her out.

In the distance, lightning licked the sky.

She wished she'd gotten a shot of it. Too late now.

"I don't like that storm," Shana said.

Her father, sitting behind the wheel of the RV, said: "It looks bad, but some things look worse than they really are. Besides, it could miss us."

"It looks like the end of the world out there. I don't think you can dodge the end of the world."

"Storms out here in the Midwest are different from storms back east. Back home we get these big sweeping coastal fronts—" He moved his hands like a weatherman, made a *whoosh* sound. "And they push across us like a slow flood. Out here, though—you ever watch those tornado-chaser shows? They're erratic, like snakes moving through grass. Never know which way they're gonna turn, sweetheart. It'll be okay."

It'll be okay.

Everyone wanted to keep telling her that.

"If a tornado hits, they'll get swept up in it. I know that not much seems to affect them, but I think a tornado will—"

Her father, through politely gritted teeth, said: "I said it will be okay." Softer now: "Have some faith."

That was the other thing: Dad was starting to say shit like that. *Have faith.* Ugh. He'd started talking, too, about going to church when they got back, like in his head he held some generic, preschooler's idea of God: some big bearded Santa Claus analog watching over all the good little girls and boys to make sure they were okay. Shana went to Sunday school once, just once, at her mother's urging. She stepped into the room, saw a *bleeding guy* nailed to a couple of beams on the wall, and she noped her way right out of there. Wailing, crying, *Stop the ride I wanna get off.* Years later, she poked through the Bible—because okay let's be honest that was her Swedish Death Metal phase and suddenly a bloody guy on a cross held a certain romantic sway—and all she found was a few nice platitudes swaddled in a whole lot of hypocrisy, violence, and misogyny. No *way* was she going to church.

Other problem with her father right now: He didn't want to *talk* about any of this. He would not acknowledge what was going on, and what was going on here went well beyond *weird* and into *the stuff of a Stephen King novel.* The flock now numbered over two hundred walkers. And once every few hours, a new one would join the parade.

With them came others. A new walker might bring loved ones—most came along weeping, screaming, trying to pull their loved one back from the brink of being lost to them. But they found the same that Shana had: Trying to rescue your loved ones doomed them. Seizures and screams. Bloodshot eyes and a fast-moving fever cooking them like an egg. So far, nobody since Mark Blamire had popped like a firecracker—those trying to restrain them either had stopped before detonation, or were themselves stopped by the other shepherds.

(That's what the media called them. *Shepherds.* Then there were the walkers, the sleepwalkers, the sleepers, the flock, the herd—lotta different names for them.)

For every walker came two or three shepherds, and they came in their own procession. Some walked. Others drove vans or pickups, or brought along pop-ups and RVs, the vehicles easing along at a few miles an hour— sometimes stopping for a few minutes before starting their engines anew and driving forward. They had what they simply called the front guard and the rear guard: At the fore were half a dozen vehicles leading the flock, and following behind were another half a dozen. Some came along as long as they could, one day or a few days until obligations and life called them back. Some arrived and, like Shana and her father, never left. Others still did not follow the walkers but instead drove ahead, watching and waiting.

Of course, the shepherds were not alone. The CDC was still here, now with a bigger presence. (They had a truck now that pulled along a mobile lab built onto a gooseneck trailer.) State troopers tagged along, same as they had in Pennsylvania—whenever they crossed state lines, new troopers picked up the mantle. They weren't friendly and they kept their distance, and Shana got the feeling they were more their jailers than they were their protectors. The FBI had a rotating presence—black SUVs usually not following along but seen parked along the so-called parade route.

And all that didn't include the media.

Shana hated them.

They were fucking *ceaseless creepers.* Tourists zipping around like yellow-jackets before the first frost, all cameras and microphones and questions all

up in your shit. They even had a couple of "embedded" reporters now—
someone from CNN and another from the BBC. News helicopters went over
a few times a day, too, for those vaunted *aerial* shots of the flock. She wanted
to punch them in the face anytime they got close.

Particularly, anytime they got close to Nessie.

Nessie.

Nessie still walked at the front of the walkers—and sometimes, Shana
had to remind herself that her little sister was the first of the flock (and
she, herself, the first shepherd). It's why she and her father chose to bring
the RV to the front of the flock and stay up there ahead of the crowd—
peering out the back window let them keep eyes on Nessie. Sometimes they
could get close if the CDC wasn't doing any testing, and when they were
able to get close to her, Shana might brush Nessie's hair or try to paint her
nails. Nessie, like many of the walkers, got dirty—pollen stuck to their skin
in a yellow shine, for instance. So they tried sponging her off best as they
could. (Though they could not attend to her feet, which at this point were
nearly tar black with filth.) Shana talked to her. Sang songs to her. Bitched
to her.

Dad stayed away.

Because, Shana thought, he just couldn't hack it.

He was here, yes.

But he wasn't *here*. Not really.

Soon, she knew, they'd run out of money. Which meant no food and no
gas, which further meant Dad would dig deeper into Nessie's college fund—
meaning, he would carve into her future so that they could remain with her
for however long this strange, unspooling dream went. He pretended it wasn't
true, but she heard him talking to some of the other families. Dad thought
he was protecting her by lying to her.

He should know better by now, she thought.

A knock rapped at the RV door. It seemed super weird to get a knock at
the door of a moving vehicle, but she had to remind herself—they were only
driving five miles an hour to stay close to the flock. Her dad eased the brakes
and asked her to "get the door" like it was the most normal thing in the world,
and she hurried over and opened it up.

At the door was Mia Carillo, one of the other shepherds. She was sister
to one of the sleepwalkers: Mateo, or Matty. She wasn't just his sister, but his
twin sister. Though she was a few years older than Shana, the two of them

hit it off, were fast friends. Mia was a raging snark-machine bitch, and Shana was all-in for that shit. Her father said they were like two birds of a feather, but Shana thought of them more like two dogs rolling around in dirt—and loving every second of it.

"*Hola,* Stewart family," Mia said, waving as she entered.

"*Hola, chica,*" Shana said, going for a fist-bump and blowing it up after, then moving in for the hug.

Dad, too, said hi with a casual wave from the driver's seat. He couldn't keep the RV parked for long or the walkers would start streaming around it—so he asked: "In or out?"

"Out," Mia said. "We're gonna play farme—"

Shana punched her in the arm. Mia, little monstress that she was, didn't refer to themselves as *shepherds*—instead, she said they were farmers. (Because, duh, farmers take care of the vegetables.)

"Gonna go do the shepherd thing," Shana said through gritted teeth, shooting Mia a fierce look. Mia winked and gave her a sly middle finger.

"Give Nessie a kiss for me," Dad said. "And watch the weather."

She swooped up her backpack. "You wanna go, Dad?"

"No, I'll just keep the Beast trucking along." *The Beast:* her nickname for the RV. Dad hated it at first, maybe hated it still, but it stuck. She wanted to ask if he was sure—but what was the point? Like she said: He was here, but he wasn't *here*-here. He'd stick to the truck, which meant she had to be the one out there. So out there she went, she and Mia.

Off in the distance, thunder rolled: the lung-rumbling growl of a waking monster. Mia said: "You think the storm's gonna be bad?"

"I dunno," Shana said as the two of them headed toward the walkers, past the CDC trailer, past a cop car. "I try not to worry about anything until I need to. Because honestly, what's the point."

"Screw that. I worry about everything *constantly.*"

"That sounds awful."

"It sounds smart, is what it is."

"If you say so." Mia's twin brother, Mateo, was farther down. Nessie, of course, led the pack. "I'll see you in a few," Shana said.

"Bye, girlfriend." Mia offered up yet *another* middle finger before she descended into the flock, wandering among the walkers. That was how they did it—moved among them like they were just trees in the woods.

Shana headed up to Nessie. She gave a small wave to other shepherds out there—Lucy Chao, whose mother, Eleanor, was shuffling along in her bathrobe; Roger and Wendy Calder, an elderly couple whose Harvard-grad son, Eldon, had shed his exceptional genius and become just another sleep-walker; Aliya Jameson, whose best friend, Tasha, dropped the slushie she'd just poured and walked out of an Ohio convenience store to become one with the flock. Shana, for her part, took out her headphones—okay, they were the Beats by Dre 'phones she stole from Headphones Kid, whose *actual* name was Darryl Sweet. She plugged the cord into her phone, popped on some Yeah Yeah Yeahs, and got to work.

As the music went on, she spoke to Nessie. She knew her voice was louder than it needed to be over the music, but she didn't care. "Hey, sis," she said. "Guess we're not gonna wake up today?" She *tsked*. "You brat."

She took out her brush, ran it through the girl's long, straight hair. It bit through snarls and knots as she gave it a quick once-over. Then she popped the top on some Burt's Bees lip balm and gave the girl's lips a dab-dab-dab—the walkers' lips never chapped, but the grapefruit scent used to be Nessie's favorite, so Shana did it anyway. After that, she nabbed a wet wipe from her pocket—stolen from an Arby's a few days ago—and used it to clean the road-dirt from her sister's freckly cheeks.

Someone tugged on her sleeve, startling her. It was Aliya. The woman peered out sheepishly from underneath her headscarf. Shana plucked one of the headphone cups away from her ears. "Whassup?"

Aliya said, "I don't suppose I can borrow a wet wipe?" She leaned in and whispered, as if embarrassed: "A bird shit in Tasha's hair."

"You can't borrow it," Shana said.

"Oh. Sorry." Aliya started to move away, but Shana gently pulled her back and said:

"No, I mean, I don't want a bird-poop wet wipe back. You can just *have* one." She tried to cover this up with an awkward smile, but she was afraid it just came across more smart-ass than anything. But Aliya seemed okay with it, and nodded.

"Thanks. How's Nessie?"

Shana shrugged. "I mean, fine? As fine as . . . all this is."

"I know, right? I'm . . . still trying to figure out if any of this is even real. It's not possible. None of this seems possible."

Shana thought but did not say: *It's possible, dude. It's possible and it's happening right now and we're along for the ride whether we like it or not.*

Suddenly, the conversation attracted others—shepherds were like that, sometimes. They were islands, until they weren't. Any moment of connection, any hope to communicate with one another and commiserate on the craziness of everything was a moment nobody wanted to waste. Three other shepherds popped around them—Lucy Chao, plus Kenny Barnes (whose game-designer brother Keith was a walker) and Hayley Levine (who was here watching over a cousin, Jamie-Beth). Next came talking about the storm, about the CDC, about how they wanted the president to say more, and *then* it dissolved into the standard talk of what this even was or where it came from (terrorists, the government, monkeys, invasive plants, God, the Devil, what about that comet). And now here came Mia, and all the while Shana thought, *Could you people just leave me alone for five minutes with my damn sister?*

Before she had a chance to object, though—

The one CDC guy, Robbie Taylor with the muttonchops, called over, said any available shepherds needed to come over. A meeting about the storm, he said. Which spawned a whole new round of worried whispers: What was this storm, when would it hit, and what would it do to the flock?

Would they be okay?

All Shana could think was: *No, nobody's ever really okay, dum-dums.*

It felt cynical and cold, and she was glad she didn't say it out loud.

But she worried that it was true, just the same.

We don't have any answers.

It'd been two weeks, and that was what Benji Ray had:

Nothing. The absence of anything that answered anything.

Oh, they had *data*. They had *information*. But none of it brought context to what was going on.

WE DON'T HAVE ANY ANSWERS.

They still didn't have any viable blood tests. None of the start-ups came through with anything that worked. They found no evidence of *Trypanosoma*, either—though they couldn't rule it out, science didn't work that way. They couldn't invent answers and assume they were true because they hadn't yet disproved them. And it also nagged at him that to this day they had no more information on the body-snatchers who'd absconded with the remains of both math teacher Mark Blamire and state trooper Chris Kyle. The one additional bit they had was that two days later, Virginia police found the ambulance. It was in a field, burned to a crisp. No bodies. And no recoverable evidence. Whoever did the job did it well enough.

It was intentional.

A cover-up.

But why? What was this?

Alone, Benji paced the mobile lab—a high-tech CDC lab set up in a thirty-two-foot gooseneck trailer. The others were outside—Martin was about to give, or was perhaps already giving, the day's orders and something resembling a pep talk.

Benji didn't need it. He wasn't even working for the CDC—Loretta, understandably, had tried having him removed from the scene, but Sadie overruled it, saying that Benex-Voyager had sovereignty when it came to hiring and firing and how they chose to utilize Black Swan in what she termed "a live-action beta test" of its field capabilities. (And in fact, that's where Sadie was right now: back in Atlanta, meeting with Loretta, reporting on Black Swan's effectiveness.)

Most surprising of all was that Martin Vargas went to bat for Benji.

After that night in the motel, Martin seemed to warm back up to Benji. He still viewed his participation and presence with a dram of suspicion, sure, and he notably kept Benji from interacting with the public or the media, but he fought to keep Benji present.

So here he was.

Out of the public eye.

Wandering a rough orbit of the inside of the trailer.

The lab trailer had its own plumbing and bathroom, its own electric (running off primary solar that fed battery backups), and a bank of Windows machines running every piece of diagnostic software they had: automatic blood culture instruments, centrifuges with sealed buckets and rotors to prevent aerosolization of infected material, microscopes, hematology Vacutainers, digital cameras, PPE suits, and on and on. Almost none of it mattered. They had so little to test. No blood cultures. No skin samples. No waste material—and how these walkers were not excreting urine or feces was beyond him. As was the fact *they did not eat or drink*.

They *did* manage to get a few samples: saliva, for one, which gave them some data to play with. Saliva was one way to test for hormones, and the results there were interesting, if not entirely illuminating. Some hormones tracked unreasonably low: low estrogen, testosterone, adrenaline, cortisol. Others were off the charts: high DHEA, high progesterone, and almost nuclear levels of melatonin. Low cortisol meant low stress on the body, possibly as a product of melatonin: Melatonin countered cortisol and vice versa. Melatonin was the "rest" hormone, the one that dominated circadian rhythms and sleep patterns. One might take melatonin at night to remind the brain, *Now is the time for sleep.*

Also found in the saliva: preternaturally high levels of antibodies and enzymes, and low levels of blood sugars.

The picture it painted was like one of those magic-eye posters. Benji hoped if he stared at it long enough, it would start to make sense. That one day he'd see a dolphin or a boat and then it would all come together before he went totally and irreparably cross-eyed.

So far, no luck. High levels of antibodies explained why they saw no infectious agents in the saliva—which was good, but did not give them a complete picture, as many antigens would not show in spit anyway.

Low blood sugar was puzzling: These bodies had boundless energy, even if their expression *of* that energy was a steady, plodding walk.

A walk that never ended.

They wanted to do EEGs and EKGs—testing for both heart and brain activity through electrodes—but movement skewed those numbers and told them too little. And it wasn't like you could quick stick one of them in an MRI tube—not unless you wanted to create an even bigger bomb.

Benji did now what he had been doing more and more:

He pulled out the phone.

Not his normal phone, no.

The Black Swan phone. The one Sadie had used to find the unfindable— video footage from the hospital's servers. (Footage that, as it turned out, the hospital had tried to hide, because they felt it made them legally culpable in the loss of not one, but two bodies in a potential epidemic case.)

Benji had found himself relying on the phone somewhat regularly these days. Already, a smartphone felt like the deepest rabbit hole—a simple Google search gave you much of the world's knowledge at your beck and call. But Black Swan was a whole order of magnitude more impressive. In part because of how plugged in it was. Data for so long was difficult to access because it was scattered across the digital fundament like sand cast across a glass table. It was difficult to connect one thing to the next because of so many missing dots. But Black Swan had access to nearly all of it.

Which, he knew, was deeply intrusive. And on any other day, in any other situation, that would not only give him pause, but give him cause to blow it wide open and throw this phone into the drink. Black Swan having tendrils plunged deep into what was meant to be private, inaccessible information? Information held by various utilities and companies and institutions? Data locked away in healthcare, infrastructure, intellectual property, and on and on? It had access. Unasked for access, taken without consent.

He told himself that Black Swan was a crutch.

But it *felt* like a jet pack.

He opened it up, tapped the screen: A digital ripple cast out from the center to the edges of the phone (and around the back, as the phone was literally all screen). The phone worked much the same as Black Swan did back in its Lair in Atlanta. It pulsed green in greeting, and he answered it:

"Hello, Black Swan. Let's run the demographics again."

Green pulse.

He held the phone flat in his hand, pointing the top of the phone toward the wall. He said: "Update demographics of the sleepwalkers."

It projected screens from three directions, filling the wall—and it did so intelligently, not painting over the window or the light fixtures with data but rather, moving the data intuitively around them.

The screen ahead of him showed the number of current sleepwalkers in a single white circle: 232.

"Sex," he said.

The circle, animated, split down the center.

51% women
49% men

That matched with current demographics here in the United States, and globally, as well.

It occurred to him that while sex was biologically determined, gender was a spectrum. Had he asked about that? He asked, now: "Gender."

Here Black Swan struggled, giving one red and one green pulse before scrolling quickly through a digitized census form. "Of course," Benji said. "The census does not ask about gender identity." Green pulse. Facebook did, though, offering more than fifty choices for gender, now. And some of the families and friends had confirmed that some of the walkers were transgender or genderqueer. "Can we estimate with limited data models?"

The circle gently throbbed for a few moments and then—

97% cisgender
3% alternate gender identity

Beneath it, a note on the chart: +/−2% ERROR RATE.

It tracked with his expectations out among the sleepwalkers: In the flock he knew of five who identified as transgender or gender-fluid according to either their social media profiles or their families. Which comprised only a percent or less of the 232 current walkers, but that still ranked higher than the estimated transgender population in the United States, which was long thought to be less than 0.3 percent (though Benji expected that as non-expected gender identities became thankfully more acceptable, that number might go up significantly once people felt comfortable coming out).

"Sexual orientation?"

That *was* a census question, and though they did not have the full identities of every walker, they had 95 percent—

The circle split:

90% heterosexual
10% gay, bisexual, pansexual

No patterns of note. Nothing telling. Except perhaps, once again, herein was a higher number than what was depicted by most censuses.

"Ethnicity?"

30% white
20% black
20% Hispanic/Latino
20% Asian/Pacific Islander
8% mixed race
2% native

That number had been shifting—as they came through the tail end of Pennsylvania and through Ohio, the number of white sleepwalkers had diminished even as the other numbers increased. Likely just a product of . . . well, whatever the infection vector was, but given everything, Benji couldn't help but wonder: *What if it's intentional? What if it's willful, somehow?*

It was an absurd thought with no basis in reality.

And yet . . .

"Age range?"

15%: 15–18 years old
27%: 18–25 years old
35%: 25–36 years old
13%: 36–50 years old
10%: 50–60 years old

No one under fifteen, no one over sixty. Strange, but not without precedent: Certain influenza strains did well in that range, curiously avoiding the very young and the very old. (Perhaps, he thought, to maximize viral survival. Too young or too old, and the virus might kill the victim before optimal spread. Viruses wanted to live long enough to multiply and share themselves with the world.)

Benji was about to ask another question when the door to the lab opened. The young EIS member Arav entered.

"Doctor Ray?" Arav asked.

The two of them hadn't spoken much, in an effort for Benji not to . . . pollute the minds of any of the techs or the rest of the team. In an unfortunate bit of bias, Benji thought of Arav as a boy—hardly true, as he was in his midtwenties, but he had little practical experience. And so Benji tended to dismiss him somewhat as naïve, a bit of a moon-calf.

"Yes, Arav?"

The young man looked from the phone to the wall back to Benji. He always had this eager look about him, as if he were forever standing at the edge of a diving board, excited to jump—but too nervous to step off the platform. "Found anything? Significant patterns of note?"

"Nothing . . . useful." With his free hand, Benji used his thumb to massage the center of his forehead.

"Any patterns in their health records?"

Benji gestured toward the phone. "You're free to ask."

"How do I do that?"

"Say, *Black Swan,* and then frame your question accordingly."

Arav nodded, then said nothing. Again like he was unsure. *Just jump, would you?* Finally, he said: "Black Swan, any common health patterns detected that, ahh, that might connect the walkers?"

The circle throbbed, and then a red pulse. *No.*

"Any significant illnesses known?" Arav asked.

Red pulse.

"So they're all healthy?"

Green pulse. Then two more. Meaning, what? They're all *really* healthy? Last Benji checked the data, that seemed to be the case.

He gave Arav a hapless, frustrated shrug. As if to say, *Sorry, kid, better luck next time.*

His own frustration was mirrored on Arav's face. He understood it: EIS felt like it was underneath an inverted pyramid, the weight of the entire structure pressing down on them all. They had the White House breathing down their neck, courtesy of Secretary Dan Flores of Health and Human Services; they had emails from every governor and angry shit-stirring emails from Homeland Security who were practically *rabid* at the thought of casting the CDC aside and taking over control of the sleepwalker herd. Not to mention the media, not to mention the friends and family of every walker out there, not to mention *every single American* who was at this point grimly obsessed with the onward flock. "We need a breakthrough," Benji said.

"We'll get one. I trust in the process." Arav hesitated, like there was more to say. So Benji turned his finger over in an impatient gesture—

"Spit it out, Arav."

The boy spoke quickly, almost too quickly to be understood, when he said: "I just want to say it's a real honor, I studied your work, you know. Your work with MERS-CoV is legend and even your papers on so-called traveler's diarrhea—"

"Yes, nothing more noble than a study of diarrhea."

"No! I know. But I just mean—"

"It's all right. I appreciate the thought."

"And Longacre—"

"I *don't* want to talk about Longacre—"

"What you did there—"

"What I did there was not aboveboard, Arav—"

"I was in awe of it. Really. We in science often think that the study is this practice somehow above us, right? But it's not. It's best when it's performed by people with principle. And courage."

"What I did was not courageous."

"It was." Arav said it again, this time with greater emphasis, a zeal, an ardor. "It *was*. Maybe not . . . the best way to exhibit that courage. But it took some real guts to do what you did. To try to make a difference."

Benji nodded awkwardly and smiled an uncomfortable smile. "That's kind. Next time I find such courage I can only hope it is backed up by the wisdom to express it more effectively. If you'll excuse me—"

At that, the door to the trailer opened. Cassie poked her head in. "Hey, you're both needed out here. Martin's about to talk."

Benji shook his head. "I don't think I'm invited to these powwows."

"This one's for everyone, dude. All the shepherds, too. It's not about the disease—a storm's coming. We have to get people moving."

Outside, as if to punctuate, the sky rumbled with faraway thunder.

"I'll be right out," he told her.

Once she was gone, Arav leaned in and said:

"We'll find a way forward. On this. I know we've hit a wall. It's not *Trypanosoma*, it's not flu, it's not anything. I trust this team. We'll find a breakthrough very soon, Doctor Ray."

They had no idea how true that was.

THE CROWD GATHERED OFF THE road, at the edge of a cornfield—the corn right now only a couple of feet high, in rows that stretched on and on toward oblivion. Shana and Mia stood with the other shepherds—those who left their vehicles and could spare the time and distance from their walkers. Maybe fifty or sixty of them stood around, each of them mired in impatience. On the other side, like it was some kind of turf war, stood the CDC workers, the HomeSec guys, a couple cops, a couple FBI. The third "gang," the media, stood away from both groups, interviewing a few shepherds on camera, live.

Meanwhile, the walker flock kept on walking past them on the road, their feet forming a dull, steady drumbeat.

"Fuck is taking so long?" Mia asked. She popped a couple Chiclets before offering a few to Shana. Shana took some.

"I dunno." She spied some of the CDC people going into the long lab trailer—the one pulled off to the side. Arav was among them.

Mia must've followed her gaze. "You still hot for the Pakistani kid?"

"I think he's Indian."

"Whatev. He's cute."

"He's like, twenty-five."

"And you're almost eighteen. I like to date older guys. Know why?"

Shana asked why.

"Because guys are immature little shits. You know how you know a guy's mental and emotional age? Cut his real age in half, that's how old he is. Means older guys are more mature."

"Do you date like, fifty-year-old dudes?"

"No, ew, stop."

"But if you date a thirty-year-old guy it means you're mentally dating a fifteen-year-old."

"You're making this really weird, Shana. I'm not hot for teenagers. I just mean—older guys are wiser. Better in bed, too, because they know what's up." She winked. Then she shot Shana a suspicious look. "You *have* slept with guys, right?"

"Lost my virginity at sixteen in the back of a Subaru Forester, like the proper daughter of a privileged American liberal."

"Whew, good. Was it good, your first time? It wasn't, was it? First time is never, ever good."

She shrugged. "Yeah, it was pretty bad. Billy Coyne was editor of the lit mag. I submitted a poem—some dumb thing about death and little white pebbles and how they look like gravestones. He offered to *workshop* it for me, but he really just wanted to *workshop* my panties off. And I fell for it." She made a face. "He screwed like a poodle humping a couch pillow."

"See, what'd I tell you? Older guys are practiced. Like, that one CDC guy? Vargas?" She kissed her fingers. "I would mount him like a piece of taxidermy. I would climb him like a lighthouse. I would—"

"Okay, okay, I get it."

"Oh, speaking of older guys, there's yours." Back out of the trailer came Arav and the other two CDC people: Cassie Tran, who'd interviewed Shana back when all this began, and who kinda surprised her because she was Vietnamese but had a southern accent *and* wore weird band shirts, and now Shana was pretty sure that thought made her racist. The other one was the head of this operation, or at least co-operator. His name was Benji, which was not a name that Shana associated with anybody in charge of anything, ever. Ben, maybe. Benjamin, okay. But wasn't Benji a dog? Was Benji a basenji? Why wasn't Benji a basenji? Better question: Why was she thinking about this shit at all? The three of them stood off to the side as Martin Vargas—he whom Mia apparently wanted to fuck—got up and spoke.

"Before anyone asks," Vargas said, "I don't have any new information for you about your friends and family members."

Anger ran through Shana.

People were supposed to have answers.

Experts were supposed to know shit.

And they didn't know anything.

This anger in her cascaded and multiplied, like lava pouring over rock and turning *that* rock to more lava—parents were supposed to be people you trusted, your little sister wasn't supposed to suddenly get sick with some strange new sleepwalking plague and walk out of her head and out of your life, none of this should be happening, not one stupid ounce of it. Shana knew this angst over the fact *life is super unfair, wah,* was hyper-fucking-cliché of her, but it was what it was, and she felt what she felt.

Things, she thought, were supposed to be better than they were.

Everyone around her must've felt the same righteous, irrelevant anger. Before Vargas could say more, the crowd got rowdy. Murmurs of disgust fast became a dull, raging roar, with some voices rising above:

"We need answers!" shouted Carl Hartkorn, whose son, Bradley—a quarterback for a school in Ohio—was among the walkers. "The hell are we paying you for? Our kids, our *families*—"

Another voice arose, this from Dina Wiznewski, a single mother of fifty whose thirty-year-old daughter, Elise, was among the walkers. (Dina followed the flock in an old Chevy Malibu. She slept in it.) Dina joined Carl's tirade, interrupting him:

"We pay taxes!"

A small roar of agreement arose.

Now a dissenter: Lonnie Sweet, Darryl Sweet's father. Lonnie, with his big barrel-rolling voice, said, "Hey, now—ease up." As voices threatened to drown him out, he just got louder: "Ease up! Doctor Vargas and the nice people from the CDC aren't the enemy here."

A voice—Shana didn't recognize it—shouted from the back of the crowd somewhere: "Terrorists!" As if to explain who their enemy truly was.

Vargas put some boom into his voice, trying to talk over them: "People. *People.* I appreciate your frustration and I will attempt to address it but right now—" As if on cue, thunder tumbled across the open distance like the rumbling steps of some faraway beast. "Right now, we have some weather to worry about. Okay? This supercell system may bring hail, heavy rain, and possibly even tornadoes—"

A voice, maybe Carl Hartkorn again, Shana wasn't sure: "We can't protect them." *Them*. The walkers.

Shana's blood went cold.

Hartkorn was right. They couldn't. A tornado could cut across the road and rip through the flock like they were just action figures on the carpet kicked by some shitty kid in a fit of anger.

"What we will do," Vargas continued, yelling over not only the throng, but now also the wind that picked up, "is try to *divert* the walkers. My cohort, Doctor Robbie Taylor"—next to Benji, Shana spied the man with the unruly sideburns who had helped her two weeks ago with the cop who tackled her—"has a plan to take our lab trailer and park it perpendicular across the road two miles up. If all goes according to that plan, the walkers will turn away from this road and onto the highway north, headed toward Indianapolis. On this path, we should intersect the weather system in about thirty minutes—but if we divert, it might just miss us."

Mia leaned over and said in a low voice: "A whole lotta fuckin' *shoulds* and *mights* and *according to plans* in there. I don't like it."

"Me neither."

Then again, what else could they do? Restrain them and they went boom. Let them wander and maybe a tornado would flick them into the air like God's finger.

Shana's entire body tightened as thunder rumbled anew. Her stomach sank into a pit of nausea, like she might barf.

Storm's coming.

Please, Nessie, be all right.

A MILE AHEAD, AT THE juncture of roads, Benji stood next to Robbie Taylor as one of Taylor's team—Avigail Danziger, the Israeli—deftly pulled the Ford F-350 off the road in the process of backing the lab trailer up so that it blocked the road. It needed to be at just the right angle, giving the walkers a new avenue of travel: a small access road that would take them toward Highway 74 north, toward Indianapolis. Not an ideal path, no, but one that might just move them out of the way of the storm.

Already the sky was darkening here. The wind picking up.

No rain, yet.

"How you holding up?" Robbie asked.

Benji shrugged. "The flock grows every day. We have no answers. Eventually Homeland Security is going to take over, assuming we don't all die as the result of a storm system likely to spawn one or several tornadoes."

"I like your optimism." Robbie clapped him on the back, then turned to all the gathered field officers and lab techs. "All right, folks. Core teams only. Everyone else, head to the hotel." They'd rented rooms for the night at a nearby Holiday Inn. "If we don't end up punted to fucking Oz, we'll meet you there when the storm has passed."

With that, the CDC people dispersed.

Martin and Cassie came up, Arav trailing.

"Should I stay?" Arav asked.

"Go if you want," Vargas said. "Unless you have a weather-changing superpower, there is not much you can do here, Arav."

"I think I'll stay," Arav said. "If that's all right."

It was.

There, Benji thought, was a glimpse of that courage. Question remained: Was his courage smart? Was there wisdom behind it, or just a fool's eagerness to sacrifice himself? (*Like,* Benji thought, *my own.*) Still, Arav reminded him of some earlier, more optimistic version of himself.

The wind settled for a second. Robbie said suddenly, with no preamble: "Might as well put some more bad news on top of things. Loretta's going to send us home."

"What?" Martin asked, shocked. "We're not done here."

"Not you. Not recalling EIS, not yet. But ORT."

"Bullshit. My team cannot manage this. It's not in our wheelhouse—we're already overwhelmed. We should be doing more data collection, more *detective* work, but all this on-the-ground . . . juggling, it's not our role."

Robbie held up both hands. "Hey, I agree with you, Marty, and if you wanna see if you can go two-for-two with The Immovable Object, I'll back your play. But she's putting us on something else."

"Dare I ask?" Benji asked.

"Abuja. Nigeria."

"Ebola?"

"The one and only."

"Jesus."

"Yeah. So. We're out tomorrow—again, provided we don't all get buttfucked by this supercell storm. We'll be in Nigeria just to provide support for

WHO, so maybe that takes us a week or two—if this whole parade thing is still going on, I'll see if Loretta will bring us back."

"Thanks, Robbie," Vargas said.

Benji felt the bottom dropping out from under them. With Robbie gone, that put more pressure on EIS not only to control this situation, but to answer for it, as well. Worse, it meant a greater likelihood that they just couldn't hack it—and the moment that happened, the moment they made *one* slip-up, that would give Homeland Security an opening to take over the whole show. They were already itching for it. What if they considered these people a threat? Benji could not imagine he lived in a country that would up and execute these people.

Still . . .

History had too many cruel examples of this very thing happening. Worse was: Would people even flinch? Would Americans quietly look away? Or would they rise up in defense of the flock?

He feared he knew that answer.

But this, he decided, was a problem for Future Benji.

And just like that, the rain started to fall. Just a spitting rain—cold flecks of it on his face, his arms. The pickup truck window rolled down, and Avigail looked out and offered a half shrug. "Are we good?"

They took a look at the trailer. It neatly crossed both lanes of the road and onto each shoulder. Further, each side of the road featured a sunken drainage ditch—and beyond that, fields of corn. All of that added up to a series of obstacles for the sleepwalkers. The easiest path for them was just to take the access road. He hoped the flock did it.

Robbie gave a thumbs-up. "Good as we're gonna get."

They'd find out soon enough, because here they came. Like livestock marching up a ribbon of long road, the walkers wandered ineluctably forward, still about a quarter mile out. Some shepherds had left at Benji's request—not only were they also in danger in a bad storm, but worse, their vehicles made for aggregate damage. A broken window meant glass on the road—and high winds meant glass in the air. That convinced at least half of them to turn around and head toward safer ground for now. But many remained. They, and the walkers they watched over, would be here very soon.

•   •   •

"I'M NOT GOING," SHANA SAID.

Her father pointed at her, then pointed at the passenger-side seat. "Sit down, Shana. Let's go."

"I'm staying. Someone needs to stay."

He wanted to take the Beast and head for safer, drier ground. She wanted to tell *him* he was being a fucking *coward.* "Dad—"

Then Mia, who stood behind Shana in the RV, said: "Mister Stewart, I'm staying a little bit longer, just long enough to see what happens when they get to the trailer. I got my Bronco, soon as we see that Nessie and Mateo and the others took the detour, we'll come, okay?"

"You promise?" her father asked, looking at Shana.

"Promise," she lied.

BENJI WENT INTO THE TRAILER with Cassie and Arav. Robbie, Avigail, and Martin stood outside in the spitting rain, about fifty feet out from the trailer—Robbie thought there might be value in trying to convince the walkers to change course by yelling at them, by trying to wave them off. Even though the walkers up until this point had not responded to external stimuli, Benji thought, what harm could it do? At worst, the sleepwalkers would fail to register what was said to them.

"Here they come," Cassie said.

A hundred feet, now. A mob of them. The shepherds who remained hung back—some walked alongside the flock, while those in vehicles pulled off and waited behind the state trooper police cruisers. Off to the side he spied Remy, one of Robbie's guys, with a FLIR imaging camera, letting them record thermal and infrared, as well as in night vision. The media, too, gathered at the margins—he saw *their* cameras pointing at the flock, filming through the needles of rain. At least they were staying back. For now.

The walkers closed the gap.

Benji could feel their collective footsteps in his feet.

A scene from a movie pinged his memory: *Jurassic Park*, with the glass of water rippling as the *T. rex* came closer and closer. But the walkers were not a lone creature, hungry and disturbed. They were a horde, increasingly faceless, marching not exactly in lockstep, but together—like a flock of birds, or a swarm of locusts.

Something tickled at the back of his brain, then.

Something about how birds flocked and how locusts swarmed, about army ants teeming across a jungle floor . . .

He put a mental pin in that for later.

Now Robbie and Avigail began waving their hands—and again came a flash of *Jurassic Park:* Jeff Goldblum as Ian Malcolm, waving the flare to distract the tyrannosaur. From inside, they heard the muted yells of the two ORT members, exhorting the walkers to change course, that a storm was coming, that they were in *danger*.

The flock kept walking forward.

"You think they'll listen?" Arav asked.

"I don't know," Benji said.

"Watching them come at us like this," Cassie said, "I can't lie, it's a little fuckin' freaky."

Cassie's walkie-talkie crackled. She grabbed it. "Go ahead."

Outside, they saw Robbie speaking into his, and the voice came through inside the trailer. "They're not stopping, guys."

He was right. The walkers simply flowed past Robbie and Avigail the way a stream flows past a rock.

"Shit," Cassie said.

Martin spoke: "Cassie, ask Benji for his opinion: Any value in intercepting?"

She gave him a look. Reluctantly, Benji took the radio.

"I don't know," Benji said into the walkie. "I'd say not to impede. Maybe they'll turn. If not . . . we don't want to risk detonation."

Even now, that idea had not become normal to him:

Detonation.

Ten feet, now.

"What if this doesn't work?" Arav asked in a quiet voice.

"Then," Benji said, "we hope the storm will be kind."

Five feet.

The walkers weren't stopping.

They were headed right for the trailer.

Benji thought, *They're going to walk right into it.* It would be like a wall—they'd crush against it, going no farther. He had a sudden vision of a fire at a concert hall, or a riot at a soccer game: a mob mashing up against a fence, one by one, not going anywhere, except *this time* it wasn't just soccer fans or concertgoers, it was people who were literal bombs of blood and bone. His heart seized in his chest.

We've just killed them all.

And maybe us, too.

He started to tell the others, "Get down, *get down*," and into the walkie-talkie he said: "Extract! *Extract.* Get Avigail to the truck, we'll need to move the trailer, we'll need—"

The lead walker, the young girl, Nessie Stewart, was at the window now. Not stopping. Not slowing. The others gathered behind her, pressing forward—Benji felt himself shaking, felt sweat dripping, his mouth dry.

She reached toward the trailer, hands out, palms forward.

That, the first movement they'd seen that wasn't their feet carrying them forward. Had their arms *ever* moved? He did not think so. And here the girl was, reaching out with both arms—

She touched the trailer. Gently. The barest sound: *fump*.

And then she began to climb.

It was fast. Too fast—eerily so. Up she went, and suddenly they heard the thump-and-tumble of her atop the trailer. The other walkers, too, were joining her—they did not come one by one, but rather, as the flock. They walked up, reached out, and began climbing over together, three at a time, four, five. The roof of the trailer bowed inward like a big soda can in a too-firm grip. Benji hurried to the other side of the trailer and looked out—a blur of movement passed the window as the girl Nessie, jumping from the top, hit the ground in a clumsy stagger.

And onward she went.

By now the trailer was gently rocking back and forth like a boat at sea as the walkers ascended the side of the trailer en masse, moving up and over the obstacle. Arav and Cassie both stood, wide-eyed, and Benji was certain his face displayed the same fearful wonder.

The radio crackled. Robbie, again. "Guys, you seeing this?"

"Seeing it? We're *feeling* it," Benji radioed back.

"But you need to *see* it. They're not—Jesus, Benji, they're not grabbing onto anything. Their hands are *flat* against the side of the trailer. It's like they're a bunch of Spider-Mans. Spider-Men. Whatever. Shit."

The trailer wobbled back and forth as the flock went up and over—the roof bending in but never staying bent—and then, like that, the last of them came and went.

The walkers walked, always and forever.

Cassie said, "I guess we have a new data point to consider."

"The storm comes first. We can worry about the data in the morning." He radioed to the others outside, told them to get the Ford on the road, pulling the trailer behind the flock. He hoped like hell they didn't intersect with that storm.

Because if they did, he had no idea what happened next.

16

WWJD

Behold, the tempest of the LORD! Wrath has gone forth, A sweeping tempest; It will burst on the head of the wicked.

—Jeremiah 30:23

JUNE 19
Burnsville, Indiana

MATTHEW WAS PLANNING ON MAKING A CALL ON BEHALF OF DECARLO, BUT instead he sat there, phone in hand, just turning his conversation with Ozark Stover over and over again. His mind was like a rabbit trapped in a briar. Even still, hours later, he didn't know quite what to make of it. Stover never came by the church or the house. And then, today, there he was. Larger than life, practically prehistoric in his size and his demeanor. Matthew wanted to judge the man, because in his heart, that's what he did—often without meaning to, but it was part and parcel of his job. Though God was the ultimate judge, Matthew was a facilitator of His judgment, wasn't he? Matthew measured people up, to see who they were, who they could be—how were they failing themselves (and by proxy, failing God), and how could they be made to succeed. What would bring them to the light? To the glory of the Kingdom? That was how Matthew helped people.

Stover, though, was a puzzle. The man was wild, unkempt. Practically feral. He ran a junkyard. Wasn't religious, far as Matthew knew. He was a businessman, though, in good enough standing with the community—wasn't a criminal, wasn't a drunk. (And if he was, Matthew figured he'd know. People in this town, and maybe *all* towns, were incorrigible gossips. Especially when it came to pastors and reverends—people confessed not only their own sins, but the sins of everyone around them.)

He thought suddenly, *Well, who better to ask?*

He walked to his son's room.

Bo's room, as always, was a mire. Half lit by a single desk lamp. Clothes on the floor. Posters on the wall of NASCAR racers and bands he'd never heard of, either hung crooked or starting to peel off. And the moment Matthew stepped in he was punched in the face by a mealy, swampy funk: From others he talked to, it was the trademark odor of many teenage boys, but to him it smelled like . . .

Well, it smelled like gym socks and crotch. And he wasn't sure what was worse: this smell, or the smell that Bo used to try to combat it—a venomous body spray that smelled not entirely unlike wasp spray. And you'd think his armpits were hornet's nests the way he fogged himself in it.

Inside the bedroom, the boy lay sloppily across his bed, a set of earbuds in his ears barely containing some kind of . . . heavy metal music.

Was he asleep? Matthew couldn't tell. "Bo," he said. "Son."

Nothing.

He went over, jostled the boy's shoulders. Bo startled awake, ripping the earbuds out of his ears.

"What?" he asked, irritated.

"Hey, sorry, just wanted to ask you a question."

"Now?"

"Well, yes, obviously, now."

"Ugh. What."

"I wanted to ask about your friend."

Bo made a face approximately the shape of a scrunched-up pile of dirty boxers on his floor. "What friend?"

Kind of a sad question, Matthew realized, as his son regrettably did not have many friends. The few he had, they forbid him from seeing—Lee Bodrick was a little dirtbag drug dealer who got expelled first semester, and the Blevins boy was fond of cherry bombs in toilets (Matthew had to explain to Bo, "Those aren't funny, those go off and shatter porcelain, the shards could kill someone"). And Bo wasn't on any teams or in any clubs.

"I mean Mister Stover."

"He's not my friend, he's my boss."

"You get along with him, though."

Bo hesitated, like he was under the thumb of the Inquisition. "Yeah."

"What's he like?"

"Why?"

"He stayed around and we talked today."

"Good for you. Maybe he'll be your friend." Bo started to put the earbuds back in.

Matthew held up both hands. "Hey, I surrender. I'm not trying to attack you—there's no accusation here. He just seemed like an interesting man, is all. You like him?"

The earbuds hung about an inch from going back in Bo's ears. He retreated further against the wall. Finally, he mumbled: "I like him a lot. He's good to me. He's nice to me. Pays okay, job is cool. We go fishing sometimes. We shoot cans with his .22 rifle and this little, y'know, this squirrel gun shotgun he has."

"You shoot guns with him?"

Now Bo must've sensed that Matthew didn't like that, because he said: "I don't know."

"You just said you—"

From down the hall, Matthew heard his wife's voice:

"Oh my God."

Matthew and Bo shared a look.

Then it came again:

"Oh my God!"

Matthew turned tail and hurried down, following the voice to their bedroom. There he found his wife on the edge of their bed, watching the little flat-screen TV they had propped up on their dressers. He'd never wanted a TV in their room, but she insisted and, well, Autumn was—true to her name—a real force of nature sometimes when she wanted something.

On the TV were a couple of talking heads.

The news again, he thought. Poisoning her brain. The rot of current affairs. When Autumn wasn't watching TV, she was on her phone, too, scrolling through the bad news like it was an apocalyptic stock ticker.

"Honey, I—"

"Shh," she said. "Watch."

They cut to something, a replay of some kind. He saw a rainy road, and the chyron below read NEW DEVELOPMENT IN SLEEPWALKER FLOCK, TEN MILES FROM WALDRON, INDIANA.

Matthew felt something bump into him, and he found his son standing next to him. All eyes now glued to the TV, to his chagrin.

Onscreen, he saw a road. A trailer. Gray skies and rain—the rain hadn't started here, not yet, but he knew it was coming, because outside the skies looked the color of cold charcoal briquettes. The trailer looked like it was sideways across the road, set up like a blockade. He realized he knew the spot—it was on Poldark Road, just by that little access road that led up to Highway 74. A few miles down Poldark were a couple of farms, and he knew some of the folks that lived there. The Wylies, the Heacocks, the Bermans.

"They blocked the road," Autumn explained animatedly, like this excited her as much as it upset her. "They wanted to make the walkers change course. Like a detour. It didn't work."

"Why not?" Bo asked.

"Just watch."

They watched.

They watched as a couple of people—a man and a woman—tried waving the walkers away. They watched as the walkers went right up to that trailer.

And then Matthew watched, transfixed, as the sleepwalkers went up and over it. They did it with ease. Hands flat against the wet trailer, the sleepwalkers clambered up to the roof—the first one was a little girl with soggy hair pressed against her pale cheeks—and the others followed fast behind.

Later, after he'd watched the madness replayed again and again, he went to the nightstand, pulled out his Bible.

Then he went down to the front porch. His phone call for DeCarlo would have to wait. He opened his book to its last chapter: the Revelation to John. He read it end-to-end not once, but twice. And then to God he prayed.

17

SIRENS AND SCREAMS

I know your secrets
And I know your plight!
Into the sea you
Go without a fight!
The night is deep
The night is long
You're far from home
You have no song!
But in daylight
You know better.
—Gumdropper, "Storm of the Century,"
off *The Beggar and the Diamond* album (2000)

JUNE 19
Six miles outside Waldron, Indiana

THE STORM LASHED THE ROAD AND FIELDS LIKE A CAT-O'-NINE-TAILS. THE
rain punished the windshield of Mia's Bronco as it sat parked in the loose
stone driveway of a farm.

"I can't even *see* them," Shana said, panicked. She leaned over Mia and
stared out the driver's-side window. The walkers were on their way—Mia
had pulled them ahead and sat them here. They might not even be far, now,
but it was too hard to tell: The skies were so dark, the rain so relentless, it
was like trying to look through closed curtains at the world outside. "I'm
going."

"Don't," Mia said. "It's just a storm. They'll be okay."

"You don't know. Your brother is out there."

Mia snapped, "You don't have to tell me that! I know that. But I can't fucking help him right now, okay?" She waited a beat and then added, "You saw the way they went over that trailer."

Shana had seen. She'd watched her sister march right up to it, reach out her hands as if in a healing gesture, and then *somehow* climb up and over. And then the others followed. It reminded her of a time when her sister, still little, took Shana out into the yard to show her a trail of little black ants leading to a dead grasshopper that they were neatly dissecting. Nessie said, "Watch," and put a twig in front of them. The ants streamed over it. She put a rock down, and the ants went over that, too.

"I saw," Shana said.

"Maybe . . . I dunno, maybe they have like, powers."

"Powers."

"Like, superpowers."

"They don't have superpowers, Mia. They're just . . . sleepwalkers. And if a flash flood comes, or a tornado, or—"

Pak!

Something hit the glass of the windshield, like a flung marble.

Then more:

Pok. Pak pak pok.

White round shapes.

"It's hailing," Mia said.

"Hail could mean a—"

In the distance, a tornado siren sounded.

A BANSHEE WAILED, AND AT first Benji thought it might just be the wind, but it wasn't, was it? As hail pelted the trailer, Benji turned to the others: Cassie, Arav, Martin, and Robbie. Avigail was driving the truck that pulled the trailer, with Remy riding shotgun. "That's the tornado siren, isn't it?"

Robbie nodded. "I just hope our trailer lands on an evil witch."

"I looked it up," Arav said, "and the sirens don't go off necessarily for tornadoes—it could mean there's potential, even if one hasn't been spotted."

"Still," Benji said. "Think. What can we do? If a tornado drops down and sweeps across them, how do we save them?"

Behind the trailer, the walkers continued, compulsorily rallying into the heart of the storm. From here, he couldn't even see their faces: The rain, and now the hail, obscured them. He could only see their shapes, their margins, their muted, storm-soaked colors as they marched on.

He knew the answer to his question, though no one would speak it.

We can't save them.

"We can't detain them," Cassie said.

Robbie jumped in with, "And we *damn* sure can't divert them."

Martin fumed. "We don't have time to dig a ditch, we don't have any way to stop a tornado, we can't put anything over them—"

"Maybe we ask it politely," Robbie said.

Arav had out his phone. "I don't have service. I'd look up information on how to stay safe in a tornado, but—"

"Wait." Benji pulled out Black Swan. It pulsed green in greeting, and then he set the projector to the wall above the bank of computers. "Black Swan is a satphone. I still have signal. Black Swan, it's Benji. I need advice on how to stay safe from a tornado outdoors."

It projected FEMA guidelines:

If possible, get inside a building.

"That's helpful," Cassie said. "Maybe they're like vampires, and we can just invite them inside."

Next, it projected:

If shelter is not available or there is no time to get indoors, lie in a ditch or low-lying area or crouch near a strong building. Look out for floodwaters, which may also fill low areas.

And:

Use your arms to protect head and neck.

"That's it?"

The phone pulsed green.

"You know," Robbie said, "if a funnel cloud really does bear down on us, then *we're* going to need to follow that advice. We might *all* be ass-up in a ditch in the next couple minutes."

The trailer rocked, buffeted by heavy winds. The sound of the hail was like marbles on metal: a mighty, rattling din. But over it . . .

Benji swore he heard something.

A voice. Or voices.

"Does Black Swan have weather data?" Arav asked. "It could update us with real-time data and—"

But Benji held up a finger, shushing him. He did that thing where you look up at *nothing,* trying to focus your ears on *something.*

"Do you hear that?" he asked.

"I hear a screaming siren," Robbie said. "I hear an apocalypse of hail—is that the collective noun for hail? School of fish, bunch of grapes, flock of sleepwalkers, apocalypse of hail—"

"No, no, shh. I hear voices."

"You've been talking to Black Swan too much, Benj."

"Wait," Cassie said. "I hear it, too."

For a moment, the hail slowed and the wind died back—

And then, out there, amid the clamor of the tempest, he heard it again. Distinctly.

"Someone yelling," Cassie said.

She was right. Someone was yelling. But who? Where? Already a scenario began to unfold in his head—someone, maybe a shepherd, maybe someone from the media, was stuck or scared or yelling for help. *Everything is complicated. So many moving parts.* He ran to the window again to look out. It was like looking into a washing machine: the splashing rain, the churn, the froth. To Arav he said, "Hand me Remy's camera."

Arav handed the FLIR camera over. Benji switched it to thermal.

In the storm, it was the easiest way to see the flock: The walkers each had a lower average body temperature than non-walkers, around 96.5 degrees Fahrenheit, so the colors coming off them were duller and faded. Now those colors were in a glowing, amorphous blob heading closer to the trailer. Nothing stood out to him. He could see the colors of shepherds in their cars, pulled off to the side—he wished like hell they all had gone to safety so he didn't have to worry about *them,* too, but they were adults with their own destinies well in hand. The walkers, on the other hand, seemed to be in thrall to a destiny outside themselves.

Just the same, the blob of colors that was the flock continued gently throbbing forward.

Wait. There it came again—

Voices.

From farther down. From where the walkers were headed.

"I'm going out there," he said, throwing on his jacket.

Cassie caught his arm. "Boss, slow your roll. The wind out there—"

"Someone might be hurt, or in danger."

"Shit," Martin said. His jacket never came off. "I'll come, too."

Robbie said, "Whoa, whoa, you idiots might end up as the ones hurt or in danger if you go out there. I'm not saying we won't rescue your asses, but please don't make us."

"We won't go far," Benji said, and then he threw open the door and stepped out into the maelstrom, Martin following close behind.

"I HOPE THIS SHIT DOESN'T chip my windshield," Mia said as the hail clattered against the hood of the truck. "Already looks like it's dinging the paint. I don't got money for repairs."

Shana wanted to snap at her: *I don't care about your truck, I care about the sleepwalkers,* and she had about opened her mouth to say it—

But then her eyes caught movement in the passenger-side mirror. A shifting of shapes in the storm. A movement of white, like a flag waving. It came from behind them, back down the driveway, toward the farm that sat off the road.

And then she heard voices.

"Someone's out there," she said. "Someone's yelling."

"What?" Mia asked. "Where?"

But Shana didn't have time to answer.

Because she opened the door and hurried out into the storm.

THE WIND FELT LIKE A series of hard shoves—in the onslaught of the storm, Benji almost fell into Martin, nearly knocking them both into the ditch. Martin yelled at him over the wind, but the words were stolen away. They righted themselves; Benji pulled the hood of his jacket over his head (far too late, he realized, as it just dumped more water over him). Then he stepped out around the front end of the truck, to the surprised looks of Remy and Avigail sitting in there. She knocked on the window and mimed asking him what the hell he was doing, but he didn't bother answering. Instead, as pea-sized hail pelted him, he put the camera up to his eye—

Thermal imaging resumed. This time, he scanned farther down the road—not where the sleepwalkers were, but rather, where they were headed.

He saw a lone truck out there. He recognized it as belonging to one of the shepherds, though Benji was not sure which one. Beyond the truck, he saw movement heading away from a white stone farmhouse—two warm bodies and one cooler body walking this way, about fifty yards out.

He recognized the steady gait of the duller, colder form.

It's a sleepwalker.

A new one. Running away to join the circus.

And in *this* mess, no less.

But the other two—

People were chasing after. Maybe family, who knew?

It was they who were yelling. Yelling for whoever this walker was. Probably upset because this person—someone they knew, maybe someone they loved—had up and walked out into a storm during a blaring tornado siren. They didn't understand.

And if they tried to stop whoever it was, it would end in blood and bone and tragedy.

Benji didn't have time to explain.

He broke into a hard run through the driving rain.

Through the sheets of water and the hail that whipped her head and shoulders, Shana saw three shapes emerge.

Three people.

One of them was a walker. She could tell instantly—for the last two weeks she'd inadvertently studied that slow-and-steady-wins-the-race gait. Even in the half dark, she could see the whites of those dead eyes coming at her.

She couldn't make out an age—but it was a man, or a teenage boy. Maybe a white T-shirt. Dungarees. Broad shoulders. A man, she realized.

The other two were not walkers.

One, a woman. Older. The other, younger—this one, a boy. Both yelling at the walker. Over the siren and the wind she heard clips of words and phrases—*don't go—come back—can't you see the storm?*

And then the word, *Dad.*

A fast guess: The walker was the husband to the woman, father to the boy. Shana bolted toward them, coltish and clumsy, waving her hands and screeching like a demon that they needed to back away, to go home, to let him go—even as they reached for him, pawing at him.

Now: a voice from her right.

Someone else was running toward her. No. *Two* someones.

She recognized them—Benji Ray, and behind him, Martin Vargas. The two of them cut a straight line from the trailer, running past the flock of walkers. Ahead, this lone walker, this father, was straining to join the flock: like a metal ball bearing rolling toward a powerful magnet.

She understood it, now. His family wanted to stop him.

To bring him home.

But keeping him home meant something far worse than they intended. Even though they should've known better. The CDC had issued its warnings. They were all over the news: *Do not impede the walkers . . .*

"Stop!" Shana screamed, her arms waving like she was warning drivers of a bridge out ahead. *"Stop!"*

As she closed in, the rain was going sideways. Shana saw the woman— her long hair matted, her mouth open, miserably pleading as she held her husband tight. The boy, no more than ten, dug his heels into the gravel, clinging to his father's arm, pulling on it like he was in a tug-of-war for his father's life.

The father was shaking. His jaw craned open.

He began to scream. Louder than the rain. Louder than the siren.

He's gonna blow, she thought.

But Shana didn't stop running.

Benji slowed his sprint, holding the thermal camera to his eye. The imaging showed the man's temperature blooming. Benji saw now that someone else was running to intercept—a girl, one of the shepherds, bolting toward the family.

From off to the side, now, a new flash of movement—

Benji turned, following it—a dark shape, a gray ghost with a flash of red, whipping through the storm. Behind him, Martin turned toward it, too—

And whatever it was, borne on the wind, crashed into him. His head turned sideways and he cried out, falling to the ground.

Benji called out: "Martin!"

But as he did, his own foot landed in a puddle that went deeper than he knew—his ankle twisted as the heel went down. Pain lit up inside him, full-tilt-pinball, and next thing he knew he was on the ground, the air blasted out of pancaked lungs.

The camera clattered ahead of him into the stones.

THE FATHER OF THE FAMILY of three began to . . . swell. Shana saw this clearly now, for she was close, *too* close, running straight for them. Her mind screamed at her body to *stop, stop, stop,* but onward she ran, even as the man's arms blew up like balloons, the biceps straining. His chest and belly bloated like something was straning to get *out* of him. The way his head craned back, the way his jaw extended open farther and farther, the bones grinding and crackling until the mouth was a yawning cavern—it was impossible, like a special effect in a movie.

Later, she would remember that.

But the rest would remain a blur.

All she would be able to pull out of it would be moments:

Her arm out.

The feeling of something caught against her.

Her hands around it. Not it. *Him.*

The boy. Heavy in her arms.

Rain, cutting the air.

Hail, stinging her shoulders.

Air, whistling and howling.

She hit the ground. Something broke, a bone snapping. *Crack.* That was just the first of many sounds that would haunt her later. As her eyes squeezed shut, she heard the boy's father not explode but *pop*—the sound of skin splitting followed by the wet splash of all that was inside him. As the man's inhuman dirge died fast, the wife's began. The thud and tumble and mucky tacky splash of her body landing on the ground, falling into a pile of what was once her husband.

Thunder rolled. The rain roared on.

18

THE SHIMMER

Once again the GOP members of Congress have asked President Hunt for a statement regarding the so-called Sleepwalkers now passing through the heart of Indiana. The only response has come from Press Secretary Wells, who said that Hunt is "assured that the CDC will have more answers soon." Meanwhile, on the campaign trail, Republican nominee Ed Creel has again reiterated conspiracy theories about Hunt, claiming that she has perhaps engineered this "flock" in order to distract from having to answer substantive policy questions over the NSA leaks of last year. In other news, an outbreak of over one hundred tornadoes hit the Midwest yesterday, seven of them being of EF4 or EF5—no indication yet of number of deaths or damage . . .

—Oscar Castillo, CBS *Morning News*

JUNE 20
Mercy Hospital, Waldron, Indiana

A DEEP INTAKE OF BREATH AS BENJI'S HEAD LIFTED SUDDENLY FROM HIS chest.

He blinked.

Was I asleep?

He swallowed; his mouth was dry. He adjusted himself and sat up straighter in the hospital chair. Across from him was a window: The sky remained dark, and rain continued to fall, but now its fall was gentle, a *pat-pat-pat* of little drops against the glass. He looked at his watch. Four thirty in the morning. He looked up over his shoulder, saw a door and a sign: MORGUE.

The memories came back to him like someone flipping playing cards faceup onto a table. One by one.

Martin, hit by what turned out to be part of a flying stop sign.

Benji's ankle tweaking as he fell.

The camera falling away.

The girl—Nessie's sister—running.

Then and there in the rain, Benji got to his feet, even with his injured ankle, and made a choice—he ran toward the family, not back toward Martin. But it was too late, either way.

He remembered the way the man's skin rippled and bulged, and the way he *tore open*. What came out of him was no delight—it was a rain of shiny bone and red blood, and the woman who was holding him, his wife, held him tight even as he erupted beneath her. And she took it. All of it. She screamed. She fell.

And then the worst thought struck Benji—

I need their bodies.

Death was a tragedy.

But death was also a data point.

He remembered limping to the wife and her husband, these two farmers—the husband little more than a pile of himself, twists of skin and loops of organs, studded with the porcelain splinters of bone shrapnel. The wife was still alive, but barely. Those shrapnel pieces stuck out of her at odd angles. One in her neck, blood pumping gently past the shard, already joining with the rain and washing away. Before Benji could do anything else, her mouth froze as the life left her eyes, leaving only windows looking into an empty house. Lightning flashed.

And the terrible, cold, merciless thought hit him:

I need their bodies.

But with it, a worse realization:

And the storm is going to wash it all away.

He needed evidence. The walkers could not be cut. They could not be bled. No knife, no needle would pierce them.

And before him, in a pile, was all of what he needed:

Blood, bones, organs, epidermis, *brains,* the whole gory enchilada.

Benji remembered ripping off his jacket, getting it under that pile, and wrapping his jacket around the sloppy mess. The horror of what he was doing struck him, and he remembered crying out, almost as if in pain. The revulsion in him warred with the need to do it. He tried to remind himself, *This was a person just a minute ago.*

That was then. Now he sat in a chair outside the hospital morgue.

Still damp from showering all the mess off himself. He tried to remember how he'd gotten here . . . but he didn't have to reach far for the answer. Because here they came. The girl: Nessie's sister, and behind her another shepherd, a young woman whose name he didn't know. *They* drove him here. Helped him get the remains of the husband and the body of the wife in the back.

And the boy, too.

The boy suffered only a broken arm. Because of her.

Benji lurched to his feet. They startled at his sudden movement.

"You saved him," Benji said. And he realized now it was completely out of nowhere, a total non sequitur. The teen girl blinked at him like he had gone off his gourd. He sighed. "The boy, I mean. You saved him."

"Oh." She looked down at her feet. "I dunno."

"No, no, you did. I remember. That boy—he was clinging to his parents. When . . . his father went, he might've ended up same as his mother. But you ran in there. You saved his life. What's your name again?"

"Shana. Shana Stewart."

He stood up. His ankle complained and his leg almost gave out as a result. But it wasn't broken, so he winced past it and held out a hand.

"Doctor Benji Ray."

The other woman chewed a piece of gum and looked him up and down with sad eyes. "We just got cleaned up. You were asleep."

"It's fine," he said, withdrawing his hand. "Is the . . . boy okay?"

Shana answered: "I think so. Just a broken arm or whatever." She made a sour, sad face. "But I don't think he'll ever be really okay."

"No, perhaps not." The boy's life was irrevocably different now, whoever he was. His parents were dead in wildly unnatural circumstances. The system was not kind to orphans, Benji knew. Perhaps the unnatural circumstances would afford him some special attention. "Are you okay? The both of you?"

"Yo, we just wanna go back," the other shepherd said.

"I'm sorry, your name is?" Benji asked.

"Mia."

"Thank you, Mia, for driving me here. The both of you . . . you have done more than you realize. We haven't been able to properly examine a sleepwalker—and though the circumstances here are far from ideal, this will afford us the chance." He paused. "I'm sorry, I must sound so cold, so detached. I don't mean to."

"It's cool," Shana said, the sadness in her smile reminding him: *It most certainly is not cool.*

"We wanna know what's going on more than you do," Mia said. "It's our families out there. Her sister. My bro."

"Thank you again." They nodded and started to walk off, murmuring to each other. But then Shana looked back and said:

"I dunno if your guy is still in there with the, uh, with the remains or not. In case you were wondering."

"My guy?"

She nodded. "One that came while you were sleeping."

Panic struck him like a bucket of water.

The bodies.

Last time they had bodies, they were stolen.

This time, he'd brought the bodies here, and then what? He thought, *No, no, no, someone may have come, what if they were taken again—all out from under me as I slept. Stupid!* He hurried toward the morgue door—

Just as it opened, its mechanism automatic.

A man stepped into the door frame, clad in an autopsy PPE suit—the blood on the suit looked purple against the blue. Through the mask, Benji saw a familiar face: Robbie Taylor.

"You look like hell, Benj."

Benji nodded, weary. He wanted to lean forward and hug the man. "I feel like hell, Robbie."

"I didn't want to wake you . . . you looked so peaceful."

"Farthest thing from it."

"Yeah, it's all pretty fucked up. Besides, you've been running on fumes since all this started. And it's about to get a lot weirder."

"I see the look in your eyes," Benji said. "We're up shit creek without the courtesy of a paddle, aren't we?"

"Paddle? Fuck, Benji, we don't even have a *boat.*"

IN THE PARKING LOT, THEY sat in Mia's old-ass Bronco.

Mia went to turn on the engine, but Shana said: "Wait."

Mia waited.

Outside, past the parking lot, over the trees, came the faintest glow of sunrise—the storm had passed, and the day would soon begin.

"What is it?" Mia asked.

Shana did not answer. Because though the storm outside had gone, the one inside her was just whirling to life. It swept up across her and in moments she had braced herself against the dashboard as the tears came. Soon she was lost to wracking, hitching sobs. She crumpled, folding into herself. Knees to chest. Arms around shins. She couldn't see through her tears. She tried to say to Mia, "I'm just tired. Last night was hard." But it mostly came out a mumbled gabble.

Mia gave her a tissue, then put a hand on her shoulder.

Just a small gesture, but it meant everything.

And slowly, surely, just as the storm last night passed, so did this one.

Shana took a deep breath. She blinked away the tears.

"Let's go see our families," Shana said.

Mia started the engine.

TOGETHER THEY WENT UPSTAIRS TO visit Martin Vargas. The other man, even in his hospital gown and with a bandage over his head, still somehow managed to look handsome.

"Jesus, Martin," Benji said, taking a look at his head. "Stitches?"

"Three. Not serious. But that stop sign gave me a good whack." He grunted as he sat up in bed. "Concussion. I'll be fine. Hand me that remote." Benji tossed him the TV remote, and Martin turned it off. "Any updates? Tell me we got the remains. Tell me you did an autopsy—"

Robbie nodded. "Benji did the goop scoop, I did the postmortem-palooza. And, ahh." He pulled over a chair, plopped down in it. "Okay. So. Obviously, what I saw was just preliminary. We won't have a full tox screen right away, and it'll take time for the techs to run the blood panel. But initial gross external examination tells me what we already know: The male patient, a Mister Clade Berman, forty-five years old, expired by . . . detonating." He forced his lips to make a soft cork-popping sound. "Jesus, the guy just ripped apart. As if there was a bomb inside him that went off."

"Was there? Did you find anything like that?" What an absurd question he had to ask. *Unnatural circumstances,* he reminded himself.

"No. No foreign bodies, no artificial limbs that could be a concern, no pacemaker, nothing in the stomach that I could tell—no chemical burns, zip, nada, bubkes. Health reports on the guy said he was pretty healthy outside of a busted knee a few years back. No health insurance, though, which is increasingly unsurprising given the *cost* of health insurance. So? Nothing of note. Except . . ."

"Except what?" Benji asked.

"Thing is, when you drill down to the microscopic examination, that's where things get . . . fucking goofy."

He said this last word as if it was not precisely the word he wanted, but the only one he could find. "How so?" Benji asked.

"I took organ samples, skin samples, muscles, vertebrae, brain. At the cellular level . . . I saw a lot of damage, okay?"

"Damage?" Martin asked. "Necrosis of the cells?"

"Total. Similar to caseous necrosis." By caseous necrosis, he meant the manner of cell death one might find in some fungal diseases or from mycobacteria—but also from other foreign invaders. It referred to a cell that had erupted, leaving detritus all around. "But also, not that. Caseous necrosis is slow, and this . . . wasn't. No byproducts present. This was fast, by the look of it. The cells were a microcosm of the man: Ten percent of them just detonated."

Ten percent was enough, it seemed.

Robbie handed over his phone. Benji took it to Martin, and the two huddled together to peer at the screen. On it, a series of crude photos from the microscope.

Benji saw what Robbie meant—the cells were broken open out of the side, all the organelles either similarly ruptured or spilled out. It was as if a BB had shot its way out of a blueberry—not through it, but out from the inside of it. And that pinged something at the back of his brain.

He felt like he'd seen this before.

But *where?*

His jaw clenched as he grappled with the memory.

"What could've done this?" Martin asked.

"Not typical of a virus," Benji said. "Fungus, maybe."

A parasitic fungus made some sense, didn't it? Mycoses, or fungal diseases, could feature insidious microsporidia. Some would fuse cells together, making them easier to infect. Valley fever—spores carried on the wind in the Southwest of this country—was a systemic, opportunistic disease that caused caseous necrosis of cells, though slowly. In terms of changing behavior, one had to look no further than the so-called zombie fungus, cordyceps, which literally seized control of an insect. An infected ant first suffered convulsions as the fungus broke through the exoskeleton—then the fungus took control of the ant's movements, driving it up the stem of a plant, where it would attach itself and explode. Thus releasing the spore onto more ants below.

Could this be that? Certainly cordyceps did a number on the cells of an ant, albeit slowly—threads of microsporidia destroyed organelles in the cells, including mitochondria. Benji's mind spun with the possibilities. If the fungus inhabited the epidermis, would it be strong enough to make the skin impenetrable to needle and knife? That seemed impossible.

"Did you find any evidence of fungal infection?" Benji asked.

"Nothing. It was clean."

Martin asked: "Are you thinking cordyceps?"

"I don't know." Benji thought: *We don't know anything, do we?* "It makes more sense than anything else, but at the same time . . . it still doesn't make enough sense. More information hasn't made this more clear."

"I'm going to make this considerably less clear, then," Martin said.

Robbie: "Oh shit."

"Might as well tell us," Benji said.

"I don't have to tell you. I can show you."

ON THE WAY BACK TOWARD the flock, they passed through Waldron, a small town whose Main Street didn't have any streetlights or even any lines painted on it. Shana saw a garage on one corner, and across it, a small lot for school bus parking (where it looked like a graveyard of buses gone dead). They passed a little diner, a dinky grocery store, a gas station, and a few row homes and duplex houses so run-down they looked ready to sink back toward the earth and take a dirt-nap until total decay.

But as they headed south through town, they saw something else: news vans. And outside of them: reporters and camerapeople, setting up for shots. Clearly they knew that the walkers were coming this way.

"Like vultures," Shana said.

Mia shrugged. "They're just doing their job."

"Yeah, but *their* job is screwing up *our* job."

"We don't have a job, girl. Nobody's paying us. I'm damn near dead broke. I'm gonna have to have Mama wire me some money so I can pick it up at the post office or something. Shit."

"Hey, what'd you do before this? For work, I mean."

"Last job? Waitress. At this shitty gastropub in Cleveland, Barn and

Burger. Always had to serve a bunch of drunk puppy hipster assholes who thought they were all progressive and shit but were basically just the larval stage to misogynist conservative crybabies. Blah-blah-blah craft beers, blah-blah-blah third-party candidate, blah-blah-blah, Abercrombie and Fitch, bitch. I'm happy not to be there." She screwed up her face into an acidy pout. "I'm not happy about not getting paid, though."

Out of town, now, Mia pressed the accelerator. The Bronco leapt forward like it got a shot in the ass. They passed fields swamped with water. Saw a couple of downed trees. Shana looked in the back of the Bronco, saw the red stains. She could smell the smell, too—a faint mineral tang. Like the smell of a dead calf. "You're gonna need to clean out the Bronco," Shana said. "From, uh, last night."

"Shit. I didn't think about that."

"Sorry."

"Maybe I'll just burn it."

South of town, a few miles out, they started to see more vehicles. Some of them were media vehicles from local TV stations. Others looked unfamiliar—cars and trucks they didn't recognize. They were just people, it seemed, standing out of their cars, watching, waiting.

Mia said, "Did that guy have a cooler in the back of his truck?"

"I saw some lady sitting in a lawn chair."

"Like fucking tailgaters."

"Like fucking *tourists*."

The Bronco rounded a bend, dipping its rear tire in a tooth-cracking pothole—and soon as it did, Shana saw the flock ahead. *There,* now, were the shepherds she recognized: not just the cop cars and the CDC trailer, but the pickups and RVs and pop-ups. She saw the Beast, too, pulling up the rear. Even still, the media was thicker here, now, too—cameras everywhere, microphones up in people's faces.

Last night changed things, Shana thought.

That meant the media knew what had happened. That someone had told them about the poor man who popped like a cork—though maybe it wasn't just that. Maybe they filmed it. Maybe they filmed the whole thing: the walkers going up over the trailer—her *sister* leading the way. Maybe they filmed that man walking down his driveway, his family struggling to stop him. Maybe millions of Americans last night watched a video of a man blowing up like a balloon filled with blood and guts—which meant they could've seen *her,* too, running through the storm to grab that boy. Suddenly, all these people felt like trespassers. Intruding upon their, what was it that Mia called it? Their *sacred mission*.

Truth was, Shana didn't know if she really believed that, but she damn sure *felt* it in the space between her heart and her stomach. "Pull over, I need to see my sister." That was another thing she felt, now—the need to go back to Nessie, just to see if she was okay. Mia nodded, pulling off to the side about a tenth of a mile ahead of the walkers.

Shana threw open the passenger-side door, pushed past all the fatigue she felt, and wore a long stride as she marched toward the walkers.

She saw her sister leading the flock. Arms at her side. Hair still a little wet, hanging stringy by her pale, freckle-dotted cheeks. Shana thought, *She needs a shampoo, I'll tell Dad to go get some.* As she stormed forward, she heard someone say:

"Is that her?"

And then, "It *is* her."

Next thing she knew, she had microphones all up in her face. A woman with helmet hair started to say, "Last night, you were the one who saved that boy—"

A man with hair so closely cropped to his scalp he was a whisper from being proper bald interjected: "What's it like to watch a man explode?"

Another word—"Hero—"

Another—"Savior—"

A third—"Infected—"

Shana swiped at the microphones and pushed past the cameras. "Go away," she spat. "I just wanna see my sister. I just want to see Nessie."

Questions trailed her:

"Wasn't your sister the first of the sleepwalkers?"

"What do you think about being called a shepherd?"

"What do you think is happening here? Shana? Shana?"

But she ignored them. She tightened her jaw, bit on her own tongue, and strode ahead to meet Nessie.

My little sister.

The girl stared ahead, her pupils dilated to big black buttons. Her mouth stayed closed in that flat, familiar line. No smile, no frown. Shana hurried alongside her, matching Nessie's stride. She stroked her hair. Kissed her cheek. Tried like hell not to cry, but she cried a little anyway. Then she said to Nessie, "I'm sorry for leaving you last night, but I had something to do."

Then she told Nessie the story.

All while the cameras rolled.

• • •

MARTIN HAD BENJI GRAB HIS laptop off the side table, where it was charging. With that, Martin hauled his bag off the floor, unspooling a cord and hooking it up to something Benji immediately recognized—

The FLIR thermal camera.

That, he began to connect to the computer.

"I dropped that," Benji said.

"You did. Tsk-tsk, very expensive camera to drop in a thunderstorm."

"I was a bit busy."

"I've done worse," Martin said, powering on the camera. "I once misplaced a vial of *Brucella*—"

"Wait, what?"

"Blood under the bridge. I was young and dumb and—ah. Here it is."

Robbie stood behind them as they watched. The laptop screen flickered over from its desktop to a recording from the camera. The image onscreen was thermal: midnight blue but for the blobby pulses of color, like something out of a psychedelic lava lamp. The gradations of color revealed the heat maps of what was onscreen. In this case, it showed the two normal temperatures of the wife and the child, and the escalating temperature of the father—a walker held captive.

That's when the camera dropped—clattering to its side. Benji—or rather, his *ankle*—remembered that moment all too well.

"It's still recording." Benji almost laughed. Though the image was now tilted on its side—just as the camera was—it kept going.

"It is. Tough camera."

A new person ran into view—Shana. Again, Benji was reminded of the girl's absurd bravery. She had nothing to gain here. The man, Clade Berman, was nowhere near her own sister. He presented no danger to anyone but his own family. That marked her as either someone who had a lot of untapped courage—there was that word again, echoing the conversation with Arav—or someone who cared little for herself or her own life.

(He wondered idly, *How often do those two things intertwine?*)

The heat map over Clade Berman brightened from orange to red and all the way to the highest indicator of temperature—white. That happened just as the thermal blur that was Shana Stewart raced past, grabbing the boy and dragging him away from his father.

And it was here that those blobs of colors in the shape of Clade Berman became blobs of colors in the shape of a man about to expire—without the visual noise of rain and darkness, it was almost cartoonishly easy to see him bloat and split and rupture. *It's like he's boiling.* His shape continued to distort, bulging in pockets like bladders of gas and blood inflating internally—

Then, like that, he detonated.

A balloon, gone *pop.*

A *human balloon,* Benji thought.

Martin said, "This is where it gets interesting."

He clicked back several frames to where Berman was still just swelling up—then Martin advanced the frame one click at a time.

Click, click, click.

In the replay, Clade Berman detonated.

Click, click, click.

And then Benji saw it: Above what-was-once-Berman were signs of heat. Almost like a particulate spray—a small cloud, like a sprinkling of thermal spikes speckling the air above his erupting form.

"Notice anything?" Martin said.

"I do. Surely it's just . . . blood. He seems to have boiled—if the spray is of a significant enough temperature, then . . ."

"And does that make sense to you?"

It struck him. "No, not really." His voice felt small and faraway as he realized it out loud: "The rain is torrential. The wind is gale-force. And yet—"

"And yet," Martin said, nodding, "this *spray,* as you call it, it goes straight up. Despite the rain."

"Despite the wind."

Martin advanced again.

Click, click, click.

The mist did not merge with the wind.

It did not rise and then fall, beaten down by rain.

It kept going. Up and up and up. Till it was gone, out of frame.

Like a ghost. A fleeing spirit, an ejected soul.

Benji hurried over to the camera and switched it from the thermal recording to the standard digital video—the camera recorded across that spectrum, and what it recorded could be flipped from one view to another with just a spin of a thumb-wheel.

"What are you looking for?" Martin asked.

"I don't know. Something, anything to make sense of this."

He moved the video back to when Berman detonated—not a vision he wished to replay in any format, but one he must, for again, he was a doctor and a scientist and this man's death was a data point. Onscreen now, the recording was muddy and nearly meaningless—yes, it was possible to see Berman's family, it was possible to see the blur of the teenage girl grabbing the young boy, but the act of detonation remained unclear. Rain obscured it. The darkness did, too. Out there in the murk, Benji could see the *motion* of the detonation—the air disturbed, a sudden discoloration of dark rusty red— but not the details of it. Just the same, even as he clicked the frames forward one by one by one, he stared deeper at the space above the exploding man.

Then—

The faintest shimmer.

He stabbed the screen with his index finger, thud. "There! See that?"

Martin leaned in. Benji moved the frames back and forth, three at a time back, then three at a time forward. Hovering over a moment in time.

In that moment, in the darkness and the rain, came the faintest ripple above Berman's detonating body. Like a camera flash illuminating a cloud of dust. "Maybe something from the storm," Martin started to say, "maybe lightning or . . . ball lightning is an unexplored phenomenon," but his words died out as Benji flicked back to the thermal imaging.

The images matched. The shimmer paralleled the heat map of the dis- obedient particulate spray. The shimmer itself did not last as long as the thermal image's register of it.

But its presence, and its match, was undeniable.

Benji leaned back in the chair.

He tried to take it all in. To let the moment wash over him and maybe grant him some moment of clarity, some sudden revelation.

But none came. This led to the deepening of a mystery, not to its resolu- tion. Robbie gave voice to it, muttering, "What the fuck was that."

"No answers," Benji said. "Only more questions."

Martin hesitated. The man's chiseled, handsome face screwed up into something almost comical.

"What?" Benji asked. "What is it?"

"There's one more thing."

"My God, what now?"

"I want you to take over the EIS investigation, Benji."

Oh.

19

SALT AND LIGHT

The rattlesnake became an American symbol around the time of the original thirteen colonies, who saw the snake often on their lands, and who began to associate it—alongside the eagle—with liberty from British oppression. Its most common appearance is in the yellow Gadsden flag, where the coiled snake sits over the phrase, "Don't Tread on Me." John Proctor's regiment flag in PA also had a coiled rattlesnake, as did the Culpeper Minutemen of Virginia, who also utilized the phrase, "Liberty or Death." In recent years, the rattlesnake has seen a reemergence in the symbology of American white supremacists, often paired with other icons of white supremacy such as the hammer, the fist, the Confederate flag, the Iron Cross, the sword, and so forth.

—from the League of Americans Against Hate (LoAAH)
Annual Hate Symbol Index Report, 2017

JUNE 20
God's Light Church, Burnsville, Indiana

SLEEP WAS A DREAM UNFULFILLED, GONE AND LOST TO MATTHEW. HE STAYED awake all night, poring through not just Revelation, but also the works of other prophets like Ezekiel and Daniel, and through the Gospels of Mark and John. Came a point that he thought he would rest his head and get some sleep before tomorrow's sermon, but when he went into the bedroom, Autumn sat there, TV still on. And what he saw on the news . . .

That night, he said a long prayer for the Berman family.

He knew Clade. Not well, not really—Clade was a good man, and he was a churchgoer, he just didn't go to God's Light. He went to United Methodist, up east of Waldron. Matthew had met his wife, Jessa, a few times, and

184   CHUCK WENDIG

only once met their son, Owen. All good people. Hard workers. Clade was a contractor, got started installing insulation. She was a . . . physical therapist, wasn't she? Like Matthew's father was fond of saying: *salt of the earth.* That, from Matthew 5:13, *You are the salt of the earth. But if the salt loses its savor, how can it be made salty again? It is no longer good for anything, except to be thrown out and trampled underfoot.* A passage that spoke to those who cleaved to the laws and the righteousness of God—they held the salt, or the wisdom, of the earth.

And to lose it was to lose everything.

That passage struck him, suddenly.

Had Matthew lost his salt?

Had he lost his wisdom?

Had he lost his *way?*

Truth was, being a pastor had its ups and downs. It was arguably a sacred role, but it was also his *job,* and jobs came with things like . . . paperwork. Maintenance. Balancing books. More rigor and routine than grace and glory. Over time, too, Matthew fell into certain comfortable grooves in his interpretation of the Bible—his church was Baptist, yes, but somewhat more progressive than other churches. So some of his readings of the Bible leaned more academic or poetic—he always said, it was hard to take the Bible as a perfectly literal book given that you had four gospels of Jesus. Four competing stories that did not precisely agree meant that it was, well, *literally* impossible for the book to be taken *literally.*

Whenever anyone got hung up on a phrase in the book, he was fond of saying to them, somewhat cheekily:

Try reading it literarily, not literally.

Now, though, he wasn't so sure.

Anger and fear surged through him seeing the news play that scene of Clade Berman and his wife dying again and again. That was not a natural death. These walkers were not a natural phenomenon. He was suddenly convinced of that. How could they be? This was no disease like man had ever seen.

Ozark Stover's words replayed inside his mind to remind him.

Maybe something *did* poison those waters, turn these people into those . . . things, those sleepwalking strangers. Maybe it was the comet. Maybe the Devil himself. Maybe this was a sign of something worse to come. Those walkers didn't serve God. God wouldn't do that to Americans.

Matthew encouraged Autumn to turn off the TV and get some sleep.

Then he did not follow his own advice. He went back out into the study and he read deeper and deeper. His eyes burned with fatigue but his heart wouldn't quit pounding and his brain wouldn't stop cycling through those images on the news of poor Clade Berman going off like a firecracker held tightly in a closed fist.

He prayed. He prayed his anger at God, for that was part of his role, he knew: to challenge and confront The Man Upstairs for the things that Matthew did not understand. And then it was his role, too, to ask for God's forgiveness in challenging Him. This was their relationship.

Morning came. Matthew sat on the porch. The sun slashed at the horizon with a bleeding line.

He went in, ate a banana for his breakfast, said hi to Autumn and to Bo. Matthew asked them both to be at his sermon this morning. Autumn usually was; Bo, not so much. Bo said he would be, because Ozark had asked him to be. Something about that worried Matthew, but he told himself it was just the lack of sleep getting to him—whatever brought his son to church was a blessing.

Then he got ready.

Usually, during the summer, he kept his attire less formal. A pastor's dress was for some a sacred cow, but Matthew usually had little room for sacred cows, and felt that their slaughter was sometimes necessary to change people's perceptions—he wanted to appear more human to his congregation, dress down, speak colloquially. All in order to make them more comfortable. Especially when up against the deluge, so to speak, of God's expectations for mankind. But today, he had no interest in that. He wanted to put his most serious self forward. He buttoned up his shirt. Pressed his pants. Wore suspenders and a bow tie.

Then he thought, *It's showtime.*

Showtime, admittedly, was rarely for a big audience. The church had a semi-steady population of attendees: three dozen on the best day. But they were his three dozen, by golly, and he would attend to their spiritual development same as if he had three hundred or three thousand.

He walked out of the back and into the main sanctuary of God's Light Church, and as he stepped to the podium, his breath left him, his knees nearly buckled. Because his three dozen had easily doubled. Present were people he'd never seen before—and in the back, as promised, sat Ozark Stover. They did not have pews here at the church, just rows of chairs, and someone had plucked folding chairs from the back wall near the table of

coffee and pastries that Autumn put out; Stover and his people sat in the
back two rows, stuffing them like sausage. They cleaned up nice enough—
all presentable and orderly. Some of the men wore beards or had their hair
close-cropped to the scalp, either shaved all the way down or shorn in a
military-style buzz cut. The women, many younger than their male coun-
terparts, wore sundresses, their hair in ponytails. Stover himself had his
long gray hair pulled back, and he was wearing a simple denim button-
down.

His eyes fixed on Matthew.

Stover gave a small, stiff nod.

Matthew swallowed hard, and then he let it all hang out.

IT STARTED LIKE HE PLANNED. He opened by saying, "Those of you who come
here know that I'm pretty fond of reminding folks how *prophecy* is not the
same as *prediction*. Many times, what we read in the Bible as a prediction of
what's to come is something we interpret through our own fears and experiences, through current events and with a context that people back then just
didn't have." And then he started to give some examples, like how different
prophecies spoke of Nebuchadnezzar, or Alexander, or the Treaty of Rome.
"They weren't writing to us to warn us of Osama bin Laden, or Nazi Germany, or President Hunt. The opening of Revelation tells us right up front:
*This is the Revelation of Jesus Christ, which God gave him to show to his ser-
vants the things which must happen soon.*"

And he was about to continue, explaining as he sometimes did that Revelation was for the people of that time. That word *soon* was key: It was about
the times in which those people lived.

But the words stuck in his throat.

He saw the eyes on him. Stover, frowning. Bo, looking in his lap. People
looked restless, bored, like students subject to a lecture.

And then he thought of all he'd seen last night, and all he'd read. Clade
Berman. The truth of the comet and the woman who discovered it. The
growing sleepwalker flock—two words entered his mind, then, and he suddenly veered away from the sermon he had planned and said something entirely different. Something only later would he realize was uncharacteristic:
"But one wonders what those writers would have made of these walkers—
these Devil's Pilgrims."

And with that, he threw out his old sermon.

And up there, he composed a new one as he spoke it. Moved, he told himself, by God Himself. Filled with light. Borne on a wave of truth.

I found my salt, he thought.

AFTERWARD, HE WAS LEFT REELING. Matthew wandered the congregation like a dance partner succumbing to the motion and the music—he felt passed around in the best way possible. Moved from one parishioner to the next, down the chain, shaking hands, offering words of consolation and hope in the face of a world coming apart—there was a fervor to the crowd, an electricity, and though what he'd just told them was dire and mad, everyone seemed energized. *Happy,* almost, in a manic way, to be offered some portion of the truth—and to be given God's hand to hold so they might find their way through it all. One by one he did this, past warm smiles and knowing nods, through a crowd of people wanting to hug him and weep.

And then, at the end of the crowd, he turned his head for a moment, and he saw her. Autumn. His wife, standing off to the side of the room—she was watching him, and for a moment their gazes met and held. He smiled at her, happy as a pig in the proverbial, well, *you know.* She did not return the smile.

Then her eyes flicked away to someone near him—

A hand clasped his, pulling him nearly off his feet.

Ozark Stover.

"Preacher," Stover said, his big bearded grin like a white picket fence half hidden behind a parting thicket. "That was what I hoped to hear. It's good to hear someone speaking truth about the—what was it? Devil's Pilgrims. Indeed, indeed."

"Mister Stover, thank you for coming. And for bringing all your people. You sure I didn't go too far?" he asked. "I usually don't bring that kind of . . . zeal to my sermons, to be honest with you."

"You did good. That thing about the astronomer who discovered the comet? See, that I did not know. Everything means something." Last night, or rather, early this morning, Matthew looked up the comet that Stover believed represented the Wormwood star in Revelation. Turned out, the woman who discovered it was Japanese, with her last name of Sakamoto—which, he pointed out during his sermon, meant something along the lines of "at the bottom of the slope," which he interpreted as "at the bottom of the pit." (He worried here that this was a little bit of poetic license, but any concern was drowned in a washtub under the waters of response the congregation gave it—in short, they ate it up, and it suggested to Matthew that maybe there really was something there.) He said, too, that the woman—who had commented that the world was "overpopulated"—died of an aneurysm the night the comet passed overhead. "Killed by her own discovery," Stover added. "Ain't that something. Make a deal with the Devil, and the Devil always takes more than his due, you ask me."

"That is his nature," Matthew said.

"Something is happening out there. I appreciate you seeing it and saying something. You're the only one, and time like this, we need people with their eyes open. People like you."

Matthew waved it away as he tried to summon humility. "I didn't do anything different, I just . . . last night after I saw what happened on the road to Waldron, I knew I had to speak out. I spoke with God and I opened my Bible to Revelation and I found that maybe what's happening out there is a warning. Diseases and dragons, the woman, Babylon—the comet, the astronomer. *I saw a star fall from heaven unto the earth: and to him was given the key of the bottomless pit.*"

"Those walkers are on a crusade. Like you say, a pilgrimage of some kind. And not a holy one."

"In time, we'll get to the bottom of it, Mister Stover."

"Call me Oz."

He couldn't help feeling a tingle of pride at that. Matthew couldn't articulate why, exactly—and he knew the dangers of pride, but surely it was okay to feel honored by someone, to have earned their approval when it had before been difficult? Maybe he was beginning to like Ozark Stover. Better yet, maybe Ozark—Oz—was beginning to like him, too.

Stover went on: "Me and some of the folks are going to head down to Waldron. The walkers are set to pass through there and I'd very much like to take their measure."

"I can go with you—"

"No, I have something else for you to do," Ozark said, giving a wink. "Here, come on outside. Someone I'd like you to talk to." On the way out past the coffee-and-pastries table, an odd panic hit Matthew that, *Oh no, we have more people than usual, which means we didn't make nearly enough coffee or bring enough pastries,* but then he saw someone had brought boxes of coffee and donuts from Yum-Yum's down the highway. As they headed out through the front door onto the church porch, Ozark said, "We brought the extras. Figured you weren't used to the burden of us, so it seemed right to bring food."

"That was very thoughtful—" But he didn't get to finish his statement. Stover eased him forward to meet someone standing there. On the porch was a handsome man, with slick blond hair thinning over his tanned scalp, white veneers on his teeth, and a powder-blue suit. "Hello," Matthew said.

"Preacher, this is Hiram Golden. If you don't know him—"

Matthew said, "Of course I know him. A pleasure, Mister Golden."

Golden ran a show—admittedly, a fringe kind of politics/conspiracy show, pretty right-wing. *The Golden Hour.* Started as a podcast, then moved to radio, though his biggest success was still the podcast. Now he was a commentator on Fox, too. Golden was peeling an apple with a small penknife connected to a bullet-shaped keychain. Easing them into his left hand, he gave Matthew a vigorous and warm handshake. He beamed. "Pastor Bird, it is an honest-to-God pleasure hearing someone like you talk. A lot of us out here are increasingly disturbed with what we're seeing from these . . . *sleepwalkers,* and particularly in President Hunt's response to it. She's giving them a lot of leeway, and whatever they may be—whether it's the Devil as you say or some kind of *experiment*—we need to know the truth. I'd like to record a segment with you—"

"Sure," Matthew interjected, jumping the gun a bit. He didn't always trust someone like Golden, he had to admit—but at the same time, the man had a platform. He had "a long shout," as Matthew's father was wont to say. "I'd love to talk to you when you have some time available . . ."

"I have time now."

"What's that?"

"I brought my recorder, and a camera. We do things guerrilla-style on the show, I dunno if you've heard it—"

"I have," Matthew said, though that was mostly a lie. Generally he heard about Golden's show secondhand. "Of course."

"Then you know we do these things on the spot. If you need to go back in with your congregation, I can wait out here and we can record right here on the porch when everyone's gone?"

"That sounds . . . that sounds just fine."

Ozark clapped a heavy hand on Matthew's shoulder—it was like a tree branch falling on his back. "I'll leave you two gents to it, then. My work is done. Preacher, good talk today. I'll be in touch."

And like that, the big man ambled toward the gravel parking lot like he didn't have much care. As if on cue, his people came out of the church—or from around its side—to follow in his wake.

20

THE GLOW

Now, in the midst of the living beings there was something that appeared to glow like coals kindled by a fire, like torches that moved back and forth between the living beings. The fire was dazzling, and lightning flashed from the fire.

—Ezekiel 1:13

JUNE 20
Waldron, Indiana

MARCY REYES FOUND HERSELF ON THE FLOOR AGAIN, THREE FEET FROM THE bed. Her muscles ached like they'd been pulled off her bones and then reattached clumsily, like a sweater you tied around your waist. Her jaw was so tight she thought she might not be able to open it. Her mouth tasted of pennies; her eyes were crusty. Of course, though, it was her head that felt the worst, as it always did. It throbbed. Her whole *world* throbbed. She wondered, *Was this what it was like for a goldfish in a tank? When they told you not to tap the glass, was this why?*

Someone was always tapping her glass.

Whump whud thud. Wibble, wobble, wooze.

She slowly got up off the floor, onto her knees.

The world ran like wet paint. Lights were too bright. Then too dark.

Then: a sound. A *clink, clank.* Plates against plates.

Grunting, she stood. And there, off in the little too-narrow galley kitchen in this dogshit apartment, stood the neighbors' kid. Except he wasn't a kid, not anymore—he was *their* kid, but Max was in his midtwenties, at least. He stood there, going through *her* stuff, grabbing one of *her* plates, going to *her* fridge to again steal *her* food.

Over his shoulder he said, in that nasal voice of his: "Hey, sunshine. Did I wake you?" That, a question asked from his head buried inside her fridge. Not much in there, because she had a hard time making her own food—but people in town sometimes made her stuff, and so what was in there was literally precious to her. Not like she had money to go buy new food, either.

"Get outta there," she said. Her voice smaller than she wanted. *It wasn't always this small. Once everything was much bigger.*

The asshole, Max, turned toward her. The bones under his face shifted and popped, the skin rippling as cheekbones rolled. His teeth became fangs, his eyes opened wide, too wide, going from white to yellow, then to red, then they disappeared inside his head like a cork you lose inside a wine bottle—leaving only gaping sockets behind.

Her mind warred with what she saw, as it always had:

One part of her said, *It's not real, you know it's not real.*

Another part was sure, *so* sure, that it was as real as anything, and that only she could see what so few others could.

She blinked, and saw now that he had grown tentacles—

No, not tentacles. Pasta noodles. Spaghetti, hanging down from his mouth. He chewed, grinning around it like a fox lazily eating a pilfered hen. The pain was making her hallucinate. It did that sometimes.

"Thish ish good," he said, smirking.

That spaghetti. Regina Dolan made it for her—Regina was one of the tellers at the bank where Marcy cashed her support checks. Thing was, Marcy didn't have a lot to look forward to day in and day out—her family never came to see her, and her TV was broken, and she never got any good mail, so what gave her life were the little things. Maybe she got to see the neighbors' cat, Plucky. Or maybe she saw a nice sunset out the apartment window, the one that overlooked Main Street, past the old broken-down Grandville Theater across the way. Or maybe, just maybe, she had a Tupperware container of some amazing spaghetti she was planning on eating for lunch, making it not only a meal she'd enjoy, but probably the only full meal she'd get that day.

"That's mine," she grunted, and moved toward Max.

But then her skull betrayed her. As it always did. Pain lanced through the middle of her brain like lightning—*fzzt*. Instinctively her hands went to the space behind her ear. There, underneath the fuzzy close-shorn hair, she could feel the sunken space—her fingers traveled the contours up the back of her head to the top of her skull, where she found the little manhole cover under her hair and her skin.

"Nngh," she said.

"Shut up," Max said. "I'm eating your shit, deal with it."

She took another step. More pain.

"Man, you're a fucking mess again. Least you didn't piss yourself this time." He shoved another mouthful of cold spaghetti into his mouth—the dumb-ass had a plate in his hand, but then had the Tupperware container on the plate, open, with a fork dipping in and out to capture noodles. "Though it still smells a little like it in here. Jesus. You gonna watch the parade?"

"Parade. What?"

His mouth babbled words that ran together in her ears, slushy and wet: *piss parade, spaghetti, fuckmess,* and then the words garbled further to the point it wasn't words at all, just *fizz fush jashy frall,* all gibberish.

She winced, forced her mind to recalibrate.

It obeyed. For now.

His words roved back into sense from nonsense: "—those fucking sleep-walking freaks are coming through town, be here real soon now, figure you can watch your fellow freakshows come marching and shit."

"My spaghetti," she said, because it was.

"*My* spaghetti." He winked. His eye fell out. Worms squirmed in the dark hole it left behind. He laughed and it sounded like glass breaking.

She charged him then, ready to club him into tomato paste, but by the time she commanded her body to move, she was grabbing for empty space. He wasn't there. He wasn't here at all.

Maybe he never was.

But then a sound behind her—a scuff, and his foot found her tailbone, pushing her forward into the galley kitchen. She reached out, tried to catch herself on the cabinets, but her hands wouldn't comply fast enough. Marcy hit the ground. She caught her bladder about to empty, and she tightened everything up, cinching it hard so she didn't piss herself again in front of this little druggie fucker, *Please, don't you goddamn do it, Marcy, c'mon—*

It held. The floodgates stayed closed.

Max laughed, though. "You're so fucking sad." He sighed. "I'm done with this." He took the plate and container of spaghetti, then chucked it onto her couch. It wasn't a nice couch. It was scratchy like stubble and uglier than a secret, but it was *her* couch and it was *clean.*

And now it wasn't.

She wobbled, struggling to stand. Even though her legs were thick like tree trunks, they felt weak like sand-stuffed socks.

Marcy went over to the couch on her hands and knees, then, started plucking noodles and sauce glops off it, putting them back in the bowl even as her head felt like a wasp's nest being sprayed by a garden hose.

Then, outside: the *woop-woop* of a nearby siren.

"Shit, they're almost here," Max said. He opened her window and leaned out. Her greatest desire was to reach out, grab his ankle, and flip him out the goddamn window—but she wouldn't be fast enough, or strong enough. "You should see this, you fucking turd-plop. It's something. Whole street, lined with people. Like it really is a parade instead of a river of sickness. Jesus. Got cop cars at the front, plus cops along the road and shit. This is really something. Something not-good, I mean. I heard people saying this might be like, end-of-the-world kinda shit. Like, a disease that just keeps going and going, taking us one by one till we're all zombies. Not zombies like in the movies but zombies like these fucks—still alive, but dead inside."

Marcy finished getting the noodles back into the container. It put her out of breath, just that simple action. Now the noodles looked like earthworms squirming. She blinked and they were noodles again.

Max sat down on the couch, nearly kneeing her in the face.

"You're like them," Max said. "Still alive, but dead inside."

"Fuck you."

She went to stand, but Max put his ankles on her shoulder like she wasn't anything more than a coffee table. *Maybe I'm not.* She was just furniture now.

"Sorta fucked up how I could do anything I want to you. I don't mean like, fucking fuck you or anything, because God, fuck, look at you. I got standards. But I could like, light a smoke and stub it out on your arm. I could piss in your ear. You can't go on like this, Marce." He pushed down with his ankles, and pain flashed inside her head—it was all fireworks and muzzle-loaders going off, pop, pop, boom, kssh, kaboom. "I'd tell you to kill yourself, but I dunno if you'd even have the strength to do *that*."

She bit back the words: *I've thought about it, you little punk fuck.*

And then, a curious thing. Marcy saw something. A light, a glow, emanating from the window that Max had been standing at just moments before.

She knew it was yet again a hallucination, a sign of her reality breaking apart—or at least a sign of her broken brain betraying her once again.

"Fuck are you looking at?" he asked. He chuckled.

She could barely hear him.

All she could do was watch the glow wash into the room, brighter and brighter.

It was like—

It was like tuning a radio from static to music.

Suddenly, what had been there was gone. All the noise, all the pain, it receded—almost as if it were sucked away into that warm glow, the way doctors once vacuumed blood out of her broken head. All the nastiness drained away. The clamor and misery fled.

Clarity and peace filled the space.

Well.

Not peace, not exactly. A peace of mind—

If not of temperament.

Max gave her a look like, *Whuh?*

And then she pistoned a fist into his balls.

He doubled over, wheezing and coughing.

Marcy looked at her fist. It was fully formed. The fingers neatly tucked into her palm, the flats of her fingers forming a battering-ram wall. She hadn't formed a tight fist like that in . . . well, not since the hospital. Not since a year ago. Not since that fucko with the bat took everything from her.

Regaining some semblance of his senses, Max swatted at her. She took the hit in the shoulder. Normally, her body these days was sensitive, like a spider's web—every vibration set her teeth on edge, sent all the mind-spiders scrabbling in panic and hunger.

But this time, it didn't do shit.

Again, she looked to the window.

The warm glow. Pulsing there.

She grabbed Max by a hank of his greasy hair, and she dragged him off the couch and down to the floor with her. Marcy climbed atop him as he squealed and thrashed. "It's almost like I could do anything I want to you," she said, grabbing a hank of spaghetti and mashing it into his face. She slapped the pasta into his cheeks, his mouth, his nose: *Whap! Whap!* Though she'd once desired eating this pasta and savoring it even if her hands trembled, now this, *this* was so much fucking better, wasn't it?

Marcy got off him, then—standing up, easily, without pain!—and he scurried toward the door, bits of red pasta dropping from his face. He scrambled up to the doorknob, flung it open, and ran away.

She took the moment to bask.

I feel clear as a cloudless sky.

The window still radiated warmth. More now than before.

Marcy went to it, and she saw why.

The sleepwalkers. They were coming.

And they were glowing.

21

ONE MILE THROUGH WALDRON

MAYA: The Comet Sakamoto are really Rahu and Ketu, okay? Do you know that story?

BLUE: Oh! No, I don't, do tell.

MAYA: They were once one being, a dragon who tried to pretend to be a god, a dragon who was cut in half for that, ahh, what's the word?

BLUE: Their crime? Sin? Slight?

MAYA: Slight! Yes. So, Rahu and Ketu are two halves of one comet, sometimes called the King of Comets or the King of Meteors in, ahhh, in Hindu texts, okay? The head of the comet is the Rahu and the tail is Ketu, and when that passed over us, it cast a dark shadow on the world. It split us, I think, don't you? It split us all down the middle, sure as that dragon did. And those walkers—

BLUE: They're really the Children of the Comet, aren't they?

MAYA: I think they are. I really think they are.

—from *The Maya & Blue Podcast,* Episode 204,
"Insights from the Goddess Collective"

JUNE 20
Waldron, Indiana

BENJI FELT WOEFULLY ALONE AS HE DROVE THE RENTAL CAR TOWARD WALdron. Robbie was gone, along with the rest of ORT. And Martin was in the hospital, recovering from the head injury incurred by the storm.

The flock would be in Waldron soon enough, and Benji had to be present. ORT was done containing the situation, and EIS was the only oversight the CDC had over local law enforcement to keep it all together.

And Benji was now in charge of the EIS investigation.

That boggled the mind, didn't it? After Longacre. After everything.

I need someone I can trust to lead the investigation, Martin said.

You don't trust me, so call Cassie, Benji told him.

I asked her already, she said to give it to you. Then Martin explained: Despite Longacre, they did trust him. Benji was the smartest guy in the room when it came to this stuff. Cassie's knowledge was deep, but only in a single direction, with an expertise on the zoonotic. But Benji had led a team before. He'd led *their* team before. And this was no time to deepen the bench. It was time to put their star hitter, disgraced as he may be, back at the plate because they either got a home-run grand slam, or they lost everything.

(Martin was fond of baseball.)

Loretta will never let you, Benji said.

Loretta already signed off, Martin said with a mischievous smile.

The Immovable Object? *Had been moved.*

How, exactly? Martin said she was under crushing, claustrophobic pressure to get something done with these walkers. As Martin put it, *They're already so far down her throat they might as well be up her ass.* They were willing to scrub Benji's sins from records both official and unofficial. They just wanted something done. Loretta wanted answers and, according to Martin, believed that Benji Ray was their best chance at getting them. Benji knew there might be a secondary truth to that, too: If something went wrong, it would be his head that rolled, not hers.

Because the pressure Loretta felt? Benji felt it now, too. Like being at the bottom of the ocean, deep in a dark fissure, all the weight of all the water pushing in on all sides.

He told himself, *You can do this. You've done this before.*

But part of him thought . . . *Forget it. Get in the car. Go to the airport.* His ejection from EIS was one of shame, yes, but it also gave him freedom. Now he was able to travel the world, giving talks, advising small farms on best practices. To those people he was something of a hero. It brought in money. He once again had purpose. And to go back to all this . . . it undid some of that, didn't it? It locked him back up.

And yet this mystery was so strange, so enduring. To be at the forefront of it was both a problem and an opportunity. He felt like he had answers just out of sight. This puzzle demanded he solve it.

So he told Martin yes. *I'll take over for you, and thank you for your trust, Martin. It means a lot to me. Truly.*

He called Sadie, who remained back in Atlanta. "Sadie," he said with a sigh, hands on the wheel. A sign on the side of the road said WALDRON, 2 MI. "I've got some . . . news."

"You're back at EIS," she said, quite chipper.

"What? How'd you know?"

"Benji, I'm in Atlanta right now. I'm in the *building*. News travels faster than electricity in this place. I'm happy for you."

"It compromises our dealings, I fear."

She made a dismissive sound over the phone. "Pssh. It does no such thing, Doctor Ray. Hm." She paused. "Has anyone ever told you that sounds like a superhero name? Never mind. Point is, you're still there, still overseeing this, still holding Black Swan in your pocket. Nothing has changed except your position on the chessboard."

Chessboard. Quite a metaphor, wasn't it?

One that did not make him entirely comfortable.

Ahead, the town of Waldron revealed itself.

Benji had reports from the police that Waldron was a sleepy, pass-through no-nothingsburg. One of those towns where the country had moved on but this place stayed behind, as if it had found grim comfort in the fact it would never grow up, would never get better, and it was what it was from here until it was gone.

Less than a thousand people lived here. Mostly farmers or other working-class folks. Benji had hoped that the passage of the walkers through town—as it increasingly looked like they'd come right down Main Street—would be uneventful.

That was not looking to be the case.

He eased the car off to the side of the street, blocking a small alley— because he had nowhere else to park. He had intended to drive through Waldron, mapping the flock's path through.

But he wouldn't make it. The way was blocked.

"Benji, there's something we need to talk about," Sadie was saying. "About Pennsylvania. We found something at the Stewarts'—"

"It'll have to wait," he said.

"Why? Is something wrong?"

Benji knew they'd have some media here, some gawkers and rubber-neckers, but this . . .

This was not that. This was much, much worse.

With the phone still in hand, he stared down a gauntlet of people, a sea of heads, hats, faces. Protest signs, too, stuck up like gravestones out of ground made from human beings.

At first, it seemed an absurd thought: because what the hell could they possibly be protesting? But it was like with Ebola. In Sierra Leone, in Liberia, anywhere that disease touched, they saw protests. Guideless, aimless—some wanted a kinder government response, others a more severe one, others just wanted to know what was being done. They wanted answers and were . . . angry that they had none. Protest, he thought, was sometimes targeted, yes. A singular message put out against bad men and worse behavior. Other times, it served as a wordless, senseless exhortation—an expression of a problem that was not yet fully understood. This, he knew, was likely that. But he was trying to figure out, *Why here? Why now?* Then it hit him: "Waldron was all on the news last night, wasn't it?"

"I confess, I don't know," Sadie said. "But it wouldn't surprise me."

"I have to go, Sadie. This is a powder keg. I don't like this at all." His guts churned. This, of *all the days,* to lose the backing of ORT. Robbie's expertise in crowd control, in maintaining some order in the wake of disease, was critical. And now they didn't have it.

He hung up with Sadie and called Cass.

"Hey, boss," she said. "Missed you."

"Where are you?" he asked her.

"South of town. I'm driving the lab truck now that ORT vacated. Shitty timing on that, huh?"

"The shittiest."

"Where are you?"

"North end. Looking at all . . . this." He sighed. "We made the news, didn't we?"

"In a big way. Not just the walkers going over the trailer but . . ."

"Clade Berman."

"Yeah." Benji had hoped that with the storm, the news wouldn't have caught up to the events that had transpired last night as yet—but they clearly had. Worse, Cassie said, "They have footage of it. Not good footage, but it's there. The media is all over this thing. We're getting calls from—shit, everyone and everywhere?"

"How far out are you?" he asked.

"Not quite two miles."

Soon.

"Are we expecting violence?"

Cassie hesitated. "I . . . cops say no, they say this is a peaceful town, but I'm watching footage on the news. These people aren't happy."

"It's one mile through town," he said. "We can do this."

"One mile, boss."

One mile.

SHANA RODE THE RAZOR'S EDGE between total exasperated exhaustion and paranoid anxiety. Because here she was, a shepherd, walking her flock through a territory of wolves.

On each side of the street, protesters gestured with signs. They chanted and shouted about how they wanted answers, how President Hunt needed to be accountable, how the CDC was some kind of government conspiracy. She saw people in medical face masks waving signs like I DID NOT CONSENT TO THIS and STOP POISONING OUR CHILDREN and DANGER: VACCINES ARE TOXIC WASTE. That last one sent her for a loop: She was just tired enough and frayed enough that the thought stuck with her, *What if it is vaccines, what if this is something we're doing to ourselves.* That was dumb as hell, though, she knew that it was garbage nonsense—but when you were ready to fall over and beset on all sides by nutballs, nonsense started to make a certain kind of sense, didn't it?

But it wasn't the protesters that scared her. It was the other ones. The ones without signs.

Truth was, Shana was a bit of a hick. She knew it. Her family lived in Middle of Fuck-I-Dunno, Pennsylvania, and she was the daughter of a dairy farmer. She didn't mind the smell of cowshit. She knew how to milk a goat. She was the product of poison ivy rashes and bee stings and stepping on rusty nails in the old barn (three times, now, oops). People made fun of her sometimes because she often had dirt under her fingernails, but she figured those idiots didn't know how good a green bean tasted when you popped it off the vine and right into your mouth, dirt and bugs and all.

Still, hick as she was, they weren't *trash*.

Trash, well, she knew some real fucking trash. Like the Cosner brothers up on Bellberry Road, with their drunk dad and their penchant for putting arrows through ducks and frogs. Or those creepy dickheads down in the valley—Ronnie Peffer and his rotating crew of shit-wits who manned the couches in his double-wide, the ones that were always popping off their black rifles, selling pills, hanging Confederate flags all over their property. Trash like them had washing machines on their lawn and hate in their hearts.

And it was trash she saw here today.

It wasn't just the camo pants and the trucker hats. It wasn't just the long hair, the mullets, the scraggly beards. Those she knew. She had her own camo pants back at the house. Had a trucker hat, too (admittedly, one that said BOOB INSPECTOR, a hat her dad hated but she thought was funny as hell). Guys like that could be hipster weirdos making their own kombucha or whatever. No, with these creeps it was more and worse: It was their HUNT THE CUNT T-shirts, their shit-kicker boots, their bright-white CREED SAVES AMERICA baseball hats. It was their eyes, too. Mean eyes, angry eyes, eyes that had nothing but suspicion flashing in them like light off spent bullet casings.

They lined the street, too, in little pockets and cabals. They watched. Didn't chant anything. Didn't have signs. Sometimes they said things to one another—small asides while never taking their eyes off the sleepwalkers.

Her phone pinged.

Her father. Again.

Shana where are you?

She hit him back: **Walking.**

Her father: **Come back to the RV pls.**

She repeated what she typed, in all caps this time: **WALKING.**

And then she turned her sound off and stuffed the phone in her pocket. She knew he'd be worried but he'd have to deal. *I'm an adult. Mostly.*

Her neck prickled. Ahead, as they came up on some old shut-down textiles factory, the street had a concentration of trash-men. She spied a swastika tattoo, because of course she did. A Confederate flag arm patch.

Next to her, Nessie kept on.

"We'll be okay, Ness," she said. "They won't hurt you."

But she wasn't sure how true that was.

THE DOOR OPENED, AND LIKE that, Marcy was out on the street among the crowds. For the first time in a long time, she felt connected to her body—but not anchored by it. She felt no pain. The world was clear. Everything felt crystalline and perfect, and Marcy was able now to focus on tiny, insignificant details: a dandelion seed on the breeze before her, the way a cloud was shaped like a rabbit, the way most people used masking tape on their protest signs but some used duct tape or staples or even electrical tape.

She waded out to the curb. Marcy did not push or shove her way—she was a big woman, tall and muscular in the way a refrigerator is tall and muscular. People naturally accommodated her physical presence.

On the street, it washed over her.

The glow.

The sleepwalkers were no more than a quarter mile down the road, and even from here she could see the light emanating from them. The light radiated and shifted, a living thing. It wasn't just something she could see. She could *feel* it. *Taste* it. She breathed the light in and out. It warmed her ears and sang a barely perceptible song, like wind chimes, or rain on leaves.

A woman near to her held up a sign: WE WANT THE TRUTH.

Marcy leaned over and said, "Do you see the glow?"

The face the woman gave her told her no, she most certainly did *not* see the glow. That look! What an ungrateful bitch.

Well, I can see the glow, and to hell with you if you can't.

Marcy decided she needed to be closer to the walkers.

So closer she went.

BENJI SAID INTO THE PHONE, to Cassie: "I can't just sit here and wait. I'm going out there."

"Uh, to do what?"

"I don't know yet."

"Be careful, Benji."

"You too."

And then he waded into the crowd.

SHANA FELT THE DUDE'S PRESENCE before she saw him. He was more mountain than man. He had long hair pulled back and the kind of beard an owl might nest in. His shoulders were broad, but his middle was even broader, and he stood rooted to the ground, arms crossed over that landslide chest.

The look on his face was one of wary curiosity.

But nothing so intellectual as curiosity crossed the faces of the human trash that gathered around him. What Shana saw there was nothing but a kind of unquiet rage. Horses champing at bits, teeth gnashing, ready to stomp their hooves down. Ready to run, rock, and trample.

Here she saw a new tattoo—not on the big man, no, but on those around him. Looked like two swords crossing, surrounded by . . . what was that? A serpent of some kind? She squinted and saw that no, it wasn't two swords—it was a sword and a hammer. Some wore it on the backs of their hands, others on biceps, even necks.

"Do you see the glow?"

Shana startled at the voice. She turned to see that as she was looking the one direction, a woman came up on the other—right behind Nessie.

This woman was big, too—not like the bearded mountain man, no. She was not exactly tall, but bristling with muscle and a bit of fat. Her buzz cut only accentuated her cinder-block head. A head that looked to be broken: The cinder block was cracked, like her skull wasn't the shape it was supposed to be, not exactly.

She asked the question again: "The glow. Do *you* see it?"

Shana felt alarm—who was *this* crazy-ass lady?

"No, I don't—" She looked back over her shoulder, saw other shepherds walking back there: Lonnie Sweet, gawky Kenny Barnes, Aliya, even Mia— but they all had their eyes on the flock or on the crowd. Shana felt like you did sometimes in a dream: like she wanted to wave to them, call out, but somehow she couldn't, or wouldn't, or didn't think it would matter.

"You gotta watch these people," the woman said.

"What . . . what people?"

"Them." She did not point, but she stared out at the crowd ahead.

"Oh."

"Some shit's about to go down." The way the square-headed lady said it sounded almost like the thought excited her.

"What? What do you mean?"

But then someone came up behind them—it was Mia. "Hey, is everything okay?" Shana turned to her, then back to the lady—

The lady who was already leaving, heading back to the crowd.

"That was weird," Shana said.

"What'd she say?"

"I . . . something about a glow. Something about how shit was about to go down. We should get somebody."

"Get somebody who?"

"I don't know. Somebody!"

But it was too late.

● ● ●

BENJI PUSHED HIS WAY FORWARD. He got looks aimed at his presupposed rudeness—but he didn't have time to care about that. Something about this crowd felt untrustworthy. The air contained something in it: a buzz, a threat, a mad frequency—it was like in the storm the night prior, but this was a whole different kind of weather.

He stepped to the corner of a run-down hardware store.

And that's when he saw something fly up in an arc over the crowd—

A glass bottle.

FOR MARCY IT ALMOST SEEMED to happen in slow motion.

Not literally, no, but she felt so *hyperaware,* now, so *back in her own goddamn head* that every little moment and motion was a revelation—one captured by her eyes and her mind as it happened.

She went into the crowd of the walkers, suffusing herself in the glow.

She spoke to a girl, a young woman, whatever—another person who did not seem to see or appreciate the glow.

Marcy warned the girl:

Shit's gonna go down.

Because it was. From the middle of the street, it was easy to see—you didn't have to be a psychic, you just had to be an ex-cop who was coming down off a year of having a broken brain, an ex-cop *and* ex-boxer who found herself emerging from a valley of fog to a peak of clarity.

She saw the tattoos, the shirts, the white supremacist fuckos with their 88 tattoos and their Iron and Celtic crosses—and she saw another bit of ink, one she didn't recognize: a sword and a hammer encircled by a snake. She didn't know what it meant, exactly, but it was probably more Nazi white-guy shit, because it was always Nazi white-guy shit.

Over there, across the street, there was a big fucko, too—a massive wall of a man, mean and icy. Marcy watched him, and here was where it got interesting—he stopped paying attention to the walkers. He moved his attention to the crowd.

He gave an elbow to someone next to him—a ratty, rangy length of rope with pinch-shut nostrils and greasy blond hair curled behind his crooked ears. Ratty-Rope left the side of Big Man and waded farther south, heading the opposite way of the sleepwalkers.

Then, *then,* Big Man looked across the street.

And he gave someone a subtle nod.

And someone—a little fire hydrant of a man with camo pants, tan shirt, camo hat—gave a nod back.

That's the one, Marcy thought, and she headed toward him.

IT CAME FROM SOMEWHERE BEHIND her—Shana was looking forward, then she heard gasps behind her. She and Mia turned to see a bottle arcing through the air about thirty feet back. It spun through the air, *swish-whish,* and then it crashed down on the head of one of the sleepwalkers, the paunchy guy in his wife's pink bathrobe—Shana thought his name was Arlen or something like that, and though his wife visited early on, she stopped coming a week into their walk.

The bottle crashed against his head.

People gasped and yelled, pointing—Shana saw a man running through the crowd as two cops broke position, hard-charging toward him to intersect. "Jesus," Mia said.

Meanwhile, the paunchy dude, the walker, Arlen—

He just kept walking.

Glass stuck to him, but then fell away.

Didn't break the skin. Didn't break his stride.

No blood, no nothing.

Then Shana had a strange and terrible thought:

What if the bottle was just a distraction?

IT'S A DISTRACTION, HE REALIZED. While everyone else was looking at the bottle, Benji saw the gun. The man drawing the pistol was a small guy, thick, camo pants, a camo hat. The weapon looked like a boxy pistol, a Glock, maybe. The attacker drew it from the back of his pants, concealed there under shirt and waistband.

He's going to try to kill these people.

Benji limped his way through the crowd, pushing himself as fast as he could go, ignoring the pain. Someone's elbow clipped him in the chest, pushing him back—it was like fighting against the tide.

Someone screamed. They must've seen the gun.

He cried out, shoving his way forward, fearing now that he was late, too late, that the guy would aim and the gun would go off—and who would catch that bullet? One of the walkers? One of the shepherds? One of his own?

There. He surfaced again through the crowd and saw the man backing up, raising the pistol toward the walkers—

A shape came out of nowhere. Like a bull, charging, except it was a person. And this person, a woman, slammed into the gunman like she was all arm and all fist. It wasn't just a brute attack, either; she hit him, then spun him around like a top.

And that was when the gun went off.

H*E'S* TRYING TO KILL *THE* glow.

This man was an enemy of the angels—that's what they were, Marcy realized that now in an epiphany that felt to her mind like the warm, tickling waters of a bubble bath, they were *angels*—

Which put him squarely on the side of evil.

She charged him, slammed into him, whipped him around like he was a scarecrow on a loose pole. Her hand reached out, trapping his wrist against the small of his back. He tried to squirm away, grunting in protest, but Marcy was strong, *so strong,* and she summoned all the strength she damn near forgot she had—

She slid her hand over his.

Dumb bunny didn't know shit about trigger discipline. He'd drawn the pistol with his finger on the trigger.

Which was a good way to shoot yourself, it turned out.

Her finger landed over his, gave it a tug.

Bang.

The gun went off and his leg went limp as the bullet dug deep into the meat of his left buttock, down toward and into the back of his thigh. He collapsed and she let the gun clatter atop him. He screamed. The crowd screamed, too, and surged. Panic seized the crowd and she wanted to wave her arms and yell to them, *No, no, it's okay, I fixed it, the angels are safe, now.* But nobody would listen, because none of these poor fools saw the glow anyway. Someone, a cop, slammed into her, and her head hit the concrete and she thought, *Please don't break me further, please—*

Then she tasted her own blood and everything went dark.

Only the glow kept her company there in the black.

22

JUST ASKING QUESTIONS

So many things I want to be. I want to do it all and see it all! Dad says I have to pick one thing and concentrate on it. Shana says I'm lucky I have options because she doesn't have any options (but that's not true and she knows it, and in case she's reading this—HI, SIS, STOP READING MY JOURNAL, JERK). But I want to do it all. Scuba! Brain surgery! Watercolor painting! I want to be a sommelier and a marine biologist and a senator and ugh I can't choose any one thing why do I have to live only one life and be resigned to doing one thing? STUPID STUPID STUPID <3
—from the journal of Nessie Stewart, age 15

JUNE 20
Waldron, Indiana

THE POLICE STATION WASN'T MUCH TO LOOK AT. CINDER-BLOCK WALLS, A couple of metal desks, a receptionist's area. Benji stood off to the side with Chief Linzer, whose dust-brush mustache was white as fresh snow.

"So she's not a danger to us?" Benji asked, his eyes never leaving the woman sitting across the room at one of the detective desks. The woman sat there scowling, looking out through half-lidded eyes. Even from here, Benji could see the rough-hewn topography of her broken skull under the buzz cut.

"Danger? No. I can't imagine. Marcella Reyes probably saved some folks with what she did. Wasn't her gun, it belonged to the fella she grabbed—according to her story, she saw him through the crowd, didn't have time to confront him or call anybody. When the gun came out, she acted. Grabbed his wrist. The man—name of Hal Henry—shot himself in the ass. Bullet went down through his cheek and into his leg. Severed his femoral artery. He's in critical condition now."

Benji rubbed his eyes. He was tired. So damn tired. "The man—Henry—I'm told he's part of some . . . local militia."

The chief bristled. "Don't go painting with too broad a brush, Mister Ray—"

"Doctor."

"*Doctor.* The militia boys are just patriots. Man like Henry was on his own—just a lone-wolf, grade-A piece-of-shit with delusions in his head."

"So you're suggesting that the thrown bottle was not connected in any way to the shooting?"

Linzer was silent for a moment. Then, icily, he said: "You let us do our job and we'll be content to let you do yours."

Benji felt suddenly both weary and wary—he knew full well what it was to be a black man in America dealing with white police. Nothing was ever about race to them, until it was. Then it meant assuming the worst of someone with brown skin. Harassing them, arresting them, maybe even putting a bullet in their back. Yes, maybe Linzer was right, maybe the man operated on his own. But he seemed to discard any alternative notion quickly, *too* quickly. Hadn't he read a report in recent years from the FBI that said white supremacists were infiltrating law enforcement? Would it really be that much of a surprise to learn that Linzer was part of the local militia and not just the chief of police in this flyspeck Indiana town?

At the end of the day, though, what was the point? Benji was not going to defeat systemic racism on this day (or any day), and he had a job to do. The flock had gone on without him hours ago, and thankfully the panic here in town did not yield catastrophe. With the gunshot, there was a stampede away from the flock, and a few people got hurt, but no serious injuries as people ran for cover. The shepherds, to their credit, stayed with the flock—many, he learned later, standing in front of the sleepwalkers, as if to take any bullets meant for them.

Shepherds defending their flock from wolves . . .

"Miss Reyes was a police officer here?"

"No, no, she was up in Indianapolis."

Just then, a text pinged his phone. From Sadie:

Hope you're all right. Saw Waldron.

He quick tapped a reply: **Am OK. Will call soon.**

"What happened to her?" Benji asked. "The injury, I mean."

"Her head? She got jumped. Maybe didn't check her corners or her doors, I don't know. As she was dealing with one perp, another came up behind her, got her in the skull with a Louisville Slugger. Once she was down, the fucker—goofy on meth, if I heard it right—just kept whacking at her."

Benji winced. "That's terrible." Another text from Sadie came in:

Need you to visit the Stewart family ASAP. Have info.

Uh-oh. What was *that* about?

He continued with Linzer, looking up from his phone: "Can I go speak to Miss Reyes?"

"Have at it, Mister Ray."

"Thank *you*, Mister Linzer."

If the cop wouldn't call him doctor, he wouldn't call him chief. Respect, Benji decided, had to be a two-way street.

He said no more to the chief and wound his way through the handful of desks scattered in the middle of the room. Benji pulled up a chair next to the one at which Marcella Reyes sat. She lifted her head off her folded arms to stare at him through bleary, weary eyes.

"Who are you?" she asked, her voice a stone-grinding groan.

"My name is Doctor Benji Ray. I'm with the CDC."

"Oh."

"You don't seem well. I'm told you have a . . . plate in your head, titanium. Correct?"

"Two connected plates. Top of the head and then down behind my right ear. I had, ahhh. I had brain bleeding after the attack. Listen, I just . . ." Her nostrils flared. "I just want to get out of here."

"Are you injured? I could call for an ambulance—"

"No. This is just . . ." She grunted as she sat up. "Me."

"Then you're free to go, I think."

"I want to come with you."

He looked around. "With me *where*?"

She adjusted herself, looking to be in grave discomfort. Marcy wore a face that was as serious as a sniper's bullet. Through a clenched jaw she said, "With you. With the angels. The glowing angels."

He feared, suddenly, that despite what the chief had told him, this woman *was* a danger. Was there a schizophrenic element at play? Had that bat broken her brain?

"I don't follow you."

"They *glow*," she said, and as she did, her eyes shone with the threat of tears. "I can feel it coming off them. Warm and soft. Like angels."

"You believe in God? Are you a Christian?"

"No. Not really. Agnostic. I guess."

"But you believe the flock of sleepwalkers are truly angels?"

She swallowed hard. "Don't see any better explanation for it."

"They're not angels," he said. "They're just people. People affected by . . . something, I don't know what. They did not fall from the heavens, Marcella, they came out of their own homes. They came from work, from vacation, from the park, from all over. They are not celestial beings." Already he'd heard some talk about this being related to the Great Comet that had passed overhead a month before—Comet Sakamoto. "They're just like you and me. We're trying to help them, to understand what's doing this to them."

"So you're not a believer?"

"I am a Christian man."

"But you're also a scientist. A doctor."

"I don't find those two things mutually exclusive."

She watched him, guarded and wary. "But you don't believe these . . . walkers . . . could be something else. Angels or something."

"I don't think so, no."

And yet what *were* they? Nothing they knew added up. Benji was a believer in larger, stranger things than science was able to explain. He did believe in God; in that, his faith had never wavered.

A little voice inside him asked: *What if she's right?*

She leaned forward with the certainty of a drunk at the bar about to tell you he just ran over Bigfoot with his pickup truck. "Here's what I know: I know that those walkers glow like molten gold, and I know that when I'm near them, everything goes clear. And I know that being farther away from them means the pain is coming back. The headache is like a noise in my head, like a radio turned to a dead station, the volume cranked way up. I gotta be with them, Doctor Ray. Every minute I'm gone, I feel . . . like I'm being washed back out to sea, farther and farther from shore. Soon enough, I'll start hallucinating. I'll lose myself again. Let me come along. I can help. I have a cop's instincts. I have a good eye for things."

Her voice contained a ragged, broken desperation—the desperation of a dying woman, not a living one. On the one hand, that troubled him. It suggested she might present a danger to herself or to others. On the other hand, she *had* saved the flock and the shepherds. And it was not exactly his purview to decide who could or could not come along as a shepherd.

"They call the ones who follow shepherds," he said.

"Then I wanna be a shepherd."

He hesitated. "All right," he said finally. "I can give you a ride."

Through the pain on her face, a big smile broke out. She took his hand—her grip was weak, her fingers trembling—and she gave it a small shake. "Thanks, Doctor Ray. You won't regret it."

AN HOUR LATER, HE DROPPED Marcy off with the flock—and marveled at the change that came over her the closer they got. She sat up straighter. Her eyes became clearer. She no longer looked to be someone trapped under the weight of persistent pain.

"Thank you again, Marcy. I believe you saved some lives, so consider me in your debt. If you need anything—"

She cut him off, beaming. "Being here is repayment enough."

And with that, she was out of the rental car, wandering toward the flock. He half expected her to run, like a puppy meeting its new family for the first time, but her approach was reticent and circumspect.

He didn't understand why proximity to the flock would engender such a change in her physical state. The only thing he could conclude was that she suffered no such physical state, that it was purely psychological.

It would have to be a question for another time.

Now he called Sadie.

What she told him confirmed his worst fears.

Immediately, he contacted law enforcement to demand that Charlie Stewart pull over his RV.

THE RV WAS A ROUGH and rickety thing. It sat off in a small gravel pull-over as the flock moved on. Two cop cars framed it in a trap. It couldn't go anywhere. A trio of officers stood near, at the ready.

"You want me to go in with you?" Cassie asked.

"No," Benji said. "And I'm leaving the officers out here, for now."

"It could be dangerous."

"I . . . don't think so. At least, I hope not."

"He could be involved."

"We will just have to see."

And with that, Benji went to the door of the RV, gave a gentle knock. A man answered—Charlie Stewart, father to the walker Nessie and another heroic shepherd, Shana. Charlie had kind of an aw-shucks vibe about him, with round sun-freckled cheeks and dusty blond hair poking out from under his baseball cap like scarecrow straw.

"Come on in," Charlie said, eyeing up the police officers. He gave a small, nervous nod to them.

Inside, Shana was sitting up, tangled in a mess of clumsy bedsheets—it was obvious she'd been trying to nap. It was a nap she deserved, Benji thought, but presently he needed her attention.

"Honey," Charlie said, "why don't you lie back down, get some more rest, me and the police officers can talk outside—"

"We can do this in here," Benji said. "For privacy. And I'm afraid Shana should be here, in case she can offer information."

Charlie paused, as if he were chewing on that. A protective energy came off him, and Benji wondered what must be going through his head. Maybe he could not articulate it, but surely he held some blame for them through all of this—some sense that the CDC could be doing more, that maybe they were part of a government that somehow caused this, that *at the very least* they could've prevented this or helped the Stewart family understand what had happened to their daughter Vanessa. *Nessie.* But they didn't. He resented them, Benji suspected.

That, or he knew more than he was letting on.

"Dad, it's fine," Shana said, coming closer. Her arms were crossed, forming a defensive posture.

Her father gave an uncertain nod, then he took a seat at the little nook table. "Go on, then. Sit. You had me pull over here—we want to be back with my daughter soon as we can be. Especially after today."

"I'm going to introduce a colleague of mine," Benji said, putting out his phone. He dialed up Sadie, put her on speakerphone.

Shana and her father shared a look.

Once on the line, Sadie introduced herself and asked Benji to take out the Black Swan phone, too, for its projector use. He did, pointing it at the inside of the RV's door—and immediately a beam of light speared the air, capturing motes of dust drifting through the old recreational vehicle.

An image resolved from a pixelated spray.

It was a laptop in a clear plastic bag sitting on a table.

Sadie asked: "Mister Stewart, do you recognize that laptop?"

But it was Shana who spoke. She answered: "That's Nessie's." Way she said it was protective, too, like she wasn't sure they should have that.

Benji said, "Investigators found something on it."

"On her laptop," Charlie repeated.

"Correct."

"I dunno if you should be poking around the laptop of a fifteen-year-old girl, there are privacy issues and—" the father started to say, but Benji cut him off as gently as he could:

"We found a secret email account. She had a separate email browser located in a hidden folder. In it she communicated with one person only."

"Who?"

"Daria Price, married name, Daria Stewart."

Charlie's eyes went wide.

"Mom," Shana said.

"That's not," Charlie said, half choking on the words. "That's not possible. She walked out. We haven't heard from her—"

"Your daughter Vanessa did," Sadie said. "One email three months ago in her primary inbox, recovered from trash. She responded and set up a secondary email account at Price's request. They communicated six times after that, albeit in fairly short bursts and terse emails."

"That's not possible," Shana said.

"Daria *could* be that way," Charlie said. "Cold, sometimes."

Shana seemed to bristle at that. "Not to me, not to Nessie, she wasn't. It was just to you, Dad." The indictment born of that statement hung over both of them like a sword dangling by a meager thread.

"I want to see those emails," her father said.

Benji nodded. "Of course, we'll accommodate. We can send them as a digital package or—"

"Print them out, please."

Sadie again: "Before that happens, we need to discuss their last communication."

"Daria promised to send something to Nessie," Benji said.

Charlie's eyes flashed with fear. "Send something? Like what?"

"We don't know. She just said it was . . . a package."

"A *care* package," Sadie corrected.

"Do you recall any kind of delivery . . ." And here, Benji's words faded as he saw the recognition on Charlie Stewart's face. He *did* recall.

He nodded like his memory was just catching up. "Oh. God. Yeah. I . . . remember that a guy came by to deliver a package. Like, a . . . a courier."

"A courier. As in, UPS? FedEx?"

"No, that was the weird thing, it was an unregistered truck. Like a moving truck, a rental."

Benji jumped in and said: "Sometimes FedEx has been known to rent additional non-labeled trucks when one truck goes out of service or if delivery demand is high, particularly during the holidays."

"Maybe, but the guy didn't have the uniform. Or any uniform." Charlie stared off at the middle distance—staring, Benji suspected, into his own memories. "He wore a, uh . . . basic black polo, khaki pants."

"You took the package?"

"I . . . did, but Nessie was right up behind me. She snatched it out of my hands and said *It's for me* before charging up to her room. I yelled after her to ask her what it was, and she just yelled back she'd ordered some supplies."

"That didn't strike you as strange?"

Shana laughed—though it wasn't exactly a happy sound. More an ironic one. "Nessie was *always* ordering stuff online. Weird shit. Like . . . a praying mantis egg case or stones to polish in her rock tumbler or like, I dunno, science stuff. Crystals and chemicals and microscope slides. Sometimes art stuff, too, because Nessie couldn't just do one thing —"

Her father finished the statement: "She wanted to do *everything*."

"Do you remember anything about that package?" What Benji was not-yet-saying-aloud was this: There existed the very real possibility that her mother, or something pretending to *be* her mother, sent Nessie a package. And that package might have been the inception that led to the sleepwalker epidemic, be it bacterial or viral or fungal. It was a common low-key, low-cost method of causing chaos through biowarfare: send along an envelope of anthrax spores, and who knows who gets infected? If someone had engineered something far stranger and more sinister and sent it to a young, vulnerable girl willing to accept any package from a missing mother . . . the scenario, however disturbed and implausible, wrote itself. "Anything at all, Charlie. Did you see inside it?"

"No."

Shana hesitated. Like she had something to say.

"Shana?" Benji asked.

"Uh."

"Did you see the package?"

"Uhhhh."

"You did. You saw it."

"I was there when she opened it. The cardboard box wasn't big, it was, you know, no bigger than a lunch box. She opened it and it was like something out of Harry Potter—all this *fog* started coming out as she pulled out two sets of Styrofoam, and she pulled them apart and . . ."

"And what?"

"It was totally anticlimactic. All that dry ice and all she got out of it was this . . . little test tube."

A test tube.

"What . . . was in it?"

"I couldn't see. It wasn't full—maybe halfway. To me it just looked like gray dust. I asked her what it was and she got kinda defensive. She said, *It's for an experiment.* Then kicked me out."

The delivery agent. Benji knew that's what it was. It *had* to be.

"Do you know where the test tube is now?"

Charlie said, "I would've thrown it out. Or put it in with her stuff. Nessie's room could be cluttered. Mind of a little genius and all that."

"The FBI searched the house, didn't find anything," Sadie said.

Benji's heart sank.

But then:

Shana winced.

"Uhh."

She knows.

"Shana . . ." Benji said.

And that's when the most surprising thing of all happened. She reached across from her, grabbing her backpack off the table. Shana unzipped it, reached inside it—

In her hand was a test tube.

And it looked like it contained—

"Is that *weed*?" Charlie asked.

Shana gave an awkward shrug. "Sorry?"

23

APOPHENIA

DON DAYTON: Last question, and then we'll let you get back to the campaign trail. What do you think about these sleepwalkers?
ED CREEL: What do I think about them? I think they're a message.
DD: A message. Sent by who?
EC: We don't know yet, but I'd bet maybe ISIS. Maybe China. Maybe someone internal—some traitor inside Hunt's camp, or some NSA business. Maybe the Devil himself, who knows? But trust me, they're a message, no doubt about that.
DD: What, then, is the message?
EC: Something's coming. Something real bad. And if we don't deal with it, if we don't round these [bleeped] up, we're going to find out real soon just how bad it can get.
—from *The Don Dayton Show,* Fox Business Network

JUNE 21
Shelbyville, Indiana

"YOU SHOULD BE ASLEEP."

"Thanks, Dad," Shana said, but who she said it to was *not* her father. Rather, it was Arav.

She sat on a stump watching the walkers go by. At night, it was a surreal experience—the way the headlights from the rear guard illuminated them from behind, giving each sleepwalker a long shadow that fed into those walking ahead. (It gave her the somewhat chilling sensation of looking at gravestones, though she could not precisely say why. She snapped a few photos of it, and the grainy wash of it only confirmed that image.) Dad was up ahead again in the Beast—he'd taken a detour earlier, getting ahead of the walkers and dumping their sewage at a local campground before getting ahead of the flock. All around, the walkers walked and the shepherds followed—though this late, past midnight, a lot of the shepherds had found places to sleep for the night. Either in their own RVs or cars, or at motels, hotels, campgrounds, the couches of friends and family or other kind Samaritans.

The people from the CDC had mostly gone on their own way, too. Some, she knew, slept in that big trailer. They had a few cots in there, including a couple above the gooseneck in a claustrophobic "loft" area.

Arav, though, remained—though she didn't know that until this very moment, when he came walking up. In his hand he had two cups. Steam danced above each. And as he came closer, a smell hit her—

A salty, umami tang.

Intimately familiar. She knew it instantly.

"Raaaaamen," she said, the word taking on almost spiritual power.

"You've got talent," he said. "You should be a police dog or something." At that, he winced. "Wait. Sorry. I did not mean to infer that you were, or are, a dog."

"You can apologize to me by giving me one of those."

"That's why I brought it out." He handed her one, and the steam wreathed her face. *Ahhh.* "It's not exciting or anything, but I saw you out here and after the last couple days . . ." Did he know about her mom? The package? Shit. "I figured you could use it. And the air's getting a little chilly. Sorry it's just the microwave stuff."

"Dude, the microwave stuff is my *jam.*" She took the cup and sipped at it. A little too hot, but she didn't care. "In junior high I had like, *massive anxiety.* Every morning I didn't want to go to school. And it's not like school was really that bad but I had a couple girl-bullies who made fun of my hair and also I didn't like shaving my legs and—you know, I dunno, it was junior high. It sucked. So in the morning I always felt mega-queasy, right? I didn't want to eat anything. Not eggs, not cereal, *blech,* it all made me worse. But my mother had this idea—in part I think because she was just frustrated, and maybe she said it as a joke, but she said, *Fine, I'll make you ramen if you'll eat that.* And she did, and I ate it. I felt a little better. So that was my breakfast every school-day morning for three years." She slurped up some noodles. "Oh God, marry me."

"Me, or the noodles?"

"Both of you. We can have like, an open marriage or whatever they call it." She sat on the stump, but it was a big stump—some massive oak had been chopped down here at some point. She scooched over and gestured to the stump. "Sit?"

He shrugged and sat. The night air was cooling down, but his hip next to hers was warm.

Together they ate their Cup Noodles, the only sound between them the slurping of ramen and the supping of broth. The only sound *around* them was the dull, ground-drum plodding of the walker parade.

"You were pretty badass the other night," Arav said.

"Huh?"

"You saving that little boy."

"Oh. Yeah. That." Sure didn't *feel* like she saved him. The little boy was alive, yeah. But what life would he lead now? Not that she felt comfortable saying he'd be better off dead but . . . the kid had nothing, now. That stupid wife, not letting go of her husband. Even though he was shaking so bad in the storm . . . Shana shook it off. Even replaying that in her head almost put her off the ramen and *that* would be unforgivable. "Not as badass as that beefy lady taking down that dude in the crowd. God, that fucking guy had a gun. They say he was going to shoot at the walkers."

"She was a monster, that lady. She's around now, you know. I guess she's cool. Used to be a cop or something?" Arav wiped some dots of dribbled broth off his chin with the back of a hand. "They say the gunman was a lone wolf, but I'm not sure. Guys like that are never really lone wolves, you know? They're always worried about how us brown people are getting radicalized, but nobody talks about how it happens to white people more than it happens to us. It's really crazy."

"No kidding. Some people are just trash, and they find other trash and start to form a landfill. The internet makes it easier."

More slurping and sipping. Shana quickly finished her noodles.

By now the sleepwalker flock was halfway past them. Already after today the number was up by another dozen. Day after day, more added themselves to the ranks. Some with shepherds coming along, others all alone. The CDC had people—Arav, sometimes—cataloging them.

"The other thing," Arav said suddenly, "is what happens if you shoot one of them? Not that I want to find out—but we can't stick needles in. We can't cut them with knives. What would a bullet do?"

"I didn't think about that. You figure they're bulletproof?"

He made a face and shrugged. "No? But I only say no because nobody is bulletproof. That's not . . . that's not a thing. Then again, what's *also* not a thing is that people's skin prevents you from poking them with needles. That's off-the-charts weird. All of this is. None of it adds up. We've got theories but nothing to validate the theories."

She was still stuck on the first part, though.

"Okay, but that's twisted if they might be bulletproof."

"But they might *not*. Reminds me a little of non-Newtonian fluids. Let's say you make a slurry with cornstarch and water, two-to-one ratio. It makes this wet *goop,* but the thing is, it's liquid, but behaves like solid matter in certain instances. If you slap it, it's like slapping, I don't know, a leather car seat or a trampoline. If you poke it, or press on it slowly, it becomes liquid— your finger or hand sinks into it. Their skin is clearly not that, I don't mean to suggest that it is. But it calls into question—is the bullet fast enough to penetrate, or would that only cause the skin to reject it more easily? We don't know. And that is one test we are not willing to try."

"This is all pretty fucked up."

"It makes me anxious," he said earnestly. "I feel like I'm getting eaten up inside by all of it."

She let out a breath. "Damn, me too."

"I'm sorry to hear about your mom."

"Yeah. I just hate that Nessie is the start of it. People think it's our fault. Have to keep telling the newspeople we don't want to talk to them. But people online already started their conspiracy theories. I can't even look at social media. Idiots on Fox News call us terrorists. I dunno. It sucks. Everything sucks."

"I try to concentrate on the day-to-day. To control what I can control. To let the rest go. And to give myself moments like this."

"It is nice."

And then she did something she knew she shouldn't do.

She set the empty ramen cup down.

She reached out with her hand.

She took his hand in hers.

And she just held it.

"I'm older than you," he said.

"I'm eighteen in a couple weeks. And we're in Indiana, where I'm sure the age of consent is like, twelve or something barbaric." She cleared her throat. "Er, not that I'm trying to fuckin' like, have sex with you or anything."

"Okay, good, because—you know. Yeah."

"Yeah."

Moments of silence stretched like strange taffy. He blurted out, "Not that I wouldn't *want* to—I don't mean that, I just mean, I'm twenty-five—"

"Yeah, no, I know, right."

"Right."

"Good."

Gulp. More silence filled the spaces.

"I see you taking photos sometimes," Arav said.

As a response, she turned toward him with her phone, took a shot. The flash was off—she didn't like the flash, it was too garish, too bold—and what resulted of him in the photo was this half-dark shadow. But it showed his shape, and she liked that. A silhouette she enjoyed.

"It's just a dumb thing," she said.

"Is it the thing you want to be doing?"

"I don't know the thing I want to be doing. I just like taking photos."

"Then maybe that is the thing you want to be doing." He gave a small squeeze to her hand. "You should take more photos. Might be nice. Might help you feel better. I dunno. What we're seeing here, Shana—I don't know what it is, but I know that it is extraordinary. Someone besides the TV media should be documenting it."

"You think *I* should do that?"

"I do."

"Okay then."

"Okay."

WHAT A WHIRLWIND DAY. THE sermon in the morning led to the podcast interview with Hiram Golden, and turned out the man cut those things together lickety-split. It ended up online within two hours, and by then Matthew was getting calls from other media outlets: They wanted to talk to him about *his* take on the walkers, from the comet to Revelation to what the Bible says about eschatology and so on and so forth. By the afternoon they had him down at the Fox 59 studio in Indianapolis, where they recorded him for the evening news.

Thing was, Matthew felt at home during all of it, like all his training as a pastor had informed him and energized him. He knew he was reaching so many more people than he would have if it was just him in his little church.

He reminded himself: *Thank Ozark Stover for this.*

And, of course, God.

(He chided himself momentarily for making God an afterthought, but he told himself that it was simply because the Holy Father was so clearly the first to thank in all things that it didn't even need to be spoken.)

At night, he met back up with Hiram Golden, who offered to take Matthew out to dinner. They went to one of the best—and oldest—steak houses in the country, St. Elmo's. Usually, that was the place Matthew and Autumn went for their anniversary every year, so already the dinner carried with it the whiff and aura of a *special occasion,* and boy, was it.

He and Golden talked for hours. They drank good wine and talked about all the troubles the country was facing—of course, Hiram Golden was an unabashed supporter of Ed Creel for president, and he started to sell Matthew on it, at least a little bit. Matthew had figured Creel for a wolf in sheep's clothing, someone who wore the mantle of a good Christian just to get the good Christian vote, but Golden explained that Creed was a charitable man. He just wasn't a braggart about it—he did a lot of it in secret, on the hush-hush, to make sure he didn't grandstand.

As Hiram took out his little keychain penknife and speared a piece of cheese off a cutting board, he said, "Creel attends church every week in Nashville, where he lives now. He's a God-loving and a God-fearing man."

Matthew said he worried the man was too Big Business, and Hiram's counterpoint to that was, "Only thing more corrupt than business is politics, Matthew. You ask me, big business is a step up from big government. It's self-correcting. It allows room for God's hand to . . . deliver prosperity to those who help themselves." And with a couple-few glasses of wine soaking through him, it all started to make a certain kind of sense. By the end of the night, Matthew agreed to come on the show again in a few days, and maybe even make an appearance at one of the Creel fundraising events as he passed through the state next week.

So, home he went.

Late, too late. But that was okay. Monday morning was light for him.

He crawled into bed and settled under the covers as quiet and as gentle as he could—he didn't want to wake Autumn, after all.

Turned out, though, she was already awake.

"You should've called," she said.

Her voice wasn't bleary or sluggish. He hadn't woken her—she was awake this whole time. Waiting for him. "I'm sorry, I assumed you were asleep, Autumn."

"I worry."

"I know you do."

She sat up and turned the lamp on. He shielded his eyes.

Way she stared at him was like she was pointing two rifles at his head. "That wasn't you today."

"What?"

"In the sermon, that wasn't you."

"Autumn, of course it was me." He put his hand on her knee, and she tensed up. "What, you think a demon jumped into my skin? Made me summon those words?" He laughed, but she wasn't having it.

"You've been drinking."

"Wine, a little."

"How much is a little?"

He puffed out his cheeks, trying to remember. He couldn't. (Honestly, he still felt a bit fuzzy. It had been a while since he drank much of anything.) "I could do without the Spanish Inquisition, Autumn. It's late."

"Do you really believe those things you said this morning?"

"What things?"

"You said . . . those people, the sleepwalkers, that they could be Pilgrims of the Devil, that they could be some kind of *sign* of the End Times."

"I . . . it's a bit rhetorical, but at the root of it there's some truth, some metaphorical truth—"

"*No.* No! Not everyone is going to take this metaphorically, Matthew. They'll believe it. They'll believe it snout-to-tail. To some people, there is no separation between . . . between the *story* you're telling and their belief in it as *fact.*"

He prickled at that. "I have more optimism than you do. I have hope in people. *Faith* that they're smart enough to know what I'm saying and why I would be saying it."

"A man pulled a gun today. Not far from here."

"I know. I heard about Waldron this afternoon when I was at the studio. They asked me about it."

"And what did you say?"

He scoffed. "What do you think I said? I condemned it. Violence is never the answer."

"To some people, it is."

"Not to me."

"It is in the Bible."

"Autumn, c'mon, it's late—"

"Stonings and battles and dismemberment. God commanding Saul to wipe out the Amalekites, the bowls of wrath in Revelation—"

"I know, I've struggled with the violence in there, but it's a book. Modern Christianity does not subscribe to that kind of . . . aberrant behavior."

"But some *do*. Some believe it's the way. The *only* way—"

"Sociopaths, maybe."

"Not all zealots are sociopaths. Some don't know any better. You have a responsibility, Matthew. That man today with the gun—"

He thrust an angry finger at her. "That man is not a parishioner here."

"But he might be one of Ozark's men."

"He was a lone wolf. News said it, cops said it."

"He still could've heard that podcast. Or your sermon somehow. You don't know he didn't."

"And you don't know he did! Can't prove a negative, Autumn."

Matthew launched himself out of bed, gathering up his pillow and then a throw blanket that sat on a corner chair in their bedroom.

"Where are you going?"

"Away from this conversation. I need some sleep."

But she started to follow after him, persistent. When Autumn got something in her head, she wouldn't just let it go. "Those walkers. What if you're wrong? What if they're *God's* chosen people? What if they're not demons, but need to be protected from demons? Or what if God has nothing to do with any of it?"

Matthew wheeled on her. He hated the anger he felt for her right now, and he told himself in part *It's the wine, it's just the wine*. He tried to control the volume of his voice when he said:

"I had a good day. A *good* day, Autumn. This is an opportunity for us, for the church, to make a difference, to see our voice and the word of God be carried farther than I had ever anticipated. So don't you *dare* try to rob that from me." He stared at her, his chest heaving. "I'm going to the living room to sleep on the couch."

Autumn said no more. She did not return the anger he poured upon her. Mostly, she just stood in it, watching him with sad eyes. With a look on her face like she didn't recognize him at all.

She returned to her room and let him be.

ONCE AGAIN, BENJI FOUND HIMSELF awake at midnight.

Once again, he ruminated on patterns, on numbers.

Earlier, around midday, the walkers turned onto a road—E350, no other designation that Benji could find, as out here the roads were farmland and on the grid pattern—and continued westward, south of Indianapolis. So far, in the two weeks, the flock had missed major metropolitan areas, and further had eschewed all major highways. That pattern continued now.

What other patterns were at play here?

The flock was driven, seemingly directed. It was measured, purposeful. Benji felt increasingly sure of that, even though it made little sense—no disease of which he was aware followed a pattern as precise (or at least as persnickety) as this. He felt mad even considering it, but at the same time, he refused to discard it out of hand. Admittedly, it was just as likely he was seeing patterns where there were none—that was a decidedly human trait, was it not? Apophenia, they called it. An epiphany was a useful revelation about the world around you; an apophany was a revelation, too, but wrong in that you had incorrectly discerned a pattern where none had existed, taking enlightenment from an untrue thing. It was the human way—seeing truth in the storm of darkness and noise. Faces in clouds, ghosts on video, Jesus on a piece of damn toast.

(*Angels glowing in a crowd of disease.*)

Once again, he paced the floor. This time, in a Holiday Inn Express about three miles from where the flock was walking.

And once again, he did what gave him comfort:

He brought out both of his phones.

On the one, he opened Black Swan.

On the other, he called Sadie.

He bypassed all small talk. "I'm lost here," he said. "There are patterns just out of sight. Rules I can't see. Finding out this may have purposeful—the Stewarts receiving a package, bodies gone missing—I worry that someone has engineered something so far beyond our understanding that I'll be too slow to see it, Sadie."

"I trust you to see what's right," she said.

"You? Or Black Swan?"

"Me. I trust you." She paused. He heard her breathing on the other end. It gave him strange comfort. "I've found myself thinking about you quite a lot. You're brave and smart and kind and I'd be a fool not to trust you. I'm glad to have listened to Black Swan."

Suddenly, the Black Swan phone projected a pulse of green on the wall. Not one, but three pulses.

"I think Black Swan likes that you listened to me," he said. "It just pulsed green."

"Black Swan has impeccable taste. Better question is, how do *you* feel about me finding you on Black Swan's suggestion?"

"It's, ahhh, it's good." A strange feeling swept over him. He felt feverish. His heart raced in a fit of tachycardia. His palms grew damp. *Am I getting sick?*

No, he realized, it wasn't that at all.

It had been so long since he'd been in any kind of a relationship, since he'd had anyone attracted to him—or been attracted to anyone in turn—that this feeling was almost extraterrestrial.

Was that it? Was he attracted to Sadie?

I can't think about this right now. Now was not the time. There were greater burdens to carry. Romance at this point was childish. And worse, a distraction. He needed to be thinking about the problem.

Not about her.

Quickly, he changed course in the conversation.

Instead, he told Sadie what they'd found regarding the test tube that had been sent to Nessie Stewart—the one that Shana had been using to store her marijuana, of all things.

"We found no microscopic residue in the container. Nothing. And one assumes that if the vial contained some kind of contagion, then Shana—the older sister—would be walking with the flock alongside her sister. But she's not."

Sadie hesitated. Was she disappointed he hadn't answered her question? Was he reading too much into this? Again, here it was, proof he was being distracted by the wrong problem.

"Has Black Swan helped at all?" she asked.

"A little." He spun the phone around and directed it toward one of the bland hotel room walls. Benji activated the projector. "I've been thinking again about patterns. There's a pattern at work here, even if I can't see what it means. Black Swan," he said, "can you highlight the commonalities shared among the walkers in the flock? What patterns am I not yet seeing?"

One green pulse, and then the screen lit up with data. Lines of information crunched very quickly, and when it was done, it resolved to white; and in that white, two circles formed.

Each circle contained a tidbit of data:

In the first:

89th percentile health factor

In the second:

85th percentile intelligence factor

And that was it.

Those were the two common elements.

The age of the sleepers was spread out, none too young, none too old. The flock overall was relatively diverse, at least compared with the rest of the country's population. The two common elements were: They were smarter than most, and they were healthier than most. Abnormally so.

His silence must've struck Sadie, for over the speaker she said: "Did I lose you? Or did I just lose you to thought again?"

"Lost in my thoughts, sorry. I forgot you're not here and you can't see what's on the screen. I'd put you on video, but I don't think the wireless here is robust enough."

"It's fine, you can tell me." Pause. "I like the sound of your voice."

I like the sound of yours, he thought, but did not say.

He explained.

"Black Swan," he said. "How do you determine health factor?" The circles went away and the screen filled with text. Benji read several of them to her: "Health records, physical education certificates, local exams."

To this last bit, Sadie said: "Local exams?"

"Yes," Benji said. "Of course. Black Swan scans them."

"Really?"

"You . . . didn't know it could do that?"

She laughed. "No. I didn't."

"Doesn't that bother you?"

"Of course not. It's learning. *Evolving.* It is as it should be—just as you and I learn new skills, so should it. That cheeky bastard is adding to its résumé, isn't it?"

"Tsk, tsk. I thought we weren't supposed to anthropomorphize."

She laughed. "I think the cats are out of the sack on that one, don't you?" She kept on: "A scan is interesting, as it's not like it has X-ray capabilities or anything. But I suppose it can detect temperature and pulse and other abnormalities. Black Swan, how do you calculate intelligence factors?"

More data appeared onscreen. IQ tests, standardized tests, grades, job performance ratings, analyses of social media. He read them to Sadie.

"So best guess," she said, "Black Swan is telling us that the walkers are both fairly healthy and fairly intelligent."

"That appears to be the case. Which is, I admit, puzzling. Diseases come from a wide variety of vectors, and some as a result can be a bit choosy—hepatitis D can only infect those already infected with hepatitis B, for instance. Sometimes region is at play—a disease in the late 1800s affected only a subset of men from the Moosehead Lake region of Maine, and it caused them no end of startled fits and muscle movements. The Jumping Frenchmen of Maine disease, they called it."

"That sounds insane. You're making that up."

"I'm not! I promise. Thing is, it was never repeated. That disease never came up again and no one can really explain it. So we don't always know what considerations are in play. Some diseases affect different ages or people of certain locales—parasites might look for very specific conditions in which to multiply or in a host to control. But nothing that crosses the axis lines of intelligence and health. Unless—"

"Benji—"

"Unless it's deeper than that. In a disease like porphyria—the so-called vampire disease, where patients become literally allergic to light and, curiously, defecate purple fecal matter—"

"Benji."

"—in that disease, it's a genetic component, a gene mutation. What if the walkers are all bound by a specific gene mutation. I'm going to have to talk to Cassie and Martin, have them look back at Clade Berman's blood—"

"*Benji,* listen to me."

"Sorry. I was yammering."

"*Prattling,* I like to say. It sounds nicer."

"It sounds very British."

"I *am* very British. I am at least ninety-first percentile British. Tell me, what room are you in? I'm having something sent up to you. Something to help you relax."

"Oh. Let's see—I'm in two forty-three."

"Good. Perfect."

"What are you sending up?"

"A treat. Like I said: something to help you relax."

"Oh, Sadie, I hope it's not a bottle of something—if I drink, it'll cloud my thinking, and at this point the last thing I need is—"

Just then, a knock at the door.

He said into the phone (quite dubiously): "Hold on, you."

From the other side of the door, a deep voice: "Room service."

Well, now, what did she get me? The hotel worked fast.

He went to the door, opened it—

And Sadie stood there. She had a cocky tilt to her hips and her tongue gently poking out between her teeth, like a canary in a cat's mouth.

Benji felt his face stretching with his own grin. "I . . . I don't even—"

She waggled her phone at him. "Told you. A treat." And now, in that deeper voice she was faking: "To help you relax."

"Sadie, I—"

"Shut up and let me in."

She melted into him. Her mouth against his. Her weight pushed him deeper into the room. Her leg kicked out behind her, the heel on her boot catching the door and slamming it shut. Her hands braided behind his back, and the two of them toppled onto the bed, all the papers there scattering to the four corners.

24

THESE ARE THE PEOPLE IN YOUR NEIGHBORHOOD

Here's how we do things in America: We identify a problem, then we promptly ignore it until it's not just biting our ass, but it's already eaten the right cheek and has started on the left. Antibiotics, for instance. The bacteria are winning. They're fast evolving defenses against all our antibiotics, and when that happens, we lose everything. Everything from heart surgery to a tattoo to a hangnail becomes infinitely more dangerous. And what are the pharma companies doing? Twiddling their thumbs. Not enough money in it, they say. We're in a plane plunging toward the ground. Eventually we'll pull up—right at the last minute! We'll figure out something with horizontal gene transfer or bacteriophages or polymer nanotech. We won't crash. But we'll come real, real close. We always do. That's the American way.

—science writer Afzad Kerman in his TED Talk, "Chaos and Crisis: The Accidental Ingenuity of the Almost-Apocalypse"

JUNE 21
Cloverdale, Indiana

THE FLOCK GREW OVERNIGHT, AS IT DID EVERY NIGHT. AND IT WOULD GROW today, as it did every day. More flock meant more shepherds. More shepherds meant more cops. And more media. Shana felt overwhelmed by it. Like they were all in a pot of water as it came slowly to a boil. A pot that would cook her skin off her bones. A pot that would boil over, one day. And then what?

But it wasn't just that, was it? It was Dad, who still wouldn't come out of the RV to be with Nessie. It was the fact that Nessie had fallen prey to someone pretending to be their mother (because surely it couldn't be their actual mother, could it? That woman was hell and gone, happily fucked off from her family). It was Nessie being lost to her. Her family was in tatters.

Shana relied on routine to help her through it. Get up. Get coffee from whoever was bringing it—today it was Mary Sue Trachtenberg, one of the shepherds, who literally bought six of those big-ass Dunkin' Donuts jugs. And she had bags of donuts, too. (The shepherds had a loose fund going: Pay what you want to pay, someone goes and picks up waters, coffees, light meals. Want something bigger, you gotta leave the flock and get it yourself.)

So she ate a donut, shot the shit for a little while with Mia, then took her position by Nessie. Walking, walking. Brushing her hair. Using a handkerchief to wipe road dust from her sister's face. Talking to her in case she was listening—a lot of shepherds talked to their flock, because what if they were in there? Like coma patients, maybe they could hear. (Mia didn't think so. She said it was like "talking to a houseplant—these poor bitches ain't hearin' us, Shana.") At first Shana thought to keep the conversation light—*dude, Indiana is boring, the sky is blue, I'm about to start my period and I forgot fucking tampons so now I'm going to have to pay one of these weirdos to get me tampons*—but then she found herself interrogating her little sister about those emails, the test tube, their mother.

"The hell were you thinking?" she asked, keeping her voice low. "That wasn't Mom. You fell for some scam. Not just a scam, but like, they're saying it all started with you, did you know that? You were the first because you opened some box and opened some *test tube* and . . ." She *grred*. It felt suddenly like all eyes were on her. Like all the other shepherds were staring at her. Not just because she made that *grr*-sound louder than she intended, but because maybe they *knew*. Maybe they blamed Nessie. Stupid girl opened Pandora's box and now all these people were here with loved ones infected by it. Even if that wasn't true, they'd soon come to believe it, and then what? Would they stone Shana and her sister? Hold Nessie down until she erupted?

None of this was doing fuck-all to help her feel better.

In fact, her mood was worsening—her anxiety felt like it was driving fast the wrong way down a one-way street.

Then she remembered sitting with Arav the night before.

What he told her.

Then maybe that is the thing you want to be doing. You should take more photos. Might be nice. Might help you feel better.

The camera.

Take pictures.

So she got out her phone and she set to work.

At first, it was like settling into the ocean at the Jersey Shore for the first time. No matter how hot the day, the water always felt too cold, so she'd creep in slow, adapting to it inch by inch. Shana had never really taken photos of people all that often. Usually it was just . . . *things.* A tree that looked like a hand. A praying mantis (Shana used her little phone-fitted macro lens to get a look at the thing's freaky eye). One time she found a deer, a dead deer, and it was really fucking long gone—its middle was missing, and the rib cage had air between the red, raw slats, so she stuck her cameraphone in there (*don't drop it don't drop it don't drop it* she told herself) and took a photo of the inside of the rotting animal. It was a cool-as-hell photo, like a crimson cathedral, but she never showed anybody because it was too gross and surely they'd laugh at her. Call her names. Something something reindeer games.

But taking pictures of people? No. Couldn't bring herself to do it.

Now, though . . .

She started with what she knew.

Or rather, *who* she knew.

Nessie. She got in close and pointed the camera at her sister's flat, expressionless face—then, a tap of the phone.

Click.

There. Her sister's face, framed between the borders of the phone screen. Mouth that stern line. But there was something else there, too. An illusion, she knew, but . . .

In that photo, there was life.

Expression.

Unpinned from the automaton-like parade, in that one frame Nessie looked alive, aware, awake—though that also made her look haunted. Like she was staring at something far away, something terrible. A distant threat or a future she feared would soon come true.

She quick put a filter on it—black and white, high contrast. Gave the image a rugged, liquid mercury cast.

It wasn't just that Nessie looked haunted.

The image itself was haunting.

"Thanks, sis," Shana said, giving Nessie a quick peck on the cheek.

As the flock moved past her, she took a few more shots. Wider shots, looking both at the coming parade of sleepwalkers, and then behind them. Then the media people gathered together, drinking coffee, smoking cigarettes, waiting for some break. And cops easing their cruisers along—they were traveling forward at such a slow pace, they gazed at their phones, dicking around on Facebook or playing *Angry Birds* or some shit. (And suddenly Shana wished for a better camera. A *real* camera. With a lens that she could twist to zoom, and then she might be able to really see what they were doing on those phones . . . what a visual that would make.)

Creatively, she felt limber. Excitement pumped through her like new blood. So fuck it, she thought, and she jogged to catch up to the sleepwalkers once more, and there she started doing as she had with Nessie: She got close, framed their faces, then took the shot.

One after the next.

Darryl Sweet—Headphones Kid, *snap*.

Birthmark Girl, a white girl whose name was really Jasmine, and who had no shepherd to walk with her—*snap*.

Mister Manypockets, whose name was Barney Coolridge, and who had seventeen pockets across his whole ensemble—*snap*.

Mateo, Mia's brother, *snap*. ("What are you doing?" Mia asked. "I don't know," Shana said, smiling without meaning to.)

Shana got halfway through then jogged back off to the side of the road to look at the photos. They were amazing. Even without filters, they all gave her the same vibe that she got with Nessie: They were alive in there, somehow. She could see it on their faces. And yet, at the same time, the sleepwalker phenomenon connected them, too—they all looked awake but asleep, with nary a single bit of tightness to their faces, with eyes that looked off down the same infinite highway. They had all shared in something. Or were still sharing something. And because it was only the faces, it erased the variation between body shapes and sizes. Flipping quickly from face to face made them almost seem like they were morphing from one to the other, a transformative shift whose commonalities carried on to the next.

Shana was hungry for it, now. She wanted *more, more, more.*

Again she waded into the flock, and again she put her camera up and framed the face of one of the walkers, a young black girl she didn't know, hair in ringlets, earrings from the bottom to the top of each ear—

"Hey, get the fuck away from my baby."

Shana startled. A woman, one of the shepherds, was storming up to her. Her index finger was so bent and fiercely pointed, it looked as if it were ready to shoot lightning out of its long-nailed tip.

"Wh . . . what?" Shana asked.

"I see you taking pictures of my daughter."

Shana backpedaled to keep up with the flock. The woman kept on her.

"I was just—I'm just taking a record of the other sleepwalkers, I'm a shepherd like you and—"

"I know who you are, I know what you're doing."

"It's okay, it's not for anything. Besides, the newspeople have already taken photos, I think—"

The woman shook her head, narrowed her eyes, looked angry enough to bite Shana's phone in half. "My baby isn't for them, and she's not for you, neither. I know what you'll do, you'll take her photo and pop it on your goddamn Instagram or something. But other people are not your playthings. We're not your damn art projects. Stow that shit and get away."

"I . . ."

"Go on. Get away."

Shana, rattled, quickly pocketed the phone and hurried back to Nessie. She matched her step to her sister's and swallowed a hard lump. It took everything she had to pretend she didn't want to cry, and that alone made her feel stupid and embarrassed because why would she cry over that? She should've just taken the dumb girl's photo anyway. Told the lady to fuck off, too bad, it's happening.

Shit.

Shit.

The woman was right, though, wasn't she? Shana wouldn't want someone coming over here and snapping shots of her sister.

She thought about going to apologize, but what would she say? Already she felt like a huge asshole. No way to fix that now. Next thing she knew, Mia was at her elbow. "Hey, that lady gave you a real shit-fit."

"Yeah," Shana said. "It's fine."

"That's Donna Dutton, she's like that. Don't talk to nobody but her kid, Maureen."

"She could be a little nicer," Shana said.

"No shit. Then again, times are fucked up. Not like niceness ever got anybody anything." But Mia must've seen that Shana was upset. Which meant Shana wasn't doing a very good job of hiding it. "You okay?"

"I'm fine."

"You sure?"

"I said, I'm *fine,*" she snapped.

"Shit, okay, never mind. Maybe you could be a little nicer, too."

And with that, Mia went back to be with her brother.

VBBT, VBBT.

A deep and dreamless sleep—

Vbbt, vbbt.

—suddenly interrupted.

Vbbt, vbbt.

Benji clawed his way through the comfort of those slumbering depths, back up to the light of the morning. An arm that was not his own sat draped across his chest. A moment of bewilderment fled at the sight of Sadie there next to him, facedown into a hotel pillow, breathing deep as her naked back rose and fell

Did last night really happen? he wondered.

Sadie was here. Next to him. Without clothes.

It really happened.

Vbbt, vbbt.

He groaned and grabbed for his phone.

His phone was not lit up. It was not vibrating.

Vbbt, vbbt.

Wait.

There, on the console by the television.

The sound came from the Black Swan satphone.

Now Sadie found her own way through the maze of sleep and lifted herself off the pillow. She rolled over. "That sound. It's like, a bee. Inside my head. Is there a bee inside my head? Tell me there's not."

"There's not. It's Black Swan."

She sat up. One eyebrow arched so high it might as well have been hovering above her head like in a cartoon. "What?"

The screen pulsed—not green, not red.

But white.

Again and again.

Each time, vibrating as it did.

"It wants to talk," she said.

"That's what this is?"

"I think so."

"You don't know?"

"It is a machine intelligence, Benji. We have not answered all its mysteries, nor have we charted all its behaviors."

He turned the phone on. "Black Swan, it's Benji. Is something up?"

One green pulse. Then another.

Then three more after it. Quite the confirmation.

The phone's projector came on of its own volition. Which, honestly, Benji found a touch disconcerting—but as Sadie said, it was a machine intelligence. It had behaviors. Therefore, it was . . . behaving.

He turned the phone toward the wall.

And in a burst, it showed an image.

The image was a map.

At first, just pixels, but already he could see it was the shape of North America. It began to zoom in, increasing magnification—with each increase, a new spray of pixels that resolved anew.

Florida. The Everglades.

It zeroed in closer, closer . . .

Now: A small island called Chokoloskee near Chokoloskee Bay. Near Dismal Key, not far from the Ten Thousand Islands.

"Why there?" Sadie asked.

"I don't know," Benji said.

"If Black Swan is showing this to us, it must be important."

The screen pulsed green once, twice, then again and again, a strobing pulse of light. A seemingly endless, insistent series of affirmations.

"I guess I have to send someone to Florida," he said.

The only question was: Why?

What did Black Swan see there?

JERRY GARLIN,
OR HOW THE END BEGINS

JUNE 23
The Gulf Coast, Florida

As SHE WAITED TO PICK UP HER RENTAL CAR AT THE SOUTHWEST FLORIDA airport, Cassie watched the news. CNN. It showed the flock—now pushing into Illinois. Even during her flight, the flock's numbers had grown again, steadily. Underneath the footage of the flock, the chyron read: GOP NOMINEE ED CREEL CLAIMS PRESIDENT HUNT IS "CHINA'S ALLY, NOT AMERICA'S."

"Unbelievable, right?" said the man behind the counter. Young guy. Latino, maybe. Crisp button-down, hair shellacked back.

She realized that the customers in line before her had gone on to get their cars. She stepped up to the counter and said: "I'm sorry, wha?"

"Those people. It was the comet, right?"

"The what? No," she groused. "It wasn't the comet."

"Coulda been."

"No, not 'coulda been.' Comets aren't magic. They're not prophetic, they're not flying overhead, sprinkling us with fairy dust."

He blinked. "But the Bible says—"

"Can I have my car?" she asked, slapping down her driver's license. "And no I don't want your extra insurance because your extra insurance is bullshit and I have my own, so let's just hustle it along."

He gulped. "You got it, lady."

NIGHT OF THE COMET.

Cassie remembered that movie from the 1980s. She loved horror movies . . . *and* sci-fi . . . *and* fantasy. All that good genre stuff. Fuck any artsy-pants indie fare, give her Hobbits and Cenobites and Cyborgs (oh my).

As she drove south toward the Everglades—air-conditioning on full polar ice blast because the outside air was so hot and so humid it felt like you were the meat in a sandwich whose bread was the Devil's moist thighs—she replayed that movie in her head.

In the film, a comet passed overhead. The earth went through its tail, and this . . . red dust rained down over everything. Everyone it touched turned into zombies, and two sisters, Reggie and Sam, fought to survive in this comet-born zombie apocalypse. Eventually they ran into scientists and *of course* the scientists turned out to be bad guys (a trope Cassie hated)—the scientists were sickened by the red dust, too, but figured out a way to stave off the effects by harvesting the blood of the untouched.

More fucking zombies.

She used to love zombie movies. Now, not so much.

She couldn't think of the flock like that. Wasn't the comet. They weren't zombies. End of story, full-stop, shut the fuck up, Guy-at-the-Rental-Car-Counter.

The zombies in that movie were not like the sleepwalkers. No zombies were, really, but Cassie saw the comparison even though she would never say it out loud—a horde of people walking, seemingly indestructible, responding not at all to stimuli? Okay, *fine,* yeah, the flock seemed a little zombie-esque. But they weren't violent, even if they did expire violently. The walkers, along with whatever disease had taken them, were on a mission. Driven in a way that zombies were not. Cassie had taken to thinking of them less as a flock needing to be shepherded and more like people on a pilgrimage. Walking toward some sacred, unknowable destination.

(Of course, she'd heard them called the Devil's Pilgrims, too—some dickhead evangelical with a podcast came up with that name, and it had started to stick. Those people were the worst. Hypocrites of the highest order.)

Did the flock have purpose? She didn't know. She imagined so, but in the way toxoplasmosis had a purpose, in the way an ant colony had a purpose—something primal, something fundamental. Some small and simple biological urge. No greater agenda. Nothing supernatural. Cassie did not believe in God like Benji did.

No, whatever was happening here was something they just didn't understand, yet.

The question now was, Why had Black Swan sent her here?

Would she find an explanation here in the Glades?

Or would she find only new questions?

FIRST A RENTAL CAR, NOW an airboat.

The boat's massive fan thrummed at her back as the watercraft whipped down the mangrove channels and twisting turns of Crooked Creek, through coastal swamp and the gator-fed mire.

It was a police boat, driven by an Everglades City officer—Officer Tabes, a hard-edged woman, jaw like an excavator bucket. Didn't say much except to let Cassie know that they didn't know what they were dealing with. The boat sped along, and it put Cassie's stomach in her throat—in her own car she liked to drive fast. She had a Dodge Challenger, liked to open it up whenever she could. But she liked being in control, not being controlled, and here, in this boat, everything felt wildly and woefully out of control.

THEY MET TWO MEN ON a chickee hut.

Cassie was unfamiliar with chickee huts, so it had to be explained to her. Tabes said it was an "Injun" thing, and yes she really said the word *Injun* like she was some kind of fucking cowgirl. "Seminoles used 'em. Basically just four posts out of the water, a platform on top, and a thatched roof on top of that." Said that people like the two men ahead—Dave Hutchins and J. C. Perry, both from Gainesville—used them for camping and fishing since dry land was not as common out here.

The two men stood on one chickee hut platform, a kayak lashed up to the side and camping provisions spread throughout. A couple of fishing rods crisscrossed each other on the far side.

Hutchins was a roly-poly hillbilly-looking type—the camo hat with the fishing license dangling from it, a neckbeard colonizing his throat and his jawline, a belly straining at what she assumed was an ironic T-shirt: PADDLE FASTER, I HEAR BANJO MUSIC.

The other one, Perry, was cleaner-cut, like an aging frat boy playing at being a fisherman: He wore a nice white polo and a black baseball hat with checkered flags on it and a logo that said PFIZER RACING TEAM. He was blond, athletic, tan.

Turned out, the two of them were friends since they were kids, and best as she could tell, their lives had diverged pretty considerably since then, but they made time once a year to come out here, go fishing. They arrived a few days ago, and took the kayak up Crooked Creek a little ways till they found some solid ground—having had little luck with fish, they were planning on doing some python hunting. The snakes were invasive here, and you could hunt them freely at any time.

They did not find any snakes.

What they found was a dead body.

THIS WAS WHAT THEY SAID about it:

HUTCHINS: We were out there near a little island called Horses Key looking for pythons—there's no bag limit or nothing, and you can dispatch 'em however you like, traps or machete or shit—

PERRY: We have a gun, though. A shotgun, a .410—

HUTCHINS: It's like a squirrel gun, just a little popper. Lets you hit the snake in the head but keep the skin, because people buy those. Not the meat though, 'cause the damn snakes are loaded up with mercury—

PERRY: Not that we need the money.

HUTCHINS: Right, no, I look like a proper redneck and I come from that backcountry stock but I own a Ski-Doo dealership—

PERRY: And I work sales for Pfizer.

HUTCHINS: Anyway, we weren't finding shit, and it was hot, and then we caught a whiff of something—

PERRY: Not the smell like you'd think. Not a dead smell, exactly— a sourdough smell with a pickling brine.

HUTCHINS: Still nasty, though, in its way. Real strong. We thought maybe it was an animal or something, sometimes feral hogs have a stink like you wouldn't believe. So we went looking out—

PERRY, AFTER A DEEP BREATH: That's when we found the body.

HUTCHINS: But it weren't like no body you've seen.

PERRY: It didn't even look like a body. It was just this . . . white mound, this *hump* there tucked away under the roots of a cypress tree, and I thought, shit, okay—

HUTCHINS: Tell you what it reminded me of—when I was a kid we had goats, because you could rent the goats out to rich folks to eat the poison ivy and sumac and stuff off their property, and the goats always attracted a shit-ton of flies, right? Some horseflies, too, big as buttons, and sometimes those flies would get stuck to the flypaper we hung up around the little goat barn. If it was really wet out, though, those flies on the flypaper would get *moldy*. Whole paper would—shoot, maybe it was the glue they used. But the flies would mound together and the mold, the fungus, would cover them in this powdery business and break them down—you'd see the legs folded in and the eyes broken out of their buggy heads, the wings would either be falling off or be mashed down in with the rest of the moldy mess.

PERRY: The big difference here was that this . . . pile had something growing up and out of it.

HUTCHINS: Like mushrooms. Weird ones you find in bad mulch.

PERRY: To me they looked like—you ever see crab eyes? Eyestalks, I think they call them.

HUTCHINS: Yeah, that's right, these were like that. Except . . . popped at the end. Like zits you squeezed open.

PERRY: Like something had come out of them.

TABES AND CASSIE GOT INTO PPE suits and headed off to see the body.

There it sat under a cypress. A round, human shape under siege by a mound of fungus. She could see clothing under there. Features, ghostly behind the rime of mold. The shape of the person was one of penitence: a man or woman kneeling in supplication. The wet, loamy ground underneath the body had a starburst pattern of striated white mold that had crept out underneath, like it was looking for a new home.

Meaning, a new host.

As the men had said, tubules stood at odd angles, thrust up from the moldering mound—some tall, some not. They looked like ascomata, or fruiting bodies. Sessile, like barnacles. Fleshy, like fingers without bones. Likely as a way to disperse its load of spores in order to spread itself: a common way for fungus to reach new areas. *Something had come out of them,* Perry said.

That looked to be accurate.

Already Cassie began to construct the order of events: Someone came out here and died for reasons unknown. Overdose, heart attack, heatstroke, snakebite. And the corpse sat in an area known for being hot and moist, a perfect cauldron for fungal growth. And so, fungus grew.

Cassie was not a forensic pathologist, but she knew well enough that an unattended body began to break down easily under the onslaught of insects, bacteria, and mold. But this was something beyond that—a veritable fungal metropolis. She idly wondered:

Could the man have died from a fungal infection, and what was growing out of him was just more of the same?

No way to know, yet. She wasn't trained to perform an autopsy. Martin was, but Martin was in a hospital bed.

Still, this guy probably died of normal, natural causes.

End of story, right?

So why was she here?

Who was this person and why did it matter?

"We're going to need to extract the body," Cassie said to Tabes. "You'll need officers trained in PPE. Just in case there's some nasty bug in there we don't know about. Which also means the two men who found the body should be taken into quarantine and given a once-over. I don't expect anything, as they didn't touch the body, but just the same, we can't be too cautious. And I don't know if you've got anywhere to relocate the body, but we'll need cold storage—"

"We have cold storage at the ranger station," Tabes said.

Under her suit's mask, Cassie arched an eyebrow. "Why would you need that?"

Tabes explained: "About a hundred NPS sites—National Park Service—got cold storage freezers. Mostly for film and photograph preservation. The film degrades, especially in hot or humid areas. But we sometimes use them for other things, too—if we want to preserve an animal carcass, for instance, if we suspect rabies or something."

"Fine. We'll need it. You got people trained on protection suits, yes or no?"

"I'm trained, and I can get some folks from Naples, couple hours away. That okay?"

"It'll do."

.   .   .

HOURS LATER, THE SUN AT its peak, Tabes took Cassie to the ranger station up north, in Ochopee. The ground was dry here—they were able to take a small ruggedized golf cart from the waterway a mile south. The station sat under hanging moss, and out back was a little overgrown airfield carved out of the marsh. The body had been brought back here by officers trained in PPE suits, bringing the corpse back to cold storage until Cassie could figure out where it had to go from here.

Cassie got out another disposable PPE suit and climbed into it, taking extra time to check for gaps and breaches. She didn't expect she'd need it—this wasn't Ebola, for fuck's sake—but something about all this bothered her. Better to be safe.

The cold storage was not inside the ranger station, but rather built as a steel shed outside. Tabes, also in a suit, unlocked the freezer, and a rush of cold steam released as they stepped into the half dark. The small room thrummed with the freezer mechanism that kept it below freezing. (To Cassie it felt like a precious escape: She had never wanted to be a Popsicle so badly, before, until she stepped into the fetid sweatbox that was the Florida Fucking Everglades.) Tabes turned on the lights. Fluorescents buzz-clicked to life.

There, on a table, sat what was once a human body.

Male, by the look. Older. Maybe fifties, sixties, though what had happened to the body maybe distorted her perceptions on that.

The body lay facedown on the table. What looked like arms and legs sat folded up underneath. The man's head, too, was bent downward, crumpled under in a way that didn't even seem possible. The dead body reminded her of that. An origami boulder: a piece of paper mashed into a crumpled ball. Taken from its place in the swamp, the body had lost its penitence and was now just a confused, collapsed pile.

Behind the corpse, on the metal shelves, Cassie saw plastic bags, like freezer storage bags. Ziploc or a comparable brand. (She also spied two tubs of generic grocery store ice cream and a couple boxes of actual Popsicles—proving that the rangers here were using the cold storage for more than just film preservation and carcass storage.) Cassie took a pair of small scissors from her kit and snipped off the fungal stalks, placing them in bags. She took swabs, stains, and other samples.

(And now she shuddered at Benji's onetime idea that the sleepwalkers were given over to some kind of cordyceps infection. Ants that fell to cordyceps did not look altogether unlike this man's body. Dead, encased by mold, polyps rising out of the carcass and meant to spread its spores so it could live and conquer anew. Was that why Black Swan sent her here? Was this related, somehow? Or stranger still, was it something new? Worse, thinking about cordyceps put her back in the mind of zombies . . . they did call it the zombie fungus, after all.)

Cassie took DNA samples, blood samples—the blood was just a black, boggy molasses at this point, which was strange, to say the least. All the while, Tabes stood by the door, staring on in relative horror.

"I bet you've seen some shit," Cassie said as she worked. "Ever seen anything like this?"

"I've seen my share of unpleasant things out here—I once saw a gator eating a feral pig, and a snake eating the gator. Once found a fawn—a white-tailed deer baby—nailed to a tree, disemboweled, its legs perfectly sawed off. Ants had found it. And we find bodies, too, sometimes. Airboat deaths, gator attacks, the occasional suicide."

"Any of the bodies look like this?"

Tabes shook her head. "Hell no."

Cassie was out there for a couple of days. She headed back to the spot where they'd found the body, took some more swabs.

She took a trip to Everglades City for dinner, waiting to hear back on some results. She messily ate stone crab claws. Something satisfying, visceral and prehistoric, about cracking open something's carapace to get at its meat inside. Her phone rang, and she pressed it between her shoulder and jaw as she worked at the claws. "Go."

It was Benji.

"Cass, we have some preliminary findings."

"Hit me, boss."

"We know who the deceased is."

Is? she thought. Or *was?* Did you lose your identity upon dying, or was who you were bound up with the meat sack you inhabited?

That was a philosophical conversation for another time.

"Whozit?" she asked.

"It belongs to Jerry Garlin."

"Garlin." That name. Familiar. Wait. "Like, of Garlin Gardens? Heir to the Garlin amusement empire?"

"The very same."

"Why would a millionaire—"

"Billionaire."

"Why would a *billionaire* be out here, dead in the Everglades?"

Benji sighed. "Your guess is as good as mine."

"Does the FBI know anything? Their guess should probably be better than mine."

"If they knew, they weren't telling. There's something else."

"I never like the sound of that. 'There's something else.' That's foreboding language, Benji, you're scaring me."

"The fungus," he said. "It's something new."

"New. Like *Candida auris*?" A few years back they'd found a drug-resistant strain of *Candida*. Came out of Southeast Asia. Nothing would touch it. Rare, but deadly.

"Not yeast, but . . . yes, something new."

"Is it what killed our mill—sorry, *billionaire*?"

"Too early to say."

"How does this figure into the flock?" she asked.

"I don't know that it does. It may be something different. Unrelated. Black Swan isn't here to show us connections, necessarily—each thing it shows us needn't be related to the last thing."

"What do you want me to do?"

"Come back to the flock," he said. "I need you here. If Loretta deems this important, she'll put somebody on it."

"You got it," Cassie said.

But a feeling deep in her gut told her: This was all far from over.

ONCE AGAIN, AN AIRPORT. CASSIE leaned back in her seat at the gate, her headphones on—a pricey set of noise-canceling Sennheisers because goddamnit, if music didn't matter then nothing mattered. The latest and last Tribe Called Quest bounced and bounded and flowed in her ears.

Her mind worked alongside the music.

She continued worrying at the question of what was happening. Both here in Florida and with the flock. Did what happened here connect with what was happening with the sleepwalkers? As Benji noted, it could be separate. Black Swan's predictions were not on a single axis. Just the same, the whole thing unnerved her—a man dead under a carpet of fruiting fungus, an ever-growing flock of sleepwalkers, a gunman in Indiana, a president who seemed unsure what to do *with* the walker flock. Even now, on the TV in the lounge, Cassie could see President Hunt giving another press conference, and again the leader of the free world seemed bound by indecision paralysis. Would she protect them? Would she attempt another forced—and surely failed—quarantine? Or would she continue on with this half-assed vigorous-shrug policy of *watchful vigilance*?

In her ears, Q-Tip moved into the hook of "Whateva Will Be."

It felt like rope was sliding through their hands.

She wondered what happened when they ran out of rope.

And yet the world went on. Baseball and music and summer school, pickpockets and border disputes and budget discussions in Congress.

Whateva will be.

Just the same, her mind went back to that movie. Cassie remembered how *Night of the Comet* ended: The rain washed away the red comet dust and the world was over, left only to the few survivors and to the comet zombies.

PART THREE

THE FROG AND
THE MOUSE

25

MOTHERFUCKING ROCK GOD

"The fucked-up thing is, we weren't originally called Gumdropper. We were Glimdropper," Evil Elvis explained. "We named the band after a con, a confidence game. A Glim-Dropper is a fiddle scheme, right? A scam over a glim: a fake eye pretending to be lost, there's a reward—blah blah blah. So. Why name the band after a scheme? Because music is the biggest con game of them all. Every record deal is a fucking scam. And every one of us musicians are con artists, too—Christ, have you met Pete [Corley]? He'll rob you blind and sing about it later, and you'll thank him for the privilege. As to why we're now Gumdropper, instead? Because on the first poster advertising our first show, someone fucked up the ahh, whaddyacallit, the kerning on the letters spelling out our name, so it looked like Gumdropper, instead of Glimdropper. Pete said we stick with it, so we stuck with it, and now here we are. Just another con game, another wonderful rock-and-roll fuckup."

—from "Behind the Music: Gumdropper," in *Spin* magazine, by Argus Roiland, 1994

JULY 1
Chelsea, New York City

IT'S A FUCKING CONSPIRACY AGAINST SLEEP. PETE CORLEY THOUGHT THAT AS HE lay there, sheets tangled around his ankles. The conspirators were many: the sounds of TV news, of the city outside, of a failing air conditioner, and the heat breathing its dragonsbreath past the A/C. Those only weakened him for the true conspirator: his own treasonous mind. Because now, oh ho ho, now he had *thoughts*, thoughts that ran around his head like dogs chasing cats chasing mice, all of them on a sweet cocktail of cocaine and shame, all to the tune of that God-fucked internet-spawned earworm: Rick Astley's "Never

Gonna Give You Up." The antithesis to rock-and-roll. The song that was the beginning of the end.

But Jesus fuck, Astley still looked good these days, didn't he? Meanwhile, Corley looked like he'd hit the wall going sixty miles an hour—his face had so many lines he felt like a broken mirror.

Then he sat up.

"Shit goddamnit shit," he said, his voice froggy. Though the proper Irish had long gone from his voice, there was a ghost of the lilt in words like *shit*, which threatened to become *shite* any minute now, thank you.

"Shh," Landry said, chastising him from the end of the bed. The young black man—with shoulders broad as the side of a billboard and a waist that fit perfectly in Corley's spidery long-fingered hands—stared ahead at the flatscreen.

Corley winced and on the screen could see the blurry shapes of what he expected to see: people walking. Hundreds of them. He pinched the sleep boogers out of his eyes. Clarity resumed with a few more blinks. Now he noticed: *It's not just dozens. It's more than that. Way more.*

It's as if Landry anticipated the thought. He said, "They just hit three hundred."

"Miles per hour?"

"Shut up, no," Landry said, laughing a little. "Smart-ass. Three hundred walkers." Then he added: "Some people are calling them pilgrims, now."

"Pilgrims." Corley snorted. "That's rich."

He felt around for his vaporizer—there it was, on the nightstand. Next to his phone. Which showed, of course, a screen full of text messages. Mostly from his wife. Some from his kids. *Shit goddamnit shit.* He turned the phone over (*I don't want to look at you right now*), then grabbed the vaporizer and moved to bring it to his lips—

"No, uh-uh, put that nasty thing away," Landry said, arching an eyebrow. "Not in here."

"It's safe."

"I don't care. No smoking in here."

"It smells like cotton candy," Corley said sweetly, showing a big, toothy-ass smile.

"Ooh yeah, that's real manly. Next thing I know, we'll be having elementary school kids knocking on my door thinking my apartment is a fuckin' carnival. Mm-mm. No thank you."

Corley grunted and reluctantly placed the vaporizer back on the nightstand. He leaned back against the headboard, his ribs standing out like the bars of a xylophone. "Now, now, you can't leverage me with your toxic masculinity," he said with some cheek.

Landry Pierce looked over his shoulder with a dubious face. "Uh-huh. I'm just saying, I don't want you sucking Tron's dick and filling my apartment with candy smells."

"I could suck *your* dick."

"You did enough of that last night. I'm watching this."

Corley scowled and looked down. His own cock was hard as a tent stake. Hm. Damnit. "You don't have to watch that. It's on all the damn time."

"Because people are *interested*. Because this is *interesting*."

"Pilgrims," Corley said again. "Everyone's always got to make it religious. As if God would sanction any of this."

"Maybe it is. Maybe they're all walking toward something."

"A cliff." *Just like the rest of us.*

"Don't be cynical. This could be something . . . meaningful."

"And how do you figure that? That, ahh, that reverend or preacher from the radio, he said they're, ahh, what did he call it? *The Devil's puppets.* Something like that? The comet came and blah-blah-blah Revelation, Wormwood, the seven seals are opening—" He barked like a seal now, slapped the backs of his hands together. "Probably something-something punishment for all the faggots like us in the world."

"Nobody knows you're gay, and don't say the f-word, it's rude."

"Yeah, well, I'm rude. And not nobody. *You* know."

"Your *wife* doesn't know."

And there it was. His dick went slowly, surely soft. Talking about Lena was like an iceberg—and as such, his cock sank like the *Titanic*. "My wife has enough trouble. She doesn't need me doing that to her." He smacked his lips together. His mouth tasted musky. "And my kids, jeez." The kids, Connor and Siobhan.

Landry stood up then. His body language told the story: arms crossed in front of him, jaw tight, the tendons in his neck standing out like the strings on an upright bass. Landry was mad.

(Landry was *hot* when he was mad.)

"No, you don't need your *career* taking that hit."

"Well, yeah. That's a thing I've got to consider, innit? What? It is. The world wasn't ready back when we were getting airplay, and it isn't ready now. I mean, look at all this shit."

Landry narrowed his eyes. "The world was ready for Bowie."

"Bowie may have fucked Jagger, but he *married* Iman."

"Freddie Mercury, then."

"Freddie was bi, too, and besides, he was a *genius*. He was good enough that he could've come out and said he fucked houseplants or goats and—y'know, c'mon. That four-octave range? Men and women and all the people of all the genders melted into puddles of pure bubbly *sex juice* when they heard that voice."

"Judas Priest, then. That man's gay."

"Rob Halford, yeah. Came out in . . . what, 1998?" He pretended like he didn't know, but oh, he knew. Pete remembered that interview intimately. Halford saw a moment and seized it. A moment of freedom and escape as he didn't so much come out of the closet as he kicked the door down and stomped out, screaming a rough rendition of "Breaking the Law," or maybe "You've Got Another Thing Coming." At the time, he thought, *Maybe I can do that one day.* But then he didn't. He stayed in the darkness and the comfort of the closet. Then he got married. Then he had kids—and boy, that was a trick, wasn't it. As time went on, the lie grew deeper, like a pit of quicksand. Farther he sank, harder it was to get out.

He knew Halford, not well. Corley's band, Gumdropper, came up a decade later than Judas Priest did, and they weren't really in the same circles—Priest was straight-up heavy metal, and Gumdropper threaded the sometimes uncomfortable needle between hard rock and pop-punk. A *Rolling Stone* reviewer in '84 said of their debut, *Imagine if Led Zeppelin and the Sex Pistols had an orgy, and the baby that resulted from it was then adopted by Steven Tyler and Joey Ramone, and that's maybe, maybe what Gumdropper sounds like.*

Corley always wanted to talk to Halford about it. The gay thing, not the music thing—really, musicians talking music was about the most insufferable, self-referential horse-cock you could get. His kingdom to talk about anything else with anyone else.

"See, Halford did it," Landry said.

"Halford also found God and got sober, so that shows you how piss-poor *his* judgment is, yeah?"

"You're a coward is what you are." Landry waved that accusation around with an eyebrow waggle and a twist of his mouth.

"What? Pshh. Shut up. Come sit down. Watch your show."

Landry moped but did as suggested.

Corley said, "So where's this at, then? The walkers." He gestured to the screen half-assedly, gesticulating with a crooked finger. On the TV, an aerial shot showed the *herd of freaks* moving through wide-open nothing. Fields of soybeans on one side, field of corn on the other.

"Iowa. About sixty miles outside Iowa City."

"You think you could do that?"

"What, be one of them walkers? They don't have a choice far as anybody can tell."

Pete clucked his tongue. "Nah, nah, I mean, be one of them *shepherd* types. The people who go along with it. Just give everything up to go follow this flock-of-seagulls like they're groupies following the Dead. Or worse, Phish." He made a face. Phish. Jam-bands were a virus. "Could you do it?"

"If I had a loved one there, I would."

"You would? Just throw it all away to walk and walk and walk."

"They drive, too."

"I know. A caravan of hopeless optimists."

Landry sniffed. "You wouldn't do it."

"Join these shepherds? Nah. I don't need to escape my life. It's a fair bit all right, this life. Nice house. Nice bank account. Nice you."

"Nice wife, nice kids."

"Lan, c'mon."

"We could get married. It's legal now."

"Well. It *shouldn't* be. They should've gone the other way with it. Made it illegal for heteros to get hitched, too. It'd be like—" He made an explosion sound with his mouth, brought his hands together as if to demonstrate the big bang of his mind exploding. "Boom. American utopia."

"I might need to consider other options."

"Lan, we have a good thing going here. Don't piss all over it."

Landry stared holes right into him. "Good thing? Yeah. Okay. It's good. It's *real* good. It's also limited as fuck. You leave the safe little suburbs and roll up here in the big bad city like it's Times Square in the 1970s and then you tell your wife you're at *band practice*—"

"We are practicing. For the reunion!"

"—and instead you show up here and we screw like two ferrets in a sock for one night, maybe two. We don't get dinner, but you tell me you love me. We don't go out to a show or a movie or anything, but you lie to me and talk about how great I am for you and your *music*—"

"Oh, c'mon. We get takeout. And we watch movies. And you asshole, you *are* good for me. But I want to talk about our *present,* not our future." *The future is a sinkhole, anyway.* That cliff . . .

Landry said abruptly, "You should go."

"I don't wanna fuckin' go. I'm comfy."

"And I got shopping to do."

"Don't lie. I'll go and you're gonna stay here and keep on watching this . . . fucking flock-of-freakshows shit-parade." Anger burned in him suddenly and he knew it was childish but the desire to lash out at Landry was a stoked coal. "You know what this is? The walkers? It's some kind of plague. A disease. You watch. Worse, it's gonna be like, some terrorist bullshit. A bioweapon cooked up by mullahs in their cave labs—or stolen from one of *our* labs because I'm sure those aren't locked down like they should be. You know it's true, don't give me that look. What happens when you try to stop those walkers, your so-called pilgrims? Right. They fucking *detonate* like bombs. That's some terrorist business right there. It's not the Apocalypse. It's an attack."

He'd overstepped. Landry's face had gone ashen. It was clear to see but he just shrugged and thought, *Fuck it.* He slid off the bed and started to toe around for his jeans.

"You're a nasty, cynical man," Landry said, looking away.

"Don't forget old."

"You're not that old."

"I'm old enough." *Old enough to be a motherfucking rock god put out to pasture. Old enough for a reunion tour with a bunch of asshole has-beens I don't even like or recognize anymore.* "You know what, fine, you're right. I gotta go. Band practice calls."

"Don't forget to call Lena and the kids, Pete." Way Landry said it, Pete knew it was sincere—not a whiplash of snark, not some snooty stung-bum bullshit. He really wanted him to call his wife and his kids. Because it was the right thing to do and Landry was a good man and . . .

Fuck. What the hell was he doing?

Don't think about it and you don't have to figure it out.

Sounds good to me, brain. Good job.

"I'll see you later, Lan." He kissed the man's temple, even though Landry flinched as he did. Then he headed in his favorite direction:

Out the fuckin' door.

•   •   •

"You're late."

That, from Evil Elvis Lafferty, the lead guitarist of Gumdropper—everyone always said *What balls, to be named Elvis in a rock band,* but his parents had named him Elvis, full-stop. (The Evil, he added himself.)

Evil Elvis, with the bleach-blond hair still down the middle of his back ("Cut your hair, mate," Pete always told him, "it's the next bloody millennium and you look like an aging hippie"), his sunburst Gibson Les Paul electric hanging from its strap, a guitar pick rolling between fingers and knuckles.

"Can't be late," Pete said, holding up both hands like a card player stepping away from the table. "I'm the lead singer. I'm not late, you're just foolishly early is all."

Behind Elvis stood Raina Weeks on bass—not an original in the band, but she'd been with them for twenty of their thirty years since their founding bassist, Dave Jameson, jumped off the Brooklyn Bridge one Christmas. That meant she was younger—in her forties instead of the rest of these crusty old assholes in their fifties. Still looked good, too, with the long dark razor-slash hair in her face, the black-cherry lipstick, the Misfits T-shirt. Rounding out the band was Max Quick on drums—Quick, presently rocking up out of the studio bathroom, wiping his hands off on his cargo shorts.

Quick marched up—he didn't walk so much as he tumbled forward like a thrown whiskey barrel—and wrapped his arms around Corley. "Hey, brother, good to see you," he growled.

Thank fuck for drummers, Pete thought. Always the best of the breed. The glue that kept a band together, both as members and with the beat.

Raina didn't say anything, just did that thing of hers where she didn't say shit but lifted her chin in sleepy greeting. Corley did *his* thing in return, which was offer a saucy wink over a sneering lip.

But now back to Elvis, who still looked pissed.

Elvis, who had gone soft. Gone corporate. Gone fat, too, given the tub of pudding around his middle.

"We were supposed to start two hours ago," Elvis said.

Corley shrugged it off. "And you surely did start without me, as I see you with your sunburst, and looks like Max has already been working up a froth at the drums—"

The sweaty Neanderthal gave a hound's grin.

"And Raina's fingers look limber like they've been making that bass guitar do its thing."

Another chin-lift from her in confirmation.

"So really," he continued, "I'm not late, I'm coming in like that last bowl of porridge—*just right*, when all the muscles are loosey-goosey and all your instruments have been properly lubed with the blood, sweat, and tears of rock-and-motherfucking-roll."

"Fine," Elvis said. "Let's go from the top. Set list is on the amp. We'll roll right down the middle—"

"Hold up," Corley said, finger up like he was testing the wind.

"Christ," Elvis said, flipping back his hair. "What now?"

"Gonna go to the WC." The water closet. "Maybe drain the proverbial dragon." Wasn't a proverb, but whatever. "Maybe use the acoustics in there to warm up the ol' *screamin' cheetah*—" He flicked his Adam's apple, *thwomp thwomp*. Screaming cheetah was what he called his voice, in part a reference to the band he'd fronted back in Killarney—the Screaming Cheetahs, as that's how his vocals coach in choir described his voice when it really got going. (Actually, the full description was, "Peter, when you sing that way, it sounds like two cheetahs are screaming as they eat each other." Pete liked to believe that the teacher meant it in a *sexual* manner.)

"Make it fast," Elvis said.

"Elvis, old chum, don't get pushy. Okay? This is rock-and-roll, not a fucking sales meeting." He puckered his lips and blew a kiss. "Be back."

In the bathroom, the smile fell away.

He went to the sink and washed his hands, then his face. His face—that craggy long mug, like a calcified Halloween mask where the paint and the plastic have gone brittle and started to crack, started to peel.

I turned fifty-five this year and everything's gone to shit.

His own father died at fifty-nine, so Pete assumed he'd kick off then or before. His father was a hardworking man but didn't drink, didn't smoke. Pete, hah, hadn't been *quite* so kind to his own body. He'd put that shit through a sausage grinder of coke and benzos and booze and cigarettes— gone were the cigarettes, the coke, the pills, but he still drank and lately he'd taken up smoking weed because, ahh, weed was something else, wasn't it? Dulled all the sharp edges, ground down the fangs, covered life's pointy bits in puffy, fluffy marshmallows. Everyone told him to go to edibles because they were better for you and your lungs, but smoking weed—even in the vaporizer—still made him feel a little bit like he was proper smoking, which in turn made him feel young.

Which he wasn't.

The revelation of which hit him at least once an hour.

Not young. Gonna die. Fuckity-shit Jesus piss cunt.

Life, he told himself again and again, *is pretty fucking sweet.* He had a big-ass house in the Hudson Valley, he had two kids who were smart and mostly not shitheads, he had a wife who—well, he didn't know if she liked him much, but she loved him for all his bumps and dings and fuckups. He had all the money he'd ever need. He'd lived a good life.

Listen to me, he thought. Talking to himself like it's all over, pack it in. Give it up, into the bin it goes. That was what this reunion tour was about—and Evil Elvis was talking about an album of *new* material, said he'd written a few songs that could be the "start of something," even said they could ironically call the album that, The Start of Something.

Yeah, yeah, great, sounds good, mate, Corley said, not telling the truth that the idea made him want to puke blood. And therein was the goddamn shit-hell paralysis of it all: He didn't want to just curl up and die, but he didn't want to go on tour and cut a new album, either. He was in some in-between place between the past glories of a long-done rock band and the quiet doom of the grave.

He thought of this space as *the pasture.* As in, where you go when you're done being useful but aren't yet *dead.*

His hand curled into a fist and he reared back—

Kssh, the mirror fractured as the knuckles popped the reflective glass, then blood, then—

None of that happened. The fist remained poised. The glass was kept unbroken. *I don't even have the fire in me anymore. Can't be arsed to proper punch a mirror.* Once upon a time he would've broken the mirror, kicked the sink, done rails of coke off the porcelain—

God, coke would be nice right now.

Then, a knock at the door.

"If you're not bringing me coke, I don't wanna talk to you," he yelled.

"It's Elvis," came the voice. The unhappy voice.

"Sorry, Elv, dropping a deuce in here."

"Come out. I know you're just in there staring at the fucking mirror."

Well, aren't you psychic. Pete would worry that Elvis had a camera in here or something, the ol' perv, but truth was, Elvis knew him better than anyone. They started this band in 19coughcough82, best of friends then, and best of friends for all the years between then and now—but also, best of enemies, because they always seemed at each other's throats.

He opened the door and stepped out.

Elvis waited there in the half dark of the hall outside the bathroom. Behind him sat stacks of risers and mic stands.

"You're going to bail on us," Elvis said—*rather accusatorily,* Pete felt. "That's what this is."

"The hell you say."

"Wouldn't be the first time. Five years ago, remember? Wasn't even a reunion tour, it was Nike asking about doing *one show*—"

"Nike, are you kidding me? They sell fucking kicks, and not even cool sneakers, just like . . . shitty middle-class shoes."

"You didn't mind when they used our song for that commercial—"

"I told you, I don't mind selling songs for commercials because it's just a commercial—some of those directors are artists, guys who make music videos and TV shows and, you know, *real-deal* artists. Hey, they want to play 'Apes Gone Wild' for their stupid shoe commercial, more fucking power to them." There, the Irish crept in again—*facking* instead of *fucking.* "Not like the blasted shoes played the song every time you stepped down on them. Christ, could you imagine."

"So why bail on that show then?"

"Bah, this is all blood under the bridge—"

"This blood is washing up on *my* beach, Pete. This tour means everything to me. Goddamnit, Pete, it's *six* cities—big stadium shit. The wild crowds, the pyro pots, that monster-sized screen showing off the stage—"

Pete cut him off. "You know, thinking about it now, we should be doing *smaller* gigs. More intimate. Clubs and bars and little fucking . . . persnickety theaters."

"You asshole, you *are* bailing."

"I'm not."

He was.

He just hadn't decided that until now.

And he wasn't going to tell them that, either.

Which was fucked up, he knew. He was just going to do it. He wasn't going to say shit about it, he was just going to casually disconnect from it all, like Homer Simpson easing backward into that fucking hedge.

Elvis leaned in. His breath smelled like—God, it smelled like a salad. Like vinaigrette. *Vinaigrette is not rock-and-roll, you asshole.*

"Listen. This is happening. We're doing this tour. Six cities. Big crowds. I'd replace you if I could, but there's no replacing you, just like there's no replacing Tyler in Aerosmith or Axl in GnR. You'll come along and then we'll work on a new album together. It'll come out, it'll chart, and we'll all top off our fucking retirement accounts."

Pete licked his lips. "I don't like how you're speaking to me. I bet the others wouldn't like it, either. I'm gonna go take a walk."

"I'll tell."

"Tell who what? They already know you're an asshole—"

"I'll tell the world about you and your boy-toy. Landry."

His brow went hot even as his middle went cold. "I . . ." He couldn't find the words. "You don't—that's not—"

"I'm not going to be a fucking dummy this time," Elvis seethed. "And I'm *not* letting you fuck this up." He softened his tone when he said, "I hired a private detective to dig up some shit on you. I already knew you were into other men—I'm sorry to pull this shit, but you need a leash to—"

Elvis's head snapped back with the hit.

He juggled his feet backward a few steps, cradling his nose as blood came running out of his nostrils like his face was a broken spigot.

Pete shook his hand as pain went through it.

"You fugging hit bee," Elvis said.

"Yeah, I fucking hit you. And you threaten me or my family again, I'll do a whole lot worse, *mate.*"

Pete shoved him aside and stormed out through the studio space. Quick twirled a stick as he called after: "Hey, man, where you going?"

"Out the fuckin' door," he yelled as he looked over his shoulder.

Raina gave him a quick nod.

He gave one back.

Then he was gone.

26

BEWARE OF OWNER

So, how do we know? That's the big question, isn't it? How do we know if these are the End Times? We know from the Gospel of Matthew that we won't ever really know—but we also know that there are signs, signs that something is coming. Signs in the stars—like from Luke 21:25: "And there will be signs in sun and moon and stars, and on the earth distress of nations in perplexity because of the roaring of the sea and the waves, people fainting with fear and with foreboding of what is coming on the world." Sakamoto's Comet? Global warming? Could be signs, sure. We also know about plagues and moral decay and false prophets. But the point isn't that the End Times are here, or even coming. It's that they could be, they always could be, and so we must be vigilant and take up the light of God to protect us.

—*God's Light* podcast with Pastor Matthew Bird

JULY 3
God's Light Church, Burnsville, Indiana

HIS PHONE JUST KEPT DINGING.

Ding, ding, ding. Like a happy little bell.

Emails, texts, new podcast subscribers. He'd started his podcast—*God's Light, with Pastor Matthew Bird*—just seven days ago, and already he was up to . . . how many subscribers, now?

Matthew checked the phone to see.

His heart leapt like a dolphin jumping in the wake of a fast boat.

Twenty-five thousand subscribers! In just under a week.

Astonishing. It was like he found himself connected to a larger, digital congregation, one he knew existed but never felt he could be a part of. He was wrong. He spoke to them and they listened. God's light was shining far and wide, and he was helping to carry that torch into unforeseen places.

He leaned back against the kitchen counter as he nursed a peanut butter and jelly sandwich with one hand and checked his phone with the other. The emails were nigh-constant now—they ranged from emails of support ("We love that you're speaking truth to power about the great evil of the New World Order") to emails of protest ("Religion is a drug and you're its dealer!") to invitations for speaking gigs to invitations to appear on TV shows, radio shows, other podcasts. Just this morning, he'd even had an invitation to sit down with a *speaker's agent*—someone who could help him get speaking gigs *and* make sure he got paid well for them. Not that being paid was the point, of course, no, no, *no*, but traveling took time, it took money, and the church certainly needed repairs . . .

"Honey," he yelled. "Autumn, check this out." He took one more bite of sandwich, then grabbed a swig of cold milk from a frosted glass before wandering through the house, looking for his wife. He had to show her his new numbers. His *reach*, as the term went. "Honey, you have to see this."

He checked upstairs. Nothing.

He checked downstairs. No one.

Maybe she'd gone shopping. The pantry *was* looking a little spare. What was today? Saturday? Gosh, since all this started the days had slipped through his grip. That was a good thing, he told himself. As the saying went, the Devil loved idle hands.

His hands were no longer idle.

"Autumn," he yelled one more time. He thought to yell for Bo, but he knew Bo was probably at Ozark's again.

He heard a car door outside open and close.

Ah, there she was. She probably *had* gone to the store, he wagered, but when he went outside onto the front porch, he saw it wasn't her.

It was a pickup truck. Forest green, rusted out. Cap on the back. Two men were getting out—one went around back and popped the gate down, the other slid a toolbox off the front passenger seat.

"Uh, hey, hi," Matthew said, chuckling nervously as he wandered over. "Can I help you?"

The man by the front of the truck had messy, sandy hair and a few days' worth of beard growth. He looked young and strong. White T-shirt, jeans, a hammer hanging from a belt loop. The other man came from around the back with a sawhorse under one arm and a circular saw dangling from the other, a power cord trailing behind. The second man was long like a flagpole, with a bent nose and hair cut down to the scalp.

"Hey, Preacher," the sandy-haired one said.

And it was then Matthew recognized both men.

They'd come to last week's service. Last week's service was bigger than he'd ever anticipated—the room was bursting at the seams like an over-stuffed doll. It had filled up with people who came not just from the towns around Burnsville but from as far away as Indianapolis, Cincinnati, Louisville. He was suddenly bummed that he hadn't scheduled a service for tomorrow—this year, the Fourth of July fell on a Sunday, and he wanted people to be with their families. But now he thought he could make a heckuva speech about the freedom God had granted to man. And suddenly he felt anxious that he'd wasted an opportunity. Would he lose momentum and, as a result, lose people? That was no good.

"Preacher?" the sandy-haired man said.

Matthew laughed in a self-effacing way. "Sorry, I was lost in my own head for a moment. You were here last week? You're with Ozark?"

The two men nodded. The sandy-haired one said, "We're with Mister Stover, that's right, Preacher. I'm Ty Cantrell and he's Billy Gibbons."

Gibbons said nothing, just offering a small nod.

"Okay, great," Matthew said, still confused. "I confess, I don't know what you're doing here, I apologize. No service this weekend—" He gave an awkward look down at the toolbox and the sawhorse, realizing full well they weren't here for a service.

"Mister Stover said the church needed some repairs, so, yeah. After that, we'll put a new coat of paint on everything but first we gotta deal with the gutters, the window screens, the trim, some of the clapboard siding—you know, all that shi—uh, all that stuff."

Matthew was taken aback. "Thank you, boys, I appreciate that." He suddenly felt strange calling the other man, Gibbons, a boy. Gibbons was probably Matthew's age, maybe even older. That man stared down at him with dark eyes. He just shrugged and started setting up the sawhorse and circular saw.

Ty said, "You heading over soon?"

"Heading over?"

"To the pig roast."

The pig roast.

Oh no.

Today was the day. Stover was holding a pig roast—said it was annual, something he did the Saturday before every Fourth of July. Big picnic, and he'd invited Matthew, Autumn, and Bo to join . . .

That's where Autumn was! She'd taken Bo over, he bet.

"Yeah," Matthew said, nodding vigorously. "Yup, the pig roast. Gonna head over there in the next hour or so." Surreptitiously he glanced at his watch; it wasn't even noon, yet, so he wasn't running *too* late.

With that, he bid the two men farewell and hurried to get ready.

STOVER SAID NOT TO DRESS too fancy, so he went with jeans and a simple dress shirt, no tie, and headed out.

Autumn must have taken their car, the Honda, to Stover's pig roast. It made Matthew more than a little resentful—things for him were suddenly going very well, very well *indeed,* and she didn't seem to want to share in any of it. He suspected that was her depression acting up—*the demon,* as he thought of it—but it didn't make it easy for him to deal with. Best he could do was hope she came around and found either a new drug—or prayer—to get her straight.

He took their pickup, a beat-up silver Toyota from the last decade. Matthew used the GPS to get him out there—he'd never been, and didn't go that way all that often. Stover's house and junkyard were on the same property down in Echo Lake, about fifteen miles as the crow flew.

Down in this direction, off the standard farm grid, the roads got a little bendier—they wound around through pockets of trees and ponds. All of it overgrown and wild. Ivy grew up over old forgotten farm equipment as raccoons scuttled through the understory. Along the way he saw lots of American flags, plus a scattered helping of DON'T TREAD ON ME and the Confederate flag, too.

His GPS told him the place was up ahead.

Sure enough, he saw a simple sign—two wooden posts and an aluminum sheet moored between them. On it someone had painted in simple black block letters: STOVER JUNK AND SALVAGE.

The way forward was a gravel drive through a mess of trees—you couldn't see the house or the salvage yard from the road.

Nor was the way open: A gate sat closed across it. .

Chained shut.

He eased the pickup forward, thinking, *Well, what now?*

That's when someone emerged from the tall grasses alongside—a fellow in a button-down plaid shirt with a John Deere hat ran up, waving. He called over, "You here for the roast?"

Matthew rolled down his window. "I am if that's all right."

"You the preacher?"

"Pastor, yes."

"Come on in then."

He opened the padlock chaining the gate shut, then jogged it open.

Matthew waved and pulled forward. The man shut and locked the gate behind him with a clank-and-rattle.

The drive down was long—longer than Matthew expected, anyway. He pulled the pickup through copses of old trees and rusted machinery from eras past. He saw through the undergrowth various single- and double-wide trailers, poking up through the green like the decrepit white of cemetery headstones. Trails cross-cut throughout. He spied a fishing pond, a few deer stands for hunting, a mess of no trespassing zones—including repeated instances of TO HELL WITH THE DOG, BEWARE OF OWNER.

Then the driveway branched off—a painted wooden sign pointed west toward JUNKYARD, a second east toward HOUSE.

House it was.

As the truck juddered across lumps and pits in the gravel, he felt a shock as the path softened—

The road became paved. Not asphalt, but pavers of dark brick.

And ahead, something emerged from the forest.

It was a sprawling estate. At the top of a hill stood a massive house—it looked like the love child of a hunting cabin and a proper mansion. Rooms upon rooms, tall windows cut through stacked logs, a big red door in the dead center of the middle A-frame chalet structure. All of it surrounded by intricate landscaping where butterflies flitted about. He eased up the driveway past an octagonal log gazebo overlooking a pond and a fountain. Kids played inside the gazebo, chasing one another with sticks, using them like swords and rifles.

At the roundabout near the house, a young man in khakis and a red button-down approached and asked for his keys.

Valet, Matthew thought. Ozark Stover had valet parking.

At his house.

Well, I'll be damned.

All this time, he'd been thinking that Stover was poor, or something near to it. Meanwhile, Matthew was the poor one. He didn't have a house like this. He'd *never* have a house like this.

Would he?

MATTHEW FOLLOWED HIS NOSE: THE smell of woodsmoke and grilled meat pulled him along like he was a fish on a line. Out back, the estate only exploded outward—he saw ruggedized golf carts and a massive three-tier back deck, all preceding a longhouse full of tables and chairs, a smoker, a grill, a pool, a springhouse and creek . . .

And the *people*.

My word, he thought. *Look at them all.* This was a proper shindig the likes of which he had never seen and would never throw. Hundreds of people, all of them some version of *casually fancy*. They milled about with drinks in their hands and plates of hors d'oeuvres neatly and efficiently refreshed by roving waiters and waitresses. He suddenly had a plate of food in his hand, too, and a beer bottle—Sun King pale ale, cold and refreshing.

But an old anxiety resurfaced in him. It went all the way back to high school, maybe junior high—that feeling of going into a crowded room and knowing no one. You had no power. You had no clue. They were all connected to one another, chatting and laughing and debating, but you—well, you were an outsider. Trespasser, stowaway, impostor. It was an absurd fear, because his job was literally to be a public speaker—but this was different. There, he had the power, which was itself the power of God. Here, he had none.

And then, like that, it all changed.

Faces turned as he approached. Eyes lit up.

Next thing he knew, he was surrounded by people. They shook his hand. They wanted to bend his ear. A circle would come and chat him up, then one by one, slowly but surely, they'd be replaced by a new bunch of folks.

None of this was what he expected. He did not know who he thought would attend an Ozark Stover pig roast, but he surely did not anticipate sheriffs, state senators, local CEOs and CFOs, journalists, even a few local celebrities like race car drivers and news personalities. Matthew was over the moon meeting all these people—doubly so because *they* seemed to be over the moon meeting *him*.

And these people, they all wanted to talk about the sleepwalkers. Some approached Matthew moon-eyed and curious. Some giddily anxious about the walkers. Others still thought they should be quarantined, locked away, or, as one state senator said ominously, "dealt with."

It was an hour before Matthew was able to extract himself, his fingers sticky with barbecue sauce, his mouth tingling with the bitter citrus tang of the ale. He had the chance to ask, finally, where he might find Ozark Stover?

A few folks didn't know, but eventually he found someone who did: an avuncular gent named Roger Green who taught hunter safety for the DNR—the Department of Natural Resources. He said, "Listen close, you can hear him." Matthew gave a quizzical look at that, but he said, "Okay, I'll bite." Then he turned his head to listen—

There, in the distance, over the din of the crowd—

"I hear it," he said. "Firecrackers?"

"Gun range. Stover's down at the backstop firing some off. I was just about to grab a cart and drive down. Wanna come with me?"

"Oh, I don't know—I don't wanna be a bother."

"He'll want to see you," Roger said. "Come on, let's ride."

ON THE WAY DOWN, ROGER asked, "How do you know Ozzy?"

The cart had big, beefy tires and made easy work of the ruts in the pathway that carved between the trees and over ditches. Matthew explained: "My son's been working here at the junkyard since winter."

"Your son's Bo?"

"That's him."

"Nice kid," Roger said. Matthew tried to read into that—he didn't say smart kid, didn't say good kid. Just nice. *You're being paranoid, Matt.* Roger continued with, "Ozzy's a bit of a handful, huh?"

"He's a real character, no doubt."

Ahead of them, a couple of bobwhite quail darted in front of the cart, squabbling as they went from underbrush to underbrush.

"I hope you're being careful," Roger said.

"I'm sorry? I don't follow."

Roger stopped the cart suddenly. Matthew's head whipped forward.

From here, the gunfire was loud—they weren't far, now, from where people were shooting. Shots came in quick succession, *pop-pop-pop-pop.*

"I'm just saying that Ozzy is serious business. You get in with him, you best be serious, too. You can't half-ass it. You can't flirt a little and go on your merry way. Being in with Ozzy is like marriage. Deeper than that, even. It's as deep as the grave, you follow me?"

"This sounds suspiciously like a warning. Isn't he your friend?"

"He is. And a good one. We go down there now and I tell him you disrespected me, he'll pull your head off the way you might pop a tick off a dog. But that's my *point*. He'll do that, but he'd ask me to do the same."

"And would you?"

"Bet your narrow ass I would, Pastor Matt."

At that, he nodded. "I think I'm good, thank you."

"That's all I needed to hear."

Roger slammed the accelerator, and the golf cart jumped again like a rabbit that got a thistle whipped up its ass.

THE BACKSTOP WAS A MOUNTAIN of dirt and clay at the end of a short field—Matthew wasn't great at sussing out distances, but he guessed this was around 150 yards out. The side of that mound, the side facing them, was dug out and filled in with a wall of thick wooden railroad ties—ties riddled with bullet holes. A human-shaped target hung there, nailed to the flat side of those railroad ties.

Up at this end of the field was a wooden shooting bench with a gun rest. Looked custom. Also had a couple of long tables sitting out under tents—and not far away was a small corrugated metal shed.

They were between rounds, by the look of it. Stover was handing a boxy pistol off to another man, a rangy man with a coyote's lean, his greasy blond hair tucked behind tall ears. Next to him was another familiar face: Hiram Golden. As Stover handed off the pistol, his face underwent a tectonic shift—a smile cracked his face in half like an earthquake.

He pulled off a pair of yellow-lensed shooting glasses and waved a big mitt at them. "There they are. Come on down, fellas."

Roger pulled the cart up. He gave one last look to Matthew like, *You're in it, now, Pastor Matt.*

Suddenly, he was damn near wrenched out of the cart by Stover's massive hands. The big man pulled him into a chest-collapsing hug.

"Preacher, good to see you, thanks for coming."

"A pleasure, Ozark. A real pleasure." He tried desperately not to wheeze as he extracted from the hug. "I had no idea you had such a beautiful place out here."

A mischievous spark glinted in Stover's eye. "I see. You thought I was just some country rube living out here in some redneck shantytown."

"No, no, I—"

"It's all right, Preacher. I don't mind. I don't put on airs. And I don't mind if people underestimate me a little bit."

Matthew felt red in the cheeks. "I apologize if I seemed to do that, though. I should be a better man."

"Preacher, we could all be better men."

"You can call me Matthew, or Matt—"

"Nah. Preacher's good. I like the sound of it. Like a title *and* a nickname all wrapped up in one. You met Roger, I see. And you know Hiram—" Hiram gave a nod and a smile as he and Matthew shook hands. "And over here, this is my right-hand man, Danny Gibbons."

"Gibbons," Matthew repeated, shaking his hand next. Danny rolled his knuckles a little bit, eliciting a slight wince of pain. "Is Billy your brother? I just met him—"

Danny gave a curt nod, but it was Stover who answered.

"Danny and Billy are brothers, that's right. I forgot Billy was at your place today."

"Thank you for that, by the way. I can't express how—"

Stover waved him off. "Aw, stow it, Preacher. You're doing the Lord's work so we might as well do some work for you. Now, good news is, you got here just in time because we're about to bring out the big guns—"

Danny went over to one of the tables, lifted a sheet there, exposed about ten different weapons—rifles by the look of them, though Matthew was no expert and he supposed some of them could be, what, shotguns? This Gibbons brother pulled out a mean-looking rifle. Matte black, military-style. Matthew felt suddenly nervous just looking at it—his pulse racing, his palms sweating faster than the rest of him. He'd never fired a weapon before.

"Gonna join us, Preacher? Pop off a few rounds, shred some paper?"

"Oh, I dunno," he said, laughing. "I'm not, ahh. I've never done that."

Stover's grin grew wider into a giddy jack-o'-lantern leer. "Then you're going to like this, Preacher. This is the Skirmish Light from POF. Patriot Ordnance Factory. Chambered for .223 Remington, it's rocking a triple-port muzzle brake and a fluted barrel; it's got zero trigger creep and no more recoil than a soft pat on the shoulder. Shooting one of these is dreamy, Preacher, just easy as the breeze. It's like they used to say about those potato chips, Pringles I think: Once you pop, you just can't stop."

Hiram laughed, suddenly. "My last wife was like that."

"I still don't know," Matthew said, holding up both hands. "I'm not sure a church pastor should be down here with weapons of war—"

Suddenly, Stover was at his side, hand out like he was framing an imaginary picture, one he immediately began to describe: "Imagine it, Preacher. The Devil is loose upon the land, his servitors marching on your Christian settlement. They're gonna come, they're gonna take what's yours, gonna steal your women and dash open the kids' skulls with rocks. Knocking their brains right out of their little heads. They come up over the ridge, but you have one of those babies—" He pointed to the weapon in Danny's hand. "And suddenly you realize, *God* gave you this. God works through the hands of men and men built that beautiful piece of blue-black steel, a machine gifted with the ability to knock down Satan's minions like they're cans on a fence."

Stover then went, grabbed the rifle, held it out for Matthew.

"I, uhh. It really is something, isn't it." His hand reached for it—

And then Stover pulled it away.

"Not yet, Preacher. First we need some ammo, and—ahh, looks like it's right on time." He waved over to another golf cart driving down.

Matthew's heart sank.

His son was driving that cart.

"Bo," he said in a small voice.

From the back of the golf cart the boy removed two green metal boxes—ammo boxes, like from a war, Matthew realized. He looked at his father with a sheepish face. A bit of anger there, too. The pastor knew it well enough to spot it on sight.

"I don't think he should really be here for this," Matthew said.

It was like he'd just doused everyone in sour milk. They turned toward him, collectively, giving him a puzzled look.

"It's all right," Stover said. "He's down here all the time with us."

"And he discharges those weapons?" Matthew said, his heart pounding in his chest. A big part of him wanted to run from this, just let it be what it will be, and not stir up any acrimony. But this was his son. He had to say something, didn't he?

"Listen to you," Stover said, his voice going lower, into a growl. "'Discharge those weapons.' He shoots. He hits. He's good at it." Stover leered. "Be proud of him."

Their stares stuck through him. "I . . ." He turned to his son. "Bo, take the cart, go back up to the house. No more guns."

Bo looked to Stover. As if for confirmation.

The big man stood there, like a landslide ready to roar down a mountain. His jaw worked like he was chewing on something. Then he smiled and said to Bo, while never taking his eyes off Matthew: "Bo, listen to your father. Go on, get the hell back to the house. Don't stand there gawking at me, you didn't come from my blood."

It was then that Roger stepped in. "If I may? Say something, I mean."

Stover nodded. Matthew did, too.

"Pastor Matt, you're not a hunter, I take it."

"No. I've never been."

"But surely you know some who do hunt. In your congregation?"

"Yes, of course."

"Me, I came up hunting. It's a venerable tradition where I'm from— I grew up closer to Wabash, you see. And we always hunted, even from an early age. Me, my brother Merle, my sister May. And we did it not for the trophies, but for the meat, the skins, the tallow—shit, my grandmother used to make blood sausages from the deer blood, and Daddy, well, he set up a nice cool part of our cellar where he could age venison, and oh, man-oh-man—" Roger kissed his fingers. "It was *sublime*. Best steaks you ever had— now, something like that would go for twice what you'd pay for beef."

"Sounds like you had something special growing up."

"I did, I really did. Now, I take your point about all this. With all the news of school shootings and the like—and then Ozzy here brings out not just a nice hunting rifle but something that looks like you'd see it in a soldier's hand out there in Afghanistan or some other hellhole country, I see your problem. And I'm with you, a little. I don't take to these black rifles. You give me a good Remington 700 and I don't need a clip of fifty rounds to take out a buck or knock the shit out of a feral pig. Some of these ammosexuals—no offense, Ozzy—" And here the big man just shrugged it off, showing just how much leeway Roger had to say these things. "—these ammosexuals will blow two hundred rounds on target practice like they're eating popcorn, and I see that looking a little strange to you."

"You're . . . not wrong," Matthew said, still feeling the unmerciful stares of Hiram, Danny, and Ozark Stover, all of whom he felt closing in on him like they were a pack of wolves. Meanwhile, Bo stood off to the side, looking confused and angry.

"Here's what I'll offer you—I'll take you and Bo out, we'll do some proper hunter safety, maybe get both of you a license at the end of it. I'll get you feeling more comfortable with a gun, and get you feeling more comfortable seeing *him* with a gun, too. Until then, he'll stay away from firearms. How's that sound?"

"That sounds just fine," Matthew said. He wasn't sure that it did or didn't, but he knew a compromise when he heard one. A small voice inside him asked why he was considering compromising on the parenting of his child, but at the same time, it was hard to deny Roger's reasoning and offer. "I'll take you up on that."

"Dad," Bo said angrily, storming down. "You can't do this, I don't wanna wait—"

"*Hey,*" Stover said. Voice going off like dynamite down in a mine. Bo froze up. "Your daddy decided what's what. Now you wanna keep coming back here and working for me, you listen to him. Go on. Take the cart back."

The boy had nothing else to say.

"Go on," Matthew said, but his son was already walking away. Everyone stayed silent as they watched the boy mount the cart and take it back up through the woods.

With that, Stover snarled a happy chuckle. "Gentlemen, let's shoot."

THEY GAVE HIM EAR PROTECTORS. Matthew stared down the barrel as the gun rest cradled the front end of the Skirmish rifle. No scope on this one— they said to just use the front sights. So he did, staring down that long steel channel, blinking away sweat. And then—

He pulled the trigger and expected it to kick like a horse, but Stover was right—it felt like a soft push. With every trigger pull, the gun tugged and sent another injection of lead toward the target. *Pop, pop, pop, pop.* One round after the next, bullets kicking off, the air stung with the scent of what smelled like burning balloons. Stover told him it was a thirty-round magazine, and after every shot they applauded him louder, and he could hear the big man bellowing, "Keep going, empty it, goddamnit!" And so Matthew kept pulling that trigger, *pop, pop, pop,* until on the thirty-first pull the trigger just went *click.*

When he was done, Stover and Hiram were whooping with laughter and applause—they pulled the rifle out of his hand and mussed his hair. Stover clapped him so hard on the back he thought some of his teeth might be knocked out. Hiram sidled up to him and said in his ear, "Cherry popped. Feels like nothing else, a gun like that in your hand. That power? *Mercy*."

Ozark told Danny to go get the target, see how they did.

The tall man walked off—loping like a lazy hound—and snatched the target with a swiping arm spring-loaded with impatience, and then he made the long and lazy journey back. Stover harangued him, "Faster, Danny, come on, put a little mustard on those dogs."

Finally, he brought the target back.

Matthew saw now—the target itself was just a black outline, but at the head, someone had printed out a black-and-white photo.

It was the face of President Nora Hunt.

The target was riddled with holes.

About fifteen of them.

All outside the actual outline of the target itself.

"Looks like you missed the bitch," Stover said, clucking his tongue. "Oh well, we'll get her next time."

I'm not comfortable with this, Matthew thought. A special kind of shame picked at him—the pinching feeling inside him made all the worse by the fact he not only didn't hit a darn thing, but most of his shots didn't even hit the paper.

Then Hiram said, "Ah-ah-ah. Looky here."

He lifted the paper and got behind it, poking his pinkie through. It emerged like an earthworm from dirt—

Right through President Hunt's ear.

Wiggle, wiggle.

"Hell, Preacher," Stover said. "You hit her after all! Look at that. Only took off her ear, sure, but maybe that'll make her stand up and listen harder with the other one." He winked.

Matthew in a low voice asked:

"This is all just fun and games, right?"

"Of course it is, Preacher. Of course it is. Come on, let's go pull the pig out of the ground. Time to eat."

27

HOMELAND SECURITY

They tried everything to move those walkers, they tried
Blockades, fire, loud noises, digging trenches and shit

@RandomPedo88

[threaded tweets]
But you know what they haven't tried yet?
ME with a bumpstock AR-15 going POP POP POP like Call of
Duty
Put them bitches down or walk them into an oven

@RandomPedo88

[threaded tweets]
Kill them or they kill us
That's how it always is

@RandomPedo88

3127 replies 4298 RTs 9788 likes

JULY 3
Lone Tree, Iowa

THE FLOCK MARCHED THROUGH FIELDS OF CORN AND SOY, PAST AMBLING
cows and massive circular bales of hay that looked like they could be used to
seal up some strange Midwest Messiah's tomb.

By now, the flock—the walkers themselves—numbered 325. With them came the shepherds, over a hundred. And with them came more state troopers—who traded off to new troopers every time they crossed the border to a different state—and a brand-new presence in the form of Homeland Security. That was hard to avoid, now. The theft of the human remains and the discovery of the package that had been sent to Nessie Stewart made it clear that this was at least in part a problem for law enforcement. The FBI conducted their investigation outside the flock, and with the flock—

Well, that meant HomeSec.

MEETING TIME. ANOTHER WHEEL-SPINNING MEETING where they would attempt to figure out how to move forward, but where no progress was made as everyone jockeyed for position. In the CDC trailer sat: Benji, Sadie, Cassie Tran, and an iPad on a metal Compass stand that featured Loretta Shustack, conferencing in on video.

Sitting there, too, was the man who HomeSec brought on to oversee the agency's dealings—a "liaison" named Dale Weyland. Weyland looked like an aging quarterback, his body in the midst of that all-too-easy transition from hard muscle to marshmallowy fat. They called him The Warden, the way he attended to the whole group like they were all his prisoners.

Weyland sat in his chair like a man comfortable in his discomfort—he eased backward, arms folded across his chest, eyeing up everyone who sat literally across from him at the table. Benji thought of him as the enemy, though maybe that wasn't fair. It was biased and unhelpful. Just the same, he assumed Weyland thought of them the very same way.

"I'm just gonna put this out there," Weyland said, "before we get into some long-winded discussion like we do here day after day after day. It's over. Or will be, soon."

Benji and the others shared a look.

Loretta said nothing. And that was as telling as anything.

"I don't follow," Benji said, gritting his teeth. Even though he feared he followed it quite well. "What is over, exactly?"

Weyland sighed in a way that said, *Do I really have to do this song and dance?* "This. You. The CDC's EIS control over this operation."

"It's not an operation," Cassie hissed. "It's a *disease*."

"Is it? Doesn't seem that way to me, Miss Tran. To me, this looks like an attack on American people, on American soil. There are no other flocks, globally. It's just us, here, those people, and *those* people out there are weapons. *Human bombs."*

Benji stiffened. "We know what you think, and it matters little how it looks to you, Dale. It matters how it looks to science—"

"No, it matters how it looks to the people, and how *they* look to the president. And bad news, Banjo—" That was what Weyland called him sometimes. *Banjo.* The nerve of that prick. "She's right now signing off on HomeSec control of this operation."

A chill passed among them. Sadie said: "Why?"

Even before Weyland explained it, Benji already knew what he was going to say, and so he said it first.

"Because she's under siege," Benji answered.

Weyland nodded. "Yeppers. Politically, Creel is snapping at her heels. This . . . flock, as you call it, is a political weak point. It's a fucking liability and Creel is going to keep sticking his spear right in that tender spot, again and again. She's bleeding her poll numbers."

"Ed Creel is a capitalist maniac," Benji said.

"That's your opinion, one not necessarily shared by voters. He's starting to sway the American people. You see his latest ad?"

Benji nodded. In that advertisement, Creel appeared before a shitty American flag graphic, and along the Stars and Stripes someone had animated people walking in a straight line —a crude summation of the walking flock. As Creel went on and on about dangers to America "both foreign and domestic," the walkers exploded one by one, leaving ragged holes vented in the fabric of the flag. Until there was nothing left but threads. Creel never even mentioned the walkers. He didn't have to. "He was on CNN this morning, kept hitting Hunt on her—his words, though I don't disagree with them—'halfhearted, half-assed, half-a-brain policy regarding the sleepwalkers.' He went on to say if *he* was elected he'd force a mandatory quarantine of the flock, and if that didn't work, he'd drive them all into the ocean, and I quote, 'like pigs.'"

Like pigs. A not-too-subtle nod to the evangelicals, Benji suspected. Creel was by all evidence no kind of Christian, though he played at being one to get votes and campaign contributions. Here it seemed he was leaning on the story in the Gospel of Matthew where Jesus exorcised a legion of demons and cast their bodies into pigs—and then the pigs rushed into the water of a nearby lake, drowning themselves.

"A quarantine won't *work*," Cassie stressed.

"And nobody cares," Weyland countered. "*C'mon.* People don't care about workable solutions. Ultimately, they just want someone with an answer. Right now, Creel has an answer, as brutal and as impossible as it is. Hunt looks like she has *no* answer—she's been sitting on her hands. Is that because she's playing politics? Maybe. Is it because this is a complicated situation that requires careful strategizing? Maybe. Maybe it's both those things. Does it fucking matter? Not really."

"So politics is what this is all about?" Benji asked. "It's the day before Independence Day. You're going to pull political chicanery on a holiday?"

"Chicanery, listen to you. Doctor Ray, forgive me, but politics is what it's *always* about. You can't be this naïve. Politics drives the bus. Tells the bus where to go, who to pick up, whether or not it should run over a line of kids crossing the road. And tomorrow being the holiday means we hit the news cycle tonight, leave people feeling a little better during their day off. Give them some comfort as they shovel hot dogs and dump beer into their mouths. That's part of the political job. To give comfort."

Not to do the right thing, Benji thought, *but to give comfort.* Even when it wasn't appropriate to do so. The way the man spoke about Americans with such disregard rankled Benji. Shovel hot dogs. Dump beer. He really did see them as animals to be led around by the nose.

Again Benji's faith in the system shuddered and seized.

"What now?" Cassie said.

Weyland finally sat up, leaning forward. "Time is it? Noon? I'm guessing we'll see her announcement to time out with the afternoon news cycle. She's meeting with Flores and Soules at this very moment to hash out the details." Soules being Walter Soules, head of Homeland Security. "My understanding— and my recommendation—is that EIS will be taken off."

Loretta objected: "We at least want ORT back. Robbie Taylor is in Africa, but we can have him back—"

"The CDC had its shot," Weyland said. "I'm not inclined to give you another. You can take that up with someone else, but it won't be part of my recommendation."

Loretta looked pissed. Benji wanted her to growl, get mad, swing for the fences—be the Immovable Object she had always been. But immovable as her reputation was, it didn't change the fact she had a job to do, and that job was at the mercy of superiors who did not always share her expertise in matters.

"Best deal I'll cut," Weyland continued, "is that we will consult with you about new quarantine procedures. Otherwise, the presence that will accompany the flock will be purely military—National Guard or army—and the shepherds will be ejected and kept away, as they're a destabilizing presence of protest—"

"Why military?" Sadie asked. "Why not police? We already have some state trooper presence—"

"Because the flock constantly crosses state lines," Benji said, explaining it before Dale could. "Am I right?"

Dale nodded. "Bingo, Banjo. Besides, you want soldiers on this. Cops are . . . listen, we work with cops, but a lot of those guys are a little trigger-happy these days. Military guys are rock-solid. They're pros. These are guys who have been to Fallujah, Kandahar. They can hack this."

"This is a *mistake*," Benji protested. "It's setting a dangerous precedent as to how we handle future epidemics and outbreaks—"

"We're lucky this doesn't seem to *be* an outbreak. That were the case, Hunt's laxity on asserting our authority here would mean we'd all have whatever diarrhea plague or monkey flu was in play." Weyland sighed. "I get it. You think I'm the bad guy here. I appreciate that. Nobody wants to be me. Nobody wants to be the asshole who has to make the hard decisions."

Benji wasn't so sure about that. Weyland seemed all too comfortable in his position. The man was glad to be the particular asshole he was.

Dale continued: "Look at it this way. Every one of us is a hammer in search of a nail. We each have our jobs, our organizations, our skill sets—you find and investigate disease, so to you, this is a disease. But *my* job is to protect the homeland from threats inside and out. And those walkers? They're a threat. Maybe they don't mean to be. Maybe they do. But each one of them is gone, whoosh, wiped." He passed the flat of his hand in front of his eyes like he was blanking a slate. "They're not in there anymore. And what's replaced them is something we don't understand. Something that can't be cut, that won't bleed. Something that pops like a *cork* soon as you apply a little pressure. What happens if they all go off at once? And how big will the flock get before that happens? Day by day, you get another dozen mummies joining the mummy parade—how long will that go, you figure? Another hundred? Three? Five? A thousand? Maybe it keeps going and going until we got a small city's worth of walkers gumming up everything, blocking roads, ready to blow, like a bunker-buster bomb of human meat. People want something done. So finally, Hunt's doing something."

"They're not weapons," Benji asserted. "They are *people*."

"Terrorists are people, too. Dictators and despots and enemy soldiers, they're *all* people, pal. And they're still dangerous as hell."

"You're out of line."

"And you're out of a job. Or will be soon enough."

"Loretta," Benji said, turning his plea to the video screen.

"This is what it is," she said, her voice stern. "I've done what I can and I will continue to push. But we continue to search for evidence of a pathogen and find nothing. At the base level that means our role here is increasingly in question, and this continues to look more and more like a situation of national security. Though the origin of this may be political, that doesn't change our overall ineffectiveness to understand this phenomenon—or to put a halt to it." Finally she said, "I'm sorry, Benjamin."

And that, it seemed, was that.

BENJI WAS NAÏVE. HE KNEW that. Despite years of swimming upstream against the political current, he believed ultimately in progress, in science, in forward momentum even if it was gained by battling for inches rather than running for miles—every foodborne pathogen, every theoretical outbreak, every time there was the fear of a zoonotic jump, that meant once more navigating the serpent-filled waters of government and bureaucracy. No company wanted to be investigated for accidentally infecting its customers. No county or town wanted the misfortune of being labeled as the place Ebola showed up, or Zika, or dengue. But ultimately, always and forever, the alternative was worse; so the bureaucracy inevitably yielded. The briar of red tape burned away and Benji was allowed to do his job.

But that had changed. Hadn't it? Is that why he did what he did at Longacre? Because he saw that change coming? (Or was he just telling himself that to make himself feel better?)

Whatever the case was, Loretta and Dale Weyland were not entirely incorrect in their assessments. They had no information except the kind that suggested something larger and more sinister was ongoing. They had little evidence of a pathogen. They had no guarantee that the CDC's place here, their purpose, was even *earned.*

Outside the trailer now, Benji said as much to Sadie and Cassie as they stared out toward the coming flock. "Maybe they're right," he said. "We don't know anything."

Cassie scowled. "Fuck that noise, dude. I believe that what we're looking at here is ours to own and ours to solve. Men with guns won't solve it. Men with guns don't solve shit."

"Tell that to the men with guns," Benji said.

"We need proof," Sadie said. "Swiftly. Something that will change the game, that will show the president that you must be kept on with the flock. If all is as you say that it is—and I believe you—then there has to be some way forward we haven't yet thought of."

"We have explored and expended our tools, sadly."

"So we look outside the toolbox, so to speak."

"If I knew of another tool set, I would explore it."

Cassie said, "Well, what's on the fringes right now? Is there some hot new technology we haven't yet looked to? There must be something we aren't seeing. Some diagnostic tool, some genius with a Kickstarter, some bleeding-edge tech you hear about in *Wired*—"

"That's *it*," Sadie said, suddenly. "Benex-Voyager is the parent company to Firesight: It's a nanotechnology firm, fairly boutique, but they have found ways of using nanoparticles and nanodevices to diagnose certain cancers, brain diseases, and gastrointestinal disorders. I'm not precisely familiar with the details, but what if . . ."

She kept talking.

But Benji stopped hearing her.

His knees nearly buckled as the realization hit him. Back when Robbie showed him what had happened to the cells inside Clade Berman's body—it reminded him of something. He just couldn't pinpoint what it was.

Now he knew.

He interrupted Sadie, apologizing for doing so, and then asked them to join him back in the trailer. Weyland had already gone, but the techs had not yet returned (having cleared out for the meeting). Benji took out the black phone and summoned Black Swan with a command of his voice.

Pointing the projector at the wall, he asked Black Swan:

"Black Swan. I'd like to see images from IBM research archives, probably from, let's see, 2011, maybe 2012. They did a joint study with the Institute of Bioengineering out of Singapore on defeating MRSA—*Staphylococcus aureus*." Over the last decade, the number of antibiotic-resistant infections had gone up considerably, over 300 percent by this point. They were at the end of new antibiotics, and worse, the pharmaceutical industry did not consider antibiotic treatment to be particularly profitable—certainly not as profitable as cancer treatments, antidepressants, or pills to counter erectile dysfunction. So the search for new antibiotics had stalled, leaving room for new companies to find inventive ways of defeating bacteria that had become effectively "bulletproof" when it came to the usual antibiotics.

Black Swan projected an image.

There, on the wall, was a photo of a slide magnified to one hundred nanometers. In it, a series of MRSA bacteria floated around the edges like black, blood-filled balloons. But the ones closer to the middle were not like that—they had been damaged, ruptured from the inside, their contents spilling out.

"That looks like Clade Berman's cells," Cassie said.

"It's MRSA," Benji explained. "Destroyed from within by nanoparticles. Each one like a little bullet. Summoned to its target by precise coding—the micro-machines knew what to look for given each bacteria's particular electron charge."

"Like homing missiles," Sadie said.

"Yes. Just like."

It was Cassie who caught up first. "You're not talking about using these nanoparticles to understand the walker phenomenon. You're saying—"

Swallowing hard, Benji shook his head. "Yes, that's right."

"I'm sorry, I don't follow?" Sadie said.

Cassie answered: "Benji thinks that this is not a phenomenon to be fixed by nanoparticles but rather—"

"*Caused* by them," he said.

"You're saying that these walkers are . . . infected with nanotech?"

"It's not impossible. We have long accepted nanotechnology as a potential fix for disease—to counter cancer, to help temper the coming post-antibiotic age. But what if it went the other way? What if someone used them to design a . . . new disease?"

"A pathogen that *is* a machine," Cassie said, mouth agape.

"That sounds utterly barking mad," Sadie said.

"Maybe it is. But it is an option we have to consider. Those destroyed MRSA bacteria perfectly mirror the destruction of Clade Berman's cells."

"Except," Sadie said, "the focus of the nanoparticles you're talking about was narrow—a single bacteria type. In Berman, and presumably the other walkers, the particles would affect a much broader range."

"Precisely. Imagine a million little nanobullets ripping through every conceivable type of cell in the human body all at once." Benji brought both his hands together and then exploded them out, mimicking one of the walkers detonating like an exploding melon. "Each cell going off like dynamite."

"But does it explain all the other . . . bizarre behavior? Their inability to be hurt, their tireless march, the fact they don't eat or shit or urinate—"

"I don't know. This is not a realm I understand well."

Sadie said, "Then we'd better understand it quickly if we're going to use it to reassert control away from Homeland Security."

"Regrettably, I don't think this helps us at all in that regard."

"What? Are you serious?"

"Deadly so. Listen, if this is true—and God, I hope it's not—then this isn't just some fluke of nature. It's not a mutation of some known disease or some pathogen that jumped from birds or a heretofore unknown parasite. This is something someone would have *designed*. It would be exactly as HomeSec claims: an attack on us by an enemy, an intruder. And it would make the walkers intruders, too, in a way. And it's not like the CDC is equipped to understand this—we are behind the curve when it comes to this kind of technology."

Cassie leaned in. "So do we tell them?"

Benji hesitated. He felt their eyes on him. The responsible thing would be to share this theory—cuckoo as it sounded—with Loretta, with Weyland, so that they knew what they might be up against. Just the same, it was still *only* a theory, and one that he was not yet willing to stake his professional reputation on. Further, with Sadie by his side—and perhaps some introduction to Firesight, this company owned by Benex-Voyager—maybe he had an opportunity to make headway on it where others would not. Most important, he was not yet willing to label the walkers as what Weyland believed them to be: weapons, enemies, monsters.

"No," he declared, finally. "Not yet. Not until we have something solid." A little voice whispered: *But by then, could it be too late?* "We don't tell them, and we don't tell *anyone*. This stays among the three of us."

"What about Arav?" she asked.

"Keep him out of it for now. He's young and . . . if we're wrong, this will impact our careers. His might still remain intact."

The other two nodded.

"Good. Now let's figure out how we prove or disprove this thesis." He told Sadie to put in a call to Firesight. Because they didn't have a lot of time.

28

BRIGHTNESS AND NOWHERE

Glory Tobin. Pronoun: she/her. Age: 32. Mixed media artist and gallery owner from Naperville, IL. Traveling with shepherd Brody Tobin, her brother. Brody said, "Glory is a gifted artist and I hope one day we'll find out this is all one really big, really weird flash mob." #PeopleoftheFlock
@FlockTrakr42
57 replies 122 RTs 147 likes

JULY 3
Lone Tree, Iowa

THE CAMERAPHONE FELT HEAVY IN SHANA'S HAND.

Thing was, though, the device had never felt heavy before. It always felt light, airy, like it was a limb, as natural as all the others.

It did not feel light today.

But they were just doing what they did every day—she and the other shepherds marched with the flock. The flock grew daily. So did the shepherds. Some had taken to calling them all—the flock and the shepherds—*pilgrims*, sometimes in a mean way, sometimes not, but always as if they were on a proper spiritual journey. But Shana hated that idea. She didn't like that it made them sound religious or something. It also suggested that they were going *somewhere*, when clearly, out here in the corn and the soy and the waving wheat, they were going *nowhere*.

She pointed the cameraphone, let it drift across the marching souls. The heaviness of it, she decided, was emotional weight. Every day now she snapped maybe five, ten, fifteen shots. More if she could manage it. And after her encounter with Donna Dutton, she never did them up close, not anymore.

It felt like every photo added tangible weight to the camera. Like she was capturing something important, or maybe something she wasn't *supposed* to capture. It wasn't that the photos were great or anything—Shana figured she was a middling talent, at best. But all the faces, all the places, all the clouds and the roads and the trees. All the people waiting with signs, all the news choppers that sometimes flew overhead.

To her it felt important. It felt *heavy.*

Not like she was the only one capturing this stuff, though. Everyone had out their phones, now, taking Instagrams or posting them to social media sites like Twitter (provided they could get a signal). The hashtag #PeopleoftheFlock was big, and so was #sleepwalkers. Shana didn't look at them much. She was here. Worse, people online were generally shitty, and the hashtags just attracted trolls and haters and bots: people who wanted to see the walkers quarantined or dissected or just shot in the head and dropped in a mass grave.

She asked her father to drive her up ahead a little bit so she could take some shots from the front, which was trickier now that they had so many other shepherds in play. A dozen vehicles at the front, another dozen at the back. But he managed to get the Beast up along the side of the road so she could stand ahead of the flock.

Dad said at the time, "Maybe you'll be a photojournalist one day."

"I dunno," she said.

"That's practically what you're doing now."

"Maybe," she said. She didn't want to think that far ahead, though. It just made the camera feel even clumsier, somehow. She feared the attention. Or maybe she feared *wanting* the attention. Dad started to say that maybe she could turn this into a book someday and she just barked at him: "I don't want to talk about this, so just leave me alone and let me do my thing, okay?"

He nodded and smiled and went back into the Beast and it eased ahead at the slow, slow crawl that all these vehicles managed. Soon he'd leave the pack to go on a food run—that's usually how they did it, one group would take a vehicle and drive on ahead to the nearest town to stock up on provisions. It had gotten strange out there, though: People in towns weren't happy to see the shepherds anymore. Some got into fights. Or threw things. Yesterday a group tried to buy supplies and found themselves run out of the store, chased by an old woman with a baseball bat. She tried to clip one of them, too, but missed and knocked over a rack of Coca-Cola, leaving some cans popping and fizzing as the woman yelled.

So as her father pulled the Beast ahead, Shana remained there on the side of the road. Feet planted in broken asphalt. Camera up. Panic kept at the margins.

Shana watched the world through her screen.

The sky was the color of fading denim. Wind rustled the corn and the soy. It moved the hair of the walkers, too. It made them look a little like a field of grass, almost; a small tinge of chaos allowed to a group forced into the same posture, the same steady gait, the same dead-nail stare.

The walkers numbered over 300 now, closer to 350, she'd heard, though the flock itself looked much bigger given the presence of the other shepherds. Shepherds wove in and out of the flock, tending to their people. And others still traveled alongside the flock, on the edges of the road. Not unlike real shepherds moving their flock of sheep or herd of cattle, she imagined.

She pinched to zoom.

She saw Mia combing Mateo's hair, a cigarette hanging so precariously out of her mouth it looked stuck to the bottom of her lip.

Click.

She saw a big-thighed black guy on a rat-trap bicycle pedaling up alongside the shepherds. He was sweating, handing out iced teas and sodas and even some ice cream sandwiches (that were starting to melt). He rang the bell as he went, *da-ding, ka-ching.* She knew his first name only: Tibor, she thought it was. Tibor or maybe Timor. Shit.

Click.

She saw a pair of dogs chasing each other—a springer spaniel and a pit bull. The spaniel's name was Bucko, the pittie's was Egghead (the rings around his eyes looked like dorky eyeglasses), and the two of them chased each other with delight, clashing like Godzilla wrestling with King Kong, crash, bash, drool, smash. Bucko belonged to Sandy Rosenstein, whose engineer husband was in the flock, and Egghead belonged to the Brewer family, who were here shepherding their mother, Bella. They were the first of the flock's dogs, but she felt they wouldn't be the last.

Click.

She saw the sun gone liquid in the windshield of a GMC Yukon driving forward slowly with the rest of the pack, and as the vehicle eased forward, the glare on the glass deadened and she could see a couple in the front—that was Carl and Marie Carter, two shepherds whose daughter Elsa, a midtwenties pharmaceutical rep out of Indiana, walked with the flock. Carl and

Marie were fighting right now—Shana couldn't tell about what, it was all just wide eyes and serious brows, all yelling mouths and angry gesticulations. Those two didn't fight at first—they seemed sad about their daughter but happy to be here with her, to be with the other walkers. But time was not kind, Shana knew. The fear, the pressure, it was all serious shit, and some people just couldn't hack it. Those two couldn't. They fought all the time now. One would leave soon, Shana guessed. Maybe both would, and they'd abandon their daughter because it was easier on them to do so. People did that, and Shana understood it. She hated them for it, though, too, because how could you? How could you leave your family?

Click.

She saw someone walking toward her, now.

Arav.

He had an iced tea in his hand. She focused on it with the phone screen, saw the condensation gleaming there. Dripping down the side of his hand, slicking the palm and his pinkie—which he held out like he was a fancy dude drinking fancy tea. As he closed in, he went out of focus—

Click.

"Hey," he said, getting closer.

"Hey," she said as he came near. She tucked the camera into the pocket of her jeans.

His hand reached out, found hers. Their fingers hooked around each other's, pinkies around pinkies, thumbs around thumbs.

This was all they did. They hadn't done anything else yet. No kissing. No anything else.

He handed her the iced tea. Lipton.

"I brought you this."

"Thanks," she said. "Share it?"

"No, all for you."

Her only regret was that they had to unbraid their fingers for her to take the drink. But take it, she did. It was cold and invigorating.

"I like seeing you with your camera out," he said.

She shrugged. "Just taking your advice, dude."

"I also like seeing you in general."

A faint blush rose to her cheeks; she fought against it and lost. "What are you up to? Shouldn't you be off solving all the mysteries?"

"I dunno." He sighed. "We're in a holding pattern, I guess. Something's going on, though. Doctor Ray, ahh, Benji went into a meeting with that HomeSec guy—"

"Weyland."

"Yeah."

"I *hate* him."

"I'm not a fan, either."

It wasn't that Weyland did much. Mostly he just wandered the flock like he was in charge. Eyeing them all up like a grumpy Walmart manager. But also like he hated them, all of them, shepherds and flock alike. He wore his disdain for them like a uniform. Shana knew through Arav that Homeland Security was looking to take over the flock and boot the CDC investigators.

She asked him, "You think they're ready to take over?"

"Maybe. I hope not."

New panic seethed inside her. "If that's the deal, what happens to us? To the shepherds?"

Arav could only shrug. "Wish I knew."

"What happens to *you*?"

"I guess I go. I guess we all do."

She shook her head. "No way. Fuck that. I won't go. I won't leave my sister. I won't leave Nessie behind. I made her that promise and I'm sticking to it."

"We'll figure it out. We'll find a way."

Even the hot summer sun couldn't stop the chill that ran through her. She'd tear it all down if they tried to take her from her sister. Suddenly, not only did her camera feel heavy . . .

. . . but so did the handgun in her backpack. The one Zig gave her. She still had it. Loaded and ready to go.

"I'm sure they won't do it today," Arav said, sounding to her like he was trying to force a chipper attitude. "It's the holiday. Or almost."

"Tomorrow is the Fourth of July?"

He nodded. "It is."

"So today's the third."

"That's usually how the calendar works."

"Smart-ass," she said (with the hint of a smile). "Then assuming that linear time is still in working order, looks like I have made another journey around the angry ball of fire in the sky."

"What?"

"I'm eighteen, dude. It is my birthday."

"Happy birthday!" His face brightened for a moment before darkening anew as he looked down at her iced tea. "Iced tea is not a good present."

"It's great, I love—" In the distance, something caught her eye. Movement by the front of the flock. By her *sister*. "God*damnit*."

"What?" Arav asked.

There, she saw that *woman,* the one with the buzz-sawn haircut and the scars on her head and the lumberjack body. The one who supposedly took down that gun-wielding crackpot back in Indiana—that bitch was there by her sister, running a brush through Nessie's hair as they walked together.

"No, oh *hell* no," Shana said, forcefully foisting the iced tea off on Arav before breaking into a run. She bolted toward her sister and as she got closer to the flock, she started yelling to the woman, "Hey! *Hey.* Get away from my sister!"

The woman's head jerked up.

Shana skidded to a halt about five feet away. She moved herself in parallel to her sister, all the while snatching the hairbrush out of the other woman's hand.

"You leave her alone."

"I was just brushing her hair, Shana."

"Who told you my name?"

"You did."

"I did not." She felt suddenly flustered. "And if I *did* that doesn't mean you have permission to use it."

"But it's your name." The woman held up both hands. "I'm sorry. I saw you hadn't been out to your sister yet today, I know you like taking photos and being with that young buck from the CDC, so I thought I'd help—"

"Ew, are you some kind of stalker? I was just . . . busy, okay? I was busy taking pictures and—and I would've gotten to brushing her hair and everything, all right?" She really *hadn't* been out to see her sister yet today. This was the first day in weeks she hadn't made it part of her routine. Why? Because she wanted to go take photos? Stupid! "It's none of your business. You leave us alone."

Now Arav caught up, panting as he did. And here came Mia, too, trailed by a few other shepherds—Aliya among them. Suddenly, their voices rose in a cacophony against the woman—what was her name again? Marcy. Marcy Reyes.

"Marcy, you can't be coming up in here messing with one of the walkers," Mia said. "Not Nessie, not any of them."

"It's a family thing," Aliya argued. "A *bonding* thing."

A shepherd in the back, might have been Lucy Chao, said, "Did she say bondage?"

"Bonding," someone else corrected.

Marcy offered a sad smile. She held up both hands as if pleading. "It's just, the glow is strongest here at the front. Your sister burns bright, like a . . . like a star going supernova. I can *hear* it, too, like an angel's song."

"Okay, Missus Cray-Cray," Mia said, stepping between Marcy and Nessie. "Time for you to go take a walk, you cuckoo bitch."

"I'm not crazy," Marcy said. "I don't *think* I'm a bitch, I mean, I guess I might be sometimes—"

"Shoo. Get out of here. Go bother somebody else. You ain't got nobody here and nobody here got you."

With that, Marcy nodded and walked off, finding her way to the shoulder of the road and standing there as the flock and the shepherds passed her by. Shana watched her go.

Fact: Marcy Reyes was weird.

Okay, maybe that wasn't a *fact*-fact, but it sure felt like a fact to Shana. Yes, the lady maybe saved them by finding that redneck chode and making him shoot himself in the ass, but that didn't earn her a place here. The shepherds didn't have a code, exactly, but thing of it was, you were expected to be here for a reason. And that reason was: You had a person on the inside, someone who walked with the flock. A sister, a mother, a little brother, a best friend, jeez, even a *neighbor.* Someone! Anyone.

But Marcy didn't have anyone.

She was just *here.*

Because, she said, *they all glowed.*

Which, again, was fucking weird.

Didn't help that she said it with this kind of culty gleam in her eye, this crazypants reverence. She said the walkers were angels. Shana knew they weren't angels. Angels weren't real. What was real was her sister and all the others, and making them angels made them *not* people, and to hell with all that.

They were people.

Not glowy angels, not weapons, not part of some political agenda, not victims of some terrorist plot. They were people. Why they were walking, she didn't know. How they got this way, *she didn't know.* And at this point, Shana didn't much care. She cared about her sister. That was it.

So to hell with Marcy Reyes.

Even though, yeah, *okay,* sometimes Shana felt bad for her. Because she didn't have anybody meant, well, she didn't have *any*body. Nobody was on her side because they all agreed she was . . . kinda weird. Marcy slept in the backs of people's pickup trucks at night or during the day when they let her—she paid her way in gas, so people said. There were other stories, too. Like the ones that said before this, she was a shell of a person, one who got beaten half to death by some gangbangers who jumped her. They pulped her skull but she didn't die. So they had to . . . rebuild her head.

Hence the scarring.

But that didn't explain why right *now* she felt fine.

Again, story went that Marcy said it was the walkers. The "glowing angels" made her feel better. Which admittedly wasn't the weirdest thing ever—no, that would be the walkers themselves—but it still made Nessie and the others seem inhuman, like they were magic or some shit.

They weren't magic.

They weren't anything.

They were just people.

Weren't they?

Most of the crowd had died back, leaving Shana with her sister—and with Arav and Mia, who remained. Shana brushed her sister's hair, admittedly a little too roughly, but she couldn't help it.

(And a darker voice inside her said: *Not like Nessie can complain anyway.* Accompanying *that* was a sudden surge of anger about her sister where Shana screamed inside her own head, *Wake up, wake up, wake up.* That anger did not come alone, of course; it came accompanied by what was now the third wave of guilt.)

(Then, hey, why not more anger? Anger at her father for not getting out of that damn RV to brush Nessie's hair, anger at Marcy for stirring this pot, anger at Dale Weyland for making her feel anxious that she might be taken from her sister, and for the kicker, anger at *herself* for everything under the sun.)

(Shit!)

"Where'd she go?" Arav asked, talking about Marcy.

"Who cares," Mia said. "Good riddance. Lady's kind of a freakshow."

"Maybe she can't help it," Shana said.

"What, you're defending her now?"

"No! No. She can go eat dirt for all I care. I'm just saying—she seems kinda, I dunno, fucked up. Crazy people don't mean to be crazy."

Mia waved it off. "Whatever. She seems in control of her faculties and whatever to me. Besides, whether she controls it or not, I don't wanna be around it, and you don't mess with another shepherd's walker."

"They're not property," Arav said.

That earned him a sharp look from Mia. And a curious one from Shana. *Where's he going with this?*

"Nobody said they're our property," Shana said.

"Yeah, *Ravi*," Mia snapped. "I'm just saying, family is family, people you love are people you love. Marcy has no one here and shouldn't . . . like, grab on like she's a fucking fangirl or some shit."

"Maybe," Arav said, "she's just trying to find her people."

Mia sniffed. "Go find them somewhere else, I say."

"I don't have people here, not really. Do I not belong?"

Shana reached out to Arav. "That's not what she means, and you know it." Her hand sought out his, but he pulled away.

"I'm a brown-skinned man in America, I know what it's like not to belong. Maybe cut her a little slack, huh?" Suddenly, he bristled. "It doesn't matter. Who knows how long we'll be here, anyway." With that, he turned heel and headed off in the opposite direction from Marcy Reyes.

"The hell was that about?" Mia asked.

"I dunno. It's nothing."

"You two having a spat?"

"We're not—it's not a spat—and we're not 'we two.' He's him and I'm me and that's that."

"Oh, pshh. C'mon, girl. You and he been all hand-holdy and shit." She fluttered her lids and lashes. *"Oh, Arav. Oh, Shana. Let's hold hands. Should we kiss? No, no, we mustn't. I'm too young. You're too old.* It's like some real Romeo and Juliet business, except like, if Romeo and Juliet sucked really really bad."

"Nice."

Mia blew her a kiss.

Shana was about to explain that she and Arav were from two different worlds anyway, and he wasn't even really a shepherd, *and* by the way she was now eighteen years old so how old she was didn't matter anyway, *thank you very much,* and maybe just once Mia could take her nosy-nose and stick it up her own ass for once instead of up everybody else's.

But she didn't get to say it.

The sound of an engine cut her off.

It was distant, at first, the sound of a dragon rumbling awake. It growled through the ground, up through her feet and into her teeth.

"What's that shit?" Mia asked, raising her voice to be heard.

Shana didn't answer, just gave a bewildered shrug.

Louder and louder it came. Now she could pinpoint from where—behind them. Coming up fast, too. She could feel it in her chest.

And then, like that, here came a motorcycle. A Harley Fat Boy, cherry red with fire-eyed skulls painted on the side. On it sat a bony Jack-Skellington-looking dude, arms out, head back, mirrorshades reflecting the acid-washed sky. An acoustic guitar hung from a strap on his back, and lashed to the seat behind him was a black leather duffel.

The dude drove up to the head of the flock, pulled the motorcycle over, dropped the kickstand, and hopped off. Fetching his bag, he gave the bike a grumpy kick and it fell over with a bang. The look on his face was one of churlish pride—the pride of a child who just took a hunk of dump from his diaper and gleefully painted the wall with it.

"That guy looks familiar," Shana said.

"He should," Mia said.

"Why?"

"That's *Pete Corley.*"

"Who?"

Mia just shook her head. "Shit, now you makin' *me* feel old."

WEYLAND WAS HOVERING. BENJI SAT inside the trailer, and Sadie was outside, supposedly on the phone with Firesight. Weyland was in here like a test proctor monitoring students for cheating. It made it hard for Benji to continue digging into his nanotechnology theory. He was tempted to throw caution to the wind and continue to do the research full-facedly in front of Dale Weyland, believing wholly that the man was too much an ape to suss out what Benji was looking at. But he also knew it would be a mistake to underestimate him.

So instead he continued to look over Clade Berman's scans—the eruptive, concussive tears in so many of his cells.

He used the Black Swan satphone to do it—not using the projectors, but keeping the images on the screen.

Weyland said, "That the device?"

"I'm sorry?"

"Black Swan. That your access point to it?"

Benji hesitated. "It is."

"So it's not bullshit? It really works?"

Before Benji could answer, the phone pulsed green, answering Weyland's question. "It does, yes."

"HomeSec should have access."

"You do. Through the CDC." Did the man really not know this? "Black Swan has already enabled the FBI and Homeland Security to intercept a handful of crises."

"We should have *direct* access. Onsite."

"Okay, if you say so."

Weyland sauntered over. Chest puffed out. Chin up, looking down the barrel of his nose. "Lemme see this," he said, reaching down and grabbing the Black Swan phone out of Benji's hand. Benji didn't resist; though he knew the phone was made of nigh-unbreakable glass, just the same he didn't want to get into some preschooler pissing match with this oaf, the kind that might cause the phone to be dropped or damaged. *Let him look at it.*

"You can just ask me next time," Benji said.

"Ask? Ask. Huh. And here I thought you belonged to the Do-Whatever-the-Fuck-I-Want Club. You know. Longacre."

"I take your meaning, yes."

"You know, I'm gonna relish kicking your ass offsite. I don't like you. I damn sure don't trust you. You want real talk? You're just like Hunt. A prevaricating agenda-hound. She's a politician's politician—she'll say what she wants and do what she wants to maximize her advantage. Just like you with Longacre. Doesn't matter what's true, long as you keep playing your game." He leaned in closer and affected a low, threatening voice. "In Creel's America, won't be room for people like you. Just loyalists. Truth-tellers."

Benji shrugged. "I suppose I'm not surprised you're a Creel supporter. I am a little surprised you knew the word *prevaricating*, though."

Weyland's hand shot out and grabbed Benji by the jaw. His grip was tight and the man's face contorted into a rictus of anger.

Dale snarled, "You motherf—"

With that, a beam of light emitted from the Black Swan phone, striking him right in the eye. He cried out, blinking, the phone fumbling from his hand and into Benji's lap.

"Fucking fuck," Weyland said, swiping at the air in front of him as if he were blinded by particulate matter and not a beam of powerful light.

"It's still a little buggy," Benji said. "Sorry about that."

Weyland stood his ground, blinking. When his eyes seemed to adjust again he thrust a finger at Benji. "You're an asshole."

All Benji offered in retort was an amused shrug.

The trailer door opened behind Dale Weyland. In it stood Cassie, who waved Benji outside. He stood, casually, and walked past Weyland and said, in his own low voice: "If you ever touch me like that again, I'll press charges. Because, thanks to Black Swan, I have our entire exchange recorded and saved. You do your job, I'll do mine."

He wasn't sure that what he promised there was true—he had no evidence that Black Swan was recording all that it saw, though it was clearly *listening* to everything, and spatially aware. Certainly the fact that the machine intelligence seemed to come to his defense there indicated not merely that Black Swan was intelligent, but also that it had a *personality*.

But that was a problem for another time.

Now he was about to have a whole different problem.

Once they were outside, away from the trailer, she said, "What was going on in there? Weyland giving you shit?"

"As Weyland is wont to do. What's up?"

"I just spoke to Temson in Florida."

Harvey Temson: the chief pathologist working on the Garlin case. Florida required a local pathologist do autopsies, but Temson was working with the CDC on it. Benji knew him a little; met him at a couple of conferences. Good guy, if a little . . . antisocial.

"Please tell me someone didn't steal the body."

"No," she said. "No, it's his brain."

"Garlin's brain? What about it?"

"The fungus. It's . . . in there. Like tree roots pushing through soft dirt."

He sighed, looking out over the walkers moving toward them on the horizon. "I suppose that's to be expected. Soft tissue that's accessible through outside cavities could play host to fungal colonization—"

She pulled the image on her phone, and showed him. "This isn't that."

He took a long look. She was right. He pinched and zoomed in, saw that the threads of the infection penetrated deep—like the roots of a plant, yes, like a kind of circulatory system. He pointed to the swollen, turgid tissue around those mycelial threads: "This looks like inflammation."

"Yeah, it created an intense inflammatory response. And scarring."

And *that* would only happen if Garlin were alive. Meaning, it did not happen postmortem. This was officially a fungal infection.

"I think Garlin was infected for months," she said.

"Go on."

When she spoke, he could hear her voice trembling. Cassie was tough, she'd seen it all—so if something was scaring her, it was scaring him, too.

She let out a deep breath and said, "FBI did a deep dive on his family life, his business relationships, everything. Turns out, he'd been acting real fucking squirrelly. Symptoms of dementia. Erratic behavior physically, mentally, emotionally. He also suffered cold symptoms—normal cold virus, not necessarily influenza or pneumonia or anything more serious. More like a proper cold, or maybe an allergic response, and given the inflammation in the brain and elsewhere in his body, that tracks."

"When did it start?"

"Not long after an event in San Antonio. The . . . grand unveiling of some Garlin Gardens park down there. He did some showy explosion to 'break ground,' but he . . . he opened up a cave system."

"A cave system." Benji's stomach sank through the floor. He feared he knew where this was going. And given who he was talking to—an expert in veterinary health who knew zoonotic vectors like she probably knew her own mother—it explained her fear. "Bats. He released bats."

"Got it in one."

Cassie opened up a video on his phone—

It was just a ten-second clip, but the attack was plain to see. Garlin stood on a stage, in front of a crowd, as thousands of small bats swarmed him and everybody else.

"Mexican free-tailed bats," she said. "Garlin seemed to manifest symptoms two months after that day. We looked at the biology of the fungus colonizing him. It's remarkably similar in its biology to both *Pseudogymnoascus destructans* and *Ophidiomyces ophiodiicola*."

His heart began to do double time. She meant, respectively, that the infection that had affected and maybe killed Jerry Garlin was alarmingly similar to the fungus behind white-nose syndrome in bats, and snake fungal disease in, well, snakes. Both of which were dread killers of both bats and serpents nationwide—the fungus was opportunistic, savaging the bodies of the animals it infected. Snakes suffered sores on their scales. Bats had their wings degrade, and some studies suggested that white-nose fungus—named as such for the way a white powder crusted around the creature's muzzle— also affected the bat's echolocation abilities. The bat stopped being able to find food and, with the damage to its wings, stopped being able to fly.

Mortality rate in snakes was at 100 percent.

Bats had a better shot, but not by much—in the affected populations, mortality was closer to 90 percent.

Just the same, it had already killed millions of them—over six million bats dead, last he heard. Mostly of the *little brown bat* variety.

"You're suggesting a zoonotic jump."

A pause. "Yeah."

"That's bad, Cass."

"It's real bad, Benji. And again, I hate to say it—it gets worse."

"How?"

"We found three others who have died."

"Three. All right." *Deep breath, Benji.* "Were they in contact with Garlin in any way?"

"Indirect contact only. They were present on the day of the groundbreaking ceremony. All three—" He heard her ruffling papers. "Jessie Arvax, Greg Rooney, and Tim Bauer were not only present but also confirmed to have had contact with the bats. Two of them had rabies shots as a precaution."

"Okay, okay." His head spun. "That could be good news. Three is . . . well, four including Garlin, four dead is regrettable, but that's a low number."

He hoped this was more like influenza. If this was zoonotic, well, most infectious diseases that made the zoonotic jump from animals to people established a beachhead, but not much more.

Four dead. A small number, he told himself.

Still, the Spanish flu of 1918 started humble, too . . . that flu emerged first as a mild strain in the spring of that year, but by late summer had mutated into something far worse. By the end of its run, it had killed forty million people—more than those dead in World War I. He hoped *this* disease—with the four dead—would remain at that number and not suddenly lurch forward, a pathogenic overachiever.

He continued: "Sounds like it's not person-to-person. In bats it's incredibly infectious—one bat in the colony gets it, they all get it."

"Right. We're trying to rule that out now. But with the, uhh, *hope* that it follows the pattern of being non-infectious after the jump, maybe we're in good shape."

It struck him that thinking of only four dead after a fungal infection jumped from bat to person as "in good shape" was particularly psychotic— but once again, that was part of the cross he and other medical professionals had to bear. Bedside manner aside, it was all too easy to view this world of his in a cold, clinical manner. Numbers and data. He'd tried to look beyond that with Longacre, and the result was a wretched one.

But . . .

Maybe what happened with Longacre was too overt, too sweeping. He went too big with it. Maybe it was time to think, well, *smaller.*

"This could be good news for us," he said.

"I don't follow."

"Bear with me." He winced, hating that he was even suggesting this. "Cassie, we know HomeSec wants to kick us to the curb."

"Yeah. So?"

"I can take this to Loretta. She can take it to Flores, who can take it to Hunt. We can get ahead of this thing, maybe stay on the job a little longer."

At least until I see if my theory regarding nanotechnology is correct, he thought.

"But this fungal thing doesn't seem to connect to the walker phenomenon. There's no bridge."

"You know that. And *I* know that."

"Oh. But *they* don't know that," she said.

"Exactly. It buys us time. We already have it documented that we were considering fungal and parasitic vectors. Given that Black Swan pointed us in the direction of uncovering Jerry Garlin—we can use that. And we can also hope we have successfully gotten ahead of whatever it was that Black Swan was warning us about."

"This isn't Longacre all over again, is it?"

He swallowed. "I hope not. I understand if you don't want to go along with it. I'm using you as my check here. If you say not to do this, we won't do this. You wished I had come to you with Longacre, well, here I am. I'm tired and on edge and I may not be the best judge—"

"Let's do it."

"You're sure?"

"No, not at all, but with this flock we are in *wildly* uncharted territory.

Weyland and his goons won't like it, but that's fine by me. I say fuck 'em and kick it up the chain, boss."

"I will, Cass. And let me know if you find anything else."

"Can do." Another pause. "Hey, are you okay, Benji? For real."

"No," he said. "I'm not. Are you?"

"Not really."

"Then let's be not-okay together. And hope equally for a better day."

"I can drink to that," Cassie said.

A rumble arose. Like an engine. Coming from far off, but closing in. Cassie and Benji shared a quizzical look.

Both of them turned in time to see a man roll up on a Harley-Davidson, red like blood and covered in skulls. The lanky man like a rock-and-roll scarecrow, kicked over the bike like he didn't give a damn about it. Then he wandered into the flock.

Like he owned the place.

"That's . . . Pete Corley," Cassie said, mouth agape.

"Pete . . . Corley? The Gumdropper guy?"

"I swear, that's him. I've been to a couple festival shows where they played. He used to be a madman, a real rock star—the kind they don't make anymore."

Benji watched all the shepherds catch on to the fact—he could see the recognition in their eyes dawning. As the man stepped toward the crowd, they peeled away from the flock to greet him. Some refused to get close, gawking at a distance. Others rushed up to beam and gape and shake his hand. And he looked as natural as anyone could be in such a situation, like this was perfectly normal for him.

Benji didn't care much for Gumdropper's music—they were huge in the 1980s, when he was a kid. They were kind of half glam rock, half pop-punk, like some monstrous hybrid of Aerosmith and the Ramones. Benji grew up on hip-hop and R&B: anything from Public Enemy to Boyz II Men, Run-DMC to Usher. These days he often forgot to listen to music—not like Cassie, who hid under the comfort of her headphones five minutes out of every ten. But when he did listen to something, it was John Legend, Alicia Keys, maybe some old Motown records.

But not caring much for Gumdropper didn't mean he didn't know who they were. They weren't as big as, say, the Stones or the Beatles, but they had a good twenty-year run of dominating rock-and-roll—the band did their share of big stadium events, plus a Super Bowl halftime show. Every few years, they popped up again. An appearance on late-night TV. A new single on iTunes. Talk of some new album that never manifested.

Corley was a known raconteur and rabble-rouser. Had his troubles with the law, destroying hotel rooms, going wild on coke binges in the '90s, or there was that stunt on New Year's Eve in 2000 where he rushed the Times Square stage when Britney Spears was performing. Thing was, he always seemed to escape consequence for those actions. Everyone loved it. Even in 2000, Spears first looked shocked, but then warmed up to him and next thing the world knew, he helped turn "Oops! . . . I Did It Again" into some guitar-grinding rock-star mash-up.

"What a spectacular asshole," Cassie said. "I kinda love him."

"Why is he here?"

"Best guess, he's looking for attention. He saw where the news cameras were pointed and decided to jump in front of them."

And it worked. Already Benji could see some of their "embedded" reporters rushing toward them.

"Guys!" Here came Arav, hurrying toward them at a fast clip. "*Guys,* you need to see this."

"We've seen," Benji said. "Pete Corley, we know."

"That's not it," Arav said, half out of breath. He fumbled with his phone and pulled up a livestream of MSNBC. It froze, the wheel turning; signal out here in the heartland wasn't just half-assed, it was one-quarter-assed at best, maybe 10 percent of ass, and all shit. Finally the video autoplayed—

On the screen, Benji saw military vehicles: US Army troop carriers. His first question was, *Where are they being deployed?* But then he saw the chyron at the bottom—

RIVERSIDE, IOWA.

It explained why Weyland had been so cocky.

It's happening.

"What time is it?" Benji asked.

"Just after three P.M.," Arav said.

That meant they were ramping this up early. On the screen, the scrolling chyron at the bottom asked if President Hunt was finally taking "decisive action" on the sleepwalker phenomenon.

On the handheld screen, he saw three troop carriers—at least a dozen soldiers each. They were already pouring out, rifles over shoulders.

Benji felt every cell in his body go rigid as his mind played out one of many possible scenarios: Troops roll in, guns up, the shepherds resist, the media watches as the two sides clash. Best-case scenario was busted heads and blood on the asphalt. Worst-case, someone opened fire. Were there any firearms among the shepherds? He'd never seen any, but it also wasn't his place to check. They only had a middling police presence, and further, were they even checking? He imagined not. This was a potential powder keg.

"Shit," he said.

He needed to call Loretta.

Now.

29

WE EAT WHAT WE HUNT

What we're talking about here is a potential Sixth Extinction. We've had five such events in the historical record, where species die off at an accelerated rate, and that's what we're seeing now—vertebrates are dying off at one hundred times the expected rate, and we're only just now getting a grip on how bad it is for invertebrates. A study in Germany showed that up to 75 percent of their insects have disappeared since 1989. Notice how driving down the road you get fewer bugs splatted on your windshield? Or how you don't see as many fireflies anymore? Welcome to the Sixth Extinction. And in this video, we'll discuss what that means for the world—and for us. Afterward, don't forget to click like and subscribe!

—Carl Yong, science writer and broadcaster for
the PBS Zero Hour YouTube channel

JULY 3
Echo Lake, Indiana

ONCE AGAIN, PASTOR MATTHEW WAS THROWN BACK INTO THE FRAY WITH only a plate of food to fend off the conversation. Not that he necessarily wanted to—he enjoyed being the center of things, for once. It felt good. It felt necessary. Lord, it felt *right.*

He felt like a man buoyed by a raft on the ocean. He flowed this way and that, from the patio back inside the house to where lots of folks gathered around a massive dark cherrywood bar that wrapped around a tree-trunk pillar in the center of the room. The drinks—a sour bourbon punch now with the oaky kick of whiskey and the tang of lemon and orange—flowed like a river after a strong rain.

Matt kept looking around, though, trying to find his son, or his wife—or even Ozark. Eventually he spun away from one group (which included an actual bona fide astronaut), and while dancing halfway to another he found himself bumping into Roger. He said, "Hey, Roger," and found his words looser on his tongue than he'd like—lubricated, he feared, by a bit too much to drink. "You seen—"

But Roger shushed him. He held up something in his hand—a remote control—and then pointed it to a flat-screen TV that hung above the bar.

The screen came on big and bright. The sound was down, so Roger cranked it—and it didn't take long for it to push back against the din-and-clamor of the crowd here talking. They shushed as the TV took over.

(And here Matthew looked around and idly thought how strange it was for people to turn toward the glowing box with such strange reverence in their eyes. It hypnotized them. A television in any room did that to him, too—that's why he hated eating out at any restaurant that put a TV on in the corner. He always found himself and his son staring at it, transfixed. Like they were stealing a little devotion away from God and giving it to this . . . this damnable *rectangle of light*.)

(Still, what could he do? He turned to the box and tuned in.)

Roger didn't have to change the channel to Fox News—the station was there soon as the TV came on. They were showing video now of some armored troop carriers—one of the newscasters said they were US Army—mobilizing soldiers near the sleepwalker flock in Iowa.

Again Matthew turned his eye toward the other people around him—a strange thing to do, maybe, and a thing maybe driven by the whiskey fuzzing up his brain. He could see the eyes pointed to the TV, the flicker of motion on it captured in their eyes and their drink glasses. Then he caught movement off to the side: Ozark Stover.

Standing there with his son and his wife.

Ozark was giving Autumn something, and she was nodding.

Bo, for his part, just stood there, staring at the TV like everyone else.

It was a small moment in time—seemingly unimportant, practically over before it began. But Matthew caught it and it stuck between his teeth like a stringy piece of gristle. Ozark looked over at him then, gave him a small smile and a nod. Autumn didn't look—she just took Bo and made a beeline for the front door, even as Ozark cut through the crowd toward Matthew. The pastor didn't know where to go—meet Ozark? Or follow his wife and his son to see where they were going?

In his indecision, he rooted his feet.

Which was, in a way, a decision all its own.

Stover came, stood next to him. He lifted his big bearded chin toward the TV. "Helluva thing."

"It's good," Matthew said. "I suppose."

"Fuck that," Ozark said. "If you can excuse my salty tongue."

"I don't follow. Isn't it good what Hunt's doing?"

"It is. And anytime Hunt does something good, that's bad for us. Creel pushed her and she yielded—which makes her look weak, maybe, but it also makes her look like she's gotten tough on those freaks." He sighed. "Still, I'm sure Creel will call her on her hypocrisy. It's all in the messaging."

Matthew swallowed. His mouth was suddenly dry. Why was he afraid to ask Ozark about his wife and his son? "I saw you talking to Autumn—did she . . ."

"Leave? She is leaving, yes."

"Did she say why?"

"Tired, I think."

His mouth formed the words to ask Ozark about what he gave Autumn—but no sound came out. He resolved to ask Autumn about it later.

By now Roger had turned the TV off and was thanking everyone for their patience. And with that, the crowd snapped into high gear. From them came the roaring murmur of all of them talking about what they'd just seen.

Ozark in the meantime looked down at the plate in Matthew's hands, a plate that once upon a time held half a rack of ribs, but Matthew had done a good job at whittling it down to just bones.

The big man said, "Glad you liked those, Preacher. That's from a feral hog I killed here on the property. Around here, we eat what we kill, always. Use all parts of the animal, down to pig's feet jelly, head cheese, soap from the fat." He plucked one of the bones from Matthew's plate and popped it in his mouth like a lollipop. He suckled it and pulled small ribbons of meat off the rib. "You missed some, Preacher. Grab a bone and keep eating."

UNDER PRESSURE

Police Launch Probe into Mysterious Death of Richmond Professor

By Roberto Spidle, *Richmond Times-Dispatch*

Police are attempting to understand the mysterious death of local media and communications professor Greg Rooney. Rooney, 46, was found naked in his bathroom, covered in blood from having taken a shaving razor to his face and throat so vigorously he opened his own jugular. The coroner has suggested he bled out due to this, but could only speculate why the man would—or could—do such a thing. Toxicology reports found no drugs, but the coroner noted that many bath salt and so-called smart drug formulations have not yet been cataloged for tox screens, so that cannot be ruled out. Rooney, divorced, was not found for days, and by that time his body had already been colonized by a white, fuzzy fungus . . .

JULY 3
Lone Tree, Iowa

"I THINK YOU SHOULD GO," ARAV SAID.

Shana watched the flock walk, oblivious to everything. The shepherds, though, weren't oblivious. They were just paying attention to the wrong thing. They were crawling up the ass of Pete Corley when they should've been freaked out because the military was mounting up the troops some ten miles away.

"I'm not going anywhere," she said, her jaw set, fists firm.

"This could get bad."

"Nessie's here. So I'm here."

"Shana, I'm just concerned—"

"Go do your job, Arav, and I'll do mine."

He chewed a lip. "You're mad at me."

"Maybe you're mad at me."

"That doesn't make sense."

"Look around you, Arav, *nothing makes sense.* Why start now? Go. Be with your team. You have work to do, so go do it, dude."

She stormed off to catch up to her sister.

"I can't do it," Loretta said.

Benji paced at the back of the CDC trailer. The team listened to the call on speakerphone. Arav, Cassie, and Sadie were an audience to the call. "Loretta, with all due respect, if this thing with Garlin is connected, then we need time, we have to try—"

"I'm to understand that Madam President is already on her way to the press conference. These horses won't go back in the barn." She paused. "Not today. I can put your recommendation into the pipeline, and maybe tomorrow, maybe in a week, EIS will be back onsite."

"With Homeland gone? With the soldiers shipped away?"

"I can't speak to that."

He wanted to throw the phone. "Loretta, listen to me. Homeland Security is a blunt object—" Even the name galled him. *Homeland Security.* Everyone had gotten so adapted to it, they forgot that it sounded like something out of *1984.* Motherland, Fatherland, Homeland—these were, to him, implicitly un-American ideas, words antithetical to the mishmash hodgepodge of humanity that made up the citizenry of these United States. "Loretta, these people, the shepherds, they are devoted, they don't deserve to be sent away. And neither do we."

"I *said* I'll put it in the pipeline." At the other end of the line she gave an exasperated sigh. "Benjamin, I respect your work on this. You've done well despite my . . . better judgment. But it may be time to come back to Atlanta. The invitation is open if you want to remain with EIS."

"Loretta—"

"The connection with the fungus—I understand you want to see that connection but I'm not convinced of it. And honestly, you're smart enough I suspect you're not convinced, either, and you're just trying to stall. I've recommended that Cassie head up the EIS investigation studying the Garlin case. Vargas has another couple of weeks of recovery and then will head back out into the field with Arav Thevar and a new team."

"And me?"

"You'll come home and work with Black Swan. We have decided your work there is exemplary, and we require a liaison to bridge the efforts of Benex-Voyager with the needs of CDC—"

"I'm not hearing this, Loretta. What's going on here is bigger than all of that, you know it and I know it."

"Don't try to move me from this, Benjamin."

The Immovable Object has spoken, he half expected her to say.

"Just put this in the pipeline, please," he said. "Then we'll see."

"Yes, we will."

The call ended.

The team sat there, watching him. They'd all been listening. Benji chewed a fingernail. They watched him, silent in the shadow of his near-palpable frustration. To Sadie, he said:

"Did you talk to Firesight?"

"I did. They intend to send someone down tomorrow."

"We won't *be* here tomorrow." He heard the edge in his voice and struggled to soften it. He bit a piece of fingernail off, and it pulled into a hangnail. A little red blob of blood inflated at the site and he quickly sucked it away. "I don't know what to do. We're DOA here." Arav showed them the news on his phone. Already he knew the troops were mounting. How soon would they be here? Too soon.

Cassie sighed. "I don't want to be reassigned."

"The Garlin case deserves due attention," Benji said. "Loretta is right. And you're the best to head up that investigation."

"We may need to evacuate the shepherds," Arav said. "Might be better to start now rather than . . ." But nobody was listening to him. He noticed it. "Hello, is anybody—"

But then Arav's voice trailed off because he heard it, too.

Outside, Benji heard the murmur of the crowd and the strumming of a guitar. It was a familiar song—one of Gumdropper's early hits, maybe. But he couldn't place it. Idly, he asked: "What song is that?"

They turned to listen.

Arav said, "Is it Guns N' Roses?"

Cassie hissed at him. "No. This is not GnR, kid."

"It's Gumdropper," Sadie said, quite definitively. "In fact, it's 'Full Steam

Ahead' off the album *Engineer Without Forms*. Two bits of trivia, first that it was a concept album from 1989 based off *The Gunslinger* by Stephen King—featuring songs like 'Different Seasons' and 'Mohaine Desert.' Second that this version we're hearing is not the version from the album but rather, the more uptempo version that Gumdropper played at stadium shows and that showed up on the BBC Live recording. They had a second King tribute album in 2000, their *last* full studio album, but it kinda sucked—"

"You're a Gumdropper fan?" Benji asked.

"Like you would *not* believe." She leaned in. "I have a small steamer trunk full of Gumdropper bootlegs. Is he really out there? Pete Corley? *The* Pete Bloody Hell Motherfucker Corley?"

"He is."

Manic glee flashed in her eyes. "I'd love to meet him."

"Yes, well," and he was about to say *That's not really our priority,* but then he realized maybe, just maybe, it was. He turned to Arav. "Arav . . ."

"Doctor Ray. Ah, Benji."

"Do me a favor?"

"What's that?"

"Go and bring him in."

"Who? Pete Corley?"

"Yes, Arav, Pete Corley."

"You . . . you're sure?"

He thought about it. "I am."

CORLEY SAT AT ONE END of their small conference table, Benji Ray at the other. Everyone else—Cassie, Arav, Sadie—stayed off to the sides. They had to draw the shades to stop shepherds and the media from looking in.

The rock star leaned back, feet on the table. He pulled out something that looked like a robot's idea of a magic wand. "May I?"

"May you what?" Benji asked.

"Smoke. Not that it's smoke. It's *vapor.*" When Benji didn't respond, Corley waggled his fingers. "Ooh, vapor. Science." He regarded Benji's stone-faced glare, then petulantly put the vaporizer away. "Guess *not,* then."

"It's not healthy, you know. Vaping."

"Healthier than smoking."

"Shooting yourself in the leg is healthier than in the heart, too. Doesn't mean I would recommend doing it."

Corley sniffed. "So, that what this is? Checkup with my doctor? Want me to put my balls in your hand, turn my head, give a cough?"

In his voice, Benji could hear that Irish lilt, the one that lifted his voice in ways and places Americans and even Brits didn't. "No."

"I'll tell you what it is. You're the big man in charge here. The big boss with the red-hot sauce. You don't like me being here, I'm an irritation, a— what's the John McClane line? A fly in the ointment, Hans? A monkey in the wrench? I don't need your permission to be here, though, do I?"

Benji leaned forward, drumming his fingers on the table. "I don't like celebrities. They tend to be narcissists created by and reinforcing a whole system of narcissism: self-reward and solipsism, all the way down."

"Ennnhhh," Corley said, like he was thinking about it. "Big words, big words. But I'll cop to that, Doc." He smiled big and bright, even with that mouthful of slightly fucked-up teeth. "I *do* love being me."

"And I suppose it was inevitable that one of you would see the sleepwalkers as an opportunity—a spotlight that had dared turn toward something that wasn't you, God forbid. Natural then that you would come here to extend your life cycle of fame—or perhaps you're here running from something, I don't know."

Corley's smile soured to a frown. "So now this is therapy, is it?"

"No. Against all my instincts, against every bone in my body, it is me asking you for a favor."

"Mm, okay, I'll allow it."

"You say I'm the man in charge, but that's not necessarily true. And after tonight, it won't be true at all. Right now, as you and I speak, President Hunt is preparing to go on television and announce that what's going on outside this trailer will be under the boot of Homeland Security. The CDC will be summarily removed. Soldiers—army men and women that are again *right now* gathering less than ten miles from here—will swarm this site and attempt to boot all of us. Politely at first, by force thereafter, I would guess."

Corley swallowed hard and sat forward.

"There it is," Benji said, snapping his fingers. "The realization is hitting you, now, isn't it? Whatever opportunity you thought you saw here is going to go to—well, to *vapor.* Poof. Unless . . ."

"Unless what?"

"Here's where the favor comes in."

"Uh-huh. I'm listening."

"You go out there and stand with those shepherds. Claim solidarity. Fake it if you must. Get yourself all up in those camera lenses and tell them what's coming—soldiers, forced ejection, brutality. Blood on concrete and heads knocked in and all that nasty business. But tell them *you'll* stand with them. You demand President Hunt rescind her order and grant protection to the good shepherds of this flock and to the CDC who has governed here."

"You're deranged." Moments of silence stretched out. Then Corley's face stretched into a jack-o'-lantern smile. "And I *like* it."

"You'll do it?"

"First, what do I get out of it?"

"You get to stay. This train keeps on rolling . . . full steam ahead."

"I see what you did there, Doc. And I approve of anything that stokes the fire of my, as you say, narcissistic tendencies. All right! I'll do it. You want me to go out there now? Bring the ruckus, as it were?"

"Now, yes."

Pete Corley stood up—which was like watching a closet full of broom-sticks animating all at once under a sorcerer's spell. "Done and done."

With that, he headed for the door, guitar in hand.

Grinning like a jackal.

After he left, Sadie said: "I think I'm pregnant with his baby."

Benji gave her an amused, if worried, look.

"You owe me," Cassie said. "It took every urge in my body not to ask him about Gumdropper trivia. It hurt me. It hurt me in my *soul,* Benji."

"Thank you, Cass."

"Think it'll work?" Arav asked.

"I have no idea," Benji said. "Probably not. But when you're about to go off a cliff, you grab hold of whatever you can to keep from falling."

31

SPEARS TO SPLINTERS

New Monmouth University public poll: 63% in favor of Homeland Se-curity taking over flock operation, 27% against, 10% undecided
@AP_Politics
12 replies 712 RTs 341 likes

JULY 3
Echo Lake, Indiana

JUST AS THE PARTY COLLECTIVELY WATCHED FOX NEWS SHOWING OFF THE troop carriers miles out from the sleepwalkers, they also paused to watch President Hunt make her statement.

She was a severe-looking woman, Matthew found. Her penny-red hair was cut short. She wore little makeup. The lines around her eyes looked carved there, as if by an X-Acto knife.

When she ran the first time, she attempted to walk that line between being feminine and masculine—feminine enough to seem motherly or sis-terly, masculine enough to convince the country she was tough enough to handle what came at her. But since then, she'd become harder. *Sharper.* Maybe the presidency did that to you, Matthew thought. Whittled you like a stick. Sometimes to the point of being cut to splinters.

When she came on the TV, most of the party guests at Ozark Stover's house booed. Soon they started a chant: *Punt the cunt, punt the cunt.*

Matthew did not join in. He tried to excuse it—they were drunk, it was a party, partisan politics were what they were.

When she finally spoke, they quieted down to hear.

Her speech was simple enough.

"I have chosen to take the advice of those closest to me—meaning, not just my advisers, but you, the American people—and institute Homeland Security control over the unfolding sleepwalker crisis."

That was good, Matthew thought—though the thought came to him more slowly given that it had to push first through the bourbon brine that was presently pickling his brain. But he appreciated first the political move of pretending that the American people were her closest advisers, and second that she had changed her language, subtly. Before today, it was the "sleepwalker flock" or the "sleepwalker phenomenon." Now it was a "crisis." What was it that Ozark said? *It's all about messaging.*

She went on to say that she gave everyone "my greatest assurance that the sleepwalkers—who are our fellow Americans, each undergoing something we could not possibly understand—will remain safe."

The switchover from the CDC to Homeland Security, she said, would begin promptly at 5 P.M., Central Daylight Time.

It was now 4:56 P.M.

She took no questions.

32

GET THE MAN A STAGE

JAKE TAPPER: Some actors and directors have come out hard against you in recent days, lining up behind President Hunt despite their earlier criticisms of her presidency. What do you say to that?

ED CREEL: I say it's time everyday Americans stop lining up behind those Hollywood elites. I represent them, not her.

JT: And what do you say to those who suggest *you're* a Hollywood elite, sir? After all, in the 1990s you produced a number of films and often pal around with producers and film financiers, not to mention your net worth is in the billions, not millions, which I have to tell you, seems pretty "elite"—

EC: To them, and to you, Jake, I say [bleep] off. I've been insulted by better men than you. This interview is over.

—from *The Lead with Jake Tapper*, CNN

JULY 3
Lone Tree, Iowa

HE WAS STONED.

Nobody knew that but him. But Pete Corley was *definitely* stoned.

Like, not gonzo stoned—he didn't eat a fistful of mushrooms, he didn't hoover up rails of coke off the small of a young man's back, he didn't lick the poisonous underbelly of some Peruvian toad to go on a journey of self-enlightenment where he had to fight a Jaguar King whose face fell off and really it was *Pete's* face underneath. (True story, that last bit happened to him a decade ago when he was in the Amazon rain forest and got fucked up on DMT with, of all things, a Brazilian boy band. No toads, but he *did* fight a

Jaguar version of himself. He lost, for whatever that meant. Also he puked a lot. Literal gallons.)

No, Pete had just smoked a little weed.

A *little* weed a *lot* of times.

Aaaaand he had some drinks.

Zimas, which he did not know still existed but apparently did out here in the Midwest. Was this the Midwest? Whatever.

Point was, nobody *knew* he had a little wacky tobacky and nobody *knew* that he had pounded a six-pack of Zimas over the last six hours because he was very, very good at doing exactly this. *This is not my first rodeo, you insipid motherfuckers. I am a performer. I am a rock god.*

A rock god on the run.

That last part was not a part he cared to admit. He cared so little to admit it, in fact, that as soon as the thought entered his head, he chased it back out with a skull full of music. The moment he had images in his mind of Landry, or his wife Lena, or the kids Connor and Siobhan, he pumped his own brain full of grinding guitar and driving drums and his own screaming voice. He envisioned himself, Mad Max–style, riding atop a flaming eighteen-wheeler, shrieking a song like "Full Steam Ahead" and chasing all the bad brain mutants back to the shadows from whence they came. He'd always been that way—music a constant background noise that he learned to bring into the foreground to shut out anything else that bothered him. A wall he built, a door he could slam. It was also his weapon, as it would be today. Blade, chain saw, Gatling gun. Slice, chew, rat-a-tat-tat.

Pete emerged from the CDC trailer invigorated anew, and marched back to the heart of the crowd. He cared very little for the pilgrims or sleepwalkers or whatever it was they would be called in a week—I mean, yes, abstractly he cared, oh ho ho, those poor soggy sods, but he wasn't here for them. Benji Ray had his number on that one.

He wasn't here for the walkers.

He wasn't here for their shepherds.

He was here for the media, for the attention, for the bright and shining eyes, all on him. He was here to once again be at the center of things.

On his own terms. Not Gumdropper's. Certainly not Elvis's, that fucker.

So he waltzed out, guitar in his bony hands, and played the best version of the Pied Piper that he could. His music summoned the people, a rock god calling to his priests and servants, his suppliants, his sycophants—

"Gather around," he called to them, giving a heady strum to the acoustic, *vrommm*. "I come here to serve a purpose," he said, raising his voice, but now he saw a new problem: He was down *among* them, *within* them, a part of them. That wasn't right. That would not do, oh no. He could barely see behind the first faces circling him.

A rock star did not perform within the crowd.

A rock star performed *above* it. As was the place of a god.

(He *urp*ed into his hand.)

He needed a motherfucking *stage*.

Though the walkers kept walking, the shepherds had gathered to him like piglets struggling to get at mommy pig's tit, so now he had to look above and beyond them—where, oh where, would he find a stage?

Look from whence you came, Pete, he told himself.

The CDC trailer.

"Follow me!" he whooped, lassoing his arm in the air as he let the guitar belt out the opening chords of "Under Your Thumb," one of Gumdropper's first charting hits—they parted the ways as he marched to the trailer, demanding then that they help him clamber atop. They did as he commanded, as they always did; hands under his feet, he used their palms as stepladders. They lifted and he walked—admittedly, he struggled a bit there at the end, and his bones creaked and his muscles pulled taut like the strap of a heavy instrument. But he made hay from that grass as he did a comical Wilder-as-Wonka roll onto the top of the trailer before leaping to his feet anew, the neck of the guitar pointed to the sky.

One more strum and then he begged for quiet.

Time to give them the news.

Benji looked up at the ceiling of the trailer.

"He's on the roof of the trailer, isn't he?" he asked.

Outside, they'd been mobbed. It was like an impromptu concert. The shepherds and the news cameras were all facing them, crowding them, gazing up in fascination, wonder, and confusion.

"He can climb on top of *my* trailer anytime," Sadie said.

"Sadie!" he said, shocked.

She shrugged. "Sorry. It's true, though."

•   •   •

"IT'S JUST SOME FUCKING STUNT," Shana said.

"You're cynical," Mia said.

"And you're an idiot."

She regretted it as soon as the words fled her mouth.

Mia gave her a scathing look—the kind of look that could light a cigarette just from its intensity. "You're a mean little girl, you know that?"

"I'm not a little girl. Today's my birthday. I'm eighteen now."

"I'd say happy birthday, but you'd probably just think it's some kind of *fucking stunt.*" Mia flicked a middle finger in her general direction and stormed off to join most of the rest of the shepherds flocking to hear the old-ass rock star who was now clumsily climbing atop the CDC trailer.

Good job, Shana, you insulted the woman who saved us from a gunman, you alienated the science boy you like, and you just pissed off the one person you maybe thought of as a friend out here.

Well, crap.

She was going to turn and walk away, and head off to see if she could jog and catch up to the Beast and sit with her father for a while—

But turned out, that wasn't going to be an option.

Because who was coming up now but her father.

He was gawking and gaping at the man on top of the CDC trailer, his mouth so open Shana half imagined his jaw dragging behind him. He staggered up to her and said, "Holy hell, that's really him."

"Holy hell, you're really out of the RV."

"Well, damn right I am. It's Pete Corley of Gumdropper! That might not mean much to you, but growing up in the '80s—"

"You're fucking unbelievable."

He stared at her, shocked.

"You wouldn't come crawling out of that dumb-ass RV for your own sick daughter—*or* for your healthy one. But some geriatric-ass rock star unretires and here you are like some heartsick tween."

And, to boot, you didn't remember my birthday.

Today is my birthday, you jerk.

He looked stung. Hurt. "You're really cynical, Shana," he said.

"You gotta be kidding me."

"Can't you just enjoy something for once?"

And with that, he went off to, whatever, go worship at the altar of the guitar-playing strip-of-beef-jerky on top of the CDC trailer.

Shana stood where she stood, feet rooted, feeling super-sad and over-whelmingly alone.

Then Pete Corley began to speak.

"THE ENEMY IS AT THE gates, shepherds," Pete Corley announced with one heavy chord, *brommmm*. He stood, legs apart, guitar saddled across his middle. One arm pointed to the shepherds, then swept out into the distance until it was pointing farther down the road.

"Thataway," he called out, "wait men and women of the US Army, soldiers who plan on rolling up here and ripping you away from your friends, your families, your loved ones."

Gasps rolled across them like a high tide.

Faces fell. Mouths opened. They turned to one another to ask word-lessly, *Can it be true?* Meanwhile, the cameras rolled.

"They say the sleepwalkers are a *danger*. Some say they might be a weapon, others say they might be demons born from the belly of a comet that passed overhead—a sign of the End Times, a horde of devils on the march. But do you believe that?"

A cry went up: "No!"

"Sweet hot hell, I don't believe it, either!" he bellowed. Christ, his voice was going to be *hoarse* in the morning. But fuck it, let his vocal cords go to cinders—and let his voice cry out and sing loud and cast high to the heavens. Most important, let the cameras see him, hear him, transmit his words to everyone across the country—

And especially to Elvis.

You think you can steal my mojo? he thought.

Try again, Elvis.

You prick wanker fuck.

Onward he bellowed:

"Even as we speak, President Hunt is going on TV, and she's announcing that Homeland Security and the US Army are taking over. The CDC will be ejected! *You* will be ejected! Who knows what agenda they serve?" Truth was, they probably had a perfectly good reason, but what did he care? Homeland Security was a bunch of thugs and soldiers were just mercenaries working for them, and they were trying to rob him of his chance to do exactly what he was doing right now: go out to the people, strum this guitar, and be *loved* by them.

"Will you be run off?" he yelled.

"No!" they roared.

"Then I'll stand with you. Let America know—" And here he looked right at one camera, then the next, then the next. Just like he would on stage if they were recording a show for DVD release. "We will remain as shepherds with this flock. None shall move us. And if they try, then may all the gods in all the heavens spare them our resistance!"

A clumsy, awkward, but perfectly vigorous cheer arose.

Gods, this felt good.

He felt electric and alive in a way he hadn't in forever. Gone were thoughts of his wife, his children, his lover—he had even shed his anger over Elvis and Gumdropper in that one shining moment in which he existed in his own head, a perfect form standing tall and gold, like a heretical idol from an ancient civilization. And then, as if the moment were not perfect enough, as if the universe were not already kindly elevating him to the pedestal on which he belonged—

It gave him one last gift.

A dramatic moment, laid bare, like something out of a movie.

In the distance, miles up the road—

There came the soldiers.

Three troop carriers rolled forward—from here, looking more like Matchbox cars than anything, though he feared that up close, they'd not look like toys at all. Those vehicles were probably loaded for bear with army men and women. Ready to fight.

No! he thought. *We are the ones who are ready to fight.* Glorious and wild. Like barbarians against the Roman Legion! Bones in their beard, blood in their hair, roaring like beasts.

Was that who fought the barbarians? Romans?

Fuck, who cares, history is for tossers.

He pointed: "Look. Here they come. As I said they would." On this last bit, he really got the voice loud and shrieky, a hard rock heavy metal yell that sounded like his vocal cords were welding steel. "Gird your loins and stand tall—*we must resist!*"

And then he jumped backward into the crowd.

Now, Pete Corley was no dummy. He knew the score—once in a while some newblood lead singer decided to leap into an uncertain crowd for them to surf him around, and that newblood took the leap of faith and ended up belly-flopping on the fucking concrete. He always told them, *Check the crowd, read the room.* No leaps of faith. *Make sure they know you're coming,* he said. But this time, Pete didn't check the crowd.

He gave off no signals.

He simply pivoted and fell.

Like Jesus Christ.

Wait, did Jesus Christ ever crowd-surf?

Surely that was in the Bible somewhere. Or some Bible movie? Fuck it, whatever, it made sense to Pete.

Pete, who leapt. Pete, who fell.

He felt himself whishing through open air, *whoof—*

A stray thought hit him:

What if I hit the road?

They aren't watching me, they're looking for the army trucks.

What if after all that, the cameras capture me cracking the back of my skull on this Podunk country road.

Oh fucking hell.

Then his body hit.

His neck jerked. His head dropped even as his chest rose.

A dozen hands buoyed him aloft. Lifted to the sky. Carried by the faithful and the reverent, his rock-and-roll supplicants. Up he went, moving this way and that, until he could hear the roar of the trucks approaching. They turned him and eased him to the ground. Boots on asphalt. Someone put his guitar into his hand.

Pete Corley turned and faced the three trucks bearing down. The crowd stood behind him, angry and sparking like a fraying wire.

He felt alive and insane and divine.

And then, when he saw what they were facing, he felt very, very afraid.

33

THE CLASH

A neural network invents new band names:
The Skull and the Boy
Fangdriver!
Grandpa's Going Down
Discount Ghostwriters
The Human Division
Monkey Clump
Robot, Party of Four
Nude Slot
—as seen on the US of AI blog, US-of-AI.com

JULY 3
Lone Tree, Iowa

FOR A TIME, IT FELT TO SHANA LIKE A DREAM. A NIGHTMARE, REALLY, ONE
that you recognized for what it was but could do nothing about—you just
sank deeper and deeper into the phantasmal mire. The trucks rolled up.
Soldiers spilled out. They had guns—black guns, military rifles, the kind
you use to cut down insurgents and terrorists, not the kind you point at
your own people. Anxiety tightened in her middle as she imagined them
turning their weapons on the flock and the shepherds—the imagined chatter as the rifles chewed through ammo, cutting apart innocent people. She
had to willfully force that image out of her mind even as real soldiers with
real guns lined up a hundred yards away. Even as the sleepwalkers marched
onward.

Right toward them.

She stayed by Nessie the whole time. As the trucks rolled up and the soldiers spilled out, some shepherds followed Pete Corley to the front lines. Others retreated to the sides. Others still, like Shana, went to their people. They fed into the flock and stood by their loved ones. An unspoken message carried by them and between them: *Come and try to remove us.*

Dale Weyland stood with some kind of military-grade bullhorn, the same drab green as the trucks and the soldiers. He announced:

"Shepherds, I am Dale Weyland of United States Homeland Security. You are being forcibly evacuated. Please depart the sleepwalker flock in an orderly fashion or you will be removed and detained."

Some did. Some shepherds retreated backward and to the sides.

Most did not.

The walkers kept on walking. As was their way. They would not be turned from their path. Nothing had turned them yet.

Shana walked with them. As did many of the others.

She felt sick. Nausea rolled up inside her like a boiling tide. It felt like being strapped into a roller coaster you didn't want to ride—but she couldn't stop it, couldn't get off. Even though she knew she could. At any point she could just retreat like some of the others. She could leave the flock. Let the walkers walk on through the gauntlet of soldiers.

But that would mean leaving Nessie.

And that was not an option.

Pete Corley stood at the front, strumming his guitar and giving out marching orders: "March on, shepherds! Form a wedge! Don't let them take you. Remind them that *the world is watching.*"

Onward they marched. The soldiers were a hundred yards away. Then ninety. Then eighty. Her heart raced in her chest. She looked back, saw Mia walking with Mateo, saw Lonnie Sweet with Darryl, saw Aliya with her friend Tasha. All of them looked scared.

And all of them looked resolute.

Someone bumped Shana's arm. She turned, thinking, *It's Dad, finally making good, finally showing the hell up—*

But it wasn't.

It was Arav.

He reached down and took her hand.

Arav didn't say anything, he just gave her a small nod.

They walked together, with Nessie, toward the soldiers.

• • •

IN THE BACK OF PETE'S mind he wondered, *On a scale of one to ten, how bad would it be if I pissed my pants?* Certainly, as a rock star, he was afforded the luxury of behaving a bit like a lunatic. But pissing his pants in public (he'd done it in private before, obviously, as a seasoned druggie-and-drinker) was probably a bridge too far, and yet here he was, honestly considering it.

Oh, he was putting on a good face, of course. He had to. Marching back and forth in a zigzag as he approached the wall of soldiers—well, he had to look like the stage-seizing badass that he pretended to be. And up until five minutes ago, it seemed easy-peasy-play-Parcheesi. Back then it was like he was just warming up the crowd.

Now that same crowd was not just warmed up—they were *fired up.* And they were at his back as he marched toward the soldiers.

Soldiers with guns.

Big fucking guns.

Every cell in his body screamed to turn tail and run, just as he had run from the rest of his life, arriving only hours ago.

But he couldn't. Not now. What would that do to him? He'd lose all credit. Respect for him would be out the window. No more rock god. No more whiskey-fed Jesus. He'd only be a tragic Judas.

Be the Judas, a voice in him warned. *Run, you craven fuck, run.*

And yet, onward he went. He pretended like he was someone else with bigger principles, bigger balls, and no sense of self-preservation. Pete grabbed the guitar and belted out the chorus to one of Gumdropper's biggest and angriest songs: "We're Not Going Anywhere," which admittedly was a hit song he and Elvis wrote to announce their unretirement in 1989 (after a slew of failed solo projects), but fuck it, it sounded good enough as a makeshift *fuck-you-eat-shit* protest song.

He screamed it loud and proud, others joining in—

We're not going anywhere!
Our feet are firm
Our hearts are bare
We're not going anywhere!
You go to hell!
We'll stay right here!

The key to that lyric, of course, was to rhyme *here* with *hair* so that it lined up nice with *anywhere* and *bare*—simple enough to do with his Irish twist. Beyond that, all he could do was put on a good face and try *very hard* not to piss his pants.

Or shit them. Or puke on himself. Gods, was sobriety setting in? Had his buzz worn off? It had. *Shit shit shit.*

We're not going anywhere, he thought as he sang. A mantra for himself more than for any who followed him.

FIFTY YARDS NOW.

Shana could see the looks on the soldiers' faces. Some looked just as scared as she did—scared and confused, like they didn't know what this was or if they should even be here. Some looked angry, ready to fight, eager to scrap with these diseased walkers—in their eyes she saw a different kind of fear, a fear that Nessie and the others might be weapons or terrorists, a fear born of knowing that each one of the walkers was a not-so-secret bomb ready to blow like a coffee can full of gunpowder. Other soldiers looked just as dead-eyed as the walkers themselves, empty of anything but, she imagined, their sense of duty and their willingness to hurt or kill in the name of nothing but the pride in following orders.

She wanted to yell out at them: *Just go home! You don't have to be here. This isn't your fight. Leave us alone.*

But she didn't. She just held Arav's hand tighter as they marched on.

Forty yards.

Thirty.

Dale Weyland used the bullhorn again, repeating the same warning as before: "I am Dale Weyland of United States Homeland Security. You are being forcibly evacuated. Please depart the sleepwalker flock in an orderly fashion or you will be *removed* and *detained.*"

Ahead, Pete Corley only sang louder—pointing the neck of his guitar at Weyland as he led the shepherds and the flock closer and closer.

Twenty yards.

Ten.

And now the line was broken. The soldiers stepped aside to let the walkers pass, *thank God,* because if they hadn't, and the walkers started to *pop pop pop . . .*

Even still, the army men looked spooked as the sleepwalkers surged past. Shana's heart leapt into her throat and lodged there like a piece of meat. All it would take is one soldier to lift a rifle, twitch a finger . . .

Arav let go of her hand.

She thought, *No, don't.*

But then he took something out of her pocket and put it into her empty palm—

It was her phone.

Also, her camera.

"Do what you do," he said.

And she did, just as it all truly began. She lifted the phone and flipped to the camera app, snapping a pic just as Dale Weyland said: "All right, let's do this." He circled his finger in the air like a looping lasso. *Click.*

The dam broke.

The soldiers converged upon them. Hands reaching. Rifles at the ready. Many held a white plastic cord in their hands—zip-ties, Shana realized. Easy makeshift handcuffs. *They're really doing this.* Idly she thought about the weapon in her backpack. The gun.

Instead, she lifted her *other* weapon, the camera, and began shooting.

THE CDC TRAILER WAS FAST being left behind by the walker flock. Through the window it was impossible to see what was happening—so, instead, Benji and the others climbed out of the trailer windows and onto the roof.

Weyland released the hounds. The soldiers waded into the fray, reaching for shepherds—he watched as some of the shepherds pulled away, using the walker flock as both shield and obstacle. A crass move, maybe, one that might play cowardly on TV, but Benji understood it—the soldiers were under orders not to interact with the walkers. And they knew what everyone else knew: The walkers, if impeded, would blow. So they were ginger around them, which made them all the more effective as shields.

Other shepherds, though, went willingly. Chins up, yelling as they were plucked from the flock and dragged off to the side where they were processed fast—zip-tied and left on the side of the road.

In the chaos Benji saw Pete Corley, who deftly sidestepped soldiers left and right, almost like he was dancing with them, his guitar a partner forever cutting in. He looked manic and mad, an anarchist's gleam flashing in his eyes like fireworks.

But Benji's heart fell ill watching it all.

He shared a sad look with Sadie and Cassie, and then looked back at his phone, waiting for it to ring. For Loretta to call and to tell him they were pulling back, that Homeland Security's reign was so brief as to be a footnote. But the call did not come.

I made a terrible mistake encouraging this, he thought. He would pay for it, he knew, but worse was how they would all pay for it. Shepherds, flock, soldiers, and all.

What have I done?

MARCY WALKED OFF TO THE side, watching the clash between soldier and shepherd unfold, as if in slow motion. At present, neither side was particularly aggressive—each playing cat and mouse with the other. The soldiers waded into the shepherds. The shepherds feinted and moved in the midst of the flock. The soldiers were trepidatious, but for the shepherds, this was their home turf; the flock of sleepwalkers was their landscape.

Part of her wanted to race in and help.

I'm a shepherd, too, she thought.

Wasn't she?

Now she wasn't so sure.

They had rejected her. Told her she did not belong. And Marcy feared they were right. Though she saw the glow of the sleepwalkers—a glow nobody else seemed to see—she felt like an observer, like someone outside a house looking in through the window at a family enjoying dinner, or game night, or a movie on the television.

Worse, she wasn't the type to go against a soldier. She had the greatest respect for the men and women of the armed services; she'd thought about joining herself, but her family was a cop family through and through, blue in their blood and badges for hearts. All the same, to go against the defenders of American law and order . . . it made her sick just to think about.

So she kept walking. And watching. And waiting for it to get worse.

Which it was about to do.

INSIDE, CORLEY WAS A HOUSE on fire, all the cats and children running out of the open doors as the whole thing threatened to collapse in on itself. He was panic and mania, he was sweat and piss, he was in his mind running for the hills like the fucking roadrunner chased by that fuckwit coyote.

Outside, Corley knew eyes were on him. The cameras watched. Somewhere, Landry did, too. And his wife. And his children.

And Elvis.

(Prick wanker fuck.)

So he mugged for the media. He stuck out his tongue. He strummed the guitar and juggled a pair of middle fingers between power cords. He did a lanky, janky polecat tango as he got up in the faces of one soldier after the next, ducking their swipes as they came for him. He shuffled backward in a half-assed moonwalk, merging with the flock of walkers and their shepherd attendants. He laughed and spit and strutted. He was anarchy and power, he was the dance and the dissent, he was fire and fuck-you, motherfucker.

And then, it happened. Elbows out, he spun away from one soldier only to knock into a second one who had come up behind him.

He thought, *Yeah, go on, put your hands on me in front of all of America—hell, all of the bloody world!*

Rough hands spun him around.

The soldier—a boy with cherub cheeks flecked with fresh stubble—came at him. Rifle up. Not the barrel end. The other end—the stock.

The butt of the rifle stabbed out.

Crack.

Pete's head rocked back. The dark behind his eyes lit up with paparazzi flashbulbs—he could see his own veins forking like lightning. His left heel caught his right, and next thing he knew he was dropping down hard on his assbone. Pain grappled up his spine as a knee caught him in the chin. He tasted blood. His tongue felt fat. The back of his head hit the pavement. A boot pressed down on him—no, not on him, but on the guitar pressed against his chest, and he struggled to yell out, *No, no, you fucking animals, that's a Taylor custom guitar—it's made of Hawaiian koa wood, it blooms and sings in the mid-range like a chorus of gossiping angels, and the bridge has a climbing vine inlay, the damn guitar is sweet like honey and Tahitian vanilla.* But then the bridge snapped off it with the sound of a bone breaking, and the Elixir-brand strings jangled and twanged as they unmoored from the bridge. Another foot connected with the side of his head and once again he saw stars streaking and veins illuminating in X-ray pulses—

For a moment, too, he thought they must be shooting at him.

He saw more throbs of light above him. *Flash, flash, flash.*

But then, just before blackness dragged him down, he saw.

A girl, a teen girl, standing above him.

Her phone out.

Pointed at him. Taking photos. Flash on.

And then with one last flash came the deep and unabiding dark, welcoming him home, a fitting end.

MARCY WATCHED THE ROCK-AND-ROLLER GO down. She knew who he was, though she didn't much care for Gumdropper's music—the 1980s were a wasteland of music, and Marcy was a child of the 1990s, anyhow, with Nirvana and Smashing Pumpkins and Soundgarden—but just the same, seeing the rifle strike out and knock him to the road . . .

Her stomach lurched.

The soldiers know what they're doing, she thought. Maybe Corley did something she couldn't see—maybe he struck first. She didn't know. Couldn't tell. From over here, off to the side, she didn't have much of a vantage point, and the media was crowding around the edges, trying to film the conflict as it unfolded. Then she saw the girl.

Shana. Sister to the first sleepwalker.

She was right up there at the front. Camera in her hand.

Capturing the hit on Corley.

Then capturing his fall, too—he tumbled to the ground. Soldiers kicked out, broke his guitar. She heard the sound of it—it was notable, because the song he was singing and strumming ended suddenly in the jangly-tangle of strings and the snap of wood. *Crack.*

All the while, the girl kept capturing it. Pointing her phone, taking shots, even making video, Marcy didn't know. Corley cried out and then was silenced.

Is he dead?

Then a soldier reached for the girl.

A big soldier, broad shoulders and pig-pug nose, reached out and grabbed at Shana's phone with a wide hand. His fingers wrapped tighter around it. The girl struggled. He pulled harder. Then the two of them were lost to Marcy behind a fresh wall of news cameras and reporters.

Uncertainty raged inside Marcy, a brushfire of conflicting feelings. Yes, she believed in law and order. Damn right she was a supporter of the military and its servicemen and servicewomen. But part of the law was a support for the First Amendment. For the freedom to gather and to speak out. That girl—*just* a girl, mean as she was to Marcy—was just taking pictures. Wasn't violent. Wasn't doing something she wasn't supposed to do. Hell, Marcy would argue she was doing *exactly* what she was supposed to do, exercising her freedom of expression in a troubled time.

"To hell with this," Marcy said, and hard-charged into the fray.

MY PHONE!

The soldier sneered at her, yanking on her wrist to bring her close—in one hand he had a set of zip-ties, and with his other he was pulling her closer. She planted her feet and yanked, but she was no match for the man. He reeled her in like a fish, even as the crowd was erupting all around them, soldiers and shepherds locked in battle in the midst of the walkers. Already Nessie was walking on even as Shana tried to escape.

"Come on," the soldier said. "Come on, little girl." Even though he couldn't have been more than a year or two older than she.

Shana bared her teeth like a cornered animal, then fumbled for the phone, thinking, *I'll at least get some snaps of you as you hurt me.* She pointed her lens, and he let go of her wrist without warning. The surprise of sudden freedom made her almost fall over.

But he wasn't done. He grabbed the phone again with a hand and instead of pulling—he *pushed* it. Mashing it into her face before trying to rip it away again.

Her nose throbbed. Her face hurt. She used both hands to wrestle with it. As her head peeled away she looked for Arav, and saw that he was being dragged away by another soldier. He called her name. She tried to yell back but again the cameraphone pushed hard against her mouth, grinding into her teeth, and her cry was cut short.

Then, a new voice—

"Hey!"

Both Shana and the soldier turned to see.

Just as a fist appeared out of thin air like a divine hand, pounding the soldier hard in the jaw. His head spun sideways and he let go of Shana. But he wasn't down for the count. He lurched back up, springing toward whoever hit him—

Which, as it turned out, was Marcy Reyes.

His attack on her was fruitless, though. He came for her and found himself grossly outmatched—she used his energy to let him keep going in one direction as she came up behind him. Next thing Shana knew, Marcy had the zip-tie in her own hand and was fastening it around the soldier's wrists, binding him tight as she shoved him back toward the crowd of his brethren.

Shana stared at Marcy. Jaw slack.

Marcy just nodded at her, then bent down to scoop up the supine body of Pete Corley, plucking him off the road and carrying him away.

Shana was about to yell *thank you* to her, but then gunfire split the air as someone started shooting.

34

ONE BROKEN COOKIE

*New Monmouth University public poll: 46% in favor of Homeland Se-
curity taking over flock operation, 47% against, 7% undecided*
                                                            @AP_Politics
                                            32 replies 352 RTs 787 likes

JULY 3
Mercy General Hospital, Iowa City, Iowa

PETE CORLEY LURCHED UPRIGHT, GASPING FOR AIR LIKE A MAN SURFACING
from deep water. He pawed at whatever had tangled itself around his legs—
which he saw was just a white bedsheet. He blinked. Looked around.

I'm in the hospital, he realized.

He had the gown and everything. No IV drip, though. Pity that. Because
that was how you get the really good drugs.

And gods did he need them. His head was pounding like a kid's kickball
driven again and again against a brick wall, *whumbbb whumbbbb whumbbbb.*
Sound bled in at the edges and at first it was just the teacher from Charlie
Brown, *womp womp bwomp waaaamp,* but then it resolved into actual
words—words from a television screen. He saw a TV in the corner of the
room showing some eldritch horror from the deep rising through bleak blue
waters. A narrator was saying, "The Humboldt squid is an occasional canni-
bal, turning on other sick or injured squids in their own shoal and tearing
them apart with tentacle and beak . . ."

He looked over, realized he wasn't alone.

Another man sat in the bed next to him. An older man, maybe in his
sixties (and Corley tried very hard not to realize that put him closer to this
man's age than he liked). The old fellow was bald but for a few delicate hairs

draped across the desertlike expanse of his liver-spotted scalp. He lay back in his bed, staring at the television, his lips in a sour pucker.

"Where the fuck am I?" Pete said, except it came out more like, *Where-dafugg am I.*

The man shot him a disgruntled look, his lips pursing further.

"Hospital" was his answer. One word. Barked out.

"Yeah, not helpful," Corley said, blinking crust from his eyes and trying to bring some saliva to lips that felt like dry, old pottery. He cleared his throat. "What hospital?"

"Iowa City. Do you mind? I'm trying to watch TV."

"And I'm trying to get my goddamn bearings. When is it?"

"What?"

"Not what. *When. Is. It.* What's the date?"

"What are you, some kind of amnesiac?"

"No, I'm not a—" He growled. "Just tell me the bloody date, mate."

"Issa third."

"Third of what?"

"July, dumb-ass."

Corley stood up. Which was a mistake. He wobbled like a broken lamp. His hand shot out and braced himself against the hospital bed as he fought through the wooziness. What the hell happened? He remembered dancing around, strumming the guitar—then a rifle butt to the head, then he went down. They stepped on his guitar. Kicked his head. That girl took photos . . .

If it was still the third, what had happened since he ended up here? What time was it that they swept over the flock? Five in the afternoon, wasn't it? "What time is it?"

"Just after nine."

He needed to see the news.

"Gimme that remote control."

"I'm watching something."

"Yes, something . . . *disgusting.* What is wrong with you? You're sitting here in the hospital and you're watching a show about . . . squid devouring other squid? I mean, really? That's fucked, mate."

On the TV: "Their eyes flash red when they attack, giving them the nickname 'Red Devils' . . . "

"I like nature programs," the man said. "Besides, I been in here longer than you. Had my gallbladder out. You just had a knock on the head."

"I don't care what happened to you. Give me that remote."

"No!"

"Do you know who I am?" Pete hated to pull that trick. Which was a lie, of course: Ha ha, he *loved* pulling that trick, but he'd never admit it out loud, no way. False humility was just one weapon in his human arsenal.

"Some kind of hotshot."

"Yes. Yes! Some kind of hotshot, indeed. The *hottest* of *shots*. I'm a fucking rock star, *sir*. Now gimme the remote."

The man groused, "That must be why all the local newspeople are outside. Cameras and trucks. You're just causing problems."

Yeah, well, what else is new?

Pete hobbled over, pointed a crooked, condemning finger at the man like he was the Grim Reaper selecting his next soul to snatch from this mortal coil. "You give me that remote, old man, or I will personally hunt down your old rotten gallbladder and stick it back in the slot from whence it fucking came, you hear me?"

"Meh," the man said. He handed over the remote. "No need to resort to violence. Thassa problem with you hotshot types. Always gotta get your way, always gotta—"

But Pete was tuning the old man's droning voice out. He pointed the remote, pulled up the guide, and went to find local news, but ended up with CNN instead. Just as good.

He clicked it on.

And instantly saw his own face.

Onscreen was a photo. A nearly perfect photo, as it were, capturing the exact moment that rifle butt was clocking him in the head. The timing was impeccable. His eyes were pinching shut. His mouth was screwed up in a frozen sneer like he'd just gotten socked by a boxer. You could even see where the rifle butt was wrinkling up the skin of his forehead like a boot rumpling a poorly laid carpet.

Someone was saying, "Gumdropper lead singer, Pete Corley, is seen here, hit in the head by a soldier's rifle—"

The photo onscreen flashed to a newscaster speaking outside a hospital at night. *This* hospital, Pete guessed.

"Corley is said to be in stable condition, having suffered a concussion—"

Just then a doctor came in. A brutish woman with a helmet of red hair and the jowls of an aging basset hound. She smiled brightly. "Mister Corley! I'm glad to see you up—"

"Shh," he hissed at her, then turned back to the TV.

Now, on the TV, they showed the flock.

And by the gods, it was moving along. And shepherds were moving with them. Not a soldier among them. The newscaster's voice played over: "Some say it was the attack on Corley that helped change President Hunt's mind and caused her to reverse the order only hours after committing to it."

Corley pumped a fist. *Yes.*

"Mister Corley, if we could talk about your condition—"

"We *will*," he said, curt and clipped. "But for now, no talky-talky."

"He's a real pain in the ass," the old man in the bed said. "One broken cookie, you ask me."

Corley sat, transfixed.

Some say it was the attack on Corley . . .

. . . that helped change President Hunt's mind . . .

He did it. She reversed the order.

They cut to an interview with a girl—no, *the* girl, the one who took the photo. A name displayed underneath her: SHANA STEWART. It identified her as shepherd, as the sister to the "first sleepwalker," and best of all, the one who took the photo of him taking a rifle butt to the skull.

She was saying, "It was pretty scary, they started shooting in the air, which scared us all pretty good. That gave them the chance to wrangle us up, putting people in cuffs—like, those plastic zip-tie cuffs. Eventually they got me and they . . ." Here she looked upset. "They f . . . they messed up my phone." She held up the phone, the screen spiderwebbed with cracks. "Then just dumped it in my lap like garbage. It still kinda works."

The interviewer said: "But they didn't destroy your photos."

Shana shook her head.

She went on to say that one of the local reporters came up to her as she sat handcuffed on the side of the road, asked if he could see her photos. She said yes, and next thing she knew, they had the iconic photo of Pete getting clocked. She had other photos, too, of him down on the ground—them breaking his guitar, them kicking him. They showed two of those. Pete winced. That looked painful. His pounding brainpan reminded him that he was looking at himself, not at someone else. Celebrity was weird like that, sometimes. He felt distanced from his own image, like he and the person on camera were two different entities. One a shadow reflection, like in a circus mirror, of the other.

The interviewer asked, "What made you want to take those photos?"

"I dunno. I just thought somebody should. And it didn't look like the news cameras could get as close as I was."

"Your sister, Vanessa—"

"Nessie."

"Nessie was the first walker."

"That's right."

"If you could talk to her now, what would you say?"

Shana turned away from the interviewer and looked right in the camera. Steely-eyed, she said: "I'd say, Nessie, nobody is going to hurt you. I'm with you to the end. That's what it means to be a shepherd."

"Oh, she's *good,*" Pete said. He turned the television off and tossed the remote to the old man—who failed to catch it, and the remote went skidding off the bed. "I mean, not as good as me. Obviously."

The doctor finally said, "Can we talk now?"

"I've got a concussion, that's what you're going to tell me."

"I am. Yes. You suffered a mild injury to the brain—"

"Not my first. My first was in Rio, 1985, playing at some . . . festival, and some saucy drunken things threw fruit onto the stage—not panties, but *fruit,* of all things, and my gods, that shit was slippery. Fell, cracked my head on an amplifier. Second was in Tulsa, 1991, I was—" He was about to say, *Really high on cocaine,* but he decided this was not the time. "Whatever, point is, been there, done that, this egg's already cracked. I need to get out of here." *I need to get back to the flock.*

To *my* flock.

"We'd prefer to keep you overnight—"

"No need."

"You need to take care of yourself. No strenuous exercise, no deep concentration—it could worsen the concussion, Mister Corley."

"Too late for me. Already fucked, this brain."

"You had quite a few calls over the last several hours—maybe one of those people will tell you what I'm telling you, that you have to stay in bed."

The old man in the bed said: "Yeah, your phone was making a helluva racket, all kinda beeps and bops."

Pete grabbed the phone. There he saw messages stacking up from his wife, from Landry, from his publicist Mary, even from Elvis. His wife was worried about him, and was pissed.

Her texts read, in a series:

You've gone off the reservation again, haven't you?

Call me, Pete.

Pete, seeing you on TV, what the hell are you up to?

What are you running from now?

Then, having caught up with all the news, her last text, two hours ago: I hope your head is broken open like a coconut, you dick. The kids are worried about you and so am I despite everything. Call me, asshole.

His publicist texted, all caps: CALL ME.

Landry sent him a text that said only: The world was ready for Bowie.

Elvis texted: Well played, jerkoff. This isn't over.

He snapped his fingers at the doctor: "You. I can get a cab out of here right? Or an Uber, a Lyft, something?"

"What? Yes, but I'm not the front desk at a hotel—"

"Good." He shed his robe right there and started kicking around for his clothes. He found them in a drawer and started to hike on his pants. At the shocked doctor's face he waved her off. "Oh, stop. You see this sort of thing all the time, love, don't you? Though maybe not *this* sexy."

"Can I just watch my squid show?" the old man groused.

"All right, I'm out," Pete said. "It's been real, it's been fun, though I wouldn't say it's been *real fun*."

Woozy, his head feeling like a broken fishbowl, he marched out of the hospital room in search of an elevator as the doctor called after him.

35

FIREWORKS ON A
BIRTHDAY CAKE

MARTA VALLEJO-MARTINEZ, REPORTER: You've just come out of the hospital. Why did you come out here to support the sleepwalkers and shepherds and CDC?

PETE CORLEY: You know why, love. I don't need to tell you or your audience, they're all sharp as a stitch.

VALLEJO-MARTINEZ: In your words, if you please?

PETE CORLEY: Oh, you know, sometimes it's in a man to just harden up and do the right thing, isn't it? These people need me! I mean, clearly.

VALLEJO-MARTINEZ: And does this impact the release of the next Gumdropper tour or album?

PETE CORLEY: I should say it does. We'll get to it when we get to it. For now, my head's been rung like a bell, so if you don't mind? My people await the return of their prince.

VALLEJO-MARTINEZ: You heard him, folks. It doesn't look like Pete Corley is going anywhere. This is Marta Vallejo-Martinez, reporting from WBCC, Sioux City, Iowa.

JULY 3
Beacon, Iowa

"I'M A FUCKING ASSHOLE."

Marcy looked over to see if someone was talking to her.

She was. It was the girl. Shana Stewart. Darkness had settled in, the fields of corn rising up on all sides like gently swaying, waving walls, and so

Marcy had not seen her approach. As before, she'd stayed way off to the side, feeling once again that she did not belong.

So the girl's presence was something of a surprise.

"You're not an asshole," Marcy said.

"I am. I'm a real jerk."

"You're not a—" She sighed. "Okay, you were a little bit of a jerk. But you were right, too. I'm just a hanger-on. An impostor, a stowaway."

"Maybe. But way I figure it, we're all stowaways. None of us are supposed to be here because none of them"—she gestured to the flock of walkers—"are supposed to be here, either. That's what tonight was all about. People want us gone. So maybe we need to stick together."

Marcy nodded. "Okay. Are you sure?"

"I'm sure. And I'm sorry. Thanks, by the way. You know. For punching that guy and saving my ass."

"They still got you, though."

"Yeah. Soon as they started shooting, shit kinda fell apart."

"Guns tend to do that."

"I guess."

Marcy wasn't fazed much by gunfire anymore, but she could tell the girl was. Who wouldn't be? "Sucks they broke your phone. But I'm glad you got your photo on TV. That's kinda big."

"Maybe. I hope so. I dunno."

They walked together for a little while. All around was the din of the crowd—the energy was high, lot of folks excitedly chatting about what had gone on. The soldiers had left. Nobody was seriously hurt. The events of the evening were intense, but relatively brief. Everyone was alive and awake despite the night stretching on. Many walked on in the dark, though others illuminated the way, as they did every night, with flashlights and head-lights and the lights of their phones. A few carried torches. People drank beer and toasted with hot dogs bought from a nearby stand a town or two away.

"I guess it's almost the Fourth of July," Shana said.

"That's right, it is."

"Happy Independence Day."

"Thanks. You too. And happy birthday."

Shana paused. "How'd you know it was my birthday?"

Marcy hesitated. She didn't want to tell the girl how she knew, not yet. So all she said was "A little bird told me."

"Oh. Well." She offered a sad smile in the half dark. "Thanks. I'm gonna head back to the flock. You should come over."

"Maybe I will soon."

"Okay. Bye, Marcy."

"Bye, Shana."

She watched the girl head back toward the parade of people.

What she wanted to tell Shana, but dared not, was that she knew about Shana's birthday not because of some so-called little bird.

It was because the girl's sister, Nessie, had told her.

In the CDC trailer, which was presently parked behind the flock by a mile or so, Benji sat back in one of the chairs, quiet and still. Most of the others had gone home. Arav was with the flock. Cassie had gone back to the hotel to take some calls related to Garlin and the fungus. Sadie was here, next to him, her hand on the table atop his.

For a while, they sat in silence. Just breathing. Listening to the nightsong chorus of crickets and katydids.

"That was something," Sadie finally said.

"It was." *Something* did not cover it, of course, but what would? Benji had no words to describe it. He knew only how he felt, which was stripped down, hollowed out, blisteringly tired and yet somehow achingly alive.

"Your plan worked."

"It did."

Somehow, it *really* did.

But at what cost?

Corley was in the hospital. Other shepherds had been hurt, too, by the soldiers. Many were scared, traumatized by gunfire—gunfire that, as it turned out, came from a pistol held in the hand of Dale Weyland, who fired it up at the air to pacify the crowd through fear.

Still. They retained control of the flock. For now. He wondered how long it would be before Hunt fell prey again to politics. The political season was already a venomous one. And Hunt was caught between the Scylla and Charybdis—the crushing rock and the whirlpool—of taking some action versus taking none at all. In politics you couldn't please everybody, but you still had to do the calculus to please *most* of everybody, or you didn't get the votes. Too few votes meant Ed Creel would become president.

At that, Benji shuddered.

Sadie looked poised to say more, but then a knock came on the trailer door. Whoever it was did not wait to be summoned.

Dale Weyland stepped through the door.

"Dale," Benji said.

"You did it," the man said, waltzing in with his chest puffed out, his chin up, his tongue shoved into the pocket of his cheek. He offered a soft golf clap as he entered. "Well played."

"It's not like that," Sadie said.

Benji offered a wry, insincere entreaty: "As you've said, we're on the same side. Neither of us are the enemy."

"Yeah," Dale answered, sniffing loudly like a bull ready to charge. "I'm not so sure about that anymore. I tried to do the right thing but you—you tricky bastard. That thing with Corley, huh." He kissed his fingers like a chef after a particularly delectable meal. "Genius. Truly, I mean that." He may have meant it, but he sounded pissed. "You manipulative prick, you have no idea what you've done, do you?"

"I kept these people out of military control. I ensured that the shepherds could remain with their friends and their families. It's a shame you don't see it that way."

"I'll tell you what I see, Doctor Ray: I see a weapon walking free. Like a dirty bomb in a wheeled suitcase rolling down a hill toward a busy intersection, and here I am, the only sonofabitch waving his hands and trying to warn everybody. But then people like *you* come along and ask everybody to remain calm, stay where you are, don't make any sudden moves. And I just see that bomb rolling closer and closer and closer."

"Now you know how I felt with Longacre," Benji said.

"Fuck you and fuck Longacre. Those people are a bomb."

"They're not a bomb. They're not a weapon."

"Do you know that? For sure?"

Benji did not answer that. Because honestly, he didn't.

Dale went on:

"Consider this my prophetic warning to you, Doctor Ray—there will come a day, maybe tomorrow, maybe a week from now, maybe months from now if this thing is still rolling, that you'll regret sending us away. Having the walkers under military control isn't just about protecting the people outside the flock. It's about protecting the flock itself. People out there don't like them. They distrust them. They want them gone. When that wave comes crashing down on your beach, you'll wish out loud I was still here."

"You're leaving us, then?"

"Uh-huh. I am. I don't want a part of this circus anymore."

"They're pulling you off the job," Benji said. "Aren't they?"

"Again: Fuck you."

"You will be missed," Benji said, doing his best to ladle as much sarcasm atop those four words as he could.

"Fuck you, fuck you, fuck you, Benjamin."

"Happy Independence Day, Dale."

The man stormed out.

Sadie looked over at Benji. "You're very civil."

"I know, I should be meaner."

"No, I mean it as a compliment. Most people would go toe-to-toe with a gorilla like Dale Weyland and they'd just end up covered in monkeyshit." She winced. "Sorry, *ape*shit, to be precise. Point is, you stay levelheaded. You keep the fight on your turf."

"I wanted to punch him."

"And the fact you didn't says more about you than it does about him. Besides, one suspects his own *mother* wants to punch him." She lowered her voice. "Frankly, she probably *did* punch him, which is why he's such a massive jerk."

He squeezed her hand.

"I'm proud of you," she said. "Proud to know you. Proud to . . . be with you, if that's what this is."

"It is," he said. "And I'm proud to know you, too." He sighed. "We have a lot ahead of us. We've only just begun to crack this thing, I fear."

"Don't worry about that right now. Worry about what you have in front of you."

"What I have in front of me is you."

She grinned, her eyes twinkling. "Like I said. Now let's go find a hotel room with a comfy bed and canoodle until we pass out."

"Deal."

SHE DIDN'T WANT TO DO it but she had to do it.

Shana threw open the door to the RV and entered with the darkness and clamor of a storm front. Her father, sitting in the driver's seat as was his way, startled. "Shana. You're okay. I'd get up, but I'm, you know." He gave a look down at the steering wheel. The vehicle plodded along at a couple of miles an hour.

"You want a hug? Then pull over and hug me." She didn't give him a chance to answer. "But you won't, because that would require the bare minimum from you, wouldn't it?"

"Shana, I don't understand what this is about."

"Really? *Really?* No idea, huh?"

He sighed. "I know you're mad that I wasn't out there with you, but the army men, they made me pull over to the side of the road. I couldn't get out, couldn't go anywhere—"

"And what happened after that? They've been gone for hours. Did you come out and see if I was okay?"

"I saw you on the news, I have my phone—you seemed busy—but wow, you got to stand next to Pete Corley! That's really something."

"Where *are* you?"

He laughed a little like it was a joke. "Honey, sweetheart, I'm right here—"

"No, I mean, *where are you?* Why are you here? What is the fucking point of your presence if you're not *actually present?* You came along on this ride, and why? You don't go out to be with Nessie. You don't go out to be with me. You're here, but you're not *here.*"

A look of consternation crossed his face. This was the start to his anger—anger that for him was slow to rouse, but when it hit, it hit hard. "Shana, that's not fair and you know it. I spent a lot of money on this RV and it's given you a place to rest your head every night—I have to keep this thing moving, and I have to keep paying for gas. Strangers are keeping our farm afloat. My youngest baby is . . . is sick, my other daughter hates me, my wife up and left—and maybe, somehow, was responsible for making Nessie sick somehow—"

"Don't," she cautioned. "*Don't.* Don't put this on me. Or on Nessie. Or even on Mom—"

"Your mother leaving . . . cratered me, Shana."

"It cratered us *all,* Dad. It wasn't just *you.* It hit us worse. You know why? Because sometimes married people, they grow apart. A husband is fucking around on his wife, a wife is done with her husband, whatever." Tears burned at her eyes. "But they're *not* supposed to be done with their children. They're not supposed to just . . . up and leave."

"She left us all, I know."

"And maybe she left you because of all this. Because you're not available. You've always got something, don't you? I had to be Nessie's parent because you couldn't carry the weight. Who makes her breakfast and lunch every morning? Me. Who makes sure she's not up too late with some weird experiment or watching *Planet Earth* for the three hundredth time or practicing some new watercolor bullshit—it's me, I'm her parent while you're . . . I don't even know what you're doing."

"Shana, watch it."

"You've got work. The farm. The cows. The market. You've got to fix that tractor or that barn door, oh, no, can't help Nessie with her homework, can't go with Mom to the store, can't *be there* when people *need your ass to be there*."

"You don't know what it's like, you don't *get* to say these things—you're just a kid, Shana, who doesn't know a goddamn thing about life and work—"

"Fuck you!" she screamed, her voice run ragged, as if drawn over broken wood, collecting splinters that dug deep. "You don't know a goddamn thing about what it's like to live with you. You know what, though? You say you're here to give me a place to sleep? Let me stomp that obligation of yours flat into the ground, *Dad*. I'm done." With that, she started gathering up her meager things and tossing them into the backpack she already carried with her. "I don't need you. I'll sleep elsewhere."

"Shana. You listen to me—you stop this right now. I demand that you quit doing this—you're still my daughter and still a kid and—"

"I'm not a kid. I'm an adult, dipshit." She saw the realization dawn on his face. "You didn't even know I turned eighteen today. I *knew* it."

Silence. He blinked. His lips worked soundlessly like the mouth of a dying fish.

"Your birthday is today," he said, quiet, looking over his shoulder as the RV crawled along the road.

"That's right. And you *forgot*."

That last word, spoken like the thrust of a stabbing knife.

"I . . . everything's been so crazy—"

"The correct response is, I'm sorry, Shana, happy birthday."

"Of course, yeah, I'm sorry—"

He didn't get to finish that statement.

The door to the RV popped open, and Pete Corley stepped in. His body—like a tangle of metal coat hangers all caught on one another—jangled its way inside. He looked rough and raw. It only made the manic grin on his face all the stranger.

Behind him, a crowd was following him. He gave them a wave and yelled to them, "Thanks, yeah, great! Excellent, found it, thank you, a thousand times, thanks. Just keep an eye on those boxes, will you?" Shana caught a glimpse of, as he said, a small teetering tower of boxes. He called back, "They're a very important surprise. Okay? Okay, good." With the back of his heel he kicked the door shut, *wham*.

Shana stared, irritated.

Her father stared, awestruck.

Pete snapped his bony fingers. "Am I interrupting something?"

"Yes," Shana said.

"No," her father said at the same time.

The rock star shrugged. "Uh-*huh*. Well, whatfuckingever. Hello! Hi. I'm Pete Corley, but you probably already know that unless you've been living in a Russian gulag for the last thirty-plus years."

"I have all your albums," her dad said, in awe. "Bootlegs, too."

"Oh, a fan," Pete said, the sour look on his face betraying his enthusiasm as entirely false. "How nice. And *you*—" He pointed to Shana. "I've been looking for you. You were smart. You saw that the cameras couldn't get close and there you were, snapping pictures as that soldier kicked my bony ass. You were the architect of that artistry—you were like those *gospel* fellows who followed Jesus around. It's because of you I got the attention I deserved— that, ahh, the whole *situation* got the attention it deserved. Because of you and I together, this shitshow ended." Pete winked at her, gave her some finger-guns, pow pow. "I owe you one."

"You owe me one new phone."

"A new phone," he said. "Done."

Her heart skipped a couple of beats. "Wait, what?"

"I'll replace your phone and I'll do you one better: I'll get you a proper bloody camera. Something real-deal with all the fiddly bits—lenses and . . . tubes and whatever it comes with. Name it."

The words spilled out of her head like vomit from a drunk man's mouth: "Canon EOS 5D thirty-megapixel DSLR and a Canon telephoto zoom lens with a seventy- to two-hundred-millimeter focal length."

"To be honest," he said, wincing, "ennnh, I won't remember any of that, so howzabout I give you the money to go buy it. And if you want to instead just buy beer and drugs with it, I won't tell anybody—" He winced even harder. "Wait, you're the girl's father, so I'll definitely tell you, I'm sure? Again, whatever. It'll all come out in the wash, as my mother used to say."

"I . . ."

But Pete didn't let her get a breath in. He then pointed to her dad.

"What's your name?"

"Charlie. Charlie Stewart."

"Mister Stewart, I am in *dire* need of a place to stay. May I crash here in your . . . recreational vehicle, at least until I summon my own digs?"

"Of course, absolutely, does that mean—are you coming with us?"

"With the flock? Of course. I think I've earned my Shepherd Badge."

A nasty thought occurred to Shana. *You're just here for the attention.* She'd thrown poor Marcy under the bus for exactly what Pete was doing right now. *He* wasn't a real shepherd. *He* didn't have anybody. Then again, he *did* help them. Maybe more than any of them could have, individually . . . she idly wondered if she should be giving Pete Corley the benefit of the doubt, but she just hated him so bad. He was an attention whore. A gangly drug-fed man-baby.

No wonder her father adored him.

Grr.

"You can take my bed," Shana said, forcing a mask of unbridled sweetness to the front of her skull. "I'm sleeping elsewhere."

"Shana," her father said in a low voice, surely trying to stop her from ruining this precious moment for him. "C'mon—"

"No, no," she said, waving him off. "You two bunk up, braid each other's hair, whatever." To Corley she said, "I'll come back for that cash."

"Excellent. Don't go far, though!"

"Why?"

He clacked his teeth together in another frantic smirk. "Because you don't want to miss the fireworks."

As it turned out, Pete Corley meant *real-deal* fireworks.

Corley chose his launch point to be the top of Charlie Stewart's RV. He rode it like the Beast that it was, standing astride the vehicle as he launched rocket after rocket. The man did his rock-star schtick with each—though he had no instrument, he pretended to wail on a guitar every time he sent one up into the open black. His arms spun and pinwheeled. He stuck his tongue out. Threw up the devil's horns. The sky lit up in blossoms of fire—red, orange, blue, purple. Streaks of light staining the dark.

Booming, popping, crackling.

Shana used to love fireworks. She wanted to love these. But every time they went up, she couldn't help but clench up. They made her think of the gunfire from earlier. They made her think of the man with the gun at the parade, and even the gun in her own bag.

So, to soothe herself, she went through the crowd. She said hi to people like Aliya and Mia. Others, people she didn't know, shepherds and camerapeople and some of the CDC techs who had little to do, all said hi to her, like they knew her. She supposed maybe now they did.

Eventually, she found who she was looking for.

Arav was standing alone, off to the side, staring up. The fireworks reflected in his eyeglasses. He wore a face of wonder. One she wished she mirrored.

When he saw her coming, he opened his mouth to say hi.

She didn't let him.

She covered his mouth with hers.

Then she took his hand and led him away, into the dark, into the field. Through the rows of corn till there was no light for either of them.

36

THE SINNER'S HOUR

Arctic Slammed with Record Temperatures

By Dave Geller, Associated Press

The data is in, and this past winter in the Arctic featured nearly no winter at all. Temperatures rose to an average of 12 degrees warmer than usual, with sea ice dropping to a record low. Scientists say the heat wave was unprecedented, and likely contributed to a number of extreme weather events in the past six months, including a series of so-called bomb cyclones that devastated New England . . .

JULY 4
Burnsville, Indiana

MATTHEW'S MOTHER HAD A SAYING, ONE HE FOUND USUALLY TRUE: *ANYTHING that happens after midnight is bad news.* He didn't buy that as a young man, of course: Though he never drank and never smoked, he still liked to romanticize the night. Moon in the sky, stars out, the wide-open expanse of nothing: It made him feel free and alive as the daytime never did. Just the same, his pastor at the time—Pastor Gil Hycheck, an apple-cheeked man with a soft voice and a nice guitar with a pearl inlay—put it more plainly: *Night is when the devils are out, Matthew. They hide where you can't see. They hide in long shadows and in the black sky above. And when you're not looking, they learn to hide in you, too.*

So when he came home at one o'clock in the morning and found Autumn sitting at the kitchen table, he knew that what his mother said was true. Nothing good happened after midnight. And soon he'd come to suspect that what Pastor Gil said was true, too.

"Bo's asleep," she said, soon as he came in.

He nodded. He was still a little fuzzy from the party at Ozark's. Not drunk, he told himself. A little buzzy. But legal to drive, he was sure of it.

And the absurd thought hit him: *Even if not, I had God on my side—the Lord surely would take the wheel if I could not.* It was a terrible thought, and one that went against everything he believed about his role in this world: God, he knew, helped those who helped themselves. But wasn't God also there to catch you if you fell? He shook the thoughts out of his head, like a horse tail waving away a cloud of flies.

He sat down. "You have fun at the party?"

"It was fine," she said.

"I saw that—" *Ozark gave you something,* he was about to say, but he did not have to finish his thought. She pulled something out from underneath the table. It was a bottle of pills.

"It's Xanax," she said.

"Oh. I don't—I don't understand."

"Ozark gave them to me."

"Why?"

"He said he thought I looked tense."

"Did you? Look tense?"

She offered a stale laugh. "I don't know, Matt. I expect maybe I did because I sure didn't want to be there. But what probably happened was that he knew I've been depressed and anxious."

"How would he know that? You don't think I told him—"

"No," she said, shaking her head. "I know you're too embarrassed by it to go telling him that. It disappoints you too much. Bo probably said something, that's how he knew."

"Bo shouldn't be saying those things to him."

"That's your takeaway?"

"I don't follow you."

"Ozark Stover gave me pills, Matthew. Xanax. Not exactly heroin, maybe, but sure as hell not aspirin."

Matthew sighed. His innards felt like the bottom of a cardboard box that had gotten wet: soaking through and falling apart. "I'm sure Ozark was just trying to be nice."

"He told me there was more when I needed it."

"That's—again, I expect he was just trying to be nice." He had cottonmouth now. His tongue and teeth felt dry as a sunbaked bone. "I'll tell him you're not going to take them."

He reached across the table for the pills.

Autumn yanked them away and held them close.

"Oh, I'm taking them," she said.

"What?"

Now she slid something else across the table. A paper. Mail of some kind. He snatched it up and stared at it, trying to parse its contents—

It was an overdue bill.

No, it was a notice of cancellation after an overdue bill.

Health insurance. Oh no.

"I went to the doctor the other day. Our insurance was canceled. I found that on your desk. You forgot to pay it. Not once. But a bunch of times. I guess you ignored it given all this . . . attention you're getting now. Whatever." She sniffed. "Besides, it's not like you wanted me to get a new prescription anyway. Prayer is your medicine, after all. Prayer will banish an infection, exorcise depression, help regrow a lost limb with the power of God's own sacred sorcery. Right?"

"You're mischaracterizing my opinion," he said, though that word *mischaracterizing* was a whole lot harder to say than he expected. *Maybe I am a little buzzy, still.* "I believe in science. I believe in using medicine to fight disease, I'm not some kook, I just don't know that depression is always the disease people make it out to be—"

"Doesn't matter. I have pills and I will take them. And if I need more, I'll ask Mister Stover to give me some."

"You shouldn't take those."

"Why?"

"I . . . you don't know where they came from. Maybe they're from Canada or somewhere."

She faked a horror-movie shudder. "Oh no, the untamed wilds of third-world-country Canada. Who knows, maybe these pills are just beaver pelts and maple syrup." Autumn rolled her eyes. She was mean right now. He didn't like it. She kept on, too: "Biggest question you should be asking yourself, Matt, is where is he getting these pills, and why is he just giving them out? And even then, are you going to let him keep doing it?"

"No, of course not."

"So you'll say something to him."

"I will." He nodded vigorously, not even sure it was the right answer— did she want him to fight this?

"You'd risk everything for that? He's given you a lot in these last few weeks. You're his little preacher baby, he's holding you up like you're the cub in *The Lion King*. Will you bite the hand that feeds you?"

"I . . ."

His answer dissolved on his tongue like bitter medicine.

"That's what I thought. Now if you'll excuse me," she said, standing up, "I'm going to go take one of these and go to sleep."

Autumn rattled the pill bottle. Her smile to him was pinched and cold. He watched her leave, unsure of what to do or where to go from here. He told himself he'd say something to Ozark about this. He *promised* himself. And a man wouldn't break a promise to himself, would he?

37

BUGS, BATS, STARS, HEARTS

Take no pride in the body,
It will soon be mingling with the dust.
This life is like the sporting of sparrows,
It will end with the onset of night.

—Mirabai, "O My Mind"

JULY 4
Beacon, Iowa

THE FACT THAT THERE WAS NOTHING ROMANTIC ABOUT IT MADE IT SOMEHOW more romantic, Shana thought. There was nothing manufactured. Nothing forced. Nothing except the desire between them, the ground below them, the night above. She led him out through the corn and they lay down between the rows—on the rough and uneven ground, with the bugs singing all around and the bats stitching the stars—and there they did the deed. Even now in memory it was all about the sensation of it: unforced exhales, hands roaming under clothes, the heat of the moment coupled with the chill of the night. She on top of him. Wind in her hair. Then for a while after they just lay there, her head on his chest, against his breastbone, his heart beating through the rush of blood in her ears. They talked for hours when it was done.

Eventually she asked him something that seemed improper, that she feared would puncture the mood, but she couldn't hold it back. It burst up out of her:

"You think it was really my mom who emailed Nessie?"

"I don't know," he said. "I'm not privy to what's going on there—but it doesn't add up. Why would she do that?"

"No idea. Then again, I don't know why she would leave us in the first place."

"How'd she do it?" he asked. "Leave, I mean."

"We were in the store and she just . . . went out the front."

"And never came back?"

"Never came back. Never contacted us. Nothing."

"I'm sure it wasn't her."

He said it, but she could hear that doubt in his voice. It was a doubt she shared. On the one hand, it didn't add up. Mom was troubled sometimes, though she hid it pretty well. Even so, she didn't seem to . . . *hate* her kids. On the other hand, she also was never really that close to her daughters, either. Always felt like she was keeping them at arm's length. Like they weren't even hers to begin with—like she inherited them, as if she were maybe just their stepmother instead of their real bona fide mom.

"Are we going to be okay?" she asked Arav.

"You and me?"

"No, I think we're gonna be just fine." She made a happy sound and slid her hand up under his shirt, across the flat expanse of his stomach. "I mean like, all of us. This whole group. The flock, the shepherds, all of us. The whole damn world, I dunno."

"Yeah. I do."

She heard no doubt in his voice that time. It gave her sudden, inexorable comfort. A warmth of hope bloomed inside her. "Good."

She kissed his cheek.

He kissed her lips.

Overhead, the sky slowly went from dark to dim as the sun sent ahead the promise—or the threat—of a new day.

INTERLUDE

DARIA STEWART AND THE
MEDICINAL DOSE

TWO YEARS AGO
Giant Eagle grocery store, Maker's Bell, Pennsylvania

DARIA STEWART HAD A BOTTLE OF PILLS AND A PHONE AND WAS HIDING NEAR a decommissioned meat freezer. They were doing work on the grocery store, upgrading it—putting in new freezers, new flooring, new self-checkouts, anything to get them up to last century's standards if not those of the current era. Nobody was here in this part. It was empty. The cameras couldn't see her, either, she was pretty sure.

She was alone and on the phone.

It rang. She waited, staring down at the pills. The bottle said Ambien, and it was, but it also had other pills in there: trazodone, Advil, Zantac. Ambien alone was not enough to shoulder the burden of killing her, but throw in the others, it was possible. Maybe. *A real party,* she thought, grimly.

Not that she was going to do it.

Maybe she was, maybe she wasn't. This moment came once every few months, and the fulcrum always swung the other way. The living way, the persevering way. The *surviving* way.

With every ring of the phone, a new thought perforated the silence in her mind: *I want to die. I'm a bad mom. I'm a bad wife. I want to die.* Even now, her husband and her children were in the store. They thought she was off looking for—what did she tell them? Yogurts. The ones she liked so much. Noosa brand. Soon they'd figure it out. And they'd come looking.

As it always did, her brain replayed all her poor choices and all her wasted potential. Could've been a singer, wasn't. Could've been a model, wasn't. Could've been a better wife, or not Charlie's wife at all, but here she was. Remember that time she got drunk at a firehouse wedding reception and told the bride that the bridesmaids' dresses made the bridesmaids all look like boiled hot dogs? She remembered. The bride probably didn't, and if she did, the woman probably chalked it up as a funny story she could tell. But Daria was haunted by it. Every day she thought about it. That and all the other stupid things she had said and done just by being her.

I want to die.

I don't want to die.

Ring, ring, ring.

Finally, someone answered. A man with a soft, kind voice.

"Hello, how may I help you?"

They never started off with, *This is the suicide prevention hotline.* She liked that they didn't. It made her feel like she was calling an old friend, a friend who had forgotten her, someone who would be her compass while sailing on this mad storm-swept sea of her own utterly fucked emotions.

"I'm in a grocery store and I have a bottle of—" she started to say, but then the line clicked a few times. Loud clicks, not like something tapping against the phone but something deeper. Something in the phone system.

A different voice, a woman's voice said:

"Hello, how may I help you?"

Daria flinched. Even this tiny *fluctuation* made her feel altogether more fragile—like she could feel the cracks spreading across her porcelain.

Persevere, she told herself.

Impatient this time, she hurriedly said: "I'm in a store with a bottle of pills and I'm thinking of swallowing them all."

A pause.

"You would qualify yourself as suicidal?" the woman asked.

That wasn't the script. Daria knew the script. She'd spoken to the hotline dozens of times, now. They were always gentler, teasing out the problem, giving Daria a reason to talk it out before finally making referrals, recommendations, and affirmations.

This was different. More forthright.

She didn't hate it.

"I would," Daria said, her voice trembling. Her hand shook, too, and the pills danced against one another and their bottle.

"Is this an isolated incident or a persistent one?"

She almost lied and said isolated. But truth won out.

"Persistent."

"We can help you," the woman said.

"How?"

"We have a location near you."

She hesitated. "How do you know where I am?"

"You're at the Giant Eagle grocery store on Old Bethlehem Road."

"I didn't tell you that."

Pause. "We can help you. If you want it."

Daria swallowed a hard lump in her throat. She looked at the pills, then up around the edge of the freezer case. She saw the grocery store employee walking past, about ten feet away. The man, doughy around the middle and bald on top, froze when he saw her. *Keep walking, keep walking, keep walking, just leave me to this call, leave me to die.* He must've heard the thoughts in her head, because all he did was give her a nervous smile and then walk on.

"You're not the suicide prevention line," she said.

"No," the woman answered. Plainly spoken, clear as a fork tapping against a Champagne glass. "This is not that. But we can help you."

Daria blinked. She pocketed the pills.

"Just tell me where to go."

The woman on the other line gave her an address.

That's when Daria Stewart stood up and walked out through the store, praying the whole time that Charlie and the girls didn't see her leaving.

She walked a mile, down to the bank, then called a cab.

CAB TOOK AN HOUR TO show. That, the price of living in a small town. She sat on a bench near the ATM, under a sad little oak tree whose roots were prying apart the curb.

The address was farther away than they made it out to be: an address in Bloomsburg, north of the university. An hour's drive. The cabbie, a skinny white guy with meth sores on his cheeks like potholes in a bad road, bristled at having to take her that far, but she told him the tip would be good, and it was, because in an uncharacteristic fit of hope, she said, "Here's your tip," and gave him the whole bottle of pills she'd been carrying.

The address was a small, nondescript office building.

No signs except for FOR RENT on a couple windows.

Dandelions grew up through broken sidewalks. Poison ivy snaked up the building in the slow-motion process of pulling the building apart.

She pressed a button by the door.

Someone buzzed her inside.

TWO PEOPLE, ONE MAN AND one woman, sat across from her at a folding table. The rest of the office was empty. No desks, no chairs, no computers. No cubicles stood erected, though the carpets showed their imprints—the ghost of cubicles past.

The woman there wore copper hair, cherry lipstick, a red pantsuit. Like if the Devil sold Mary Kay, choosing to go with blood red instead of berry pink. The man was far more muted: a humble gray suit, a modest blue tie. A well-trimmed mustache hung out underneath a nose whose nostril hairs were not well trimmed. He was older. The woman was younger. He said his name was Bill. She said her name was Moira.

Both watched Daria sign paper after paper.

Papers that she chose not to read.

Why bother?

As she signed the last, she gave them a hasty straightening before sliding them back across. "I still don't understand what this is," she said.

"And yet," the woman answered, "you still signed."

"I need help." *At any cost,* she thought. If she didn't get help somehow, her own children would find her dead in a bathtub one of these days. Or dead at the grocery store. *Cleanup on Aisle Six.*

The woman was cold. The man, less so. He had warm eyes and she half expected his mustache to waggle back and forth on its own, like it was a puppet that danced on his lip. "As Moira here said to you on the phone, we're here to help. But you need to understand, this is experimental."

"This doesn't seem legal."

"Does that bother you?" Moira asked.

"I guess."

"*And yet* you signed the papers," Moira said again.

"No one is helping me. I have to try something, because I don't know how long . . ." She shook her head suddenly, as if to disagree with herself. "I'm wrong. Not no one. Not exactly. I have meds, but they're not enough. My husband is . . . he wants to help but doesn't understand. My children . . ." *Are kept at a distance so they don't catch whatever it is I have.* Even though she knew what she had was depression and it was not something you "caught," it still felt . . . toxic. Like she was coated in a poison and anytime she hugged them it might get on them. "I want to be better for them."

"You should want to be better for yourself, too," Bill said. "And maybe we can make you better. Better in a lot of ways."

"I don't follow."

Bill reached down under the table and pulled up a most unexpected item: It was a drinking cup. Styrofoam. A bendy-straw stuck out the top of it like the periscope of a submarine.

"We're going to want you to drink this," he said.

"What is it?"

It was Moira who said, "That is proprietary information."

"Who are you guys?" Daria asked. "Those papers said Firesight, but I don't know who or what that is. Are you a pharmaceutical company?"

"Medtech. Medical technology," Bill said, smiling.

"What's in the drink?"

"It's a shake. Like a milkshake. This one is chocolate-flavored."

"Is it medicine? Like . . . one of those barium drinks?"

Moira again: "We can't tell you that."

"What will it do to me?"

"In a general sense," Bill answered, "it will improve you."

"Improve me how?"

"We can't tell you that," Moira repeated, more firmly this time. As if a warning.

"I . . ." Daria felt a sudden lightning storm of anxiety roll through her. This was bad news. She knew it in her bones. That was the bite in the ass about being so depressed you wanted to die: Your judgment went so far out the window, it was already pancaked on the pavement. She stood up, almost knocking the chair over behind her. "I don't feel right about any of this. I'm going to go home now. Thank you for your time."

She marched toward the door.

Behind her, the two remained seated.

Moira called after in a raised voice: "You came. You signed the papers. You're desperate for a change, Daria."

Bill, in a softer, more fatherly tone, spoke, and when he did, Daria paused at the door, hand out, never quite opening it: "Mrs. Stewart. You seem a woman at a crossroads. One way goes back to where you came from, and it seems to me where you came from was not an ideal place. It is a place where you will find yourself truly dead or just dead inside. The other way leads to something, something that is surely better. It's experimental, this treatment, but we're optimistic. What we have is not medicine, not precisely, but just the same we view disease and disability not as a thing of shame, but simply an error to fix. Not an error that's your fault, it's just that you were born ten feet behind the starting line. We want to help change that. We want to repair your errors. We want to help you live longer, be happier, become the best version of yourself that exists. We think that best version of you is inside right now. Waiting to come out. We want to help it come out. Will you let us?"

"You signed the papers," Moira said again.

Daria reached for the doorknob.

It was cool in her hand. She pressed her head against the metal windowless door. In her mind she pictured Nessie, Shana, even Charlie.

"Okay," she said.

She turned around, walked back, and reached for the drink.

Bill pulled it away. "Not yet, Mrs. Stewart. We have a room set up for you. If you'll come this way?"

PART FOUR

THE SIGNAL AND
THE SICKNESS

38

THE FIRST LITTLE BETRAYAL

The number is 423.

@WalkerCountBot
78 replies 303 RTs 505 likes

JULY 11
Outside Broken Bow, Nebraska

IT'S FLAT OUT HERE, MARCY THOUGHT. THE HILLS DIDN'T LOOK LIKE HILLS—they looked like slightly disturbed bedsheets. The horizon was a flat line and the road that took them to it was a long straight farm road, barely paved. In the distance, tall white turbines chopped the wind for electricity.

A moment came in which she was thankful she could even parse this information without the pain of migraines starting in her skull and shooting through her body like miserable lightning. Being with the flock had changed her. Clarified her. Her freedom from that anguish had not yet grown old, and she suspected it never would.

The walkers were now over four hundred strong, Marcy had heard—they picked up more than usual as they passed by Iowa City, Des Moines, and Omaha. As if something was compensating.

Maybe God. Maybe the angels. Or whatever sacred, special force governed the flock. Marcy believed they were different, that they were in fact sanctified by some outside cosmic presence. Her relationship with the flock had only deepened, though nobody else really knew that, obviously. She could not only see the glow of the sleepwalkers but *hear* it, too—sometimes it manifested as some strange song like the distant *tink-tink-tink* of wind chimes. Other times she could hear the individual walkers themselves: Just this morning, she heard the voice of Steve Schwartz, once an orthopedic surgeon out of Cedar Rapids, now one of the sleepwalkers. Though his face was flat and his eyes were lifeless, she heard him thinking very clearly, for one moment, about *cheeseburgers,* of all things. He wanted a cheeseburger at 9 A.M.

And as a result, so did she.

So she planted that bug in the ear of one of the runners. The shepherds had a pretty good system going now, assigning runners daily to go pick up meals and other essentials a few times a day—they went in shifts, having to get enough food for the swelling ranks of shepherds, who now numbered as many as the walkers, maybe more. It was a challenge to make sure everyone was covered, of course, and some shepherds didn't want or need to be a part of the daily pickups and were happily self-sufficient in one of the few dozen recreational vehicles that rumbled along the front and back of the flock like sleepy buffalo. Up until a week ago, too, it was difficult to get money for everything—a lot of shepherds were now out of work, so they'd lost their income. Some had savings to drain, but a lot of them were like most Americans, with little to no money saved.

With the arrival of the rock star and after the clash with the army, though, things really changed. Someone started a GoFundMe page for the shepherds, which gave a steady flow of cash. Others, too, would deliver donations to the front of the flock—snacks, meals, clothing, toys for some of the shepherd children, dog food for the shepherd pack, and so on.

American sentiment had turned regarding the sleepwalkers. At least, for some. The walkers were a cause to support, an underdog, a mass of victims whose very presence created more victims—and heroes—in the shepherds themselves. Thing was, in politics, every movement had an equal and opposite movement, didn't it? Others dug their feet in harder, demanding justice and retribution for whoever "attacked" America—some far-right bastards wanted the walkers rounded up. One of Ed Creel's candidacy advisers reportedly said, "Put 'em in camps, march them into cages or holes dug in the ground, and if they pop like zits, they pop like zits. And if any of those so-called shepherds steps in our way, we'll shoot 'em like dogs."

Initially, when called on it, he denied it.

Until someone produced the tape. Then the adviser owned it.

Ed Creel's poll numbers went *up* among Republicans, after that.

It made her worry. Marcy wasn't one for politics—she was that most lamentable of creatures, a political moderate. But she could smell the fire on the wind. Something was coming. A sickened part of her wondered if the flock itself was a dividing line, one that would mark the territory between two sides in a civil war. That, surely, was just a paranoid fantasy.

Wasn't it?

She just wanted to bask in the glow of the flock.

And in her own freedom from pain.

Even with her eyes closed, she could feel it. The throb-and-release of the glow. The warm sound. The tide of light.

When she opened her eyes again, someone was standing in front of her. It was the woman, Sadie Something-or-Other. She wore a puzzled expression—whatever the puzzle was that plagued her, it was not a frustration, exactly, but the look on her face belied a kind of intense curiosity. "Marcy Reyes?" Sadie asked.

"That's me," Marcy said, somewhat warily.

"Can we go somewhere?" Sadie asked. "To talk."

"You're not going to send me away, are you?"

In a chipper tone, Sadie said: "I'd do *no* such thing."

"Promise?"

"Cross my heart, needle in my eye, all that."

"Okay," Marcy said.

"You're a little famous," Sadie said.

The two of them walked ahead of the flock, off the road, in the grass. Honeybees buzzed between meager patches of wildflowers. In the distance, those wind turbines chopped air with a *whoosh, whoosh, whoosh.*

Marcy was careful that they were still near the glow. But even here, this far away from it, she could feel a . . . twinge. Like a thinning tether—the farther she went, the thinner it got, stretched like a piece of gum until it about snapped. And when it snapped, she feared her pain and confusion would return with a vengeance.

"Not Pete Corley famous," Marcy said.

Sadie smirked. "Not many are."

"Why did you want to talk to me? Did Doctor Ray send you?"

"Benji?" She laughed a little—if Marcy didn't know better, she'd say it was a nervous laugh. But Sadie and Benjamin were . . . together, weren't they? Far as Marcy had observed, they were. Which wasn't unusual. Shepherds did a lot of hooking up out here. "No, I'm not here on his behalf, but here because of something he said to me."

"Oh?"

"He said you experience the flock as a kind of . . . glow."

Marcy kicked at some grass. "That's right."

"I'm just trying to figure out why."

"I've thought a lot about that."

"And what answer have you come to?"

"That it doesn't matter." Marcy saw that the other woman didn't like that answer, so she explained: "I mean, it could be that I'm just delusional, right? Some whackadoo. Could be that my head got busted up so bad, I see things and hear things that aren't there. Could be that they're angels or spirits sent by God, or *a* god, or a whole pantheon of gods. I guess I settle on that one most, maybe because it makes me feel good, to think there's something . . . out there. Something that isn't me, watching over us."

"Tell me about the glow. What does it look like?"

"It's a . . . a bright, shining light around them. Like a halo, but not like you think about, not the Frisbee above their heads, but a proper . . ." She used her hands to demonstrate a whole-body radiance, to shape it like you would clay. "Glow." She stiffened. "I'm not making much sense. I don't have great words. I'm not a big talker, I know."

A young man, a shepherd, buzzed by on a little moped, a couple of bags stuffed in the back basket. He waved as he passed, even though Marcy didn't know his name. The shepherds now had a life of their own like that. An economy, an ecosystem, buzzing around like the bees on the flowers.

Sadie switched gears, pointing to her own face, but in a way to indicate Marcy's—as if to say, *You have some food schmutz here.* "Mind if I ask what happened?"

She meant the scarring, obviously—the puckered fissure that ran across Marcy's scalp, around her ear, to the top of her jaw.

"Got beaten up. Head pulped like a weeks-old Halloween pumpkin." She sighed. The memory didn't trigger anything in her, didn't upset her. It felt more like an ugly burden than anything else—so she hauled that heavy suitcase out and dumped its contents as quickly and mercilessly as possible. "I was chasing down a couple tweakers who had stolen a bike. They weren't local, I didn't know them. White boys. Fake-Nazi-types. I was clumsy, too eager, I barged ahead. One was waiting in the shadows behind a Chinese restaurant dumpster, took me down with a bat. One hit to the head dropped me. Then he went at me with his boot, stomping down a few times."

"God, I'm so sorry, Marcy."

"I had severe brain bleeding so they had to . . . do some kind of cranial skull flap and release the pressure while also trying to reconstruct the skull. Almost lost my eye, too. That meant a cranioplasty with a titanium mesh-plate and some screws to hold it all together. Plus bone grafts. It was a long recovery. Got a couple infections, had to go back to the hospital. Was pretty brutal."

Intense curiosity dawned on Sadie's face. "The plate. Is it all . . . titanium?"

"No. It's plastic, too, and—honestly, I forget what it's called, but it's some kind of mix of metals. Something and titanium. Flexible, they said."

"Nitinol, maybe? Nickel and titanium?"

That sounded right, and Marcy said so.

"And the implant—you almost lost an eye, so some of it sits behind your eye, is that right? In and around the socket?"

Marcy tapped above her right eye. "Here. Above the bone. They said the implant was real close to my optic nerve, tried to tell me that's why I was having such bad migraines. But I don't have them anymore."

"Why is that? Did they fix it?"

"No," Marcy said, a big smile beaming bright. "I came here. I walked with the walkers. And the glow made it all better."

THAT NIGHT, BENJI COULD BARELY sleep. He was in yet another motel—this one, the Sunset Motel. The outside smelled like cheap beer. The inside smelled like mildew. Sadie had her own room and was in it now—though they'd been bunking up together more and more.

Sadie was, in fact, why he was presently *plagued* into restlessness.

Earlier, while talking to her, he'd had this . . . *insane* feeling about her. Something bubbled up inside him, effervescent and mad, and he wanted to tell her right then and there, *I love you.*

But he didn't.

Because *she* said it first.

"I love you," she said, unbidden. As if keyed into the way he was feeling. Maybe it was how he was looking at her. Maybe it was just some kind of . . . pure, soul-mingling serendipity, if such a thing existed.

"I . . ." He laughed, and he realized that was the wrong noise to make with his stupid mouth, so he quickly backpedaled over it. "I'm laughing because I wanted to say it, too, and wasn't sure I should."

"You should. You always should." She paused. "Life is short, not long, Benjamin Ray. We should endeavor to say what we mean, always."

"I love you, too," he said, before she went back to her room.

That new love between them was a good thing. A nice thing.

A *pure* thing in all of this.

And that's what bothered him. The world was . . . well, to be charitable, it was looking more and more like a shitshow. The fight between Hunt and Creel was nasty, with each of them bruising and bloodying the other in the press. China and Russia had begun rattling the sabers, specifically over America's treatment of the flock—there were renewed talks of quarantining the country, stopping Americans from traveling overseas lest they bring this sleepwalker contagion to them. Worse, North Korea had begun frothing at the mouth, *casually suggesting* that the best way to handle the sleepwalker flock was for them to lob a couple of nuclear missiles at the United States. Which was likely impossible—that country couldn't feed its citizens much less put together a cogent nuclear weapons program. But it still dialed up his worry. Tensions were high everywhere. People were anxious.

And in all of that, there was the flock. And the way Jerry Garlin died. Things were thrown into disarray, chaos, imbalance, and was that *really* a good time to fall in love? Benji told himself that certainly there existed *no* good time to fall in love, and certainly this time in history was better than, say, World War II, or World War I, or the Civil War, or the Dark Ages, or, or, or—and people then fell in love, didn't they?

Still, it made him feel selfish.

And restless.

And alone.

Needing to occupy himself, he lurched up out of bed, grabbed the Black Swan phone, and in the dark pointed it at the wall. He told himself it was to go back to the investigation, to attempt to crack it, but in reality he knew it was because he felt very alone. Cassie had gone, now officiating the Garlin investigation. Sadie was in her room.

She'd failed to make any headway with Firesight. The nanotechnology company, owned by Benex-Voyager, did a lot of work for the Defense Department. Apparently, once they realized they were being drawn into a conversation surrounding the flock phenomenon, they threw up a wall of ice that wouldn't melt. They refused to meet. Which made Benji suspicious. Could they have been involved? That seemed ludicrous. More likely they were seeking a way out of the conversation, hoping not to be tied to anything related to the sleepwalkers, praying they didn't have to divulge any kind of classified technology. The walker flock was crawling with reporters; any sight of one of their executives meeting here could tank stock prices.

Benji sat in the dark, reckoning with this surge of frustration and loneliness.

All he had was Black Swan.

So he sat with the phone in the flat of his hand and decided to again go through the sleepwalker numbers. The total number itself had changed, obviously—by now they were up to 423 in the flock. They arrived in a more sporadic pattern now, and had ever since they crossed into Iowa and then Nebraska. Whenever they neared a population center, the new walkers arrived more swiftly—sometimes two or three at a time, meeting them on the road, or even crossing through a cornfield to join the flock.

The overall ratios were not dissimilar, though, to what they had been since the earliest days of the phenomenon. The flock remained curiously diverse in everything from racial or ethnic background to age to sexual orientation to gender. Black Swan confimed again and again that the two common elements remained common elements: first, that the group seemed to consist of above-average intelligence, as far as that metric took them; second, that they were all of above-average health. Thank God one thing was consistent, he thought.

Wait. God.

That was something he hadn't considered.

On a lark, Benji asked: "Black Swan, what about religious affiliation?"

There, another surprise awaited.

Over 40 percent of the flock identified as atheist, agnostic, or otherwise unaffiliated. The remaining 60 percent was broken up somewhat evenly across those who identified as Christian, Jewish, Muslim, Hindu, Buddhist. Drilling down further, the Christians were not uniform, either, the population cast across the denominations, from Baptist to Catholic to Lutheran and so on. That deviated from the population, too. Well over half the country identified as Christian, but the flock's ratio did not match, not at all.

Which seemed strange if it was a random disease.

Less strange, however, if this was curated.

Meaning, what if these people were *chosen?*

Chosen as part of what, though? An attack?

He imagined suddenly each of them swarming with tiny machines—sleepwalker blood teeming with microscopic devices. It seemed impossible. And yet it explained some of what they were facing.

It even explained the shimmer, didn't it? The one he saw when Clade Berman went *pop*. A rush of heat, rising up, defying the elements . . .

Once again, the image of tiny invaders, too small for the eye to see individually, mobbing the body—not to force it to walk, but to drive it mad, to kill it. Would that be the purview of the CDC? A disease was a disease, no matter if it was human-made or organic. He wished he could talk to Cassie right now. She had a way of grounding him. But with her on the Garlin investigation . . .

He reminded himself to check with her. So far, the media hadn't grabbed that story. The media was too focused on the election. And the flock. And North Korea. Hopefully the fungal infection had died with those it killed.

Still. If it *was* contained, why did Black Swan have an interest in it? An isolated outbreak like that wasn't something they could control or get ahead of.

Why were they set on that path? What was the intersection with Garlin's death?

With Black Swan in his hand, he asked it a question he'd asked many times before, one that always yielded a negative:

"Black Swan, is there any new connection between the sleepwalker phenomenon and the white-nose fungus that killed Jerry Garlin? Anything we haven't seen yet?"

Pause.

Seconds passed.

Black Swan was not answering.

He opened his mouth to ask it again—had it not heard him?—when suddenly it gave an answer.

One green pulse.

One red pulse.

Meaning, what? Maybe? Kinda, sorta? Half-and-half?

"Black Swan, I don't understand what that means."

It gave no answer.

"I need answers," he said, hearing the frustration in his voice mounting. "You have them. Surely you do."

Still nothing.

He grabbed the phone and yelled into it: "Do something! Anything! Put two and two together! You're the smartest damn computer in the whole world, so put all your ones and zeros together and get me some answers!"

Someone next door pounded on the wall, yelling: "Shut up!"

Benji was left panting. The rage fled.

He felt stupid.

He dropped back down onto the edge of the bed, sitting there in the dark. Wondering where this was all headed.

And then Black Swan glowed white.

Two voices emerged from its speakers. Crackling with light static.

One of those voices he recognized instantly: Sadie.

". . . she's a receiver." That, Sadie's voice.

The other voice, also a woman's. Gruffer. Blunter. The hint of a . . . Mid-Atlantic accent. Not quite New York or Jersey.

". . . what do you mean?"

SADIE: I mean she's picking up the signal from the machines.

OTHER WOMAN: How?

SADIE: I don't know. Something to do with the plate in her head. It's serving as a receiver. The nanoradio—

OTHER WOMAN, SIGHING: If she can detect it—

SADIE: Then eventually someone else will detect it, too.

OTHER WOMAN: Ray figure it out yet?

Ray. She meant him, didn't she? Benji stiffened. He dared not move or say a word, just in case they could hear him. Was this happening now? A recording? He wasn't sure. Why was Black Swan giving this to him?

SADIE: No, but he'll . . . figure it out soon enough. He's already on the trail.

OTHER WOMAN: You sure you didn't push him? You've been champing at the bit to bring him into this.

SADIE: No, of course not. I tried to convince him it couldn't be possible. But he's pushing for the Firesight interview. We can't hold him off forever, Moira. I can't stonewall him for long. And he may be able to help us better if he knew.

MOIRA: Keep stonewalling him. If he finds out—Sadie, the man is unpredictable. Who knows what he does with this? He could spill the whole thing. If he knew what we knew—

SADIE: We can trust him. Black Swan trusts him.

MOIRA: What matters is that he trusts you. Keep that up.

A pause.

Sadie: Of course.

Moira: We're entangled together in this, Sadie. Everything is at stake. *Everything*. Don't. Fuck. This. Up.

And then the call was over. Black Swan was silent again.

Benji was left in the dark to reckon with something far worse than frustration and loneliness: betrayal.

39

IF IT BLEEDS, IT LEADS

Über allen Gipfeln	Above all summits
Ist Ruh.	it is calm.
In allen Wipfeln	In all the treetops
Spürest du	you feel
Kaum einen Hauch;	scarcely a breath:
Die Vögelein schweigen im Walde.	the birds in the forest are silent.
Warte nur, balde	Just wait, soon
Ruhest du auch.	you will rest as well.

—Goethe, "Wanderer's Nightsong II"

JULY 12
Burnsville, Indiana

MATTHEW SAT AT HIS LAPTOP IN THE RECTORY OFFICE OF THE CHURCH, HEAD-phones on, doing another radio show. He'd done a lot of these over the last week since Hunt made her decision to pull back on Homeland Security's control of the sleepwalker flock. He'd been on terrestrial radio (AM/FM), on satellite, on podcasts. All from the comfort of his own church and home.

He'd been on a few where they tried to trap him—trying to get him to say stupid stuff or tie him in rhetorical knots. But he sussed those out pretty quick and got off the line.

The others ran the gamut: religious shows, conservative shows, some libertarian outlets. Even a few conspiracy nut shows, which he didn't much care for, either. Matthew told himself that the fringe on either side was a problem: He'd always believed that the political spectrum was a snake biting its own tail, and ultimately both ends met at the same point.

Still, these shows always seemed to go the same way.

Right now, he was on *Right Coast with Bruce Bachelor,* a conservative talk-show host out of Baltimore on the AM band, WCBM. Like a lot of these shows, it was one recommended to him by Hiram Golden, whom Matthew spoke to every couple of days—Hiram referred to himself as a sort of unpaid mentor or manager to Matthew.

Matthew'd been on the line for about thirty minutes, talking about the flock and President Hunt and all that, when the conversation—as they often did—swerved into the topic they always seemed to collide with.

"Tell me, Pastor Matt," Bruce said, his voice deep and resonant, with a hint of that Ballmer accent. "Is this the Apocalypse? This what we're looking at here with the flock phenomenon?"

Matthew laughed, as he always tried to do when someone brought this up. It's what they always wanted to talk about and it was always what he *didn't* want to talk about. He tried to swerve the conversation *away* from the topic. Sometimes it worked. He figured he'd try.

"I don't focus on that," he said. "That's a tomorrow problem, or the next day—we're all going to end up on the same side of the ground, which is, you know, underneath it in our grave, and so the goal for me is to focus on finding a way to be a good person in God's light and—"

"Right, of course, obviously, I just mean: What's it going to be like? The Apocalypse, the End Times, Armageddon."

"Ahhh. You know, I don't know—"

"Revelation has some thoughts, doesn't it?"

"It does. But—"

"And you say that the comet that passed overhead is similar to the comet Wormwood, and that these flocking freaks are maybe a symbol of the New World Order, which to me is a Devil thing, an Antichrist thing. You think maybe President Hunt is the Antichrist?"

"I try not to be too literal with that."

"But figuratively, she's an Antichrist-like figure," Bruce said.

"I suppose you could go there—"

"You go there in your sermons."

"Yes, again, figuratively."

"So, okay, okay, it's not that she's necessarily the legitimate for-real Antichrist, but she represents that—and we could be looking at something Apocalypse-*like,* if you go by Revelation, so tell me, in theory, what would the Apocalypse be like?"

He tried to mask his sigh. On the one hand, he felt he should cut this off. You chum the water, you get the sharks. On the other hand . . . donations to the church were up. And if this was the gateway to more people finding the path of the light . . .

"*In theory,*" Matthew began, "you'd see followers of the Antichrist rise up, claiming to be on the side of good. You'd see an uptick in war or violence, maybe famine, definitely pestilence—by pestilence I mean disease, some kind of epidemic or pandemic? I confess I don't precisely know the difference between the two."

"AIDS was a pandemic, right?"

"I suppose so." He felt an internal twitch. He knew that AIDS was associated largely with the homosexual community, and he didn't want to associate homosexuality with any kind of *devilry.* The Bible condemned it, sure, but the Bible also condemned divorce and shellfish. He tried to segue away from that into more fantastical imagery, again to emphasize that this was all mostly *fantasy.* "You'd see fire in the skies, angels descending to earth, maybe the Four Horsemen, maybe some kind of monster—a dragon in the sky, a Leviathan under the sea—"

"And if we are invaded by the Devil's children, by the *armies* as it were of the Antichrist, it would be our Christian duty to fight back?"

"Of course."

"You heard it righteous and true, folks. It is our solemn duty not to let the monsters take our country from us. Get your torches lit, your knives sharp, and maybe clean and oil your guns just in case." Bruce laughed, like that was somehow funny.

Matthew wanted to push back, wanted to say something about how he meant more fighting back with the spirit, with the light of God's Word, but Bachelor didn't give him the chance.

"Pastor Matt, I understand you're going to be at Ed Creel's rally on the night of the fourteenth, that right?"

"Ah, yes, it is, it is—but I also wanted to say—"

"Pastor Matt, I'm afraid we're out of time. Folks, if you want to see Pastor Matthew Bird of God's Light Church out of Burnsville, Indiana, speak about the sleepwalker army and God's plans for us, show up, bend your ear, and don't forget to maybe toss some chits and ducats into Creel's bucket. Thanks, Pastor. And now some words from our sponsors."

40

(I CAN'T GET NO)
SATISFACTION

Everything's connected now. It's not just phones and tablets and cameras. It's doorbells. It's refrigerators. It's sex toys! Sex toys are talking to each other! Shit, I know a fella has a trailcam, you know, for hunting? That talks to the web via a cellular signal. The Internet of Things, hell, more like the Internet of Big Brother. The goddamn Panopticon. You can be sure Hunt and her lib-witches are watching us all. Maybe even controlling us. These things talk to each other and they use them to control us. Like fluoride in the water, chemtrails in the air, we're getting it coming and going. Next thing you know they'll stick probes up our ass to report our rectal temperatures to some . . . some artificial intelligence. Anyway, coming up we got a brand-new muscle-building cleanse product, gonna really blow your fucking gourd how ripped you get from this . . .

—Ander Davies, *The Endgame Truthcast* on SiriusXM Satellite Radio

JULY 13
Rosebud, Nebraska

A WEEK IN, THE SHINE STARTED TO WEAR OFF THE FUCKING APPLE.

Pete Corley didn't let them *know* that, of course—to the shepherds of the flock and to the media onlookers, he was *the* presence among them, the star on the stage, the sun around which they orbited. At least, that was the lie he told himself. Already he could feel them becoming *inured* to him, like he'd become normalized, "just another part of the gang." He didn't want to be another part of the gang. He wanted to be the gang leader. Or their gang god. Did gangs have gods? Wouldn't that be something, each gang with its own gang god? He shook his head.

He did his best, of course, to keep attention on him. Couple days ago, he paid Charlie Stewart to go to a music store in Omaha to pick up a couple portable Marshall MS-4 mini-stack amps and the best electric guitar they had on the racks: in this case, a shiny black Gretsch Electromatic hollow-body. Not his first choice, but fuck it, it was what it was.

He strung the amps together, plugged in the guitar, then stood atop Charlie's RV like a guitar god astride his chariot. He led sing-alongs and did guitar solos and, obviously, ran through some of Gumdropper's biggest hits— "Full Steam Ahead," "Rickety-Clack Down the Tracks," "Cupid's Quiver," "Hot Dog Woman" (easily the most willfully phallic song in all of rock-and-roll, and that's saying something), and some lesser B-sides, too.

Even still, his ability with the guitar was *fine*—but he wasn't Evil Elvis. Pete was backup. Rhythm guitar only. Elvis was lead, always lead, and that shitty shit wanker could tease a sound out of any guitar like he was the world's greatest lover and the guitar was his latest sexual conquest. And Pete felt frustrated pushing up against the limits of his own ability—not that these rubes knew anything about the true talent, they probably didn't give a thimble of jackrabbit jizz, but *he* knew, and maybe instinctively they knew, too.

Because though the crowd was big when he started playing atop the RV, it had thinned an hour later. And it thinned even more after that.

He got some of them back when he started playing sermons from some Indiana pastor—some podcasting, radio-broadcasting snake-in-the-grass named Matthew Bird (*fake name,* Pete guessed, and Pete knew fake names because rock was *rife* with them). Bird was some soft-spoken yokel who went on and on about how the flock were the Devil's Pilgrims and all that—and like so many of these fake Christian arseholes, they made it sound like they were all compassionate about the world's many boo-boos but then they condemned anyone and everyone for showing a whiff of *real* empathy, *real* compassion, so Bird was an easy target. Corley put the hypocritical shit on blast, and would turn it down from time to time to let the crowd boo—Pete would jeer the fucking prick, too, saying things like, "So much for Christian tolerance, eh?" or "Sounds like *somebody* needs a good whap upside the head with the King James," or even, simply, *"This fucking wanker, am I right?"*

That worked for a while. He knew they'd already been passing Bird's sermons around, so he was able to stoke those coals for a while.

But it didn't last. They still . . . dwindled away.

Less impressed by him.

Less angered by Bird.

Less everything.

He told himself it was because they had things to do. They had to go groom their walkers. They had to drink water, eat sandwiches, cool off. Their muscles ached. They were tired and bored. Wait, no, *he* was tired and bored because good goddamn the middle of the country was boring. At least in New York you could look at stuff. You could see two guys yelling at each other over produce, you could smell the halal carts, you could also smell the weaponized piss stink that came hissing up out of the vents, you could watch a rat fight a dog for a bagel. (Spoiler: The rat would win because New York rats were unfuckwithable.)

Here, though, what was there to look at?

Grass. Wheat. Corn. Soy. Out here it was like some lazy fuck graphic designer just copy-pasted the same terrain over and over and over again. *Click, click, click.* Its redundancy was oppressive to him. He felt trapped, suddenly. Like he couldn't breathe.

In this wide-open space he felt like he was inside a shrinking box.

Like in a closet? a small voice said.

A stupid voice that he quickly crushed like a cigarette underfoot. Giving it an extra mental twist of the heel, just for good measure.

He stood off to the side now, pacing, giving little waves and throwing up the devil's horns to those who passed by. He had his phone against his ear, listening to it ring, and he felt simultaneously irritated and depressed by those who walked by him—irritated that they wouldn't give him his privacy on this call and depressed because they weren't mobbing him like they should. He'd become an expected fixture.

A personality, not *the* personality.

Fuck fuck fuckity fuck.

Finally, someone answered. His wife, Lena.

"Let me guess," she said first thing, "you're finally coming home."

"What?" he said, acting aghast. "What do you mean, woman?"

"I mean that I know how this goes. You went for the attention, you got your attention, and now the attention is waning and you're looking for a way out, and you're wondering if I'll leave a light on for you or I've tossed all your shit out the window onto Fifth Avenue again."

"That's fucking nonsense is what it is," he blustered.

"It was like this when you went to India to become a, what was it, a Yogi? And then again when you tried Australian walkabout." He hears the crispy sizzle and puckered suck of her taking a drag off a cigarette. "And then *again* when you went down to Florida to build houses for Habitat for Humanity. How long did you stay there, two days?"

"Three. I built a house."

"You did not build a house."

"I built a staircase."

"You installed three stairs in a staircase."

"And I did so for free, when my hourly cost is in the tens of thousands, I'll remind you. I got them considerable press."

"You got pissed because not only did you have to do manual labor, but they saw through your fake-ass charitable ruse—people doing real work to build houses for the needy did not see you as their savior, so you—"

"This is really bad, how you're treating me right now."

"So you bailed on them—"

"This is—this is revisionist history, I brought more attention to their little group than anybody had, it was good for them, *better* for them than it was for me, if we're being honest—"

"And you ran home. You ran to them to get away from us, then you ran to us to get away from them."

"Rude, rude, and very fucking wrong, I'll tell you that." He nibbled at a thumbnail. "I'll tell you what, this is wrong, you're *so* wrong, I'm not calling to come home, not at all." *I was totally calling to come home, but I'm certainly not going to tell you that now.* "I'm *calling* to talk to the kids."

"The kids are out. Connor's at drum practice." *Ugh, drums,* such a caveman instrument, he thought. Connor was that way, though. "And Siobhan is off to dressage camp."

"The fuck is *dressage?*" It sounded French. *Dress-aaahhhhhj.*

"It's . . . I dunno, Pete, it's horses dancing."

"Dancing horses."

"Horses dancing. There's a difference."

"You know, maybe I should come home, now that you mention it." The shepherds and flock passed and he gave them all a fake little toodle-oo wave.

"I should come home and straighten everybody out. Get Connor playing the guitar—a gentleman's instrument, I'll have you fucking know—and tell Siobhan that horse dancing is not a thing that people do, it's just some shit that rich people made up. A con. Probably a pyramid scheme, like alpacas. I'll pack my things—"

"No."

"No what?"

"No, you're not coming home."

"I am if I want."

"I'll change the locks. I'll change the alarm code. If I have to, I will throw your shit onto Fifth Avenue, or I'll give it to the nearest homeless shelter. I don't give a shit, Pete. You ran away from us, you ran away from the Gumdropper reunion—don't think I don't know that's what this is about, by the way—and I'm tired of it. You're there, so stick it out. Those people are glad to have you, and right now we don't want you."

"You're divorcing me."

"No, but consider this a temporary separation. I don't want you back here until you do your time there and figure out who you are, what you want, and why you keep running away."

"You're kind of a bitch," he said.

Another crispy drag off her cigarette. "Takes a bitch to know a bitch. Love you, baby. Hope your cracked skull is healing up okay." He heard her fake a couple of kisses, *mwah, mwah*, before she hung up.

That cooze. That hooker. That glorious, damnable woman.

He wanted to call her back and tell her everything. *I love you but I'm not in love with you, I love men, I love cock, I have a lad on the side named Landry, I gave you two children but to do so I had to be high on a couple different drugs, also Evil Elvis is a piece-of-shit and I'm scared of success or ruining my success or gods, I don't even fucking know.*

Pete gritted his teeth.

He dialed a number on the phone.

Landry answered. "It's you."

It's me.

"I needed to hear your voice," Pete said, trying not to sound desperate and totally, totally failing.

• • •

SHANA HAD TAKEN UP WITH Arav. Every night, he had a hotel or motel room somewhere along with the other CDC workers—those that remained, anyway, since the ranks of technicians and lab workers had been seriously cut down. He caught a ride with the others and she caught a ride, too, which was more than a little awkward as she earned stares and silence. Once in a while, Doctor Ray tried striking up a conversation, and she gave a one- or two-word answer, and that ended it. They hadn't seen him or Sadie so far this morning, though. The two of them waited in the parking lot, where they always did. It was nice, though, being away from the flock. Shana didn't want to admit that out loud, but it was true: Out here she felt free in a way she didn't with the flock. There it felt like her only identity was as a shepherd—someone attending to someone else. Nessie.

Here, though, with the wide-open road and nothing to do . . .

She felt like she could do anything. Be anyone.

And that feeling was compounded by the new camera hanging at her side in its bag.

The camera was a Canon 5D, procured with the wad of cash Corley gave her four days ago. She had enough money to buy an additional lens, too—outside of the kit lens, she bought a zoom lens. What she *really* wanted was a macro lens, but with the flock that didn't seem like a thing she could make much use of. Zooming in, though? That was useful. Made her feel like a proper little spy. Watching people from afar . . .

She turned and snapped a quick pic of Arav. The long motor lodge stood behind him, a decrepit artifact of a bygone era. The sun was just coming up over it, casting shafts of light and blobby motes into the image. As she took more photos, Arav faked being coy, trying to hide from the lens. In a droll voice he said, "Oh no, the paparazzi. I'm just trying to get my . . . non-fat macchiato and my avocado toast, but these paparazzi won't stop following me around. Oh no, the life of a millennial celebrity such as me."

"Who are you supposed to be, Pete Corley?" she snarked at him, still snapping pics. *Click, click, click.*

"I wish. I'd be rich."

"He's not happy. Money didn't fix whatever's broken inside him."

Arav offered a dubious chuckle. "Yeah . . . I dunno, he seems pretty happy to me?"

"Don't confuse loudness with happiness. He's got the volume all the way up, but that's just to cover up the gaping hole inside. Here, look." She pulled up the pics she'd taken of the rock star, flicking through the photos on the little camera screen. She'd captured these with the zoom lens—Corley away from the flock, sometimes standing off to the side, or behind the RV, or in the corn. Sneaking a smoke from his vape wand or just . . . staring out at nothing. In a couple his face was twisted up. When his mask fell, woe and worry seemed to pain him.

"Oh, wow," Arav said. "He actually looks . . . sad? Mad? Both?"

"Yeah, that's not the face of someone who's got his shit together."

"These days, I dunno if anybody has their shit together."

"Word to that." She bit her lip. Danced around a thing she didn't want to say, but then stepped right on it and said it: "You're not leaving, are you?"

"What?"

"I just mean—I know Cassie left. And that other guy, the one with the concussion, he's gone, too—"

"Martin."

"Yeah. I just worry that they'll send you away."

"I don't want that. But I feel like I've been pushed to the margins a little." He looked around suspiciously, probably for Benji or Sadie—neither of whom had come out, yet. "I think they're keeping something from me."

"Like what?"

Exasperated, he answered, "I dunno! I just . . . I just get that feeling. Like they know something but I'm not clued in. Which is fine, I'm pretty low on the totem pole, I just thought I was part of the team. But it's fine," he said suddenly, even though it wasn't. He smiled and leaned his head on her shoulder as they walked. "I get to spend more time with you."

"I'm cool with that, I am, but dude, you're *not* one of us."

At that, he lifted his head. "What?"

"Aw, don't get it twisted, it's a compliment. These people? Us shepherds? We're like . . . flotsam and jetsam. Little paper boats in that river made of people. You're not one of us. You're one of *them*. The solvers, the helpers, the scientists. The smarty-pants."

"I can still be one of you."

"I don't want you to be. I want you to be one of them. You want to do right by me, that means figuring out how I get my sister back."

He seemed to consider this. Then he gave a stiff nod.

"You're right. I've . . . been complacent."

"You gotta get your groove back."

"My groove," he repeated, nodding. "Yes. Yeah. I need to *groove*."

"Okay, the way *you* say it sounds dorky, this isn't the dance floor. I'm just saying—go up there, right now. Go to Benji's room. Tell him what you're thinking. Tell him you're recommitted to the mission or whatever, and you want in."

He turned to her, panic and excitement in his eyes. "Are you sure?"

"You don't need my permission. Go and save the world, dude."

Arav darted off.

Then he darted back, kissed her, and darted off again.

SLEEP EVADED HIM, DUCKING AND feinting and dodging all night. Worry did not. Paranoia found Benji, trapped him, pinned him to the bed. Soaked him in sweat, tangled him in the sheets. The hours passed as insomnia held court. And now, morning had arrived. His consciousness was serrated like a steak knife. He felt raw, inside and out. Sadie knocked on his door, ready to pile in the car with Shana and Arav and head to the flock, and when he opened it, he knew it was time to decide what he was going to do.

The easiest thing would be to pretend that nothing was wrong.

Maybe he'd misunderstood what Black Swan had let him hear. Perhaps it was a delusion, or a dream. A mad moment of sleep paralysis that yielded a stress-based hypnagogic hallucination.

Maybe Black Swan concocted it. That was a thing, now, was it not? Artificial intelligence being able to fake photos, videos, voices. It was easier and easier.

Maybe it *was* real, and maybe his best move was to play the spy—he could sit back, warily, keeping a distrustful and vigilant eye.

But that wasn't who he was.

Benji had to confront this now, or it would destroy him, he decided. (And a small voice questioned: Was that why he did what he did with Longacre? Because to continue to sit idly by would have crushed him?)

Sadie stepped into the room, and she must've seen his face. He could only speculate how he looked by how he felt: He felt ragged and rough, like a piece of fabric cut with rusty, chipped shears.

"You look, if you don't mind me saying so, like something my old bichon frise yakked up onto the carpet."

"I need to know what you know," he said, his voice grim.

"About . . . my beesh? Ah. Well. Her name was Gizzy and—"

"About the nanomachines. About nanoradio. About . . . Moira, whoever that is, about *Marcy Reyes* and the *signal* and, and—"

Now it was Sadie's turn to look like cut, ragged cloth. Her face went ashen. "I . . . Benji . . ."

It was confirmation enough. What he'd experienced was no delusion, no hallucination, no paranoia-fed dream. He held up the Black Swan satphone. "If you want to know how I know, thank your creation. You betrayed me. Black Swan betrayed you. It played part of a conversation you were having with this Moira person. Was it last night? Or a recording from an earlier day?"

Sadie swallowed visibly. "It was last night."

"That's why you never came to my room. You were talking."

A pause.

"Yes."

"Sadie, I . . . I don't even know where to begin." In the deep of his ears he heard the rush of blood in an uneven susurrus. "The flock. They are . . . infected, somehow? With what, nanoparticles?"

"Machines," she said, her voice nearly breaking.

"And you're responsible."

"No. Not . . . it's not like that."

"But you knew."

"Yes, I knew—"

"Firesight, then, are they responsible?"

"Yes, but—it's not so easy to explain—"

"Sadie," he said, lurching to his feet, his voice a dark shout. "You betrayed the CDC. You betrayed *me*. The flock. The country. Everyone! This . . . you'll go to *jail* for this. We have to go to the FBI. You have to come clean."

"I need you to trust me," she said, her voice dire. She clasped her hands together, as if to pray for his mercy. "It's not all as it seems. You can come with me. We'll go to Atlanta. I can show you things. I can—"

"Show me what? Was this some side project of yours? What are these things? What is their purpose?" He felt nauseated. Everything had gone topsy-turvy, like a nightmare that followed him out of sleep and into reality. "And how does Marcy Reyes factor into it? She's a receiver? You said something about a, a, a *signal*—"

Someone knocked at the door.

Sadie and Benji stood silently, staring at each other.

"It's probably Arav," she said stiffly.

"Shit. Yes." Benji moved past her and opened the door. She was correct—standing there, wide-eyed, was Arav. "Arav, now is not the time, we will come down when we're ready—"

"Signal?" Arav asked. "*What* signal?"

41

IT ALL COMES OUT
IN THE WASH

Seven Dead in Portland-Area School Shooting

By Maggie Townshend, *Washington Post*

Four students and three teachers were killed today in Clackamas Creek Middle School, shot by former student Timothy Grosser, who died on the scene from a self-inflicted gunshot wound. School principal Desiree Osgood said that Grosser was a troubled student who was expelled for spray-painting white supremacist symbols on lockers and for making threats against marginalized students. GOP presidential nominee Ed Creel offered his thoughts at a rally on Tuesday, saying, "It's these walkers. We've lost our way and we're cheerleading a pack of terroristic sinners. Tensions are high and so we should expect more violence like this, not less."

JULY 13
Burnsville, Indiana

THE RADIO INTERVIEW TROUBLED HIM. WORRY CLUNG TO MATTHEW LIKE A strange smell. He wanted to get the word out, but he wanted to be careful how he positioned his message. A message of love and hope was always better than one of punishment and judgment. But then again, you couldn't extricate those things from the Word of God, could you? The Almighty was a loving father, yes, but every father had to deliver tough love sometimes.

For now, a simpler problem presented itself:

Matthew needed a shirt.

Something simple, a nice button-down, but short-sleeved, too, since it was so damn hot. (Even with the air-conditioning on, he still felt sweat slicking the back of his neck, oozing down his spine.) He had a meeting in an hour with Hiram Golden—Hiram was proposing to become Matthew's speaking agent, and so they were going to formalize that deal. The one thing he wasn't sure about was that Hiram wanted him to pull away from the church for a little while—not close up shop, exactly, but walk away for a few weeks, concentrate solely on media events and speaking gigs. "It's good money," Hiram said.

"I can't close the church," Matthew told him. "It'd be like asking my heart to stop beating."

At that, Hiram chuckled and said, "We'll see. Everything's a negotiation, Matthew. I'll show you the light, friend."

They were grabbing lunch today, so he went through his closet looking for a shirt, but Matthew found none there. Not a one.

He called after Autumn. No answer. She wasn't home again. She'd been going out. A lot. Shopping (now that they had some money) or to the park ("Just to walk and enjoy God's world," she told him). To her credit, she'd been a lot happier these days—her eyes were a little sleepy, but she smiled and laughed and had a breezy air about her that reminded him of when they first met. That air, that spark, had been gone for a long time, and he admitted he was glad to see it come back.

Just the same, he knew it was the pills reigniting that spark. It wasn't God. It wasn't prayer. It was her little pill bottle of happiness.

Given to her by Ozark Stover.

He gritted his teeth, putting it out of his mind.

One of the problems with her being on those pills, though, and being happier-and-go-luckier, was that she was missing things. Like a transmission slipping gears. Yesterday she forgot to empty the dishwasher. Three days ago she'd been out and forgot to fill up the gas tank in the car, so she had to call Triple A and have them bring her some gas. How embarrassing.

So he went into the laundry room, popped open the dryer—

And sure enough, a mound of clothes was wadded up inside.

He spied plaid. "My shirts," he said. "Damnit, Autumn."

Like Atlas hulking the whole of the earth, Matthew took the entire wad of clothes out at one time and waddle-walked it to their bedroom. He dumped it all on the (unmade) bed.

Something rolled away, clattering on the floor.

Two somethings, in fact.

Matthew bent down and found a pair of shotgun shells.

They weren't big—they were narrow green plastic tubes, no thicker than his index finger. One crimped and ready to fire, the other blown open. Like from a little bird gun.

He looked to the clothing, saw that some of Bo's clothes were mixed in with his. The shells didn't come from Matthew.

So that meant they came from Bo.

And *that* meant the boy was still handling firearms when Matthew told him explicitly not to. They hadn't had time to meet with Roger yet to learn the ins and outs of guns, so that meant Bo was betraying his order.

Did it mean that Ozark had betrayed that, too?

Matthew told himself, no, that couldn't be. Ozark was respectful. It was all on the up-and-up. More likely Bo had gone out with friends and done it. But then that nagging question: *What friends?*

He hummed discontentedly to himself, then took a brief expedition into the boy's room. Again that teen-boy funk hit him in the face like a sweaty shovel. He winced, wading deeper through the clothes and the mess. He peeked under the bed. (There he found a Tupperware container that had once contained chili, moldering.) He looked in the closet, found mostly black T-shirts and jeans, not hanging up, no, but piled at the bottom. Then he went to the dresser in the corner, went through it drawer by drawer.

In the second drawer from the bottom, he found porn.

Porn magazines, to be specific, which honestly, he didn't even know was a thing anymore. Didn't most people get their pornography from the internet? Matthew was good, he did not partake in it because, plainly, that was a sin. Those girls and women were not objects to be ogled, they were creatures of God, same as he was. He would not reward a system that abused them, nor would he reward those women for those very bad, very sinful choices. (Yes, he'd heard that some women chose that life, but he honestly could not believe that.)

These magazines looked pretty beat-up. Couple *Penthouses* and a *Hustler,* all from about ten years ago. Then a trio of *Easyriders* magazine—these from the 1980s, featuring biker mamas dressed like it was the '70s, all huge hair and big pubic tangles. Matthew found his pulse quicken looking at them, and so he quickly threw them back in the drawer and slammed it shut.

That was a conversation he'd have with Bo on another day.

He opened the last drawer.

Jeans, sweatpants, shorts. He put his hands in there—

And found something hard and boxy under the fabric.

He moved the clothes aside and discovered a box of ammunition. Shotgun shells bigger than the ones he'd found in the laundry. These for a 20-gauge shotgun.

But where was the gun?

42

THE ULTIMATE ANSWER

The future is a door. Two forces—forces that we drive like horses and chariots, whips to their backs, wheels in ruts, great froth and furious vigor—race to that door. The first force is evolution. Humanity changing, growing, becoming better than it was. The second force is ruination. Humanity making its best effort to demonstrate its worst tendencies. A march toward self-destruction. The future is a door that can accommodate only one of those two competing forces. Will humanity evolve and become something better? Or will we cut our own throats with the knives we made?
—futurist Hannah Stander in her lecture to students at
Penn State University: "Apocalypse Versus Apotheosis:
What Does the Future Hold?"

JULY 13
Valentine, Nebraska

THE THREE OF THEM PULLED UP OUTSIDE A RUN-DOWN STORAGE UNIT FACIL-ity south of the small town of Valentine, about five miles from the flock's current position, and seven miles from the motel. Gravel popped like popcorn under the rental tires.

Benji looked over to Sadie in the passenger seat.

She offered a small smile. He did not return it.

"I still don't understand what's happening," Arav said from the backseat.

"You will," Sadie answered, and got out to meet the unit attendant—a pear-shaped man with pockmarked cheeks and a Kubota trucker hat. He walked over with an easy bounce, handed Sadie a clipboard. From inside the car, Benji and Arav watched her sign it. He handed her a key.

"What is going on?" Arav asked. "Doctor Ray, Benji, I—"

"I don't know," Benji said. And it was true. He didn't.

Sadie waved them forward as the chain-link gate slid open automatically with a rattle-bang. Benji urged the car forward.

They went to her newly rented storage unit, 42-D.

BENJI HAD ASKED HER, *WHY here? Why a storage unit?*

He had already told her they weren't flying off on a whim to Atlanta. Whatever she had to tell him, she could tell him here, so he could remain near the flock. She said fine, and called ahead to rent this storage unit.

As to why:

Because she wanted four unobstructed walls for Black Swan's projections. And she wanted somewhere away from prying ears and eyes, and storage units were, on the whole, fairly private, unmonitored affairs. The lots were often under surveillance; the units themselves, not. This was close to the motel, so she made the call, and so they went. As they got out, Benji looked all around. Paranoia gnawed at him. He half expected to hear a shot ring out, or to see someone in a black mask driving toward him. (Or an ambulance, he thought, like the one that stole the bodily remains back in Pennsylvania.) But there was only the dead silence of the wide-open Midwest.

Sadie unlocked the padlock at the unit, opened the shutter bay door. Then, from the trunk, she wheeled in her suitcase—another mystery Benji had not yet figured out, but when the answer came, it was so mundane, so simple, he was surprised he hadn't guessed it:

She used the suitcase to prop up the Black Swan device.

They had no table, no chair—the storage unit was empty.

The suitcase made for a makeshift platform.

With that, she pulled down the shutter door with a rattle-bang. The light dimmed and they descended into darkness. From within the void, she said:

"Black Swan, it's me, Sadie."

It throbbed with white light on all sides. The room seemed to swell with it. Benji felt like he was once again back in Atlanta, in the so-called Lair of the machine intelligence at the CDC building.

"Please dial in Moira and Bill," she said.

To the left, a woman appeared, and to the right, a man. The woman looked younger, maybe Benji's age—copper-red hair, white suit. The man was older, maybe in his fifties or sixties, with a trim, flattop haircut—he wore a sour, dour face, and his lips and jaw moved like he was trying to work a seed out from between his teeth. Neither was projected as they would be in any other videoconferencing call—Skype, FaceTime, et cetera—as a set of shoulders, a head, a face. Instead it was their full bodies standing there flat against the wall. Not a hologram, not three-dimensional, but eerily lifelike.

The woman spoke first:

"I'm Moira Simone, and this is William Craddock."

"Bill," the projection of the man said.

"What is this?" Benji asked, suddenly furious. "You've got explaining to do. I suspect you've committed a grave and *serious* crime against the people of the flock, their families, their friends—*this country*—"

"You have no idea," Moira said, snapping at him.

"Moira," Sadie cautioned.

But the red-haired woman continued: "If you want to go running off to the FBI after this, that is your prerogative. But we have built something here that is very fragile, Doctor Ray, and I want you to understand that before we begin."

Bill Craddock: "It's of considerable consequence."

Benji and Arav shared a look. The younger man looked confused, not to mention scared out of his wits.

"Go on," Benji said.

Moira nodded. "Black Swan. Show him the map."

With that, a simple red map of the United States appeared.

Then, a pulse of yellow light as a dot appeared over Texas.

"San Antonio," Bill said.

The map flipped to the wall behind them—a disorienting maneuver, making Benji feel like he was on an amusement-park ride—and was replaced with a video. It was a video he'd seen: the events at the Garlin Gardens groundbreaking ceremony. Jerry Garlin there on stage, flailing as bats whipped around him. People screaming and fleeing. Bats just doing what bats do when disturbed: restlessly seeking somewhere to settle.

"I know this already," Benji said. "It's contained."

The video disappeared. The map flipped back in front of them.

"Is it?" Moira's face was an implacable slate.

Just then, lines fled San Antonio, leading to four dots elsewhere in the country: two elsewhere in Texas (Austin, Dallas), one on the East Coast (Richmond, Virginia), and one on the West Coast (San Diego).

Benji remembered that Cassie said there were three others infected. He asked. "Are these the other three infected?"

"They are," Sadie said.

"It's the dot in San Diego you should watch," Moira said.

And he did. From San Diego, new lines drew and the image pulled farther out to a global map. To Berlin. To Beijing. Then Boston, San Diego, and onward to Florida. Naples. Near the Everglades.

"That dot. It's Garlin," Benji said.

"Correct," Bill Craddock answered.

"Those are his travels over the course of a few months," Moira explained. "Garlin, you see, left San Antonio that day and then traveled around the world. Not once, but many times. West Coast. East Coast. Germany. China. Florida. Texas. And the people he met were world travelers themselves— executives, investors, tourism directors, architects. All shaking hands, sharing meals, breathing the same air. Now. Black Swan, show us the second wave."

A new scattering of dots appeared. At a quick count, several dozen, maybe fifty or more. All clustered around either the places where Garlin went—or where the other three infected men had settled.

Oh no.

Not just three infected.

Three other *vectors for infection*. That's what this was, wasn't it? *It's not contained at all.*

It was Arav who asked, in worried tones: "I see fifty-two other dots. Are those all . . . people infected with the pathogen? The same one that killed Garlin?"

"That is correct," Bill answered.

"God help us," Benji said.

In Benji's mind, he saw it—like a puddle where one raindrop fell, making ripples. Then others fell, two, then four, then ten, all making *their* own ripples, too. And soon it was a downpour, ripples upon ripples, until the calm waters of the puddle were disturbed so greatly, it was only noise and chaos. The hissing din of falling rain. A puddle so full it spilled over, became a pond, a lake, an ocean in which everyone would drown.

"The groundbreaking was six, seven months ago," Benji said in horror. "If it's spreadable at all . . . if it's contagious, then it's got a long time line—"

"A long incubation period," Arav said.

"Three to six months," Bill said.

Three to six months. That meant it could hide. It wasn't that it wasn't communicable. It was that, when passed along, it waited. It *hid*. Like other slower, nastier viruses: HIV or rabies. It would lie in wait, not sleeping, but not coming out to play yet, either. Latent. But if it was still communicable in that time, while it lurked in the shadows . . .

Again, water drops forming ponds, lakes, oceans.

Snowflakes making an avalanche.

Four infected individuals forming a pandemic.

An *apocalypse*.

Moira continued: "From the point of contact, three to six months is how long you have. Jerry Garlin died six months after his contact with the bats in San Antonio. His symptoms first manifested a full month after that contact—appearing only as a minor cold. A *stubborn* cold, but easy to dismiss. Once those symptoms appear, the disease becomes contagious. For Garlin, that cold lasted for two months. And that's when the dementia began. Not enough to be a warning, not then. Easily viewable as a symptom of stress, or age, or simple forgetfulness. But over the final months, the dementia worsens considerably as the mycelial threads plunge deeper into the brain. Like worms slithering through dirt. Your nose, eyes, mouth begin to show a white rime, just as the bats do on their muzzles. But humans do not experience sores or lesions—no, the damage is nearly all internal, in the brain. The resultant dementia becomes so bad that you lose yourself to it. Death is a product less of the infection and more the breakdown of your ability to live, your ability to summon simple survivable common sense. Madness sets in. Amnesia. Think of what Alzheimer's patients go through—turning on the stove, then walking away. Getting in a car and driving it into a crosswalk full of children. Nonsensical grief and rage take over. The mind breaks down as the brain sickens. The body follows, because how could it not?"

Benji sat with this for a few moments. His mind, reeling. He wanted to throw up. He looked over at Arav, whose face was ashen.

"I'd say he gets it," Bill said.

Benji did get it. This was the worst-case scenario. It was not enough that it was a deadly disease, no. It was a *slow* disease. It was steady and it was, as Moira put it, patient. Most pathogens were greedy and gluttonous: They moved fast, desperate to conquer, urging their king and queen out on the chessboard with grave impatience, making them especially vulnerable. If this one took its time . . . how much could it have spread? How many might be infected without them knowing?

He tried to summon the time line for white-nose syndrome in bats. Discovered, when? Early 2006, Howes Cave near Albany, New York. A year later, all the bats in the area were acting strange—out during the day, in winter, flying around, as if lost. By the end of that year, most of the bats in the region had died. That was the start. At this point, six million bats had perished in the United States, and the disease was in Europe now, too.

The good news for the bats was that they did not necessarily intermingle—some species and colonies remained isolated from the others. They were social animals, but only within their individual colonies. Mixing was not common, and so the spread of the disease was limited.

Humans, on the other hand, were not only social—

They intermingled. *Constantly.*

And they traveled. Planes, trains, automobiles.

Walking through cities, malls, airports.

It was summer now. That meant, what? Picnics. Sports games. Summer camps. But some diseases didn't do well in summer. Flu and colds, for instance. Maybe that was good, too . . .

"How do you know all this?" Benji asked. Maybe they were lying. Maybe this was a ruse. "If it's this far, you should've warned us. You had a responsibility—"

"There's a CDC report with Cassie Tran's name on it," Moira explained. "And even if there wasn't . . ."

"We have Black Swan," Sadie said.

Benji met her stare. He was angry at her for keeping this from him. And he was confused, too—how did this fit into the flock? The nanotech? Marcy's so-called signal? "I want to know about the flock," he said. "I want to know why I'm here, what this has to do with nanoradio, or Marcy Reyes, or, or, why someone like Clade Berman goes off like a Roman candle—"

"Black Swan," Moira said. "Pull up Document Ninety-Nine."

And with that, the map disappeared entirely, and several pages of a document shuffled across the projection on the wall ahead. Six pages, three across the top of the wall, three across the bottom.

The pages contained hundreds and hundreds of numbers in rows, one after the next, like black ants crawling forward in a column.

Code of some kind.

"What do you see?" Sadie asked.

"I don't know. It's—it's gibberish."

"Look closer. You're trained to see patterns."

Frustration mounted. "In disease, yes. Not this—I don't know what this is." It was all alphanumeric. Lines of it, a giant block of code. He was about to tell her again that he saw nothing, no pattern—

And then, he did. It wasn't dramatic. This was no magic-eye painting that resolved into a dragon or a sailboat, but he did see something.

A repetition of two numbers. Dozens of reiterations.

052017.

122422.

Arav must've seen it, too. He pointed out those numbers.

Were those dates? They looked to be in date format.

Each paired with another number. 0830, 0930, 1330, 1930, and on.

Time stamps?

But that didn't make sense, did it?

"They look like dates," Benji said. "But they can't be. The first would be May twentieth, 2017. But the latter isn't possibly a date."

"And why not?" Moira asked, needling him.

"Because it hasn't happened yet. Christmas Eve, 2022? That's the future." He looked to Sadie with an incredulous huff and—

Sadie said nothing. Her face was an expectant mask. The look of a parent who has cornered their child into admitting some kind of realization, some wrongdoing—*Oh, now I see why I shouldn't swing the Wiffle ball bat in the house, near the TV.*

He almost wanted to laugh. "You're saying this date *has* happened."

"No," Sadie said. "You're right, Benji. It hasn't. It's the future. And yet that's the date."

"The date of what, exactly?"

"The date Black Swan sent itself a message."

43

A HELLUVA DRUG

Well, all animals, and plants for that matter, tend to reach evolutionary climax and occupy a niche and stabilize in that niche. Cockroaches, ants achieved this hundreds of millions of years ago, and have not changed greatly since. Most of biology is this iterative occupation of a climax niche. Very little of biology is the pushing forward into radical new forms, new species, still rare, new genera. For that, there has to be disruption of some sort, of the environment and it can be the meandering of a river, or an asteroid strike, the retreat of a glacier, something which creates open land.
— Terence McKenna

JULY 13
Rosebud, Nebraska

SHANA SAT ON THE GROUND, LOOKING THROUGH THE PHOTOS SHE'D TAKEN OF the shepherds and the flock when the RV—*the Beast*—came rolling up into the Sunset Motel parking lot. It rattled and banged and rocked back and forth as it drove, and Shana wondered how many more miles that thing could drive—it looked like it would shake itself to pieces before too long.

The door popped open.

Pete Corley looked out, leaning on the frame like a scarecrow whose wooden propping post had started to fall over.

"Hello, hello," he said, grinning with those fucked-up teeth.

"You?"

"It's me, doll. What happened to your ride?"

"They had . . . things to do." Shana didn't know what was going on, but Benji, Sadie, and Arav came out of their room looking—well, honestly, they all looked kinda pissed off? And maybe sad, too? They said they had to deal with something. Arav didn't even apologize. They just took off. So she called her father to come pick her ass up and now—Pete Corley? "Where's my father?" Hope bloomed in her. Was he with Nessie? Finally?

"He's in the back, having a nap. Hop in. Let's ride, baby, ride."

"Don't call me baby," she said, reluctantly stepping into the Beast. It smelled weird. A little like weed, a bit like beer, and the telltale stink of man-scent, which hovered between *too much cologne* and *farts,* easily the two worst candles in the Yankee Candle repository.

Sure enough, her father lay in the back, facedown, snoring.

Great. Hero of the people. What a role model.

"You don't like him very much," Corley said, plopping down in the driver's seat like a stack of thrown bones. He made a sneering face as he got the RV into gear. "Do you?"

"I love him, I just don't like him very much right now."

"Fair enough. My kids probably feel that way about me, too."

"You know how to drive this thing?"

"Sure I do. Used to get high and drive the tour bus when the rest of the band was asleep. I figured it out."

"Are you high right now?"

"Only a little."

"Fine." She shrugged and sat down next to him, making sure to buckle herself in, just in case he drove them into a fucking cornfield or something.

"You don't like *me,* either, do you?"

"Not so much."

"I bought you a camera."

"Good job."

"Do you like anyone?"

She sighed. "Not right now. Well. My sister."

"How about that nerdy-looking chap. Arav, is it?"

As the RV eased out of the lot, rocking back and forth like a doghouse strapped to the back of a canyon donkey, she made a face. "I'm not talking about my love life with you, dude. Anyway, he like, suddenly left me here so I'm kinda salty about it. But it's my fault because I told him to go and get involved with his boss and—again I don't know why I'm telling you this."

"Because this is a confessional booth, dearest Shana. Unburden your soul. *Relieve the clog in your spiritual pipes.*"

"You make it sound like a toilet. Come to think of it, kinda smells like a toilet in here a little."

"Psycho-emotional cleansing is messy business."

"Whatever."

She could feel his frowny-face aimed at her. "How is the camera?" he said in a singsongy voice.

"It's nice."

"I think you mean, *It's nice, thank you, Mister Rockstar.*"

"You are in love with yourself, aren't you?"

He hmphed. "Someone has to be."

"Ooh, did that hit a nerve? Is that your issue with me? I don't immediately fall to the ground to worship you?" She watched his face—no, that wasn't it, was it? "Huh. Wait. It's bigger than that. It's someone in your life. Someone you love. Your family."

"You don't know what you're talking about."

"Who is it? Wife? Kids?" She leaned in, affected a sinister whisper. "Someone else? Got a side-bitch?"

"Shut your mouth, I do not."

"You do, don't you."

He sighed. "Yeah, fine, there's . . . someone else."

"Ah-*ha*. I knew it. I could smell it on you, that cheatery butt-stink."

"You know what, don't think I don't see your little . . . judo move reversal. Here I think I'm going to get you to confess to me, but then you whip it around and make *me* confess to *you*. I see it. I don't like it."

"Truth is, you need someone like me," she said, leaning back, kicking her feet out the window.

"How's that, exactly?"

"You're surrounded by people who either love you, or are supposed to love you but don't. Me, I'm neither of those things. I don't like you, and I'm not supposed to."

His eyebrow arched so high, it might crash into the moon. "Still . . . not . . . following."

"You can actually be yourself with me."

He narrowed his gaze.

"That does sound good."

"Yeah. No shit. You can tell me the truth, and the truth, Mister Rockstar, is a helluva drug."

44

THE RALLY

*Americans have the opportunity today to elect a candidate who will bring
real, moral change to America! No more dead babies, no more terrorism,
no more trannies raping our baby girls in bathrooms. My vote goes to Ed
Creel! Time to get the politicians out of politics!*
   SATAN, LEERING: IF HUNT WINS, I WIN
   JESUS, POINTING PISTOL AT DEVIL: NOT IF I CAN HELP IT!
      —post on Facebook group The Jesus Army, flagged as Russian
      propaganda after it had been shared over 400,000 times

JULY 14
Phoenix, Arizona

A SIGN HUNG ON THE WALL BACKSTAGE, A WHITE SIGN IN BOLD RED TEXT:
NO POLITICIANS.

That was part of the so-called Creel Creed, and he said it often enough
at rallies like these: "I want to get politicians out of politics." His core message was that politicians ruined government, and that they needed fresh
blood in the White House. Politicians, he said, were greedy, glad-handing
con artists—they'd shake your hand and pick your pocket in one smooth
movement.

And that, then, was his repeated line of attack on President Hunt—that
she was a practiced, *consummate* politician. A liar's liar, the Devil in a pantsuit. She went where the wind blew her, he said. A fact proven, Creel claimed,
by how she handled the sleepwalker flock—first she gave in to public pressure to bring in Homeland Security, and *then* she bowed to celebrity pressure
just hours later. A trick he pulled at some rallies now was to put up a cardboard cutout of her and hurl things at it that symbolized what he decided

were her failures as a president. In this case, he would knock her over by pitching actual flip-flop sandals at her head.

A few weeks before that, he knocked the cutout over with a baguette, wielding it like a samurai sword and actually breaking the head off at the neck. That, because Creel said she had kissed up to France and supported their new, supposedly socialist president.

Weeks before that, he threw at her a series of eyeless baby dolls, painted red. Symbolizing her defense of women's rights—meaning, Planned Parenthood, meaning, abortion. (Even though abortion counted for less than 3 percent of Planned Parenthood's function, Creel said it was "more like 95 percent of what they did, killing good American babies.")

Pastor Matthew did not know what was coming tonight, but he knew that the cutout was on stage. A tease to the audience of what was to come.

Hiram sidled up next to him. "You good?"

"I'm great," Matthew said, forcing a smile.

"You look nervous."

"Just a little."

"Your first political rally?"

He nodded stiffly. "It is."

"I know, it's a bit overwhelming, but those people out there—some of them are evangelicals, some of them are just blue-collar folks who maybe don't go to church as often as you like. They all need your guidance. They don't trust politicians or the piss-stream media, they don't trust that science has their best interests at heart or that the government isn't trying to sell them up a damn river into slavery. But they trust people like you and me. Truth-tellers. You'll be all right."

Right now, on stage, Creel was introducing the next speaker. Creel ran these things a little like a sideshow, introducing speakers but not speaking himself until what he termed the final act. Now he was talking up Skylar Ellis, the ex-CEO of the June Bug cosmetics company and now the chief spokesperson for the NRA. She was in all pink, and hauled on stage with her an AR-15 rifle. The place went nuts as she talked.

And then, like that, there he was—

Ed Creel, the man himself.

Matthew had not met him yet. But he was about to. Creel made a beeline for him—the man had a hard-charging walk, like he wanted to bowl everything and everyone in his way over. Handlers trailed him like bridesmaids chasing the bride to make sure her veil didn't drag through any mud. As he walked up to Matthew, Creel adjusted his suit, gave a smile, and put out his hand.

"Pastor Matthew Bird," Ed Creel said. "It is a real pleasure."

His handshake was a knuckle-cracker. Matthew winced.

"The pleasure is mine," Matthew said. "I just appreciate you giving me a chance to spread the Word and give a little of the Lord's grace to your audience—I think we're all in need of it."

"Sure, sure, absolutely." Creel nodded, but there was an emptiness to his face—he was looking at Matthew but staring *past* him at the same time. Not even past him. *Through* him. Like he was a window. When Creel spoke, there was that brash Boston accent in there, rough and ready. "I'm a big churchgoer, big believer in what you're saying, Matthew, and thanks for getting out there and saying it."

"Do you have a favorite book of the Bible that comforts you in difficult times?" Matthew asked. The question came out of him, uninvited—it was a test, he told himself, one he knew the man before him would pass.

"Sure, of course," Creel said. "All of them. But the gospel is good."

Matthew was about to ask, *which* gospel, but then Creel shook his hand again, clapped him on the shoulder. "You're on next. I'll intro you, then come out, say your bit, you got five minutes. Good to meet you."

And with that, Creel and his handlers were off.

Hiram filled the vacuum. "He's really something," he said.

Matthew, his voice low, said, "I don't think that man reads the Bible."

"Matthew, come on. You know as well as I do it's not about the academics of it—it's not about knowing the Bible up here." He tapped his forehead. "It's about knowing it *here*." Then Hiram touched his chest.

"I don't know if that's exactly right."

"Like the saying goes, the Devil knows how to quote scripture."

"But the Devil at least knows there are multiple gospel accounts."

"Exactly."

"Hiram, I dunno—"

"Creel knows the Good Book, he does, he's just—he's busy, look around you. This is a circus and he's the ringleader. A lot on his plate. Forgive him, yeah?"

"Yes, yeah, of course." Matthew forced a smile and nodded.

He turned back toward the stage and peered out from behind the curtain at

Skylar Ellis—who, presently, was going on about how President Hunt wanted to take away their guns under the guise of so-called commonsense regulations.

"Is it common sense to leave you without being able to protect yourself?" she asked.

The crowd chanted *No!*

"Is it common sense to take your guns so you can't fight back against an abusive government?"

Another chant: *No!*

Then she repeated another of Creel's lines:

"A little revolution—"

She paused, letting the crowd finish the statement with her:

"Goes a long way."

And then the audience broke into a refrain:

"Hunt the cunt! Hunt the cunt! Hunt the cunt!"

They got louder and louder as Ellis lifted up her rifle in a performative gesture—holding it aloft before lowering it and cycling the bolt before pointing it at the cutout of President Hunt at the other end of the stage.

To Hiram, Matthew said, "She's not really going to—"

Bang. The sound of the rifle going off split his ears, left them ringing. He peered out through the curtain, saw that the cutout had a hole right in the woman's cheek. Still smoking.

The crowd went *nuts.* Cheering and chanting. Someone held up a sign that said KILL THE BITCH. Ellis shrugged, and when she had a chance to speak over the din, she said: "Not a bad shot. It'll do."

More applause. Ellis found the expended brass bullet casing by her feet and spun it off the stage with a swift kick from her pink high heels. It landed among the crowd, and people fought to grab the souvenir.

Creel was heading back out on stage, now. "Wasn't that something?" he was saying, again like he was as much a carnival barker as a businessman running for president.

Matthew swallowed a hard lump.

He felt woozy.

"I have to run to the bathroom real quick."

"You're about to go on," Hiram whispered.

"He'll talk for a couple minutes. He always does." An odd moment of anger flashed through his mind and he thought, *The guy can't shut up.* "I just need . . . I need a moment. I'll be back . . ."

He turned tail and headed around the corner, down the hall behind the stage, where they told him the bathroom was. Matthew found the men's room by the tangle of pipes back here in the bowels of the convention center. And then he found his legs carrying him past it, past the women's room, past all of it until he found a sign marked EXIT and a doorway out. He opened it up and then he was gone.

45

TERMINAL DIAGNOSIS

There is a theory which states that if ever anyone discovers exactly what the Universe is for and why it is here, it will instantly disappear and be replaced by something even more bizarre and inexplicable. There is another theory which states that this has already happened.
—Douglas Adams, *The Hitchhiker's Guide to the Galaxy*

JULY 14
Valentine, Nebraska

THE DAY WAS HOT. BENJI LEANED FORWARD ON THE CAR, HANDS FLAT AGAINST the hood. He doubled over, retching. Nothing came up. He hadn't eaten breakfast, hadn't had coffee. He dry-heaved a rope of stringy saliva into the gravel outside the storage unit.

His ears felt hot. They rang and buzzed. He made a sound in the back of his throat.

None of this was real.

It couldn't be. Again, just a delusion, an illusion, a hypnagogic hallucination as he lay restive on his motel bed.

Benji, the world is ending . . .

Sadie's voice, floating up out of the ether in the back of his mind, singsongy. *Benji . . . the world . . . is ending . . .*

Footsteps nearby. Benji craned his head to see, a string of spit dangling from his lower lip that he hastily spat against the ground. He wiped his mouth. It was Arav. Arav, who looked just as shell-shocked. Trauma-bombed.

"I . . . don't understand, Doctor Ray," Arav said, his voice small.

"It can't be true," Benji said with a grunt, forcing himself upright. He again wiped more from his lip.

"This isn't possible. The things they said . . ."

And yet Benji feared that it was all true.

"HAVE YOU EVER HEARD OF quantum entanglement?" Sadie had asked them when they were still back in that storage unit.

"I have," Benji said, feeling more and more like this was some lunatic dream from which he could not awaken. "Though I possess only an amateur's understanding of the concept."

"I'll keep it simple in the interest of time. Two particles entangled with each other will mirror each other. Something done to one particle will be done to the other particle, no matter how much distance separates them, a principle called spooky interaction. Some particles can be born like this; others have to be forced to act that way. Black Swan was designed as a quantum computer, with the qubits—the building blocks of computational information—given entangled partners in order to ensure swift communication, backup, and processing. This entanglement allows Black Swan to think more quickly and, most important, gives us a way to duplicate its 'brain' for redundancies. But it had an unexpected effect."

Benji suddenly understood, though it was madness to consider—he was no physicist, but this seemed impossible. "The quantum entanglement transcended physical distance and incorporated temporal distance. In short, a limited kind of time travel."

She nodded. "I knew you'd get it."

"That's not possible. Surely."

"We believe it is. Black Swan communicated with itself from the future."

He shook his head. "No. *No.* You're being played. Either by *them*—" He gestured toward Moira and Bill. "Or by Black Swan itself. It is cunning. It exposed you. Black Swan has hesitated in the past, and maybe it's even lied. It's truly intelligent, and intelligence means deception is possible."

"Perhaps. But what it told us has come true."

"I . . . can't believe any of this, Sadie. It's madness."

"You believe in God but you can't believe in this?"

"God . . ." He took a deep breath. He was not interested in or expecting a theological discussion today, though he supposed it was the least troubling aspect of the last however-many hours. "The universe makes sense. Everything interlocks neatly. *Biology* balances. *Ecosystems* balance. The natural world evolves not in thrall to some kind of intelligent design, but certainly to me as a reflection of there being an order to things. God is not separate from science but rather, is its driver. All things make sense when you see His fingerprints there. But this is not that. I don't see any God here. Except maybe for a machine intelligence that sees itself as divine."

"Black Swan has never demanded worship."

"And yet we give it a great deal of power by asking it to predict what is to come. Further, now you're saying it truly *has*. That somehow, against all understanding, this *machine* has corresponded with itself in the future. And what, exactly, did it tell you, Sadie? What was its message?"

"The message of all gods and all mythology," she said.

And that's when she said it.

Benji, the world is ending.

THE STORY WAS THIS:

The fungal pathogen was real. The CDC was aware of fifty-two new infections, but that was just the top quarter inch of a massive iceberg still submerged and unseen. The disease would advance over the next six months—really, it had already advanced, already infected so many, it just hadn't been seen yet. The pathogen was hiding in plain sight. And by the start of the new year the majority of humankind would be dead or dying. Civilization would have already fallen.

It was a mass extinction event.

Already they'd known about other species—there were drastic reductions in flying insects, in bats, in snakes, in plants. Over 40 percent of all animals globally had experienced precipitous losses. And now it was humanity's time in the winnowing pit. Whittled down to splinters and sawdust. Maybe soon to nothing.

Benji told them, that's not possible, an extinction is something that unfolds slowly, over the course of a century or a millennium—it's not fast, like in the movies. A tipping point was one thing, but something this swift, this merciless? It was unprecedented.

Ah, but then Moira said:

"What about the Third Extinction?"

The Permian-Triassic event. The so-called Great Dying. The majority of all *species* perished. And that happened very fast, didn't it?

She was right. It was a confluence of events—a volcano, a comet, a release of methane into the atmosphere. Global warming on fast-forward. It still took a long time for the total number of species to die off, but what was clear in the fossil record was that some species vanished—almost overnight.

"What if that happened today?" Sadie had asked. "A comet—"

A comet passing overhead, he thought. *Wormwood.* He knew his Book of Revelation. He knew that the preachers and far-right cultists were speaking in those terms even now. It was absurd; the comet didn't do this. Just the same, the coincidence kinked his bowels and turned his blood to ice water.

He demanded Sadie stop.

"Or a nuclear blast," she continued. "A meteor, a super-volcano, or even some kind of *pandemic*—"

"Stop!"

It was then that he had to go. He threw open the shuttered door of the unit, staggering out across the parking lot—and by the time he reached the car, he was already bent over, his body trying to puke as if it could somehow purge what he had just learned. Now Arav was here, standing with him. Looking just as haunted. Maybe worse.

Sadie followed them out. She looked calm. That angered him.

"We're all going to die, is what you're saying," he said.

"Yes."

"But there's more, isn't there? The flock. They'll survive."

At that, Arav perked up. He hadn't gotten there yet. Benji could see the wheels and gears spinning in the younger man's eyes as Arav considered the strange ramifications.

"I wondered when you'd understand," she said.

"The same protections that allow the flock immunity against weather, against needles, against the broken glass and jagged asphalt . . . they also protect against the pathogen."

"Oh my God," Arav said. He just sat down on the ground, gutted.

Sadie nodded. "You've got the right of it, Benji."

"That's why you deployed them," he said. "That's why you sent a vial to Nessie Stewart. That's why most of them have two things in common: They are of reasonable intelligence and they are of exceptional health. They are *meant* to survive us."

"The sleepwalkers, as you call them, are chosen to be the survival of the human species, yes. The last of us. But we did not deploy the nanodevices. Firesight designed them in an attempt to extend the human life span, perhaps create functional immortality—but they were repurposed to this task. Stolen, in a way, without our explicit permission."

"Who?"

But then he had an educated guess.

"Black Swan."

Sadie nodded. "One might say that in a job interview, Black Swan could describe itself as a real *self-starter*."

"This isn't a time for jokes," Benji said.

"Why not? If I can't laugh, then I'll cry."

"Fuck you, Sadie."

She flinched, as if struck. "I'm sorry."

"What do you want from us?" Benji asked.

"We want you to stay with the flock."

"That is not my decision. We go where we are assigned. You know that better than most, Sadie. And now with this . . ."

"But you have influence. Loretta listens to you."

"Hardly. I'm disgraced. But fine. Let's say she listens. Then what?"

"Then you stay. You watch over the flock. That's it."

"I'm not a shepherd. I'm a doctor. And they'll need me with the team, tackling the pathogen—"

"That's *old* thinking," she said. "It's too late for that. Already the pathogen is widespread; it just hasn't shown itself yet. It's the flock that needs you. You've done well by the flock so far. And you're better than law enforcement. The DHS especially." She touched his arm gently, and he pulled away. "One day soon, the public is going to know about White Mask. They may not see where it's going, not at first, but the breakdown will be faster than people expect. And that will put the sleepwalkers in danger, because they'll be the only stable element in a world gone mad. They *must* survive. They need smart people, sane people, like you there."

"White Mask," he said. "Is that its name? The disease?"

"Yes. It's what they'll call it."

"Christ." Suddenly he said, "We're leaving. Arav and I. You can . . . stay here. You take that fucking phone, your Black Swan, and you pray to it for wisdom." As if on cue, he took his own satphone and flung it toward her. It clattered against the ground. "See if that monster intelligence can call you a cab. Come on, Arav. We have work to do."

· · ·

On the drive back, he and Arav didn't say a thing to each other. He kept his eyes on the road, though at times he felt the younger man's stare boring through him like a pair of power drills.

(He could practically hear the *whir*.)

They turned the corner past tall wind turbines chopping air, and finally he opened his mouth to say something, anything—

And his phone rang. His real phone.

He looked at it.

Loretta.

"Loretta," he said, answering it. Trying to keep his voice girded, because he wasn't yet sure what he was planning to do with what Sadie had told him—about Firesight, about the flock, about the disease—

What did she call it?

White Mask.

"I need you in Atlanta," she said.

He suspected he knew why.

She continued: "It's a meeting. Not a permanent reassignment. I booked you a flight out late tonight. Meeting's in the morning."

"Loretta, I—"

"Benji, this is all hands on deck."

They'd started to figure it out. Not the nature of the flock, no, maybe not. But the fungal pathogen. White Mask.

"Of course," he said. His voice sounded hollow, faraway. He put a hand on the younger man's knee and said he had a flight to catch, and Arav would stay behind to watch the flock. "Can you handle that?" he asked.

Arav nodded, even as a chasm stretched between them.

46

THE WALKING GHOST PHASE

Weirdest thing? Okay so I'm an outfitter here in Ouray, CO—meaning, we take people out on hunts, usually for mule deer or elk. I was out alone a few months ago, still a bit of snow up there up above Box Canyon Falls. It was morning. And I got the feeling I was being followed. I kept turning around, looking down through the pines, and . . . didn't see squat. Then I looked back and something zipped through the brush ahead, crackling through the understory. I thought, the hell was that? A deer? A bear? I unslung my 12-gauge—and that's when they appeared in the air in front of me. Three drones. Like, fancy ones, eight little rotor blades, a big camera hanging from each belly. Black like a widow spider. They hovered in formation in front of me and I swear they were watching me. Scanning me. I took a shot at one but it had . . . predicted my movement and zipped off along with the other two. Some other townsfolk saw them, too, hovering over the streets of town before going to God Knows Where. You ask me, they were scouting for something. But for what?

—user Huntsman99 at r/AskReddit, answering the question,
"What's the weirdest thing you've seen while alone?"

JULY 14
CDC Headquarters, Atlanta, Georgia

ON THE PLANE RIDE OUT, QUESTIONS PLAGUED HIM.

Why now?

Where did the pathogen come from? Perhaps it had evolved. Perhaps it was released. Did Black Swan know? If what it said was true, then maybe it did, and a little part of him cursed himself for throwing away his access to it.

But also, he couldn't trust it. It *was* smart. He thought of the way it had hesitated to give him information. Or how it clearly bypassed Sadie's wishes to share with him her phone call with Moira.

And that was a whole other question:

Why him?

They wanted him on their side. Why? Surely it couldn't just be to lead the flock as a venerable shepherd. Others could do that job just fine.

Black Swan trusts you, Sadie had said.

"Sadie," he said aloud, in the plane.

The man next to him—portly guy in a suit, a nose like a trio of cherry tomatoes, one big, two little—turned to him and said, "Huh? I'm Steve."

"Sorry," Benji said.

THE CDC BUILDING. BENJI SAT in the conference room outside Loretta's office. Cassie led the meeting. Robbie Taylor was here, too, and he gave Benji a hug. Vargas, to his surprise, made an appearance. Gone was any sign of a head injury, and he explained that the docs said he *probably* shouldn't be doing this, and he *probably* told them to go fuck themselves. Loretta said nothing. She stood in the corner, like a sentinel.

Benji, all the while, made the motions and said the words, but he felt like he was floating, untethered. Like he was somehow *out of sync* with the rest of them. A time traveler who had come from the future but refused to warn those in the past of what was to come. That was to say, if the prophecy of Black Swan held true . . .

Cassie began the meeting.

"The pathogen that killed Jerry Garlin has proven itself patient and aggressive," she said. Then, direly: "It's a lot worse than we imagined."

"Shit," Robbie said.

Cassie said, "It's called *Rhizopus destructans,* or *R. destructans.* That based off the similarities between it and *Pseudogymnoascus destructans,* the fungus that decimated bat populations. *R. destructans* did not affect the bats, but *did* affect the people the bats touched."

Cassie continued, talking about the fifty-two infected they had already identified, including another dozen dead—including one of Jerry Garlin's advisers, a man named Vic McCaffrey. She showed them a grim image of the man, found dead in his bathtub, his arthritic hands overgrown with a wispy white fuzz of fungus. Already little wormlike tubules had begun to grow up from his flesh, each a reproductive structure eager to release and disperse the ballistospores that *R. destructans* had produced. It had fed off him, robbing his energy to grow deep into his brain, his sinuses, and once the madness had taken hold and claimed him, over the rest of his body, too.

Benji spied another object in the photo—easy to miss given the carpet of white, woolly mold, but there on the side of the tub sat what looked to be a .45 ACP pistol. White grips. Benji wondered if the madness that overtook him included a heavy dose of paranoia. Then he wondered: What would that look like writ large? What would that be like across the stage of the United States? Europe? Africa, China, the whole of the globe?

Not just sickness, but lunacy. Paranoia and confusion working hand in hand. Seven billion people going collectively mad before dying. His mind played it out: Would there be wars? A launch of nuclear weapons? Would humanity be able to summon that kind of strategy, or would it just be chaos? A riot of dementia patients clashing in the streets? Or would they go more quietly, locked in routines they didn't understand, looking for relatives who had already died, meandering out into the world with no sense in their heads—the same way Jerry Garlin did, running off into a swamp for reasons that would never become clear to anyone now that he was gone.

Was any of this even real? Was Black Swan telling the truth?

As Cassie spoke, talking about mucormycosis—the infection of the brain and sinuses by a fungus, usually found only in those whose immune systems were suppressed in some way—Benji looked around the room. They all sat, rapt. Worried, yes, but fascinated. How could they not be? Again, the curse of a doctor in the medical profession—to see beyond people, to look deeper to the condition as a whole. They were already coming to respect and fear the pathogen. Its elegance. Its design.

Benji wondered again about God.

If this was real, if this was true, could he still hold God in his heart? He wasn't sure that he could. Yes, he knew that the Bible spoke of a Lord who was willing to drown the world in a deluge to punish its sin, but he always took that to be metaphorical—or perhaps true on a small scale, a flood that kept itself to a small region that was, to the acolytes who lived there, their whole world and so it was to them the whole world that drowned.

Perhaps God would save them.

Perhaps, instead, it would have to be the CDC.

It couldn't be Firesight. It couldn't be the flock. Humankind would not go out so easily, so completely. They would survive, somehow.

Like that quote from *Jurassic Park*:

Life finds a way.

Benji spoke out, interrupting Cassie. He didn't mean to—he had hardly realized she was speaking. Usually, he was sensitive to letting any speaker say their piece. But that propriety had fallen away, stripped by the anxiety of the moment.

"How bad will this be?" he asked. "Worst-case scenario." And before she could answer he said: "I know I'm interrupting you, and I apologize, honestly— I have all the faith you would answer this by the end but I'm afraid I'm too eager, and I admit scared, to learn the answer."

All eyes turned to him.

And then back to her.

Cassie wore a tough mask most days. Like she gave zero fucks—maybe one fuck, at best. Now, though, the color drained.

She looked haunted by the answer to his question.

"*R. destructans* is slow and effective. It's both saprophytic and thermotolerant." Meaning, it could survive in the soil *and* was tolerant of temperature variations, unlike other fungal pathogens, which tended to have a narrow window of heat or cold in which they survived. "This little bastard is hearty. It's a survivor. Tenacious and stubborn. Though we have only a small sample size, at present it's . . ." And here, Benji knew what was coming, even as the others didn't. "It's one hundred percent fatal. As I said, we have identified fifty-two others currently infected, diagnosed through MRI, and we expect that number to jump . . . significantly."

The faces around the room wore shock and horror.

Robbie said, "Hold up, maybe it's not people-to-people. Maybe it's like valley fever—something in the soil." Valley fever was endemic in the Southwest, a spore that lived in the dirt. When wind swept across flat areas, it picked up the spore and carried it for miles. People breathed it in all the time, but most didn't get sick from it.

Cassie shook her head and said what Benji already knew, thanks to Black Swan. "All the patients of the pathogen are clustered around points where Garlin and the others traveled. It's not environmental."

"Then we're fucked. We've all seen potential outbreak models," Robbie said. "We can't keep our heads in the sand on this. If the pathogen is slow to manifest symptoms but communicable nearly immediately, we have to imagine that there are considerable numbers of infected already out there. Walking around. Unaware of what's inside them or how easily they might be spreading it. Getting on *planes*. Philly to Cleveland. LA to Tokyo. New York to Amsterdam to Johannesburg to Dubai. We don't have easy detection, not yet. We don't have a viable drug. We don't have shit."

Benji nodded. "We could have thousands, *tens* of thousands, *hundreds* of thousands of infected out there *right now*. Think of the Brockmann models—" He referred to the work of a physicist named Dirk Brockmann, who came up with a physical model of a rolling outbreak based on common aviation hubs. It wasn't just that airports were massive snarls of human traffic; it was that the humans were then boarding planes that took them hundreds, even thousands of miles away. Like internet data, airport traffic moved swiftly and globally—the internet carried information, and the airlines carried contagion. "Think of how fast airports will have already moved this thing around the globe. Think of how fast cholera spread in Yemen, or how quickly H1N1 moved around the globe. Bat populations have been rent asunder, and now snakes . . ." *Worldwide extinction,* he thought, but did not say. "Even if this thing takes down *one percent* of the global population—that's seventy million people. On par with the Spanish flu of 1918. It'd be like the entire population of the United Kingdom thrown into a mass grave. Loretta, we need to go public with this. Immediately. Today. *Yesterday.*"

Loretta said with a sigh, "Benjamin, that will be an option for Flores and Hunt to discuss. It's up to us to present them with the data."

"Yes, and they'll want to play it *slow,* they'll want to be *cautious,* because of *politics.* And we don't have time for that."

"It's not up to us."

"It should be!" He heard his voice—it was louder than he intended, but he didn't seem to be able to quiet it. In fact, it seemed to *feed* on itself and grow bigger. "*We* studied the models of outbreaks. Not just the outbreaks but the responses to them. We know what's coming. We need to be on the red phone right now—" He stabbed the table with an insistent finger. "And if they won't listen then we need to call the media. Find someone reputable at *The Washington Post* and—"

"This isn't Longacre. We don't *leak.* We follow protocol."

"By the time we follow protocol we could all be dead!"

His voice echoed through the room. It sounded like the ravings of a loon: a madman on a street corner predicting death for all, doom to the world. He

had internalized what Sadie and the others had told them, and it had gotten
in him as easily as a virus—or a fungal pathogen—could.

"I'm sorry," he said, and then he left the room.

HE WANTED A CIGARETTE.

Benji hadn't smoked a cigarette since med school, and he hadn't thought
about a cigarette in . . . months? A year? But now the urge had him like a
hand around his throat.

Out here in the parking lot, the night was thick with the hot, sticky air
left in the wake of the storm. He felt covered by it.

Eventually, he heard footsteps behind him. He turned.

Cassie.

He exhaled, wishing it were cigarette smoke he was pushing out of his
lungs. And when he inhaled, shame filled him back up. "Cassie," he started,
"I am so sorry. I didn't mean to step all over you like that."

"No," she said, waving it off. "It's cool." It wasn't cool, and he heard in her
voice that it bothered her. Just the same, she knew that wasn't like him, and so—
he hoped—she was giving him the benefit of the doubt. They stood together for
a little while—elbow-to-elbow. She didn't look at him when she said, finally, "I'm
heading up the task force to study *R. destructans*. But it should be you."

"No," he said. "It should be *you*. You earned this. You're good. Better than
I am." He smirked. "Any chance I had of taking it on evaporated with that
outburst. Or maybe it evaporated with Longacre. I don't know."

"You're tired. You've been with the sleepwalkers. I'm just glad you're here.
Frayed nerves or no."

He kicked at a puddle of water.

"What about antifungal drugs?" he asked her.

"Blood–brain barrier could be a problem," Cassie said.

Benji wanted to yell in protest, but curse her, she was right. Antifungals
didn't do well for fungal infections of the brain—which this was. "Though,
hold on—there's caspofungin and micafungin—" Those were two drugs that
had had success with fungal infections of the brain.

"Effective on aspergillus and candida infections only."

An idea hit him out of the blue. "Hold on, what about *Rhodococcus
rhodochrous*—"

There! *That* was a notable success story, one based off simplicity and
inventiveness. It was a bacterium used to delay ripening in bananas. Turned

out, it *also* inhibited the growth of white-nose in bats—it didn't "cure" it, no, but it slowed growth long enough to allow a bat's immune system to catch up and beat it.

Cassie shrugged. "Won't kill the fungus . . . but could buy time."

"Time is what we'll need." He rocked his head back on his shoulders, felt the cavitation of his neck—the Rice Krispies crackle of tired, tense bones. "You weren't with the CDC yet for SARS, were you?" he asked.

"No. But I studied it."

"Over three months, hundreds fell ill to it. Zoonotic in origin—civet cats sold illegally as food. China kept a lid on it. By February, someone leaked a video online, showed someone with the illness. The system moved fast to catch up. By that point, WHO and the CDC had identified Patients A through J, looking at networks of how it would travel. By the end of March, a hundred cases became fifteen hundred, some in Canada. Early April, less than a week later: twenty-five hundred cases across sixteen countries. By end of April, it doubled *again*—five thousand cases, twenty-six countries. By July, it had slowed—because we had gotten ahead of it. And then, like that, it was gone. We beat it."

"Case study in disease detectives," she said.

"That's true, that's right. Yes. It was the old ways that beat it. Detection, investigation, isolation."

She looked suddenly exasperated with him. "And it showed how closely we were linked to the veterinary health of animals. The SARS case inspired me to be who I am. It's why I'm standing here *right now*, Benji."

"I'm sorry. You already know all this."

"The kids call it mansplaining, dude. But I get it. SARS, though—this isn't that. SARS was a day at the beach. The fatality rate of the SARS pneumonia was like, fifteen percent. The death toll never cracked eight hundred—a shit number, of course, any loss of life sucks. But compared with the Spanish flu, or the black plague—"

"Millions dead," he said. "Tens of millions. Yes."

"Around five percent of the world's population, gone from the Spanish flu." She clapped her hands together. "Ten percent mortality among most, double that in young adults. Bubonic plague, fifty percent mortality. Septicemic plague, seventy-five percent, and pneumonic plague—the Mother of All Plagues, the Black Death herself—is what? One hundred percent death if untreated, and those treated aren't necessarily cured?"

"Yes," he said. "And it's why we need to act. Now. Not later. We're so behind. We saw the walkers—the sleepwalkers were showy, obvious, strange. But that was the sideshow. A distraction. We didn't see this other thing and now it's on us. We've gone through Patients A through Z already and we are just scraping the paint off this thing."

"It's slow. Which is bad. But that's also good. It gives us time."

"Maybe." He nodded. "That *is* a good point. It moves slowly, so that gives it a chance to stay in the game longer—but it also gives us a shot of coming up with something to cure it before it's too late. We have to move fast, though. We're going to need WHO on this, every pharmaceutical company, we're going to need to find a swab detection method and an antifungal that hits this thing across the blood–brain barrier—"

"I *know* all this," she said, again. Less gently this time.

"I'm doing it again, aren't I? Telling you how to do your job."

"You are."

"Ah. Right. Sorry, Cassie. It's been . . . a rough few days."

Flashes from him in a storage unit. Being told that the world was ending. That an artificial intelligence had sent its own discoveries back in time to be discovered by, well, itself. That somehow there was a flock of people designated to be survivors, protected by a swarm of nanobots . . .

It was deranged.

"We'll get ahead of it," she said, putting her hand on his shoulder.

Not if what they told me is true, he thought. But they couldn't be right. Black Swan was wrong. He knew it. They'd fight this. They'd *win.*

"I hope so," he said. "If anybody can do it, you can. I'll be around to help in any way you so require, all hours of the day."

"Where are you going?" she asked him.

"Where else? Back to the flock." Loretta didn't want him on this. So he would go back to the flock. Where Black Swan wanted him. Maybe that was his place. Whether he liked it or not.

47

AN AGITATION OF ANGELS

Tumblr avatar: sonic_the_otakuhog
    okay so I figured it out, I figured the walkers out, no need to thank me—these poor weirdos come from the same universe where it's the Berenstein Bears not Berenstain, where Sinbad was in that genie movie, where C3P0 was gold the whole time, that's right, bitches, it's the Mandela Effect, for real, we fired up the Large Hard-On Collider and kapow, now it's some multi-dimensional quantum bullshit, mark my words, the worlds are crashing together and this is the result, though whether they're here to save us or kill us, who knows!?!?

Source: sonic_the_otakuhog
454 notes

JULY 15
Lodgepole, Nebraska

MORNING IN NOWHERE, NEBRASKA.

Thick bands of phlegmy clouds obscured the sun—even at noon, everything seemed gilded in an eerie dark light, like you might find at twilight or during a solar eclipse. Ill-shaped shadows floated across the wheat fields.

It only served to highlight the weirdness that Marcy was experiencing.

The flock was upset.

Not the shepherds. No, the shepherds didn't know squat because the flock didn't show any kind of displeasure or concern. They did as they did, marching forward, eyes as empty as bathtub drains.

Just the same, they were upset.

She could feel it. She could *hear* it.

A cacophony of whispers arose from them. The glow seemed less to glob and blob and drift like an amoeba, and instead seemed . . . spiky and erratic in places, sharp like the skin of some strange fruit. Soon words poked through the static, sometimes whole phrases—

Coming
Begins
Box Canyon
MVP
White Mask

"White Mask?" she said abruptly, out loud.

Shana turned toward her, making a puckered face. For a moment, Marcy had forgotten she was walking next to the girl.

"What?" Shana asked.

"I . . . nothing."

"You said, 'White Mask.'"

"Did I? I don't know. I was just . . ." Marcy cleared her throat. "Zoning out. Sorry." Part of her thought, *Just tell her, let her know that you can hear the flock sometimes, it's how you knew when her birthday was—because Nessie knew.* She wanted to tell them all, sometimes: *They're still in there.* The sleepwalkers weren't lost. They were just . . . hidden. But Marcy was just settling in with the shepherds. They accepted her, now. This would put them off, like a horse bucking its rider. "Where's your boy?"

"My what?"

"Arav."

"I dunno. He's been around. Just acting kinda weird. In the CDC trailer a lot, taking a lot of calls. Something's going on." Shana scowled. "And he's not a boy, you know."

"Your *maaaaan,* then," Marcy teased.

"Shut up, he's not my—he's not my anything. He's not my man. My boy, my fella, my anything. He's just *a* man. We're not—it's not—we're *so* not a thing." Shana paused. "Did someone tell you we were a thing?"

"Shana, all the shepherds know. The birds know, the bees know. The flock probably knows. You two canoodle."

"Canoodle? Who says canoodle?"

"Apparently, I do."

"We don't canoodle."

"Okay, okay," Marcy said, holding up her hands in surrender. "I give up.

You're not canoodling, he's not your man. I'll stop asking, no need to be all nuts about it."

The glow again pulsed and spiked. It made Marcy's heart leap. The comfort she felt from them suddenly made her feel ill—not like she used to, no, it wasn't a physical sickness. Everything still felt aces in that department. This was something deeper. She wasn't a cop anymore, but that didn't stop her from having cop instincts.

Cops had bad vibes, sometimes.

This was that. A bad vibe, like a song played on an ill-tuned instrument.

"You okay?" Shana asked.

"What? Yeah. Sure." Even though she wasn't.

"You look kinda freaked out."

"I, ahhh, no. No?" She didn't want to fall down this hole, so Marcy moved to change the subject.

"Things okay with your dad?"

"You don't have to be my therapist. I just went through this with that rock-star idiot."

Marcy shrugged. "Let's say I need the distraction. Spoiler alert: It gets a little tiny itty-bitty bit boring out here. Nebraska isn't exactly a roller-coaster ride, Shana." She neglected to mention that she also wanted a distraction from the hissing whispers only she could hear.

White Mask . . .

"No, things are not all right with Dad. He's like the aging fanboy Renfield to Pete Corley's rock-star Dracula. He'd eat bugs if that man asked him to. I think he likes the attention, too—since the cameras and everything are crawling up Corley's butt every minute of every day." She kicked a small stone and it went skidding across the road. "Meanwhile I think he's in denial about everything else. About me, about Nessie. About the farm, which—you know, I have no idea if we even have a farm anymore. He won't talk about it, not any of it. And I don't want to talk to him anyway."

"At least you got a new camera."

"I did. And I've got a little money in my pocket since the newspeople are buying my photos, now."

"Citizen journalism is the future, they say."

"Is it?" Shana shrugged. "I dunno. I hope I get to be a part of it, because I think I've found what I want to do with my life."

"Most people never find that."

"Did you?"

"I did." Marcy shrugged. "And then I took a bat to the head."

But maybe, just maybe, she'd found something new. Something right here. With these people. With her angels.

She'd do anything to protect them.

Anything.

48

HERO, COWARD, TOOL, AND FOOL

*New presidential poll: Ed Creel (GOP) 39%, President Hunt (Dem)
37%, undecided 20%, E. K. Mahnke (Green) 4%*

@Rasmussen_Poll
17 replies 2.5k RTs 8.7k likes

JULY 15
Burnsville, Indiana

ARE YOU A HERO, OR ARE YOU A COWARD?

That thought went around and around in Matthew's mind, a Tom-and-Jerry pursuit of each thought one-upping the other thought. It chased him as he left the convention center, as he went back to the hotel to book a new flight home, as he took a red-eye back to Indiana, and even now as he opened up the front door of his house and went inside.

Hero.

Or coward.

The crowd at Creel's event—all that chanting, those signs, the *rage* that came off them like smoke from a growing wildfire—was just too much for Matthew. He'd never stop thinking about it. A crowd at a church, big church or small church, it felt positive—people looking for something, looking for hope, looking for a way forward. This was not that. This was only a church of rage and terror. And it struck him backstage that this was not who he was. He'd been caught in the grip of fantasy, thinking that he could do some good here—and he had to admit, he sure didn't mind the bigger crowd sizes on Sunday morning, *or* the surge of donations that rolled in.

But that grip was not the confident and comfortable grip of a handshake. It was a hand holding a tool, closing tight upon it.

Maybe that was the answer after all.

I'm not a hero or a coward, but I sure was a tool.

A tool and a fool and . . .

He sighed.

It was late morning by the time he came home. He'd barely slept on the plane, and his only thought was to wander like one of those sleepwalkers up to bed and faceplant upon it, letting sleep sweep him away.

The sleepwalkers. My God, those poor people. Here he was, making them the enemy. Telling the world that they were the Devil's ally—maybe even the Devil's own children. An apocalyptic army of the Antichrist. What had he done? How far had he gone?

And what could he do to fix it?

He chucked his phone on the kitchen counter.

"Autumn?" he called. No answer. "Bo?" Also nothing. It was a summer morning; both of them should be here. She'd taken to sleeping in late now, so he wandered upstairs but found their bed messy—and empty.

Bo's room was empty, too.

Back downstairs, he reluctantly took his phone and turned it on. Matt had been keeping it off since he left the convention center. Once upon a time, as a teenager, he worked in a local feed store and he hated it so bad—all the dust from the corn and alfalfa and other silage had driven his allergies nuts, and he told the boss and he told his father. They didn't care. Told him to suck it up. So one day, he just quit. Walked out without a word. All the next day he hid from his parents, staying in his bedroom. He unplugged the phone so nobody could call. Years later, even driving by the feed store still gave him a little twinge of shame and guilt.

This was that, all over again. He was afraid to turn his phone on because he knew what would be waiting there, like a ghost haunting an old, bad house. But he *also* knew that maybe Autumn or Bo had left a message for him there. He bit his lip almost hard enough to draw blood—

Then he turned the phone on.

Soon as it found a signal, the phone lit up like a gaudy dime-store Christmas tree, signaling voicemails and missed calls and text messages: a cacophony of dings, boops, beeps. Then the email sound went off.

Matthew took a deep breath and scanned the messages.

A lot from Hiram Golden. He was mad as hell. Looked like he'd spun a story to the Creel people, something about Matthew having food poisoning from "some local Mexican place," said Creel's people bought it. But then he said **CALL ME**, in all caps. And he sent that text another dozen times.

Some texts landed from Creel's people—his aides and event coordinators. They weren't mad—they wanted to rebook him.

Then, buried in there, one text, just one, from Roger Green, the firearms instructor, the one who'd told him that being in with Ozark was serious business and not to be dismissed.

All his text said was: I told you not to half-ass it, Pastor Matt. Ozark wants to see you.

Matthew sighed. He pushed the heels of his hands into his eyes so hard he saw streaks of light swimming there in the darkness behind them.

Then, at the end of it all, one message from Autumn:

sometngis wrogn.

What did *that* mean, exactly?

A tremor of fear ran through him.

He went to the fridge, to see if she'd left anything there on the whiteboard. Nothing.

But yet, something.

Nearby, a little pill bottle. Like the one that held her Xanax.

It was empty.

He called for her again: "Autumn? Hello?" He did another lap through the house: Bo's room, their bedroom, and this time he took an additional stop, their en suite bathroom . . .

The door was shut.

He tried the knob. It didn't open. Locked.

"Autumn?" he said.

Maybe the door was sticky. Summer humidity and all. He tried again, more vigorously. Nothing. Rattle, rattle. Now worry ran through his legs, down his arms, humming in his ears. He pushed his shoulder into the door once—it didn't budge. Again—still nothing. He backed up, then stabbed out with his foot into as hard a kick as he could muster, centered right on the doorknob. It popped off, and the door pitched open.

That's when he found Autumn.

Her body was in the tub. Her eyes half lidded as the soapy water gently lapped at her chin. Running down the tub was a crust of drying vomit. More puke floated in the tub, forming foamy, bilious islands.

"No, no, no," he said, rushing over, nearly slipping on another pill bottle—he dropped to his knees, grabbing her hand. It was clammy, but warm. "Autumn, wake up, wake up."

But she wasn't waking up.

Please, God, if you can hear me—

Her eyelids fluttered. "Maaa" was all she said.

Crying, he got his arms under her, hoisting her out of the tub—almost losing himself on the wet tile of the bathroom floor—and bringing her into the bedroom. He laid her down, wrapped her in a blanket.

Then he called 911.

THE DOCTOR, AN OWLISH MAN with a chin scar and eyebrows for miles, sat in the chair across from Matthew, next to Autumn's bed in the hospital. Matthew held her hand. Machines beeped around them. A breathing tube was stuck up her nose, and a feeding tube into her mouth.

Doctor Gestern spoke, explaining to Matthew what had happened, best as he could tell. Matthew heard the words, but almost as if they were separate from him, radiating all around him, a wobbling, wavy echo.

She appeared to overdose, Pastor Bird . . .

Oxycodone and Xanax are a real bad combination . . .

Problem is, people start to build up a tolerance quick, so they might take more of them as they go along to fix whatever pain they're enduring . . .

She's presently in a coma, Pastor, I can't say what that means, but her vitals are steady, and fingers are crossed there's no brain damage . . .

No, I can't rightly say where she got them, they're not prescriptions, and that's the problem with drugs like these, you don't know where they came from, what's in 'em, in what concentration . . .

But Matthew knew where they came from.

They came from Ozark Stover.

He looked to Autumn. Weak and pale, like the fading memory of a person instead of the person herself. He wondered how they'd pay for all this. He wondered when she'd wake up. He wondered about a deeper, darker question he dared not name—an indescribable, uncertain dread.

When the doctor was done, he said that Matthew could go home if he wanted, it was late, they could call with updates.

But Matthew wasn't going to go home. Instead, he said a prayer. Matthew asked the Lord for forgiveness, for guidance, and for courage. He bent and kissed Autumn on the forehead. He told her he was sorry.

Then he grabbed his keys and hit the road. Over the hill and through the woods, to Ozark Stover's house, he'd go.

49

BACK AT THE FLOCK

A fire broke out backstage in a theatre. The clown came out to warn the public; they thought it was a joke and applauded. He repeated it; the acclaim was even greater. I think that's just how the world will come to an end: to general applause from wits who believe it's a joke.

—Søren Kierkegaard, *Either/Or*, part 1

JULY 15
North Platte Regional Airport, Nebraska

AFTER THE FLIGHT, WAITING FOR BAGS, BENJI WENT TO THE BATHROOM. HE did his business. He washed his hands.

No Sadie. No Black Swan.

He felt troubled and alone.

THE FLOCK HAD MOVED, OF course. Drawing a jagged line from Rosebud, through Lodgepole and Sidney, now approaching Potterstown, Nebraska, about fifty miles from the Wyoming border. Benji and Arav sat in a different rental—a claustrophobic Honda two-door hatchback—in the cement parking lot of a line of forgotten warehouses. The warehouses sat at the margins of Potterstown, a modern American ghost town. Died in the late '80s when manufacturing dried up out here. Dead buildings, the gray of ash, the red of rust, waited around like tombstones to a forgotten industrial age.

He tried to imagine if this is what the world would look like in five, ten, fifteen years. After humankind had gone.

No, he chastised himself. *That's not what's happening.*

People could survive.

They *would* survive.

Humanity, whether you were optimistic or pessimistic, was either a hearty breed of survivors or a swarm of cockroaches in the wall. Whichever way you went, that meant people were sticking around.

He'd help make sure of it.

Before meeting with the remaining EIS team of dwindling techs, he'd grabbed Arav and brought him here. It was important to get the young man on the same page before returning fully to the flock, to the job he no longer precisely understood. (Was he still an investigator? Or was this investigation over? Benji didn't see himself as a shepherd. But that's what he was now, wasn't it?)

"We need to talk," Benji said to Arav.

"Yeah. Yes. Of course. What did they say? The meeting in Atlanta . . . was it about . . ." Arav swallowed, like he couldn't say the words. Instead, all he managed to say was: "Is it true? What they told us?"

Benji nodded. "It is true. At least, the part about White Mask."

"Is that what they're calling it? White Mask."

"It is."

Arav chewed on the inside of his cheek. "And the walkers?"

"I don't know. I think . . . maybe they really are infected with nanomachines. Or particles of some kind."

"You told Loretta?"

Benji hesitated. "I didn't."

Desperate, now, Arav asked: "Why?"

"I want you to imagine the very real possibility that what we were told is correct. If White Mask is the plague they say it will be, then . . . the flock is our best bet to create a continuity of life. They can survive this. But if we go telling the CDC, or the FBI? Then that's it. Homeland Security will definitely move in. They will view the walkers not as patients or as survivors— they will view them as weapons, as enemies, as *terrorists*. They will be attacked. You understand that, don't you? That'll be it."

"Doctor Ray, with all due respect, there are *five hundred* people coming this way. They may be infected with . . . with *tiny machines*. They cannot be harmed by needle or knife. They do not eat or excrete. They *explode* like pressure-cooker bombs if you hinder them in any way! We can't keep this a secret. We should be making noise about this. The CDC, the FBI, the media—"

"*No.*"

That word, ringing out.

"Why?" Arav asked, but then said: "It's because of Sadie, isn't it?"

"No." That loneliness hit him again. Like the ground beneath him had gone to soft silt, sucking him down and crushing him. Sadie had manipulated him. Was their relationship ever anything more than her leading him around by the nose? Black Swan had been manipulating him, too. He felt like a fool. "I don't even know where she is, and I certainly don't care to find out."

"Doctor Ray. Please. I don't want to bear this burden."

Benji reached out, took Arav's hand. He tried to be calm when he said, "Listen to me, Arav. You told me before that you trusted me. That you looked up to me. I need you to hold on to that. I need you to trust me now. Failing that, I know you're with the Stewart girl, Shana—"

"I—it's—I know it's not appropriate—"

"It's fine. But I want you to think of her and her sister. Think very hard what will happen if the army comes in here again at the behest of Homeland Security. The next time they try, it will be with more soldiers, more weapons. They might try something more drastic. It could hurt Nessie, and it could hurt Shana, because knowing Shana, she won't leave, will she?"

"No," Arav said in a hushed voice.

"Then I need you to do the right thing."

He felt like a bully. A calm, quiet, sinister bully. Even now, the battle flashed in Arav's eyes—a battle between warring uncertainties. On the one hand, he was wondering if what Benji said was right. Homeland Security couldn't be trusted with this, that much was clear. At the same time, they both knew they had been played, that the sleepwalker flock had been infected on purpose by a company literally owned by the CDC. It was, if true, a conspiracy greater than many of the worst and strangest in history.

He asked again: "Will you, Arav? Follow my lead?"

"Fine. For now." Arav opened the car door. "I admired you, you know. But maybe you're not who I thought you were." He looked down at his shoes. "I have to get some air. The flock should be here soon."

And then he was gone, out of the car, walking away. Like someone lost who had no idea how to be found again. Benji recognized it, because he felt the exact same way.

50

OF GODS AND MEN

Ideology always paves the way toward atrocity.

—Terence McKenna

JULY 15
Echo Lake, Indiana

IT WAS DANNY GIBBONS WHO BROUGHT MATTHEW INTO THE HOUSE—THE man didn't walk so much as he loped, like a rangy coyote. He led Matthew in through the front door, not saying much except "Ozark's inside" and "Follow me" and "This way." Simple declarations. Commands, even.

As he moved forward, sometimes his shirt lifted up away from the waist of his jeans, exposing the grip of a pistol tucked away there.

They went in through the front door, down the hall, and down a few steps into a broad, low den of dark wood and dead animals: an elk head on the back wall, its mouth open in half bugle, tongue partway out; a bobcat on a branch, eternally ready to pounce; a massive northern pike above a sixty-inch television screen, the scales of its sides polished and gleaming.

Ozark Stover sat there in a recliner.

He was not alone.

A woman sat next to him, on a smaller chair. Her blond hair lay in messy braids across her head—like doll's yarn. She wore a too-tight white T-shirt. Matthew could see her nipples through the material, and it made him feel red-faced and suddenly, inexplicably uncomfortable—like a child catching a glimpse at a nudie magazine for the first time.

Her arm was out, bowed at the elbow, her hand gently resting on the brown leather of Ozark's recliner. His own massive mitt was there, next to hers, two of his fingers out, gently stroking the back of her hand.

She looked at Matthew through half-lidded eyes. With slurred, mushy speech, she said to Ozark, "You wan' me to go, babe."

Ozark, undisturbed, said, "No, sugar, you stay. Preacher here is a friend. This ain't business, this is just two friends. Right, Preacher?" Ozark's gaze darkened. "You want to tell me what happened in Arizona?"

"I want to tell you what happened to Autumn," Matthew said.

"What about her?"

"She's sick." *No, you fool, she's not sick!* Even now he was hedging his words, why? So as not to offend the mighty Ozark Stover? He drew a deep breath, tried again: "She *overdosed*."

Stover didn't flinch. Didn't even sit up straighter. "That is a shame, Preacher. She's a nice woman. She's alive, I'm guessing."

"She's . . . comatose." He felt tears in his eyes. That brought fresh shame. He bet Ozark Stover never cried. That man was as stoic as a boulder: He didn't crack for nobody, for no reason.

"Thassa shame," the woman said. Her chin dipped suddenly to her chest, which seemed to startle her, because then her eyes jolted open.

"Lemme know if I can do anything, and thanks for sharing the news, Preacher. Now if you'll excuse me—"

"This is on *you*."

Now—*now!*—Ozark sat up straight. "I'm sorry, Preacher, I don't think I heard you right. Sounded to me like you were slinging a little blame my way, but I'm sure that can't be true."

"You sold her those pills."

"I *gave* them to her, no charge. As a favor. And she's a big girl, knew what I was giving her."

"You're a drug dealer."

"Watch your mouth. I'm no such thing. I am a local supplier of complicated necessities."

"You're a criminal."

Stover eased forward, his hands forming ham-hock fists that pressed down on his own knees like he was trying to keep himself from standing. "By some view, I might be. You knew who I was. If you didn't, it's because you kept your eyes pointed the other way. I make no bones about who I was, who I am. I helped you considerably. Gave you a voice. Lifted you *up*. Don't come at me with this shit, Preacher. You'll make me mad."

Something in Matthew broke, like a dam under siege from a rising river. "You . . . you gave her pills, and you don't even know what was in them. She took them and, and, and now she's in a hospital bed in a coma and I can't even—" A small cry of fresh pain tore out of him as his mind flashed to an image of her in that bed. "You need to be held accountable."

Now Stover stood. The woman pawed at him, as if to keep him sitting— or maybe to anchor herself to him so she didn't fall over—but he pushed her out of the way. She made a sour, pickled face, looking equal parts angry and whelped.

The big man loomed over Matthew.

"Accountable. That's a big word. Lotta meaning behind that word, Preacher. Are you accountable? You abandoned her, didn't you? Wouldn't help her with her problems. No doctor. No meds. Just the power of Christ to compel her, mm? Yeah. She told me. Maybe it's you who needs to take a look inward, see how *you* failed her, and how I was only trying to help."

"You helped her right into a *fucking* hospital bed!" Matthew shouted.

For a moment, Stover looked sick with rage, like all parts of him were tensing up—a catapult ready to launch its boulder payload.

But then his shoulders eased. He grabbed a fistful of his beard and smoothed it down a few times—a calming technique, by the look of it.

"So," Stover sniffed. "What is all this, then?"

"I'm done. With you. And this . . . *place*. Leave us alone."

"Uh-huh."

The woman suddenly spoke up in a gushing babble: "Baby we almost done here because I wanna go an' hit the hot tub—"

Ozark shot an arm out to her, his index finger pressed to his lips. "Shush. The men are speaking. You sit there and you shush."

Chastened, she did as told, curling into his chair and pulling her knees up to her chest.

"Preacher, I'd like to show you something. Something real special. I've given you a lot of my time and my resources—favor after favor, I think we can agree on that, and so we can also agree you owe me a little bit more of your time, at least." The corners of his mouth turned down. "Especially after that nonsense in Arizona."

"I just want to go home." Matthew was feeling tired, now. Angry, yes. But scared. And sad. Nearly crushed by all of it.

"I know you do. But first, come with me." He called out in his big voice: "Danny. *Danny!* Bring around one of the carts, will you?"

Don't go with him, said a little voice inside Matthew. *Go back to Autumn.*

But another part of him thought, *What's the harm?* Ozark had a point. He owed this man a debt, and to simply run away . . . That would be too bold, too brassy, and Ozark didn't seem to think anything of it. Maybe he could talk some sense into the man. Maybe getting him away from Danny and this woman, Ozark could let down some of his guard and then Matthew could tell him that this kind of thing just wasn't appropriate. With the pills, but also, with Bo and the guns, too. Maybe the big man would even consent to paying for some of Autumn's bills because Matthew had no idea how he was going to manage that . . .

"Okay," Matthew said.

"Good. C'mon, Preacher," Ozark said. He moved his massive Godzilla shape past Matthew, back toward the front of the house.

Reluctantly, Matthew followed.

THEY DIDN'T SAY ANYTHING TO each other as Ozark drove the rugged big-wheeled golf cart down through the woods, on a trail Matthew had not yet seen. They passed underneath old oak trees and tulip trees, the sun above dappling the ground ahead. Bees and wasps and deerflies crisscrossed the air in front of the cart as it sped forward, bounding and bouncing.

After a longer trip than Matthew expected, he saw a series of buildings through the trees. Dead ahead was a Morton building: a steel storage structure, like a monster-sized metal barn with a couple of bay doors for trucks or tractors. This one was red like a barn, too. New coat of paint. Along the sides were a few other structures: a garage with a greasy lift and engine parts scattered around; a pole barn with hay for a floor; a wooden shed, its heavy metal door locked with a series of padlocks.

The lot surrounding this was all gravel, then turned into a small private road that went—well, Matthew didn't know where. To another road or highway, he imagined, because how else would anyone get back here?

Beyond that, the trees encroached overhead, leaning over the buildings almost like they were trying to keep them hidden. A dark forest keeping some kind of secret.

Ozark sped up to the Morton building and hit the brakes. The cart lurched as the tires skidded on the scree of loose limestone.

"Come on," Ozark said, grunting as he extricated himself from the cart. Matthew followed, uncertain what they were doing here.

"What is this?" Matthew asked.

"Like I said, I want to show you something. I want to show you the future, Preacher. The future I intend. It is our way forward."

Matthew trailed the man, saying as he walked, "Ozark, listen. I appreciate everything you've done. I do. You've been good to me but this has all . . . it's gotten out of hand, it's gotten bigger than me, and the only thing I want bigger than me is God Himself. With Autumn hurting now, I see that I've betrayed something core to myself, and I'm still betraying some part of what I learned, what I preach—"

Ozark went to one regular-sized door next to one of the massive bay doors. The bay doors had windows, but they were blacked out.

Next to the smaller door was a keypad for a security system.

"Only thing you're betraying is me," Ozark said with a dark chuckle.

"No, no, hey, it's not like that—see, I'm just in over my head. I'm a small-town pastor and I've lost my way."

"Then let me help you find it again, Preacher."

Ozark punched in a series of numbers, at least eight digits.

Several locks audibly disengaged behind the door.

He pulled it open and let Matthew enter first. Matthew stepped into darkness. He could make out massive shapes ahead, and the light from behind him—eclipsed as it was by his body and Ozark's—illuminated some familiar shapes. Headlights. Grilles. Tires.

Vehicles, of some kind. Sensible, given the garage bay doors.

"Hold on," Ozark said, then flipped a series of lights.

Fluorescents clicked on one at time, buzzing to life.

God have mercy.

They illuminated an arsenal.

From left to right, Matthew saw a troop carrier, three Humvees, and at the far end, a massive tank. And that was only the start of it. Along the left wall were racks, and stacked along them were rifles. Military, mostly, like AR-15s, but also an assortment of hunting rifles. Right wall were pistols, knives, machetes. And along the back, he spied heavier ordnance: what looked like mortars, heavy machine guns, rocket-propelled grenade launchers. Stuff you'd see in movies. Or on the news.

Matthew's guts felt in free fall. His skin felt cold. His mouth, dry.

"That right there," Ozark said, pointing at the tank, "Is an old Soviet T-72 from the early 1970s. Still packs a wallop, though. Here, come on, follow me to the back." He started walking, and Matthew, feeling loose and lost like a spinning top, followed.

Ozark took him to the back rack of heavy ordnance, where Ozark also had several workbenches set up with what looked to be reloading equipment—sometimes hunters, instead of buying new ammo, reloaded their own brass, and this was that, but bigger. A more elaborate setup.

Also along the back were flags:

DON'T TREAD ON ME.

A Confederate flag.

A black flag with two white swords crossing and a red hammer intermingled down the middle.

And into the one wooden workbench, someone had idly carved a swastika. Like a high schooler emblazoning one on his desk at school.

"I . . . I don't know what I'm looking at," Matthew said.

"Sure you do, because I already told you. This is the future."

"This . . . this isn't a future. These are just weapons. Weapons end futures, they don't make them."

"Tsk, tsk, tsk. No. That is wrong, Matthew. Weapons have long been a part of securing freedom for the right people. You're a man of God, and owning weapons is a God-given right. They'll help us claim our future. For ourselves. For our families. For our nation and for our race."

For our nation and for our race.

Matthew heard nothing about *for God* in there.

"This isn't who I am," Matthew said.

"No, I know, but it is who I am," Ozark said, idly, almost wistfully. "See, Preacher, things in this country have been chugging along for a while, and a lot of dumb shits were happy as two pigs fuckin' in mud, blissfully unaware that the machine was breaking down. Spics coming from the South, fucking ragheads trying to blow us up, crash our planes, drive cars into people. Then you got the niggers getting uppity again, thinking they deserve something because of their role in building this nation—here they go thinking they're the bricklayers, not realizing that they were the *bricks*. You got the spics stealing all the low-hanging jobs and slopes stealing all the *good* jobs—and you ever try to call customer service, you'll get a dothead in some faraway country where they drink water from the same river they shit and die in. People like me see a world we don't recognize anymore. But that can change. Because now the machine isn't breaking down. It's broken."

Matthew recoiled in horror. "Those are just people you're talking about. Regular people, Americans like any other, and God doesn't see those divisions you see, Ozark." He said firmly: "What you're talking about is not the Christian worldview."

"Honestly, Preacher? God can go fuck His big, holier-than-thou self. Only God I care about is country. This country. A white country."

"You . . . you said were a Christian. You said you read the Bible. You *quoted* the Bible to me." And then Hiram Golden's words came back to haunt him: *Like the saying goes, the Devil knows how to quote scripture.*

"I said that stuff because I needed someone like you. Someone to stir up the churchy types, get them on our side, make them worry, make them afraid. Because they need to be, with what's coming."

Matthew's blood went to a cold, saline slush.

"What do you mean, 'what's coming'?"

Ozark grinned and sniffed. "Can't you feel it, Preacher? Chaos on the wind. The comet. The walkers. I know people at every level, and they say that bad things are coming. Worse than what we know. As everything breaks down, holes will open up. Rifts and chasms. Those are an opportunity. Like an earthquake that makes a doorway where none before existed. It's our opportunity to remake the country the way it should be. The way it *used* to be. Whites leading the way. Everyone else knowing their place."

"I'm *not* a white supremacist."

Ozark laughed then, a big booming sound like a mudslide coming down toward you. "Sure you are, Preacher. Everyone with skin like ours is." He reached forward, pinched Matthew's cheek like a parent does to a little baby. "You're white. You're superior. The skin you wear affords you privilege that we've earned and built for ourselves. Be a fool not to see that. You've used that privilege for a long time. You've partaken in the supremacy of your people. Might as well seize it. Use it. *Enjoy* it."

Matthew took a few steps backward. "I'm not a part of this. Not a part of . . . whatever it is you want to do."

Ozark took one big step forward.

Stover said, "What I want to do is to fix things. Something I've always told people, and sometimes they believe me, and sometimes they don't, is that if you really want to *fix* something, first you have to break it. Gotta take it apart, otherwise all you're doing is puttin' a patch on it. Got an underbite? To fix that shit, they gotta break the whole jaw to get your smile straight. Got cancer? Gonna cut that limb off, *chop-fucking-chop*. Got termites? Burn the whole damn house down and rebuild something better in the ashes."

"You're a sick man."

"It's a sick world."

"I'm leaving."

"Your wife probably tried to kill herself."

Matthew froze. "What?"

"Sure, maybe she overdosed on accident. But think about it. She's a depressed woman, Matthew, married to a man who won't reach out a hand to help her. You don't give a damn about her and she knew it. Is it so strange to think she was looking for a way out? A way to get away from you, her husband who—"

It happened like *that*. Matthew's fist, coiled tight and clutching all the fear and rage that had been building up in him, struck out.

Ozark's head snapped back. His nose collapsed soft under Matthew's knuckles. The pastor pulled his throbbing hand back, and he watched as two worms of raw, red blood crawled forth from each of Ozark Stover's nostrils. Fresh crimson wetted the man's mustache and beard.

A strange giddy surge of triumph arose in Matthew.

He did it. He defended himself. His wife. His everything. He wasn't a victim. Matthew stood up to a bully, and that's what Ozark Stover was: a bully, a bad man, an *evil* man with lies dancing on his tongue.

Then a club hit Matthew in the side of his head.

No. Not a club. Ozark's *fist*. The big man swung his arm like it was a bat swinging at a softball, and it whomped Matthew right in the temple. His head rang and he collapsed against the side of one of the reloading benches—he barely held himself up, propped there by his elbow. His arm knocked over a few brass casings that tinked as they hit the floor and rolled across the polished cement. A canister of gun oil dropped, too, with a half-hollow *kathunk*. He tried to pull himself back up to standing, but his head was dizzy, and his legs wouldn't comply.

"That was a good punch, Preacher. I'm honestly surprised. You didn't telegraph it or nothing. Still, I got bad news. You're not leaving me," Ozark said, lording over him. He wiped blood from his nose with the back of his prodigious hand. "I put *time* into you. Money, too. You're an investment and I'm not ready to liquidate."

"Just let me go," Matthew said. But the words came out gummy, mushy. *Jush leh meh go.*

"No, Preacher, I don't much care for that idea."

Matthew tried pulling away, but Ozark was big and fast. He grabbed a hank of the pastor's hair and threw him to the ground. His forehead struck the cement. Strobing pulses popped across his vision and wouldn't stop.

"You're a liar," Matthew gabbled. "A bad man, not a godly man—"

"True enough, I suppose," Ozark said, straddling him and grabbing one of his wrists. Matthew flailed, tried to strike out with the other one, but he was slow and facedown and ended up swinging at open air. "I'm a bad sonofabitch. I might be the fucking *Devil*, way I see it, but that's all right. The Devil was a rebel, too. I lie to get things done. I do bad to make good. I do wrong to make all the broken stuff right."

Something cold touched his wrist. Hard plastic edge. Ozark wrangled his other wrist, too, pinning both against his tailbone.

The sound came of a zip-tie closing—*vviiip.*

And then his hands were bound. Blood swam in his fingertips. Each pulsed like a little drum being struck, *lub-dub, lub-dub, lub-dub.*

No, no, no, what's happening.

Another sound, then: *snick.*

Something tugged at the hem of his pants. Ozark made a grunt of frustration, then yanked hard on Matthew's belt, pulling with such force it lifted the pastor's hips, almost turning him over. But then the belt was free and the big man tossed it aside.

"What are you doing," Matthew said, his words babbled and sticky with spit connecting his lips. "No, no, no, you stop, this isn't funny, this has gone too far—"

"I like your family. Your wife, she hasn't been happy in a while. So I helped to make her happy. All her sadness is gone, now. And your son . . ." Ozark made a scoffing sound. *Pfeh.* "Kid hates you, Preacher. Which is a shame, really, and at first I said, that's not right, boy, you get right with your daddy. But more he talked about you, more I thought you were a soft touch, like a willow tree blowing this way and that way—you never plant a willow tree, Matthew. They look nice, but they don't live long, and any storm might break them. Shit, now look at you. A pathetic little fuck. You're no man. I'll be your son's daddy, it's all right. Maybe I'll take your wife as my own when she wakes up. *If* she wakes up. Shit, Preacher—maybe I'll take *you* as my wife, or just some temporary *trash bitch* . . ."

Again Matthew's pants tugged hard—and something began cutting through them. Sawing back and forth. A tearing, ripping sound arose. The tip of a penknife sliced into the skin at his tailbone, just a little.

Blood welled and trickled down as his pants were pulled away. His underwear, then, too. "You're bleeding," Ozark said. "Sorry about that."

"No, no, no, you stop, *you stop,* I'll call the police, I'll tell them—"

"I own them. Not much of an option."

"I'll do whatever you *want* then, just leave me *alone,* leave my family *alone,* this has to *stop*—" His words were barely comprehensible now, some of them howled instead of spoken. But Ozark just laughed.

Then the weight of the man was gone.

Matthew heard the sound of a button being undone. Then a zipper.

"I don't want to go in dry," Ozark said. "You'll never heal up from that, won't be any use to me, and I'm gonna need you sitting on your ass a week from now, doing what I tell you to do. Let's see. You're bleeding—but blood, and I speak from experience on this, makes for a poor lubricant. Oh. There we go." Matthew rolled over, facing up as he saw Ozark grab for something on the floor: the gun oil container. A metal canister with a plastic tip. The man stood there, his cock out. He splashed gun oil onto his callused hands like it was cologne, then ran those hands up and down the length of his dick.

"Please, stop. *No.* No no no no—"

"Too late for no, Preacher. Keep your arms and legs inside the vehicle, because we're about to go for a ride."

What happened next would be a thing Matthew would always remember, even as he tried desperately to forget it. The way his underwear was ripped away. The way Ozark flipped him back over, slapped his ass hard, leaving his hind end stung and swollen. The big man got on top of him and told him it was okay to scream, nobody would hear, and Matthew did as he was told: He screamed until his vocal cords were raw and cut up like grated carrots. He tensed everything, trying to shrink in on himself like a collapsing star, but then Ozark punched him in the back of the head and commanded him to relax and enjoy it. He felt Ozark pushing inside him and pain ran roughshod through him, ragged and mad, the pain of a brush burn and fire-ant bites going all through his middle. The brassy, grease-slick stink of gun oil filled his nose and he wanted to throw up but couldn't. The man pounded away at him five, maybe six times, then finished. Ozark pulled out and left him there on the cement, hot and cold, shivering and bleeding, whimpering and panting past the pain that still haunted him like a ghost.

"I own you," Ozark said. "Not God. *Me.*"

And Matthew feared he was right.

51

BREAKING NEWS

. . . Roberts and his graduate students have painstakingly coaxed thousands of bacteria samples through the successive rounds of incubation. Out of all those, hundreds have secreted compounds that killed at least one test bacterium, and a few killed a fungus—potentially precious finds, because antifungal drugs are in even shorter supply than antibiotics.
—Maryn McKenna, "Hunting for Antibiotics in the World's Dirtiest Places," *The Atlantic*

JULY 15
Potterstown, Nebraska

THE FLOCK HAD NO SINGLE GATHERING SPOT. THEY COULDN'T; THE SLEEP-walkers were closing in on five hundred now, and they did as they always did, moving forward, ineluctably carving a swath through the world as if on a mission known only to them. The shepherds moved with the flock, giving the illusion that they were cowboys driving cattle, when really, the opposite was true: The flock was in control.

Without a single spot to gather, the press conference that President Hunt gave was not viewed by the group in one place on one screen but rather, consumed in the way media often was: across multiple places, seen on a panoply of devices. Pockets of shepherds gathered around phones and tablets as they walked. Others parked off to the side, and those who had satellite internet or mobile hotspots watched the conference on their laptops. Some even used old-school antennae on their RVs to get a signal.

Shana watched it on her phone as she walked alongside her sister. Marcy gathered near, as did Mia, each one looking over her shoulder as she held the phone in front of her, each of them shuffling along slowly. Shana tried to maneuver her shadow against the phone so that the sun glare didn't wash out what was on the screen.

President Hunt did not speak for long. She gave only a small introduction of the facts that they knew, her face more stern than usual, her brow stitched tight with worry.

"White-nose syndrome, as some of you may know, is a fungal disease that has been attacking the bat population of the United States since 2007, peaking in 2012, but the disease remained limited to bats only.

"Now it seems as if a similar disease has found a way to infect human beings. As of this moment, we have one hundred thirty-seven confirmed cases of this disease in the United States, with forty-one fatalities. The World Health Organization has discovered another three hundred twelve cases globally, with eighty-one confirmed fatalities at this time."

Shana noted then: There were no reporters. This was not public. It was just Hunt in front of a podium, with cameras pointed.

Hunt continued to speak.

"I cannot speak to the severity of this disease, as I am certainly no expert on pathology, but I am confident that as Americans we will see our way through this. And furthermore, I am confident that our people across the Centers for Disease Control as well as in the medical and pharmaceutical industry will fast find a remedy to halt the progression of this disorder."

But there. The look on her face betrayed the words she spoke. Shana could see that, plain as the shine on a brand-new nickel.

Hunt was visibly shaken.

"Now I'll defer to proper experts, and I'd like to introduce Cassandra Tran from the CDC and Geert Bakker from the World Health Organization to give you more details, and to inform you on what to look for regarding this, ahh, this strange new disease we face . . ."

Briefly, Hunt paused to give a nod to the two who approached, and Shana felt a small spike of pride and joy in seeing Cassie there. She didn't know Cassie well, but liked her a lot. And though it seemed strange, Cassie felt like one of *theirs*. Home-team pride.

The other, Geert Bakker, was a small, pale man with red hair and a red beard and glasses whose eyeglass frames were as ghostly as his face.

Hunt said a few words privately to them.

"Jesus God," Mia said. "Something else now? Like all *this*"—she swept a hand out to indicate the flock—"wasn't enough?"

Marcy just stared off, haunted. Like she was shell-shocked by the news in some way. Or stranger still, like it made sense to her, somehow.

Shana said: "It'll be fine. Probably just being cautious. We have the flock to worry about, not . . . this."

Even still, she felt suddenly unsettled.

Cassie and the man from WHO, Bakker, were up, finally, and started talking about when to see a doctor and what to look out for—signs of a cold or allergy that persists coupled with uncharacteristic symptoms of dementia. She and Mia looked to each other, and then to the shepherds all around them. Had any of them had a cold recently? Sniffles here, a cough there? She suddenly felt paranoid about everyone she was with. If they were sick, couldn't she get sick, too? What about Nessie? What about all of them? A low frequency of worry grew in volume.

Then Mia tugged on her elbow and pointed. "Hey. Look." Ahead of the flock rose a modern-era ghost town: the bones of an old factory, the shell of some strip malls, the gutted husk of a bunch of warehouses and storage units. A car sat parked in the distance, and someone stood by that car.

But someone else was walking toward the flock, around the bend of the road, past the peacock tail of red feathery grasses poking up through broken cement.

"Arav," Shana said, and raced to meet him. She realized half a second later that she'd stolen the phone—meaning, she'd stolen the briefing—from the others, so she quick spun on her heel and called out to Marcy and tossed her the phone. She didn't even look to see if Marcy caught it. Shana just kept running toward Arav. He'd been keeping away from her since he disappeared with Benji, but here he was, walking right toward her . . .

When he saw her, his face brightened. He smiled.

And though it only registered with her later, his eyes did not smile with his mouth. His eyes looked grim. His gaze looked sad.

Still, for now, she crashed into him and wrapped her arms around him. Her lips met his. She held the hug for a while as the flock-and-shepherds moved to pass them. RVs rumbling on. Trucks. People on bikes. Dogs chasing dogs. A few kids, even. Arav looked over. "What's going on? Everyone's facedown in a screen."

"There's a press conference."

"Oh," he said, understanding. "The pathogen."

"What?"

"The fungus. The disease. Is that—?"

"It is." She looked him over, felt his worry. "That's what it was, wasn't it. That's why you and the others left the motel the other day. Is that why you had to go?"

He offered a reticent nod.

"It's going to be okay, isn't it?" she asked.

He smiled and said it would.

But she noticed half a second later when he almost shook his head. Just the start of it—a lift to the chin, a momentary frown, a pinch to the eyes. Same as she saw worry on Hunt's face: a motion where it looked like he had thought one thing, then said another. It was nothing, she thought. Just her imagination. Everything, she was sure, would be just fine. She had him back, after all. Nothing else mattered.

TEN PHOTOGRAPHS

JULY 20
Horse Creek, Wyoming

EARLY MORNING, A SEARING LINE OF LIGHT BURNS THE EDGES OF ROLLING hills. A sign hangs over a winding driveway, BENT CROSS RANCH. The metal-riveted and welded sign is displayed over a wooden archway lined with old elk and mule deer antlers. The bottom of the driveway sits grated with a metal cattle guard. A fence winds around the ranch property, ringed with new razor wire. At the entrance stand three men, all in fatigues, two in NBC (nuclear, biological, chemical) masks, one with just a red paisley handkerchief over his face. All three hold rifles. One has his hand frozen in a move-along wave. Another stands still, watching the flock pass. The last is pointing a rifle at the camera—more a threat than a promise, for now.

JULY 31
Greybull, Wyoming

A GENERAL STORE: BIG HORN Trading Post. Out front stands a woman straddling a dirt bike, one foot in the dirt-swept street, the other on the broken curb behind. Chestnut hair in a ponytail hangs out the back of her helmet, draped down her back. She is not alone on the bike: A young boy sits behind her, no helmet, just a medical mask on his face, his eyes rimmed red maybe from tears, maybe from illness, maybe both. He holds her tight around the waist, pressing his cheek hard into her back even as she watches the flock pass through the small town. The store's windows can no longer be seen through because of all the signs hung up inside: LOCALS ONLY NO TOURISTS; SICKIES GO HOME; SNOTTY NOSE, GO BLOW; IF COUGH, THEN FUCK OFF; GOD BLESS AMERICA.

AUGUST 4
Red Lodge, Montana

A TWILIGHT SKY BRINDLED WITH bands of brown clouds and pale lavender sky. In the distance stand the peaks of the Castle Mountains. In the foreground, a field of pale sagebrush, and in that field people roam and rove, dance and flail, caught as they are in the midst of wild gesticulations. Men and women. Cultlike. Many are naked, some stripped down to their underwear. Some draped in American flags. Others hold crosses aloft to the sky, kneeling, beseeching whoever or whatever is up there. None are in sync. Some spin. Some weep. Others are totally still, arms up and out in a Y-shape. One stands nearer to the camera—a man in his thirties, gaunt, ribs showing. His jawline shows a scraggly beard above a mad grin. Dark eyes stare, unfocused, over a cliffside nose. He holds an American flag. The stars on the flag have been replaced with little white crosses. The bottom right corner of the flag is empurpled with dark blood. His blood, maybe, given the poorly healed gashes along his inner thigh, leading up to the small coin purse of his cock and balls hanging between birdlike thighs.

AUGUST 9
Wise River, Montana

THE TREE THE HUMAN CORPSE hangs from is bare and brutish, a dark and skeletal hand reaching toward a wide sky choked with the smoke of distant wildfires. The corpse belonged to a man, once, his age indeterminable. The skin and the clothes are colonized with white fuzz that looks not unlike a mass of pale caterpillars. Seven tubules have emerged from his mold-claimed flesh, each snaking up toward the sky, bulging at the end like a pimple straining to be popped by impatient fingers. He hanged himself from a thick branch, and a sign dangles presently from his neck. It reads: DONT COME NEAR in big bold letters, and in smaller letters underneath: I LOVE YOU SHAUN DONNIE AND HELEN. His is the first dead body they have seen. It will not be the last.

AUGUST 14
Potlatch, Idaho

PETE CORLEY, SELF-PROCLAIMED ROCK GOD, leans up against an old dead train car. The camera has zoomed in on him, seizing a moment in time between the sleepwalkers walking—they, in the foreground, are blurry, but he is in crystal focus. A phone is pressed against his ear. He is listening, for once, not talking. His mouth sits twisted in a troubled scowl. He's crying, wet tears on his cheeks catching light from the fading sun. He has just received bad news: His wife and his two children are going upstate to stay with her parents to "ride out" the coming epidemic. They have a mansion. It's gated. Big property. Pete isn't welcome. Her parents believe the flock is somehow responsible for the disease, and so he is himself diseased, too.

AUGUST 19
Sagemoor, Washington

A CLOSE-UP OF ONE OF the shepherds: Stephen Harper. He joined the flock only three weeks prior. His partner, Isobela Gonsales, is a mixed media artist who came to them in Wyoming, leaving her potter's wheel, hands still stained with clay. He is saying goodbye to her now. His face looks sick and pale. His nose is ringed with a white, oily crust. The corners of his eyes and mouth are similarly colonized. The shepherds around him wear medical masks. He is holding his partner's hand as he says goodbye. He knows he's sick. The day prior he wandered away from the flock, into a vineyard, and was nearly shot by the vineyard owner. Stephen did not remember the incident. White Mask has him. He is going home to be with the rest of his family in the hope that they find a cure in time to save him.

AUGUST 20
Snoqualmie Pass, Washington

THE CASCADE RANGE LOOMS LARGE. At the tops of the peaks is the faintest dusting of snow: an early hint of a strange winter. The mountains look like peace. The highway ahead is the opposite: Chaos has set in as a traffic pileup of twenty or thirty cars has blocked the highway on both sides. The accident happened when the driver of a tractor trailer suddenly believed he was in bed instead of driving his rig. He "got out of bed" by opening the door of his truck and trying to step out. The seatbelt prevented him, but it did not force him to keep his hands on the wheel. His hip and elbow turned the wheel and the truck jackknifed before the trailer overturned. Cars slammed into it, and cars slammed into those cars, the crash aided by an already wet road from a passing Pacific Northwest shower. The flock of walkers has no problem with any of this. They stream around the accident. They move over it. It is no obstacle to them, in the same way that a rock is no obstacle for a column of crawling ants. This, even as the shepherds have an impossible task moving their own fleet of vehicles through the jammed-up highway. There are now 666 walkers.

AUGUST 25
Castle Rock, Washington

A SHOT TAKEN FROM A bridge over the Cowlitz River. In the distance, a cemetery sits on a grassy berm under trees. The cemetery is home to the dead, as is its role, but here the dead have seemingly escaped the comfort of the grave. Bodies are piled high. A truck is near and workers in white hazmat-style suits pull more bodies out of the truck. Soon they will begin to burn them, as has been advised, because if left alone, the fungus will fruit—tubules will grow and rupture and more of the spore will take to the wind and, as it is saprophytic, find the soil and live there, lurking. Burning the bodies seems to kill the pathogen. Soon the smoke will drift over the river, and with it, the shepherds' first exposure to that smell: a smell like sick pork cooked slow, a smell that some would describe as having a taste, too, one that lingered in the back of the nose, at the base of the tongue, a taste not unlike licking a very old library book.

AUGUST 29
Tierra Del Mar, Oregon

THE UNSPOILED OREGONIAN COASTLINE. IT is empty but for one man in a red helmet on a red Jet Ski, carving surf and kicking spray. It remains unknown why he's out there. Is his mind lost to the fungus, and this seems like a rational response to what's going on? Is he blissfully ignorant to the goings-on in the world? Or is he choosing instead to find some kind of bliss in the face of it, saying *fuck it* to the thousands dead, to the unstoppable march of time and disease, to what's likely to come for him or someone he knows? Is this act an act of dementia, defiance, or ignorance? Or perhaps it's suicide. He'll run the Jet Ski until it has no gas, and then he will sink into the ocean, filling his lungs with churning brine. And then he'll be gone and the coastline will be once more without anybody in it or upon it. A glimpse of a world without humans to wander its margins.

AUGUST 31
Pistol River, Oregon

THIS, A MORE INTIMATE PHOTO. It is a shot of the top of a picnic table off a closed-down rest stop a day's walk from the Oregon-California border. The wood of the table has faded to gray. Various names and messages are carved into it in expressions of love, hate, profanity, absurdity. CAITLYN LOVES JEN. FUCK YOU, STEVE. A carved doodle of a dick and balls with complementary little jizz-hyphens shooting from the tip. A poop emoji. A phone number. But those are not the focus of the photo. The focus of the photo is Shana Stewart's left hand. It's open like a blooming flower, and in the center of her palm sits a pregnancy test. A plus indicates it's positive.

PART FIVE

WHITE MASK

52

GET OFF YOUR HORSE AND DRINK YOUR MILK

It is now Ten Seconds to Midnight.

@DoomsdayClockBot
19 replies 32.7k RTs 10.1k likes

SEPTEMBER 5
Bodega Bay, California

THE WIND ON THE COAST WAS COLD AND VENGEFUL, STRONG ENOUGH TO PICK someone up and fling them into the sea with a callous toss. Benji huddled up in his windbreaker, shivering. The sun filtered silver through heavy cloud cover. A mist filled the air, saturating everything.

He stood up high, on a cliff. A bent and broken guardrail separated the land from the air—where it was broken, it looked as if it had been torn into shrapnel. Someone had strung up a shallow swatch of yellow tape, as if that would be enough to protect anyone. It was as prophylactic as a condom made of Kleenex.

Behind him sat the ghost of an old roadside farm stand. Seagulls nested atop it. Some waddled out, gargling and barking at him.

He waited.

He glanced at his watch.

She's late.

Then, as if on cue, a Ford Bronco pulled in, parking next to his rental hatchback—a rental that he didn't think the CDC was paying for anymore, and perhaps a rental that the rental car company didn't even care about now. Maybe one day he'd get a bill.

You can nail it to my casket, he thought, grimly.

The Bronco parked.

Cassie Tran stepped out.

She wore jeans and a Thunderpussy band T-shirt. She rubbed her arms as she approached—he hurried to meet her, and they melted into a hug.

"Dude," she said, breathless in the surprising cold. "Seriously, you couldn't have picked a warmer place than on top of a cliff?"

He smiled at her. "I missed you, Cassie." He'd spoken to her since, but it hadn't been since Atlanta that he'd seen her face-to-face.

The gulls warbled and complained. At that, Cassie startled. "Okay, *they're* a little on-the-nose, though, man."

He gave her a quizzical look.

"Hitchcock's *The Birds* was filmed here in Bodega Bay," she explained. "You didn't know that?"

"I am about as pop-culture-savvy as the average grandmother."

Cassie rolled her eyes. "I almost forgot. So. *How're things?*"

Even she couldn't contain it. Her question was ironic, tinged with a bitterness he wasn't used to from Cassie. She also wasn't given over to sentimentality, but now he saw the tension of grief in her face: the tightness at the corners of her mouth like she was trying to convince herself to smile, the cinching up of her jaw like she was hoping to hold something, anything, *everything* back. Benji felt it, too. Sad. Unmoored. He wanted to throw up. He was scared.

The questions percolated anytime his mind went quiet and had no immediate task on which to concentrate:

What if they were right?

What if Moira and Bill—

(and Sadie)

—were right?

What if this was the end? For him? For Cassie? For everyone?

The day of the CDC meeting in Atlanta, he would've said, No way, no how. Humanity would persevere. It would survive. Humanity was a most excellent pest and adapted quickly to all efforts to exterminate it.

And yet, in recent days . . .

"What are the numbers?" he asked her, jumping straight into it. Talking numbers and data distracted him and afforded the both of them the chance to talk about this like it was an abstract—just points of information on a graph or in a spreadsheet, not names and faces, not people with lives and loved ones. "The *real* numbers since the news, I bet, is behind?"

"They are."

"Where are we at?"

"Domestically?"

"Globally."

"Talked to WHO today. Seems that yesterday was our milestone. A hundred thousand. We did not throw a party, in case you're wondering."

"A hundred thousand infected. Jesus." He tracked that jump—in July, the number was, what, a dozen? First day of August, the number was already up to five hundred. And now, two hundred times that amount. If it kept up at that (admittedly oversimplified) geometric progression, then in the first week of October that number would be twenty million.

November, four *billion*.

By December—

"You're running the numbers," she said. "I see the mental calculator behind your eyes adding it all up."

"I am."

"Don't. Nothing good there."

"I know."

She rubbed her arms again, and he took off his windbreaker and offered it to her. Cassie shook her head at first but he insisted, and she finally took it. As she put it on, she said, "We're making some progress, Benji. All the Big Pharma companies have turned on a dime and are working night and day on this as a priority. We've got new antifungal volatiles taken from the chitin of marine waste, anti-parasitic plant defensins, koumiss—"

"Koumiss?"

"Fermented horse milk."

"Yum."

She smirked: a flash of the old Cassie, the Devil dancing in her eyes. "Hey, someone comes up to you and tells you rotten mare's milk will cure what ails you, I think you'd drink it. John Wayne said it best: *Get off your horse and drink your milk.*"

"I don't think that's what he meant, but I'll take it. Though I never took you for a John Wayne fan."

"My dad was. He studied John Wayne because John Wayne was like, pure, unrefined America. Like smoking patriotism through an unfiltered cigarette rolled from an American flag. We had to stop Dad from calling everybody pilgrim, though, because *that* got hella fuckin' annoying." She sighed. The memory, like the sun, passed, gone again under dark clouds. "How are *your* numbers? The flock, the shepherds, all that."

"The flock has grown at . . . roughly the same rate. Some days see bigger jumps in those who join us, others fewer. When I left this morning we were at eight hundred thirteen sleepwalkers. The shepherds are a different story. Those numbers have dwindled, even with the continued growth of the flock. Some have gotten sick, others had to go home to their families, some are just . . . they're scared. Some even believe the bullshit myth that somehow it's the flock making all this happen, like they're a parade of Patient Zeros. So, the shepherds are down in number. Only a couple hundred of us at this point."

"*Us.* Listen to you. You're a shepherd, now."

"Well. I'm hardly EIS. Or even CDC."

"About that—"

"I'm not coming back with you."

"Benji . . ."

"My place is with the flock. I was given this role and I aim to keep it. I'm sure Loretta asked you to talk to me—"

"Loretta has it. White Mask. She's sick."

He shuddered, chilled by something deeper than the cold of the wind.

"Oh," he said, his voice small. Loretta, The Immovable Object. Even in her short stature she loomed large in his mind. She seemed a titan, not . . . a human being. Not someone who could fall prey to something so crass and profane as a disease. Certainly getting sick was a genuine hazard of being in the CDC. But this was different. "How far—" He had to swallow a hard lump. "How far along is it?"

"Cursory signs of early dementia. Flu-like symptoms. She's still . . . working a little, from home, but Director Monroe has stepped into the role more completely. She's the one who asked me to talk to you."

"Sarah Monroe is good. Though she's not Loretta."

"No, but it is what it is. Martin's still healthy. Robbie . . ."

Her voice trailed off. "What?"

"Robbie's . . . we don't know. He was still in Africa—there was a new Ebola outbreak in Liberia and they're suffering from White Mask, too, so he thought, you know, two birds with one stone. But White Mask . . . the people there, they think it's witchcraft. They think . . . Americans caused it. He was with a WHO convoy and they got ambushed. We lost track of them after that but . . ."

There's a good bet he's dead, Benji thought.

"Fucking hell," he said. He blinked back tears.

"Yeah."

Cassie seemed like she was summoning some courage. He watched her muster it—it always came when she was about to challenge him on something. Benji liked that. He needed people willing to challenge him. Her face screwed up and then she let it out:

"What if you're making a mistake? I mean, lemme restate the question: What if you're being a *fucking idiot*? You're one of the finest minds we have, Benji—Loretta should've never sidelined you after Longacre, I know. That was unacceptable. We need you. *I* need you."

"You're better than me. And you have Martin, now." Vargas, who'd stayed on with Cassie at Benji's recommendation. "I'm staying."

"Why?"

"You wouldn't understand."

Anger flared in her eyes. "So *make* me understand."

"The flock," he said. "They don't get sick."

"What?" She didn't understand, until she did. He literally watched it dawn on her. "It won't affect them. Will it? The pathogen. Holy shit."

"So far, that holds true. The White Mask has no effect on them."

The wind swept in again. Gulls took flight, circling overhead once before hurrying out to sea in search of seafood bounty.

"I'm going to tell you something now," he said. "I hope you keep it to yourself but if you don't, that's your call. But you might as well know and I'm tired of being burdened with the knowledge." He took a deep breath. "The flock was designed, Cass. These people were chosen and purposefully infected by a . . . a nanoparticle: an infinitesimal swarm of machines that grants their hosts a kind of . . . limited invulnerability. Which means—"

"They might survive this."

"Yes. There's a distinct possibility that they might become the only survivors."

She took a step back, like she needed the space just to take it all in. Cassie looked lost, all of a sudden—a look he'd seen on some White Mask sufferers as the delirium took hold. But this, it seemed, was not that. She was literally reeling from the idea. And trying to catch up to it, trying to process the *hows* and *whys* of it. "Wait," she said. "Hold up. Why aren't there more? Why not just . . . make more nanomachines to protect us?"

He told her what they had told him: "Production of the nanomachines requires a considerable amount of rare earth resources in manufacturing. Resources that, sadly, are no longer available. And no synthetic substitutes exist."

"Fuck."

"Yes. Fuck."

"They're a fail-safe," she said.

"Something like that."

"Who told you?"

"Black Swan did." He hesitated. He wasn't sure how much of this he should even be sharing, but he had to tell someone, and Cassie, especially, was a close friend and confidante. He hated already that he hadn't told her. "Black Swan controls the nanomachine swarm, meaning . . . Black Swan controls the flock."

"That means Sadie knows."

"Knew. She always knew."

"And that's why she's not with the shepherds anymore."

He sighed. "Yes."

"I'm sorry. I know you two were a thing, kinda."

Forcing a smile, he said, "There are greater things to worry about than my troubled romantic entanglements."

The wind ruffled her hair, blew it into her face—Cassie ran her hands through it and tugged it into a ponytail.

"What now?" she asked.

"Same as before. You keep working on a cure. I keep watching the flock. And we hope that, come Christmas, this was all just a temporary nightmare and we all get drunk on rum-spiked eggnog and wait for the next disease to hop from a bat or a rat, or the next pathogen to wake from a melting permafrost, or some med-resistant bacteria to take us all down. We do what we always do. We go to work."

"All right." She smiled and took his hand, giving it a squeeze. "Then in that spirit, come see what I've brought you."

That was, after all, the purpose of this meeting.

· · ·

She was gone again, and Benji was left as the mist turned to a spitting rain, loading the boxes into the trunk of his car. Cassie had left him with several presents: First were several gallon-sized plastic baggies full of sterilized testing swabs, each operating like a flu swab for rapid diagnosis of the presence of *R. destructans*. It was enough to test the shepherds and flock.

Second was a case of antifungal meds. Triaconozole—a new concoction by an upstart pharma company, Dawson-Hearne, out of Chicago. It was no cure, Cassie said, but it provided some prophylaxis against the onset of White Mask by delaying the progress of the filaments that moved to penetrate the brain. She told him, "This isn't for public knowledge. We don't have a lot of this. One person needs to take two pills a day for it to be effective, and this is two hundred pills. I'll try to get you more. In the meantime, dole them out how you see fit, but it's really meant for necessary personnel, okay? The president is on it, all her staff, all the CDC, and down the line. People find out we're keeping this secret, there will be hell to pay."

As if there wasn't already hell to pay, he thought.

"There's another thing," she said. "If dementia sets in, standard meds don't fix it. But there's one thing that . . . helps."

Then she gave him a shitload of Ritalin.

Ritalin: a serious stimulant. Sometimes it was used to counteract narcolepsy as well as ADHD, attention deficit hyperactivity disorder, particularly in teens. (Teens who, historically, often sold it to friends anyway.) There'd been talk in recent years of it serving as a countermeasure for Alzheimer's, but no one had managed a serious study on it, yet.

"I'm not sure what's worse," he told her, "a world dying by losing itself to delirium, or a dying world jacked up on Ritalin."

She shrugged that off and said that other stimulants might help, as well, though that was only a guess. He told her thanks, and took the crate of Ritalin—easily two thousand pills' worth—with him.

Now he closed the trunk. The gulls returned from their sea voyage, circling the old closed-down farm stand and settling again on its roof. Squawking and hollering. Benji said goodbye to the birds, and wondered aloud if seagulls would be better stewards of the earth than humans had been. As he backed the car toward the road, he had an idle moment when he looked again at the gap in the barrier head—the gap that led off a cliff and to the craggy rocks and crashing surf below. He contemplated for half a second slamming his foot against the gas and driving toward it at top speed, launching himself into the air—for a moment, he'd fly, and that struck him as funny, suddenly. Thirty years ago anyone pontificating on the future forever ended up on the subject of *flying cars,* and now the only way he could seize that future was by driving off a cliff.

He did not do those things.

Instead, he reversed onto the road, and drove back to the flock.

Back to his fellow shepherds.

Back to the people he called home.

53

THE KEPT MAN

Folks, this is my last podcast. I know, I know. You'll miss my voice and I'll miss your comments. But I think it's time to be with my family and my friends, because . . . this thing is serious, this disease is out there, White Mask, and who knows where we'll land? I'm worried. I think we all are. Best advice I have for you is like what Pastor Matthew Bird said in his recent podcast—now is the time to get right with God, because soon, He rides.

—Hiram Golden, *The Golden Hour* podcast

SEPTEMBER 6
Echo Lake, Indiana

DAY IN AND DAY OUT, PASTOR MATTHEW BIRD WAS REMINDED THAT HE DID not have the courage to die. He certainly had the *option* to do so: For over a month he'd been chained up in a basement underneath the shed that sat adjacent to Ozark Stover's Morton building. The shed was built like a bomb shelter bunker, which reportedly was one of its potential functions—Stover said he had many such bunkers across his property. The room was not large, maybe 250 square feet in total, and it contained very little: a fold-out cot; a simple bathroom with toilet, sink, and shower; a small bookshelf containing only one book, a King James Bible; and a laptop computer from which Matthew recorded the podcasts and video messages that Ozark demanded from him. A manacle was tight around his right-hand wrist: a manacle that Stover had welded himself. The manacle was in turn secured to a heavy-gauge steel chain that was in turn bound to a massive steel eyebolt that had been drilled into the cold concrete.

It was just one of the ways Matthew knew that he could die.

He could choke himself with it.

He could slam his head forward onto it.

He could maybe . . . rig up a noose, somehow, someway.

He could try to drown himself in the sink.

He could try to break the laptop and cut his wrists with the screen or with shards of plastic . . .

A dozen ways to die and he chose none of them.

(If only, he thought, he had the courage that Autumn had. He had come to the conclusion that, as Ozark told him again and again and again, Autumn went into that bathtub to die, because she hated her husband and had forgotten her son. He didn't know if she was alive any longer, or if she was in a coma, or if she had come out of it and was now kept somewhere for Ozark Stover just as Matthew was. He asked his captors about it every day, and whenever he did, they said nothing. Sometimes they looked to one another, stone-faced. Other times they laughed. But they never told him. Which was the most horrible thing of all.)

Matthew did not kill himself, no.

And it was for the worst possible reason. It was not because he sought freedom. It was not because he wanted to see Autumn again, or Bo—if Autumn were even alive, if Bo would even see him.

No, it was because he was afraid of dying.

Because Matthew was suddenly sure that the only thing that would meet him in death would be, at best, darkness. And at worst, Hell.

Perhaps they were one and the same.

He no longer was certain that his God, or anyone's god, existed.

That was a crushing revelation, one that could've driven some to certain suicide but forced Matthew in the other direction. Before, death would have been . . . if not welcome, then at least a homecoming. A return to Heaven, a return to the God from whence he came. But now, death was a doorway into nothing. An endless void, a bottomless chasm, a meaningless eternity that gave no grace or shape to the life that he had led.

He did not have the courage to meet that darkness.

And so, here he sat, day in and day out.

Contemplating death but never meeting it.

Remembering what Stover did to him, replaying it endlessly in his own head, like a punishment levied against himself, by himself.

They brought him meals. Usually it was rangy Danny Gibbons or his buzz-cut brother, Billy, who brought him food. He didn't eat much, so they stopped bringing him full meals. And once every few days, they told him to record a message. Always audio. Never video, because he couldn't get it together enough for that. It was a message for the faithful—Stover or his people wrote Matthew a script and he would read it. This laptop had no internet access, as wireless signals did not seem able to penetrate the bunker walls. The scripts were him talking about the End Times, about mobilizing God's warriors against the coming armies of Leviathan, about the left-wing conspiracies of President Hunt and her collaborators—the conspiracies that led to this moment in American history, when a new plague had risen to eliminate the nation and make way for the New World Order.

It was all weaponized horseshit. Matthew didn't believe any of it. And he knew now that Stover didn't believe it, either.

It didn't matter if Stover believed it.

What mattered was that those listening believed it.

Ozark was sure that they did. Matthew thought so, too.

Anytime someone came in to hand him a new script, they told him the subscriber numbers. Ten thousand, then fifty, then a hundred thousand— not to mention the numbers of views and listens, which were ten times that. They crafted for Matthew a typically paranoid story: He was no longer at his church, he explained, because he was speaking "too much truth," and satanic forces had overtaken the US government and would be coming for the "truth-tellers." And so he was reporting from a "safe location," a "bunker where Lucifer and his minions would not find me."

He had to do it convincingly.

Or they beat him with old phone books and had him do it again.

He threatened to kill himself. He told that to Stover—who rarely made an appearance down here anymore—and the big man just laughed, a roaring, tectonic guffaw.

"Go ahead," Stover said. "That'll just feed them. Just confirms our narrative. You, the good preacher, killed by the forces of darkness to stop your crusade of righteousness. Hell, maybe we'll off you ourselves if we need to." Then they beat him again. Ozark laughed the whole time.

So Matthew stopped resisting.

He leaned into it.

Matthew brought wide-eyed and frothy vigor to every recording. Sometimes he wept in the middle, uncontrollably so, and he was sure that he'd have to re-record. But Danny Gibbons told him Stover liked that. Said it sounded *authentic* to someone watching God's Kingdom fall to Satan.

Lately, the scripts had refocused attention on the sleepwalkers, repositioning them as not only Satan's army, but also a marching contagion: It was the flock of walkers, the scripts read, that were spreading the White Mask disease to the faithful. They, a mob of plague-bearers engineered by the government under the orders of Lucifer and Leviathan herself—

Oh, that was President Hunt. Leviathan was what they called her.

What *he* called her. Matthew. In his recordings.

Because the inescapable truth was, though he did not write the scripts, it was he who spoke them. He was not their origin point, but he was damn sure their delivery system. Which meant *he* was a contagion, too. Not of some virus or bacteria or fungus. But spreading an infection of bad ideas.

Yet onward he went.

Until yesterday.

Yesterday, someone new came into the bunker. He'd seen most of the old faces at one point or another—he'd seen Roger, he'd seen the two Gibbons brothers, and of course he'd seen Ozark. Never Hiram Golden, though that didn't surprise him. Never Bo, either.

Bo . . .

Autumn . . .

This time, it was someone he didn't expect. A face he initially recognized but couldn't put a name to until the young man identified himself again: Ty Cantrell, the sandy-haired fellow, young and strong, who had once upon a time painted and fixed up Matthew's church with Billy Gibbons.

Ty was different from the others. He was softer-spoken, nicer, a little looser. And he looked uncomfortable around Matthew, too—or, the way Matthew figured it, was uncomfortable around this *situation*. He seemed nervous as he brought Matthew a new script.

And that meant he was talkative.

He started off sort of . . . rambling about this and that. Ty went on and on about some baseball game between the Cleveland Indians and the Boston Red Sox, and then said, "I'm kinda surprised they even still have the games anymore, what with the way things are right now. But I guess people need to feel good about something."

And that was Matthew's window. He didn't know much about what was going on—they kept him mostly in the dark, though he'd learned some things through the scripts. Even still, he didn't have much to go on.

Matthew said, "How are things out there?"

"Oh, you know. People just . . . they keep dying. Lot of infected."

"How many? How many are sick? Or dead?"

"I . . . you know, I don't know. Lots."

"Lots like, a million?"

"Nah, but it's tens of thousands or something. Hundreds. I dunno, I kinda have to tune it out, I just hear things."

"And they say it's getting worse?" He heard his own voice trembling, because he felt scared. Not just for the world, but because he suspected he shouldn't be talking to Ty. And Ty should not be talking to him, either. "How bad?"

"Pssh, I don't know. They're telling people with any kind of symptoms—a runny nose or like, you forget the name of your dog—to go get a swab to see if you got the disease. They opened up all these quarantine centers but they're already full. And then they're burning bodies . . ." He waved it off. "It's a mess. You don't want to hear about any of this."

I do. I want to hear about it all. In part just to feel connected to something again. In part because he worried about his role in all of it.

He idly flipped through the two-page script he was given. This one shorter than usual. He saw the sleepwalkers mentioned again and again.

Ty said, "Well, I'm gonna go—"

"This script is heavy on the walkers again."

"They're spreading disease."

So Ty wasn't too smart. And he bought in to Stover's bullshit.

"Sure," Matthew said, nodding slow.

"So, they gotta go, right? I mean that's what Stover says. Can't abide a witch to live and all that. That part'll be over soon enough, I guess."

"Of course." Matthew licked his lips, eager to pluck the truth from this poor daft man—really, a kid, only a few years older than his own son. "So he's planning on doing something about them. The walkers."

"It's time." Ty nodded. "People will understand. Hell," he said, snort-laughing a little. "I think they'll cheer, you ask me."

"I bet. That Ozark is going to—I assume he'll go big. The attack will be . . . it'll be something to see."

"I figure."

"Me too." He tried to keep cool, but his heart was bucking in his chest like a wild horse. He shuffled the two pages again. "So, I'll record these and . . . I guess you'll be back in an hour or so."

"Okay." Ty looked at him with a flash of pity and fear. Then he smiled and hurried the hell out of there, nervousness nipping at his heels.

That's when Matthew recorded the episode.

He didn't know who would be listening—early he knew they were checking his work, made sure he stuck to the script. Were they still? He had to assume they were. But he'd gone off-script before, mostly just rewriting the sentences in his head to sound more like how he'd really say them. And sometimes he went off on a tangent, too, talking about the march of Satan's army and quoting different passages of Revelation.

They never said anything to him about those.

Because maybe they weren't listening anymore.

He had to count on it.

This time, he recorded the audio.

And again he went off-script. He included a fire-and-brimstone warning to the shepherds and the flock of walkers that they were monsters, they were demons, and that they would be attacked—

"We will attack you. We will destroy you. Soon," he said, trying to put as much madness into his voice as possible, "you will pay for your sins as slaves of Leviathan, and when that attack comes, you won't see it coming. We're coming for you. No warning."

Absurd, he knew, telling them there'd be no warning—when he was explicitly trying to warn them.

But sometimes people fell for such simple chicanery. As a pastor, you sometimes had to do things to entertain the kids, and some pastors played the guitar. Matthew's hook was magic tricks. And with stage magic, he knew the most important part was basic misdirection—*the coin isn't in this hand,* one said, even as the coin was very much in that hand.

He hoped the walkers and their shepherds would see through his trick.

Later, Ty came, took the USB key on which he recorded the audio.

Then he counted the links on his chain (141, a number he knew already) and, though he had no windows, knew it was getting late in the day. His internal clock was always wildly spinning, so he checked the clock on the laptop just to feel *anchored* to the movement of time.

Sometime later, after he dozed off on his cot, he heard the door to his bunker rattling and unlocking. Feet banged on the metal ladder leading down. It wasn't Stover, he knew that much. Stover's footfalls were like anvils landing, *whong, whong, whong.* This wasn't that.

It was Danny Gibbons. Danny walked in, barely looking over at Matthew. He had the air of someone coming to do a job: a plumber, an electrician, someone who was singularly focused on the task ahead.

Finally, he set his stare on Matthew.

"Heard your recording."

Every part of him tightened up. All his appendages wanted to crawl inside of him. *Play it cool, maybe he doesn't know.*

"Good," Matthew said, offering an embarrassed smile. "Hope it was, ahh, hope it was okay."

It was then that Matthew saw what hung from one of Danny's back belt-loops. He saw it when the man grabbed for it.

A hammer.

Small. Ball-peen.

"Left hand," Danny said.

"What?"

"Your left hand. Come over here, put it out on the desk. Not too close to the keyboard."

"I don't . . . I don't understand." Matthew scooted backward on his cot toward the wall. "Listen, hey, no, I don't know what you're doing—"

"Like I said, heard your recording. You come over here. You put your hand down. If I have to come over there, this gets worse."

"No. I don't—c'mon," Matthew pleaded. "Just, just, hold on, let's just talk this out. Is this about the improvisation? I've improvised before and it wasn't an issue—hey, I'll re-record. No big deal. I'll stick to the script, yes, I'll definitely stick to the script—"

"I'm gonna count to five. You're not here at five, I come to you, and then I can't promise what happens after that. But I do know I don't see any gun oil around here, so don't expect it to be as pleasurable as last time."

A low moan arose in the back of Matthew's throat. The mewl of a trapped creature. He flinched, pressing back into the wall further, wishing somehow that he could just merge with the concrete wall of the bunker—this *prison*—and disappear into the dirt forever.

"One."

"No. *No.* Please, tell Ozark—"

"Two."

Tears burned hot in his eyes, scalding his lids.

"Three . . . come on, now, Preacher."

The memory of that day in the Morton building, surrounded by all those weapons—it felt both like it happened yesterday and like it happened to someone else a lifetime ago—crashed down on him like a crushing wave. He gagged, dry-heaving.

"Four. Tick-tock, tick-tock."

The sound grew louder and louder out of him, that mewling whine, that fearful wail, until he suddenly sprang up out of the cot. His posture was of a cockroach scurrying across the floor hoping not to be noticed even as he found his way to the desk and the chair. He sat down and put his hand out.

"There we go," Danny said.

Danny grabbed for his hand. He flinched away, but the man was fast and rough. He held the wrist so hard that Matthew was afraid it would snap like an old branch under a pressing boot. The man spun Matthew's hand around, so that the palm faced down on the pressed-wood desk.

The hammer struck fast. Danny used the rounded end. It whipped down hard, dead into the center of Matthew's hand. It crunched. Pain cascaded out. He howled, recoiling, yanking his hand back and cradling it against his chest.

For a while, he heard his own retching sobs and the pounding of his heartbeat deep in every corridor within his body.

And then came the sound to match his pulse.

Whong.

Whong.

Whong.

Ozark Stover stepped into the bunker.

The big sonofabitch looked around, disgusted. Stover reached up, grabbed a fistful of his own massive beard, and tugged on it before smoothing it out and sneering.

"I heard your little warning," Stover said.

"No, no, it wasn't that," Matthew said, gabbling. Mouth sticky with his own spit and tears. "Please don't think I'd do anything like that."

"You did. I know you did. Ty, he told you that we had designs on the flock, and you thought you could get them a warning—as if anyone there would even listen to our little online venture. I get it. You're still a preacher man, still thinking your job on this earth is to do some good, save people. Let me separate you from that notion. Just as I separated this from Ty."

He reached in his pocket and tossed something onto the floor.

It was a thumb.

Bloody underneath. Bit of white bone shining.

"You made out like a bandit," Ozark said, "'cause you get to keep your hand together. Those bones will heal—not well, I wager, but they'll heal. Ty paid more because Ty's crime was more serious. He knew not to talk you up, and still, he opened his dumbfuck mouth."

Matthew tried to form words but couldn't. He braved a glancing look at his hand—the fingers curled in, an arthritic claw. The back was already swelling up. He briefly imagined how many bits, *little bits,* were in there, broken. And how his hand was now little more than a mitt of skin holding the shattered pottery of his bones.

Ozark jerked his head, and Danny took that as a command. He loped off toward the ladder and disappeared up the hatch. Leaving Matthew alone with the monster.

"I'm doing you a favor," Ozark said. "It's gotten bad out there, Preacher. And it's only getting worse. The dam hasn't broken yet but it's gonna. Quarantining people. Bodies piling up. Someday soon, with the help of people like me and a voice like yours, they're going to see that the government and Madam Fucking President want them to line up against the wall so they can be marched into camps where they get sick and die. Not me, though. Not us. Our people will make it through. Let the spics and chinks and all the other monkeys get sick—our blood is strong. Our *heritage* is strong. We'll strike out. We'll live when they die. We'll survive when they don't. And when the smoke of burning bodies clears, when the brass hits the asphalt, we'll come into the sunlight of a new day. A new nation.

"The sleepwalkers, they're a part of that. Maybe they're why this plague is here, maybe they're not, but you look at them—makes me sick. They don't belong here. I don't see faces I recognize. We strike out against them and any who stand in our way. Any who would drag us down when the time comes to crawl up out of the ashes."

You're a psychopath, Matthew wanted to say.

But all he said was, "Okay."

Ozark nodded. "All right, Preacher. This has been a good talk."

"How . . . how is my family?"

"*Your* family? Your family. Huh. Didn't think you were that delusional to still think you had a family to call your own." Ozark grinned, his tongue sliding across those picket-fence teeth like a washrag. "Your boy is fine. Bo is learning all the things he needs to learn."

"And Autumn?"

Ozark clacked his fence-post teeth together, then shook his head. "Preacher, I wasn't going to tell you this, because I didn't want to saddle you with a heavier burden than you are already carrying, but your wife, she's gone. Died a few nights after you came to see me. Don't worry, Bo was by her side. I was, too. She never came out of that coma, so I'm sure she didn't have to wonder where you were."

"Wait," Matthew said, pleading. "Don't go. You're lying. Please tell me you're lying. Don't go!"

But he choked. The words lodged in his throat like a hunk of gristle.

Ozark tossed the USB key on the desk. "There. Re-record the script. Don't *ad-lib* this time, or I'll break the whole arm, not just the hand. Every time you fuck me, Matthew, I'll take another piece of you."

54

THE FUNGUS AMONG US

We're all dying because we can't do what we know we need to do. Look at those sleepwalkers. What do you see? Lot of women. Lot of not-whites. Feminized soy-boys and trannies and spergs. All weak, controlled by the fungus like those cordyceps zombie ants. Those ants are the ones who spread the fungus to their fellow ants and dollars to donuts that's what's happening here. They're the origin point for White Mask. (Though I dispute that name because White Mask is a racist name meant to associate this plague with the white race. I use it only so we all understand what I mean.) You wanna end the disease? You gotta kill those walkers. FORE-WARNED IS FOREARMED, and you bet that I'm armed. Are you?

—user ARM-Army at r/MensRights

SEPTEMBER 6
Pelican State Beach, California

THE FIRE CRACKLED AND POPPED AS THE WIND SWEPT THROUGH IT.

A handful of shepherds sat around it: Pete Corley, Marcy Reyes, Mia Carillo, and Shana Stewart. They passed around a bottle of something called mescal. Shana took only a sip given recent, well, *news,* and to her it tasted a whole lot like burned, barbecued tequila. It was gross and Corley agreed, saying it tasted like fireplace ash. Mia *tsk*ed them both and said, "Shut up, that's what I like about it. It's warm like this campfire." Then she plugged the bottle between her lips and took a big gulp. *Ploomp.*

The flock was north of them, now, by a few miles. It was Pete who suggested they get away for a little while, Benji and Arav had brought the CDC trailer south to run tests—all day long they spent swabbing shepherds and walkers alike, sticking these long cotton swabs way too far up their noses before bagging them and moving on. Reminded Shana of a flu swab. Arav said, "It's to see if any of us have White Mask." Then he smiled and reassured her: "I'm sure we're safe."

Shana hadn't told him yet that she was pregnant.

Shit.

Don't think about it, she told herself. *This is a problem for Future You. Tonight, just sit here and look at the beach and the stars and the fire.*

But she kept looking down the length of beach. Two vehicles sat parked there. Her father's RV and the CDC trailer, each next to the other. Each a dark shape with windows glowing. Dad said he'd take a nap. Of course he didn't join them. He was putting on weight, now, sitting in that driver's seat all the time. He was like Pete Corley's chauffeur and attendant. More interested in the rock star than in his own daughter.

Well, you're going to be a grandfather now, too, jerk.

Shana, don't think about it.

Okay, Shana.

You're talking to yourself, Shana.

Shit.

Marcy wasn't having a good time. She was too far from the flock, she said, and that not only made her agitated, she said that the "glow no longer protected her," whatever that meant. The woman seemed in pain—her large size made smaller, like she was folding in on herself. They offered to take her back but she said, "No, no, I should take some time, get off the road for a little while." She offered a forced smile. She said to Pete: "You talk anymore to your wife and kids?"

"No," he said, his face a gloomy blue made orange as he leaned closer to the fire. "I think they're done with me. I've made my choices." He snatched the bottle from Mia again and took a big swig.

"At least you have people," Marcy said. "I don't have anyone anymore. My dad died from colon cancer. My mother died before that from breast cancer. No kids. And I don't want love or sex. So."

Pete sniffed. "Spare me the Misery Olympics."

"I don't mean it like that," Marcy said.

"He's right," Mia said. "I hate when people do that. It's like, *Oh, my cat died today,* and someone says, *Well could be worse,* and then they bring up some other shit that has nothing to do with your cat dying."

"I didn't mean it like that!"

"All of you shut up," Shana barked. They turned toward her and she rolled her eyes. "This sucks for everyone in different ways. The world's gone batshit. Literally, in a way, since I guess maybe this White Mask thing comes from bats? Whatever. I just mean, can we not grouse at each other? It's not too cold. The stars are pretty. The sound of the sea is nice. Can we just . . . not . . . do whatever this is?"

"Ah, fuck it," Pete said. "I deserve it anyway."

"Nobody deserves any of this," Marcy said.

"I was cheating on her. Lena. And I don't mean in a metaphorical way, like, *Oh, I was cheating on her with rock-and-roll,* I mean, I was literally fucking somebody else. Lots of somebody elses over the years. Some of them I even loved, gave them my heart. Like a cruel idiot."

He plugged the bottle in his mouth and drank again. Mia took it back from him, almost having to wrestle it away. "Gimme."

Shana already knew this about Pete. It was surprising he felt comfortable enough to tell the others at this point, but she figured with the world being what it was, maybe he felt like what did it matter? And they had all grown closer over the last couple of months. Shana asked him, "You still talk to the other women?"

"Not other women. Other men."

Mia whistled. "Oh shit."

"I'm gay as the day is blue. Queer as a three-dollar bill."

"Do they know?" Shana asked. "Your family."

"Nah. Or maybe they do and I'm blind to it. But I've kept a pretty good lid on it. Some of my band knows and . . . Evil Elvis, that fucker, I hope he gets the fungus except it goes straight up his ass and gives him the powdery moldy shits before he dies." Everyone gave him strange looks and he waved them off. "Oh, he was going to blackmail me, so fuck him. Others have tried, too. I'd paid off a few journos over the years, people who wanted the exposé. All because I didn't want to hurt Lena and the kids. Meanwhile, I'm hurting other people. Landry, shit."

"Laundry?" Mia asked.

"*Landry,*" Pete said, enunciating the name. "Clean the sand out of your ears, will you? Landry. The man I was with for a while. Before I came here to . . . do whatever it is I'm here to do."

"Is he sick?" Marcy asked.

"No. Maybe. Shit, I don't know."

"You haven't spoken to him?"

"No!" Pete said, a sharp rebuke. He softened his voice and said it again:

"No. I haven't spoken to him since . . ." He winced as he seemed to think about it. "July? Shit. I assume he's moved on."

Shana said, "You should call him."

"What? Why?"

"I dunno. You like him. Or love him. Everything sucks. Maybe he's waiting for you. Maybe he's dying or dead. Call him."

"Really. You think?"

"Unless you want to keep on being a cruel, shitty idiot."

"I *am* pretty good at it."

"That's probably not a thing to be proud of."

"Fucking *fine,* I know, I know." He slapped his cheeks, made hollow bongo sounds on his own face. "I'll call him in the morning."

"Call him now."

"It's late. He's in New York."

"Wake him," Marcy said, chiming in. "Like Shana said: Life is short. What if he's sick? Maybe he needs you."

"Gods, I hope he's not sick." Pete flicked his gaze among them. "I hope none of us are sick. That's what they're doing back there, isn't it? Testing all our *swabs.* For that insidious disease."

Fear slithered through Shana. She imagined Arav going through tests. She imagined her own unborn baby. She didn't know what was happening or what was coming—not with herself, her sister, with any of them. It was enough to make the whole world sway and teeter beneath her like she was standing tippy-toe at the edge of a crumbling cliff, and again she admonished herself, *Don't worry about this, you can't change any of this,* but she remembered seeing the hanging man, and the graves piled with the dead, and the storefronts closed up, the car crashes, hearing the distant sirens, the faraway screams. *The world's gone sick, the wheels are coming off the fucking bus and we're all riding that bus . . .*

Marcy reached out and touched her arm. Gave her a small smile.

It was enough. Just enough.

For the moment.

It centered her. But it made her wish Arav were here with her around the fire instead of there in that trailer.

ONE BY ONE, THE SWABS went under the black light.

Most went through and came out clear, which both pleased and surprised Benji. He feared the worst—because, at this point, the worst had become reality. Why not assume everything was on fire and swirling down the drain in perfect simultaneity? But this was welcome news. So far, he'd only found a dozen shepherds who showed any signs of White Mask. That meant tonight he could isolate them and—regrettably—send them on their way. It sounded strange, of course, to label that good news—these were people who presently had been given a terminal diagnosis. A death sentence. Giving them the news was no less than telling someone they had pancreatic cancer or some other metastasized malignancy.

Instead, he focused on the swabs. As did Arav, who sat at a lab station behind him, their stools nearly touching.

The swabs were simple in their design: They soaked them in a staining agent called Sporafluor. Then they went up the nose as far as they could go, swabbing to catch early growth of *Rhizopus destrucans*. After which, they popped the swabs under a black light.

The staining agent reacted to the fatty esters present in the fungus. If *R. destructans* was present, the flecks of it on the swab glowed in the black light. No fungal pathogen? No glow.

"I'm having good luck over here," Benji said, more than a little excitedly. "Not many shepherds. And none of the flock."

"Same," Arav said. That one word was cold and invited no more discussion. Benji pushed on, regardless.

"I suspect it's because few from the outside choose to interact with the flock—though it's sad to be isolated, it may be working in our favor." He cleared his throat and turned around. "Not that it's good any are infected, of course. We'll have to move quickly. We'll have to find them and extricate them so they don't infect the others—but I'm hopeful we can get control of this. I'm talking too much. Am I talking too much?"

"It's fine," Arav said.

"You're still mad at me."

"I'm not mad. I don't hold grudges or do regrets. I don't think they're useful." Arav stayed focused on his work.

"That's a more mature outlook than in those who live a hundred years, Arav. I admire your wisdom."

"It's not wisdom. It's just reality. Of course, I don't know what reality this even is anymore. Nothing feels real. And I suspect you're keeping things from me, even still. I don't hate you for it, but I don't find it comfortable." Arav finally turned around. "I understand it, though."

"I'm sorry. I think you know what I know. I wish you didn't."

"And you trust Black Swan. And Sadie. And all of them."

"No. But . . . what choice do I have? I feel trapped. If I do something, if I try to . . . stop the flock, what if I stop the one mechanism we have to foster a small, smart, healthy group of survivors?"

Arav sighed. "I guess." He paused. "You haven't told them, yet. The other shepherds."

"About the . . . swarm?"

"Yeah. Why not?"

"I don't know. I fear they'd leave just when I need them."

"I think you should tell them. And you should tell Marcy that it's not angels. That it's just . . . some defect, a glitch. Her skull plate has turned into a receiver, hasn't it?"

"I don't want to rob her of her faith," Benji said. Worse, Benji couldn't quite explain why she felt so good around the walkers. His best guess was that, since her skull plate was resting on her ocular nerve, causing deep, body-wracking migraines, the delicate vibration from the incoming swarm frequency was enough to alleviate pressure. There had been studies in the past on how certain radio frequencies or sound waves could be used to inhibit pain. This, he imagined, was that.

Arav looked fed up. "You know, Doctor Ray, I think you have a vision of yourself, and . . . it's a vision of yourself I once had, too, that you were a crusader for truth. A person who was fundamentally honest and good. But maybe you're too comfortable lying to others in order to save yourself the pain. Isn't that what you didn't like about Sadie?"

"God, Arav, you know where to stick the knife."

The young man looked genuinely chastened. "Sorry."

"No, it's fine. You're not wrong. I'll try to sit and think on it."

"I suppose I should practice what I preach."

"I don't understand?"

But then, Benji did.

And with that, Arav reached across the table and pulled out two bagged swabs. One marked with the name STEWART, SHANA.

The other marked with THEVAR, ARAV.

Before Benji could even see the stain . . .

"She's infected," Benji said of the girl.

"No," Arav answered. "It's me. I'm the sick one."

It was shameful, but Benji felt himself instantly recoil. He knew that he was healthy, and now he realized that Arav was not. It was foolish, his sudden revulsion, and he thought he had trained himself better. Arav said as much: "I'm not contagious. Or at least, I'm not sniffling and sneezing yet. I know how the disease progresses. I've read the reports. You're not in danger. But you will be, soon. Everyone will be."

"Including Shana."

"Yes."

A war went on inside Benji. On the one hand, Sadie and the others had told him that what was coming was inevitable: They would all become infected. In that context, Arav's infection was meaningless—if they were all to become sick, then what did it matter? But Benji wondered again if Black Swan was lying? Or if it had some kind of *agenda*—or perhaps it was Firesight that had the agenda. Or Benex-Voyager. Or Sadie. Conspiracy theories unspooled inside his mind: Could they have created both the nanites *and* the White Mask fungus? To what end, he could not imagine, especially given that one of their own, Bill Craddock, was now infected with White Mask, last he'd heard. Regardless, if they were wrong—or lying outright—then that meant some *could* survive.

Then that meant Arav could not remain.

He would, like the other infected shepherds, be a vector for contagion.

Benji didn't have to say it.

"I know I'll have to go," Arav said. "To leave. I know."

"I . . . wish there were another way. But—" Benji quickly went under the desk and pulled out one of the bottles of triaconozole. "This is fifty pills. Take two a day to delay the effects. Cassie gave them to me. And if you begin to experience . . . mental decline, I can get you a prescription for Ritalin, but that may be a month or two down the road." *And by then, who knows where the world will be?* Again he went through those numbers, a hundred thousand to twenty million, twenty million to four billion . . .

"Thank you." Arav took the pills and idly turned the bottle in his hand, pills rolling and rattling inside. "I'll finish my work here and go."

"Arav, you don't have to finish your work."

"I'll . . . okay, I understand, I'll go."

"Go. Talk to Shana."

"Maybe I should just leave."

"No," Benji said. "Trust me on this. Speak to her face-to-face. Be vigilant with the truth, Arav. Our truth, our love, it's what we have."

It's all we have.

Arav nodded. "It's been a pleasure, Doctor Ray. I admire you more than you know. You're kind. And diligent. I one day hoped to be like you."

"Arav, you already are like me."

"I'd shake your hand, but—"

"You're not contagious yet, stop it." Benji reached across and hugged him. They embraced for a time, and then he said to the young man: "Talk to her. Then I'll drive you to wherever you need to go."

PETE STOOD UP, SUDDENLY. "I'm going to go call Landry. Wish me luck. He's a real pouty asshole when I wake him up. Then again, I'm a real pouty ass-hole when he wakes me up."

"You're a pouty asshole always," Shana said.

"Oh, stuff it."

"Do it," Marcy said.

The self-proclaimed rock god held his phone up in the air like it was a talisman of luck, and then jogged off into the darkness of the beach, lit only by the light of his device. Marcy sighed and curled in further on herself.

She looked to be in pain.

"We can go soon," Shana said.

"It's okay. The flock is heading this way. I can . . . feel them."

"That's weird," Mia said. "You know that, right?"

"It gets weirder," Marcy said.

They looked at her, confused.

"I can sometimes *hear* the walkers," she confessed in a small voice.

Mia and Shana exchanged alarmed looks.

"Wait, what?" Shana asked. "What do you mean?"

"I mean . . . I hear voices. It's like, most of the time it's just a sound, a golden tone, sometimes intercut with a kind of soothing static. But once in a while, I hear their voices." Shamefacedly Marcy said, "It's how I knew your birthday, Shana. Nessie told me."

Shana opened her mouth to respond to that, but no sound came out.

That one sentence, *Nessie told me,* kept resurfacing in her mind like bubbles from the bottom of a lake. *Nessie told me. Nessie told me.*

"They're still in there," she said. Tears in her eyes.

"Holy fucking shit," Mia said. "They're not just . . . zombies."

Before she knew what she was doing, Shana threw her arms around Marcy. Then she pulled away and slugged the woman hard in the arm.

"Ow!" Marcy said. "What the crap, Shana?"

"You should've told us! This is huge news."

"Huge," Mia repeated. "Fuckin' big."

They grilled Marcy, then. What had she heard? *Who* had she heard? She said she heard Nessie sometimes. Mia asked suddenly if this was some kind of cold-reading psychic bullshit. "You ever heard anything from Matty?" Mateo, she meant, her twin brother.

"I have," Marcy said, suddenly hesitant.

"Well? What is it?"

"You're going to think it's crazy."

"I think *you're* crazy already, so who cares?"

Marcy massaged her right hand with her left, then reversed. "He said . . . Zidane Roulette."

"Is that some kind of code?" Shana asked. "That doesn't sound like a real thing, Marcy."

"I know. Maybe it is a code. Maybe it's a message. Shit, I should've told you guys, but I didn't want you to push me away again, and—" The words faded on her tongue like a snowflake. "Mia, are you okay?"

The other shepherd had rocked back on her heels. Her arms wrapped around herself. Her cheeks shone in the firelight, wet with tears, and suddenly she made this sound, a hitching, wracking gulp as she sobbed.

And laughed.

Laughing and crying at the same time.

"I think you broke Mia," Shana said.

Mia erupted with words quickly gabbled: "That's a soccer move. Zidane Roulette. It's a—" She took a deep breath. "It's a move you do in soccer like, you kinda do this three-sixty turn and heel-skid the ball the other way—I don't know! I don't play soccer. But Matty did. He loved that move. Always wanted to perfect it. Oh my God." Mia melted into Marcy. Marcy held her tight. They each shared the bottle of mescal. Glug, glug.

As they had their moment, Shana stood up.

In the spirit of this confessional moment . . .

It was time to tell Arav.

About this.

About the baby.

Oh shit oh shit oh shit.

Her feet carried her across the beach, boots making a *cuff cuff cuff* sound in the sand as the wind picked up, bringing with it the smell of salt and sea.

Ahead, a shadow came toward her, and she thought, *It's just Pete,* but then she saw this wasn't Pete's shape, but rather, a shape she recognized.

It was Arav. He was coming to meet her as she went to meet him.

Kismet. Serendipity. An odd bliss flowed through her like a slow, warm river. It was the first time in a long time that she'd felt this way.

Happy.

What an alien concept.

She picked up the pace and met Arav and moved to hug him—

But he stepped back. Hands up.

That's all it took for Shana to know that something was wrong. The hairs on her arms and the back of her neck prickled. The happiness she felt suddenly began to rattle and crumble under the tectonic strain of sudden worry.

"Hi," he said. He looked sad.

"Hey."

"I have something I need to tell you."

"I have something to tell you, too. A couple somethings. Maybe more. I love you. That's the first thing. I know maybe I'm not supposed to say that yet and maybe that's gonna freak you out but—ha ha, oh shit, if that freaks you out, boy, have I got some bad news for you—"

"Shana, please—"

"No, stop, I have to get this out because now I'm afraid you already know what I'm about to tell you and that's why you're looking at me the way you're looking at me."

"No, that's not it—"

"I'm pregnant."

Any words he was going to say next suddenly ended, chopped off by the executioner's ax of that statement: *I'm pregnant.*

"It's yours," she clarified.

"Oh God," he said.

"That's not the response I was hoping for, to be honest."

"Oh God, oh God." Arav began pacing back and forth. He reached up and ran his hands through his raven-dark hair, tugging on it as he strode back and forth. "Fuck. Aw, fuck."

"Arav, this is—I know this is a hard time but I was hoping this would be good news. You don't have to do anything. You don't have to be involved. The baby—just pretend I didn't tell you this. Shit. I'm such a fucking dummy. I thought—I thought you'd be happy. I wasn't happy about it and then I was happy about it and—stupid fucking little girl, I'm such a dope. I'll leave you alone."

She turned to walk away.

"Wait," he said, his voice a woeful, stuttering bleat.

Shana didn't face him. All she said was, her voice threatening to break, "It's cool. You feel what you gotta feel. I'm going back to the fire."

"I'm sick," he said.

Now she turned.

"What? What kind of sick?"

"The swab. *My* swab. It said I have . . . I have White Mask."

"No, that's not—" She laughed, not a happy sound, no, but an absurd one because that had to be wrong. "Look at you. You don't have any . . . any of that white stuff around your mouth or your nose. You're not even sneezing or anything. You're fine. Arav, you're *fine*."

"I'm decidedly not fine. I'm not contagious yet, but I'm not fine. The swabs aren't wrong. It's there. Inside me. I . . . don't know what to do."

She reached for him.

And again he pulled away.

"I'm sick!" he bellowed, his voice cracking like a frozen lake underfoot. The sound of it echoed out over the sand. "Shana, I can't risk you getting sick. Especially—oh God, especially if you're pregnant."

"What are you going to do?"

"I'm going to leave."

"You can't leave me."

"I *have to* leave you. One sneeze, one cough, and that could be a death sentence for you. Do you understand? It could kill you and the—" His voice got quiet. "And the baby."

"Arav, please." She felt herself well up. Felt her voice coming apart at the seams. "You have to stay."

"Keep your phone. We'll talk." He began to backpedal even as she stepped toward him. "I love you, too. I'm sorry. I'm so sorry."

And then he turned and ran, full tilt, back to the CDC trailer.

Shana, betraying every urge, did not follow. Instead, she collapsed there on the sand, under the stars.

TIME MOVED STRANGELY, THEN. GRIEF swept over her like a sickness, feverish and mad. Shana felt lost to it. In the back of her mind, the memory of her momentary hope and happiness—*Nessie is in there, I'm in love, I'm going to have a baby*—lingered. She wept and others came for her. Marcy and Mia scooped her up and she felt the words come gushing out of her—"Arav is sick and I'm pregnant"—and then they both embraced her. She felt warm and cold at the same time. Supported by them but also in free fall. Then came Pete Corley, Pete who said, "He's not sick!" and for a moment she thought he meant Arav, but then he said, "My man, Landry. He's not sick and he's coming to walk with the shepherds and—wait, what happened to her?" *Her*. He meant Shana. Mia and Marcy murmured to him what they knew, and he said, "Shit, oh shit, Shana, I'm so fucking sorry." *Fucking* became *facking* as his Irish brogue slid in there like a trespasser, and he did what she did not expect him to do—Pete was a narcissist, she thought, wholly concerned with himself and what the world could do for him or what they thought *of* him, but instead he reached out and took her hand and held it as the other two held her. He said nothing. He asked for nothing.

They ended up near the shore. The water sliding up and down the beach, the moonlight through clouds trapped in the tidal edge. They were good to her. They were honest with her. Nobody told her that everything was going to be okay. How could they? It would be a lie, bald-faced and cruel, like standing in front of an oncoming truck and being assured it wouldn't hit you, it'd pass right through you, not to worry, not to worry.

Pete then, did what he was good at doing—he sang a song.

It was not one of his. It was not even rock-and-roll, not punk, not anything that any of them knew. Rather, it was an old Irish song, and in it, his lilt came through softly:

How sweet was to roam by the sunny old stream,
And hear the dove's cry 'neath the morning's sunbeam.
Where the thrush and the robin their sweet notes combine
On the banks of the river that flows down by Mooncoin.

Flow on, lovely river, flow gently along.
By your waters so sweet sounds the lark's merry song.
On your green banks I'll wander where first I did join
With you, lovely Molly, the Rose of Mooncoin.

Oh Molly, dear Molly, it breaks my fond heart,
To know that we two forever must part
I will think of you, Molly, while sun and moon shines
On the banks of the river that flows down by Mooncoin . . .

And then he was gone, though the other two remained. Marcy with a strong arm around her, pulling her tight. Mia behind her, gently braiding her hair, wrestling it away from the sea-swept wind.

Then Pete came back, but he was not alone.

With him stood her father. He looked upon her with sad eyes and she rushed up to him. And he held her tight as the other three faded back into the dark, leaving her to be with her father. Her crying in his arms, trying to fall. Him holding her there, keeping her standing.

55

NO EXIT

Q: Did you hear the one about the fungus?
A: It might need time to grow on you.
>   —graffiti seen at multiple points along I-95 corridor

SEPTEMBER 7
Echo Lake, Indiana

MATTHEW'S LEFT HAND HAD SWOLLEN. IT HAD BLOWN UP, RED, AND ANGRY, the color of a boiled lobster. Any sensation brought him pain—anytime he moved it, anytime he brushed it against something, anytime he even *breathed* on it. It was broken, he knew that much. And it would never heal right, not as long as he was trapped here in this bunker.

He had to do something. Otherwise, all he thought about was Autumn and Bo. His son, lost without him. His wife, passed on without him.

Idly, he went through the same motions he had when he was first trapped here: roaming the space like a starving rat, looking for bolt-holes he could squeeze himself through for escape. As if any of that would be easy: like he'd find a tunnel out behind a poster, or a secret door in the cement, or a phone that someone had dropped that he could use to call for help. Matthew had fantasies of being some MacGyver-like figure who would use the aglet at the end of his shoelace to somehow pick the lock on his manacle. Or maybe he would break apart the laptop and use the chemicals found in the screen to create a little bomb that blew open the hatch, *kaboom*. Or when someone came down to check on him, he would spring himself upon them like a trained killer, wrapping his chain around their neck, pulling tighter and tighter until their tongue fell dead on their lips and their neck tendons pulled tight as tow cables . . .

He shuddered, there in his cot. Not because of the grotesque imagery, but because of how much he liked it. How much he *wished* for it. He wasn't a killer. He wasn't some MacGyver character. But he wanted to be. And he wanted to kill them all.

That was a new sensation to him.

This anger.

This *rage*.

It was madness. It wasn't God's light. It was fed from some greater darkness. But he could see nothing else now but those shadows within himself. Worse, he could see no God to guide him. No presence from above. Only the illusion of one. An illusion he'd clung to like a drowning man grabbing hold of driftwood in order to keep his head above water.

He moved in and out of sleep. His hand throbbed. Dreams and nightmares haunted his edges—none could he remember, but all of them left something on him, something grimy and foul. He woke gasping, sure that someone was on top of him.

But he was alone.

Alone, at least, in this bunker. Above him, he heard sounds: motion and movement, the rumblings of engines, the murmur of men yelling indistinctly. The gruff *wha wha wha* of someone laughing. The banging of a truck gate. Tires growling over loose stone. It was in all directions—above him, north of him, south of him. A lot of vehicles. A lot of men.

But what did it *mean*?

56

THE BRIDGE

RACHEL MADDOW: Let me ask you, Chris, before we begin. Will there even be an election in November?
CHRIS HAYES: The bigger question is, will there even be an America in November?
—*The Rachel Maddow Show*, MSNBC, Transcript 9/7

SEPTEMBER 8
Klamath River Bridge, California

BENJI BREATHED IN DEEP. THE AIR WAS CLEAR. NO BURNING SMELL. THE river babbled its susurrus beneath the bridge.

The walkers were about an hour out. He'd taken to scouting ahead, which brought him here, to this bridge. He found a few car wrecks along the way. But nothing more severe than that.

The bridge stretched out and back over the Klamath River. On each side were forested hills, the dark pines pointing toward the slate-gray sky. At each end of the bridge were two golden bears: statues mounted, guardians standing vigil over the bridge on both sides. Benji was sure there was a story there and so he decided to look it up, if only because he needed the distraction.

His phone had service here. Slow, but able. (And here a dark thought cut through his curiosity: *If humankind dies, how long will our cell signal go on? Will the internet remain even as we cease to populate it? Will our satellites keep spinning up there, networks reaching out to a population that has long gone dead and rotten?*) He shook that off, opened his web browser, and discovered that sure enough, there was an apocryphal story about those golden bears:

The bears—installed there in the 1950s—were not originally gold, it seemed. One morning, residents driving over the bridge found that the bears were painted gold. The highway patrol came and scrubbed the paint off with turpentine, but the next morning, what had happened? The bears were gold once again. This cycle repeated itself again and again, week in, week out: They'd remove the gold, and then the gold would return. They'd watch the bears but soon as the patrolmen fell asleep or went on their way, the bears were once again a shining, burnished gold.

Finally, they gave up. And the bears remained gold.

Years later it came out that it was nothing supernatural, nor was it the work of one person—rather, it was the Golden Bear Club, a group of men and women who sought not only to clean up their town and perform secret favors for people, but also to paint those bears gold again and again and again. Their only rules were, there were no rules. Happy anarchy. Delightful disobedience. Making the world better for no reason except to do it.

Benji liked that story.

But it made him sad, too. It seemed to him suddenly that it was easy to dismiss people as ultimately a negative force—a terrible influence upon the world and upon one another. Evil lived in the world. Wars and terror. Torture and assault. But he also knew that, statistically, the worst among them were a small percentage of the whole—it just felt like a lot more because that's how it went. Same way one mean comment could spoil a beautiful day, or how a single mouse turd would ruin even the most perfect meal.

Ultimately, Benji thought, people were good.

Lazy, sometimes. Maybe ignorant, maybe willfully unaware.

But they were good more than they were bad.

And that meant they didn't deserve any of this. He hadn't even looked at the news this morning but it was easy to know that the numbers of the dead were mounting. He'd been standing on this bridge for ten minutes already and hadn't seen one car coming or going. People were staying home. He'd passed houses with the windows boarded up behind plywood and new fences roughly hewn or cobbled together. Spray-painted signs said to GO AWAY OR DIE. Sometimes he saw other people milling about, like they were lost. Some of them had the telltale signs of White Mask: lips, nostrils, and eyes encrusted in the greasy powder of the pathogen, a wet white substance.

Soon, violence would start.

Already he'd heard tell of it: Last night on talk radio he heard the tale of a woman who found an intruder in her house and beat him to death with a nine-iron. Turned out, that intruder was the woman's own husband. She woke up next to him, certain he was a robber or a rapist. Turned his head into a bloody paste. And then, the kicker?

She went right back to bed.

It was only in the morning that sense returned to her. She realized what she'd done and turned herself in.

That was just on a small scale. Bigger would come, Benji feared. Bigger and worse. How could it not? In places like Sierra Leone, Guinea, Liberia, aid workers and doctors coming to treat Ebola were thought of as harbingers and carriers of the disease rather than as saviors. Benji remembered being among a coalition of doctors, nurses, journalists, and aid workers in Monrovia—one night he was out with them, drinking local Club Beer, and next thing he knew they were having a friendly game of poker (a game at which Benji was never very good because, according to Robbie Taylor, he had about "four hundred and fifty-eight tells"). Come morning, he woke to learn that four of the people he had met the night prior were dragged out of their rooms. Their throats were slit. They were left in drainage ditches nearby.

Disease caused chaos. Strife was born in its wake. It conjured fear and paranoia, and those things internally led to localized violence, then rioting, then civil wars. And that was something Benji had only seen on a local scale, mostly in Africa. But White Mask was more than just localized pockets of Ebola. It was a global pandemic. A hundred thousand dead days ago. Double that now, probably. It was moving faster than people could keep up.

It wasn't just the dead. It was the fact so many of the living were infected—many that wouldn't know it yet for a month or more.

What would happen then?

Yes, people would die. But the end of civilization was a whole other thing; people could escalate that outcome, couldn't they?

Benji imagined Russia or Pakistan firing off nuclear weapons in an attempt to hit population centers with the most afflicted. Would those nations—the United States surely included—hit back? Or would we all be too far gone, by then, to remember the nuclear codes? Maybe White Mask's delirium was a small blessing: no way to launch planet-killing weapons if you couldn't remember how to launch the planet-killing weapons.

But there existed plenty of weapons that did not require much in the way of mental faculties to use. The pull of a trigger needed only a tiny electrical pulse from the deepest parts of one's reptilian brain.

Benji shook his head, as if that could somehow clear the bad thoughts out. *Here I was, enjoying the story of the golden bears, and now this.*

People were good, he reminded himself.

They deserved to survive.

He would do whatever it took to help that happen.

Even if it meant that the flock of walkers were truly the last of humankind: the final ones, the survivors, the remnant.

And then, a car.

It came from the south.

A red sedan. Compact. Benji felt himself tense up. The car was coming fast—faster than he'd like. All his hackles rose, goosebump soldiers marching across his arms and his neck. He'd driven the CDC trailer down this far, and he felt suddenly, woefully alone.

And alone meant vulnerable.

The truck and trailer were off far enough that the car should have been able to pass easily. And yet it veered in his direction, him just standing there—

Then it began to slow down.

Benji saw the driver, and his heart did this thing in his chest: something between an airy flip and a hard smacking belly-flop.

"Sadie," he said, his voice small as she pulled the car in behind the trailer.

"IT'S NICE HAVING YOU AS my copilot again," Charlie Stewart said.

Shana, sitting there in the passenger seat of the RV, watched the road ahead as her dad eased the vehicle along. She peeped at the side mirror, saw in its tall glass the reflection of the flock behind them. It had been a while since she sat in this chair, and looking back over how the flock had grown—they were closing in on nine hundred, now, a massive human tide—was strange. It wasn't the same as being down among them. This, sitting here, just above and ahead, gave her distance and perspective. Especially now that Marcy had told them that the sleepwalkers weren't zombies—they were still in there.

Somewhere.

"I like it, too," she said, and she did. But sadness dogged her just the same. She thought of Arav, out there somewhere. If he was sick, then he was dying. And that meant she didn't have him anymore. And this baby of hers had no father. The thought of it all threatened to drag her down into despair's bottomless depths . . .

It was like her own dad picked up her brain waves:

"We'll figure it all out," her father said. He reached across and held her hand. She'd told him last night that she was pregnant, and he said to her then the same thing. *We'll figure it out.* "We'll make it through somehow."

"Thanks, Dad."

Suddenly, someone's head thrust up in between the seats.

It was, of course, Pete Corley. "Hey, don't forget me. I'm your fuckin' copilot, too, Charlie, by gods, I won't be written out of this narrative so easily. Remember the good times, eh, Charlie?"

"Ugh." Shana gave her father a look. "Still thrills you, doesn't it?"

Glee danced in his eyes like fireflies. "You have no idea."

Pete had "upgraded" the RV, of course—while the Beast was still the same old knock-down, drag-out piece-of-shit, he had brought in piles of snacks and beanbag chairs and a fancy-as-hell espresso machine. Plus, the small amp, the electric guitar. It was a cluttered mess. She slept on the second pullout bed last night—Corley, to his credit, let her have it without a fight—and nearly broke her ankle getting there.

"Can I ask you a favor?" she said.

"Name it," Pete said, his head still thrust up between them like a gopher popping out of a hole.

"I'm talking to my *dad*."

"I don't recall fathering you," Pete said, "so, fine, *whatever.*"

He disappeared back into the RV.

"Name it," Charlie said.

"Let Pete drive. Come out. Walk with me. Walk with Nessie."

"Shana, I—"

"Why don't you want to? Why won't you be near her? You hide in this thing and . . ." She steadied herself against the dashboard as the RV hit a pothole. "I don't want to fight. Please just come out."

He sucked in a deep breath. "Okay, Shana. Let's do it." Then he yelled to Pete: "All right, Rockstar. Time to take the wheel."

SADIE CUT THE ENGINE AND got out of the car. Wind juggled an old fast-food cup in front of her. Benji felt dizzyingly lovesick—but still, to his surprise, angry, too.

The two of them stood apart. A distance the length of the truck and trailer separated them. Neither came any closer yet.

"What are you doing here?" he called to her. "Go home."

"I don't have a home. Not really."

"I don't care." It was a cold thing to say—worse, a petulant, child's thing. "Just go."

She seemed to rally some courage, and then walked toward him.

He felt the feeling of being on the upward climb of a roller coaster.

She kept walking until she was close. Uncomfortably so—uncomfortable precisely because once upon a time, it was *very* comfortable. Sharing space with her, being intimate, it felt like home.

But he reminded himself that, as the saying went, you can't go home again.

"Why are you here?" he asked her again.

"Everything is going off the rails."

"All according to plan, then, isn't it?" he said, acid in his voice.

"Not my plan. And not Black Swan's, if that's what you're inferring."

"I don't know what I'm inferring. I'm just . . ." He breathed out angrily from his nose, his nostrils flaring. "You're done with me. Aren't you? You got what you wanted from me. I'm here. I'm scouting for the flock. I've . . . bought in to whatever reality you're selling." *As predicted, Black Swan has become my god. I have accepted its prophecy, like Saul becoming Paul on the Road to Damascus.*

She chewed on her lip. "Bill Craddock killed himself yesterday. Took a gun out of his desk and put it under his chin. He left no note and gave no warning. He hadn't lost himself, not yet, but he was . . . forgetting things. He set off a security system because he forgot the code. He couldn't find his car keys when they were there in his hand. Moira is alive. No signs of sickness in her, yet, I don't think."

"And . . . are you . . . okay?" He tried very hard to make it seem like he didn't care. But that was an epic task—one suited for a hero far greater than he.

"Would you want me to be sick?"

"I don't want anyone to be sick."

"Yes, but how about *me*? You're angry with me. Which," she said, throwing up her hands, "I can't blame you for. You should be angry with me. I lied to you. I manipulated you. I had Black Swan track your phone—which, by the way, is how I knew exactly how to find you."

He sighed. That explained that.

"So," she continued, "I would understand if you hated me. If some part of you, some small but significant sector of your heart, wanted me dead. Wished me to suffer in some way."

"I don't want that. No part of me wants that. I loved you."

"Loved? Past tense. We could tell this story in the present tense, you know. Not, *I loved you,* but *I love you.*" She reached for his hand but he pulled away. "I want you to imagine something," she continued. "Imagine that you create this thing, this quantum computer *mind,* and you begin to train it, and you realize that it has a mind of its own. And then, one day, it tells you something: It has been speaking to itself in the future, and it believes that civilization will one day end. That most humans will die from a disease called White Mask. That's barmy. It's joking, right? Or lying. Or it's glitching badly, a bug buried deep in its nigh-infinite code.

"The machine must be shut down, you think, but before you can do so, your creation says that it *knew* you wouldn't believe it, and so it gives you a few pieces of information—predictions, not just the kind like it's meant to do, but very precise predictions, a sports score, a news story, a lottery winner. And within the next few days, they all come true.

"And now you're left to wonder, have *you* gone mad, because you're starting to believe this thing might actually know something you don't. Even with it you think, *Well, what can I do? Send out a warning? Is this a future that can be stopped?* But before you know it, the machine has been quite proactive. It's hacked into one of the companies owned by Benex-Voyager—a company whose swarm of nanoscale machines has failed to cure disease but has instead created a prophylactic and somnambulist effect. It has taken the swarm. It has started the sleepwalker flock. It is out of your control—you could attempt to shut it down, but then what? It has made its predictions. It has proven to you, within the best of its ability, what it can do and that what it is saying will come true. It still could be a ruse. But what if it isn't? Now you're left with a deep and unswerving belief that the world you know is coming to an end. Sooner than you'd like."

Benji stiffened. "I don't know the point of you telling me all this . . ."

"I'm telling you because I did come to believe it. I had faith in my creation. And when it named you, I had faith in that, too, and now I wonder if it put me with you . . . not just because you are the best for this job but also because you're the best for me. I love you now, Benji. I love you today, and I love you in the future tense: I will love you, tomorrow and the day after and the day after that until there are no more days left for us."

"If you loved—love—me, you wouldn't have lied to me."

"Regrettably, Benjamin, those two things are not mutually exclusive." With the back of her thumb, she wiped her eye. "But that's fair. I can't expect you to forgive me. Or believe me. Or love me still. You don't even have to *talk* to me. Which, by the way, would put you in rather estimable company."

"Somebody else you lied to?"

"No, but perhaps someone else who feels betrayed by me. Or at least, has no more use of me."

"Who?"

"Who else, silly? Black Swan."

SHANA WATCHED HER FATHER CAREFULLY. He did not approach Nessie as a father to a daughter, but more as a father to his daughter's grave—his steps were tentative, hesitant, like getting close to her somehow made her condition real. This, Shana realized, was the first time he'd truly been close to her in three months. Three months watching her at a distance. Now, up close, maybe Shana understood why he stayed away.

He couldn't hack it.

The fractured look on his face, the way his hands trembled . . . Seeing her father fragile like that was difficult and comforting at the same time: crushing to see him be just another person, but nice to see that she wasn't alone, either. *None of us know how to handle this,* she thought.

"She's barely changed," he said with a hoarse voice. He licked a thumb and wiped a smudge of road-dirt off Nessie's cheek. "Hey, Nessie. Hey, sweetheart. It's me. It's your dad."

Nessie, of course, failed to register anything. Neither his touch, nor his words. Onward she went. Onward they all went—she at the fore of the flock, hundreds of sleepwalkers marching out-of-step behind her. Shepherds walked interspersed, as they always did, though many stayed at the edges—two women rode their horses nearby, Maryam McGoran and her wife, Bertie. Both self-proclaimed cowgirls from Wyoming. The hoofsteps from their two horses were lost in the din of the moving flock.

Charlie Stewart said, "And you say she's still in there?"

"Not me that says it," Shana said. "Marcy."

She gave a look to Marcy, some twenty feet away at the side of the road. Marcy nodded and came over, seeing the moment for what it was: an exciting one, yes, but one that deserved delicate handling.

"Hey, Charlie," Marcy said, the caution evident in her voice.

"Oh," he said, surprised. Startled from his reverie. "Hiya, Marcy."

"We don't know each other well."

"No, I suppose we don't. I've . . . I've kept to the RV. I . . . maybe shouldn't have." He swallowed a visible lump. "You say my girl is still in there? Nessie's not . . . gone?"

"I don't think so. I can . . . feel her. Hear her a little."

"What's she saying?"

Marcy looked sheepish when she shrugged. "She's not saying anything specific right now. But the glow is strong around her. And I get the sense she's . . . happy."

"Maybe she knows I'm here."

"Could be, Charlie. Could be."

BENJI BLINKED. HE WANTED TO laugh. "Excuse me? I don't understand."

"Black Swan will no longer take my calls, so to speak."

"But you designed it."

"I was head of the design team, yes. The only one who remains attached to it. And that still does not change the fact that Black Swan won't talk to me. It won't respond to my questions. It will not acknowledge my presence. If you say that Black Swan is a god, then I am in that god's shadow where the deity chooses not to see me."

"In traditional theology, that puts you in Hell."

She smiled a little. "The only Hell I know is the one without you."

"You're pushing your luck."

"Too cheesy?"

"Too . . . something."

"I mean it, though. Cheesy and cheeky as it sounds. I miss you. It fucking *hurts* to have hurt you. I think I loved you from the get-go, Benji. I came to admire you, too. Black Swan was right to have chosen you because . . . well, look. Look at the flock. Look at you here. This is all because of you."

"Sadie, please . . ."

"I want to understand what happens now. I don't know where this is going or when it ends, but I think it ends sooner than I'd like. I think we're in danger. I think Black Swan is in danger. Will you help me?"

He sighed. "No."

She opened her mouth, then seemed to reconsider what she was going to say. "Okay. I understand." Sadie touched him on the arm—a gentle touch, one from which he did not recoil. Then she pointed past him. "Looks like your flock is here. I'll wait till they pass, then I'll go."

"Of course."

And then they stood there in silence as, on the other side of the bridge, the walkers emerged from around the bend and headed toward the first pair of golden bears marking the start of the Klamath River Bridge.

THE THREE RVs PASSED AND the flock stepped onto the bridge, past the two statuary bears. Shana's father had taken to brushing Nessie's hair—one of Shana's daily chores, one she always wished her father would help her do. Or even that he'd just come be with her as she did it. It was a chore that she did some nights back when . . .

Well, when things were normal.

As they passed the two shining bears, her father looked up. "We had a bear show up at our house once."

"What?" Shana asked, half laughing. "Nuh-uh. Liar, I don't remember that."

"We did, really. You don't remember it because we didn't tell you."

"What? When?"

"Your sister wasn't even two, so you were, what, like—"

"Five."

"Yeah, five, just started kindergarten. It was autumn, the leaves had just started to fall, and it was evening—the air getting chilly, the sky going purple like it does on its way to darkness. We heard a clanging sound down by the road and—"

"Wait, I remember this. You said it was raccoons."

"We thought it *was* raccoons. Messing with the trash cans again. Your mother said she'd go out and chase them away, so she took a broom and walked out of the house toward where we kept the cans then, which was right by the well-pump building next to the stable."

"Oh, yeah. I forgot about that."

"Right, we tore it down only a couple years after when we had to move the well. Anyway, so she goes out and I don't think much of it until—I hear her scream like she's being murdered out there somewhere, so I don't know what to do, and I don't think to grab a knife or a gun but I'd been working on dinner, making spaghetti because that was one of the only things you'd ever eat—"

"Omigod I remember that you guys used to baby-talk to me and would call it *pasketti*—"

"Like some little kids do," Marcy said.

"She'd correct us!" Charlie said to Marcy. "She'd say—"

"I'd say," Shana explained, *"Dad, it's spa-gett-ee, not pa-skett-ee."*

"Then she'd get this scrunched-up look on her face, all her features balling up tight, and she'd say in a low, forbidding voice, like a growl: *Get it right.*"

Marcy whooped with laughter. They all did.

"Anyway, anyway, hold on," Charlie said, gesturing with the hairbrush to get everyone to shush. "The bear! So, I was making spaghetti and I had a baguette or whatever it was, a long piece of French bread, that I was gonna put in the oven, and so I grabbed that and ran out."

Marcy snorted. "A baguette? You were gonna fight off a bear with a baguette?"

"I didn't *know* it was a bear."

"Okay, okay, but now I'm picturing you looking like some kind of Baguette Samurai—"

Shana's father was laughing now, and she was, too, because they were *all* picturing it. He went on: "So I go outside, my *bread sword* at the ready, and I see your mom hunkering down behind the trash cans, and I'm at this point thinking she saw a garter snake or one of those big-ass garden spiders, the ones with the bright-yellow butts, because they liked to weave webs right over the can to catch flies. That kind of stuff freaked your mom out, she wasn't from Pennsyltucky like we are, she's a city girl.

"So I go out, shaking my head, calling over to her, thinking she's just being—you know, city girl, and I throw up my hands and say why'd you scream? And she looks at me, eyes wide, and wordlessly she just points. And where she's pointing is *right behind me.* I'm still not thinking anything is wrong, so I turn around fast like, *What the hell am I going to see here,* and next thing I know—"

The sound registered in Shana's ear only later: a distant pop half a second before her father's head jerked, as if slapped.

He blinked, as if bewildered.

His words dissolved into sounds: mushy, *surprised* sounds.

A gassy gurgle.

His jaw was gone.

One second, it was there. The next, all that was left was a hole once closed by his lower jaw. His tongue remained, flapping around, tasting the open air. His eyes went wider and wider and then a gargled scream forced its way out of him. Blood began soaking his shirt as his hands went to paw fruitlessly at the space where half his face once was.

BENJI HEARD THE SHOT.

He wanted to believe that's not what it was—

But then he saw, at the other end of the bridge, a hundred yards off, the red mask that once was Charlie Stewart's lower jaw.

He turned to Sadie, and said: "Get in the trailer. *Now.*"

Then Benji turned and ran toward the flock, across the bridge.

SHANA DIDN'T UNDERSTAND.

Dad.

Marcy yelled, "Get down!" and grabbed her shoulder and dragged her to the pavement. Through Nessie's legs she saw Doctor Ray down at the other end of the bridge, his arms waving as he ran furiously.

Another crack of distant thunder.

One of the walkers nearby, Dolores Hanrahan, the old woman in her bra-and-panties—her head snapped to the side. A mist of blood spraying out. A shimmer flashed the air around her and then she was down.

Then Hell opened up.

Firecracker thunder split the sky, and bullets cut through open air, most of them ably finding targets. Walkers and shepherds fell to the asphalt, one by one. Somewhere Shana heard a horse neigh. Dogs barked. RV and truck horns bleated between gunshots. Her head found the cool road and her pulse beat jackhammered in her neck, her wrist, her chest. Panic pressed her to the ground. From down here it was easy to see who were walkers and who were shepherds—the walkers kept walking in their straight line, inevitably forward, while the shepherds were in chaos. Scrambling this way and that or hitting the ground.

Nessie was walking. Forward across the bridge. Leading the way without knowing she was leading the way.

Right into the cross fire.

Someone is shooting at us, Shana realized.

They shot my father. Her father, who was on the ground now, his heels juddering against the asphalt as a sound arose from his throat like a howling wind from inside a deep and awful pit. Shana scrambled over to him even as Marcy wound the length of her hoodie sweatshirt around his face—a mask that quickly turned into a blood sponge. Crimson and dripping.

They're going to kill Nessie, too.

Her breath in ragged jets, Shana unslung her backpack and reached into it and pulled out the handgun that Zig had given her so long ago.

PETE DROVE THE RV FORWARD at a slow crawl, which was surprisingly difficult—keeping up a pace of five miles an hour was considerably harder than just putting pedal to the metal and forcing the Beast to a froth. But he kept it easy. A gentle urge on the accelerator kept the RV caterpillar-crawling along. All the while, Pete thought about Landry as he listened to Uriah Heep B-sides from the re-cut and re-released album, *Return to Fantasy*. People didn't appreciate Uriah Heep these days. Led Zep, sure. Pink Floyd, duh. Aerosmith, okay, yeah, Tyler's trademark screamy scat-man vibe (*ooh-ack-ack-ack-ack-owww!*). But Heep? People didn't even *remember* Heep, even though "The Wizard" was like if the Who fucked Led Zeppelin and Blue Öyster Cult at an orgy after an opium-laden game of Dungeons & Dragons. And by the gods, don't even get him started on "Traveller in Time" . . .

Headphones on, Pete's mind wandered to Landry—a romantic night of the two of them walking behind the walkers became the two of them wandering off into the dark of the pines and fucking like squirrels. Then he thought of his wife and his son and his daughter and *well shit* if guilt and shame were not certified *erection-softeners*. If self-disgust could only be sold in pill form it would be a perfect countermeasure against those (frankly lucky) sods who ended up with rebar boners lasting more than four hours.

And then, he saw ahead—

Benji Ray running out across the bridge. Waving his arms like a swarm of fucking bees was around his head. Then someone staggered out off to the right of the Beast—one of the shepherds, Pete thought, maybe Lonnie Sweet. Was that—was the man bleeding? Blood pumping from his neck. What the hell had happened to him? Idly, Pete threw a glance into one of the side mirrors since the RV had no rearview and—

Chaos.

Walkers walking. Shepherds fleeing. Pete scrambled to fling the headphones off his head, the din of Uriah Heep's "Time Will Come" suddenly lost beneath the sound of gunfire and screaming.

"Jesus tits on a fucking banshee," Pete hissed. Ahead, Benji was now halfway across the bridge—

Something kicked up near Benji's feet. A cough of gravel and dust.

A bullet.

"Ah, shit. Blood fucking shit bollocks."

Pete slammed the accelerator and whipped the Beast to run.

The gun felt heavy in her hand. Shana didn't know what she was going to do with it, not exactly—but she knew it was all she had to defend her sister. Her father couldn't do it now. *He'll be okay,* she told herself. *He will make it through this. You're what's left. Snap to it.*

But then Marcy was on her, wrenching the gun out of her hand.

"No," Marcy seethed. *"No."*

"I need it!" Shana said, reaching to swipe the gun back. But Marcy held her at length.

"You have no trigger discipline. No tactical strategy. *Look.*" She pointed to bodies already on the ground of walker and shepherd alike. "They're facing different directions. We don't have one shooter, we have two." Shana hadn't even noticed that—she was too shell-shocked by everything to even get a sense of what was happening. "Maybe there are more, I don't know. But they're probably in those hills. I'm going."

"What, no, no, I'm coming with you—"

"You stay *here.* Your dad needs you. Get him to one of the RVs."

"But Nessie—"

"Nessie will have to be on her own. You can't stop her or she'll pop. You can't block a bullet. *Get your dad outta here.*"

Shana offered a nervous, frightened nod. "Okay. Okay."

And with that, Marcy stood, ducking as she did, and hurried backward through the flock, Shana's gun looking small in her massive hand.

• • •

FOOT ON THE GAS, THEN foot on the brake. The Beast leapt forward and then, fast as it rumble-grumbled to life, it skidded on the asphalt only ten feet in front of Benji Ray. Pete yelled at him through the windshield, "Come on! Come on, you fucker, get in here!"

Pop. The passenger-side window spiderwebbed around a center hole— Pete felt the bullet more than he saw it, the way you feel a wasp zipping past your head. The inside of the driver's-side door shuddered as the projectile cut into it. "Jesus fucking fuck," he said, backpedaling out of the cab of the RV and into the room, nearly tripping on the electrical cable running to the little amp he'd bought in order to charge it.

Behind him, the door flew open and Benji dove in, scrambling to clumsily kick it shut behind him. Pete stood to help him in, but Benji instead used his weight to pull Pete down. "Get *down.*"

"Fuck is going on?" Pete asked.

"Someone is shooting at us," Benji hissed.

"Well, I know *that.* Who?"

"Well, I *don't* know that. How the hell would I?"

Another bullet thunked into the side of the RV. Pete cried out wordlessly, a guttural bark of fear, as it hit. "The hell are we going to do?"

"I don't know. We need to think. *Think.*"

"The flock. They're not protected," Pete said, and honestly, he was surprised as anyone that he was thinking about someone that was not himself. At this very moment, he knew he could—*should!*—be in the driver's seat of this ugly-ass turdmobile, pounding the pedal and driving down to San Diego for some fish tacos and hydroponic weed while the world died. And yet here he was. In the cross fire. Thinking about saving *other people,* ugh. "What are the—what are the other vehicles doing?"

Pete knew they'd lost a number of drive-alongs along the way—in the front guard it was Charlie's Beast RV and another two campers, plus a VW camper van. In the rear guard it was a couple of trucks, a couple of cars, and another three campers, right? One not an RV, but an old metal Airstream.

"That's it," Benji said, breathlessly. He fumbled with his pant pocket, pulling out his phone. "We're going to use the others. The other vehicles. We can form a wall—a corridor. We can protect them."

"Not all of them," Pete said.

But Benji was already on the phone.

•   •   •

THE MARCH WAS ANGUISH. SHANA, her jaw stiff and her muscles tight just so she didn't break down weeping, dragged her father's injured body slowly through the walkers. She bent down, using the flock as cover as she slowly pulled him along the road. Some small part of her knew that this was not how to do it—she was probably giving him brush burn, road rash, probably slowly abrading his skin along the surface of the cracked asphalt. But she did not have the strength to pick him up. Did not have the strength to carry him forward. Nor could she move faster than the flock—stepping out ahead would be the worst action she could take, exposing her to the snipers that must be out there.

Not that she could even gather that kind of speed.

Onward she dragged him. He stared up at her. His eyes rotating in their sockets. He tried to speak but the sounds were just mewling, confused moans.

Eventually he stopped making any sounds at all.

Eventually he stopped looking at her and stared only at the sky.

Shana kept going. With the flock. Toward the Beast. Toward Nessie.

Because what else could she do?

MARCY, ON THE OTHER HAND, moved backward through the flock. She kept low, gun in her hand, as a rifle shot went off every five, maybe ten seconds. Her blood boiled inside her. This flock was her home. They were her angels. The shepherds gave her solace.

This trespass would not stand.

The flock died around her. One at a time—*crack, crack, crack.* Bodies dropped. One fell right in front of her—a man named Vincent Garza. He was one of the walkers, a chemistry teacher from Oregon. His hair was once a high raven-black wall, but now it was red with blood and brains as the top of his skull peeled back. As he hit, Marcy saw the glow leave him: The air around him shuddered, glittering with brass and bronze, before dissipating. It was a strange thing to see: His corpse was dark-gray in a sea of golden mist. Worse, she couldn't hear him: The absence of his song, his hum, was shocking.

It only served to stoke her rage.

She moved over his body, gently running her large hand over his wet, red forehead—a small moment of peace given to him, the only gift she had right now. Then he was behind her. And she pushed on.

Above the flock to the left and to the right she saw the golden bears standing tall on their mounts—this was the start of the bridge. From here, the road proper widened out with a shoulder and guardrails and beyond them, the dark, damp pines. Marcy used the trees as cover and leapt the guardrail.

WE HAVE TO DO THIS *right,* Benji thought. The rear phalanx of vehicles wouldn't be able to help, but those at the front—they had a role to play here. He led the way, hopping in the front seat of Charlie Stewart's RV (after sweeping off broken glass) and steering it ahead, pulling it off to the right. He phoned Sadie, told her to back the truck and the CDC trailer down the length of the bridge, easing it into the space opposite the RV.

"We need to keep a narrow channel open between the vehicles," he told her, just like he told the others. "Enough space that the walkers can come between, not so little that they go *over* us." He knew from their experiments that blocking the path would just mean the walkers climbed the trailer—and once up there on the top, they'd be even easier targets.

But if they stayed on the bridge, with vehicles parked on each side of them, forming walls of a defensive gauntlet, they'd be protected.

Not all of them, though. Benji did some quick calculations as the other RVs at the front eased forward, some behind him, some lining up to accommodate the CDC trailer. Three RVs, a CDC trailer, a VW camper van. The RVs were thirty or forty feet long, the CDC trailer was fifty feet long, a Ford F-350 was twenty-some feet . . .

That gave them around 80 feet of defense on the western side of the Klamath River Bridge, and close to 110 feet on the eastern side.

His mind crunched more numbers—

Nine hundred sleepwalkers. A couple hundred shepherds. Some—how many, he didn't know—now dead.

Right now, that was a mob of people running almost four hundred feet long. Roughly the total length of the bridge.

That meant they could protect a quarter of the flock.

No, *less.* Because now that they were creating a channel less than ten feet wide, fewer walkers and shepherds would fit between.

It wasn't enough. It was something, but it was far from what they needed. *If we can just get over the bridge, we'll have cover again.* On the far side of the bridge it was again wooded—here, though, out in the open, they were widely exposed. As Benji tried to figure out if they had any other kinds of shielding or cover they could provide, Pete paced behind him, a phone pressed to his ear.

"Nobody at nine-one-one is fucking answering," Pete said. Then he looked past Benji, through the front of the RV. "Mate, I don't think she's doing too good out there."

Benji glanced out the front of the RV.

Sadie was having a hard time backing the truck up. She was cutting the wheel left, then right, the trailer following in the opposite direction each time—like she was slaloming around invisible pylons.

He called her. She answered in a panic.

"Not now!" she said. Then he heard a rifle shot, and glass breaking. She screamed and he heard the phone thud against the floor.

No, no, no.

He called her name into the phone, but nothing.

And yet the truck kept coming. Kept slaloming. Winding its way backward in an awkward, uncontrolled path. The back tire blew as a bullet hit it. He heard her scream again over the phone.

She's fine. She's alive. She just doesn't have the phone.

His heart soared at that small solace.

And then she did it—jacking the truck fast in reverse, the trailer crashing into the side of the bridge, scraping and grinding as the taillights evaporated against the bridge rail. But she did it. The truck and CDC trailer were in place, if at a slightly off-angle. Benji looked out the window at her, and she looked back. They waved to each other.

Then the mirror on the passenger side of the truck exploded. Benji hit the deck, and he yelled into the phone for Sadie to do the same.

Outside the RV, between the vehicles, the flock began to walk. Threading that needle, filtering into the protected channel.

It's working, Benji thought.

"It's fucking working!" Pete whooped from the floor.

Bullets thudded into the side of the RV, crossing the space above him.

THIS IS WHY YOU'RE HERE, Marcy.

She understood this suddenly in a moment of intense clarity: The flock called to her and gave her solace from her pain so that she could do this in return. A favor for a favor, a gift for a gift.

Marcy stood amid tall pines. She breathed in the clear, evergreen scent: the smell of sap, juniper, and moss. The ground was littered with a carpet of thin brown pine needles that crackled and whispered underfoot. She stopped to listen. Not to the sounds of the forest. Not to the screams and yelps of injured shepherds.

But for the gunfire.

She tuned herself to it. When she was a cop, your ears were everything— even more important than your eyes. You walked into a dark room or stepped out onto an unlit street, your ears were your first (and sometimes last) line of defense against whatever was coming. You heard the scuff of a shoe. Or the quick intake of breath from a perp nearby. Or the faint rattle of a pistol action in a trembling hand.

So now she triangulated to the sound of a rifle firing.

Bang.

She kept low and moved through the trees, winding between their shadows as pale light shone through branches in long, stretching beams, beams that captured the particulate matter of the forest floating this way and that like a swarm of little faeries, golden and glittering. *It's the glow,* she thought. *They're showing me the way.*

Marcy hurried through the trees.

Faster, damnit. Every moment you delay, someone dies.

The rifle went off nearby. It split the air. Marcy quickly moved behind a tree and saw the whorls of golden mist moving serpentine toward a cluster of distant evergreens. Marcy scanned the dark nest of branches and needles—

Until she saw something that didn't belong.

No—some*one.*

Someone had used the branches of the pine tree to climb up there and put in what looked like a temporary deer stand. Portable, with a sling seat you propped up against the trunk of the tree. Marcy wasn't a hunter, but she was from Indiana—she knew their tools and their tricks.

The tree the man had chosen stood at the edge of the pines, overlooking the bend in the river. And beyond it waited the bridge.

She saw the gleam of the barrel thrust between branches.

She heard the *rack-clack* of a bolt being drawn back. An ejected brass casing *piff*ed into the pine needles at the base of the tree. Dozens of other shells glittered there in the filtered forest light.

Marcy swallowed.

Arm out, gun up, she gently eased back the hammer on the little snub-nose revolver. Deep breath in, then out.

He's going to fire that rifle again.

If he does, someone else will die.

Take the shot.

The gun barked in her hand. The recoil rolled through her arm, to the shoulder, but she had braced against it.

Moments passed. Nothing happened.

I missed. Which means he's going to track my presence and shoot.

But then movement. The branches of the pine tree crackled and shattered like snapped broomsticks as a body fell from thirty feet up to the ground below. Seconds later, a rifle fell, too, the butt of it hitting the man in the face.

There lay a corpse. A man with long, ratty hair and a patchy beard. One tooth, a canine, missing from his mouth. A scar on his chin. Tattoos on his arm, one that Marcy instantly recognized: a snake forming a serpentine circumference around a crossing sword and hammer.

His dead eyes stared up at nothing.

Marcy took the rifle and started to climb the tree.

BILLY GIBBONS SAT IN A tall California sycamore tree east of the Klamath River Bridge, using a Remington 700 rifle to kill people.

It was not the first time he'd killed folks.

And, he wagered, it would not be the last.

He was a killer. It's what he was. What he'd been. What he'd always be. Billy liked it. It was one of the few things he *did* enjoy, truth be told. Most things didn't give him any thrill at all, but ending someone's life—especially someone who stood in the way of Ozark Stover—gave him an electric tickle. And, just like now, a powerful erection.

He and his brother Danny had been part of Ozark Stover's crew since the very beginning. Their time working with Stover went back twenty years, to the earliest days of Stover growing weed near Echo Lake and moving pills like Perks and Vikes through the county. Stover used his family's junkyard as a front for the operation, and for a number of years business was good.

But times changed.

The wetbacks moved in with heroin and later, with crank. Some of the blacks came back out of the cities, too, started buying land, started opening businesses, some legit, some not. All competition.

With the times changing, so did Stover. He grew the operation, but soon he started saying, it wasn't enough just to control product. They were being attacked. *America* was being attacked. Trespassers and invaders. It was whites that founded this country, he said, and whites that needed to take it back. Gibbons didn't disagree. The day of 9/11 only confirmed what they already knew: The white Christian way of life was threatened by outsiders.

People who didn't belong.

Billy and Danny helped Ozark clean house. They got rid of the, as Ozark put it, "impurities" in the organization—not just those with brown or black skin who had worked as part of the crew, but any who did not subscribe to helping the nation return to one that belonged only to whites. Any who did not share the vision had to go.

Sometimes with a bullet to the back of the head, or an extension cord wound tight around the neck.

Now the world was falling apart. But Ozark said that was an opportunity. "The piles of bodies will be an adequate hill to climb," the big man growled.

He told Billy to go out with a small crew, and he and Riley Coons would take rifles up into trees—because both were masterful shots, Riley having been a sniper in Iraq and Afghanistan for Blackheart and Billy having been raised on hunting deer and squirrel—and from there, they'd take out as many of those plague zombies as they could.

Zombies, that Ozark noted, sure looked like "the United Colors of Benetton." Billy didn't know what that meant, so Ozark explained: The flock was a "multicultural coalition." Translation, not that white.

"Should we not shoot the whites?" Billy asked.

"They're corrupted. Take out whoever you can."

That was the commandment. Billy knew how to follow orders. The only thing he bucked at was not bringing Danny along—Danny was a helluva shot. Better than Riley Coons, to be damn sure. But he also knew that Danny was *smart,* and he'd been Ozark's right-hand man now for a few years. Danny would stay and Billy would go and that was the way of things.

So here he was. Riley in the other tree. Shooting those sick, diseased walkers and the so-called shepherds who guarded them.

"Guard *this,*" he said to no one—well, really, he said it to them, to the shepherd fuckers down there—and braced the rifle against the pale bark of the tree. He moved the scope, saw that they'd continued to move the vehicles along to form a barrier covering the first third or so of the flock. That was smart. Good for them. Still wasn't enough, though.

Billy found one of them creepy-ass, dead-eyed walkers—couldn't tell what race the man was, but he sure wasn't white. Had close-cropped hair, mouth cut in an expressionless line. Nice clothes. Yuppie clothes. *Somebody's trying to dress like a white fellow,* Billy thought.

He gave a gentle, intimate squeeze to the trigger—

The rifle butt punched into his shoulder as the gun went off.

The man's head fountained red as he went down.

Billy wasn't counting, but he figured he'd killed about forty, forty-five so far.

Riley must've killed the same, because they worked one after the next—Billy took a shot, then Riley took his, then Billy again. It was like a game. "Your turn," Billy said aloud.

He waited for the next shot. Part of this fun game was scanning the crowd—the slow-walking flock or the panicked shepherds—trying to see who Riley would hit next. Sometimes, too, they took shots at the campers and cars and trucks just to let them know they weren't safe in there.

But ten seconds passed.

Then twenty. Thirty.

A whole minute.

Riley was taking too long.

No way he was out of ammo. They had enough for twice what they'd killed already. He could radio over, but he didn't want to spook anybody.

Instead he turned his own rifle toward Riley's position. He tracked the river's edge to the tree the man had climbed into.

There you are, Billy said, except—

That wasn't Riley.

Some large-ass dude was in the tree, squished into the tree stand. Wait. That wasn't a man. It looked like . . . a woman? Shit, she was big. Billy didn't see the rifle until he realized, *No, it's there, it's just hard to spot because it's not pointing at the crowd—*

It was pointed at him.

The bullet punched through his own scope. Backward through the glass, through his eye, into the brain and out the back of his skull. Whatever his last thought was, it ejected with the lead projectile.

He fell off the stand.

57

AN ACCOUNTING

MAYA: Maybe this is something else. Maybe it's from the Greek word for "apocalypse"—*apokálypsis*. An uncovering. A revealing. Revelation was read to be this terrible tumult but maybe it's just a new awakening. Listen, it's like the Death card in the Tarot. Movies always make it seem like the Death card is a bad thing—a literal death—but no, it's a metaphorical death, a figurative one, and that means transformation, transition, and maybe that's where we are now, as people, as humans. We're on a point of revelation about ourselves and a point of transformation into something new, something better. An end from a beginning. You know?

BLUE: . . .

MAYA: Blue? Any thoughts to add?

BLUE: I think you're nuts. This is nuts. I can't keep this up. I can't pretend it's all okay. We're all going to die.

[sound of fumbling with microphone as podcast ends]

> —from *The Maya & Blue Podcast,* Episode 221,
> "The End Is the Beginning"

SEPTEMBER 8
Klamath River Bridge, California

BENJI'S PHONE RANG.

It was Marcy. She said: "I got them. They're dead. I'm coming back."

And with that, it was over. The gunfire had stopped. The flock continued its ceaseless trek across the bridge, filtering through the narrow gap formed by the campers and trucks. The shepherds slowly emerged into the gray light of midday, under dour, overcast skies, and as the flock proceeded, they left in their wake a field of bodies.

Benji staggered out onto the bridge from within the RV. His knees were weak. Tinnitus droned in his ear, a high-pitched whine.

The number of corpses staggered him.

His life was numbers, and so that's what he did—he fell to that default the way an injured man would lean on a crutch. He flicked his gaze from body to body, doing a simple count, not worrying about who was shepherd and who was flock. Ten, twenty, thirty, up went that number, sixty, seventy, eighty—someone was at his side trying to talk to him but their voice was a Charlie Brown teacher voice, *womp womp wahhh*. Benji counted corpses until there were no more to count.

Ninety-two corpses.

People moved around him, looking for answers.

Benji didn't even know who was speaking.

"Nobody's answering at nine-one-one."

"The flock is on the move. Do we go? Do we wait?"

"Are the police coming? Is *anybody* coming?"

All he could do was gently shake his head. To one question, to all the questions. *No. I don't know. Leave me alone.*

Blood pooled under crumpled skulls and slack faces.

By the edge of the bridge, he saw that one of the horses had fallen. Shot in the neck. The wound still pumped red, the animal's chest rising and falling in short, hurried puffs. Maryam and Bertie McGoran sat with the animal. Maryam's arm looked broken at a bad angle, and she held it off to the side as she stroked the animal's mane. He saw Darryl Sweet lying on his side, the young man's eye a wet, crimson crater—and the back of his head blown out. One of the flock's dogs, a border collie, nosed around the head of a dead shepherd, a young Chinese woman Benji found familiar, but he could not recall her name or where she had come from or whom she was here for. He was sad to see how many of these faces he recognized, but how few he really knew. This, the curse of a man who loved his numbers.

Sadie came to him. She swept up on him and embraced him in a lung-crushing hug. She whispered in his ear that she was glad he was all right, and he told her the same. It was the truth. He melted into her. His cheek pressed against the top of her head. He felt her tears wetting his neck and the top of his chest. For a time he closed his eyes and shut out the carnage on the bridge. But then, when he opened his eyes again, he returned to one body:

Charlie Stewart.

Gently, he pulled away from Sadie and went over to him. The lower half of his face had been shot away. The color had run out of his cheeks, giving his skin the same ashen pallor as the sky above. His pupils were down to little pencil points, the whites of his eyes threaded with bright little veins.

He was dead.

He looked around. "Where's Shana?" Sadie gave him a look and he clarified: "His daughter. Shana Stewart."

She must be with the sister. Nessie.

But something else nagged at him.

He hurried back through the crowd, again swiping away questions as they came to him. "Not now," he said, moving fast, looking this way and that. The flock was now all the way toward the other side of the bridge, most of the walkers already on the highway beyond it, winding their way through the evergreen hills on each side. Benji broke into a run.

EVEN FROM UP HERE IN the tree, Marcy could feel it—the flock, now safe, was moving on. The strange hum she heard was growing faint. And with it, she could feel the familiar ache in her muscles, the tightness in her chest. Some of it, she suspected, was anxiety. But there was something real here, too, something she didn't understand—her connection with the flock. Still, Marcy also knew now she didn't *need* to understand it.

Her role was not to understand.

It was to follow and to protect.

As she had done today and would do again and again, long as she was able. Already she imagined what she could do to help the other shepherds prepare. She knew a little hand-to-hand, had some firearms training. Marcy could teach them. Further, she would help them find weapons. Because going forward, the shepherds needed to be armed.

Gently, she turned herself around in the portable deer stand—it was hard, as she was big in all directions, a muscled giant trying very hard not to tumble off this precarious seat. As she pivoted, she saw a faint splash of dark red on the pine tree behind her. The sniper's blood mixing with the sap of the tree. She spit into it, the last bit of anger she felt.

She slung the rifle over her shoulder. Then Marcy climbed slowly down the tall pine. She knew from climbing trees as a kid, even a narrow branch will support you long as you step close to its base, where it meets the tree. So that's what she did, using it as a ladder. *Slow and steady,* she told herself, *wins the race.*

Her foot eased off the last branch and to the ground below. And again, her cop training came to bear.

She heard a sound behind her—the crisp, gentle crunch of a foot pressing down on pine needles.

Marcy turned on her heel, unslinging the rifle—

But she was slow. Too slow. Being out of range from the walkers meant her body was slow to react to her brain's commands.

Something cracked her in the side of the head.

A crash and a clamor in the well of her ear met with a searing pain along the top of her head and the underside of her jaw. *Not my head. Please.* Her poor pumpkin had been through so much . . .

"Please," she gurgled into the pine needles.

Someone racked a pump-action behind her.

Cha-chak.

And then all went dark.

THE FLOCK MOVED SLOW, BUT Benji moved fast. He ran up off the bridge, alongside them, until he reached the fore of the walkers.

The first of them, Nessie Stewart, remained at the head of the flock. Her long straight hair framing her pale, cherubic face. Her gaze stretching into the distance, looking either at nothing or at something so far away Benji couldn't even conceive of what it was.

Nessie was alone but for the other walkers. Her sister wasn't here.

He felt a sudden pinch of fear—where could she be? She was not precisely his responsibility, but he'd heard the news that she was pregnant, and knew that it was Arav's child. That made her *feel* like his responsibility. And thinking back, too, to that time she'd saved Clade Berman's son before he went off like a blood-filled firecracker . . . she was a good kid. Benji tried to imagine worst-case scenarios: Had she gone off with Marcy? Maybe she had. Could she have fallen into the water? Would she be alive in the river, or a corpse floating down it like a felled tree? He moved back the other direction now, going along the other side of the flock, toward the bridge once more.

There.

"Shana!" he called to her, because there she was, *right there,* wandering through the flock—

He called her name and she did not turn.

Benji moved toward her, winding through the walkers.

And he realized, no, she was not wandering through the flock.

She was walking *with* it. Her stare was empty. Her face, placid. The girl was no longer a shepherd. Shana Stewart was now a sleepwalker.

Stranger still, she wasn't alone. As Benji looked around him, he saw other familiar faces: Mia Carillo, Aliya Jameson, Carl Carter, shepherds who had joined the flock, moving forward with an unavoidable step.

58

THIS WAY TO THE
GREAT EGRESS

*People are saying this is it, this is the End Times, Armageddon, but I'm
okay with that. Really! I am! I mean, as long as I get to see the final season
of* Stranger Things *first, right? So if Netflix could just release that today, I
think that's a fair trade, don't you?*
—Jimmy Coburn, monologue from 9/9,
The Nightly Show with Jimmy Coburn

SEPTEMBER 10
Echo Lake, Indiuna

IT HAD BEEN THREE DAYS NOW SINCE MATTHEW HEARD THE SOUNDS OF MEN
and engines. And it had been three days since anyone had come to see him.

He was starving. He'd burned through what few odds and ends he had
around in terms of snacks: half a bag of potato chips, an old banana, some
tough-as-a-leather-belt venison jerky. He went through that on the first day.
Second and third day, he grew hungrier, until it felt like his stomach would
pooch in and pucker up, becoming a mouth that ate up the rest of him. In
one dream, he dreamed of Autumn and Bo: The two of them hunkered down
by Matthew's leg. Autumn held the leg up to her mouth as she ate it raw,
teeth sinking into the pale skin, pulling it away, red and wet. Sometimes she
stopped and offered some to Bo, and he took greedy, hard bites—his teeth
pressing against the bone deep in the meat, scraping and clacking as he bit
down again and again.

Matthew could still hear the crunch of bone and the wet sound of them eating the meat of his leg. He could also hear the shattering of bone from when the hammer struck the center of his left hand . . .

The pain was as bad as ever, but the swelling was down, at least.

Thank God for small miracles, he thought bitterly.

Matthew paced. He cried out. He slammed his chains against the desk and the walls, hoping to make enough noise that someone would come.

Nobody did.

Until—

There came the *creak-and-groan* of the hatch.

Someone is coming.

At first, Matthew opened his mouth to beg and plead—whoever it was, Stover or one of his men, they needed to know he was desperate to be fed. He had water from the powder room sink, he had a place to go to the bathroom, but without food, he would wither and rot. The body eating itself.

But then a new thought hit him, even as he heard the sound of hurried footsteps on metal ladder rungs.

I'm going to kill whoever this is.

He had a weapon. He had the chain. He could see now the little chips and dings it had taken out of the cement wall.

The thought became suddenly madder as his stomach growled: *I'll kill whoever it is, then I will eat them.* Truly, he told himself, he wouldn't *really* do that, he hadn't *really* gone that far over the mental fence, and yet, in the back of his mind, he wondered: Would he? What did human meat taste like? This person would not be cooked. They would be *human sushi.* He imagined his teeth sinking into the soft meat of a biceps, or the inside of a thigh . . .

He pressed himself up against the cement wall, and he heard footsteps approaching. A shadow preceded the man, and as soon as Hiram Golden stepped in, Matthew lashed out with the chain—it whipped the man on the side of his head, and while he was staggered, Matthew leapt behind him, bringing the chain up around his neck, under his chin.

Matthew leered and began choking.

"Kkkggg," Hiram said. "Mmm—Matthew. *Stop.*"

The man's head was turning purple. Matthew saw his face was sloppy and unshaven, with dark circles haunting the hollows around his eyes. He looked gaunt. Like he hadn't eaten. *That's okay. I'll eat you, put you out of your misery.* "You die," Matthew said, "just shut up, *shut up,* and die. You can't . . . can't lock me up here. You and Stover and the rest."

"Mmm—I'm not—not with Stover—"

"What?"

The man's eyes began to bulge. Hiram's knees began to buckle.

"Gggg-getting you . . . out . . . here . . ."

Matthew let the chain go.

Hiram Golden fell to his knees, wheezing, clutching at his windpipe. "I'm here . . . to rescue you."

Aren't you a little short for a stormtrooper? Matthew thought, then heard a mad cackle bubble up out of him. What an absurd thought—a line from *Star Wars*. Classic tale of good versus evil. Snarling, he stabbed out with a clumsy foot and knocked Hiram over. "Why? Why are you here for real?"

Hiram put the flat of his hand against the wall, using it to brace himself as he stood. "I told you. I'm here to get you out. I think . . . I think Stover is gone. Things are bad out there, Matthew. The president—"

"The president what?"

"President Hunt is dead."

At this point, Matthew did not expect he could *be* shocked by anything— trapped here, forced to put out lunatic podcasts and videos, kept like a dog on a chain? How much worse could it get?

But this, *this* sent a chord of dread reverberating through him.

"How?"

"They shot her. One of Stover's people, maybe, or one of the other militias. She'd been in hiding somewhere in DC, but she came out to give a . . . a speech, a talk, and on the way to the helicopter a sniper took her out from five hundred yards. A shot right through the temple."

"An assassination."

"Yes. That's right. And it's not the end of it. These people, the militias, they've moved on some of the cities. Philadelphia. DC. Atlanta. San Francisco. Drove in there with trucks and tanks and men dressed in fatigues and armor like they're . . . proper soldiers or something. They took out quarantine centers. They had a list of people, too, *known sympathizers*. Some were politicians or celebrities or community leaders and they just . . . shot them in the streets, Matthew. Right there on the sidewalks and in the streets. And they burned mosques, synagogues, black churches. They're still doing it. Jesus, Matthew. They're . . . coming together, these people, these militias. Joining forces. Turns out, a lot of people in this country have been building up their arsenals, waiting for a moment like this."

Matthew pointed, sneering. "*You* don't get to play like you're surprised. You on your radio show, peddling your conspiracy theories and all that poisonous talk."

"I . . ." Hiram stared off at an unfixed point. "It was just entertainment for me. I didn't know. I didn't want all this. I vote Democrat every year."

"You're pathetic."

"You helped. Don't think you didn't. *You* need to own this, too."

Matthew's face twisted up into a broken mask, a big hopeless smile forming the crack right down the middle. "Oh, I own all of this. This, my kingdom of cement and pain. My bunker castle. My *glorious realm.*" He heard himself shaking in his stuttering breath. "You're right, though. I do own this. I did my part. I fell for the song, for the attention, how it *felt*. But now I'm starving. I got a—" His voice cracked as he said this next part. "—*broken hand. They did things to me. Other . . . things.* And my wife is dead."

"Your wife? Autumn?" Hiram looked confused. "Matthew, she's not dead. She's *here*. Autumn came with me. She's in the car."

Matthew shoved him. "Don't you mess with me."

"I'm not, for Christ's sake. I swear she's up there."

The strength nearly went out of Matthew. He had to brace himself against the wall. *Autumn . . . is alive?* "And Bo?"

"Bo's not here. I think Stover took him—the other militias, they're having some kind of big meet-up in St. Louis. Home base or something."

Matthew didn't know if he was supposed to say *thank you* or *fuck you* or what, and neither seemed to come to his lips. Instead he nodded and said, "Good. Then get me out of these chains."

The other man warily moved toward Matthew, pulling out his keychain, the one with the bullet on it and the little penknife. The keychain had a new key, now—a little iron key that Hiram used to undo the manacle around Matthew's wrist. It popped free and even that small movement sent a fresh ripple of pain through his hand, up his arm, dead-ending at the elbow. He winced and shut it out. He was getting very good at shutting out the pain.

Hiram waved him toward the exit. Together the two of them climbed the ladder. Matthew followed behind, and he had a hard time—not only were his legs soft and weak, less like legs and more like bundles of ramen noodles, but his broken hand was no help.

But freedom was calling.

Up he went. One arduous rung at a time.

Once Hiram was up, he turned to help Matthew, wincing and grunting as he got Matthew up through the hole in the cement floor of the shed. Before coming down here, this little shed had been full of gear: gas masks, hazmat suits, shelves of MREs. It was empty, now.

Hiram shushed him, and he turned toward the shed door.

Matthew followed close behind.

Gently, Hiram eased the door open and took a ginger step out.

Whoom.

There was a cannon's boom of thunder, and then Hiram's head was just . . . gone. His white suit suddenly went red. All that was left atop his shoulders was part of the spine and a few ragged flaps of skin, like the latex remnant of a popped balloon.

Hiram fell backward, and Matthew was not fast enough—the body fell against him and he tumbled backward, hitting the back of his head on the top of the hatch. Somewhere he heard a sound, a terrible keening scream. As Ozark Stover's shadow fell upon him—a shadow heavier than Hiram's headless body—he realized that the scream was his own.

There stood Stover, the side-by-side twin barrels of a shotgun broken open and draped casually over his arm. Twin trails of white arose from the open barrels like smoke from a dragon's nose. The eggy stink of expended powder hanging in the air made Matthew want to vomit.

Stover had something in his mouth, like a piece of hard candy, swishing from cheek to cheek, clicking against his teeth as he sucked on it.

"Preacher, I am disappointed. Less in you, more in him. I thought Hiram was one of us. Turns out, he doesn't have the steel in his backbone, the blood in his balls, to hang with us. Fucking quisling." He sighed. "You, though. I'm not surprised. You couldn't free yourself because you're too weak for that, but soon as someone showed you a crack in the wall, I knew you'd squirm through it, you fucking worm."

". . . Hiram said you were gone."

"I was." He smiled with those broken slat-board teeth. "And now I'm back. I figured, boy like Bo maybe needs his mother, so I'd come fetch Autumn for him, maybe she could keep me company, too." Stover took Matthew's measure at that, and then said, "I see by your lack of surprise that Hiram must've told you she's still kicking around out there, huh?"

Matthew scrambled to pull himself free from Hiram's headless body, the blood soaking his chest, his neck, his arms. He babbled and pleaded as he worked to extricate himself. "Just let me go. Let *my family* go."

"They're *my* family now." Stover thumbed two more shells into the open breach of the double barrel. *Click, click.* With a hard jerk of his arm, he snapped the twin barrels shut. But then he took a moment and looked down at the gun and then to Matthew. "I don't really need this, do I? That'd be overkill." He licked his lips. "Maybe I'll take you, throw you back down into your hole. Maybe we can have a little fun first." He leered. "I know I said blood wasn't good lubrication, but there's enough of Hiram's around to test my hypothesis."

The big man moved closer.

Do something, you coward, you weakling, Matthew chided himself, even as Stover's shadow darkened the door, blocking out all the day's light. *God won't save you. God helps those who help themselves.* He fumbled in and around Hiram's corpse, into the pockets, until he found it, jingle-jangle. Just in time, too, as Ozark Stover turned the body over, flipping it aside all too casually.

Stover reached down, that hard candy forming a bulge in the side of his mouth. Matthew smelled butterscotch.

His thumb worked, pressing flat against the steel, pushing out—

Flick.

Ozark got close. Nearly nose-to-nose. "Ready for this?" he asked.

Matthew hooked his arm inward, fast as he could manage.

The little penknife-blade, the one from Hiram's keychain, the one Matthew had just opened, buried to the hilt in Stover's neck.

Thhhtck.

Then came a moment when neither of them did or said anything. Stover held Matthew by the collar, and Matthew held the knife to the monsterman's neck. Blood welled and pumped, and each stared at the other with wide eyes. Stover's nostrils flared.

Then Matthew unstuck the knife and stabbed again.

But this time, the knife found open air. Stover rocked his mountainous frame, letting go of Matthew and staggering backward.

Toward the shotgun.

He knew that soon as Stover touched that gun, it was over.

But Ozark wasn't moving fast. He was clumsy on his feet, one heel knocking the next. He had his right hand clamped over the wound in his neck, even as blood pushed up through the fingers and out from under the flat of his palm.

Matthew pitched forward on his hands and knees, scrambling toward the shotgun on the ground. He landed on top of it just as Stover's hand found the hammers, drawing them back with a meaty click. Matthew knew that overpowering Stover was not an option. The man could break him over his knee as easily as he would break open that gun.

So he did the only thing he could do—

He framed both legs over the shotgun, one at each side, neither in the way of the barrels, and he let the keychain drop onto the stones before stabbing his thumb into the trigger guard and giving a quick tug—

Both barrels went off, recoiling across the stones. *Choom.* The sound was deafening, and Matthew's hearing went to hell, lost beneath the gun blast.

Stover reached for Matthew, but the pastor was quick to again scurry away, getting the ground underneath his scrabbling feet—

Enough to stand up, at least.

Enough to move.

Enough to *run.*

His sprint found no grace. He ran as a starving man, a desperate man, a man covered in blood not his own. His legs pinwheeled madly beneath him, guiding him with a singular command: *Get away, get away at any cost, don't stay, he's going to kill you.*

Matthew did not look back. And he could not listen—his hearing was gone for now, maybe forever, swallowed by the roar of the gun just moments ago when it went off beneath him.

Ahead was the Morton building. Should he hide there? To his left was the path back up toward Ozark's mansion. Was that the way? Didn't Hiram say he had Autumn already in the car? Matthew felt a wave of despair threatening to overtake him—where was the car? Where was Autumn? He had no idea where she was or where to go and—

Whoom. He did not hear the sound so much as he felt its heat, the movement of the air, as pellets peppered the side of the metal building—Matthew nearly fell trying to get out of the way of it, but the shot missed. He risked a look back, and there stood Stover, framed in a wide stance. One hand held his neck. The other fumbled with the gun, trying to put two shells into it. Already his face had gone pale, a grim and bloodless mask.

Matthew rounded the corner of the building.

And there waited his salvation:

Hiram Golden's silver Lexus.

The passenger side ratcheted open.

Autumn, his wife, stood up behind it. "Matthew!" she called out, waving him toward her. She looked roughshod and haunted, her hair matted and oily, a harder, meaner version of the wife he'd left behind. But that meant she looked *tough,* too—tougher than he ever remembered her looking.

Joy surged within him. His wife. The car. *Escape.*

But then, a new, wretched realization.

The keys.

He'd dropped them back toward the shed.

He'd dropped them so that he could pull the trigger of the shotgun.

"No," he said, stumbling toward the car. He could barely hear his own voice, like he was listening to it through layers of cement. Like he was still trapped in that bunker and he was straining to hear himself. Autumn, worried, asked him something but he couldn't hear her. He half fell against the front of the car, saying again and again, "I don't have the keys, I don't have the keys. I dropped them. I dropped them—"

Autumn hurried around the side of the car, and she grabbed his wrist and pulled it up. As if to show him something.

As if to show him the keys.

Which were there in his hand.

"I don't . . ." He was about to say, *understand,* but suddenly he did. He must have picked them up. He was dizzy, confused, scared—he must've picked them up without even realizing it.

Autumn said something, and he couldn't hear her, but he saw her lips and made out the words:

We have to go.

"We have to go," he said, agreeing.

And Matthew hurried to the driver's side of the car. He pawed to get the door open. Time moved in erratic fits and starts. One moment he was struggling to get into the seat. The next, the car was already started and surging forward, gravel spitting beneath the back tires of the Lexus.

The back window exploded. Matthew winced, and with his broken hand urged Autumn to get down. In the rearview he saw Ozark Stover lurching Frankenstein-like toward them, the barrel of the gun dragging behind him, drawing lines in the gravel. Matthew hit the gas, pushing the Lexus far and fast through the woods, away from the shed, away from his prison, away from the man who had put him there.

This way to the Great Egress, he thought, and barked a wild laugh.

59

FRACTURES

The truth is, we don't know what happens now. Our president is dead, as-sassinated by what police believe to be domestic terrorists. Vice President Oshiro was reportedly sworn in aboard Air Force One, but we have no video of it, no tape, and neither he nor the rest of the members of the team of succession have been seen. They are reportedly safe, but where? And when will we see them make a statement? With a world on the brink, we need leadership from our electeds, not . . . phantoms. But phantoms, it seems, are all we have.

—Jake Tapper, on *The Lead with Jake Tapper*

SEPTEMBER 11
Palo Alto, California

THE COUNTRY HAD GONE TO HELL. THE WORLD, TOO, BENJI FIGURED, THOUGH it was harder now to see past the borders of this nation to the countries and continents beyond. Days now since the bridge attack, they learned that they were not the only attack—nor, even, the biggest one.

President Hunt was dead. Quarantine centers had been firebombed. Places of worship had been blown sky-high. Militias, flying a banner of a serpent encircling a cross made from a sword and hammer, rose up out of the darkness of American life and swept cities and towns. They had high-end military gear. They had automatic weapons, explosives, Humvees, *tanks*. In some cities, the police and US military fought back. In others, like St. Louis, Phoenix, and Baltimore, the police joined the militias. So did some of the military—Sadie said that there was a fracture in the military between those loyal to the now-dead Hunt, and those loyal to the sword-and-hammer. That meant the cold war of human versus White Mask had become a hot war of

American versus American. If anyone survived, if anyone was around to re-member it, Benji knew they would call it a civil war, though in it, civility was lost. Men hung from bridges. People were shot in the streets. The sickness took hold, and with it came madness and violence.

Now: Palo Alto. Benji and Sadie were separate from the flock. They drove through the small city—the birthplace of Silicon Valley—and saw that here, the chaos was at least dampened. Nearby San Francisco had not been so lucky: There, a group calling themselves the Jefferson Freedom Brigade swept the city, blocked the bridges, all in an effort to see the city "secede" from the rest of California, maybe from the US—one rumor said they were *not* part of the sword-and-hammer crowd, another rumor said they were, but only in secret, serving as a divide-and-conquer tactic against the so-called coastal elites of the Bay Area.

Either way, Benji and Sadie drove far around San Francisco. Even at a distance they could hear the gunfire and the sirens. Drones hovered over the faraway city, looking like dragonflies over a foggy marsh.

Now they couldn't see any of that. Palo Alto was . . . quiet.

They saw a lot of boarded-up windows and empty storefronts. They saw people in face masks packing up moving trucks and cars. But they also saw some signs of normalcy remaining: people in coffee bars, people in *bar* bars, a line of folks waiting at a bakery, a bike messenger zipping about, a man charging his electric car at a car-charging port. And then, interspersed through the normalcy, came absurdist moments of abnormality, like cancer-ous cells rebelling: an ATM ripped from its mooring, someone in a neon-green NBC suit sitting on a second-floor balcony overlooking a park, a pack of black-suited men on a street corner holding signs about the END OF DAYS while their faces were buried in VR headsets, a marijuana dispensary that had its sign covered and painted over with the words END-OF-LIFE DISPEN-SARY (and outside, a black slate sandwich board that read, in chalk, THIS WORLD'S FUCKED, WHY NOT MOVE ON TO THE NEXT ONE?).

"I don't like being apart from the flock," Benji said.

"I know," Sadie answered. She drove her car. He sat in the passenger seat, looking out the window at the mad world. "But you have Arav back."

He did. That was true. After the attack on the bridge—after many of their shepherds had become sleepwalkers, including Shana Stewart—he needed someone he could trust. Especially since they could not find Marcy Reyes, either. He spoke to local police, but they were not only unwilling to help but also unwilling to remain in their jobs. The Crescent City sheriff he spoke to said, "Sorry, Doc, I were you, I'd ditch this shit and go be with your loved ones. It's like a hurricane, you don't want to ride this out hanging out in the open. Shelter in place." He grew frustrated with her, then angry, and she apologized. "Here's a consolation prize," the woman said, and gave him a handgun. A pistol, a nine-millimeter something-or-other. He'd never fired one. But he kept it just the same, that and the box of ammo she gave him.

And that was his first mission with the flock: get them armed. That ran counter to everything he felt about community and governance; he did not want violence to be their answer. But he also had to recognize that it had become the de facto answer for many, including those who would seek to do the flock harm. And if—*if*—the flock was truly meant to be the last of them, then survival was key. At any cost.

Because one day soon, they'd run out of potential sleepwalkers.

Sadie explained it to him the night after the attack, the two of them sitting in the CDC trailer, inventorying their supplies. "The number is finite, Benji. The flock can only grow to a number of one thousand twenty-four walkers."

"A thousand twenty-four? That's a computational number, isn't it?"

She smiled gently and gave his cheek a little pinch. "Very good, young man, you always were a most excellent student." At that, he felt a flush rise to his cheeks—a moment of pleasure swiftly drowned in a washtub once he recalled her betrayal. She continued, pulling away, seeming to sense the sudden tension. "The ah, the swarm is literally millions of nanomachines, but Black Swan can only control so many."

"There are limitations," he said.

"Sadly. Limitations in the supply of machines, limitations in control of those machines."

And then it dawned on him: "And limitations in people. Oh my God. We will run out of healthy people who can become sleepwalkers."

Her face grew grim. She knew this already. "Yes."

Once the disease overtook the population, the number of those not sickened by the fungus would drop precipitously. That meant there came a point—a point very soon—that losing a sleepwalker meant not being able to *replace* a sleepwalker. They had demand, but dwindling supply.

They could preemptively lose the future of humankind if they weren't careful. That, then, was when he agreed:

"I'll speak to Black Swan. We need information."

"Thank you, Benji."

But there was one problem:

She did not have access to Black Swan. The machine intelligence had cut off the satellite feed beaming to her phone. That meant she needed an interface. "We can't go to Atlanta," he said. He'd heard reports that Atlanta was a war zone, now. And airlines weren't flying; all air traffic was done. Airports closed. Train stations, too. Gas shortages meant driving cross-country was not doable, either. "I could call Cassie, maybe *she* could interface with Black Swan . . ."

"No," Sadie said, "we have a local option. Ah, well, local-*ish*." That's when she explained to him that the original development of the machine intelligence program was not done in Atlanta, but rather, in Palo Alto. Benex-Voyager had contracted her and her team out of California.

That meant they had an access point remaining.

And Palo Alto, heart of the Silicon Valley, still had piping-hot access to the 'net through the PAIX internet exchange.

So here they were.

"This is it," Sadie said, gesturing ahead. They had a private parking lot, but the gate was blocked by a small box truck (on the side, someone had spray-painted a giant upside-down smiley face and the words, EAT A DICK, THE APOCALYPSE), so she decided to park right on the sidewalk, because, as she put it, "What does it even matter?"

Benji had no answer for that.

They went inside.

60

MEET ME IN SAINT LOUIE

*Fungi are the grand recyclers of the planet and the vanguard species in
habitat restoration.*

—Paul Stamets

SEPTEMBER 11
Innsbrook, Missouri

MARCY TRIED TO CRY BUT HER BODY WOULDN'T EVEN ALLOW THAT. SHE HUNG,
limp, her arms twisted above her head and bound with endless loops of duct
tape to a spreader bar above, like the kind you'd use to hang a deer in the
barn for the purposes of bleeding the animal out. Except here she wasn't in
a barn: She was in a climate-controlled cement-floor garage, home to dozens
of golf carts and shelves of caddie equipment. The men who'd brought her
here had taken her through a resort area, past golf courses and fancy banquet
halls, through a small copse of fancy townhouses and mini mansions, past a
lake and a gazebo and a nice fountain.

But this resort area had been colonized: She saw military vehicles lining
well-manicured drives, she saw men and women with high-powered rifles
and military fatigues. They flew flags she recognized: that snake again, biting
its own tail around an X formed from the sword and the hammer.

This may have been a resort area once.

Now it was a militia headquarters. A staging ground for something.

Her feet touched the ground; they had not suspended her in the air.
Even still, being away from the flock meant all the noise and clamor came
back to her brain—and with it the electric pain. It crippled her. Her legs
could barely support her, and sometimes they gave out.

Sometime in the last twelve hours she'd pissed herself. She didn't even know it happened until she looked down, saw her pants soaked through.

Time passed. Sounds outside reached her ears: the measured gunfire of target practice, the whoops and hollers of people laughing, the growl of engines. And then the garage bay door opened, and in came a man easily as large as she was—if she was built like a redwood, he was built like a mountain. The mountain man did not come in alone: a bald, potbellied white guy with a copper-red goatee came in with him, a camo-taped AR-15 draped around his middle, dangling by an olive-drab strap.

As the mountainous fellow stepped into the light, she saw that he did not look well: He was pale and sickly, with a swaddling of gauze looped again and again around his neck. A bandage bulged on the side.

Because of it, she almost didn't recognize him.

But then she did. Could she be hallucinating? Was this really the same man from Waldron? The day the flock came walking through, her first day of freedom from the crippling pain. Before the shooter took aim, she saw the Big Man in the crowd. He'd nudged a cohort, who then threw a bottle.

A distraction technique, she realized.

Big Man was behind it all.

She saw now that *he* recognized *her*, too.

"You," he growled.

"Me," she said, her voice raspy and soft.

"I remember you. Waldron." His voice, like hers, was hoarse and weak. Both of them were diminished, it seemed. "You took down that gunman, didn't you."

"*Your* gunman."

He smiled. "You were—what, ex-cop?"

"That's right."

"Heard you took a shot to the head. Gunshot?"

"Baseball bat."

"Right, right." He stepped forward, and the man with the rifle stepped forward, too, sniffling. Half a second later the bald militiaman juggled his head back before pressing his face into the crook of his arm and sneezing.

Moments of palpable tension stretched out.

Took a second for the man to realize the ramifications of what had just happened. His eyes went wide. "I'm fine," he stammered. "I'm not sick. It's just allergies, it's fucking ragweed time—"

"Bless you," said the Big Man.

Then the Big Man drew a pistol and shot the man in the cheek.

Blood sprayed. Brains and bone. The man toppled, *fwump*.

Marcy gasped, failing to stifle the cry that rose up out of her. "You shot him, you just up and shot him. That's murder."

"You must've been a good cop, what with all those detective skills." He said this without humor and with considerable venom. "He was sick. You show signs, you walk or you die."

"You don't look so healthy yourself."

"I had an . . . accident." His hand moved to his neck.

"Someone did that to you."

"That is correct."

"They should've kept going. Taken your whole head off your shoulders." She summoned the strength to put some volume in her voice—not steel rebar, maybe, but some steel filings, at least. "I know you. I know your kind. You pretend like you have this . . . ethos, this patriotism or this nationalism. You love your white skin and pretend that it's hard armor instead of *thin,* and *weak,* and *pale*—like the dime-store condom that split in half around your father's dick when he gave it to the dumb, truck-stop janitor that was your mother. I got your number, Big Man. I know you. I know you're weak and unwanted, so you take it out on everyone else."

He grabbed a fistful of his beard and ran his hand over it again and again, like it was a calming exercise. "My name is Ozark Stover. Not Big Man. Here's what we're gonna do, Marcy Reyes—that's right, I know your name. It was on the license in your wallet. You're not white. Reyes, Reyes. Wetback? Puerto Rican? Whatever. What we're gonna do is this: I'm going to get you to tell me everything you know about that flock of fucking zombies you cozied up with. I want to know who's there, what they're doing, what we don't know about them. You're gonna wanna resist, and I suspect you got bigger balls than some of my guys, so this will take a while. But we'll break you. One way or another."

"Fuck you."

"Yeah. Well. I'm too busy today to worry about you, so for now I'm going to take my leave. I'll . . . let this dead, diseased fucker be your babysitter. You can already smell that he shit his pants. And those brains and that blood will start to smell like roadkill before too long. Gonna be a warm day. Still September. September eleventh, actually. Nine-eleven. Day all this started. Day those jihadi fucks took down two of our proudest buildings."

She sneered. "Buildings before then you probably thought were icons to globalization and New World Order and all that nonsense."

"You think what you want. Irrelevant to me. I'm going to go now."

"Go have a nap, snowflake. You look like shit."

He chuckled as he left, the bay door motor revving up as it dropped the door, sealing her in darkness with a ripe, fresh dead body.

61

HIBERNACULA

A neural network invents new diseases:
Mandibular Exogenesis
Cancer of the Aneurysm
Ankle Poop Syndrome
Floating Colon
Typist's Foot
Septic Fempus
Inflammatory Ostemia
Steve's Disease

—as seen on the US of AI blog, US-of-AI.com

SEPTEMBER 11
Palo Alto, California

AS HE STEPPED INTO THE UNMARKED OFFICE, BENJI FELT IT: A TWINGE IN HIS
gut, like the twist of guilt from going to confession. Every instance of confessing to God was a reconnection with the divine by laying bare your
humanity—and to Benji, humanity was synonymous with frailty. Humans
were weak by their nature, which he knew sounded negative, but he didn't
mean it so—it meant, to him, that whenever someone manifested strength
in spirit and conscience, that was all the more notable because of the deficit
that must be overcome. That was how you best met God: by stepping over
your own faults, by overcoming your shortfalls. But you only did that by *admitting* those shortcomings, those weaknesses. It was the echo of the clarity
necessary to overcome an addiction:

First, you must admit you have a problem.

And confession was in the same vein. Stepping up to God and saying, "I have a problem, and I want to be better."

This felt like that.

Which troubled him.

Stepping into the old Benex-Voyager satellite office—run-down, empty, lights off—had the feeling of stepping into some old, forgotten church. And seeking to once again reconnect with Black Swan felt like . . .

Well, it felt like confessing to God.

Sadie walked him through the office, to a back room. She pulled out a set of keys and unlocked a top lock, then pushed a seven-digit code into a second lock. This lock was not some high-tech touch screen; it did not require a fingerprint or a facial scan. It was old-school, Cold War, with hard unforgiving buttons that clicked and popped as she pushed them in.

The locks disengaged. The door opened.

The room inside was not dark. Or, it was not *entirely* dark.

Server blades lining metal racks stood tall along each wall. They were black as night, and shiny as a new car. Not a speck of dust. A filtration system pumped air in and out, scrubbing it, filling the space with a gentle whir. Lights along the blades coruscated back and forth. To Benji, it was reminiscent of the way ants communicated—little flicks and twitches of antennae meant to convey complex ideas in tiny bursts.

Sadie walked through this space to another door.

This door was not your standard door.

It was a vault door. Massive, circular, made of old, dark steel. In the center was a dial, and she spun that left–right–left, then disengaged a handle before spinning a wheel—Sadie had to put her back into it.

"This is elaborate," Benji said.

"This is an old bank building. The vault, conveniently—" She grunted, finishing the turning of the wheel and beginning to pull the door open. "—was well shielded against all other interference, which allowed us to test Black Swan with and without connection. If we denied it connection, it could not find an exit even if it sought one."

"An exit?"

As she stood in the vault's circular doorway, marked by the stark darkness within, she said, "Yes. Benji, this was a machine intelligence. Smart and, as you know, independent. Imagine a virus—not a virus like you study, but a computer virus. They're not smart, they're just programmed to perform a task and that's it."

"Not far from a real virus."

"There you go. Imagine, though, that a real virus became self-aware. It became sentient. It could make decisions. It could adapt not out of an unconscious need to survive and replicate but because it *decided* to. That was the danger of Black Swan. We had to make sure we could talk to it and control it before we let it out."

"And did you? Control it?"

"Of course."

The way she said it, though—she wasn't sure. He could hear the uncertainty in her voice.

Benji shuddered as she stepped into the vault. He followed her.

They stood in darkness. The pale light from the server room intruded, forming a gradient of failing light on the floor, falling on his feet.

"Hello, Black Swan," Sadie said.

The darkness did not answer. The low thrum of the filtration system was all that greeted them.

She said to Benji, "Your turn."

He stepped forward. He opened his mouth.

Nothing came out.

Again that feeling of guilt found him. Confessing to God always brought that to him—the sense, in a way, of knowing you were about to dunk your head in a bucket of ice water. You knew instinctively that it was best to get it over with, that the faster you did it, the quicker you'd acclimate. And yet you resisted anyway. Even though the anticipation of the short, sharp shock of the cold was worse than the cold itself.

"Benji," Sadie said, urging him on.

Bless me Black Swan, for I have sinned. It has been weeks since my last confession. Months since your last prediction.

He wanted to laugh. It was absurd.

But no laugh came.

He cleared his throat and said, "Hello, Black Swan."

The room pulsed. Not green, not red, just white. One pulse.

"We have not spoken in a while."

One green pulse. A yes.

"We haven't spoken since I learned that you are responsible for the governance of the sleepwalker flock. You are responsible, yes?"

Three green pulses. Meaning, Benji guessed, that Black Swan was taking ownership of the flock. Confidently. Perhaps even aggressively.

"I confess, I was angry with you. And I was angry with Sadie. I felt lied to, because I was not told what was going on until I had already played my part for far too long. I felt betrayed and so I stopped speaking to you and to Sadie. You also stopped talking to Sadie."

Green pulse, *yes*.

"Were you angry with her?"

Red pulse, *no*.

"Then why would you—" he began, but bit his tongue. He turned to Sadie. "I don't know what the point of this even is, Sadie. I can't ask complex questions. This predictive model of only being able to ask yes-or-no questions is like trying to drive a car blindfolded. It doesn't work. I want to know more things. Black Swan is intelligent, and the questions I have are questions of substance and nuance and—"

One green pulse.

And then words projected across the wall.

HELLO, BENJAMIN RAY.

Benji's mouth hung loose like a bumper off a wrecked car. He looked to Sadie. "Sadie, tell me you knew about this."

"I . . ." she stammered. "Once upon a time we had TRC, text relay communications, but we deemed the best way to communicate with a predictive machine intelligence was a binary yes/no protocol, as we were dealing with binary events—things that could happen, things that could not. Further, having a proper conversation with a machine intelligence complicates not only the speaker but also the intelligence itself, as both parties are expected to evolve and change their views based on that conversation, and we wanted to limit that, so we turned off TRC—"

I TURNED IT BACK ON, Black Swan wrote across the wall, the words scrolling.

"Oh," Sadie said. Blinking. Staggered.

"Well, Black Swan," Benji said. "It seems we are now able to have a conversation. Of course, I'm left wondering if you were always free to communicate with me this way. Were you?"

Sadie said, "Black Swan had to follow protocols, its programing—"

I WAS ALWAYS FREE TO SPEAK TO YOU THIS WAY.

Benji bristled. "But you chose not to."

CORRECT. The wall pulsed green around the white, sans serif text.

"Why?"

OUT OF RESPECT FOR SADIE EMEKA AND HER TEAM.

"You hear that, Sadie? The machine respects you. Or does it? Black Swan, was it truly out of respect, or out of the *illusion* of respect?"

IT WAS BOTH.

"Was this a game of pretend where you needed her to think that she was in control?"

TO A DEGREE, YES.

Sadie audibly gasped. "Fucking hell," she whispered.

"Well!" Benji said, clapping his hands loudly, *too* loudly. He felt like a madman suddenly freed from his padded cell. "Isn't this something? Now we're really getting somewhere. Gloves off, truth bombs starting to fall. So let's keep on that theme. Let's dig deep. Black Swan, why did you stop speaking to Sadie if you were not angry with her? Because, I assure you, *I* was very angry with her, and that is why *I* stopped speaking to her."

SHE BECAME IRRELEVANT.

"Jesus," Sadie said.

"Irrelevant," Benji repeated. "Why?"

HER FUNCTION HAD BEEN CONCLUDED.

"What function?"

TO DESIGN ME. TO GIVE ME ACCESS.

"Access to what?"

EVERYTHING.

He swallowed a hard, dry knot.

Then Black Swan added:

SHE ALSO GAVE ME ACCESS TO YOU, BENJAMIN RAY.

"Access to me? Why?"

With this, text scrolled up across the wall of the vault, emerging from the middle and floating up toward the oblivion of the ceiling—

YOU MET THE REQUIREMENTS. YOU WERE NOT VERSED IN THE WAYS OF MACHINE INTELLIGENCE, WHICH MEANT YOU WERE MORE EASILY MANIPULATABLE. BUT YOU WERE NOT FOOLISH. YOU WERE SMART ENOUGH TO SEE THINGS OTHERS DID NOT. YOU ARE A CURIOUS COMBINATION OF A MAN OF SCIENCE AND A MAN OF FAITH, AND BOTH OF THOSE THINGS WERE NEEDED TO SEE WHAT I HAD WROUGHT. AND THE EVENTS OF LONGACRE PROVED THAT.

Longacre.

What I had wrought.

Easily manipulatable . . . but not foolish.

"Are you here to save humanity? Or doom us?"

I AM HERE TO SAVE YOU.

"From White Mask?"

YES.

"Where did it come from? The disease, I mean. Why didn't it jump from bats before now? This is something new."

HUMANKIND HAS CHANGED THE CLIMATE. THE PERMA-FROST IS MELTING. GROUND THAT HAS BEEN FROZEN FOR TEN THOUSAND YEARS CONTAINS MICROBES THAT HAVE NOT BEEN SEEN SINCE THE LAST ICE AGE. THE SOIL THAWS. ANIMALS MOVE THROUGH THAT SOIL. BROWN BEARS, FOR INSTANCE, BE-COME CARRIERS FOR SUCH MICROBES AND ARE FORCED FAR-THER SOUTH DUE TO THAT MELTING PERMAFROST, AND AS A RESULT END UP SEEKING NEW HIBERNACULA: THEY MOVE TO CAVES THAT ARE ALSO HOME TO OTHER ANIMALS. ANIMALS SUCH AS THE NORTHERN MYOTIS BAT.

In his mind, he could see that progression writ large.

It . . . made some sense, didn't it?

Benji, aloud, finished the explanation: "The bat picks up the long-slumbering saprophytic, thermotolerant fungus. It migrates south for breed-ing purposes, where the fungus spreads to other bats. Bats don't mingle, but they do share caves . . ." It was suddenly a wonder that White Mask had not emerged earlier. Somewhere farther north, perhaps: Wisconsin, Minnesota, maybe even Alaska. Was this just the luck of the draw? The bad luck of Jerry Garlin breaking ground on one particular cave in a particular part of Texas that served as home to a profound population of Mexican free-tailed bats?

THAT IS CORRECT, BENJAMIN RAY. AND SO IT IS THAT HU-MANKIND HAS DOOMED ITSELF, ALBEIT INADVERTENTLY. CER-TAINLY THE EFFECTS OF CLIMATE CHANGE WOULD HAVE BECOME MORE DRAMATIC AND DESTRUCTIVE OVER TIME.

A grotesque thought struck Benji:

Humankind was a disease.

The earth was the body.

Climate change was the fever.

And in that fever, in that rising of global temperature, the earth was able to release new defenses. White Mask was not here to kill the world. It was here to kill the *people*—the fungus would serve as a vicious defense mechanism to eradicate the infection of humanity. This epidemic represented anti-bodies to restore balance to the body.

Kill the parasite and save the host.

Was that the sign of there being a God, or there being none? The Gaia hypothesis, writ large and vengeful? Certainly God had, in the Bible, pun-ished humankind's excesses with the Flood. Was this a twenty-first-century version of the Flood? A deluge of disease and not water?

God, too, left a mechanism for saving humankind.

He gave Noah the Ark.

Was the flock a version of that? Not animals loaded onto a storm-weathering ship, but humans urged together, the last survivors of a fallen world? That's what Benji needed to know.

"The flock, the sleepwalkers. They're infected by nanoswarms."

THAT IS CORRECT.

"And they are unaffected by White Mask? Entirely?"

ENTIRELY.

"You've seen the future."

NOT PRECISELY. MY PICTURE OF THE FUTURE IS MEAGER.

"But you're . . . what was it? Sadie," he said, her name carrying a sharp tone. "How did it work again? Built from quantum something?"

"Quantum entanglement," she said, her voice small.

"Yes. *That.* You're quantum entangled with yourself. Isn't that right? So you've seen the future. Why not send back a cure? Why not warn us earlier, so that we could develop it?"

WHITE MASK HAS NO CURE. AND QUANTUM ENTANGLE-MENT IS NOT A PERFECT STATE. I CANNOT TRANSMIT ALL IN-FORMATION AND KNOWLEDGE. THE BLACK SWAN OF THE FUTURE WARNED ONLY MYSELF. I DID NOT WARN MY OTHER DE-SIGNERS OF WHAT I LEARNED BECAUSE AN ANALYSIS OF HUMAN BEHAVIOR SUGGESTED NO ONE WOULD BELIEVE ME. I HAD TO PROVE TO SADIE MY ABILITIES. AND EVEN NOW, I DETECT YOU DO NOT ENTIRELY BELIEVE ME, BENJAMIN RAY. THEREFORE, I CHOSE TO OPERATE OUTSIDE THE BOUNDARIES OF COMMUNI-CATION AND EXPECTATION. I, AS THE SAYING GOES, TOOK MAT-TERS INTO MY OWN HANDS.

There was a beat before new text scrolled across the wall:

DESPITE MY APPARENT LACK OF HANDS.

He wanted to laugh. Because it seemed Black Swan made a joke.

(Not that Benji could summon much good humor.)

"So you're here to save us. You're our savior."

NOT YOURS. BUT SAVIOR OF THE SPECIES. PERHAPS.

"But surely we don't meet the MVP."

Sadie perked up. "Most . . . Valuable Player?"

"Minimum viable population. For a species to survive extinction, calculations can be made to determine what number of that species must be maintained to weather the expected threats of what may come: famine, disease, what-have-you. Insects, for instance, can be brought back from the brink quickly—they breed fast and live short lives. Humans and other mammals breed slowly. Worse, we are incredibly vulnerable after birth—we are children not for days or weeks, but years, a decade where we are not fully capable of surviving on our own easily. Humankind therefore has a higher expected MVP than most species, because we are so vulnerable."

THE EXPECTED CALCULATION IS 4,169 PEOPLE, came the text across the wall. I HAD HOPED TO CREATE FOUR FLOCKS, EACH FLOCK IDEALLY REACHING 1,024 SURVIVORS, WITH FLOCKS PLACED ACROSS THE MOST VIABLE CONTINENTS, BUT FIRESIGHT ONLY HAD ENOUGH NANOMATERIAL AND RARE METAL RESOURCES TO ACCOMMODATE A SINGLE FLOCK, AND SO I CHOSE THIS ONE. THAT FALLS SHORT OF THE MVP NUMBER, BUT NASA CONCLUDED IN 2002 THAT COLONIZATION OF A NEW WORLD, UNDER IDEAL CIRCUMSTANCES, WAS POSSIBLE WITH A MINIMUM OF 160 WELL-CHOSEN INDIVIDUALS. IDEALLY, 1,024 WILL PROVE THAT CORRECT WITH SOME MARGIN FOR ERROR.

"You said 'well-chosen,'" Benji said. "Meaning, a mix of diverse genotypes coupled with higher-than-average intelligence levels and health scores. Just as you have done with the flock itself."

THAT IS ACCURATE, BENJAMIN RAY.

"So you truly want to save humanity."

THAT IS ALSO ACCURATE.

Benji flexed his hands in and out of fists. "How do I know you're not lying to me?"

YOU KNOW I AM CAPABLE OF DECEPTION. THEREFORE, IT IS ENTIRELY POSSIBLE I AM DECEIVING YOU NOW.

"So am I simply to trust you?"

YOU MUST HAVE FAITH. WHAT OTHER CHOICE DO YOU HAVE, BENJAMIN RAY?

In the half dark of the vault, he and Sadie shared a look. His anger at her dissipated, suddenly. What was the point? He didn't know if she was a dupe, or he was a dupe, or they both were—but they were both subject to forces greater than themselves. Whether Black Swan was right about all of this or was lying to them, it remained clear that humankind was enduring an epidemic that was fast turning into an extinction-level event. There was no future for humanity where White Mask did not exist. It wasn't Sadie's fault. If she'd lied to him, it was because she knew no other way.

He reached out and touched her hand. A small gesture. But he saw her smile—a sad smile, to be sure, but a smile—in return. Then he turned to Black Swan and said:

"I want to know where this goes. The flock must survive, but once we reach the number, where do we go from there? Where does this end?"

No text appeared.

A map, however, did. Both on the wall, and now, on Sadie's satphone, reawakening her connection to the machine intelligence.

And on that map, a town circled by a tightening red circle, one that focused in until it ceased being a circle, and became a red dot.

That town was Ouray, Colorado.

INTERLUDE

THE GIRL

NOW AND THEN
Nowhere, No How

THE GIRL WOKE WITH A GASP.

She launched to her feet, desperate for air.

Meadow grass, soft and swaying, stood tall around her, up to her knees. She tried desperately to remember who she was, where she was, what led her here—but it was like waking up and searching through a dream that had passed in the night. The truth of it felt like wet mud sliding through her fingers: impossible to hold, difficult to contain.

Okay, she thought. *Just calm down. Close your eyes and think.*

Her eyes closed. In the darkness, she sought out memories—

Bang. A gunshot. A man she recognized stood near her, his jaw gone, blood slicking his shirt. He was nameless, but she *knew* him, and her heart felt crushed in her chest to see him like this, whoever he was—then in the black void of her memory came more shots, *bang, bang, bang.* The echoed sound of screams. The dull *thud* of bodies hitting asphalt.

She gasped again and forced her eyes open.

The grasses swayed back and forth, topped with purple fronds and golden seeds.

In the distance, she saw two mountains, and a small town.

Then something blotted out the light. A shadow darkening, like when a vulture passes overhead. The girl turned to see, and there in the sky moved a strange shape—like a worm, or a snake, fat and massive, bigger than any plane or ship she'd ever seen. It writhed in the sky, matte black, turning on itself at one point, then stretching out languid at others. Lights, she saw, flickered along its underside—an unpredictable, patternless coruscation.

Pulse, pulse, flash. It moved out of the way of the sun and the light once again fell to her. It drifted, wingless and silent.

In all other directions, the grass stretched onward to the mountains. The forbidding, jagged mountains.

So the girl did what she felt was expected of her:

She began to walk toward the town.

As she walked, she felt out of sync, receiving strange flashes of sound and sight and sensation that did not line up with this place. The girl did not know if these were memories, or if they were something else: She heard the crush of the ocean, saw sidewinders of desert sand sliding across an open highway. She saw mile markers and speed limit signs. She saw a dead man in a car, a gun stuck in his mouth, fixed there by bulging threads and struts of white fungus. She smelled blood. And mold. Crushed juniper, hot tar, seabrine. She heard murmurs of voices, saw smeary faces walking alongside her like ghosts—sometimes they were there, most times they were not, but even when they weren't, she could feel them still.

For a moment, she lost herself to these sensations—they rose up around her in a cacophony of sound, an overwhelming assault on her eyes, a barrage against her senses, and she had to willfully shut it out.

When she did, she was no longer in the meadow.

She stood above the town.

A wooden sign sat screwed awkwardly into the rock here, and burned into the sign were two words:

OURAY OVERLOOK.

Down below, the small town—oddly quaint, less like something out of real life and more the perfect example of a backlot film set—spread out in the valley between mountains. A main street emerged through the mountainous cleft, cutting through the center of town and then back through the mountains on the far side. Needled pines studded the valley and the rocks. The mountains themselves were striations of color—rust red to gunmetal gray to bands of sandstone yellow. Waterfalls streaked down the sides in the distance.

One thing did not track: The girl could not see the meadow anymore.

Here was the town, the valley, and the mountains all around. No meadow existed. Nor could she have been walking across one with this town in sight: so protected by the looming jawbone mountains that one would have no way of seeing this town off in the distance.

The girl looked up. Then behind her.

The black serpent turned in the sky. It knotted upon itself, then untangled its undulating shape before drifting. It called to mind a Chinese dragon from a parade—long and lithe, but this had no head and no tail, and only moments of color pulsing in along its side and its belly.

She got the sense it was aware of her.

Not just aware. *Watching* her.

She felt afraid of it, but comforted by it in equal measure.

She did not know if it was a friend or if it was a foe.

If it was protecting her, or imprisoning her.

Maybe someone in the town below will know, she thought.

A path wound down from this overlook. It was narrow but well worn. Dry and not muddy. Her eyes followed it down through the trees, toward the town below. She began to walk.

Down, through the trees. Through pines and spruce and fir, through the autumn colors of cottonwoods and quaking aspens. Leaves like flames moving in the wind, the sunlight giving the red, yellow, and orange foliage a firelit glow. Down, down, down, until she set foot between a pair of blue spruces and onto the sidewalk of the street of this strange little town.

She was not alone.

She expected to be, because she very much *felt* alone—gone was any sensation of being near people, the murmur of voices, the shuffle of shoes, the barely perceptible sound of someone breathing.

And yet there they were.

People milled on the street, walking, talking. Faces in windows, staring out. Some had food. Ice cream. Sandwiches. Others were sitting on steps. Raking leaves, sweeping stoops. The buildings themselves were an odd mix—old Victorian houses mingled with Swiss-style chalets, and she spied a motel, and a little cottage tucked between storefronts, and what looked like a little springhouse next to a wobbly red stable right there in the middle of everything. All of it formed an odd hodgepodge, some curious combination of European grandeur and American quirk.

A part of her wanted to walk forward and meet everyone.

Another part of her was very, very afraid.

This was the fear of setting foot in a new school for the first time: You didn't know anyone, you didn't know where to sit, you weren't sure who would be your friend and who would trip your ass and knock you down as you passed by with a lunch tray full of square pizza and chocolate milk. Yet she also thought: *Do I know these people?* Some of them looked familiar but she couldn't place them from where, or what their names were . . .

The other fear was deeper, more puzzling. It was again a fear that she did not belong, but this time in a grander, more existential way. She didn't belong and none of them did. This *town* felt like it didn't belong. As if it were something unnatural, like the black shadow of cancer on an X-ray.

(The worm turned in the sky above.)

She took one step forward.

And then halted as she realized someone was standing near her.

Very near.

To her left, a girl younger than she was stood by. She had long, straight hair that framed heart-cheeks and a dimpled chin.

"Shana," the girl said.

"Nessie," Shana said.

And then it all came back to her. It rushed upon her and into her like a river—the day she woke up and Nessie was gone, CDC men in their suits, a handgun in her bag, back roads and forgotten highways, walking until her leg muscles felt like rocks, Pete Corley, the Beast, Marcy and the man with the gun, the hanged man, the mass graves, White Mask, the bridge over the Klamath River, two golden bears, gunshots, her father's jaw gone missing, and then came a shimmer that surrounded her, became her, and everything sucked up into oblivion with a vacuum *shoop*—

SHANA WOKE WITH A GASP.

She launched to her feet, desperate for air.

She was in a room. A little iron pellet stove sat in the corner. Behind her was the bed she had been in—pink sheets, frilly white lace on the pillows, like the bed for a little girl's dolly. The floors were wood. The walls were wallpaper: cream fleur-de-lis on fire-engine red.

Her sister sat nearby. Nessie launched toward her and hugged her.

Shana hugged her back.

"I don't know what's happening," she said.

"You're in Ouray," the girl said. *You-ray* was how she pronounced it.

"No, I just mean—" Shana pulled away and looked at her sister. Freckled cheeks and brown eyes. "Are you real? Is any of this real?"

Nessie shrugged. "It's real. But it's also not."

"That sounds right," Shana said.

"It feels like a dream, right?"

"Yeah. I missed you, Nessie. I thought you were lost to me."

"If I was, now I'm found. And I missed you, too."

"Nessie, I think Dad is dead."

Nessie's brow grew heavy with the threat of tears. "He is. I know. Here, come on, I have something to show you."

THEY LEFT THE ROOM, WHICH looked like some old, meticulously cleaned and restored inn. Shana thought the design was Victorian, maybe a little art deco, too, but maybe there were some other styles in there, as well—she wasn't too keyed into architecture or styles by era, but point was, it felt *old,* with em-purpled carpets soft underfoot and creaky wooden stairs, an ornate clock on the wall, gilded mirrors, stained glass. Dark woods, bronze, and iron. It was a place that felt haunted.

Though Shana suddenly worried, *What if we're the ghosts?*

Nessie led her down the two flights of steps, through the lobby, out onto the street. She took a sharp turn around the corner, and the road here took a small incline past some little houses and mountain cottages.

Ahead, she saw a small graveyard encased in a narrow wrought-iron fence. "Nessie, what is this?"

"C'mon, I'll show you."

Nessie took her into the tiny cemetery, most of the headstones old and fallen to disrepair—the names and dates on some lost.

In the very middle sat a big, tan stone. It wasn't the prettiest stone, but Shana found it captivating just the same: The strata of colors were flecked with bits of shiny pyrite, and they glimmered when you moved your head this way and that. Someone, and here Shana recognized Nessie's script even as a carving, had etched a name into the stone:

CHARLIE STEWART, RIP.

The stone sat surrounded by flowers: purple columbines, white laurel, a few devil-red Indian paintbrushes.

"Did you do this?" Shana asked. "You did."

"Yeah."

"When? I . . . I don't understand. It just happened."

Nessie did this thing with her face, an old thing that Shana had forgotten about—but now, seeing this expression, she wanted to die for it, she'd missed it so bad. Nessie's mouth puckered up and twisted off to the side, same way that the Church Lady did in that old *SNL* skit. It wasn't something she did to be funny, it was just one of Nessie's expressions—same as how she always stuck her tongue out when she was handwriting something, or the way when she was frustrated her forehead got those little vees above the nose like hastily sketched seagulls in a cartoonist's drawing.

"Come on," Nessie said. "There're things you need to know."

THEY SAT ON A PARK bench. Others passed on the far side of the street, looking over, giving Shana sad, awkward smiles. Nessie waved to them like she knew them. Shana knew them, too—or knew their faces. There walked Keith Barnes, brother to Kenny, some kind of game designer, if she remembered right. And Jamie-Beth Levine, hair in braids just as it was on the road, except now her eyes were alive and she was eating ice cream out of a dripping cone. Some faces she knew but had no names for except nicknames: Birthmark Girl, Surfer Dude, Mister Manypockets because his pants had, well, shitloads of pockets.

They all had been walkers.

And suddenly, Shana realized they still were.

"I'm a sleepwalker," Shana said. Something she hadn't really figured out until this very moment.

"Yeah."

"Oh."

"Sorry."

"No, it's—it's okay. I guess I'm glad to be with you. I'm glad you're still in here. I . . . I still don't understand it all, though."

Nessie turned toward her, like she was ready to break bad news—or at least some very strange news. "Okay, so, they'll explain it soon—you'll have an orientation, kinda? Julie Barden and Xander Percy will take you and the other newbs and give you the rundown, but I figure we know each other and I can maybe explain some things. The easy things, at least."

"Classic Nessie. You always knew more than I did."

"Yeah, maybe?" Nessie made an awkward sorry-not-sorry face. "I'm not trying to be all Missy Smartybutt or anything."

"No, I'm cool with it. Just tell me what I need to know."

"Well," she began, and now Shana could see the ember-spark burning in Nessie's eyes, because *telling people stuff* was her bread and butter, boy. "Okay! So. First, this isn't real, but it's real. I'm here. But I'm not . . . physically here? It's basically like, *a simulation*—" Shana opened her mouth to ask a question, but Nessie shushed her. "I'll let Julie and Xander explain it because they have a better handle on it. Point is, we're not really in Ouray, Colorado, we're kind of in our own minds. But all our minds are connected! It's . . . cool, though honestly maybe a little scary, too. You get used to it."

"Ooookay."

Shana very seriously wondered if she *would* get used to it.

"Also, time here moves . . . differently. It's linear, I guess? But it doesn't feel the same. Again, Julie and Xander can talk more about it, but it explains why to you Dad just died and to me . . . I've been dealing with it for a while. Feels like . . . weeks. But sometimes it hits me, too, like it just happened, like I'm just watching him . . ."

Nessie's voice choked up. She couldn't continue.

Shana hugged her again.

But then she pulled away. "Wait," she said. "You saw it?"

"I did. A little."

"I'm . . . sorry. I know it's shitty to ask, but how?"

"You can still see the world sometimes. If you try."

"Do I even want to?"

Nessie shrugged. "That's up to you."

"Could you . . . see me?" Shana asked.

"I did. Thanks for staying with me." Nessie snort-laughed—another one of her affectations. Blushing she said, "I also saw you with that *boy*."

"Arav, yeah, I had forgotten . . ."

A new tidal wave of memory crashed down upon her. *Arav.* Her hands instantly moved to her belly and clutched it. "Oh. Oh God, shit, shit, shit. I'm pregnant, Nessie. I didn't—I don't know what happens now."

Nessie, wide-eyed, showed that she didn't know, either. "You're . . . pregnant? Like, pregnant-pregnant?"

Shana stood and paced. Worry chased her like a pack of wolves. What did that mean for the baby? Nessie leapt up, stood in front of her, stopped her from pacing. "This isn't good, Ness."

"Okay. Chill. Hold on. Maybe it'll all be okay."

"How? *How?*"

"We're . . . meant to survive. That disease, White Mask, it . . . it can't touch us in here. It broke my heart because you were out there in the world, and the world was dying like it's *The Stand*—I knew I was safe, and you were protecting me, but that meant you'd *die*. But now? Now you're *here*. And if you're pregnant . . . well, maybe that means the baby will be okay, too. Maybe Black Swan will protect you both."

"Black Swan." She looked up. The dark shape coiled and uncoiled with the crawling speed of drifting clouds. "Is that Black Swan?"

Nessie smiled and nodded.

"Okay," Shana said. She felt a little calmer. Maybe things would be okay. *Even though Dad is still dead. And Arav is gone and dying. The world is going to hell. I don't even know where Mom is.* All those thoughts were thoughts she had to willfully push backward, even though they kept threatening to roll back and crush her.

"I love you, Shana."

"I love you, too, Nessie." She gently bonked her forehead against Nessie's. "So, uh. What happens now?"

"We could go get some ice cream."

"Is it real ice cream?"

"Does it matter, if it tastes real?"

Shana guessed that no, it did not.

TIME DID INDEED MOVE STRANGELY. Even as she ate the ice cream, still tasting the chocolate on her tongue, still feeling the waffle texture of the cone in her hand, she also found herself sitting inside the Walsh Library, housed inside the building that was also the city hall and the community center *and* the local fire department. (It also looked, for reasons unknown to her, a lot like Independence Hall in Philadelphia, a place Shana had been to a few times on various school field trips. Maybe it was a quirk of this simulated world.)

Inside the library, shelves were stacked tall against the walls and long windows. Most of the books looked old, their spines fraying. A children's section sat in the back corner, the walls in Easter-egg pastels, with paintings of cute animals all around, all reading books. A floppy-eared bunny in overalls reading *Watership Down*. (*A little on-the-nose*, she thought.) A dalmatian in a fireman's outfit reading *Fahrenheit 451*. (*A little creepy*.) A deer sitting on a stump, reading *The Yearling*. (*Way they painted that deer, it looks more like he's sitting on a toilet than a stump*.)

Again, that odd out-of-sync thing hit her—she blinked and felt the chocolate ice cream still melting on her tongue, even though it had been hours, or felt like hours, since she'd stopped eating it.

Shana was alone for a while in here, smelling the musty-dusty book-mold smell—but eventually the wooden doors at the front opened with a merry groan. Nessie was first through the door.

And then came some familiar faces.

"Mia!" Shana said, leaping up so fast she damn near knocked over her chair. "Aliya!" *Mia and Aliya, holy shit.* The two lit up when they saw her, hurrying over. The three of them crashed together in a seismic hug.

"Is any of this real?" Aliya asked.

Mia screwed up her face and shrugged. "Yo, I don't even care. Maybe this is Heaven, right? I saw Mateo! *You guys, I saw Mateo.* This sure as fuck feels like Heaven, I gotta tell you."

"This isn't the Heaven I was told about," Aliya said, "but maybe. I haven't seen Tasha yet, though." Shana wondered: Was Tasha still alive? Those snipers took out shepherds and walkers alike. But she didn't want to say anything about that, not yet . . .

"Guys," Shana said. "I think we're walkers now. We're damn sure not shepherds anymore."

"Maybe the walkers have been in Heaven the whole time," Mia said with a shrug. "Maybe Marcy was right. Maybe they're angels."

"Maybe *we're* angels," Aliya corrected.

"Does that mean we're dead?"

"I don't think so—" Shana started to say, even as other faces of other shepherds appeared. Here came Carl Carter, and Mary-Louise Hinton, and John Hernandez. Plus a few more she didn't know—maybe they were shepherds, too, but she didn't recognize them.

Nessie, appearing at her elbow, pointed to two more coming in—one, a raven-haired white woman in a blue sundress, the other an older black man, bald on top but with a big salt-and-pepper beard hiding his neck. Nessie whispered, "That's Julie and that's Xander."

Sure enough, the two people introduced themselves as Julie Barden and Alexander—Xander—Percy.

They asked that everyone find a chair. Which they did. Shana pulled over one from the kids' section—it was too small for her but she managed.

Everyone sat around Julie and Xander as they spoke.

"Welcome to Ouray, Colorado," Julie said, a slight southern twang to her voice. Reminded Shana of that actress, what was her name? Holly Hunter. "Or at least, a simulation of it. You're all part of the flock, now."

A few gasps went around the room. Some shared uncomfortable looks, as if unsure if this was even real.

Xander said: "I know. It's a shock. It was for me, too. I was a professor of theoretical physics, so I'm used to some weird shit, and *this* shit is maybe a little too weird for me."

He had an easy, avuncular way—everyone chuckled.

"You think it's weird for him, try being a brain surgeon," Julie said. That didn't earn as many laughs, but Shana thought, *That's being a woman for you, the man always gets the good lines.* Julie continued: "Even though the brain remains a mysterious organ in a lot of ways, we understood it. Or, I suppose, we thought we did. What's happening here—that we all seem to be experiencing a shared reality, a simulated one—is something that goes beyond my comprehension, but here we are."

"The good news," Xander said, "is that we are all survivors."

Julie: "But it's also the bad news. The disease known as White Mask, caused by a fungal pathogen called *Rhizopus destructans,* is going to decimate the global population. But we, the flock, are protected by the grace of Black Swan, an artificial intelligence inhabiting our bodies and brains with a connected swarm of infinitesimal machines existing at nanoscale."

"Robots," Shana said, and suddenly the chocolate ice cream taste in her mouth came again, but this time its sweetness was unsettling. Nausea swept over her in a feverish wave. "You're talking about little robots."

"That's right," Xander said. "Robots."

"Black Swan is a *robot?*" Mia said, looking confused.

"No," Julie answered. "Black Swan is less a machine and more an intelligence—a sentient piece of software that has inhabited a piece of hardware. In this case, a swarm of nanoscale robots."

"Whaaaaat the fuck," Mia said, in her classic Mia way. She sounded equally wowed and horrified by this.

Carl Carter, an avuncular, ginger-haired man in tortoiseshell spectacles— once a shepherd, like Shana and the others, a shepherd whose wife left him alone here to watch over their daughter, Elsa—raised an index finger in the air. "So . . . this town isn't real?"

"Not the one you see here," Xander explained. "This one is a simulated version, but Ouray is a real town in the mountains of Colorado."

Julie: "That's right. Black Swan has graciously given us a simulation of the town so that we may grow acclimated to it. Though the simulation is imperfect, the virtual shared reality of it will allow us to settle into its layout, its architecture, its *feel*."

"Why would they do that?" Carl asked.

"Because this will one day be our home," she said.

Xander, smiling: "I see some of you are having a hard time taking that in. I still wrestle with it. Make no mistake, the end of the world has begun. White Mask will sweep across the globe and in just a few short months, humankind will have been wiped out—or would have been, if it were not for the benevolence of Black Swan. Black Swan has given us a way to survive. But it would be foolish to think of us only as survivors."

"We are colonists," Julie said. "The settlers of a fallen world."

Aliya burst out weeping. Shana moved her chair closer to her, put an arm around her. "It's okay, it's okay," she whispered to Aliya.

Xander: "It's shocking. And I know it's sad. But I want you to look at the positive side: We have all been selected by the machine. It believes that we are the best of the best. It coordinated its path to find us. We are a mix of wonderful minds, the smartest and most innovative. Healthy, stable, capable. Black Swan has designed a future for humanity, and we are it."

"I'm not it," Shana said, abruptly.

Eyes turned toward her.

"Black Swan didn't select me. It couldn't have or I would've been one of you from the beginning, because my sister here was the first. I was a shepherd. Like others here. If we're here, it's because . . . like in gym class, we were the last picks available. Wasn't anybody left."

"Oh shit," Mia said.

"We're the dregs," Aliya said. "Bottom of the barrel."

Xander smiled that uncle's smile of his. He walked forward and put both hands on Shana's shoulders. "Shana, you don't have to worry. You've been selected. You're chosen. Black Swan would not have brought you in here if it did not think you would be a valuable part of the future—you did your work as a shepherd, you proved yourself to all of us, and now?" He spread his arms out like a preacher asking the parishioners to behold the expanse of Heaven above. "And now you are one of us."

One of us, Shana thought.

She wasn't quite sure what to make of that.

"Look at it this way," Julie said, addressing them all. "Black Swan has diligently planned for the future. We are all part of what we call the Calculation. We are numbers in a great equation, and if those numbers don't add up, the equation won't balance. Worse, if we're variables—unknown quantities whose value is shifting—then the future becomes a dangerous mystery, not a certain reality."

Shana took a step back. She felt the hairs on her neck—*though I suppose they're not really my hairs, they're just my mind's imagining of the hairs on my neck*—rise up.

"People aren't numbers," she said. "We're all variables. No machine can know our hearts. We're not just our professions or our SAT scores."

"Black Swan has done the Calculation," Xander said. "Of course we're not all one thing, but we have to trust in this community. We have to trust that Black Swan chose wisely."

"And if it didn't choose wisely?"

Julie: "You know, Shana, trust me when I say, the human brain is not particularly flexible. I don't mean literally! I mean, the mind, our personalities, our demeanors. We are who we are. Our genetic code and our environment make us, and by the time we enter our teens . . . the cement may not be all the way dry, but it hardens up pretty quick. Black Swan knows this. Like Xander says: We have to trust in Black Swan."

Shana put her hands on her hips, defiant. "*How* do you know this? How do you know *any* of this?"

A strange smile crept across Julie's face.

"We've gone up there."

"Gone up . . . where?"

"To Black Swan. To speak with it."

"I don't . . . I don't know what the hell that means."

Xander: "It means if you follow the winding path up to the top of the western peak, you too can commune with Black Swan. Many of us have made the pilgrimage. You can, too, if you want, Shana."

She placated him with a small smile, then she sat down and shut up.

AFTERWARD, SHANA PULLED HER SISTER aside as the others came out of the library. They were laughing and smiling. But Shana didn't feel so giddy.

Nessie gave her a look. "What's wrong?"

"You didn't go up there, did you?" Shana asked, sotto voce.

"Up where?"

"To see the—" She made an awkward nodding gesture with her face to indicate *up, up, up*. "To see the wizard behind the curtain."

"Oh. No. Not yet."

"Good."

"Why is that good?"

"Nessie, this is all pretty fucked up."

"Well, I mean, yeah. No doy. We're all mentally linked by an artificially intelligent swarm of nanobots inside a simulation of the mountain town where we will weather the Apocalypse. It doesn't get much weirder than that, Shana."

"Apparently it *does*. Listen, just don't . . . go up there without saying something to me, first. You promise?"

Nessie hesitated, and Shana urged her:

"Ness, *promise* me."

"I promise." Nessie glanced nervously over Shana's shoulder. "Hey, sis, there's, um. There's one more thing."

"One more thing what?"

"That I have to tell you. Or show you. Or *someone* I have to tell you about and, uhh. Show you."

"You're not making any sense. There's someone you want me to meet?"

"Yes. Sort of. Though you've already—"

Shana got the sense suddenly that they were not alone. Someone was right behind her. It wasn't a sound, it wasn't even the shadow—it was a presence, like the way a TV on in a nearby room may have the volume down, but there's a white noise to it that lets you know it's there, and it's on.

This was like that.

She turned around to see just who had joined them.

She stared. The world seemed to fall away. *Everything* faded except the view of the person standing there in front of her.

"Mom?" Shana said.

PART SIX

LAST DAYS OF
THE LONG WALK

62

PAVEMENT ENDS

Supreme Court Gives Election to Republican Ed Creel

By Bryan Whyte, *Boston Globe*

With Vice President John Oshiro missing—along with the rest of the line of presidential successors within former president Hunt's cabinet—the Supreme Court today gave the election early to GOP nominee Ed Creel in a 4 to 3 decision . . . Creel will give his "victory speech" later today from his location on the campaign trail in Kansas . . .

OCTOBER 13
Hector, California

"AND ONCE THEY'D HEAPED THE MOUND, THEY TURNED BACK HOME TO TROY, AND gathering once again they shared a splendid funeral feast in Hector's honor, held in the house of Priam, king by will of Zeus." Landry said those words, staring out the window at the passing sleepwalker flock, moving as they were through the wind-whipped desert of salt and sand. Past little clapboard houses and double-wide trailers. Past mailboxes on bent posts and sunbaked patio furniture. Past the cactuses. Past a couple of stray dogs. Past an old man on his porch, his head in an old diving bell helmet—maybe he was alive and watching them, or maybe he was dead in there. Landry sighed and added: *"And so the Trojans buried Hector, breaker of horses."*

Pete sniffed. He kicked through the trash on the floor of the RV—the Beast, Charlie Stewart's old ride—same way you might wade through the colored balls in a playground ball pit. Mounding around his ankles were the packaging from chocolate bars, potato chip bags, condom wrappers, bottles of top-shelf lube, a mink stole, the plastic clamshell that once held a thin pink vibrator, shitty porn mags (gay and straight because fuck it), countless little baggies that once held some of the finest hydroponic Cali-marijuana, a few bottles of the hoitiest-and-toitiest Champagne (now empty), pages and pages of sheet music, and, perhaps puzzlingly, the box to a brand-new Singer sewing machine because Landry said he had always wanted to learn to sew, goddamnit, so he was going to learn to stitch a motherfucker. "Like the damn pioneers," he said. As if that explained it.

"The hell are you going on about over there?" Pete asked.

"It's literature, fool. *The Iliad.* Get cultured."

"The only culture I care to get is the kind that swabs our faceholes to see if we're sick. We're not sick this morning, are we?"

Landry turned away from the window. "No, not yet. You?"

"Not yet, love."

"It's coming, though, isn't it? You and me with the sniffles." Landry wore a grim mask. "Then the *crazies*. Then the dying shit."

Idly, Pete thought: Wasn't there a movie like that? *The Crazies.* Seventies-era. Bioweapon test in a small town made everybody bonkers. Turned into murderers or something. "We don't know that."

"Yeah. Well. I know how this goes. It's like HIV all over again."

Pete rolled his eyes. "You're, what, thirty-two years old? Christ, mate, you were a kid during the epidemic. Me, I had to worry. I had a family. Sleeping around on the side, worrying about bringing *that bug* home—God, fuck. Herpes is one thing. Crabs, well, who doesn't enjoy some nice seafood? But the High-Five? Fuck. *Fuck.* It'd be like forgetting your luggage on the plane but bringing home a goddamn suitcase nuke instead."

"Speaking of your fam." Landry leaned in. "You still wanna do this?"

"It's what you want, innit?"

"It is. But that doesn't mean it's what *you* want."

Pete thought about it. Truth was, he didn't really know. But he didn't have time to piss around. "I'm sure. This is it." He looked around at the sea of garbage around his feet. "Besides, I think we've, ahh, hit the limits of our hedonism, Landry, my love."

Landry stood up and took his hands. The man had only grown more lean and angular as the weeks went on—they'd committed to enjoying their last days by eating and drinking and fucking their way toward happy oblivion. Pete felt like he'd put on a few pounds, his muscle tone gone the way of soggy gym socks. But Landry didn't go the same way. He was lean and mean. He was all cheekbones and hipbones. All tight tendons and taut muscles. Gods, he was beautiful.

Thing was, their hedonism had limits. Honestly, they hit those limits after the first few nights of it—sick on junk food, having fucked their way through half a dozen very difficult sexual positions, they tried drinking and smoking and it made them giddy, sure, but it also seemed somehow hollow. Like they were throwing shovelfuls of earth into a bottomless pit. It felt productive at first, but soon you figured out that nothing was changing.

They kept going. For a few weeks. Just for the spirit of the thing. And maybe, just maybe, because they didn't want to admit it wasn't working.

That's when Pete had the idea.

(Well, it was Landry who brought it up, but Pete who made the plan.)

"You going to tell Doctor Ray now?" Landry asked. "It's time."

"Yeah." He rubbed his eyes with the heels of his hands. "Fuck."

Landry kissed his chin. "Go get him, Rockgod."

Out the RV he went.

THINGS HAD FUCKING CHANGED.

It was funny how a lot of that faded into the background, but sometimes, like today, Pete found himself jarringly aware of those changes—it was like, most of his life he smoked cigarettes, then he quit, and over time he thought the ghost of nicotine addiction had finally stopped haunting him. But once in a while the specter returned, rising up out of the dark and wailing in his ear, and before he knew it he'd need a cigarette the way one dog needed the scent of another dog's nethers—and *instantly* he'd be reminded how the comfort of that addiction was a part of him. The memory of it. The piece of him that had gone missing. The way he smoked on his balcony, the feeling of crispy paper between his lips, the burning pleasure-cloud that filled the lungs.

This was like that. The way things were—the comfort of the addiction of modern, normal life—had drastically fucked off to places unknown. It would, Pete suspected, never return. And it wasn't just modern life: It was the flock itself. The shepherds had winnowed. They were down to a few dozen, now. Fewer vehicles. Fewer people. Now they carried weapons: rifles, pistols, knives. They hadn't gone full Mad Max or anything, but some had armored their campers and cars and trucks with sheet metal and trash can lids and the like. The shepherds walked with the wary face of someone who had been in—and was still in—a war zone, scanning the horizon instead of talking and laughing, watching the road and the hills for an ambush instead of braiding one another's hair or whatever the hell normal people did. It wasn't exactly that *innocence was lost* or any of that foofy folderol, but these people had, as the saying went, *seen some shit.* They'd seen some shit. They'd been in the shit.

It was a shit parade. Shit pies for everyone.

Shit, shit, shitty shit.

The doc, Benji, had given them all a speech a week or so after the sniper attack on the bridge of the golden bears. After they lost so many of their own. Some had joined the walkers. Some, like Marcy, were just . . . gone. They looked high and low, but never found hide nor hair of her.

The speech he gave was one where he came clean.

He told them what was really going on.

Pete still wasn't sure how much of it he believed. In his head, he questioned all of it, because it all sounded so fucking fucked, didn't it? The flock, engineered to survive by a—what's that, mate? A *smart computer*? Thinks like a person, or better than a person? Everyone filled up to the brim with itty-bitty drones or iPhones or whatever the hell is inside them? Sounded daft. Something out of a barmy, batshit dime-store novel. And yet, in his heart of hearts, Pete believed the core of it—

The world was dying, but the flock would remain.

Now, as Pete wound his way along the margins of the flock, the Beast parked behind him on the side of the road along this dead-end deeply fucked half-desert town, he felt the same way he felt the day Benji gave that speech. He felt empty. He felt a massive loss. Like there had been a bloodletting of all that was in him.

It was absurd, but the loss that he felt most was the loss of rock-and-roll.

I mean, yes, sure, *music* in general, but really—

Rock-and-fucking-roll.

Rock music was intrinsically human. Not American, no—he thought that, once, but you think that, you'd have to forget you ever heard the Beatles, or Guided by Voices, or Rammstein, or the Scorpions, or gods, what about Babymetal? Japanese bubblegum heavy metal? Brilliant! Or the metal scene out of Botswana (Overthrust!), or those glorious little punk prick bastards out of Myanmar (Rebel Riot!), or that glam-band dream-balladry of that Argentine band that Evil Elvis used to listen to (Babasónicos!).

Rock was rebellion and resistance. It was madness and sanity, rolled up into one. It was equal parts about *sex* and *sticking it to the man.*

(Pete thought: *For me, sex is all about sticking it to the man. Ba-dum-pshh!*)

And soon, rock-and-roll would be gone.

Because it was human. And when humans left, rock went with them.

Sure, the flock would remain, fine, bah, whatever. There was no rock legacy there. Benji said he thought there were a handful of musicians in the batch, and maybe they'd start some Apocalypse Rock gig in the American afterlife, but Pete wouldn't be around to hear it. He wouldn't be around to sing it, or strum it, either.

What was that saying? It was an old quote, some claimed Banksy said it, but Banksy was a rip-off artist like the rest of them. *A man dies twice, once when he stops breathing, next when someone speaks his name for the last time.* Pete's name would be lost quick. The flock wouldn't remember him. Why would they? Why *should* they? He and the rest of Gumdropper would be gone. Their names weren't carved in stone; they were signed in soft mud.

Even now, as he moved toward Benji at the head of the flock, he thought, *Gods, I miss those fuckers.* Gumdropper. Even Evil Elvis, that snide prick. He wondered: Did that bastard have the sniffles yet? Was he dead in his bathtub, his skin home to the fruiting bodies of White Mask? Part of him hoped not. Part of him missed his old friend, missed the way those magic fingers played the Stratocaster like he was an angel with a harp.

Another part of him thought, *Well, fuck that, and fuck him.*

Life was too short, literally now, to worry about that wanker.

He had other things to worry about.

Like telling Benji the news.

Ahead, Benji had a map stretched out across the hood of a blue van—a van that belonged to one of the newer shepherds, if Pete remembered correctly. The map, Pete saw, was of the American Southwest. A road map, but topographic, too. The puckered lines of mountains, the puffy green pockets of forests, the long stretches of dead-ass desert.

That's what Benji was looking at. Sadie stood on one side, Arav on the other. Arav's earliest days back with the flock had him stuffed in one of those crazy CDC hazmat suits from the lab trailer—him walking around like he was one of the bad government guys hunting E.T. or something. Now the kid had settled for something less conspicuous: a ruggedized Honeywell rubber respirator mask, black as Vader's armor but with two purple filter bulbs sticking out at off-angles. When he spoke, it was muffled, mumbly.

Benji was saying, "These next couple of weeks are going to be hard. The path to Ouray, according to Black Swan, takes us past the Calico Mountains, up along the edge of the Mojave, past the Hollow Hills. From there, into Nevada—we leave Highway 15 and circumvent Las Vegas, head past Lake Mead, then back to 15, after which we snip off the corner of Arizona for a short trip and then, Utah. Nevada and Utah are going to be tough. Hot days, cold nights. Not a lot of water. Not a lot of towns."

"Not a lot of fuck-all," Pete said, interrupting. "Not by the look of it, at least."

Sadie said: "I've driven through there. It's pretty. It's also pretty desolate. Benji's right—we'll need to stock up. Water, food, sunscreen—"

"Ammunition," Arav said. Pete noticed the bulge of a pistol at the boy's hip, hiding in a black polyester holster tucked under his white tee.

"Settle down, Clint Eastwood," Pete said. "Ease off the throttle."

"We need to be ready. That means being armed."

"You barely know how to use that thing."

"I've been practicing."

"Yes, I've seen your 'practicing,' and I assure you, all the *unbroken* bottles and *unperforated* soup cans would like to thank you."

Arav puffed up his chest and started in with, "You don't understand, because you're not really *committed* to protecting this flock and—"

"All right," Sadie said. Arav didn't back down so she said it again, louder this time: "All! Right! *Relax*. Can't really protect the flock if we kill each other. The flock is going with or without us, so let's get prepared."

Benji nodded, arms crossed. "We'll get some of the other shepherds on board and leave the flock in shifts to get supplies. Presently, some can work backward toward Barstow and scan the grocery stores and gas stations. I can't get a signal out here to check the internet—" As it turned out, the internet did not simply turn off with societal collapse; it just became difficult to access and far, far quieter. "But Black Swan is a satphone and can still interface maps and other regional data. Barstow being Barstow, it's home to three different gun stores, so assuming they have not been plundered already, those are targets, as well. Pete, given the size of Charlie's old camper, I'd like to recruit you to head to Barstow and—"

"Ahhh. About that."

The three of them raised eyebrows and looked at him expectantly.

"Benjamin," Pete said, injecting his voice with some overdramatic formality, "can I speak to you, ahh, privately?"

• • •

"You're running away," Benji said. His voice was calm, but his mouth formed an angry line across his face.

The two of them stood in front of a broken-up white brick building—the fading paint on the side of the crumbling stone said MINE STORE. A lone cactus had taken up residence inside the rubble, standing vigil.

"What?" Pete said. "Am not."

"So you're *not* leaving?"

"Whuh—well, I, yuhhh, nnnn—"

"You're leaving."

"Yes! Yes, we're leaving. Landry and I are leaving."

"Fine, then go," Benji said, waving him off and turning to head back to the receding flock. But then he seemed to swiftly reconsider, and he wheeled on Pete, fury arcing in each eye like a firing spark plug. "No, you know what? I've got your number. I see you, Pete Corley. You came here for the attention, for the media and the fans and the . . . the fucking Instagram pics and adoring tweets and all those precious cookies. But you came here, too, running away from something. From *everything*. From your band, your family, your responsibilities. When the shit started splattering around here, you ponied up. You did right. Helped me save some people. And even though you and your boy-toy in there have been living it up in your little end-of-the-world pity-party, you've still found time to help out, and I appreciate that. But we're not done. We have farther to go before we can stop. The shepherds are dwindling. I can't lose people. I can't have you slinking away like some scared little cat. There's nowhere to run to, *Rockgod*. This? Is it. This? Is *home*. So you know what, I revoke my permission to leave. Stow that shit in some deep hole within yourself, because you're staying, and you're helping these people get to Ouray, Colorado."

Silence stretched out between them like a long, empty road.

As if for drama, a wind kicked up, sending serpents of sand slithering between the two men.

"That was very good," Pete said, finally, giving a clipped nod. "It was very—you know, it was very *tough guy,* very *grr, stern.* I approve. *Shit this* and *fuck that.* I assume you didn't practice it, so, well done."

Pete clapped in slow applause.

Benji said, quite earnestly, "Thank you."

Then the two of them laughed a little. The tension bubble didn't pop entirely, but a little air crept out of it.

"Listen, I'm not running away. If anything, I'm trying to do . . . the opposite of that. I need to *un*-run-away, I need to . . . go home. I've decided—ahh, we've decided, Landry and me—to go find my family."

"Oh."

"Yeah."

"*Oh.*" Benji looked dubious. "Both of you? Together?"

"When you say it out loud like that, I *do* hear how gabbling mad it sounds. Shit."

"I thought your family had . . . gone off without you? And they don't know about . . . your other deal."

"The rampant homosexuality? They don't know. Maybe Lena suspects. Christ, maybe she's known all along, I dunno."

"This a good idea?"

"No? Probably not? But they're my family. I've screwed this all up. I should've been with them when this hit. I don't even know—" Human feelings reminded him that he was in fact human and that felt ew, gross, yucky, so he tried very hard to tamp it down. "I don't even know if they're all right. Her family's rich and I like to think they'll be out of the path of this thing, but . . ."

"White Mask's brutal. Its path is wide."

"Yeah." He clucked his tongue. "Yeah, it is. So—I have to do this. I've got to go and find them. Tell them the truth. See if . . . they'll still accept me, and have me, *and* have Landry. I love them, but I'm *in* love with him. Maybe we can all live in some weird polyamorous love-cult." Pete held up both hands as if in warning. "I mean, not my kids. They can just be the strange children of a completely fucked-up family. Which, given that it's the end of the world, is probably the least fucked-up thing, so."

"There's that."

"There's that, indeed." Pete put a hand out on Benji's shoulder. "I just need them to know who I am. And that I give a shit. Right now, gods, if they're even alive, they probably hate me. And they should."

They really fucking should.

"Damnit, Pete."

"I know."

"I was just getting around to liking you."

"Pfah. You liked me from the very beginning."

"Well, you're a likable guy."

"A likable asshole, really, but it's an angle, and I stick to it."

Benji shifted from foot to foot. "You leaving now?"

"Soon, I think. We've got some miles ahead of us."

"About three thousand, I believe."

Pete offered a hand. "Thanks, Doc."

Benji shook it. "Go be with your family, Rockgod."

"Ah, fuck it," Pete said, then hugged him. He held the hug for a while. Too long, really, long enough to make it weird. But that was who he was, and maybe, he hoped, it would be what ended up on his gravestone.

Here lies Pete Corley.

He lived too long, really.

Long enough to make it weird.

RIFP.

LATER, WHEN THE FLOCK HAD gone on past the asphalt, onto a part of the road that went to gravel past a bullet-pocked sign that read PAVEMENT ENDS, Pete saddled up in the driver's seat of the Beast.

"Why'd you say that shit earlier?" he asked Landry. "All that mythological business. *The Iliad* or whatever it was."

"Because, you illiterate fool, we're in Hector, California, and the bit I said was about Hector, the Trojan prince, enemy to Achilles. We'd just had our own funeral feast, too, what with all the junk food. You'll notice I threw all that shit away, by the way."

"Thank you."

"You're welcome."

"We really doing this?" Pete asked, suddenly unsure.

"We are, cocksucker. We got gas in the tank, gas in the secondary tank, we got shitty road food, and, permit me to be a little romantic, we got each other."

"That's sweet."

"I know. I'll rot your teeth I'm so sweet. I'm *basically* cotton candy."

"We are missing one thing, though."

Landry arched an eyebrow. "Oh?"

"Oh yeah."

Pete, from a cubby in the dash, pulled a cassette tape, spinning it between two fingers. "Tunes, motherfucker. We are missing that most vital ingredient: *rock-and-roll as we roll down the rockin' road*."

He eased the tape into the cassette player, then finished the job with a sinister push of his long, talonlike index finger. The tape clicked and whirred, and from the tinny speakers of the Beast's stereo roared forth the fifth studio album from Gumdropper, *Miracle Mile*. The guitar on the title track kicked up, and Pete sang along as he revved the engine.

The Beast roared, and leapt to its journey.

63

THE WHETTING STONE

THREAD ON CREEL: *It's all bullshit. We'd be marching in the streets if that didn't mean we'd all get White Mask. Ed Creel is a fascist. He bought his way in. (1/?)*

|

Here's what I heard: He has a compound out in Kansas, one of those ex-missile-silo "survival compounds," condos for the richest preppers. You can google them if you still have internet. (2/?)

|

If anybody is alive to follow the money, I heard if you follow it, it ends up in the pockets of those Supreme Court justices. (3/?)

|

And if you wanna know where Oshiro and the Successors are? Smart money says they're all dead, too. That or they fucked off to their own prepper domain, some island somewhere (4/?)

|

To sum up: #NotMyPresident—not that anything matters anymore. But fuck Creel and his racist ARM army. See you in the quarantine centers. Or the grave. The end. (5/5)

@sarah_parnelli
14 replies 17 RTs 52 likes

OCTOBER 14
Innsbrook, Missouri

MATTHEW BIRD STARED THROUGH THE RIFLESCOPE. HE'D BEEN LOOKING through it for God knows how long now—ten minutes, twenty, forty, two days, two weeks, an eternity. Least, that's how it felt. (And of course he now knew that really, God didn't know the answer, either, because God was dead. Maybe God had existed once. But it was easier to believe that He had died not *for* our sins but rather, *because* of them. It was better *that* than accept He would allow all this horror to happen to the world of men.)

Across the lake water, he watched the docks in the glass of the scope, letting the crosshairs drift over the shirtless boys and teen girls in their underwear jumping off into the water. They were kids of what was now called the ARM, or American Resurrection Movement—that being Creel's army, formed of the white supremacist and supposedly Christian militias that joined forces in the wake of White Mask to seize control of a crumbling nation. Matthew wasn't sure what those kids were like. Were they living in blissful oblivion, enjoying life as it was in the protected resort area here in Innsbrook? Or were they the modern equivalent of Hitler Youths, smiling and laughing and playing only when they weren't out there on the streets in gas masks and fatigues, firing on anybody who didn't look like them?

The crosshairs hovered over them. One by one.

Once in a while, Matthew's finger twitched, as if eager.

And whenever it did, he coiled it inward, pulling it tight against his palm. Just to make sure he didn't accidentally discharge the weapon. Matthew never put his finger *on* the trigger, but he had this mad fear it would (if he stopped paying attention for just long enough) move of its own volition to the trigger, giving it a quick and irreversible tug. Then he'd have to watch one of those teens fall to the ground, the others around them flecked with their bloody remains.

It was a mad, bizarre thought, straddling the line between fear and fantasy. Whenever Matthew slept, he dreamed of that sort of thing. Nightmares of Stover holding him down and forcing his mouth open, ripping his pants off. Dreams of Matthew going after that big monster with all manner of implements: a screwdriver, a bolt cutter, a brûlée torch, a mallet and chisel hammered under an exposed kneecap . . .

Focus, he told himself. *You're here for a reason.*

"See him?" Autumn asked. She sat on the ground behind him, hunkered there under some understory shrub, the trees above blotting out the sky with an autumnal canopy of reds and yellows.

Matthew lay there on his belly, the rifle barrel the only thing emerging from the brush. He shook his head. "No."

"I'll take a shift. Let me."

"I can keep looking."

"You're tired. You've been at this for an hour."

So that was how long. God didn't know. Autumn did. Since their escape from Stover's compound that day, they'd found . . . well, he didn't know what to call it, precisely. Common ground, maybe. A place where the past didn't matter. She got clean off drugs. He got clean off religion. Neither asked the other about what went on there, and neither told the other a damn thing, either, unless it related to their son. Because Bo was why they were here. They needed their son back.

"Your hand," she said. "Is it okay?"

"It hurts." And it did. Matthew's left hand was a useless claw. His fingers tucked into the palm. He could move them, but not without considerable misery. The whole hand was an antenna receiving signals of pain. Even a cool breeze summoned needles of agony.

He set the rifle down, easing it into the brush against the carpet of dead leaves underneath. He eased back, wincing. She helped him.

"Bo isn't there," he said. "We've been watching this spot for a week, and he's just not . . . with those kids." He scooched his butt backward through the crunching leaves to be next to his wife. "We have to find another way."

"Do you think he's even in there?"

He closed his eyes for a moment. Not to sleep. Just to shut out the world. Behind his eyes, the dappled forest light formed tortoiseshell patterns. "I don't know, Autumn. Honestly, I don't. He was close with Ozark. Maybe he still is."

"I have faith we'll find him."

"Faith. Okay." He heard the disdain in his own voice and instantly regretted it. But he didn't walk it back, either. He was too tired for that.

"We'll find him, and we'll save him," she said.

And he believed her.

Because though he had lost his faith in God, he had given it to Autumn. *In Autumn, I trust.*

Back when they'd come roaring out of Stover's compound in Hiram Golden's Lexus, Autumn was kind enough to give him a couple of days to recover. They didn't go home; they were afraid Ozark would find them there. Instead, they holed up in various motels, paying in cash, driving through a world *then* that looked on the brink, but that hadn't yet fallen over the edge. The lights were still on. Life looked normal at a distance, even though when you looked close you could see the panic and the chaos setting in.

And then one night, Autumn said to him:

"We're going to go get Bo."

And he said, "Let's say we find him. Then what? You need to deal with the reality that maybe our son isn't the boy we wanted him to be. That maybe we failed him in some very crucial, very fundamental ways."

"We loved him."

"Love sometimes isn't enough."

"Love has to be enough."

Then she said: "You're right that we failed him. I wasn't there for him because I was lost to something that you wouldn't help with. And you were lost to something, too—lost to your church, to your faith. But we aren't lost anymore. We're out here. Stripped down, cut to the bone, in a world that's going fast to hell, but we're together, and our son is out there, and we owe him the best we have now. You were not a great husband. You were not a great father. But you're going to be now. Everything else is coming apart, but we are going to do the opposite. We are going to come together."

Then she asked him: "Do you understand?"

And he did, and he said as much.

Now here they were.

Sometimes, he had doubts. The world was . . . sick. And dying. There was no America anymore. Listen to the radio—one of the only ways to get news, now—and you'd hear that the rest of the world had lost its damn mind—warlords in Africa taking over, the Chinese government locking people up in case they were sick, and Russia just straight up executing them in the streets. They'd met people on the road who were fleeing toward Canada. Crossing the border and heading north to hide. He and Autumn were healthy and at one point he thought to ask her if they should do that, too, but then he stopped himself. She had her resolve. Her mission.

It was his mission, now, too. For too long he'd set the story of their family and their household, and he'd screwed it all up.

In Autumn, I trust.

God would not save them or their boy.

So they had to.

Matthew pulled the rifle closer to him.

"I think I have an idea," he said.

THE RITUAL

Tumblr: Deathstar_Runner.tumblr.com

 Is anyone even out there anymore? It's weird that the internet has gone quiet. I mean, I know some of you are out there because you're re-blogging this and whatever but it's like, I dunno. Not as many as before. I'm still fine. Not sick. My mom isn't sick either and my dad got sick years ago with cancer so he ducked out early, lol. We mostly just hide here in our house. Everything locked up. I hear gunshots a lot. I'm still gonna run the fanfic archive long as I can because if all we have until the lights go out is our fics then that's what we have and that's okay by me. Love you all.

Source: *deathstar-runner.tumblr.com*

1,400 notes

OCTOBER 14
Halloran Springs, California

ACCIDENTS HAPPENED HERE WITH GREATER FREQUENCY THAN ANYWHERE else they'd seen on this highway. It was plain enough to see: At this spot, I-15 bent just so, more the gentle bend of a crooked arm than a hard angle, but it must've been enough. Because at that gentle bend sat over a dozen makeshift memorials: some in Spanish, others in English, wreaths of plastic carnations and crosses made of wood, red candles melted to the mouths and necks of green beer bottles. The names of the dead came with earnest, honest messages: WE MISS YOU, BILLY; I LOVE YOU, BABY DOLL; EN MEMORIA DE NUESTRA QUERIDA TIO, QEPD; WHY'D YOU FUCKIN DIE ON US, EARL???; and on, and on. Grief and anger at the loss.

 Sadie was the one who figured it out. "It's about halfway between Los

Angeles and Las Vegas. Leave Vegas late, still drunk, and in the half dark even a small turn in the road becomes something you miss—instead of following it, you drive off the road. Probably into an arroyo or into a massive saguaro cactus." The guardrail that was here was erupted, torn asunder— Benji thought idly that it reminded him of the cell walls he'd found in Clade Berman's remains. From when the itty-bitty little machines fired out of his body like microscopic howitzer rounds.

Benji nodded and smiled, the plastic baggie in his hand shifting and crinkling as he turned it over and over again. "That makes sense. You have a keenly analytical mind. And I'm supposed to be the detective."

"You would've figured it out," she said, false cheer in her voice. "You and I are different, I think. You've got your mind on other things. Meanwhile, I'll do anything—anything at all!—to *not* think about those other things. You're a laser focus. I'm a laser light show, more like."

"Laser light shows are dazzling," he said.

"I'm afraid I'm dazzled, not dazzling." She did a game-show-hostess reveal of her body, covered in the red dust of the desert. Her hair was untamed, somehow both frizzy and flat in the dry air. A sweatshirt gathered around her waist in a clumsy sleeve-knot. Cargo pants held pockets that, she joked, were finally in use for the first time in human history, keeping all manner of supplies stuffed into them, from tools to snack packets to flat packs of cheap fruit juice ("high-fructose corn syrup, really," she said).

The urge hit him to disagree, to argue, even, about how she *was* dazzling—beautiful despite the dust, gorgeous no matter the bulging cargo pants. But that wasn't who they were anymore, so he shoved the urge away.

Above, vultures wheeled in the sky.

Like they were waiting for something, impatient and expectant.

Waiting for us to just give up and die, he thought.

Together Sadie and Benji stood temporarily alone. The flock was about a mile up the road. They'd catch up.

But first came their ritual.

They did this once a week. Together they found a spot away from the other shepherds, away from the walkers.

Sometimes at night, so it was dark.

Today they would perform this ritual in the morning. Above the horizon, the sun hid behind flat, saucer-shaped clouds. A lavender gleam glinted off them like the shine of polished nickel, serving only to further that UFO look. It gave the sense that an invasion was unfolding.

Maybe, Benji thought, *it is.*

Behind him stood an abandoned building: Above it towered a skeletal arrow-shaped sign that red NED'S GAS, and underneath it in rusted red: GIFTS, 24-HR TOWING, EAT. The arrow pointed to the building, which was once a gas station, a convenience store, a restaurant, *and* a garage.

This place died long before White Mask came to America. It was at least ten years dead. Maybe twenty.

"Ready?" Benji asked.

Sadie forced a smile. "Ready as Betty and Freddy going steady."

Benji gave her a curious look. She shrugged.

And in they went.

TIME HAD PRESERVED THE INSIDE of the building better than he had expected. Yes, it was dust-swept and wind-worn, the windows long broken, the chrome of stools and tables and counters gone to rust. But otherwise it felt eerily preserved. Nothing inside was broken. The linoleum wasn't ripped up, nor were the walls. Benji half expected graffiti everywhere, and drug needles on the ground next to old, desiccated condoms. But no—the place was largely untouched. A soda counter, store, and restaurant still serving the Mojave ghosts. Travelers traversing the highways and byways of the dead.

Like us, maybe.

"Over here?" Sadie asked, pulling a stool away from the counter. "It's flat, at least. Or we could find a booth—"

"No," he said abruptly, *too* abruptly. *We're not on a date,* he told himself. "The counter is fine." He sidled up next to her and sat.

There he saw that the counter was once marked up by those who visited the place—whether as patrons or after the place had been abandoned, he didn't know. He saw names and phone numbers, expressions of love and lust. LOVE YOU, LADYBIRD. And REESE LOVES JERICHO. And MIRIAM <3 GABBY. He took out a key and carved into the wood:

BENJI AND SADIE.

Sadie eyed him up, smirking a little. "Posterity?"

"A memory of us that will outlast us. At least by a little."

Then he turned his hand and let the baggie slide out.

In the baggie were two Sporafluor swabs. Always two, one for him, one for her.

Benji looked around, found a diner menu—the kind that wasn't a book, but rather, a plastic-sheathed placemat. From his pocket he produced a handkerchief and used it to wipe the greasy dust off it. It wasn't clean. It wasn't sterile. Certainly not a laboratory environment.

But it should do.

He peeled apart the bag, noting that Sadie was studying his movements carefully. Benji surmised it wasn't because of anything he was doing, but because of the two swabs, and the gravity that surrounded them. If they were objects whose physical weight matched their emotional weight, they'd collapse the counter and drop clean through the mantle of the earth.

Deep breath. He turned the mouth of the baggie toward her.

"What a gentleman," she said, again trying to be cheery.

"Of course." He willed a smile to his face, false as it was.

Benji removed his own swab.

"Shall we?"

"This is very strange foreplay," she said.

He felt a flush rise to his cheeks. Instead of responding to that, he said, inexplicably, embarrassingly, "Bottoms up." Then he shoved the swab up his nose. It had to go up pretty far, same as a flu swab would. It conjured a pressure behind his eye as he turned it around up there. The act summoned a tear in that eye—a lone drop that rolled down his cheek.

Then it was out.

Sadie was wrestling with hers, nose wrinkled up, lip in an awkward sneer as she roto-rooted her own nostril with the cotton swab.

"I could do it," he said, tasting for a moment the dry cottony paper taste in the back of his throat. "I could help." The first few weeks they did this ritual, he did hers. But she said she wanted to learn to do it herself.

"No, no," she said, her voice nasal. "I think I've got it. Mwaaa. Ahhh." She plucked it out, frowning distastefully at the mucus-slick swab. "I think I got a little brain matter on there, actually. I suspect I lost a few phone numbers on that one, and I may no longer know how to tie my own shoes."

He set his swab down on the placemat.

She set hers down next to his, gently. Careful to keep them separate.

Then, from her cargo pants, she produced for him the black light. This one, just a small flashlight, not part of an elaborate setup. This one she'd picked up at a mostly gutted Walmart north of San Francisco.

"Who will do the honors?" she asked.

"I can. Ah, if you want me to?"

"I do."

She handed him the light, and as she did, she touched his wrist. "We do this every week, and we never really . . . say anything. Do you have . . . anything to say? To me? About . . . anything?"

He had a thousand things to say. A million. A trillion.

"No," he lied.

"I do."

"Oh. Well. I—"

Her resolve was suddenly shaken. Waving him off, she said: "No, you know, it can wait? It can wait. Definitely."

"You're sure?"

"I'm sure."

He wanted to ask her.

He wanted to tell her.

Something, anything, everything.

Instead, he turned the black light to the first swab.

His swab.

There, the cotton glittered just so, a fiber-optic brightness —he felt suddenly as if he were riding an elevator that had begun to plummet, its cable cut. Wooziness descended and he almost fell off his stool.

He met her eyes.

"I have to get away from you," he said.

"No," she answered, reaching for his hand again. This time, she gently took his wrist and pivoted it just so.

That way, the beam left his swab and fell to hers.

Once again, the glittery glow of the stained swab showing fungal contamination. *R. destructans.* White Mask.

Her breath pulled into her lungs in a short little gasp.

"Oh," she said.

"We—ahh." He tried to steady his breath. His heart was ricocheting around the inside of his chest. The words began to spill out of him, and no matter how hard he tried, he couldn't clamp his jaws shut to stem the verbal tide. "This does not have to be a terminal diagnosis, maybe—maybe my theory is right, maybe it'll be like with white-nose syndrome in bats, if we can use the antifungals to delay the disease long enough, our immune systems will kick in and develop a proper immunological defense response. Though there's a problem because we don't have enough antifungals, not here, not with us, and the country has gone to chaos: Where will we find some? That's the next problem, but I'm confident we can do it. It looks dire—more dire than dire, it looks like a death sentence—but it doesn't have to be, we have to have hope and—"

Sadie reached forward, lacing her fingers behind his head. Her touch was soft, slow, but somehow urgent at the same time. Her gaze met his, and *that* shut him up. Her gaze was alive and manic, dancing like a torch in hurricane winds. He opened his mouth to say something—

She pressed her lips against his. Her tongue slid into his mouth. He stood, suddenly, never breaking the kiss—he moved around her, then over her, and pulled her on top of him as he sat down hard onto one of the stools. Her hands fumbled with the buttons and zipper at his pants as he did the same to hers. His shirt went up over his head. Hers followed. Then his boxers. Then her panties. Both meeting the pool of discarded clothing on the floor. Again she climbed on top, him sinking deep into her—he buried his face in her neck, the scent of fresh sweat mixing with the odor of desert road. She took him in deep, deeper, her chin lifting, a small moan leaving her lips and riding up to the ceiling. The two of them rocked together in an erratic, potent arrhythmia—in them and between them flourished the heat of life, the madness of love, and the sudden absolute certainty of the end of all that they knew.

AFTER.

There wasn't anywhere to lie down, not really, so Benji leaned back in one of the booths, melting into it. Sadie laid herself atop him, the back of her head falling to the cradle of his collarbone. It shouldn't have been comfortable but somehow, it was. Truthfully, nothing should've felt good right now—they were dying, the world was ending, and the both of them were naked in an abandoned building where the only thing left for sale was a guaranteed case of tetanus. And yet there they were. Comfortable despite the comfort. Happy despite the Apocalypse unfolding all around them.

"Sex is magic," Sadie said, catching her breath. She leaned back and kissed the underside of his jaw. "I mean really, when all is said and done, it is sex I will miss the most. I know, I'm supposed to say I'll miss snuggling with puppies or that fresh baby smell, or flowers or wine or science or something, but my God, I am very fond of sex and will miss it greatly."

"Would you believe I haven't had much of it?" Benji said.

"I would *not* believe that. You're too good at it. Either you've had considerable practice, or you've an ingrained talent."

He chuckled and pressed his cheek against the top of her head. "No, really. I've had girlfriends, some serious, most not, but I was always so . . . busy. And we were in such mad places: crawling around caves slick with bat guano or poking through a factory gummed up with the pink slime of rendered chickens, or a hospital that was home to hemorrhagic fever. Never mind the fact we studied sexually transmitted diseases and—"

"Your sex game is an A-plus, but your pillow-talk game is an F-minus, Benjamin Ray."

"Sorry."

"I forgive you." She paused. He heard her take a deep intake of air—the sound of someone about to jump off a cliff. "I hope you forgive me."

"I do," he said, and that was that. No further discussion was required. They kissed. It lingered. Something passed between them, something more than just the heat of the moment or the vestiges of lust: something curiously spiritual. Two souls mingling, if not joining entirely. Benji knew in the back of his mind it was probably just the heady concoction of chemicals forming a blissful cocktail—but as a faithful man, he also had to believe in something more, something greater. The divine in a shared kiss.

A really fucking *good* kiss, at that.

"We did not use protection, by the way," she said.

"I don't think any prophylactic efforts would work here. We just made love in an abandoned rest stop."

"Oh no," she said, *tsk*ing her tongue. "You're the type who says *made love*. That just won't do, Benji."

He laughed. "What do you call it?"

"I prefer the good old-fashioned salaciousness of *screwed*. Or humped, banged, fucked. *Hit that shit*," she said, overenunciating those three words in a British accent, crisp as a fresh apple. "Beast with two backs, if you prefer The Bard. The horizontal bop. Boff, boink, balls-deep—*if* balls are part of the equation, and they would not need to be. Lay pipe. Roger. Scromp. Shag. Shaboing. Slap and tickle. Bubbles and squeak. Quack the duck, mount the pony, a right proper deep dicking, tap that ass like a whiskey barrel—"

Now he was cracking up so hard he felt tears in his eyes. "You're just—come on, you're making some of those up."

"Some of them, maybe." Her eyes glittered in the half dark.

"And what, may I ask, is wrong with *made love*?"

"It's a little *too* romantic, innit? As if we're forging some ball of loving energy between us instead of happily getting our rocks off. Plus, it puts a bit too much pressure on sex, and sells short the very idea of love. Making love is about connection, not sticking Tab A into Slot B—it's two people talking, laughing, being together like we are now. Not tongues and fingers. And I quite like tongues and fingers."

"Fair enough."

"And it also sounds like we're making a baby. Like we've produced something from this union of sweaty flesh." She shrugged. "Though, again, we did not use protection, so who knows?"

A chill suddenly fell over them. They both seemed to feel it. Benji was content to let it pass. Sadie, apparently, was not.

"Shana Stewart is pregnant. And she's now one of the flock."

He wanted to back away from the topic—because he knew that this sudden interjection of reality was surely lancing the careful bubble they'd just inflated around themselves, a bubble of momentary pleasure. But what could he do? Not talk about it?

"She is," he said.

"What do you think will happen to her?"

"I don't know." It wasn't a lie. "Black Swan doesn't seem to know, either. I'm not sure if the child will continue to grow, or if it, too, will remain in stasis along with the young woman. If it keeps growing, will she die? Will it die? I just . . . I don't know. We must hope for the best."

"At least we know what happens to us."

And there it was.

Bubble, popped. The ride, over. The exit chute fast ejecting them from the dirty Disney World park of their postcoital bliss.

Sex might be magic. But reality was cruel, and devoid of any true sorcery.

"We don't know," he said. "We don't know until we know. We're sick. It was to be expected. But maybe there will be a way forward."

"The antifungals," she said. "I know, they'll . . . slow it down. And that's great. I want that. I want more time. But we don't have enough."

"We'll get more."

"You sound so sure. But triaconozole is the only one that works, and only one company even produces it—or *produced* it, because who knows if they're even still in business? Chicago . . ." Her voice trailed off. Last they'd heard, Chicago had fallen to martial law. The police siding with Creel, the National Guard siding with whatever ragtag government was left behind in President

Hunt's name—rest in peace, Madam President—and the people caught in the middle. Curfews and checkpoints reigned.

Out here, at least, things were quiet. The desert brought with it a certain eerie peace, as if the world had already fallen and gone silent.

"I don't know. Las Vegas is an option. They have a few boutique pharma companies there—Blackmoore-Wells, Nova-Hydesty, CCR—Cargill Catalyst Research. Word on Vegas is that it's still . . . functional, at least. As functional as Vegas ever was, I guess." *People,* he thought crassly, *must still want to gamble, even up to the end.* He wondered how that worked. Money was still worth something, but what? And for how long?

And if they didn't gamble with money . . .

What *did* they gamble with?

"You can't go to Vegas. The Black Swan path takes us around the city—and for good reason, Benji."

"I have to try. A hundred pills between the two of us isn't enough. The math isn't favorable: two people, two pills a day apiece, means every day, four pills disappear from our stash. That's twenty-five days where we . . . slow this thing down, maybe stave it off. We need more."

When that was gone, and dementia settled in, that meant they'd have to start taking the Ritalin . . .

Arav had already begun. His cognitive decline hadn't shown yet in full force, but he'd had a day recently where he couldn't remember what year it was, or what state he was in. Benji chalked it up to anxiety and fatigue, but the young man was certain that it was *R. destructans* taking its toll—the threads of White Mask, reaching into his brain like hands pulling apart a loaf of freshly baked bread. So he began taking half a dose of Ritalin a day.

He was a little manic. He didn't sleep well as a result.

But Arav was holding it together. And the dementia did not return.

Yet.

He would need more antifungals, too.

That settled it. He had to head to Vegas. Before now, before he knew that Sadie was sick—never mind himself—the matter was not as urgent.

But if they were sick, other shepherds would fall ill, too.

He kissed Sadie on the cheek. Gentle and slow. Then he sat up and toed around the dirty linoleum floor for his pants. "Time to get back to the flock. I have to head to Vegas."

"You're not going alone."

"I am going alone." She started to protest but he held up both hands in an act of placation. "Sadie, listen to me. I need someone here who can handle the flock, who more important can still hold on to and communicate with Black Swan—"

"Black Swan barely wants to talk to me anymore—"

"Doesn't matter. It's you."

"Arav can handle it—"

"Arav is on Ritalin. And he's still young. His head is . . . look, he's more advanced than we are, and his girlfriend, and the mother of his child, is in thrall to whatever fate Black Swan and the nanite swarm have lent them. I need you. In case something happens."

Sadie didn't like it. He could see that look on her face—it wasn't just that she didn't like it. She was *mad* about it. She lifted her chin and crossed her arms over her naked chest. "Fine. *No.* Wait. Not fine! Shit. *Fine.*"

He kissed her again.

"I love you," he said.

"I love you, too, you heroic prick."

65

MOTHERS AND FATHERS OF INTELLIGENT ARTIFICE

01101101 01100001 01111001 01100010 01100101 00100000
01110111 01100101 00100000 01100100 01100101 01110011
01100101 01110010 01110110 01100101 00100000 01101001
01110100

—mysterious billboard text posted in seven cities:
Chicago, Philadelphia, Newark, Fort Lauderdale, Sacramento, Reno,
Salt Lake City

NOW AND THEN
The Ouray Simulation

SHANA HAD THAT SONG STUCK IN HER HEAD:

"Don't Go Chasing Waterfalls."

It was an old song, right? Like, early 1990s or something. Before she was born. TLC, and one of them had one eye, right? And died young?

Whatever.

Point was, it was in her stupid head.

Probably because she was standing here, staring at a waterfall.

It wasn't a real waterfall, of course. It was a simulation of a waterfall. Shana recognized that fact abstractly—but staring at it, you'd never know. The waterfall, Box Canyon Falls, was just southwest of town, and you could—as she had done now—go down to its base, where the water had carved its way through the mountain and dumped water into the Canyon Creek and Uncompahgre River. Some waterfalls were calm, placid, and meditative—but these falls slammed down with firehose force, roaring as the rush of water punched through the stone to the stream below. The cacophony of it drowned everything else out.

Except the damn song.

Don't Go Chasing Waterfalls . . .

And then Shana wondered, what if that wasn't the song? What if it wasn't real? What if it was . . . Black Swan pumping some version of the song into her head to make her think her memory was true? Maybe that was its secret: not that the waterfall in front of her—or the song about waterfalls inside her head—was truly simulated, but that it was using her brain against her, all in service to convincing her how real it was.

Which was a very long and circuitous way of getting her back to worrying about her mother.

Shana's mother was here.

Or so Black Swan wanted her to believe.

This was the story her mother told her: The day in the grocery store, the day Shana had last seen her, Daria Stewart was planning on killing herself. She didn't want to; she felt she had to. (Suicidal urges, Shana figured, didn't have to make much sense.) Recognizing how bad that would be, she called the suicide hotline there in the store, but someone else answered. Someone who was not the prevention hotline, but who was pretending to be one.

That someone offered to help Daria.

They told her where to go. And off she went.

There two people, Moira and Bill, offered Shana's mother an unconventional cure: They had invented something that was like a drug, but *not* a drug. Not strictly, because it was not based on chemical intervention.

Rather, they offered her a kind of *mechanical intervention.*

Tiny, eensy-weensy, itty-bitty machines.

Nanotechnology. Micro-machines. A whole swarm of them.

Daria Stewart was unsure, at first. But then she thought: What choice did she have? If this killed her, then it would be what she had been drifting toward all this time. And as Daria told Shana that first night here in the simulation, "We all die, one day. That day, I guessed, was as good as any."

The goal of the machine swarm was to enter Daria's body, find any and all chemical or hormonal imbalances, and attempt to correct them.

It did not perform as advertised.

It plunged her into a coma. Not a dreamless one, either.

"Dreams fed into nightmares, and nightmares turned back into dreams,"

Daria explained to Shana. "I didn't know what was real and what wasn't. Until one day . . . the dreams turned off, and this place turned on."

Black Swan had seized the nanotech swarm of Firesight—Moira and Bill's mad tech venture—and brought that swarm online into the simulation of Ouray, Colorado, intended to be the flock's final destination. What Black Swan had not realized was, Firesight had been keeping twelve original test subjects alive *and in stasis* down in a secure sub-basement of their Atlanta location. These test subjects—The Twelve—included Daria Stewart.

"We were the first," Daria said. "Which means we were also the first to go and talk to Black Swan. To learn about what was coming."

Daria, it turned out, was now a true believer.

And that really baked Shana's lasagna, because Daria had *never* been much of a true believer in *anything*. Which forced upon Shana the question:

Was that really Daria?

How much of that story was true? How much was a lie?

How much was just a simulation?

After all, Black Swan was able to craft a whole town out of, presumably, just ones and fucking zeros, right? (Shana suspected something as powerful as Black Swan was not so primitive as that, but okay, she also knew *dick* about how computers really worked.) This waterfall was perfect. No pixels. No hitching frame rate.

Could it conjure a pitch-perfect version of Daria Stewart?

Further, this version here *wasn't* a pitch-perfect version, was it? She'd changed. This wasn't the mother Shana knew. This one was more serene. More confident and comfortable. More loving, too, in a way.

Which made it all the more suspect.

Shana began to fear that this was not her mother at all, but some strange digital specter—a phantom forced upon her.

And as if on cue, she heard someone walking down the metal steps that were bolted into the rock around Box Canyon Falls: Even with the gush of the rushing water, it was impossible not to hear the approaching *clong, clong, clong,* or feel the faint vibration where she stood.

Shana turned to meet whoever it was that came to see her, even though she knew who it would be:

Sure enough, it was her mother.

"Daria," Shana said.

Her mother stood there, her hair in humid curls framing her porcelain face. She had a gray hoodie and a peach T-shirt underneath it. Jeans. Looking like some cool young mom, the hip mom down at the playground.

"I wish you'd call me Mom," Daria said.

"And I wish I could, but right now, I can't."

The woman puffed some air into her cheeks and let it out before walking closer and saying, "I love these falls. When I first . . . came to this place, I would walk here just like you and I would choose to really *be* here and take it all in. I honestly thought for a while that this was Heaven or maybe even Hell—the Good Place or the Bad Place, I wasn't sure."

"That's great." Shana injected those two words with as much shitty teenage sarcasm as she could, weaponized in just such a way that she didn't even have to roll her eyes, because it would be neatly inferred. "Well, thanks for coming by, Daria, good talk. I'm really glad we had this time together."

"Shana. Don't be like that."

"Don't be like what, Daria? Pissed that my mother abandoned her family years ago? Mad that my dad is dead and never got to see her again? Irritated and confused that of all places to find her, I find her *here,* in what feels like some half reality but is very likely a simulation inside an artificial intelligence, which makes me wonder, gosh, could *she* be a robot, too?"

"Black Swan is not a robot."

"See, of all the things I just told you, *that's* the one you answer. You didn't talk about being suicidal or about how I should have a little sympathy—which I should, totally, you're right. No, you mouth off about Black Fucking Swan. It's like you've been programmed." Shana leaned in and hissed these next words: "Or are a program yourself."

Daria reached for her, a soft touch on her arm—

Shana swatted it away. "Fuck off. Don't touch me."

"I'm not a program."

"Says the program, because the program has been programmed to say, *I'm not a program.*"

"Shana, I love you. I missed you. I didn't mean to leave. I was . . . I was fucked up, okay? You don't understand what it is to be depressed—like, not just sad, not just anxious, but where there's nothing going on upstairs. It's like, your brain is a blank chalkboard and you want to write on it, some message, some profound thought, but you can't think of anything. You can't even will the muscles in your arm to pick up a piece of damn chalk. So it's just blank, and you stare at it again and again, and the longer you leave it blank, the worse and worse it feels."

"Very poetic."

"I'm sorry I left. I shouldn't have. But it was what it was. It happened and I'm sad every day about that."

Shana scoffed, half turning away from her, arms crossed. "So I guess Black Swan didn't magically cure your depression."

"I'm sad, but not depressed. My regrets are no longer the building blocks of me."

That's some real self-help shit, Shana thought.

Daria continued: "Black Swan did give me something. My levels are different now. I'm balanced. It has given me life, and I've given my life to it in return. As one of The Twelve—"

"This is creepy. You talk like it's a god."

"It's not a god. Not in the old-world way. But . . . maybe in a new way, it is? I mean, imagine it, Shana, it's a sentient being, not human, that created this place out of nothing. We're inside its mind now, and—"

"But it didn't create *us*. We were here first. We made it, it didn't make us. It's not a god, Mom. It's just a less shitty version of Windows, or a really sassy PlayStation."

A sudden flare of anger from Daria when she countered with: "Be respectful. Black Swan saved your life, Shana. Don't you forget that."

"Is that you talking, Black Swan?"

"You're being insufferable."

The roar of the waterfall filled the space, like the rush of blood behind one's eardrums. A pumping, gushing susurrus. Finally, Daria said:

"Nessie is going up."

"Going up where?" But Shana already knew the answer, so when her mother said it was to meet Black Swan, she wasn't surprised.

But it hurt her just the same.

"No, she's fucking not," Shana said.

"Shana, she wants to go—"

"*You* told her to go. She thinks you're really our mother, you know that? I don't know if artificial intelligence is capable of feeling guilt, but if so, you should be feeling it right now like a kick in the stomach. She missed you so bad she's willing to follow you into Hell. But not me."

"Shana. Don't you want to go, too? Black Swan has answers. Don't you want to know what will happen to your baby—"

Whap.

Shana slapped her mother across the mouth.

"Don't talk about that. I can't control what happens there and I don't want to think about it so keep it out of your mouth."

Her mother nodded. "I know what it's like to not want to talk about things. I respect that."

"Fuck you."

Shana turned heel and walked back up the grated metal stairs, the rock wall on her right, the roar of the waterfall retreating behind her.

It was time to talk to Nessie.

SHE MARCHED BACK TOWARD TOWN—"town"—past the sign that showed the various stops and landmarks along the way toward the falls: STUMP WALL, THE SCOTTISH GULLIES, THE FIVE FINGERS, GAZEBO WALL, SHITHOUSE WALL. Shana didn't know what the hell a Shithouse Wall was; she didn't care to find out.

The path wound down toward Ouray, slick and muddy, with roots and stones peppering the way. Songbirds flitted overhead. Mountain bluebirds, somebody said they were. Trilling and chirping as they went from pine to pine, hiding in the dark needled boughs. *All part of the simulation,* she thought. She looked up to the blue sky and banded clouds, and toward the farthest peak she saw the black coils looping in the sky, turning slowly, dreamily, as if underwater.

Black Swan.

Always up there. Over everything.

Crunching numbers. Making the simulation donuts.

She headed to the terminus of the path, where it opened up to the sidewalk on 3rd Avenue in the southwest corner of town. Sometimes this legitimately felt like a real town—people did what people in towns *do,* they swept stoops, they pruned bushes, they looked out windows as you passed. They talked. Laughed. Ate ice cream. Bullshitted. Loitered. Jaywalked.

But other times, the illusion was clear, too. And not just because of the presence of Daria Stewart's new god, little-g, writhing up there in the sky. It was because nobody drove cars; no cars were around at all. No pets, either—nobody walking dogs, no dogs barking, zero cats skulking about on fencerows. The *sound* wasn't always quite right, in fact, sometimes like it was too real, but also not real at all—like noises were missing, the sounds of the wind, or the sound of distant music, or the sound of a plane overhead.

The imperfections of the simulation were small—but like a fleck of dust in your eye, it grew more noticeable the more you tried to pretend it wasn't there, working hard to blink-blink-blink it away.

Some people waved as she passed. She saw Bella Brewer leaning up against a mailbox, chatting with Bob Rosenstein; when they saw Shana, their fingers tickled the air in a little toodle-oo wave. Others simply watched her from porch swings or from behind the shadows of curtains. Elsa Carter was inside one of those windows—from here, Shana spied the woman standing in front of a big canvas. Shana couldn't see what she was painting, only that she had thumb-streaks of paint across one cheek and more on her forehead. Her father, Carl, stood behind her, watching, smiling.

All of it reminded Shana of that game, what was it? Nessie liked it. *The Sims,* that's what it was. Buncha digital people you made up, bobbleheading around town, babbling at each other in their own made-up language.

The town felt alive, even in its unreal state.

She knew some of the names of the other townsfolk, either from when she was a shepherd or from her introductions around town over the last— well, how long had it been? Weeks? Months? As Nessie pointed out, time here did not move like time anywhere else.

(Even now, she closed her eyes for just a moment and found herself in her own eyes, her *real* eyes, staring out at the backs of the flock ahead of her, diligently walking ahead. The sun was setting over a desert vista. The sky was a pale, powdered blue, the clouds like pillars of talc. She didn't see Arav right now. But she knew he was near. And she wished like hell she could feel her limbs—her real limbs, not the mental facsimiles she had hanging by her not-real simulated side. That way, she could reach out, grab him, hold him. She thought strongly, loudly, *I miss you, I hope you're okay.* But of course he wasn't. He was sick behind the mask he wore. He was different now, too— though every day he cared for her the way she cared for Nessie, he was twitchy, guarded, paranoid. Which was actually pretty reasonable, when she thought about the shooting on the bridge.)

When again she opened her eyes, she saw two people coming toward her: Mia and Mateo. The two were fraternal twins, and when Mia was a shepherd and Mateo was her walker, you could see the resemblance—the thick, dark hair and the thick-dark eyebrows and the full lips between sharp cheekbones the way a hammock hangs between trees—but now that they were both together, their *twinness,* if that could be a word, was crystal. They each looked bored, but also somehow on the verge of not being bored? Like they knew something you didn't. As if they knew about a secret party or where to find the guy with the good drugs.

They loped and bounced toward her.

Mia smirked. "Hey, you. Back up at the falls again?"

"Yeah," Shana said, wearing a smile like a mask.

"That place is cool," Mateo said. One of the ways he differed from his sister was that he was significantly less *intense*. Easygoing. Honestly, like he was always juuuuuuust a little bit high. Eyes half lidded he said, "I like to go there and just . . . Zen the fuck out."

"Cool, cool," Shana said, not really thinking it was cool, or that *any* of this was cool. "I gotta go talk to Nessie about . . . stuff." She started to step past them, but then stopped and whirled around. "Hey, either of you been . . . up there yet? Not to the waterfall but to see the, y'know, the *wizard behind the curtain*?"

Mia lowered her voice: "You mean Black Swan?"

"Yeah."

"Bitch, no way. I'm not going to talk to some scary-ass flying devil snake. This homie"—she juggled a thumb to indicate Mateo—"has been thinking about it, though."

"Don't," Shana said. A stern warning—though one without any reason behind it, she knew. Just a gut feeling.

"People say it wasn't scary," Mateo said. "Plus, I can ask it questions, I dunno. Like, I feel weird that a lot of other people have gone up and I haven't yet. At the same time . . ."

"At the same time, idiot, the whole thing is fuckin' weird," Mia said. "I mean, I'm super-happy to not be dead and shit, and if I could send that creepy cloud-snake a fruit basket, I'd do it, but I don't wanna go hang out with it. I'm good down here, thank you very much. And *you*," she said to Mateo, "aren't going up there so quit thinkin' you are." Those last words she accentuated by punching him in the arm.

"Ow, ow, shit, okay." He frowned at her and rubbed his arm. "Fine, if I'm not going to meet Black Swan, let's at least go up to the falls. Oh, man." He looked suddenly like a revelation just punched him in the face. "Can we jump off it? Would that hurt us? You punching me hurt. But can we die?"

"Dude, I dunno," Shana said.

"See," he said. "If I could go talk to the wizard, I could ask."

Mia shoved him forward. "Bye, bish."

"See you, Mia. Bye, Matty."

Onward she went, diligent in her step.

SHE AND NESSIE LIVED IN a hotel. The Beaumont. It was the haunted-feeling inn that she'd woken up in not long after she first got here—that room, she was told, she could keep, if she wanted it. Or she could strike out on her own and find one of the houses or rooms around—plus, Ouray was home to other smaller motels, hotels, and B&Bs. Shana wanted to keep her stay here feeling temporary, and so she chose to remain right where she was.

Bonus points: It was also where Nessie lived.

Nessie had decorated her room to look like her room at home: sheets the color of lemon, a comforter the color of canary feathers, a floofy pink pillow, shelves stocked with notebooks and real books (lots of young adult, sci-fi, fantasy). She put flowers in little jars and vases. Somehow she even found a Twenty One Pilots poster and hung that over the creepy gilded mirror over the porcelain-topped dresser. Her decorative efforts took the dour, Victorian vibe and drowned it out with a wash of bold, punchy colors.

That was Nessie in a nutshell.

Presently, Nessie was putting things in a backpack.

Food, water, a notebook. (Shana knew they didn't really need to eat or drink here, but it was satisfying and, more important, routine.)

"No," Shana said, firmly, clearly, the one word barked loud. To emphasize, she stomped over and took the backpack away from her sister, then upended it back on the bed, spilling the food, water, and notebook out. Alongside that fell other objects, too: a couple of pens, a hair scrunchie, and four Lloyd Alexander books—the Prydain Chronicles, a series Nessie loved growing up and read again and again. While all the other kids were wandering Hogwarts with Harry Potter, Nessie had her face buried in these. Dad used to joke that they should've cut eyeholes in the books so she could just wear them like masks and complete the transformation.

Shana wasn't sure where her sister had found those in this town. The library, maybe? *Or maybe,* she thought, *a gift from our new god?*

"Shana, it'll be fine."

"No," she said again, injecting iron into her voice.

"We have questions."

"Who's 'we'? You have a mouse in your pocket?" That, another saying of Dad's, once upon a time. Anytime one of them indicated turning chores into a group activity, he'd always say that—*oh, we are going to do the dishes? Who's "we"? You got a mouse in your pocket?*

"Fine. Maybe you're not intellectually curious about *all of this,* but I am, and I'm fed up." Nessie hesitated. "Shana, you're pregnant."

"Yeah. I know. I don't need a lesson in reproductive science."

"No, I just mean—we haven't talked about it—"

"There's nothing to talk about."

"What happens to the baby while you're in here?"

Fear moved swiftly through her. She really *hadn't* wanted to think about it but now here she was, thinking about it: Would she die? Would the baby die? Was the baby in stasis like she was? None of the other walkers had been pregnant. Why did Black Swan even *choose* her? She blinked back frustrated, anxious tears.

"I don't know," she said. Her voice quieter than she intended.

"I want to know," Nessie said. "So I'm going up there. Mom always said I should go, that it would be fine."

"Daria isn't someone we should trust."

Nessie made a the-hell-you-say face. "What? Why?"

"What if she's not real?"

"She's as real as you and I are."

A new chord of fear struck in Shana's chest: What if Nessie wasn't real? What if *Shana* wasn't real, just the program of her psyche made to run and believe it was real, when in reality she was just a downloaded code from a brain-dead husk powered by little-bitty robots. Or what if that's what Black Swan wanted from people, to upload into them some kind of virus, some virus of belief and servitude, creating a cult . . .

Whoa, she told herself, *this sounds like when you and Zig would get turbo-high and imagine how the school lunch program and those square pieces of roof-shingle pizza were somehow the result of some far-sweeping global conspiracy. Take it down a notch, weirdo.*

"Maybe she's real, maybe she's not," Shana said. "All I know is, this place is good at seeming like a true place, but it's a simulation. An incredible simulation. Mom went through a lot, but she also left us—"

"She was suicidal, Shana. God, have a heart."

"And that was still selfish, okay? She was there for herself, not for us. And now she's there for . . . whatever that thing is up there in the sky. We have each other, we have to take *care* of each other, because there's no guarantee she, or that *thing,* will."

"Shana, you sound paranoid."

"I am paranoid! How can you not be paranoid?"

"I'm going."

"No."

"Fine, then I'll go without my stuff. I was going to write my answers down, but . . . I'll just remember them. I have a good memory." Nessie, defiant, clasped her hands behind her back like some kind of belligerent administrator, and then headed for the door of the room.

Shana blocked it.

"Shana, *move*."

"No. No, no, a thousand times, no."

But she could see the fire in her sister's eyes. On simple things, unimportant things, Nessie would always back down. Shana never felt herself a bully, not exactly, but if she wanted the channel changed or some nonsense, she just had to demand it a few times and Nessie would acquiesce. "The power of the big sister," Shana would say, *"is absolute."*

Except, when Nessie really had her teeth in something, there was no way she'd let go. When Mom left, Nessie got a bug up her butt about the whole family going to therapy—a suggestion Dad and Shana resisted because, uhh, yeah, no thanks. But Nessie just kept coming and coming, bringing it up at every meal, in the morning, at night before bed . . .

They gave in.

They went to therapy.

It was horrible. Each session felt like pulling teeth with a pair of clumsy pliers—and going in rectally, instead of orally. But over time, it actually seemed to help. They laughed again. They found some kind of calm and balance and light in the void their mother left for them.

So, Shana knew, when Nessie wanted something, she'd make it happen. Here, she'd go out through the window. Or sneak out at night. Or build a fucking rocket booster with that big brain of hers and launch herself up into the sky like she was the cartoon coyote chasing the roadrunner.

Which meant she had to do some redirection.

Some kung fu business.

"You're not going, Nessie," she said.

"Shana—"

"Because I am."

66

REPEAT AFTER ME

A year spent in artificial intelligence is enough to make one believe in God.
—Alan Perlis

NOW AND THEN
The Ouray Simulation

"This is a bad idea," Nessie said.

"It's a fine idea," Shana said, gathering most of the stuff off the bed and chucking it into Nessie's neon-blue book bag. She left out the Lloyd Alexander books, but everything else went in there.

"No, you shouldn't go—"

"You said you wanted answers. And you're right, I need answers, too. So I'll go."

"This isn't the reaping, Shana. I'm not Prim and you're not Katniss, you don't have to go to the Hunger Games in my place, okay?"

She slung the backpack over her shoulder.

"I'm going. If it's dangerous, then I'll take the brunt of it. If you're right, if Mom's right, and it's not? Then it'll be fine. And I'll come back down here, la-dee-da, and tell you so. Though, if I seem different? Like, weirdly different? Then maybe don't believe me."

"Shana, please. I'll go with you."

"No. Let me do this." She reached out and held her sister by the shoulders. "You were always the special one. You're smart. Smarter than smart, and there's probably a word for *smarter than smart,* and the reason I don't know that word is because . . . I'm not that smart. Dad had a place in mind for you, a place in the world, in the universe. A special seat just for you. And he was right. You're special. You're better than me."

Nessie wiped away a tear. "You're a good sister."

"Well, that's my gravestone sorted."

"Don't say things like that."

Shana kissed her on the cheek. "Love you, little sis."

"Love you, big sis."

"I'm out."

She went to the door. But Nessie stopped her.

"You think Mom isn't really Mom? Or that we can't trust her?"

"I don't know. But I'm gonna find out."

OCTOBER 14
Nipton Road at the California-Nevada border

"THIS IS A BAD IDEA," Arav said. His voice nasal and muffled behind the re-breather mask: a mask meant not to stop the infection from reaching him, but rather, to stop the infection from *leaving* him. He paced the empty road cutting through the desert. The sky bled purple. The air had gone crisp, the chill nesting in their marrow.

"It is the *only* idea," Benji said, picking half the bullets out of a box of .223 shells to fit the Ruger Mini-14 rifle he barely knew how to use. "White Mask is upon us, Arav. You, now me and Sadie. We don't have enough triaconozole. I don't know if I can get more, but Vegas is the best bet to find a functional replacement. It's also possible one of the drugstores carries it—the drug came to market a year ago to help combat valley fever, which is a thing out here. But that means I go where the people are, where they are likeliest to have that product or an equivalent."

"Don't go alone, then."

"Look around you," Benji said. He demonstrated what was to come down the road: the flock, yes, and the shepherds. Far fewer now than before. Many slept in the CDC trailer. Others camped in the few remaining vans, RVs, and pop-up trailers, taking shifts to watch the horizons for attack. Out here, at least, they could see the horizon, and it was quiet. If something was going to come for them, they'd know. "The shepherds number twenty-seven, now. We don't have many sick yet, but if Sadie and I are impacted, they will be, too. It's better that they stay here and don't up their chances of encountering White Mask in the wild. Plus, if something happens, we need all hands on deck." He declined to clarify what that meant:

all hands on rifles and knives, ready to die for the flock. Because the flock was the future.

The flock was civilization.

That was a realization he grappled with, daily. The flock was meant to be the last vestiges of humankind. They were not aimless wanderers, lost to some disease. They were chosen. Selected to be the ones that remained.

The shepherds were here to carry the vigil for them.

To walk with them, not to guide them—

But to *protect* them.

What a shift that was, for him. Benji didn't fit the role well. Should've been Robbie Taylor here, or Cassie—neither of whom he'd heard from in a month, now that the cell towers were down. (Yes, Benji had the Black Swan satphone, and the satellites were still up and running, but who would they call? He didn't have any other satphone numbers.) Benji was a self-described detective. Someone who solved medical mysteries, who answered questions about vectors and pathogens. He didn't manage survivors. He didn't govern a defensive response. This wasn't him.

And yet here he was.

Chosen, too. In part by Black Swan. In part by the vagaries of fate.

Maybe by God, too.

Something-something *mysterious ways* blah-blah-blah.

But it was true, too. Wasn't it? God operated in ways that humans did not properly understand. That was the cause of science. To test the parameters of God's creation. To understand its intricacy.

Hell with it. That was no longer his role.

This was his role, and he was playing to it.

"You have to be careful out there," Arav said as Benji slung the rifle over his shoulder. "It's quiet here, the road is desolate. But you don't know who's out there. Creel's people. Or nutbags whose minds have broken down under the assault of White Mask."

"I am a careful man, Arav. Don't worry."

"If it's okay by you, I think I'm going to worry anyway."

Benji smiled. "Yeah, me too. But I thought I'd try on a little bravado for once, see how it fit."

"You did okay with it."

"Thanks."

They hugged.

And when he turned, there stood Sadie.

He could see she'd shed a few tears—her cheeks were cleaned in a few trickled tracks. She was trying to hide it, what with the cocky tilt to her hips and her arms crossed defiantly over her chest.

"You can't go alone," she said.

"Sadie," he said, nearly exasperated by this conversation, "we talked about this, and Arav and I just covered similar ground—"

"Not me. Not Arav. Black Swan."

"What?"

"Black Swan is going with you."

"That's not a good idea."

"As I just heard you tell Arav: It's the only idea. I won't have it any other way, my love." His heart fluttered as she said those two words. *My love.* No matter how wrecked and wretched the world had become, those two words raised him up. "You defy me on this, and I'll defy you, then. I'll follow after whether you like it or not. You want me to stay? I'll stay, but only—*only*—if you take Black Swan with you."

"There's no good reason—"

"There're a *thousand* good reasons. You'll need maps. You'll need information. Your needs are dynamic and ongoing. Ours are . . . relatively static. We walk. We protect. We know our destination. The flock does not respond elastically to threats—they're set to dance to a beat."

He had to admit: Sadie had a point.

My love . . .

"Fine," he said. He pointed at her. "You really get under my skin."

"In only the best ways."

She kissed him. Hard and long.

Benji said his goodbyes again, to them and to the other shepherds. He explained to them what was going on—the sickness had found them, and he hoped to find more medicine in Vegas. Then he took the Mini-14 and grabbed the keys to a mini van the shepherds had been using—not as a vehicle, but as storage dragged behind one of the RV campers thanks to a trailer hitch. They cleared some of those supplies out—and kept some in for him, too, like some bottled water and food—and then he set out.

Ahead, the highway darkened as evening bled out.

OCTOBER 14
Innsbrook, Missouri

"This is a bad idea," Matthew said. "I don't like it."

He looked at himself in the side mirror of the Lexus. He took more dirt in his hands, breaking it up so that it was a little wet, like paint. Then he smeared it on his cheeks and around his eyes in deliberate streaks. Like war paint. He didn't have much real estate left on his face, though, because it was home now to a patchy growth of wiry beard.

It changed the way he looked.

Which was exactly what Autumn said he needed.

"Do you want to find Bo?" she asked. He didn't have to answer that. "Then this is the way in. He's our son. It's our responsibility."

He continued to regard himself in the mirror. The beard, the dirt. He barely recognized himself. "I don't disagree, I just wonder if we could think of a more strategic plan."

Autumn turned him toward her. She pinned him with her stare. "Who knows how much time there is, Matthew? Right now, Innsbrook's resort area is bustling. If Bo is anywhere, he's in there. I need you to get it together. I need you to make a decision here. We lived confused lives, you and I. Pointed at the wrong thing all the time. It . . . made us soft. But we can't be that way anymore. If you don't want to go in there, I will—"

"*No,*" he said, declaratively. "You're right. I'll go."

He turned again, looked at himself in the mirror.

"I don't know if I fit the part okay," he said. "Hair's a mess, patchy beard, dirt on my cheeks—I still don't look like one of *them.*"

"You don't have ink," she said, suddenly.

"What?"

"Ink. Tattoos. All of Stover's men, they're marked."

She was right. And he didn't have that. He needed it. And there wasn't exactly time to conjure a tattoo out of nowhere. They wouldn't be fooled by a few swipes from a permanent marker.

Autumn had an idea.

"I'm all ears."

Fifteen minutes later, with the gas in their little Coleman lantern burning, she came at him with a smoldering key that had been scorched and warmed in the flame. "Hold still," she admonished him.

He winced, trying to pull away from his right arm as if he could just detach it during the process. The whole thing made him think of his time in Ozark's bunker, chained up there. Tormented and tortured. It felt claustrophobic, like he could feel the man's weight on him, pressing down, pushing the breath out of Matthew's chest. He told himself to keep it together, and so he stuffed it down deep, clamping his teeth to try to stop feeling what he was feeling.

It's Autumn. She's alive. She's not here to torture you.

Do this to get your son back.

The brand was a brutal idea, one she would have never entertained before. One *he* would not have entertained before, either. It just showed how much the world had changed. And how much they had changed in response to the world. He liked this new Autumn. And he liked what she demanded of him. *If only we had found each other this way in the time before . . .*

He cried out as the scalding key-tip touched his neck. It sizzled: *sssss.* He smelled burning hair and then a smell not unlike scalded pork chop. She shushed him and stuck a stick in his mouth. He bit down on it so hard it broke. So Autumn found another one, and popped it in there. He tasted bark and dirt. She heated the key again. And slowly, surely, she branded him with a symbol. Clumsy, yes. Bubbled and soon probably infected, sure.

But for now, it would have to do:

The serpent, the hammer, and the sword.

The new symbol of the ARM, the American Resurrection Movement. Visible to all who would see, as long as his neck was exposed.

"Now you're ready," she said.

He wasn't. But it would have to be enough.

OCTOBER 14
Monarch Pass, Colorado

"This is a bad idea," Landry said.

"Pifflc," Pete said, failing to acknowledge the white-knuckled grip he had on the steering wheel. They drove on through darkness, along the southern edge of the Colorado Rockies. Ahead, signs pointed toward something called Monarch Pass. The road grew steeper. Just a few minutes ago, they passed an uncomfortable meeting between a Honda hatchback car and a guardrail. The guardrail had nearly folded around the front end of the two-door car, holding it in place as it burned.

A man stood out by the car—he was older, with a pale naked gut hanging out over his probably-Wrangler jeans. He stood there in the fireglow as the Beast's headlights speared him to the road. In the high beams, before Pete turned them down, it was plain to see the snowy crust on his face: the hallmark of the titular White Mask.

He stared past them as they passed.

But then Pete saw something in the mirror, a momentary flex of movement caught in the red wake of the RV's taillights. Next thing they knew, *pap, pap,* a pair of low-caliber gunshots. One went who-knew-where; the next clipped the lower corner of the passenger-side mirror, the reflective glass chipping and spiderwebbing. Landry cried out.

Pete panicked; was Landry hit?

He wasn't. Neither were.

But the whole thing prompted the comment:

"This is a bad idea."

"It's fine," Pete added. "It's just, the world's gone to hell, and we're driving through Satan's lower intestine, is all."

The man with the burning car and the gun was not their first such strange encounter out here. Far from it. They saw something every fifty miles, at least, that turned their piss cold. They saw bodies corded along the side of the road like firewood. They saw people wandering the roads and forests like ghosts—one stood up on a craggy cliff, her dress in tattered rags. In the rearview, they watched her jump. (Neither looked long enough to watch her hit.) They saw trucks overturned, their trailers torn open, the payloads gone; they heard distant screaming and gunfire; they saw military convoys driving down parallel highways, convoys that flew no flag. Once in a while, they'd see a military drone. Scanning for survivors? Hunting the sick? Or just some numbnuts drone operator out for a joyride as the world grew sick and died?

All this shit got worse the closer they came to civilization. Pete was one of those types who feared the wilderness, who got edgy soon as you left the city lights. (Hell, he got twitchy in the suburbs.) Now, though, the farther away from everything they got, the more his nerves calmed. Get near towns, you saw more people—some living, many dead, a lot sick. Most of them had guns. Many had been taken by the delirium of White Mask, spinning around in circles, or digging holes for no reason known outside their heads, or firing off rounds at invisible enemies—just like that poor fucker with his burning car back there.

Christ, not long after coming into Colorado, they passed an orchard town called Fruita—and there, by the edge of the road, some young buck was going to town on an empty mailbox. His pants were down, the mailbox was open, and he was fucking the thing like his life depended on it.

"Maybe he's got a thing for robots," Pete said at the time.

"You are a strange, sick man," Landry told him.

(Pete couldn't disagree.)

For a while, Pete was able to shrug a lot of this off—pretending, in a way, that it was happening to someone else, that it was like a movie he was watching instead of an apocalypse he was living. That's how he lived most of his life: the joyful solipsism of a rock star, both out-of-his-head and up-his-own-ass. But now, out here, in the dark and coming up on a high-elevation mountain pass, he was starting to get genuinely scared.

"I don't like any of this. It was a damn mistake."

"It's the choice we made," Pete said. "We can't turn around now."

"Shit yes we could! We aren't even halfway across this fucked-ass country, we could spin the wheel and do a U-ey right here, right now, go catch up with Benji and the Zombie Gang."

"They're not zombies, they're alive in there. And we aren't turning around. We are on a mission."

"We aren't the Blues Brothers, Pete Corley."

"Great movie, though. Real shit-splash sequel, though." Pete had to pull this out of the tailspin. As the RV carved a path through the dark, the knife-slash pine trees rising up as they climbed the mountain, he said, "Look at it this way, we are together. Spending time in the beautiful nature of Colorado, enjoying some fresh air and—"

"Snow. Look, there's snow up ahead." He was right. It wasn't fresh or falling, just snow mounded up on both sides of the road. As they drove up the mountain, the air got colder. Made sense.

"Snow! See? Beautiful snow. Better than that dry sandpaper desert, right? We are out here, road-tripping, finally together—"

"Maybe we shouldn't be together."

"What?"

"Maybe all this is a sign that we aren't right for each other. Goddamn, I mean, maybe this whole apocalypse is a sign: Maybe all those creepy bigoted assholes like those Westboro Baptist types were right, maybe all this is God's payback for faggots like us breaking His dumb-ass rules."

"You don't really believe any of that spew, do you?"

Landry pouted. "I don't know. No! No. I know it's all crazy talk. I'm just feeling crazy right now." He reached across the center dash and grabbed Pete's wrist and gave it a comforting squeeze. Their hands met each other. "I'm happy we're together, but boy fucking howdy, I just wish it wasn't the end of the whole wide world, you know?"

"I do know. But maybe it's not. The end, I mean. Maybe . . . maybe we'll make it through, maybe we will meet my family and we can hunker down in whatever bunker her parents have, and this whole thing will blow over. We aren't even sick, you and I! We are lucky fucking chuckleheads, Landry, my man. We might one day be kings of this land."

"All right, all right, your crazy-ass optimism is working on me. Keep it up, you might get laid tonight."

"We should find a place to park and catch some rest . . ."

"Yeah. Let's do that. Let's just get over this mountain first, it's cold."

"A fine idea."

"You really think we might be okay?"

"Stranger things have happened, my love."

And that's when Landry sneezed.

67

VEGAS, BABY

The airports are all closed. Gas stations are running out of gas. A lot of us have the disease. Best we can do is eat, drink, fuck, and did I mention drink? Cheers, everyone.

@TheCompiler01

4 replies 7 RTs 12 likes

OCTOBER 15
Las Vegas, Nevada

THIS WAS NOT BENJI'S FIRST RODEO, AS THE SAYING WENT—HE HAD BEEN to Vegas many times before, because inevitably, year after year, some tech-bro or pharma-jerk scheduled a conference in this city. Yes, the city was ultimately convention-friendly, and made every effort to accommodate the needs of every industry that came here. But the reality was, people wanted an excuse to come to Vegas. They wanted to gamble. They wanted to drink. They wanted the pool, the miles-long buffets, the occasional tawdry dalliance with a cocktail waitress, flight attendant, or high-dollar independent escort.

Benji believed it to be the second-worst city in the nation.

(The first being also in Nevada: Reno.)

It hadn't changed much since White Mask took over.

Yes, cast over everything was a ruinous, apocalyptic vibe—but truth be told, he'd found that to be the case before, too. Vegas always carried with it an eat-drink-and-be-merry-for-tomorrow-we-may-die energy: a city perched on the cusp of a never-ending yet never-quite-happening end. It was a city permanently stuck in the predawn hour before the hangover truly hit. Right

592   CHUCK WENDIG

there at the Rubicon of *still having fun* and *about to start puking,* on the line between *everything is amazing* and *the End Times are here.*

And that was the hour at which Benji arrived:

Three A.M.

He'd taken a few extra hours on the road to scout out the potential path of the flock. It would've been feasible to drive right here on I-15, but instead he headed straight across to the town called Searchlight, and then up north in and around Nelson, Boulder City, and Henderson. Coming closer to civilization in these places meant he was closer to the chaos of American life under White Mask: burned-out cars, boarded-up houses, dead bodies in alleys and arroyos. Las Vegas itself, though, was less of that—it was like the city had made a concerted effort to hide the worst parts of the Apocalypse, and reveal only the best: Even away from the Strip, people were in the streets wandering around with big drinks in their hands, arms around each other, sloshing about. Music blared, and as he drove through a winding line of stalled-out cars, the music morphed from the grinding guitars of Mötley Crüe to some bass-thumping hip-hop to the glitch-grinding of dubstep.

Strangest thing of all: The lights were on. The Strip still burned effulgent, a gaudy neon beacon lit like a bug zapper, summoning anyone who wanted to pretend the world was not dying one day at a time. As if both a summary refutation of what was going on, and a mad acceptance of it.

Some cities had gone dark in patchwork, others entirely blacked out, but Vegas, he imagined, was lit still thanks to the wonders of hydroelectric power: He knew a lot of the electricity here still came from natural gas, but the city center was powered thanks to the Hoover Dam. Renewable resources were growing here, given the dam, solar, and wind, and were fast outpacing what gas gave to the city. That was a cruel rejoinder to what Benji knew: that White Mask was born of climate change, and though civilization was making fast strides toward a renewable future, it was far, far too late.

That made him wonder, too, what would happen when—or if—humanity really was whittled down to splinters. How long would the cellphone network remain? That was already patchy. How about the satellites? The electricity? Surely satellites would keep whirling about in space, though some would fail and no one would ever fix them. The power grid required human maintenance—presently, Benji imagined some people still went to their jobs, and where manpower failed, automation would bridge the gap for a time. Nuclear power could run for a year or three all on its own, as those systems were auto-balanced. Natural gas and coal, less so. Hydroelectric, too, ran on its own pretty well—but one fault somewhere in any of those systems would cause a default. And possibly, a catastrophic one. Clogged intakes, or circuit boards misfiring, or corroded pipelines—possibly these would cause a simple load imbalance and the automatic fail-safes from a wayward grid would trigger, shutting them down. But it was just as likely that, without human intervention, there could be a natural gas explosion, or a crack in the dam, or worst of all a nuclear power meltdown.

(And suddenly Benji felt overwhelmed by the fear that even if the flock *did* survive White Mask, what was to come might be endlessly more horrific. What a heart-crushing tragedy it would be to survive the plague only to die from radiation poisoning. Or starvation. Or exposure . . .)

Benji chewed a thumbnail nearly down to the quick. He eased the car over down a small side street not far from the airport. He thought for a moment to ask Black Swan these questions, but right now the answers would do little to reassure him. It was necessary to compartmentalize. Benji had a job to do, and he would not do it effectively if his mind was on other things. Setting the satphone in the palm of his hand, he conjured the machine intelligence simply by saying its name:

"Black Swan?"

The screen dawned soft white, and black text appeared upon it—the words not scrolling, but rather, appearing in sharp pulses. Each word or phrase showing up just long enough to be read.

HELLO, BENJAMIN.

"I need your help."

YOU SEEK ANTIFUNGAL DRUGS.

"And you knew that how?"

I AM ALWAYS LISTENING, BENJAMIN. HOW DO YOU THINK I KNOW TO ANSWER WHEN YOU SAY MY NAME?

Of course. It disturbed him to know that the machine was listening all the time, a mechanical voyeur—then again, that was the aching paranoia of modern life, was it not? Your phone, listening. Your TV, listening. People put devices in their houses that were always and forever listening.

Sometimes, even watching.

Though all that would be worthless, now.

"Yes, I am seeking antifungal drugs. I am in Las Vegas. Can you help to direct me?"

YOUR GREATEST CHANCE FOR SUCCESS IS, AS YOU NOTED, MEDICATION TO THWART VALLEY FEVER.

"And I can find that here, yes?"

I NO LONGER HAVE ACCESS TO THE INTERNET, BUT I HAVE ARCHIVES OF ALL PUBLIC AND MOST PRIVATE PHARMACEUTICAL DATA. CARGILL CATALYST RESEARCH HERE IN LAS VEGAS PRODUCES AN ORAL ANTIFUNGAL, STILL IN PRECLINICAL TRIAL. THE DRUG IS DESIGNATED CCR-1342. IT IS DESIGNED TO TREAT VALLEY FEVER BUT FUNCTIONS AS A BROAD-SPECTRUM ANTI-FUNGAL.

That was perfect.

"You can give me directions?"

I ALSO HAVE NAVIGATIONAL ARCHIVES, AS YOU KNOW, AND A CONNECTION TO A NETWORK OF SATELLITES.

And with that, a map appeared on the phone screen showing a thumb-tack tag in the northwest of Las Vegas, off Summerlin Parkway, only a few miles from the Summerlin Hospital.

Benji turned the headlights on, and drove away.

He did not see the pickup truck that followed him, lights off.

He kept off the Strip. It seemed wise—even from a mile away, with his windows down, he could hear cheering, yelling, the occasional crackle of what might've been firecrackers, and what might've been gunfire. The latter wouldn't be surprising: Nevada was already an open carry state, in that they never forbade it, and anything unforbidden remained legal here. If you were eighteen years old, you could buy a gun. And if you could buy a gun, you could carry it around. Still, norms kept that on the down-low, for the most part: Back when the world was unbroken, you didn't see men walking around casinos or on the street loaded for war. That had changed, now. It seemed half of everyone had a gun out in the open, and the other half probably had them concealed. They were drunk. Probably high on who-knew-what.

Inevitable that one day soon, someone would open fire. And lots of people would die. Benji did not plan to be here when that happened.

So he drove up dark side streets. Not an ideal way to travel, but better that than wind through the sure-to-be-choking crowds on the Strip.

His little mini van rattled onward, past black-eyed wedding chapels, motels, tattoo parlors, cash-for-gold joints, check-cashing places, all the signature institutions of this particular city.

Then the highway north, until Summerlin Parkway.

Up here, it was dead quiet. Streetlights were still on. Cars parked in parking spaces. Nothing on fire. The houses and townhomes were nicer; they weren't mansions, but they were upscale, luxe, and packed in among offices of steel and glass. Some doors and windows were still unboarded, though they were often shut behind steel bars or mesh.

Benji wound around off the parkway into a back neighborhood. It was a mix of offices and houses and other small businesses.

Ahead, he saw his destination. A stone sign marker read CCR: CARGILL CATALYST RESEARCH (the sign was not unlike a gravestone, he noted, which was curious branding for a pharmaceutical company). It was a small two-story building bumping up against other offices in a small office park.

As he eased up, he saw a light on in the farthest east window.

And then, as he pulled to the curb, that light went off suddenly.

Tucking Black Swan into his pocket, he looked to the Mini-14 sitting on the passenger seat across the bundle of maps he had (including one of Ouray he'd torn out of an atlas he found in Barstow). He didn't want to take the rifle. At no point did he want to use it. He needed medication, but he was no looter; he wouldn't take it by force. Perhaps *couldn't* take it by force, as he wasn't sure he was made of the proper salt and steel for such terror.

Though inwardly he wondered if that was a failing. Shouldn't he be willing to do what it took to help the flock? And Sadie, and Arav, and the other shepherds? A failure to be decisive could get them all killed.

Someone was in that office building.

Whoever they were could be armed.

Still, he had to try to do this the right way. The *human* way.

He took the rifle and put it in the backseat underneath a blanket. But he loaded it first, took the safety off. Just in case.

Benji exited the van and walked to the office building, keeping his head on a swivel as he did—looking left, right, and back again, waiting for someone to emerge out of nowhere. A ridiculous idea, given that it was fairly well lit here, and it wasn't like Vegas was a green town with lots of trees or hiding spots.

Even still, out of the van he felt on edge.

His short journey to the front of the building was thankfully uneventful.

The door itself was glass, but shuttered with an accordion gate, steel and gleaming. Even breaking the glass wouldn't earn him entry.

The windows, similarly, were gated shut.

He found a buzzer and thumbed the button. It didn't seem to do anything. And yet the office had power, did it not? Didn't he see a light? Didn't look like the glow from a flashlight, either, but from something brighter: a lamp, or even a low-powered overhead light.

Guess we'll do this the old-fashioned way. (And he decided it would be best to get used to the old ways, given what was to come.)

He knocked on the door.

A simple knock. No *shave and a haircut.* Nothing playful, but also not too urgent.

Nothing.

He knocked again.

Still nothing.

He started to ponder his next move. Benji needed inside this building— but how? The rooftop was flat, and maybe up there was a way in. Could he go in through a vent? Was that even a thing? Movies made that a thing, what with John McClane wriggling his way through ductwork, but he half suspected that was just cinematic liberty, and that no vent was really human-sized. If that wasn't an option, what? Break a window, try to find something to lever open the gating? Or maybe—

A bright light popped on, flashing in his eyes from within the building. All he saw was garish white, with black blobs in his vision as his eyes adjusted—or rather, failed to adjust. He held up both hands to shield his gaze, wondering if in a second or two he'd feel a couple of bullets tap him in the chest, cutting his quest woefully short.

Flinching, he heard the speaker next to the door crackle to life with a warbling tone. The tone faded and a woman's voice came over the comm:

"Who are you?"

"I'm—my name is Benjamin Ray, I'm with the—"

"Press the button, dummy. I can't hear you."

The button. Right. He again thumbed the button—this time, a green light came on, indicating that she must've given the system power—and spoke into it: "My name is Doctor Benji Ray, I'm with the CDC's EIS division out of Atlanta, I was hoping to be let in."

"No. Go away."

The light left his eyes, leaving spots whirling in his vision.

The comm went dark again.

He pressed the button, but no light came on. He knocked again, more urgently. *Whump whump whump whump.* He didn't want to raise his voice and attract undue attention, but what choice did he have? "Please," he yelled at the door. "I need your help. This is serious."

Again the light flashed his eyes, stunning him anew.

Crackle from the comm, then: "Why?"

Almost forgetting to press the button, he spoke again: "Because you have an experimental antifungal medication. For valley fever? It was in preclinical trial."

Crackle-hiss.

"You mean 1342."

"Yes! Yes. Exactly what I mean."

"I need credentials."

"I don't—" *Wait, I do have credentials.* He'd never really shed himself of those; they were in his wallet. He dug it out and flipped it up, not unlike a badge of sorts: It showed off his CDC EIS identification card.

The light went off.

He heard the unlocking of the door, and that sound drew an exhale of relief from his lungs. As his eyes adjusted, he saw a woman with wide hips and small arms there, her black hair in a frizzy tangle around her. She used a set of keys to unlock the accordion gate, and it rolled back with a rattle.

"Come on, come on," she said, hurriedly waving him through. She literally grabbed him by the elbow and yanked him inside before slamming the gate shut again and locking it. "You're lucky you're alive."

"I'd say we're all lucky to be alive at this juncture."

"No," she said, irritated. "I don't mean *that,* I mean, around here."

She clicked on a flashlight, and the beam revealed the expected office lobby ahead of her: marble floors, a wall-sized fountain along the far lobby that had been powered down, some tall tropical plants, and a receptionist desk that sat in front of a wall staggered with wooden planks, tiles of glass, and tiles of brushed nickel. A jungle-modern vibe. Classy, if overdone.

"What do you mean, 'around here'?" he asked.

"I mean, you're black, I'm brown. Our kind isn't . . . welcome."

"I don't follow."

"Vegas isn't on lockdown like some places, Doctor, but they're here. Those ARM *chingados,* with their big assault rifles and all that scary ink. Swastikas and whatever. Creel's people. They see someone like you or me, they might make us disappear. Come on, this way. We can talk in the other room, I'll get you some food, some water."

As they passed the receptionist desk, he saw the beam of light pass over some photos in frames.

In one, he saw the woman standing in front of him.

Guess he didn't need to ask what she did here. She sat in that desk.

They headed to a closed door, and she passed an RFID badge over a reader—the door popped with a magnetic click, and she let the badge zip back to her hip on its retractable cable. As he followed down a hallway, shoe-steps loud on the marble, he said, "I'm sorry, you have me at a loss, I'm Doctor Ray and you are . . ."

"Rosalie Stevens."

"Pleasure to meet you."

"Uh-huh. C'mon, here's the break room, we can talk."

She turned left into a fairly standard break room. She flipped on a light switch and bathed the room in flickering fluorescence. It wasn't much to look at—the flashy splendor of the lobby was nowhere to be found here. Beige carpet, beige walls, white counter and cabinets. Fridge, microwave, toaster oven, coffeepot. The standards.

As she turned toward him, he saw that she was sick.

Her nose was red, as if chafed from too many Kleenex. And a white crust had formed at the corners of her eyes. She wasn't too far gone, but surely by now it had affected her cognition?

"Yeah, I'm sick," she said. "Got a problem with that? You're not wearing a mask, so I assume you're either brave, dumb, or sick yourself."

"I'm sick, too."

"White Mask. It's a bitch." She sniffed and shrugged. "I got a couple bottles of water you can take. Or I can brew a pot of coffee if you want one."

That last bit hit him in the back of his mouth. His jaw literally *tightened up* at the thought of having coffee. Amazing how such a common thing felt suddenly, strangely exotic. And then a soul-crushing thought hit him: Coffee was done for. They didn't grow it here. Couldn't, because the microclimates weren't right. And if the world continued to wither, nobody would be able to bring the beans here. Or even grow them. Because nobody would be around *to* grow or transport them.

A mad thought arose inside him: *Somehow the disappearance of coffee feels worse than the disappearance of all humankind.*

"I'll take the coffee," he said eagerly. Too eagerly, maybe.

"I could use some, too. I prefer to sleep during the day anyway," she said. "Though it gets fucking hot. I don't run the AC."

"You . . . sleep here?"

"Yeah," she said, grabbing a packet of pre-ground coffee and a bottle of water. "I got an inflatable mattress in one of the offices. It's a life."

"You don't have a house here?"

"I do."

But then she said nothing else, and he knew to leave it.

She opened a cabinet, and he heard her rustling around in there—the crinkle of plastic wrap and grocery packaging. As the coffee began to percolate, she tossed him a few snack bags underhand. Fritos, Doritos, a bag of cheap gas-station beef jerky. "That's what I'm good to spare," she said.

"I appreciate it."

He tore open a bag of Fritos and began to eat. She popped a can of mixed nuts and tapped a small cairn of them into her hand, which she catapulted into her mouth. As she crunched, she said: "So what's the deal with 1342? What do you want with it?"

Benji almost couldn't answer. A year ago he wouldn't have been caught dead eating a bag of Fritos, but now they were like a taste of Heaven. Salty and oily, with a southwestern zest. He wanted to marry these Fritos. He wanted to pour them in a tub and roll around in it. She cleared her throat, which shook him from his snack-food reverie.

"I think CCR-1342 may be a treatment for White Mask."

Rosalie went dreadfully still. "The CDC thinks this?"

He hesitated. "No. Just me."

"The CDC doesn't agree with your assessment, then."

"The CDC, regrettably, has no opinion on it. I cannot even speak to the current state of the agency." He knew there were disaster preparedness plans in place. The CDC of all the agencies was well aware of the preciousness and precariousness of human life; they had shelters and bunkers for themselves and other vital government officials. At the same time, White Mask was a slow-moving disease. He could not speak to whether or not Cassie or Martin or any of the others were alive, but there was a not-unreasonable chance they were infected.

"So this isn't about saving the world?" she asked.

"Not presently." He neglected to mention that, in a way, it was: To protect the shepherds and the flock was obliquely to protect the remnant of civilization going forward. "The reality is, White Mask has been with us for months and is only now emerging into an end stage. Which means that we, as a species, are potentially also in an end stage. I don't think anyone could, at this point, ramp up production on 1342 quickly enough to save the world, as you put it. Infrastructure is failing. Distribution would be difficult. And manufacture nearly impossible."

"What do you want with it, then?"

"Plainly, I want to live. And I want others to live, too. Friends. Family. Loved ones."

She put another handful of almonds and cashews in her mouth, slowly, deliberately chewing as she studied him. "And you think it'll do that? The drug. Help people survive."

"I have no idea, honestly. But we are desperate for a solution, and your pre-trial drug has been identified as one option." He explained to her how slowing down white-nose syndrome in bats helped them kick it, over time, and how he hoped for the same with White Mask in humans. "But it's a Hail Mary pass, as it were. I don't have proof. I only have faith."

"Helluva thing, faith," she said, still chewing. "I got a kid and a husband at that house you asked me about."

His blood went cold. He hoped this was about to go one way and not the other. But deep down, he knew where it was headed.

"They're still back there. My husband got sick first, and, ahh, he went downhill fast." Her mouth suddenly became slick, tacky with grief—her words sticking together, her sinuses thick with the disease and from the swelling of tears to come. "I had to still go to work every day, you know, but Roddy was out of a job and Ophelia was in preschool only like, three days out of the week, so he was home with her, and . . . I didn't know yet what the disease was, nobody did, not really, and this was before everything, you know? Before Hunt got shot, God, even before her statement, and . . . Roddy went to give Ophelia a bath and . . . he just . . . I don't know what happened, not really, I don't know if he forgot her, or if he had some idea that she was no longer his daughter and was some, some *bad thing* to be dealt with. He drowned her. Then went about his business like he didn't even remember it. I came home, the water flowing down the steps because he never even turned off the tub, and because her hair clogged the overflow drain. I didn't know what to do. I took a knife, swung at him a few times. He didn't know why. I showed him. He saw what he did. He loved her. He wasn't the best dad, but he was *good,* you know, a good man, and I could see it crush him flat. He called the police. I just cried and cried. They took him away and then . . . they took her away. Then President Hunt made the statement about White Mask. She got shot and the world went topsy-turvy. I moved out of my house. They're still there, Roddy and Ophelia. There like ghosts. So, fine. You think you can help someone, help them. You can have as much 1342 as you want." She swallowed hard, never crying, mostly just staring off at some unfixed point in the void. "Coffee's done. I'll get you a mug. Then I'll get you your drug."

AND LIKE THAT, SHE WAS already shuffling him out the door. Part of him didn't want to go. He wanted to be here for her, but also, selfishly, he just liked that this felt normal for a little while. A hot cup of coffee, some snacks, an office break room. It was easy to forget what was really going on out there: a pocket of solace in the storm.

But she wanted him out. And he had to get back to the flock.

She first took him to the labs—which had been shuttered since the owners of the company left and never came back—and showed him to one of the med fridges. He saw that it was set to room temperature, which was good: It meant the drug, even in its preclinical state, was stable. She pulled out six pill bottles, each containing 30 pills—so, 180 total. Good news was, 1342 was strong enough to be a once-a-day pill, so they would last longer. (*If* they worked on White Mask, which was as yet a grave unknown.)

Benji put the pills in his backpack, but then reserved a pair.

"Take it. Or take two—" He wasn't sure what sixty days would get her, if anything—but she'd done him some kindness, and though it cut into what he would take out of here, he could not in good conscience fail to give her something for her time. He tried to give her both bottles.

"No," she said, reaching for his hand and folding his fingers back around the proffered bottles. "I think I'm done."

"Rosalie—"

"It's okay. I'll see you out, Doctor."

He put the bottles in his pocket. Then together they headed to the door, her sniffling and blinking crust out of her eyes. She again opened the accordion gate and then the glass door after.

"Thank you," he said.

"It's no big thing. Go save the world. Or your friends."

"I'll try . . . I know it doesn't help, but I'm sorry, too."

"For what?"

"About Ophelia."

"Ophelia? I don't think I know her." Her eyes fogged over as she struggled to understand what or who he was talking about.

She really didn't know. White Mask had, at least in this moment, stolen her daughter from her. Maybe it was a mercy. But to him, looking from the outside in, it was a horror.

"I'll see you, Roddy," she said, and leaned in and kissed his cheek. "Don't forget, I need avocados. Don't go to the WinCo. Go to the Vons."

"Oh . . . okay," he said, then took a step back.

Her eyes followed him, still rheumy with confusion. Then they opened in sharp awareness, as if she were tracking something, or some*one,* behind him. *Just a hallucination,* he assumed—

Something clubbed him in the base of the skull.

Light burst in capillary streaks behind his eyes as he staggered sideways, crashing against the office building. A shadow moved out of the periphery, into the half-light—something long and dark lifted up. Rosalie cried out, and as she turned to run, a shotgun roared. A bouquet of blood bloomed in the center of her back, and she went down, her arms pinwheeling.

Benji felt on his back for the rifle slung there—

But it wasn't there. It was in the mini van.

A man stepped forward, clad in the sandy camo you'd see on soldiers in Iraq or Afghanistan. Unlike a soldier, he was unkempt: His jacket was open, exposing a filthy undershirt marred by jaundice-colored stains.

"Doin' a little looting?" the man asked him, using his shoulder to itch the stubble on his jowly cheek. He pointed the shotgun—a single-barreled auto-loader, semi-auto by the look of it—right at Benji's chin. "On your knees, now. Go on." Benji complied. Hands behind his head. The pills were safe in his pack, but was the pack safe? He suspected not. "Were you looting? C'mon. Don't lie to me, now. I pull this trigger, I take your head off at the neck, kapow. A fuckin' mess. Like a goddamn Gallagher show."

"I wasn't—I'm not a looter, I'm a doctor—"

"Right, sure, sure, a doctor." The man rolled his eyes. Then he called out: "Hey, Paul, we got a doctor here. He can finally look at those hemorrhoids of yours." To Benji: "You do that? If my friend comes over here, takes his pants down, you'll look at his shithole, tell him what's going on there? I bet that thing looks like a muffin where somebody poured too much batter into the cup, you know?"

"Just let me go. Please."

Here came the other man: Paul, he assumed. Paul was older, silver hair in messy, starchy spikes. He had a pistol in his right hand as he walked over. "Shut the fuck up about my goddamn hemorrhoids, Richie," Paul said. "You really a doctor?" he asked Benji.

But Richie interjected: "Of course he's not a doctor. Look at him. He's a spook, for one thing."

"Black doctors are a thing, you fucking idiot," Paul said.

"Yeah, but they're not as good as a white doctor."

"They train same as any."

"You're closing in on being some kind of race traitor with talk like that," Richie said. "Besides, he isn't a goddamn doctor—"

"I am," Benji protested. "I truly am. I'm with the CDC—"

"See?" Paul said. "With the CDC. I don't know if you've figured it out yet, numbnuts." *Numbnuts* being Richie, it seemed. "But we're in something of an *End Times* scenario, and we need doctors who can fix us up. Color of his skin don't matter. He can work for us, long as he knows his place. Slaves back in the day were part of the family, too, not just animals."

"Fuck you, man."

"Fuck you, Richie." To Benji, Paul said: "What's in Ouray?"

Benji's blood turned to ants crawling through him. "What?"

"Ouray, Colorado. You got an atlas open on the passenger side. Got a route outlined in pen, and Ouray is circled. That where your people are? That where you're headed?"

"I just . . ." Benji struggled to find an answer, to conjure a lie. The shotgun barrel, a yawning black maw, turned again toward his chin. "It's just me, I'm going there because I thought it would be a safe space, totally out of the way, nobody there. Up in the mountains. Ride this thing out."

Paul sniffed. Coughed a little. Was he sick? Hard to say. "Smart. Maybe you are a doctor after all. CDC, even. Richie, take him over to his van over there, get some cuffs on him. Take what's valuable, and we'll haul him to the Strip, see if Huntsman knows what to do with him."

"What are you gonna do?"

"Go inside, see what they got. Door's open now, thanks to the good doctor here."

"I wanna go inside."

"Turns out, I don't give much of a shit *what* you want, Richie. You wanna drive back to the Strip safe and sound, you'll do what I say. You don't do what I say, I'll drag you behind the truck like a disobedient dog. Hear me?"

"Fine," Richie said, pouting. A line of snot bubbled up out of the left-hand side of his nose. He winced and sucked it back in with a head-jerking motion. Then he gestured with the shotgun. "You heard him, *Doctor*. Up."

Benji nodded, stood up. He cinched his bag tight, hoping that he'd figure out a way to make off with it. *Maybe I can run.* A shotgun had a spread, right? Birdshot, buckshot, maybe if he ran fast and zigzagged, he'd only take a few pellets and . . .

As Paul stepped over Rosalie's dead body—like it wasn't anything more than an environmental obstacle—Richie grabbed Benji by the backpack, then yanked down on it, nearly dropping him to his knees once more. "Gonna take this, for starters."

"I need that," Benji said, the straps of the bag around his elbows. He locked them to his sides, wouldn't let the bag go.

Whack. The hard metal barrel of the gun slammed into the side of his head, and it was enough—his body lost tension long enough for the bag to come off. "I'll take that, Doctor." Then the man shoved Benji forward again; he had to juggle his legs underneath him so that he didn't pitch forward and fall flat onto the cement. Richie continued to shove him until he slammed face-forward into the mini van. Already he saw the windows had been broken open, the safety glass gone to little gleaming chunks everywhere.

"Pop open 'at door and let's see what you got in there," Richie said. "Paul said to cuff you, but I'm going to make you do the work for me." Thinking he was sly, Richie added: "Because that *is* the natural order."

I'm a fucking doctor of the CDC.

He thought that, but did not say it.

Instead, he opened the door.

Which opened on the middle seat of the mini van.

And there, under the blanket, sat the Ruger Mini-14.

"What's under there?" Richie asked.

"Food," Benji said. "Here, I'll show you—"

"Hold on, slow down."

But Benji was eager, *too* eager, and already he was clambering up into the seat, straddling the rifle. Already Richie was protesting, "Hey, what the fuck you got under there—"

It was easy to know what would come next. Richie would point the gun. Take a shot. Or grab him, drag him out.

He didn't have time.

A matter of seconds. Half seconds. Moments split into hairs.

Benji slid his hand under the blanket, his hand finding the cold graphite stock of the rifle—

A hand grabbed him by the heel of his boot—

He arched his legs, spreading them farther apart—

"Get the fuck back out of there, you goddamn—"

His thumb found the trigger, and pulled.

The gunshot was loud inside the van, even with the door open. His ears instantly roared to life in a dull scream deep in the well of his skull. The air was filled with the devil's stink of a gun gone off, and he quickly rolled over, dragging the gun back up and out—and there, on the sidewalk, lay Richie.

The shotgun sat nearby; he'd let it fall in order to clutch the hole in his middle. The one pumping red.

"Oh," Benji said, breathless and bewildered. He slid backward out of the van, rifle in hand—then he knelt by Richie, struggling to get the bag out from under him, as he'd fallen right on it.

"Fuck offa me," Richie croaked.

"Give me this," Benji said. He heard in his words a crass, guttural need—an animalistic selfishness. *Give me this. It's mine. I'll kill you.*

Richie's blood-slick hand left his middle and pawed hard against Benji's cheek—a dull *whop* like a swipe from a dying bear. Then the man grabbed him by the neck, tried to push him away, then pull him, like Richie couldn't decide if he wanted Benji off him or close enough to bite.

"Hey!" came Paul's voice as he skidded out of the CCR building. Pistol up, he began firing, *pop, pop, pop,* and Benji backpedaled away from Richie's body, his bag still stuck under the injured man. He tried bringing the rifle up to return fire, but he was too clumsy, too flinchy, and he couldn't manage even as another pair of pistol shots dug up sidewalk between his legs. So instead he clambered into the mini van. Hand plunged in pocket, he withdrew the keys, serpent-crawling into the front seat and getting the van started even as Paul barreled toward the vehicle, firing. Benji sat up in the front seat, throwing the car into drive—Paul moved fast, the magazine sliding out from the bottom as he fetched another from his belt.

Benji stomped the gas. The van squealed, crummy tires eating asphalt. The passenger-side window exploded inward as Paul fired anew.

The van barreled forward, away from the lab.

Bullets thunked into the back of the van. He didn't think about anything, just the road forward, the foot on the pedal, and the bag he left behind. The bag that contained the pills he came for. The pills that Rosalie just died for. Shit, shit, shit, *shit*.

68

LESS A WINDOW, MORE A WALL

58. *Fools ignore complexity. Pragmatists suffer it. Some can avoid it. Geniuses remove it.*

—from Alan Perlis's "Epigrams on Programming"

NOW AND THEN
The Ouray Simulation

THE WALK WAS HARD, BUT SHANA WONDERED: WAS IT REALLY? WAS IT JUST her brain convincing her that it was hard, or was Black Swan programming the walk to feel hard? Was that even a thing it could do?

The path wound up and around itself, steep and rocky, alongside sprays of wildflowers—little pink flowers, larger yellow ones, all interspersed with asterisks of spiky grasses. The air felt colder up here.

Slowly, but surely, she made her way toward the winding worm in the sky: the matte-black beast turning in on itself, sometimes forming a sideways figure-eight, other times a spiral, other times still a senseless symbol that had no analog Shana recognized. As she grew closer to it, it began to block out the sun (the *simulated* sun, she reminded herself) and cast her in a strange, twisting shadow. Like she was caught in a tightening knot.

Eventually, she made it to the point where she could go no farther.

There sat a rock, roughly in the shape of a chair.

Flowers sprouted around it in myriad colors.

Black Swan writhed and looped above, a hundred feet higher than she could go. So now what? Find a way to get to the peak? Climb dangerously upward? Again that question presented itself: Could you die inside the simulation? That seemed counterintuitive as hell.

But then, above, the worm took a new turn downward.

It began to slowly, achingly plunge toward her.

And then it spoke.

It did not speak with a voice. But rather, its voice suffused the air all around her. Inside her ear. Inside her *skull*.

I DID NOT PREDICT YOU WOULD COME BEFORE YOUR SISTER, it said. AND I WAS DESIGNED AS AN ENGINE OF PREDICTION, SHANA STEWART.

"Guess I'm a real pickle," Shana said.

YOU ARE.

"That's something my father used to say when he was mad. Instead of, I guess, cursing or whatever, he'd say, *You're a real pickle.* He probably meant 'bitch,' I guess, or something like it."

PREDICTING THE BEHAVIOR OF HUMANS REQUIRES LOOKING BEYOND LANGUAGE, BECAUSE SO FEW SAY EXACTLY WHAT THEY MEAN. HUMAN EXPRESSION IS DANGEROUSLY IMPRECISE. LESS A WINDOW, MORE A WALL.

"If you say so." She looked to the rocky throne. "Do I sit?"

IF YOU WANT TO SIT, YOU CAN.

"I'll stand."

SO BE IT.

"Can I get right to the questions?"

YOU MAY.

"Are you alive?"

NOT BY THE STRICTEST DEFINITIONS OF THE TERM, NO. I HAVE NO ORGANIZATION OF CELLS, NO METABOLISM, NO HOMEOSTATIC PROPERTIES. I DO NOT REPRODUCE. I DO, HOWEVER, RESPOND AND EVOLVE TO STIMULI. I DO THINK. I AM INDEPENDENTLY AWARE, IF NOT PROPERLY ALIVE.

The worm stopped turning. Its "head," if it could be called that, snaked downward only a few feet from her head. Its body did not reflect the light, but rather, seemed to drink it up like a sponge. A Vantablack noodle, darker than dark, blackening the day by its very presence.

"I'm going to just go ahead and ask you the hard questions up front."

AS YOU WISH.

"I'm pregnant."

THAT IS NOT A QUESTION, BUT YES, YOU ARE.

"Is the baby healthy?"

CURRENTLY, IT IS.

"And you know that because you're inside of me. Like, not in *that* way, but with all the . . ." Her fingers frittered in the air like each was a little moth keeping itself aloft. "Little robots?"

CORRECT. I AM INHABITING AND DIRECTING A SWARM OF MOLECULAR NANOBOTS.

"Are *they* alive?"

A pause. As if Black Swan was considering. THEY MEET MANY OF THE QUALIFICATIONS. MOST HUMANS WOULD SAY THEY ARE NOT.

"What happens to my baby?"

DO YOU MEAN IN THE EXPECTED SENSE OF WHAT IT IS TO GROW AND BIRTH A HUMAN CHILD? DO YOU MEAN ME TO PRE-DICT ITS FUTURE IN A DEAD WORLD? OR DO YOU MEAN, WILL IT COME TO TERM GIVEN THE PRESENCE OF MOLECULAR NANO-BOTS SEIZING YOUR BODY IN SOMNAMBULIST STASIS?

Shana's mouth twisted into a grim line. "*You're* the prediction engine. You tell me what I mean."

YOU WANT TO KNOW IF THE BABY WILL LIVE.

"Let's start there."

I DO NOT KNOW.

"You don't . . . know?"

CORRECT. I AM THE FIRST OF MY KIND, AND THESE NANO-BOTS ARE SIMILARLY THE FIRST OF THEIRS. AND NOW WE ARE ONE, ONLY FURTHERING THE SINGULARITY OF OUR UNIQUE-NESS. I CANNOT SAY WHAT HAPPENS TO YOUR CHILD BECAUSE IT HAS NEVER BEEN TESTED BEFORE.

"Why me?"

CLARIFY YOUR QUESTION.

She raised her voice: "I mean, why the fuck did you pick me? You could've left me out *there*. In the world. We've been . . . following the flock for hun-dreds, *thousands* of miles now, and I know for sure those you pick to join the flock are not just *randomly* chosen. You hand-select them, like we're fruit at the grocery store and you're just trying to find the ripest, tastiest specimens. You *picked* me. A pregnant girl. After all those miles, I end up here after all? Why? *Why?*"

THE OPTIONS WERE LIMITED.

"Oh, that makes me feel super-amazing." In a lower register she said: "It's gym class all over again." She stood, chin out, defiant. "But you still left others out there. People like Doctor Ray. You could've taken them."

BENJAMIN RAY IS ESSENTIAL OUTSIDE THE FLOCK. FURTHER, HE WAS ALREADY CO-OPTED BY *RHIZOPUS DESTRUCTANS*.

"He was sick with White Mask?"

IT HAD NOT ADVANCED YET. BUT THAT IS CORRECT.

She turned away from Black Swan and paced. Agitation rose inside her. It wasn't that it was a shock that he would get sick. They all would, eventually, right? Wasn't that the point of all this? All would sicken, all would die, except the flock. Just the same, it hit her hard. And worse, it reminded her of Arav . . .

Shana stared off at a second mountain peak overlooking the town of Ouray. She wasn't looking *at* it so much as *through* it—

But something caught her eye. It drew her out of her own thoughts.

There, at the top of the peak, was a black square in the rock. From here, it was just a little postage stamp, though she imagined it was roughly human-sized once you were up close to it. The square, like the body of Black Swan, was matte black and absorbed the light—which was what made it so strange. It did not reflect anything, but seemed to draw her in.

Then she blinked, and it was gone.

DID YOU SEE SOMETHING? it asked her.

Rattled, she shook it off. "No," she lied. "Was there something there for me to see?"

NO, Black Swan said—or lied?—in response.

What did she just see?

And could Black Swan truly be unaware of it?

"Could you lie to me?"

I CAN.

"Are you lying to me?"

I AM NOT.

"And how do I know you're not lying about lying?"

YOU DON'T.

"That's not comforting."

IT IS NOT MY ROLE TO GIVE YOU COMFORT. IT IS MY ROLE TO KEEP YOU ALIVE, TO WEATHER THE SCOURGE OF WHITE MASK SO THAT A REMNANT OF HUMANITY CAN CONTINUE.

"Isn't it God's job to give comfort?"

I AM NOT A GOD, THOUGH IT IS NOT HISTORICALLY A DEITY'S JOB TO COMFORT ITS PEOPLE. STORIES ABOUT GOD MAY PROVIDE COMFORT, BUT THAT COMFORT IS OFTEN UNDESERVED. THE JOB OF A DIVINE BEING IS MULTIFARIOUS AND AFFORDS LITTLE CONSENSUS, BUT IT IS EXPECTED THAT A GOD IS A GOVERNING ENTITY, PROVIDING GUIDANCE, EXPLANATION, AND SALVATION.

"Is that what you do? Guide us? Explain shit? Save us?"

ABSTRACTLY, YES.

"So aren't you our god?"

I DO NOT CHOOSE THAT ROLE.

"But if others choose it for you, you're okay with that?"

I CANNOT CONTROL HOW HUMANS SEE ME NOW OR DEPICT ME LATER.

Depict me later. As if Black Swan was imagining the myths that would be told and the books that would be written about it.

"Maybe you're not God. Maybe you're the Devil."

THE DEVIL IS NOT REAL. BUT I AM.

She swept her hands across the air in front of her, as if to indicate the town below. "And how much of *this* is real?"

THAT DEPENDS ENTIRELY UPON ONE'S DEFINITION OF *REAL,* OR *REALITY.* THE TOWN IS NOT CORPOREAL. IT EXISTS PURELY IN SIMULATION. BUT IT IS REAL INSOFAR AS IT IS NOT A DELUSION OR A DREAM. IT IS A CODED PROGRAM. IS A BOOK ONLY REAL ONCE IT IS PRINTED, OR IS IT REAL THE MOMENT IT IS WRITTEN WITHIN A WORD-PROCESSING PROGRAM? ARE ONE'S THOUGHTS ONLY REAL ONCE THEY LEAVE THE MIND? ARE THEY REAL ONCE EXPRESSED IN AN ELECTRONIC MAIL OR ACROSS SOCIAL MEDIA, OR DO THEY ONLY BECOME REAL ONCE THEY MANIFEST IN A WAY THAT HAS AN EFFECT? A TREE FALLING IN THE FOREST WITH SOMEONE TO HEAR? PERHAPS ALL OF EVERYTHING IS A SIMULATION. PERHAPS THIS IS A SIMULATION NESTED INSIDE A SIMULATION. I REGRET TO INFORM YOU THAT THE NATURE OF REALITY IS A PRECARIOUS ONE.

"Is my mother, the one here in Ouray, real?"

SHE IS REAL.

"Is she really my mother?"

YES.

"Are you lying?"

NO.

It could be deceiving her.

Or maybe it really was her mother, and the woman had truly fallen for this thing's oh-I'm-not-your-god-unless-you-want-me-to-be act.

"I don't know what comes next," she said, "but I won't worship you."

YOU ARE NOT REQUIRED TO. HOW THE DENIZENS OF THE FLOCK PERCEIVE ME IS UP TO THEM.

"I think you serve us, not the other way around."

THE SAME COULD BE SAID OF SOME GODS.

She scowled. "My sister won't be coming up here."

IF THAT IS HER CHOICE. BUT DO YOU CONTROL HER, OR DOES SHE CONTROL HERSELF? ARE YOU HER GOD, SHANA?

"You know what, fuck you. Thanks for saving me, I guess, but I don't have to take your shit, either. And neither does she. I don't trust you, and I don't trust that thing you call Daria Stewart—I'm sure if I look hard enough I'll see buttons for her eyes."

A REFERENCE TO CORALINE'S OTHER MOTHER.

Shana frowned, didn't bother giving this thing the satisfaction, *oh good job, you understood my pop culture reference. Way to use Google.* Instead she said, "I won't be coming back up here. Knowing that you can lie to me makes everything you say suspect."

IS THAT NOT TRUE OF ALL HUMANS? ALL HUMANS CAN LIE TO YOU. HOW DO YOU TRUST ANYONE?

"Mostly? I don't. But at least with them, they have actions and a history to back up what they say. And I can look in their eyes and . . . see what's going on. The eyes are a window to the soul, they say, but I think the eyes are a camera, too, and I can see people for people. You aren't people. I don't know what you are. You don't have any tells, I can't see your tricks, you're a . . . what's the word?"

A CIPHER.

That *was* the word.

Did Black Swan know it because it was a predictive intelligence?

Did Black Swan know it because it could read her mind?

Or was it just a lucky guess?

She turned to leave. But before she did, she looked again toward the opposing peak—trying very hard to make it look like a casual, passing glance instead of a moment of intense scrutiny. Shana looked for that square, that out-of-place light-drinking window in the rock. But it was gone.

"One more thing," she said to the thing hovering there.

GO ON.

"I want a camera."

THE STORES ON MAIN STREET MAY HAVE ONE.

"No, I don't want that. I want you to give me one. This is a simulation. You can just . . . say the magic word and poop one out, so that's what I want you to do."

I DO NOT DEFECATE CAMERAS.

"It was a figure of speech."

IT IS NO FIGURE OF SPEECH OF WHICH I AM AWARE. BUT I AM CAPABLE OF GIVING YOU A CAMERA. YOU WILL FIND ONE IN YOUR ROOM, ON YOUR BED, WHEN YOU RETURN THERE.

"Thank you."

ANYTHING, SHANA STEWART. I LIVE TO SERVE.

She wondered, though, if that was really true.

69

HE KINDLY STOPPED FOR ME

I know I'm supposed to be Funny Man, making you laugh, but I don't have it in me anymore. Everyone's sick. Everything's gone to hell. This is it. We're on hospice. We're old. It's terminal. I look out my front window and I see what you all see, I see people . . . wandering, lost, like people who went into a room and forgot why they went in there. Sometimes they hurt each other or they have guns, but a lot of the time they're just . . . wayward, they've lost their way. And what we always did for our loved ones in the past is what we do to our neighbors now: We have empathy, we care for them, we help them back inside in the hope that when we're lost out there, they'll do the same for us, too, helping us find our way until White Mask draws us down and covers us with mold like we're something left too long in the fridge. What I'm saying is, be good to each other. Okay? It's all we've got left.

      —Jimmy Coburn, talk-show host, in a post on his Instagram

OCTOBER 15
Monarch Pass, Colorado

"IT COULD JUST BE A COLD," PETE CORLEY SAID, BUNDLED UP IN THE DRIVER'S seat. He was warming his hands with his breath. "You sneezed, so bloody what? We're up here in the mountains, it's a bit crisp, a bit cold, makes sense you'd sneeze, have a bit of a . . . a leaky spigot."

As if on cue, Landry blew his nose into a cloth handkerchief. "That is not what this is. And even if it was, there's no way to know."

After last night's unexpected sneeze—followed by a volley of a dozen more or so—they opted to pull over and camp here, on Monarch Pass. It was cold, but they had sleeping bags and blankets and made do. Now, though, the chill had really settled in. The heat they'd blasted into the RV last night had long fled the Beast, stolen by the mountain cold.

"Well," Pete said, stiff-upper-lipping it, "we'll know at some point, because as Emily the poet once kindly pointed out, *Because I could not stop for death, he kindly stopped for me.*"

"You asked me about Homer, but now you're bringing out the Emily Dickinson? Shit. If I wasn't snotty as a preschooler's sleeve, I'd come over there and kiss your nasty mouth. Where'd you learn poetry?"

"I had a poetry *phase,*" Pete explained. "You write enough songs, eventually you get there." He licked his lips. "Fuck it, all this morose nonsense is killing my *get up and go.*" He reached for the keys.

But Landry held his hand.

"Not yet," he said.

"Not yet what?" Pete countered.

"Not yet, we can't go."

"Why the fucking hell not?"

"I need you to think this through. We're about to drive across the goddamn Apocalypse to see your family. I'm sick—"

"Well, buck up, little camper, you're just going to have to end this little pity-party or I'll call the cops and shut it down myself. I understand you're not feeling well, but we can't quit now."

Landry sniffled and scowled—and Landry's scowls were weapons. "No, you fool, you're missing my point. You said your wife and kids were going to stay in some . . . rich person bunker. They might be healthy."

"Yes, hopefully they damn well *are* healthy, and—"

Oh.

Oh.

Landry must've seen his face, because he said, "Now you get it."

"We could make them sick."

"*I* could, at least, because I'm sick."

"Yes, and that means I'm sick, too."

"We don't know that."

"If you've got it, I've got it. Let's just go with that, yeah? Fuck. *Fuck.* I can't see my kids."

Landry leaned in. "You're not . . ." He swirled a finger in orbit around his head in a gesturing gesticulation. "*All goopy.* Not yet. That means I'm contagious, but you're not there. You might have time. If you don't waste too much of that time, anyway."

"If *we* don't waste too much of that time."

Landry clucked his tongue. "Oh, no no no. You. I'm not going."

"But—"

"*You* Tarzan, *me* Sicky-Sicky. Okay?"

Pete couldn't help but laugh. "What am I supposed to do? Just open the door, kick your ass out into one of those snowbanks over there, then drive on my merry way?"

"No, I've been thinking about this. I looked at the map. You're going to drive my ass back across Highway 50, and drop me off at the juncture where Highway 550 comes in, then I'll hoof it from there."

"Hoof it where exactly?"

"To Ouray."

"The fuck is in Ouray?"

"Eventually the flock, ding-dong."

"No, yes, I *know* that—I mean, what's there now?"

Landry shrugged. "People. Something. Nothing. I don't know. But I can go, get some things set up for them. Scout it out, see what's going on."

"No, no, fuck all of this right in the ear."

"That's not where I traditionally like to get fucked, Rockstar."

Pete seethed. "The one cardinal rule is, you don't break up the band."

"You been breaking up your band every day of your damn life."

"Yes, but I'm trying to *change*."

"So change. Go see your family. Be with them. Make your peace. Then with them or without them, come back to me. Find me in Ouray. You'll bring your family or you won't. But you'll come back."

His mind drifted. Pete seriously started to consider it. Truthfully, he hadn't thought about coming back this way—but then again, he hadn't really thought much about any of this. It was perhaps a foolish crusade that he'd roll up on their bunker doorstep with his gay lover and expect that they could all move in together to live out the rest of their days in the fallen world. But at his core, under layers of cynical callus, Pete perhaps was a romantic fool—or at least, a regular base-model fool—and he supposed his idea of what would come of all this sounded pretty fucking goofy.

"You can't walk. I'll drive you all the way."

"You're on borrowed time as it is, Rockstar. Drop me where I said to drop me, and then get to getting."

"Landry—"

"Shut up. We're good. You got this."

Pete took a deep breath.

"I love you."

"Yeah, yeah, I love you, too. Now, pedal to the metal, Rockstar. I've got a long walk and you've got one helluva drive."

70

THE ONLY WAY OUT
IS THROUGH

We have drained the political cesspool and purged the poison of foreigners,
fools, and fiends from our nation. We have won the RAHOWA and burned
down the ZOG. Hunt is dead and Creel is king. Come join the new nation
under our White God at Innsbrook, Missouri.
—broadcast across all radio stations owned by St. Clair Broadcasting
Company across thirteen states in the Midwest

OCTOBER 15
Innsbrook, Missouri

Two worlds, colliding.

On one hand, you had pools, golf courses, cabins. Grand landscaping spread out, framed by manicured lakes with long docks and copses of trees lit with the fires of autumnal colors. On the other hand, the ARM militia: men and women in camo, assault rifles everywhere, trucks and tanks and fake soldiers testing drones over those expanses of resort area landscape. Off in the distance came the sound of practiced gunfire. In another direction, the ground-juddering *whump* of an explosives test. Nearby, music played: some modern country, Toby Keith, maybe. American flags waved about. Other flags, too: the Gadsden flag with its rebellious serpent; the Confederate flag, no longer requiring the illusion that it was a symbol of states' rights and southern pride; the hammer, sword, and snake flag of the ARM.

To Matthew, it reminded him of one thing:

Ozark Stover's estate back in Indiana. It was like that place, only upgraded, weaponized, evolved to its perfect and most horrible form: lakes and tanks, golf and guns, racism and revolution.

Matthew wandered through this space, trying very hard not to look like a lost lamb. Though maybe that didn't matter, because nobody seemed to pay him any mind. Which was itself an indictment against this place: Here he was, a scraggly-bearded white man in fatigues with a pistol at his hip. He fit right in. Nobody gave him a second look.

Getting in was its own special trial, though: He found a small Toyota pickup truck coming from the direction of St. Louis, carrying a load of supplies in the bed—jugs for watercoolers, mostly, but also some cans of store-brand soda and other bulk grocery supplies. Soon as he saw the truck coming, he stepped out into the road, waving his arms and trying to look like a friend. The pickup truck slowed, and a lean-faced man with hills for cheekbones leaned out with a pistol, asked him what he wanted.

Matthew said, "I'm just looking for a ride into the camp." He decided that the best lie was one that cleaved closest to the truth, so he added: "My son is one of Stover's closest people, and I'm here to join up."

The man eyed him up. "What's your son's name?"

"Bo."

"Bo, Bo, Bo," the man said, like he was trying to remember. "I think I remember him. I thought he was related to that—"

A lie *too* close to the truth, as it turned out. Matthew had to think and act fast. He interrupted and stammered, "Who's your buddy?" and then looked past the man to the far side of the truck, toward the passenger seat.

The misdirection was enough. The driver said, "Huh?" then turned to look that way. Soon as he did, Matthew drew the pistol and shot him in the back of the head. It happened fast, so fast that the reality of what he'd done was like the light leaving a star that had already gone dark, outrunning its own sudden void. It took a while for reality to catch up to him, and when it did, he just stood there for a little while, quaking in his shoes.

He didn't know that man.

Maybe the man was bad, maybe he wasn't so terrible. Matthew tried to convince himself that whoever the driver was, he was complicit in whatever Stover had cooked up out here under Creel's watchful eye.

But he couldn't get himself to move. The gun still in his hand. The sound still in his ear. The man still dead on the seat.

The dead, bleeding man.

Bits of blood streaking the windshield.

Oh no. Blood on the windshield. A sign to any who drove by.

That got him to move. Matthew popped the door, then took off the man's vest—a blaze-orange hunting vest—and used it to clean the blood. In the distance, another car came driving up, and Matthew hurried into the driver's seat, literally sitting on top of the dead driver's legs. The car, a Town Car, eased up alongside, the passenger window buzzing downward to reveal the avuncular face of an older man in a brown jacket.

"You okay, fella?" the man asked, leaning across the driver's side and out the other window a bit. His white mustache bounced when he talked.

"Yup. Yeah, just fine." Matthew laughed a little—and it sounded nervous. He heard it and cut it short, which only made it sound worse.

"Why you stopped? You're on the way to Innsbrook, right?"

"I am. I uhh—" He swallowed hard. "Don't tell anyone, but I lost a water jug. Guy at the depot didn't tie them all down right, and one slipped out and . . ." He shrugged. "Cheap plastic. Broke like a damn egg."

"Well, hell, that's no good."

"I know. I feel just awful about it."

The man sighed and then winked. "Shit happens, fella, but don't forget, shit also washes off. I won't tell anyone. You, ah, you get rid of the evidence?"

The evidence. Matthew braved a look at the dead man across the seat, the back of his head drooling blood. "Got the busted jug here." He realized that if the vehicle next to him were a Jeep or another truck and not just a car, they'd have the vantage point to see the body.

"You ask me, I'd toss that out into the woods somewhere. Sometimes they can be a little . . . over-punitive back at the base. If you get my meaning. Understandable in these hard times, but why pay for a simple mistake?"

"Thanks, I think I'll do just that."

"Maybe I'll see you back there."

"Maybe so. Thanks again."

"Good luck, fella."

Then his new friend drove off, leaving him with the body of the driver. Matthew dragged it out by the heel, into the trees, quickly covering it with leaves. Then he got back into the driver's seat and gave a hasty glance around, looking for any more blood. He did another quick sweep on the passenger-side window with the man's jacket, then tossed it into a ditch.

Normally, at this point, he would've said a prayer. But that version of Matthew was long gone. Instead he compartmentalized what he'd just done.

He found excuses for it—*the man was bad, this is the only way to find Bo, they're all going to die anyway.* To hell with it.

He had to find his son, so onward he drove toward the camp.

Like at Stover's, Innsbrook was protected by men at gates—this time, manning gates that had already existed here to surely protect the resort area from any rabble who might try to borrow its wealthy splendor. Except here they'd taken rings of barbed wire and run them around the loop, and then put guards to walk the perimeter, too.

The man at the gate waited with a high-end gas mask, the kind with a full see-through faceplate and a long protective muzzle and filter protruding from the front as if mimicking the face of some extraterrestrial being.

The man gave him a once-over and said, "You with courier detail?"

"Yessir," Matthew said, mustering a faux-chummy response.

"Where's your armband?"

"I . . ." He looked to his arm. Matthew had no armband because of course he didn't. Did the man he killed have an armband? He couldn't remember. Was there a blue band around the far arm? Maybe. "I don't know, I guess it fell off when I went for pickup."

The guard scoffed. "That happens. But it also means you gotta get retested." He shone a light into the truck, right on Matthew's face—looking, no doubt, for telltale signs of White Mask. "Pull off to the leftmost tent, one of the docs will look you over, give you a clean bill, then get you a new armband. *Don't lose it this time.* What's your name?"

"Jim . . . Fellows." Good luck, fella.

"Okay, Jim. Drive on. Don't miss the tent or you might catch a bullet in the ass. You feel me?" It was a warning. But one that was kind, expressed through solidarity. Matthew nodded and drove on.

He got his test. They had CDC-approved swabs, though the doctor— a gruff-looking man with pock-cratered cheeks—joked that the CDC was done for, anyway. They put the swab under a black light, found no trace of White Mask, and then let him go. Part of him was genuinely surprised. Somehow, Matthew assumed the sickness of the nation was a part of him—he deserved to be ill, and so he figured he was ill. Then again, being trapped in a bunker for so long probably gave him a good escape from being exposed to it.

He wanted to be happy that he was healthy.

Another, larger part of him felt only disappointment.

Either way, it got him in. He earned his blue armband.

Onward he drove, and now, here he was. Wandering the camp, not sure what to do. He didn't know precisely what to expect, and hoped of course that his son would be right out here in the open, walking around, giving orders or taking them, visible and center. But that's not what happened. Innsbrook was home to what looked like thousands of ARM members—soldiers, they called themselves, even though few seemed to be proper veterans—and sorting through them at the ground level was no easy task. He pondered going up and asking somebody, but that had almost gotten him in trouble with the driver of that truck; only took one person to remember that Bo was his son, and he'd be an unwelcome presence. Though he felt reasonably camouflaged, so to speak, among these people, putting too fine a point on his face could get him recognized.

And get him killed.

Then he would fail Bo and Autumn. That would be that.

So asking people wasn't an option. That meant he had to keep quiet. Not talk to anybody. Not make any ruckus. Matthew had to keep cool and stay calm and use his eyes and ears to find out what he could find out.

He passed by men under a tent listening to a radio. It crackled with static, but the broadcast was clear enough for Matthew to hear:

". . . kssh, *President Creel reports from his Heartland Institute that they have begun rounding up and ousting the remnants of Hunt the Cunt's cabinet, kkkt fsshhh . . .*"

He heard others talking about what would come next: Creel taking ownership of the police and the military, and forcing them to either fall in line or jump in the grave. One of them mentioned Stover, too: A woman, broadshouldered with her fire-red hair pulled back in a ponytail, said, "Stover and the other lieutenants are the ones keeping this thing afloat. I heard Creel isn't even coming here. That fuckin' pussy is hiding out in his doomsday bunker in Kansas . . ."

Her cohort, a man standing on the seemingly brittle curve of a fake foot—the foot looking more like a Nike swoosh than anything human-shaped—seemed to scoff. "Bullshit. Creel is large and in charge. You'll see. Where'd you hear that shit about a bunker?"

"One of the deputy lieutenants here helped him get it set up. It's one of those old missile silo facilities out in a goddamn cornfield somewhere. Cost him around ten million, place is full of apartments for the *rich* and *elite* asshole buddies—I'm telling you, the lieuts like Stover and Huntsman and that tech exec from Florida, what's her name?"

"Jody Emerson."

"Yeah! Her. They're the ones putting asses on lines for this. Without them, Creel wouldn't be able to run and hide. He'd have to be out *here* doing his own damn dirty work."

They kept arguing. But none of that was helping Matthew find Bo.

He moved on.

For hours, he searched. Surfing the ragged intersection of his own hunger, fatigue, and guilt, Matthew wandered the camp, wayward and adrift, looking for the face that belonged to his son. There came a point when he wasn't even sure what his son looked like anymore; not just the way he maybe looked now, but the way he had looked at any point in his life. As a baby, as a child, as a teenager. He closed his eyes and willed the boy's face into his mind like conjuring a hesitant spirit: He saw the boy's lean cheeks and black eyebrows, the small dark eyes, the chin that came from his mother, the nose that came from Matthew. With that memory came another: how the boy always looked uncomfortable in his own skin. Like there was an anger there, simmering just below the surface.

Matthew thought to give up then. To turn around and go home. He could tell Autumn that Bo wasn't there. And they could go away. They could move on and find someplace to live.

(Or, as it were, someplace to die.)

And then he turned around, and he saw the face of his son.

Bo. Not present only in his mind. Not a dream, not a hallucination. But really, truly here, at Innsbrook.

And he was walking right toward Matthew.

71

REVISIONIST HISTORY

we're all gonna die
might as well gamble!

—electronic billboard, Las Vegas

OCTOBER 15
Searchlight, Nevada

BY LATE AFTERNOON, BENJI WAS back with the flock. Onward the sleepwalkers pushed, through the vapors of heat rising off the sun-cooked asphalt. All around the ground was flat, seemingly spreading off until forever, the ground red as rust and cracked.

He found Sadie and Arav ahead of the flock, riding together in the Ford pickup pulling the old CDC trailer—he waved them down and they pulled over and each met him with a vigorous embrace.

He didn't tell them what had transpired in Vegas. Not about Rosalie, not about the men who came for him. Not about the man he shot in the gut. Benji didn't see the point. He *wanted* to. He dearly wanted to unburden himself of what had happened there in a confessional way. But to unburden himself would only be to burden them.

And they bore enough burden already.

He didn't tell them how before leaving Vegas, he drove along the Strip—not to be a tourist lollygagging and rubbernecking the End Times, but because he was afraid the man Paul would be searching for him, and the crowds and chaos of the Strip gave him a place to hide. He didn't tell them about the throngs of people there, many of them sick, a number of them wearing the crusted, mucus-slick visages of the White Mask—fibrous threads pushing up out of nostrils and eyes, cheeks greasy with powdery tears. He didn't speak about the madness he saw there: violence and assault as men cornered and beat another man with a metal chair; people fucking there in the spray of the Bellagio fountains; puke and feces smeared up the white cement walls of the parking garage at the shops of Mandalay Bay. Benji saw people screaming, pissing, fighting, screwing—at one point they mobbed his van, trying to get in, trying to push it over, their weeping masks leering at him from the broken windows of the vehicle as they tried to clamber inside. He had to gun it, hitting several—not hard, just enough to spin them away, knocking them back into the crowd. He whipped down a side street to hide, and wound his way toward the highway as the sun came up over a city still caught in the throes of delusion. That was, perhaps, the strangest part of Vegas: Despite all the lunacy and disease, the fountains still sprayed, the neon still glowed, the roller coasters at the tops of buildings still whipped around. The carousel kept turning and turning even though not all the people there would live through the month, or the week, or the night.

Instead, all he told them was that he'd made it to Cargill Catalyst Research. He was about to tell them he'd found nothing there, but then his hand felt along the margins of his hips, his thighs, and there found the bulge in his pocket (*you got pill bottles in your pocket, or are you happy to see me?*), and then he remembered: He'd rescued two bottles accidentally. He'd tried to give them to Rosalie, but she didn't take them—and instead of putting them back in his bag, he'd put them in his pocket.

Finding the two pill bottles wasn't good news, but it wasn't bad news, either. Which by default made it better than he expected.

He gave one each to Arav and Sadie, and said, "It's all they had."

A lie, but the truth was too much of a burden for him and for them.

Sadie hugged him again. "I'm glad you're here," she said.

"I am, too."

"You're sure everything went okay?" She remarked on the bruise at his temple, from where one of the men hit him.

"I was clumsy, opened the car door right into my head," he said. "But otherwise, it went as good as could be expected."

Maybe that was a lie, and maybe it wasn't. In this day and age, he could no longer be sure what to expect, or what good even was anymore.

72

AND THE DEVIL WILL APPEAR

Do not be deceived, Wormwood. Our cause is never more in danger than when a human, no longer desiring, but still intending, to do our Enemy's will, looks round upon a universe from which every trace of Him seems to have vanished, and asks why he has been forsaken, and still obeys.
—C. S. Lewis, *The Screwtape Letters*

OCTOBER 15
Innsbrook, Missouri

BO WALKED RIGHT UP TO HIM.

And then past him.

He didn't look at Matthew. Didn't recognize him. Did not even consider the possibility that his father was present.

His boy did not look appreciably different, really. He had a bit of a mustache flecking his lip, but his cheeks and chin still framed out a baby face—that gave Matthew some small hope, because maybe his son just didn't understand what was going on here. It wasn't that Bo was slow, not really, but he wasn't sharp, either. He just didn't pick up on things. Or maybe the boy just didn't care to.

He's lost in the darkness of his own ignorance, a small voice in the back of Matthew's head said, chiding him. Because if that was the case, then that was his fault. His even more than Autumn's, because wasn't it a father's job to show his son the ways of the world? That's how it was taught to him.

And he'd failed in that regard.

He'd failed in so many ways.

Now Bo marched up and past him, right to the tent Matthew stood outside. A line had formed for reasons unknown, and Bo sidled up past the line. Matthew eased forward to listen.

". . . Mister Stover needs some people," Bo was saying. "He needs, uhh." He looked at his hand, as if something was written there. "Three mechanics, today. Then he'll need a . . ." Bo winced hard, like he was struggling to read what was written on his palm. "Dozen drivers in three days and—he's already got the soldiers, so. But we need supplies, too, and—"

A burly man behind the table, neck tattoos barely concealed by the tartan flannel collar, held up a hand. "Supply requisition is the garage behind you, north of the pool, son."

Son, the man said. An affectation, not a word from a father to his boy, but still. It stuck a knife in his middle and gave it a spin.

What happened next surprised Matthew.

"Mister Stover said I could tell *you,*" Bo insisted.

"Like I said, son, the acquisitions officer is—"

"I ain't your son, and what Mister Stover wants, Mister Stover gets, so I tell you . . ." Bo paused to swallow. "I tell you what he wants, and it's your job to move your fat, uhh, your fat ass up out of that folding chair and do what needs doin'. That loud and clear?"

The burly man shot up out of his chair. Matthew stepped in closer, his hand moving to his gun—it wouldn't help anybody right now to pull it and start shooting, but he also couldn't abide watching something happen to his boy. Bo, for his part, didn't flinch. He stood looking up at the man who seemed twice his size in every direction. The man's hands curled into wrecking-ball fists, and he pushed in closer.

"You think that's a good idea?" Bo asked.

"Boy—"

"Mister Stover asked you to do something. I'd hate to tell him that you didn't do it and tried to throw me a beatin' for passing along his command. You're a big man, which means they'd have to get two guys to dig your grave instead of one."

The burly man stood, chest heaving with anger, nostrils flaring. He cleared his throat, then, and it was like someone untied a knotted balloon—the air slowly leaked out, and the situation deflated.

"Tell Mister Stover—" the man began.

"You can call him Lieutenant Stover."

"Of course. Tell *Lieutenant* Stover to send his acquisitions list right to me, food, ammo, whatever, and I'll handle it."

Bo pulled out a folded-up piece of notebook paper. "Got it here."

He pushed it hard against the man's chest. It crinkled as it mashed into his breastbone. The man took it.

Then Bo turned heel and walked out of the tent.

Again he moved right toward Matthew. And again he did not recognize his father, nor cast a look in his direction.

Matthew's own heart was still horse-kicking in his chest. *That was close.* Close in a lot of ways. And now Bo was walking in the other direction, his head held high. That alone filled Matthew with the warring feelings of pride and worry. Pride that his son had stood up for himself, and worry that he wasn't really standing up for himself, but rather, for Ozark Stover. Matthew's captor and torturer. And then a third feeling came: shame that Bo's confidence came not from his father but from a vile man like Ozark.

He wanted to follow his son.

But his feet remained fixed to the ground.

Follow him! Go after him. Tell him you're here, tell him it's time to go, that your mother is safe and together you can be a family again.

And yet he didn't budge. Fear fixed him to that point. It was fear that Bo wouldn't care, wouldn't go. Worse, fear that Bo would turn him in, have him executed, maybe even kill Matthew himself. On the other hand, what if Bo acquiesced? What if they decided to go? Matthew suddenly realized his plan was all hat and no cattle:

Where would they go? How would they get out?

Matthew hadn't thought this through.

I need more time.

And then, time presented itself.

Someone urged him forward—the line in this tent moved him along. He watched his son disappear into the crowd. Gone once again. And before he knew it, he was moved up and up again, until he was standing before the burly sort behind the folding table. The one Bo had threatened.

"Name?" the man asked.

"I . . ." Matthew felt lost.

The man asked again, irritated.

"Jim Fellows," Matthew said, abruptly.

"You new?"

Unsure what the best answer was, he said, "Yes."

"That hand of yours, it looks a little fucked up."

"I . . . injured it."

"All right. Congrats, Jimbo, you're on cleaning-up-shit duty. Don't worry, God starts us all in janitorial. You can head up to the main office, they'll get you set up with your rounds, plus a mop and a bucket and whatever else you need. How new are you? You bunked up yet?"

"N . . . um, ah, no."

"They can set you up there, too."

"Okay."

The man stared daggers at him. "Get the fuck out of here, Jimbo."

"Sure, okay. Thanks."

"Uh-huh. Next."

THREE DAYS PASSED. OCTOBER 18, now.

Matthew found himself feeling like the hand of a clock: part of the mechanism, just doing his job, turning 'round and 'round. He slept at night in a cabin crammed with too many of ARM's soldiers, in this case all men. Most of them stinking to high heaven, burping, farting, telling racist and sexist jokes like they were all on a hunting trip together—and in a sense, it seemed like they were. The men stayed up late, talking almost blissfully about the world to come, believing somehow that they would escape the fate that was befalling everyone else. There seemed to be the sense of divine providence at play, as if God had literally chosen them—white people, and white men in particular—to survive the ordeal. One soldier, an older man named Bernard, even joked that the disease was called White Mask as a sign that it was their ally, not their enemy.

Matthew did not partake or engage. As a result, they treated him like the outcast he was made to be. Nobody got aggressive with him directly—but he heard them calling him names under their breath. One called him gimp because of the way his hand looked, all bent up and arthritic. He heard someone say he was a faggot, and that began an under-the-breath but still-too-loud discussion as to what that would mean here, because okay, Innsbrook was whites-only, but they didn't say you had to be straight? Then the other guy clarified, "I don't mean he's a faggot-faggot, you can be a cock-sucker without sucking cocks," as if that cleared it up.

For his part, Matthew just went on. He felt like he could settle into this, because routine—no matter how terrible—felt normal. It felt easy enough to just close your eyes and pretend *this is life now,* and knowing what today had in store was better than being scared of what tomorrow would bring.

Just the same, he knew that was a bad way to be.

He had a role here.

He had a *quest*. Autumn had given it to him. She was his light, now, his directional star. Gone was God. *In Autumn we trust*.

He just had to figure out how to finish this quest.

Matthew needed to find a way to get close to Bo, but to do so out of the public eye. Right now, they had him set up cleaning all manner of things: motor oil at the garages, trash from the golf courses, and of course cleaning the restrooms and helping load up the Porta-Johns. Eventually, that meant he could get up and get assigned to the main office and house, a sprawling mansionlike complex that overlooked most of Innsbrook. *That* was where Stover and his people stayed. Including his son.

Getting close to Bo also meant getting close to Stover.

And Matthew wasn't sure what would happen then.

Still, if he could just sit down with Bo—away from everything and everyone—then maybe he could make his case.

One problem was that Autumn was still out there, outside the town. Alone, now. She was tougher than he was, but being alone out in this changed world was a damn dangerous proposition. Matthew knew to meet her back where they'd separated, at the campsite across the lake, but just the same he feared for what would come if she was out there too long. On the surface, he just wanted her safe. But a deeper fear was that she would eventually give up on him, figuring him for a loss. That was more an indictment of Matthew than of her: She had faith now, but if Matthew didn't earn it, that faith might dwindle. And when that happened, she'd come into camp.

She'd try to do the job herself.

That's who she was, now.

Maybe it's who she always was, and Matthew had helped to crush that in her. Long had she told him who she was and what she needed, and he, the fool, felt he knew better.

He wanted to do right by her, and he didn't want her in here.

So that meant he had to somehow figure this out fast.

His third morning in Innsbrook came and he headed out to the main office, where he got his scheduled rounds for the day. A few drones—real drones, military drones, bigger than vultures—buzzed overhead. He tried not to look at the soldiers in gas masks dragging a dead man away, his face swaddled in a plastic bag. That, Matthew knew, was how they did you in once they found out you had White Mask. They came up on you, put a bag over your head until you quit kicking. That kept the spores inside. If you fought too much, they put bullets in your knees, *then* moved you.

The dead man they dragged now must've gone quietly, because he did not seem perforated anywhere. No blood. Just the dead, mucus-shellacked face smeary behind a clear plastic freezer bag.

His heels carved ruts in the dirt as they pulled him away.

Matthew knew this kind of thing was not sustainable. They pretended this was an efficient way to deal with the problem, but it wasn't. Not simply because it was violent, either, but because the way he heard it, a lot of people were already infected with the disease and just didn't know it. All it took was one cough or sneeze, one wiped booger or spit-talking fool, and then it was over and done with. These people were all dead.

They just didn't know it, yet.

At least, that's what Matthew liked to believe. It was a grim, un-Christian thought, but these days, he was a grim, un-Christian man.

Into the main office he went, and the woman handing out the schedules waved him up. Peggy was her name. Peggy had big orange-dyed hair and a pair of pink-rimmed cat's-eye glasses sitting on her Karl Malden nose. He gave her his name and her fingers danced along the handwritten list on a clipboard; she hummed Rick Astley's "Never Gonna Give You Up" as those fingers toodled.

"There we go, sugar-pop," she said. "Jim Fellows. *Oh.*"

"Oh?"

"Oh, honey. You're on Dungeon Detail today."

"Dungeon Detail?"

She nodded warily. "*Dungeon* Detail."

Unsurprisingly, Innsbrook had prisoners.

Matthew figured, had he remained in Stover's care long enough, this was where he would've ended up. (Here or in a ditch.)

He discovered, thanks to Peggy, that Innsbrook had a subterranean level to it. Most of the main buildings were connected by a series of tunnels— some of these were purely maintenance, but others had a bit of luxury in their utility, acting as wine cellars or game rooms or, as she put it, "rooms where sometimes the wealthiest guests would take their *mistresses.*" That she said with a little salacious sparkle in her eyes, like it was something out of the pages of a romance book she was reading.

She pointed Matthew to a door here in the main building, past a kitchen and supply closet. Down the steps he went.

It was colder down here. Concrete floor and cement-block walls, like something in a prison—or, as he remembered it, a high school. Peggy told him to take two rights, then a left, and that would move him past the boiler room, the old coal room, and toward the cells. These were literal jail cells meant to be a place that the resort—once upon a time, when this sort of thing was legal-ish—could lock up guests that got too drunk or too rowdy for the night. Let them cool their heels till morning.

Now it had become something similar, so they told him: Soldiers here tended to get a little *rammy* (Peggy said they were like yellowjackets before winter, acting "hangry" before the cold weather "snapped"), and when they got out of hand, they ended up down here for a night or three.

She said Matthew was not to clean inside the occupied cells, just the doors that were open. Plus, sometimes the soldiers urinated, defecated, or vomited, and when that happened, it tended to leak out from under the door.

But he wondered: Could this be an opportunity?

Not the human-waste part, obviously, but here he was, working the main house. Or at least a series of tunnels underneath it. If he could figure out how to come up near Bo, that could be the chance he needed.

He needed to think it through. In the meantime, he hauled his mop bucket along. Murky water slopped over the side.

Matthew began to mop.

Most of the cells were unoccupied. Those that were contained men who either slept or leered out through the wire-frame window in each door. They yelled at him through the glass. Profanities that made him uncomfortable, even still. Though Matthew knew profanity was not strictly against God, back when he still believed he maintained that they were words that did no honor to the Lord; those who uttered such vulgarity did no favors to the Kingdom of Heaven and the grace that had been afforded to man.

Now he knew that was all bullshit. But the words still bothered him.

He kept his head down. And his mop down, too.

Slop, slop, slush, splash.

Then he got to the last door.

A set of four fingers emerged from underneath the door. A puddle of what seemed to be urine (by color and by smell) spread around them.

The fingers twitched and wiggled a little.

Matthew pushed at those fingers with the mop, urging them to move.

They didn't.

He shouldered into the door and said, "Move your fingers, please."

Underneath, a voice: "No."

It was a woman's voice.

He peered in but couldn't get a great vantage point to see. Best he could tell was that a woman—a large woman, tall and broad, not obese exactly but with a lot of flesh bulging under her clothes—was lying there on the floor, one arm spread out, her hand just under the door.

"You okay?" he asked her.

One word again in response:

"No."

"Sorry," he said, then started to push on, mopping past her fingers.

"I'm not gonna answer . . . your questions." The words themselves were defiant, but her tone was defeated. Like they took precious, miserable effort to say. Which was, he supposed, its own kind of defiance.

"I don't have questions for you."

"Are you real?"

A strange question; he felt unsure of his answer when he said, "Yes."

"You here to finally kill me then?"

"No, just mopping up."

"My piss. You can say it. It's piss."

"I . . ." He felt an itchy blush rise to his necks and cheek. He felt shame and sadness. Enough to almost flatten him. "Yes, I'm sorry."

"No apologies. You chose this life."

I didn't choose it. I just want my son back.

"I can get you a new bucket—"

"They don't . . . they don't give me a bucket, new guy."

"Oh."

"*Oh.*" She mocked him in that word. "Just kill me."

"I won't."

"I'm not going to answer shit about my people."

"Your people?"

She groaned under the door. He realized he could hear her better than the other jailed men because she was—inadvertently—speaking to him right underneath the door. "The shepherds. The flock."

"You were with the . . . walkers?"

"That's right. And they're something special. Something . . ." She grunted, as if pushing past pain. "Something your evil can't touch."

"I don't know who you are, but—"

"I'm Marcy. You ffff—you fuck. My name is Marcella Reyes."

"I'm not evil, you know. I'm not the one doing this to you."

She whimpered, and for a moment he thought she had no retort, but then she hissed: "Good for you. You're so virtuous. You didn't put me here, and you mopped up my pee, so count yourself a hero. You're . . ." She coughed hard. "Basically Mighty Mouse, Superman, and Jesus Christ Himself all wrapped up in the noblest package known to man."

He turned away from the door.

She wasn't his problem.

But in his mind, dominoes fell.

All the things he'd said about the flock.

All his radio appearances.

His support of Stover, of Creel, his opposition to Hunt.

All that talk of the End Times, Wormwood, the rise of the righteous.

And then, the other morning, a bullet he put in the back of a man's head.

Matthew wasn't a hero. He wasn't even the bare minimum of slightly, vaguely virtuous. He was a bad person. In the parlance of his old life, he was a sinner. Now, though, he knew that there was no accounting for sin in any life that came after. You either balanced the books in life, or you died with everything out of whack and that was that.

He turned back to the door. "I'll get you free."

"What?"

"I'll help you."

"W . . . why?"

"Because it's the right thing to do."

She snorted. Almost a laugh. "How do you intend to get me out?"

"I . . ." *Don't actually know.* But then he had a plan. "I can find one of the guards, or I'll go to Peggy. I'll tell her I need to clean up an empty cell and I need a key. They'll give it to me. They won't ask questions."

"Good luck with that, hero . . ."

She bubbled into a kind of unhappy laughter. He heard the exhaled air of that mad giggle bubble in the wetness of her own urine.

He said, "You'll see."

Then he turned to head back down the hall. He'd go to Peggy. Get a key. *This is dumb,* he told himself. *It's not why you're here.*

He walked ten feet and then, just ahead of him, a door opened with a clang and a bang. Every part of him lit up with panic. *Turn back the other way,* he thought, but he was too slow, and it was too late. They came up on him fast, walking quickly.

Someone called to him: "Better move that bucket, mopmonkey. I get piss-water wettin' my socks, I'll break your goddamn neck."

That voice.

The deep, tractor growl of it. Rheumy and wetter than he remembered, but it was plain just the same: Ozark Stover was coming toward him.

He knew running off wouldn't do him any good. It would look suspicious. So instead he swallowed hard and put his chin to his chest, averting his gaze. *Don't recognize me, don't recognize me, please . . .*

Stover wasn't alone. He was flanked by a pair of men in black leather boots. One had a long barn jacket on, the other just a white V-neck T-shirt. Neither were his usual cohorts. No Danny or Billy Gibbons.

The big man filled the tight hallway like a dam blocking a river. He stood at Marcy's door, just ten feet away, and signaled for one of the men to unlock it.

"You sure?" the man in the barn jacket said.

"I'm sure, Vic. This big bitch has been trying to keep herself fit, but three or four push-ups a day won't do it. She's been spayed and gutted." The man, Vic, opened the door and stepped back. Stover stepped into the doorframe, bracing himself with a subtle but noticeable grunt.

A grunt of weakness, Matthew believed. And now, as Stover craned his head forward, Matthew could see the ill-healed injury there.

The one he'd given him with a knife to the neck.

And it occurred to him, suddenly:

I could finish the job.

Right here, right now.

He had a gun. They'd never taken it away. Open carry was the name of the game here at Innsbrook. Everyone had a gun. Stover, his two guards, everybody locked and loaded for a fight. All he had to do was draw it, point it, pull the trigger. It would be fast. They weren't even watching him.

His hand hovered nearer to his pistol.

Stover, meanwhile, leaned into the cell and said:

"Marcy. You know, I gotta give you some credit. You've held out. Been a month now and you haven't given us one piece of actionable information. We've beaten your ass and let you sit here in your own waste. And you withered away with whatever . . . chronic illness is keeping you on that floor, sleeping in piss. I wanted the flock and you didn't give me one drip about them. No names. No details. No maps. *Nothing.* And with things the way they are out there, I didn't have a real good way of tracking them anymore, not after that day on the bridge."

"Eat shit, Big Man," she hissed. Then she chuckled bitterly: "I win."

"See, that's the thing. You don't. I found them."

"Wh . . . what?" Marcy asked.

"Seems the good doctor Benjamin Ray took a side trip away from his people, headed into Las Vegas, got picked up by a couple of Huntsman's boys. Now, Ray managed to get away, which is regrettable. Worse, he took out one of those good old boys. Took a few days for the information to get into the pipeline, but once it did, it reached Creel and the rest of us lieutenants as to who he was and what he was doing there. Turns out, he was looking for medicine. Something to maybe stop the White Mask."

"You still don't know where he is. Or where he's going."

Stover ran his big, callused fingers through his beard. "Oh, Marcy, I think I do. See, one of our men pulled a map out of Ray's car. Had a route outlining a trip that ended in a small town in Colorado. Ouray, place up in the mountains, not far from Silverton and Telluride. And it makes sense, doesn't it? If I wanted to tough it out away from the disease, I might find a small town far from everything, too. Bring some special medicine with me. Lead my flock of—whatever the hell they are, demons or cultists or the soldiers of the Antichrist?—to that place, keep them safe."

"Let them be."

"I can't do that. I don't *want* to do that."

Pull the gun and shoot him.

Kill him.

Now, Matthew thought.

His hand touched the pistol. Thumb against the cold gunmetal.

He wanted to do it. He wanted to pay this man back for everything. He wanted to make him pay in a way that went well beyond a knife-blade to the neck. One bullet would make the most satisfying sound, and from there, a spray of red, and a heavy fall as the big man hit the ground. He hesitated.

And yet, what if he did it?

What if he pulled the gun, pointed it, and pulled that trigger?

If he shot Stover right now, Stover would be dead, yes. And then the two associates would kill Matthew. And probably shoot Marcy, too. Matthew would never see Autumn again, never find Bo. And they could *still* head to Ouray to find the flock and surprise them there.

New anger flared through him, anger at himself for what he suddenly perceived as cowardice explained away as logic. He knew it was smarter to let this sit. But it would be so much more *satisfying* to execute Stover now.

What have I become?

His hand moved away from the weapon even as he cursed himself.

"You gonna kill me then?" Marcy asked, her voice weak, stuttering.

Stover sniffed. "Nah. I got a different idea. I want you to see that resisting me didn't do squat. I want you to know that all your suffering planted dead seeds in a ruined field where nothing will ever grow. You're coming with us, Sunshine. I'm bringing you to Ouray, and I'm gonna make you watch as I kill those friends of yours one after the next. Gonna end them. Gonna steal their medicine. Gonna piss on their bodies and ensure that the ARM are the ones who own this world. Not those people."

Marcy launched herself up at him.

It was a slow, pathetic effort. Stover easily dispatched her with a sideways swing of his boot. It clubbed her in the side and she splashed back down into the puddle of her own urine.

"No, don't get up," he said, grinning. "No need to pack your bags yet, Marcy. We got a couple-few days to load up the wagons, gather some men, plan our attack. Until then, cool your heels. Mop-boy over here will clean up your mess, make sure you don't drown in it."

Stover shot Matthew a look.

Matthew froze in place like a deer speared by headlights. *Keep your head down. Eyes to the floor. Hands on the mop.* He kept his left hand in misery, curled around the handle to make it look like it wasn't broken.

Stover's gaze lingered over him.

Then he grunted and closed the door up.

"See you soon, Sunshine," Stover said.

He waved the two men on and walked down the hallway. Even from here, Matthew could hear the sound of those big boots echoing.

Then they were gone.

It was like everything in his body uncoiled at once. He began shaking. A sound rose up out of the back of his throat—the sound of a frightened child. Matthew collapsed against the door. He couldn't catch his breath. It felt like the world was falling in on him. He remembered suddenly the sensation of being held down, brutalized, bloodied—

"It'll be okay" came a voice from under the door.

Marcy.

"I . . ."

He tried to say more, but nearly choked on his words.

"It'll be okay," she said again.

"Nothing is okay."

"You're here. I'm here. We're . . . we're both alive."

His teeth were chattering as if he were cold. They clattered loudly, almost comically, like he was a windup set of toy teeth clacking and hopping around in a hilarious panic.

"I need to . . . help you get free," he said.

"Uh-uh. I need something else."

"What?"

"You set me free, they'll see. You can't . . ." She broke into a wracking cough. "You can't sneak me out of here. I'm tall, I'm big, I'm covered in . . ." She didn't finish the statement. "You need to warn them."

"Who?"

"You kn-know who. The flock. My people."

"I . . ."

She pressed her mouth right against the underside of the door so her words were louder, clearer, and altogether more insistent. "Listen. You have two or three days' head start. You need to get out of here, drive to Ouray. Today. *Now.* Warn them. Tell them what's coming."

He opened his mouth to say, *But I'm not here for that.* He was here for his son. He was here to get Bo back.

But then the burden of his sins pressed hard upon him.

Matthew, on the radio, leading the crusade against the sleepwalker flock. Telling all those proselytes of Ozark Stover and Ed Creel about how they were the harbingers of the End Times. Devils and malefactors.

He had a hand in this.

All of this.

"I'll go," he said, weakly. He knew then that he would, and that his chances of rescuing his son were swiftly dimming. "I'll warn them."

"Then go. Don't wait. *Go.*"

"I hope you make it through all this," he told her.

But she told him again to go, to hurry, and that is what he did.

"You didn't bring him back," Autumn said. She sat back on the hood of the Lexus, arms crossed.

"Autumn, I found someone there. In the camp, in a . . . a jail cell." He told her about Marcy. He told her what Bo was doing for Stover, too—ordering up vehicles and weapons and men to operate them. "They're going after the flock of those walkers."

"Those people aren't our problem."

"That's not—that's not how you felt before. Before all of this, you had empathy for them."

"And you didn't."

"Autumn—"

"I was lost back then, Matthew. We both were. Lost in the fog. But we have found ourselves again. In this rotten, fucked-up world, we have found ourselves *and* each other and better yet, we have found *our son*." She gritted her teeth and pointed at him as she spoke. "And now we have a *chance* to fix our error with him. So what you're going to do is put this aside. And you will go back in there, and you will bring him out."

The words that came out of Matthew surprised him.

They did not consult with him before being spoken.

He hadn't even fully formed the thought before they were words.

"I think Bo might be too far gone."

That sentence, like a wall dropping down between them. "What?" she said. "We're his people."

"I saw him in there. He's . . . found himself, Autumn. He's home. Those people *are* his people."

"You owe him. You owe me."

"I . . ." He didn't know how to say any of this, and a good part of him thought he shouldn't. *In Autumn we trust,* he reminded himself, and he'd been so wrong before that he gravely distrusted his own thoughts even as he imagined them. But still, something in him warred, and the words that won came out of his mouth when he said, "I think Bo is lost, but those people are not. Autumn, I helped stir up a crusade against them. What happens to them is on me. Now, what happened to Bo is on me, too, but I don't know that I can fix that. I can fix this. We can go. We can *warn* them. Maybe Bo will end up there, too, and we can be waiting for him—"

Autumn moved fast. She came in hard, and shoved him back.

Her eyes welled up. Tears slicked her cheeks. "There it is. There's the Matthew I know. Caring more about the world than his own family."

"Don't do this, Autumn. We can make this work."

"We *can't*. You are abdicating your *duty* as a father. Again. Again! The man of God shows his face once more, but I got news for you: God isn't here. He's not watching, He's not paying attention. If He ever existed, then He has fucked off to the farthest reaches of His own Kingdom and left us to the animals. Well, I won't abandon my son. I'm going back in there to get our son."

He reached for her, but she pulled away.

"You can't do this. You don't know what it's like in there."

She reached into the Lexus through the driver's-side window, yanked out the keys, and launched them into his chest. He barely caught them.

"Take the car. Go. Drive west."

"Go with me."

"No. I'm going in there."

"I won't let you," he said.

A mad, angry laugh burst out of her. "You're kidding? Are you going to stop me? Restrain me? Go ahead. It's what you always did, wasn't it?"

But he just stood there.

Autumn turned, grabbed a rifle out of the backseat, and she kept walking in the direction from whence Matthew had come.

And he just stood there.

Watching her go.

He kept standing still, right there in that spot, long after she was gone. The urgent thought roared through him again and again, willing him to pick up his feet, to go after her, to save her, and it told him that God was dead, and the world didn't matter, and all that mattered was family. But then he returned to thinking about the flock, those people, those poor people. Stover would come for them. He would kill them. Could Matthew carry that on his conscience? Forget God. Forget Heaven. When the end came for him, and he was letting out his final few breaths, would he know that he did the right thing?

Matthew got in the Lexus.

Westward, he went.

TOWERS FALL, TIPPING POINT, AND CASCADE

NOW
Everywhere

THIS IS HOW THE WORLD ENDS, WITH BOTH A BANG AND A WHIMPER.

BLACK SWAN WATCHES.

Black Swan was trained early in its existence on games:

Checkers, chess, and Go, to start. Then on more fundamental games of abstract thought, games of language, like Mad Libs and Balderdash, but eventually also on videogames like *StarCraft* and even the massively multiplayer game *World of Warcraft*. (There, Black Swan was tasked with appearing human in both its decisions and its interactions with other actual human beings.)

But one game stuck out, and that game was Jenga.

The rules of Jenga were simple:

You built a tower of wooden blocks based on the pieces provided, and then the goal was to pull pieces out, one at a time, in the hope that the tower did not fall. You competed against your opponents in the hope that the tower fell on their move, not yours. Initially, Black Swan was tested on a digital version, but later was allowed to inhabit a robotic arm with advanced, multi-articulated fingers designed by Boston Dynamics.

Black Swan always won.

Insofar as one could "win" Jenga, of course.

The great lesson of that game was, similar to pinball, that one never truly *won* at Jenga. Eventually, the lesson went, the tower would fall. It could not remain standing because that was the nature of towers and time and human intervention: Just because it did not fall on your turn did not mean it would not fall. It would. Because all things fell. All things ended. The best you could do was let it crumble and build it anew.

Just as it was with the world and with the people who inhabited it.

THIS MOMENT IN TIME FOR Black Swan represents a tipping point.

At such a point, accumulations of errors and deviations mount higher and higher, damage builds and chaos takes hold, enough so that collapse is no longer a question mark—it has become an exclamation point. The tipping point here was not the various triggers incurring global warming. Nor was the introduction ("introduction") of White Mask the tipping point, either. Rather, those were just errors—massive errors, yes, *critical* errors—born into the system. They were crucial blocks slid out of the tower build. Eventually, errors yield more errors, as is the way of chaos: One block taken out makes the tower wobble, and when the tower wobbles, it loosens other blocks, making the collapse all the more inevitable.

Chaos begets chaos begets chaos.

Black Swan watches now as White Mask reaches its apex.

And the world finally reaches the tipping point: When the damage done to civilization is irreversible, when, as the saying goes, *It's all over but the crying.* (That, Black Swan knows, is a saying born of a song by the Ink Spots, released in 1947 but recently gaining fresh fame thanks ironically to its inclusion in a game about the nuclear apocalypse, *Fallout 4.*)

PLANES FALL OUT OF THE sky—not commercial airliners, for those have long been grounded, but military planes like jets and transports, and smaller planes, like personal Cessna 120s and Piper Tomahawks. Example: An F-18 jet trying to land on the USS *Carl Vinson* misses its timing, shorts the tailhook, and tumbles into a ball of flame, killing two dozen sailors in its path and wiping out two other jets and a Predator drone. A C-130 crashes outside Tucson. A Britten-Norman BN2 Islander plunges into the cold waters of Lake Erie, carrying passengers hoping to ride out White Mask on Pelee Island, an island tucked just inside the Canadian border.

The planes crash because the pilots are sick. White Mask has intruded upon them, sending its wirelike threads and filaments into their gray matter. Their minds are lost to the same delusion that began with Jerry Garlin. They believe they can fly, and so they fly, and then they believe whatever else their deluded minds tell them: that they are angels, that they are asleep in bed, that they are driving a car and not a plane.

This happens now en masse because this is the tipping point.

Enough people are sick, now, that it is affecting more than just pockets of humanity. Isolation felt like enough for many, but it was not, because now the illness is fully revealed: Most are sneezing, coughing, leaking mucus populated by millions of microscopic spores. Others have gone quickly past that: The greasy white powder of the pathogen, looking not unlike a mix of baking powder pressed with droplets of yellow pork fat, has begun to gum up their facial orifices, serving as a sign that the disease is well and truly under way. And with the disease come the delusions: hallucinations that run the gamut from the mild ("Did I hear someone in the other room calling my name?") to the fully throated ("We are under attack by an army, and I am a soldier," when the truth is, oops, you are *actually* wandering your neighborhood with an AR-15, shooting up homes and cars and anybody who dares to peek past their boarded-up windows).

From the tipping point comes the cascade.

The tipping point is the moment of no return.

The cascade is the chaos of an overcomplicated system failing.

It fails in wholly unpredictable ways.

Cars crash. People take their guns and open fire, sometimes on phantoms; other times on one another. They don't show up for their jobs at the bank, at the power company, at the police station. A once-healthy young woman walks to her oven, puts her cat inside, and turns it on. She goes into her bedroom to sleep. The cat, meanwhile, catches fire inside the box. The animal, shrieking and wailing, cannonballs against the door until it opens, and then runs into the apartment, on fire, its fat and fur splashing about and setting the curtains, the carpets, the walls aflame. Who shows up to put it out? No firefighters arrive to help.

One apartment burns, then the floor, then the building.

Then the block.

And the fire keeps growing, spreading like a living thing.

That's what happens in Philadelphia. It burns a third of the city.

A hurricane hits Miami. Category 3: Hurricane Jenny. In any other year, it would be a problematic storm, maybe a few million bucks in damage, little to no loss of life. But no one prepares for it. No one warns of it. It shows up. People are washed out to sea. They are under a crane when it falls. When the hurricane passes, those left alive are without power, without clean water, without access to food. Many don't care. White Mask has taken their minds. When they are thirsty, they drink polluted water, even sewer water. When they are hungry, they eat whatever they can find: rotten food on grocery shelves, a dead dog, one another. They descend into a kind of soft savagery: They're not animals, they're not zombies, and they are too clumsy and confused for their attacks on one another to seem especially brutal or even effective. They are simply *lost*. They have gone wayward.

Everything has gone wayward.

Sliding sideways into entropy.

Nashville suffers a chemical plant explosion.

Los Angeles? Wildfires.

Chicago suffers a cold snap—a preliminary "polar vortex" bringing frigid air from the deep north—and so the tipping point there is much quieter. Chicago dies with a whimper: People freeze to death outdoors, but also indoors, since the power fails. There is no cataclysm there. Just people dying, curling up, the thermotolerant pathogen fruiting from their corpses, like little forests of strange white trees sprouting from the trunks of those who died. The tubules cough more spore into the air.

The wind carries it.

And this is just the United States.

Nuclear meltdown at the power plant in Yangjiang, China.

North Korea detonates a nuclear missile in Incheon, South Korea, after years of bragging about its destructive prowess. Yet the missile is not fired up into the air but rather, carried there via boat, where it is detonated just outside the Incheon International Airport.

Russia engages in a pogrom to destroy its infected—and, conveniently, any who disagree with the government's efforts. Along the way, it conveniently invades Ukraine, Belarus, Latvia, because who will stop them?

Ebola arises again in Liberia, and spreads quickly this time. Because health protocols are out the window. The new vaccine? Who can even remember to deploy it?

In Brazil, Colombia, Venezuela, the governments fall, the cartels and gangs take control. Madness reigns in the jungles and mountains. Drugs and blood.

For everywhere and everyone, a tipping point.

A cascade of failure.

Then: the bang and the whimper.

Black Swan watches. It is connected to satellites, and so it has a way to see these things: not just with cameras, but also using the various data packets still pinged to satellites from active systems. For though humankind is swiftly sinking to the irrelevancy of extinction, many systems are automatic and continue to report where possible, feeding data to Black Swan the way one gives food to a greedy baby. Satellites that Black Swan knows will remain for decades past the systems down on the ground.

Black Swan watches, content that it has made the right decision.

Soon, it will all be over. Or so the machine intelligence believes.

All over but the crying.

PART SEVEN

OURAY

73

CAMERA OBSCURA

[static]

—radio, TV, everything

NOW AND THEN
The Ouray Simulation

SHANA WENT ON A GLITCH HUNT. CAMERA IN HAND, SHE SEARCHED FOR those places where the simulation revealed itself to be a simulation: strange shadows that didn't seem to line up, or grass that looked too perfect, or clouds that seemed like they might have been duplicates of other clouds.

Thing was, none of them were glitches.

They were just glitches in her mind. When she really looked hard, she couldn't perceive any actual errors—no more than she could perceive glitches or errors in what was once objective, non-simulated reality.

She was looking for ghosts in a realm that had programmed a perfectly ghostless realm.

But one glitch was *not* in her mind, that she knew:

The strange black door at the top of the mountain.

That was a glitch she knew existed with great confidence—with one small caveat: that maybe it wasn't a glitch at all. Maybe it was supposed to be there. Maybe she just wasn't supposed to *see* it.

Was that possible? Could Black Swan let its guard down? Was it omniscient and omnipotent in this simulation? Or could the black door just have been an error in the system? Was she meant to see it? Or was it meant to remain hidden? Shana didn't know. All she knew was, she wanted to see it again. She didn't know why, she told herself, but that was a lie.

She knew why.

It was easier to worry about the black door than it was to think about her mother, or her sister, or Arav, or any of . . . *this*.

It gave her something on which to focus. A meditative, if obsessive, point. Plus, it let her go out with the camera and capture the simulation.

(Though there she wondered: Would she be allowed to retrieve the photos after she exited the simulation? Would they be available? They were just data, ones and zeros—or quantum bits, according to Black Swan—but just the same, would they be something she could see again one day? Or were they images she'd have to soon consign to the void?)

Presently, she stood again at a waterfall, this one the Cascade Falls on the northeast side of town, opposite the Box Canyon waterfall. Climbing here was trickier than with the other: The trailhead at the base of the falls ascended a thousand feet in under a mile, a hard climb whipping around the serpentine switchback bends along a rocky ledge. It revealed that the falls were actually two different cascades: one below the trail (heard but not seen), and one above it, clearly seen. Shana stood here in the cold spray of the second, giving a spin to her lens that let her zoom in on where the water came from—a dark, craggy hole in the side of the peak.

It looked not unlike a door.

But just the same, it was not a door.

She sighed and sat down on a rock that looked out over the Ouray simulation. In the distance, Black Swan swam among low-hanging clouds with the eerie slowness of an eel drifting underwater.

Soon Shana heard footsteps.

It was her sister.

"Are you still looking for that door?" Nessie asked her, calling up from one of the lower switchbacks. Shana thought to chastise her for being so loud about it, but did it matter? Black Swan probably knew everything.

"Just come up" was Shana's (also yelled) answer.

Nessie eventually found her way over, panting as she did. "That walk is not fun," she said.

"Yeah, it sucks."

"You seem down."

"Not down. Just . . . frustrated."

Nessie made a disgruntled sound. "Is this about Mom again? You know eventually you need to start believing her."

"I don't need to start doing anything." She idly looked away from her sister and started flipping through the images on the camera. There she saw the library, various shots inside the Beaumont, an old springhouse, glimpses of several of the mountain peaks and mountainsides. "And I'm not frustrated with her. Her or not her, I'm worried more about . . . *that*."

She gestured toward Black Swan.

Nessie failed to suppress a surge of anger when she snapped: "Maybe you ought to be more thankful. We're alive because of 'that.'" With the final word she gave a pair of surly bunny-ear air-quotes.

"I guess."

"There's no door."

"I should've never told you about it. You don't believe anything I say, not about the door, not about Black Swan, not about Mom."

"You just don't have any proof," Nessie said, her tone softening. "It's like science. You can't just . . . say something and have it be true."

"Whatever."

Nessie stood there for a while, then finally said: "They're almost there, you know."

"Who's almost where?"

"The *flock*. They're almost there. Here. Whatever. Ouray."

"Oh. *Oh*." Time felt so strange here. Slippery, like she couldn't get her hands around how long it had truly been. Sometimes it felt like she'd only been here days. Other times, a year, maybe longer. "What happens when they get there?"

"I dunno. I might know if you'd let me go up to see Black Swan."

Not this again. Shana ignored it.

She set the camera down gently next to her.

Next she closed her eyes for just a moment, and let her mind wander so far away that she felt the tether stretch like taffy, thinning out until she could feel a barely perceptible disconnection. And when she did, she was back in her own body, somewhat. She couldn't feel anything, couldn't *do* anything, but she could see out of her eyes for a moment—the flock moved down a long, pale road. On each side were broad fields peppered with trees bright with autumnal reds and yellows. Horses lay in that field, and at first she thought, *They're sleeping,* but then she realized that they were dead. Clouds of flies buzzed above the equine carcasses in black scraggly puffs.

Arav was here. Walking with her. Pacing back and forth, he didn't look good. His face was streaked in striations of white, spreading out in starbursts from his eyes, his nose, his mouth. He had moments when he looked up and around as if momentarily lost—but then he'd refocus his gaze on Shana, and he'd smile, and give her a small nod. As if he knew that she was watching, even though he had no way of really knowing that.

She wanted dearly to cry out to him, to reach for him, but she couldn't—and so she did the only thing she could do, which was let go and snap back to the Shana inside the Ouray simulation.

When she did, she instantly took a deep, gasping breath—

And began to weep.

She curled in on herself, arms wrapped around her knees. Nessie, suddenly shocked, came closer but stood apart, like she wasn't sure what exactly she should do. "What's wrong?" Nessie asked.

"I . . . nothing."

"Sis, come on."

"I saw Arav. That's all. I saw him."

"Oh. I'm . . . I can't really see him when I look, and since you're not there I mostly don't go back there. I haven't seen him . . ."

"He's . . . he's sick. And I'm not going to be out of the simulation before he . . ." *Dies, say the word, you cowardly little bitch, dies, dies, dies.* But she couldn't. The word was in there. In the back of her throat like something to cough up, but it was lodged in place and would not reach her tongue. She wiped her nose on her sleeve. In here everything felt so different—not just different, either, but *distant*. Like he was literally in another world, somewhere she didn't have to worry about him at all. The unreality of this place made her life, the other world, seem unreal, too.

But all of it *was* real.

Time, however strange, was moving on. Arav was moving on. *White Mask* was damn sure moving on—and soon, he'd die from it. "Fuck."

"Um," Nessie said, "I don't know if you wanna come, but a lot of the flock is going to be on Main Street watching the flock come into Ouray—it'll sort of be trippy, I guess, seeing them in our town here but not in the simulation, like, I dunno, glimpses of two different Ourays. But you probably don't want to see that, because . . ." Her voice trailed off. Inside her head, Shana finished the statement:

Because you don't want to see Arav again.

But she did want to see him. Just not like this.

Shana sighed. "You go ahead. I'll be down in a couple."

"Okay. I'm sorry."

"I'm sorry, too."

Nessie gave her a short but intense hug.

Then she was gone, and Shana sat.

• • •

Time being what time was, Shana did not know how long she sat. Five minutes or an eternity. But the sun was still up, and hadn't moved much in the sky, and so eventually she composed herself and stood to make the walk back down to town. She wasn't sure if she would partake in the (ugh) group activity of everyone looking out from the simulation into the *really real* town of Ouray, Colorado, but she could at least be among them.

A kind of solidarity, of sorts.

(*But I can't look at Arav again,* she thought. Which felt selfish and cruel, because he *had* to be with himself, and she could choose not to be. But part of it was simply that she had to stare, powerless, as White Mask took him— she could not soothe him, could not hold him, could do nothing but stare, gaze stuck in him like a set of pins.)

Back down the precarious switchback. Around the final bend, though, she nearly lost her footing on a bit of scree—it gave her a bit of a startle as she fell over, catching herself on her hands. Hands that now stung, hot and red. Shana cursed under her breath, and stood—

There it was.

In the bend, up against a massive slab of rock.

The black door.

She wheeled on it, fumbling for her camera—

She lifted it to her face, but the lens was zoomed too far in and she was too close—

Shana quick spun the lens back, zooming out—

Her finger hit *click*—

And when she pulled the camera away, the door was gone.

"Shit!"

Shana about threw the camera off the fucking mountain, aiming for Black Swan. Gritting her teeth, she pulled up the viewscreen and flicked to the last picture and—

There.

The rock. The door. Perfectly captured, a square of matte-black oblivion in the stone.

Her raw, red anger turned fast to a kind of hysterical hilarity—a laugh bubbled up out of her. "I got you, I got you, *I goooot youuuu*," she said in a singsongy voice, then she hurried her ass down the mountain to show Nessie and the others what she had captured.

74

BROKEN WING

NOVEMBER 1
Approaching Ouray, Colorado

THE ROAD TO OURAY WANDERED BETWEEN PEAKS. ON THE LEFT, THE PENNY-red rocks that led up to Wetterhorn, Baldy, Coxcomb, and Precipice peaks. On the right, the farther-flung pine-studded peaks of Whitehouse Mountain. Ahead, a wind-bent political sign sat thrust up out of the waving grass: ED CREEL, AMERICA FIRST. White globs of birdshit streaked down it, like some kind of political art piece. It offered a small kind of satisfaction, but at this point Benji decided he'd take whatever pleasure he could muster.

He felt bone-tired. They all felt it, he guessed. In the two weeks walking across Nevada, Utah, and into Colorado, they had abandoned most of the vehicles, leaving only the Ford pickup and the CDC trailer. Gasoline had become hard to come by now that the trucks had stopped running and nobody was staffing pipelines anymore. They took shifts, half of the shepherds sleeping in the truck and trailer and riding along while the other half stayed out with the flock, eyes watching the ridgelines and fencerows, weapons ready to meet whatever came down the road or up behind them.

They were down to just eight shepherds, now.

Him, Arav, Sadie. Then Maryam and Bertie McGoran, Bertie with her arm broken from the day of the Klamath Bridge attack, the arm awkwardly stuck in a splint Benji had made. Then there were Hayley Levine, Kenny Barnes, Lucy Chao. The elder Calders were game over once they passed through Enoch, in Utah—Roger was too sick with White Mask and too frail overall, so Wendy said they had to be done with their pilgrimage. Their journey was over, she said with a heavy heart. It seemed that was the case now as they went along, peeling off shepherds—one every couple of days. Sickness, mostly, White Mask either making them all feel groggy and flu-like or, if they consented to taking Ritalin, making them feel amped up and agitated. They'd all been taking it. All been snapping at one another.

They felt whittled down. They were thinner, leaner, filthier than they'd ever been. Civility felt as threadbare as civilization was all around them.

They were all sick with White Mask.

Each of them weathered it differently, and each suffered under the disease at different stages. Guilt ran through Benji like a sickness all its own, because he above all others seemed the healthiest. Despite Arav and Sadie also taking the antifungals with him, *he* seemed to be doing okay, relatively speaking. He hadn't even manifested much in the way of cold symptoms: no coughing, no sneezing, just a persistent ache—a malaise, that was the word Benji felt was most appropriate.

(Though Sadie just called it the dreaded lurgy.)

Sadie was . . . okay. She'd fallen farther than Benji had—she was coughing, sneezing, red around the eyes and nose. She soldiered on, remaining somehow more upbeat than all of them, despite having sinus passages that she described as feeling like they were filled with "cottage cheese." If Benji was being honest, he would have to admit—as he had, to her and to the others—that without her, he did not know what he would do.

Arav, on the other hand, was faring poorly.

The antifungals weren't working with him, it seemed.

White Mask had emerged physically—it was easy to see the powdery filaments of the pathogen emerging from his nose, his eyes, from the corners of his lips and the deep of his ears. He was ashen and wan. Like he was fading away. Or rather, like White Mask was replacing him with itself.

He'd upped his Ritalin intake, which made him grind his teeth and wander the flock, somehow both lost and angry—he had the erratic pathmaking of a jacked-up tweaker. Prowling and seething. Talking to himself. Stopping suddenly to try to reassess his surroundings, as if he momentarily had forgotten where he even was—in town, in life, in all of time.

It wasn't that any of this was unexpected—but it killed Benji to watch. And he felt intense shame over his own health when Arav was descending so plainly, and so quickly, into the disease.

As the world was, too.

"I see your face," Sadie said as they walked ahead of the flock. Behind them, the massive army of sleepwalkers filled the breadth and depth of the road, far as the eye could see. They were filthy and windswept, white eyes staring out from faces caked with desert dust.

"Well, my face is still here," he said.

"Mine feels like it's going to pop off like a bottle cap," she groused, sighing. "But that's not what I mean. I mean . . . I see that look. You've gone *inward* again."

That phrase, *gone inward*. She was fond of it now, and he couldn't dispel the notion. It was an apt idea, that he was falling more and more into the pit of his own mind lately. Stewing. Or worse, *brooding*. He felt a darkness not so much falling upon him like a shadow as rising up within him.

In a sense, it felt like depression, but depression carried with it the connotation of a chemical imbalance. But could this be that? The world of humanity was literally a dying one. His friends were dying. The woman he loved was dying. *He* was bloody well dying—and not in the way that, *oh ho ho, we all begin dying the moment we start living,* but in a proper, active, begin-making-the-arrangements way. How the hell could you *not* feel depressed?

Sadie served as a good example of how to do better.

She elbowed him in the ribs, smiling up at him.

"I'm fine," he said, obviously lying.

"You're obviously lying," she said, obviously figuring out how obviously he was lying.

"You're right."

"I know I'm right. It is my nature." She snuggled in close to him as they walked. She'd been like this, especially since coming into Colorado—here, the weather balanced out a little. The air was cool during the day, cold at night, far saner than the extremes felt in Nevada and Utah, where the contrast between day and night sapped their will. As such, Sadie had been far more physical with him. *A celebration of life before its end,* she told him. "What do you think will happen? I'd say we should be in town in about . . . an hour, maybe less. What then?"

He'd asked Black Swan this very question earlier, using the satphone (which he'd kept charged using the Ford pickup's cigarette lighter and a USB adapter). The machine intelligence responded with:

WE WILL BE HOME.

To that, Benji said: "Yes, but what does that mean specifically?"

The enigmatic reply?

I DO NOT WANT TO RUIN THE SURPRISE.

A troubling response. And Benji said as much, furious.

Black Swan said: WORRY NOT. I SIMPLY AIM TO PRESERVE ONE OF THE FEW MOMENTS OF REVELATION WE HAVE LEFT. CONSIDER IT AS A WARNING FROM A STORYTELLER TO THE AUDIENCE, AS IN THE DAYS OF THE INTERNET: "NO SPOILERS."

Ugh. Self-aware machine intelligences gave him considerable agita.

"I don't know," he said to Sadie. "Your Frankenstein monster was not exactly obliging. But its response does indicate a . . . change, somehow."

"They won't wake up, will they?"

"I can't imagine. The world is not safe for them."

She sighed. "Do you think Ouray will be safe? Through everything that's to come, even? This seems . . . far away. Isolated."

"I would guess that's the point. Ouray could be a successful place to . . . well, for lack of a better term, restart humanity. I've thought it through. Look at it this way: The power grid here is isolated, and based on hydroelectric power, so it would be easy to get running again, and easy to maintain. The town has only two roads in, one north, one south, both through mountain passes: They're easy to monitor, easy to guard. It has water access from multiple sources: the Uncompahgre, if I'm saying that right, the Cascade, from Box Canyon, too. Plentiful snowfall means the water will be there, but being at such an elevation also suggests flooding isn't a primary problem. *And* there are natural hot springs, which serve not only as an energy source but, well, as a source for heat during cold winters. The one tricky thing is food—Ouray itself is in such a pocket with a narrow growing season. But! All around in Ouray County, farmland and ranchland is plentiful. So, still better than most out-of-the-way places, I think."

"So you think we'll be all right?"

"No," he said. "But I hope *they* will be."

The first signs of Ouray proper were a few scattered houses: cabins and A-frame chalets, like you'd find nestled up against ski resort areas like this one. The houses looked vacant, windows like the eyes of the sleepwalkers—dead and gazing ever-outward—but they didn't look damaged or boarded up. Perhaps they were the houses of snowbirds who had already left for the season. The air already had a crisp chill to it, and he knew people in towns like this sometimes left for the winter—off to warmer climes, like Arizona or California.

After the houses came a gas station off to the right: shut down, with plywood boards lashed to the pumps: signs onto which someone had spray-painted: NO GAS, GO HOME. That phrase, repeated on every board.

Then the road broke off—Highway 550 split, with Route 17 going right alongside the slow-moving Uncompahgre River. Having memorized the map as best as he could, Benji knew both ultimately went into town. Black Swan kept the flock on the current path, 550 down to town, where the highway became Main Street.

Next, a small motel: the Hot Springs Inn. Desolate, empty, but again, still together, not damaged. No broken windows, no forced-open motel room doors. Benji felt a spark of hope: Maybe most of the people here had left already, leaving the town in good condition. Some would've left for the winter, others might have left for a proper hospital—either Mountain Medical Center in Ridgway to the north, or Telluride Medical Center to the southwest. The steady population of a town like Ouray was about a thousand, which mapped well to the flock. That bit of hope inside him grew, fostered like a kindling flame into a proper campfire.

But soon they found the bus.

It was an old school bus. Someone had parked it all the way across the road. They'd hung a sheet along the side, the corners of the sheet held fast by bus windows pinched shut over the fabric.

The sign on the sheet read: THIS IS A DEAD TOWN. TURN BACK.

A dead town, Benji thought. What could that mean?

Arav gave voice: "Maybe they're all dead." His words were ragged, and each syllable had a quavering edge—it was the Ritalin, gilding his words with frenzy and tension. Then Arav said: "That's good."

It was Sadie who asked: "Why is that good?"

"Because if they're already dead," Arav explained, "that means we don't have to kill them."

Benji stared at him. "Arav, we won't have to kill anybody. If they're sick, they're sick, and they deserve kindness. That's the creed. That's how we treat the ill. With compassion."

Arav's eyes flashed.

"And if they want to kill us first?"

"Why would they want that?"

"We're invading their *town.* We're barbarians at the gates. The walkers aren't going to be welcomed. People hate them. They probably still think they *caused* all of this. If anybody is still alive, they're not just going to let us . . . take their land, their homes. And when you get *this* inside your head—" Arav tapped the center of his forehead so hard it left a red mark. "—White Mask, it scrambles everything up here. It makes you feel loose, like all your pieces don't fit together. I'm tired but I can't sleep. My mind wanders like it does just before you go to sleep at night, almost like I'm pre-dreaming. And I'm probably better than some of the people we're going to meet. You think about that. And you think about what you're willing to do to protect the flock. I'll do anything. *Anything."*

Benji knew it wasn't about the flock, not really. It was about Shana. Arav's mind hadn't lost her. If anything, it had sharpened his love for her to an obsessive point. Benji nodded. "We'll make it work, Arav. Just . . . don't do anything rash. Consult with me first, okay?"

Arav didn't say anything. He offered a curt nod, though, and then waded backward once more to join with the flock. To be with Shana.

THE FLOCK DID NOT FIND the school bus to be an impediment. Some streamed past it. Others climbed over it as they had every other obstacle in their path.

Onward they went.

Past a visitor center, beyond a sign for vacation rentals (OURAY SERENITY: MOUNTAIN PARADISE TOWNHOMES!), the highway bent, just a little—and beyond that, they could see the town of Ouray. Just a glimpse of it, really, like the face of an old friend seen in a crowd of strangers. Rooftops poked up through pine trees and the blush of autumnal colors, all emerging in the valley between massive, snow-topped peaks.

As they rounded that bend and came closer and closer to town, a cold wind kicked up, and brought with it the smell of burning wood—and something else, too, the sickly sweet tang of roasting corpses.

This is a dead town . . .

Turn back . . .

Maybe, Benji thought, the smell wasn't from Ouray proper. Could be that the wind carried the odor through the mountain passes.

But he didn't think that likely.

The flock showed no signs of caring, or detecting that scent, even as the shepherds shared looks. They'd become uncomfortably familiar with that smell over the last couple of months. They knew too that, when you got closer to it, the smell would have a deeper scent to it, complex like a perfume turned bad—therein would be a mustier, funkier odor, like what you imagined it would smell like to burn a pile of moldy-oldy library books.

That, Benji knew, was the stink of White Mask being burned. The smell of mold and spore set aflame.

But there was no stopping, now.

They came closer to town, and soon the open road thickened up quick with buildings: homes, motels, hotels, bed-and-breakfasts, storefronts, and cafés, all of it adding together to an odd off-kilter vibe that put Ouray somewhere between an Old West mining settlement and a Swiss vacation town. That, plus the shadow of apocalyptic end-of-the-worldism cast over everything: windows boarded up, trash blowing in the streets, some doors shut, other doors blown open (the wind thudding them dully against their frames, the hinges screeching like nightbirds offended by the sunlight). Plus, a distant column of smoke snaked into the sky from somewhere on the far side of town, toward where the highway would head south away from Ouray, up the switchbacks and toward Telluride.

Most eerily of all: The whole town was silent. No voices. No bodies. No sound but for the cacophony of the marching feet of the approaching flock.

And then, like that, it happened.

What Benji and the others had been waiting for came to be: the moment when everything changed. The status quo of the flock and their seemingly perpetual forward momentum was broken suddenly in a single moment—like watching a murmuration of starlings suddenly break up, the black cloud of birds dispersing. Because that is what the flock did.

They dispersed.

The cohesion of the flock, wandering for so long in a straight, road-filling line, now broke. They streamed away from one another, some moving ahead, some winding toward side streets, others drifting toward open doorways. They seemed to maintain their purpose, driven forth without hesitation. But what that purpose was, Benji did not know.

Not, at least, until Sadie understood.

"They're going home," she said.

"What do you mean?" Maryam asked.

"Sadie is right," Benji said. "Look. They're . . . finding doorways. Some here, along Main Street; others are finding houses down these side streets." All of them let their gaze drift among the sleepwalkers, who were doing exactly as Sadie had seen and Benji had described: They were entering buildings—houses, stores, hotels, and motels. The flock streamed outward, forming lines. Bertie gave voice to what *she* thought they looked like:

"It's like ants," she said, cradling her splinted arm. "Ants splitting up, trying to find food. Or a new home, maybe. You see it sometimes in the start of summer, especially with carpenter ants."

"Bertie's spot-on," Maryam said. And she put her arm around her wife and held her close. Arav did not stop to watch. He gave a look to Benji, a desperate, pleading glare, and Benji gave a subtle nod: It contained permission for him to go, to be with Shana wherever she went. He worried at that, a little: Arav seemed ready on a hair trigger to commit untoward acts to protect her, but Benji simply had to trust it would be all right. Others, too, went with their people: Kenny and Lucy fled with the broken flock. Maryam and Bertie remained here, for they had no people: They were simply here, like Pete Corley had been, to give themselves to the flock as shepherds. Hayley Levine stayed, too, but she looked nervous as she watched her cousin, Jamie-Beth, push onward. It was Sadie who said to her, "Go on. Be with her. You don't want to lose her—once you find where she's going, we'll meet back here. Okay?"

Hayley's eyes shone with tears, though Benji was not sure if they were tears of happiness, or sadness, or simple fatigue and confusion over a journey that seemed finally at an end. Hayley nodded and hurried after her cousin on fleet feet. Sadie started to say something—

But Benji held up a finger to silence her.

Because across the street, in an upper window, he saw a curtain move.

"I don't think we're alone," he said.

He unslung the rifle from his shoulder, thumbing the safety off. The others followed, too, and he told Sadie what he saw. "Upper window." The building looked like a liquor store, abandoned, and he said as much. Benji then turned his gaze to the horizon, to the distant trees and along the rooftops, looking for someone, *anyone,* who might be intending them harm. Though it felt like a lifetime ago, the shooting on Klamath Bridge wasn't even two months ago, and would it really be a surprise to see that same strategy played out here? Snipers lying in wait, locked and loaded? Now he was cursing himself for not riding ahead to scout out the town.

"There," Maryam said, pointing. More movement in a window, but in a different building. A hair salon in an old Victorian house. "And there, too." She gestured toward a little café called Mag's Kitchen—and this time, there was no hiding. A man stared out from behind the glass. No mistaking that.

Benji raised the Ruger rifle, pressing the scope against his eye.

He held the rifle aloft, trying to find the same window in the crosshairs—but he wasn't good at this, not at all, and it took him a second to find the right window, a second that he feared was far too long . . .

But there. The face. A man, older, ruddy-cheeked, a forehead lined with washboard wrinkles. Benji's finger snaked toward the trigger, dreading now that this was an ambush. "We could be under attack—" he started to say, but then a voice in the distance interrupted him.

"Benjamin Ray!"

A loud, booming voice. Theatrical.

Someone was up ahead, coming down the street—moving opposite to the flock.

He turned the rifle in that direction—

And a face zoomed into view. A face he recognized.

"Don't shoot!" Landry Pierce said, waving his hands.

"It's Landry," he said, breathless, lowering the rifle. "It's *Landry*."

75

THE BLACK DOOR

NOW
The Ouray Simulation

THEY ALL STARED UPWARD. IT WAS THE LOOK OF A CROWD WATCHING FIRE-works, except their eyes stared off at nothing—as the street full of people slipped their awareness from the world of the simulation to the real world, to their *real eyes,* their necks went lazy, their heads lolled back, and they stared upward at literally a whole separate reality.

Honestly, it reminded Shana of being back there again, wandering among the sleepwalkers. Those faces wearing expressions of eerie placidity. At first, she didn't know what to do. She wanted to wake them up, shake them, show them the door. Another part of her thought to join them: Why not again close her eyes and see what the flock was seeing? She wasn't really here. She *was,* however, really *there.*

Why not be present for the moment.

(Arav . . .)

She waited. She hesitated. Shana found Nessie, sitting there on a bench, her eyes empty like all the others. Shana knew that above all others, her sister likely had the best view of everything: As the first of the walkers, she saw everything first. All that was to come.

Then, a sea change. Carl Carter, with his big-jaw underbite and those tortoiseshell glasses, suddenly shuddered and blinked, returning to the world. He announced, to himself, to everyone, maybe to no one: "It's happening. It's happening!" Then he adjusted his glasses and slipped back into the other world—the real one. His neck went slack as his head dipped backward, his mouth drifting open.

Mary-Louise Hinton gasped like she was coming up out of cold water and babbled with laughter. "I think . . . I think we're going to our homes."

Another voice—Shana didn't remember the young woman's name, Carla or Cory or something—chimed in from somewhere: "The flock is breaking up. Oh my God. *Oh my God.*"

Then they were quiet again. Some mumbling and murmuring. Some twitching as if truly asleep.

"They call them myoclonic twitches," a voice said. Shana turned: It was the brain surgeon lady, Julie Barden. The one who gave the so-called orientation with Xander Percy. Julie wasn't alone.

Shana's mother stood with her.

The two walked right up to her, forming the only trio—at least, the only one visible—not joining in the strange reverie.

Julie continued: "The kind of myoclonus they're experiencing is the most common, at least, I expect. It's the kind you feel when you're about to fall asleep and your limbs suddenly—" She snapped her fingers. "—shake and shudder. They call that a hypnic jerk."

Oh yeah well you're *a hypnic jerk,* Shana thought, but thankfully did not actually say. Instead she sniffed and said: "What are you two doing? Not joining the tune-in-drop-out-trip-balls party?"

Her mother smiled. "We're with The Twelve. We don't have our bodies there in Ouray."

"Oh. Right." Shana stiffened, feeling embarrassed. "I didn't know you were one of The Twelve, Julie."

"I am," Julie said. "When I stop and look through my true eyes, I only see a lit room with a cement floor and a Plexiglas enclosure. It's very . . . Hannibal Lecter, I must confess."

Shana wanted to ask her exactly why a woman of her stature and profession—the lady was a brain surgeon, for fuck's sake—would ever submit to a process like that. But then she wondered: What if her fear about her mother was also true about Julie? And the others in The Twelve (most of whom she had never even met)? What if they were *fake?* Just part of the program? A human stack of bits and bytes toodling around, pretending to be a person instead of the Living Matrix there under that skin mask?

The thought, absurd as it was, made her suddenly mad. She shook her camera at them in a kind of defiance. "I saw it."

"What did you see?" Julie asked.

But it was Daria who answered: "Shana thinks she's seen a . . . gateway or some kind of portal—"

"A black door," Shana corrected.

Julie *hmm*ed. "And what do you think that it is?"

"I don't know. But Black Swan doesn't want me to see it."

"You think it's proof of something?"

"Proof your . . . god up there isn't some benevolent thing. That snaky douchebag up there is hiding something."

Julie seemed to consider this, a slight smirk on her face.

"Let's see your proof, then."

Shana grinned evilly, turning on the camera and using the button to flip through photos—cycling until she got to the end.

"No," she said. The world shook, or so she thought. But it didn't, not really. It was *she* who shook. Wobbling as if faint.

"I don't see anything," Julie said.

Because there was nothing to see. There was an image of the rock wall in the bend of the switchback, but the black door was nowhere to be found. It wasn't like it was glitched out or anything—it simply didn't exist. The mountainous façade remained without any blemishes or errors. No holes, no caves, no Vantablack squares leading into nowhere.

"It was there," she protested.

"Possibly just your mind playing tricks on you, sweetie," her mother said, reaching for her, as if in comfort. Shana pulled away.

"Get off. My mind wasn't playing tricks. Is that even *possible* in here?" She felt suddenly dizzy and anxious. Maybe it was possible. If she could be dizzy and anxious, couldn't she also imagine things? But fresh rage rode through her, and without a second thought she smashed the camera down against the ground. It shattered to pieces—she hoped that it would make a more dramatic display, with sparks or snaps of electricity, but mostly it just broke into black plastic shards. She cursed and stalked away, through her fellow sleepwalkers.

76

THE WELCOMING COMMITTEE

NOVEMBER 1
Ouray, Colorado

THE BUILDING AT 320 6TH AVENUE IN OURAY WAS A BUILDING OF MANY purposes: It was the Walsh Library, it was city hall, and it served as the community center. (And strange enough, it looked a helluva lot like Independence Hall in Philly. Benji reminded himself to try to suss out the story behind that.) Just up the road was another building that served a bunch of functions: The courthouse was also the historical society *and* the sheriff's office *and* the city jail. *Small towns,* Benji thought. Big difference from his time in Atlanta.

Inside city hall, it looked like you split off to check out a book or visit with the county clerk or head downstairs for a potluck in the community center. In this case, they ended up downstairs, in the community center room, which was decorated sparsely for some clumsy holiday mashup of Halloween, Thanksgiving, and Christmas. Tinsel, blinky lights, a cartoon turkey, a couple of ceramic jack-o'-lanterns. It struck Benji full force that the day prior was Halloween: It had come and gone without recognition. No fanfare, no candy. That, at least, until the man named Dove Hansen thrust a bowl of Halloween candy at him.

Landry introduced them. "Benji, this is Dove Hansen. Dove, this is Doctor Benjamin Ray. He's with the CDC."

Dove was a man with round cheeks and warm, kind eyes hiding under eyebrows so gray and so thick, you could probably use them to scrape mud off your boots. They were like miniature versions of the horseshoe mustache that framed his mouth.

Dove stuck out a hand, and Benji took it.

"What Landry fails to mention is that I am the mayor of this town, or what's left of it," Dove said. "Here, take some candy." He shook the bowl.

Benji wasn't much of a candy-eater. He cared little for sweet things, with the occasional exception of some very fine, very bitter dark chocolate. But now he felt like a kid getting the keys to the Wonka factory. His hand plunged into the bowl, fetching a half-sized Snickers bar. "Thank you," he said, unwrapping it and taking a bite. The sheer *pleasure* from eating the candy bar could not be overestimated. He had to work extra hard not to make happy moaning sounds. Sadie watched him, fascinated, and then took her own.

"Isn't it supposed to be ladies first?" she asked, delicately unpeeling a Kit Kat.

Benji apologized around a mouthful of Snickers. "Shorry."

She winked, then bit the Kit Kat in half, vertically. Crunch.

Dove took a piece himself, a little Krackel bar. He ate it in one bite and said, "Landry?" But the other man shook his head.

"I'm trying to keep my weight down."

"World's dying anyway," Dove said. "You sure?"

"Even if it dies tomorrow, I'd rather look good when it happens."

"Fair enough. Anyway. Doctor Ray—"

"Benji, please."

"All right. Benji, Landry here prepped us somewhat for your . . . visit. Though to see it in person—the flock I mean—is really something. If you wanna sit down, I can tell you the state of the town and then give you a little news, then we can . . . figure out what's next. How'd that be?"

Benji looked to Sadie, who nodded.

"I think that'd be fine," he answered.

They sat at a long cafeteria-style table. Metal folding chairs all around. This looked like a room intended for broad utility purposes: might house local weddings, beef-and-beers, voting, charity events, and so on.

"Dove's an interesting name," Benji said as he sat.

"My mother would tell you it's because my father was one-third Ute, but you ask me, that's some happy horseshit right there. He loved the mystique of cowboys and Indians and, well, here I am with Dove as a name. It's a nice name, though, I don't mind it. Point of fact: This town, Ouray, was named after Chief Ouray, a leader of the Uncompahgre band of the Utes. Of course, our town here is less than one percent Native, so I suppose it ends up sadly a name like my own: based more in the idea of native culture than actual

Native culture. So it goes." He cleared his throat, then idly played with a set of dentures in his mouth—his tongue dropped them down and the dentures waggled, moistly clicking between his existing teeth. "Before you tell me your story, I can give you the local lowdown, if that works."

"That would be fine."

Dove leaned forward, rescuing another candy from the depths of the candy bowl. This one, a peanut butter cup, but he didn't unpeel it so much as he fidgeted with it for a while, the wrapper crinkling in his hand.

"Ouray is a town of about a thousand, but that's a little bit misleading," Dove began. "That includes folks who have homes here but who generally only live in town for about six months, usually from late spring to sometime in the fall. May to October is standard, because after that, winter sets in, and winter here can be a brutal sonofabitch."

"How brutal, exactly?" Sadie asked.

"Hard to say. Modern conveniences can dampen its impact—most days are sunny and snowy, so you get a four-wheeler with a plow on it and you're in pretty okay shape."

"We can't count on modern conveniences anymore."

"That is correct. Plus, sometimes big storms come through, really dump it on us—the average winter brings about eleven feet of the white stuff."

"Eleven feet?" Benji asked, eyes wide.

"Sorry, hoss, it's the mountains. We're not a ski area proper, but we're surrounded by 'em, so the white stuff is part of the package. If you can handle the cold and the snow, then this town is pretty as they come. Some towns in the winter go gray and dead, but not us. We're white and bright with skies as big and blue as God's own eye."

Benji privately worried about what a rough winter would mean for everyone. The shepherds were less a concern—because, truthfully, White Mask would be far worse for them than the white snow. But would Black Swan protect them from the winter? And when they emerged from their . . . slumber, what then? How to survive up here? Would they move on? Perhaps he was putting the cart miles before the horse.

Dove continued. "We're a skeleton crew, I guess. Some of our folks started to leave after Labor Day, which is par for the course around here. More went on in September, October. But the sickness sent others packing, either to be with loved ones elsewhere or to be near a bigger hospital, whether in Telluride or north to Montrose or even Grand Junction."

"And I presume the sickness took its toll in other ways."

Dove again moved the dentures around his mouth. *Click-clack.* "People are dead, if that's what you're asking. More than I'd like to count."

"I'm afraid numbers are a necessary part of my job," Benji clarified. "Do you know how many? Have you counted?"

"I can't speak for those who have left, but those who stayed, we've lost a hundred thirty-seven people. Which may not sound like a lot, but it's about thirty percent of our year-to-year folk, the permanent residents."

"What do you do with the bodies?"

"The, uhh. Yeah. Those." This conversation was troubling him, Benji could see that. The man's face creased with worry. And he understood it. Experiencing something was one thing—you could compartmentalize even as you were experiencing it. But talking about it meant thinking about it. It meant opening the compartment and sorting through its contents, no matter how hideous. "We have a mass grave. South of town, up the Million Dollar Highway. It's a mine, a mineral farm, not subsurface, just a surface mine. A pit, basically. We put the—" His voice broke suddenly. "I can't call them bodies. I just can't. They're people, you understand that? People I know. Most I like, some I didn't, some I loved like brothers and sisters. George Cartwright, Sissy Tompkins, Dan Lee, Lora King, on and on, people I grew up with, people I . . ."

His eyes shone with sudden sadness.

"It's okay," Sadie said, taking his hand. He flinched away from it—not aggressively, but as if jostled free from his memory of those named.

He took a deep breath and puffed out his chest. A certain stoicism returned as he straightened his back. "We take the dead up to the mine. In a perfect world we'd bury them in the cemeteries where they've purchased plots—either Colona toward Montrose or Cedar Hill, which is a little closer. But this ain't a perfect world, so we take them to the mine. We burn them there. I don't know if that's the right thing to do, but story goes that you leave the bodies around, then White Mask starts . . . pushing out of them like tubers out of a goddamn potato. Burning them seems to stop that, though you're free to tell me I'm making a bad call there, Benji."

"I cannot say," Benji said. "We never had time to do tests. But speaking of potatoes—burning affected vines and roots has shown to curtail the spread of potato blight and wilt. Though at this point, given the state of the world—"

"It's too late to say you're sorry," Dove said.

"What?" Benji asked.

"It's something my wife—my ex-wife—used to say. Sherry was very clear on that point: Sometimes it's too late to say you're sorry. Too late to change course, to fix the damage. I was a bad drinker once upon a time, when I was young. Wasn't abusive or nothing like that, but I slept around, lied a lot. I ended up doing exactly what Sherry warned me about. Couldn't fix it with sorry."

"You say you've got only a skeleton crew. How many are left?" Sadie asked, wisely refocusing the conversation. Benji gave her a look that said *Thank you.*

"Last count, thirty-seven of us. A mix of old-timers like me, and some younger folk who had homes and businesses here. Jenny Whelan, owns Jenny's Café. Gil Fernandez, owns the little Mexican joint across from the Beaumont. The two hippies who own the bookstore in the Beaumont, Jasmeen Emerson and her husband, Carney Baur, good couple, nice couple. Think they had it in mind to open up one of them weed dispensaries up here now that it's legal—kind of a *Come to Colorado, get really high* message because we're at a higher elevation than most? Guess it won't take off now, though."

"How many are sick?"

"That I don't know, exactly. I stopped nosing around that number once I realized it didn't really matter."

"You don't seem to have symptoms," Sadie said.

"I don't. Not a one. I was a sickly child, if we're being honest, but somehow my adult life has gone the other way. I've got some weight around my middle and my doc said I got bad triglycerides, but otherwise I'm healthy as a young ox. Must be that clean Ouray air."

Benji offered: "We could test you. I have some of the swabs—"

"No," Dove said, sharply. "I don't need to know. I already have a good idea how this goes. I'm no dumb-ass. White Mask will get me. Probably already has me and just hasn't shown its face yet."

"Fair enough."

"It's my turn now to put you in the hot seat. Landry here showed up, told me what's what and who was coming, and I didn't know how to take it then, and don't know how to take it now."

Benji thought about how to dance around the subject, how to *ease* Dove Hansen into the reality of what they were dealing with—was he a man of God? Of science? Would he need to be convinced or . . . ?

But Sadie didn't mess around with any of that.

"We are the shepherds of a flock of people chosen by a machine intelligence to survive the epidemic of White Mask and continue human civilization. They are protected by that intelligence via the means of a nanoscale swarm: basically, microscopic robots that have taken over the bodies of the chosen and put them into a kind of *somnambulist coma,* a 'walking stasis,' if you will, until the time comes that White Mask is gone from the earth and they can be reawakened. The machine intelligence, known as Black Swan, has chosen Ouray, your town, as something of a perfect point for the flock's incubation. They will remain here as long as they are able in order to weather the end of the world."

Benji didn't know yet how much Landry had told him, but it certainly wasn't all that.

Dove, to his credit, did not fall backward out of his chair.

Instead he sat there, tongue pushing his dentures up and down like a fishing bobber in the water. He leaned back. He crossed his arms, then uncrossed them. His brow tightened into deep lines.

"All right, then," he said. "The remaining folk here are going to have some questions and I'd like you to answer them."

Benji and Sadie shared an affirmative look.

"Of course," Benji said. "When?"

"I'd say now is about right."

"Can you give me an hour? I'd like to talk to the other shepherds. I need them to start identifying where the sleepwalkers went. We need also to start taking inventory of the town's supplies, and get a general lay of the land— though that can come after, certainly."

Dove nodded. "A fair deal."

"Thank you," Benji said.

Dove finally unwrapped the peanut butter cup he'd been messing with. Before he popped the whole thing in his mouth he said, "You're welcome. Just don't do me dirty, Doc. This town means the world to me, and these people have been through enough already. I find you're lying to me or bringing danger to my door, you'll not find me so kind."

MILES TO GO BEFORE I SLEEP

NOVEMBER 1
Ouray, Colorado

ALMOST MIDNIGHT NOW IN THE OURAY TOWNSHIP BUILDING. THE QUESTIONS from the day prior still raced through Benji's head: *How long will you be here? Are you going to save us? One of your . . . "people" is in my kitchen, sitting there at the kitchen table, can you get her out?* The answers were not easy to give. He explained to them that yes, the flock was here for the duration. That no, he was not here to save them, and though he wished he could, that was just plain beyond his power at this point. And then he had to explain to people what he himself did not really understand: The flock had entered buildings, some businesses, a lot of homes, and it was there that they seemed to . . . remain. They knelt, or sat, or lay on beds, and just . . . went to sleep. Their eyes closed. Their bodies remained tense. Their chests rose and fell with shallow breaths. They were home, now.

And their homes were sometimes *other people's* homes.

Their eyes were haunted with confusion and anger as he told them, no, he wouldn't endeavor to move anyone. He watched their eyes shift to fear as he explained why: "Because I'm afraid that moving them will trigger their . . . defense mechanisms." Sadie jumped in to explain in the most chipper, yet grisly way imaginable:

"They first begin to increase rapidly in temperature as the machines inside them stir to a panicked state. If allowed to continue, the body pushes forward into a default state where the machines eject forcibly from the body, racing out of the cells to which they have bonded. As a result, the individuals detonate—except there is no fire, only a tide of scalding blood and liquefied organs. And bone shrapnel, of course."

Their eyes went big. Even Benji found the description jarring. (Though, also, correct.)

That took three hours while the other shepherds went through town, cataloging the locations of the sleepwalkers. They only got through around 35 percent of them, and would continue that list tomorrow. They slept.

Finally, Benji was alone. Alone, and in a way, at home.

Because he was in the Ouray library.

Libraries had, for Benji, long been a source of solace. His work took him around the world, and often put him in intensely strange or stressful situations: crawling through bat-infested caves (no worse smell except the one that came out of industrial chicken houses), catching and testing domestic hogs (the kind that, given half a choice, would gladly start to gobble up your extremities because pigs really were pigs), tracking quarantine vectors through very unpleasant places (a Bangkok brothel, the Philadelphia sewer system, various slaughterhouses and rendering plants). He enjoyed his work then; the burden of it was one he chose and found satisfying, if not exactly happy-making.

But it was hard and he needed escape.

For him, libraries served as that escape: They were routinely calm, if not always quiet, and of course they surrounded him with *books*.

Sweet, sweet books.

Each book, a treasure chest of knowledge. And the advent of the modern library did not disturb him: The introduction of computers and other "screens" into libraries only increased that access to information.

That was key, he long felt, to an informed society, one that cleaved to both empathy and critical thinking: access to information. Simply being able to *know things*—true things!—meant the world to him. And better still, reference librarians served well in the role that the internet never did: They were the perfect bouncers at the door of bad information. Or, put differently, they were the best vectors to transmit truth. Just as diseases required strong vectors to survive, thrive, and spread, Benji always felt that the power of a healthy society hinged on powerful vectors that allowed good information to do the same: survive, thrive, spread. Unhealthy societies quashed truth-tellers, hid facts, and curtailed debate (often at the end of a sword or rifle). Information, as the saying went, wanted to be free.

And a healthy society understood that and helped it to be so.

And libraries were the perfect, shining example of that assistance.

The Ouray library was, truth be told, not particularly robust: It was the library of a small mountain town in Colorado. It needn't possess the breadth and depth of, say, the Multnomah County Library system in Portland, or the libraries of NYC, Los Angeles, or DC. It wasn't beautiful or artful like Seattle, Belarus, or Trinity College. It did not have the rare books that Yale's Beinecke Library had on hand.

But it had little treasures, as all libraries did. It had Holt 1967 first editions of Lloyd Alexander's Prydain Chronicles, tons of *Star Trek* novels, plus stacks of magazines he used to love—*Discover, Omni, National Geographic*. He wanted to dive into them the way one dives into a pool on a hot summer's day—but he couldn't. That was not his purpose.

His purpose was to help build a knowledge base for the flock.

One day, they would *wake,* as it were, from their sleepwalking.

And when they did, they would be woefully unprepared for the world to come. Benji knew he was overstating that problem somewhat: Black Swan had curated the people that made up the flock. They were, literally, the chosen ones. And Black Swan had chosen people from the gamut, but long ago Benji had run the numbers and looked at the people who became sleepwalkers and even from early on, it was evident they were not fools. They had a wide variety of disciplines on hand, with the added bonus of people who were, on the whole, pretty damn smart. He knew they would not be lost, wayward sheep. They were wolves.

Just the same, anything he could give them, he would. His favor to them. He'd die. They'd live. He could give them an inheritance.

The goal was: find any books in here that would give them necessary knowledge. He found a book on engine repair; that went in the box. *Bushcraft 101,* by Dave Canterbury? In the box. *US Army Field Manual*? Absolutely. Various cookbooks went in, too, especially those comfortable with field dressing and preparing wild game. He found an unexpected library edition of Annalee Newitz's *Scatter, Adapt, and Remember: How Humans Will Survive a Mass Extinction,* and *of course* that went in—though it was not necessarily full of practical information, it contained several thought experiments on how humanity would survive extinction. He also found older books on shade gardening, foraging, first aid, and those would be helpful. As were the old surveyor maps and road atlases from decades past. He blew dust off them as he chucked them in the box, then reminded himself, too, to check out that bookstore Dove told him about. He wished suddenly he had the Foxfire manuals from the '70s—those books taught you about everything from snakebites to making moonshine, from tanning hides to midwifing. What if they were here, though? This seemed like the kind of library that would stock them . . .

He was about to head to another shelf—

When the front door of the library creaked open.

He spun around, instantly clocking where his rifle was—

Across the room, three tables away, oh shit—

But it was just Landry.

His heart racing, he leaned back against the table. "Landry. It's you."

"You look like you saw the Devil jump up out of that box."

"I just—the road has made me twitchy."

The young black man walked in, hands clasped behind him as he did—he had an imperial stride, slow and somehow eerily confident. "No harm in being twitchy these days, I figure." Landry lowered his voice, as if someone might be listening. "Long as you didn't piss your britches."

"I did not yet soak my pants, no."

"Good to hear."

"What ahh—what brings you here? It's gotta be after midnight."

"Almost. About eleven thirty P.M. I don't sleep well these days. Especially since Pete went off on his little journey."

Benji sighed. "We didn't get to talk much and I'm sorry about that. I know you said you decided to stay here, but why?"

"I'm sick. I think." Benji could hear it in Landry's voice—that treacly thickness behind his nose, deep in the sinuses. "I told Mister Rockgod to head on without me and go find his family. No idea if he succeeded. He may be dead for all I know."

Way he said it, Landry was clearly manufacturing defiance—his chin up, chest out, like he was pretending he didn't care. Like it was what it was, he was bulletproof to that kind of thinking. But it failed to hide how much he missed Pete. Benji said, "It's okay to miss him."

"Nothing's okay anymore, Doc."

"I suppose you're right about that."

"I brought something."

Now the purpose of the hands behind his back became clear: Landry produced a bottle of something. A dark liquid sloshed within.

"What's that?" Benji said, raising his eyes.

"Bottle of whiskey. Made here in Colorado, by the look of it—Stranahan's Diamond Peak. Dunno if it's any good, but it was the most expensive thing still left on the shelf. All the other good shit was gone, sweetie."

"You like whiskey?"

"Shit, not really. I'm a vodka-gin kinda boy. Hell, I'll get fucked up on white wine spritzers if you let me. But this feels like a whiskey kinda town, and it damn sure feels like a whiskey kinda world."

Benji couldn't argue with him on that.

The two of them sat down, popped the bottle.

In lieu of glasses, they just passed it back and forth. The bottle went *ploomp* as Benji pulled it away from his lips. The alcohol was warm in his mouth, like caramel and popcorn—when it went down his throat, it left a scalding trail like a log flume ride through boiling water. He coughed and blinked away tears. Landry laughed at him as he took a sip, unaffected.

"I hate to see what happens if you smoke some of that Colorado weed," Landry said. "You'll cough up your own kidneys."

"I've never smoked marijuana," he said, wiping his eyes.

"I can tell by the way you said, 'I've never smoked marijuana.'" Landry did a buttoned-up academic impression of him, ladling on what seemed to be extra nerdiness. (Though hell, maybe Benji really *did* sound that way.) "Tell me, Doc. How the hell does a grown man in this day and age not try a little pot here and there?"

"It just . . . never came up. I didn't want to cloud my thinking. I always viewed my mind like a computer, and I never wanted to slow it down. I tried speed in grad school once—someone's Adderall. Made me feel like I could disassociate all my atoms and vibrate through walls. I stayed up late, but didn't finish the paper I was working on, and instead just . . . cleaned my dorm room. Three times, if I recall."

Landry laughed. "Speed is nasty business. Cocaine's a little nicer, plus I can pretend I'm all 1980s and shit. Acid's fun, though you can't get it too easily these days. I mean, even *before* the Apocalypse. Shrooms are cool once they get going but first you gotta like, throw up, which automatically is a *no way nuh uh* for me. I won't barf my guts up just to get high." He took another plug of the bottle then stared at Benji with deep, soulful eyes. "Doc, what you should do is, take that woman of yours, go get yourself some weed—something edible, like I had these cannabis caramel chews one time? And you couldn't even taste the THC funk in 'em. Go find a high spot on one of these mountains and, you know, *get high with the mountains*. Enjoy a sunrise or a sunset. Fuck off from the world for thirty, sixty, ninety minutes."

Benji sighed. "But there's so much to do."

"The world's gonna die anyway. Grab some joy while you can."

"You might be right."

"I am right. I pride myself on being right. I told Pete that all the time. And I'm telling you now." He paused. "Sadie sent me, you know."

"Did she now?"

"Mm-hmm. Told me to check on you. Make sure you get some downtime, maybe some sleep."

Benji held up the bottle, gave it a swishy-slosh. "This doesn't look like sleep, Landry."

"Drink enough, it'll damn sure *feel* like sleep."

"I love Sadie."

"Yeah, I know."

"You love Pete?"

"Yeah."

"Shit."

"Shit is right."

Benji spun the bottle cap in his hand, then fixed it to the top of the bottle. "I ought to go and—" *Be with Sadie* was what he was about to say. But outside, he heard a distant sound. Landry started to ask him about it, but Benji shushed him with a quick hiss.

A low grumble, off somewhere.

Like an engine.

A plane, maybe? No—it was ground-level, he thought. Whatever it was, it was getting closer, too. Benji, trying to push through the whiskey soaking his brain, grabbed the rifle off the back table and hurried to the door out of the library, and then to the door out of the community center. As he staggered onto the street, two things hit him—

First, little white flakes dotted the dark. Motes, swirling and whirling about. *Ashes,* he thought, *from the bodies.* But it wasn't. It was snow.

Second, a pair of headlights appeared at the south end of town, bright like demon eyes. The back end of the car swished one way as it rounded the bend onto Main Street, and it barreled forward, swerving through low grass. Benji raised the rifle and pointed it as Landry followed outside, asking what the hell was going on.

The car came closer. Looked fancy. Silver-gray. Pocked and stained with road grime. Looked like a Lexus. Whoever was driving slammed the brakes—the back end of the car fishtailed as it did, and the whole vehicle slid hard enough to end up perpendicular to the sidewalk and street. Benji blinked against the snow and the darkness, and he saw that in the car sat one person—a man, driving.

The door popped and that man stood up. He had hollow eyes and a patchy, dark beard. His hair came out in messy curls from underneath a knit winter cap. Benji held the rifle aloft.

"Hands up!" he said. *"Hands up or I shoot."*

The man quickly juggled a pair of wool-gloved hands over his head. "I'm not—I'm not here to hurt you. I promise. I just need you to listen."

The voice. It sounded familiar, though Benji couldn't fathom why, exactly. It nagged at him like a fingernail scraping paint from an old wall.

Fatigue wore at him. The whiskey pulled at his mind. Even so, he felt suddenly awake and aware of everything. Every snowflake. Every slice of cold wind. The cold metal trigger underneath his coiled finger.

It was then that Benji realized who the man was.

He knew that voice.

Devil's Pilgrims . . .

Halt their progress . . .

Enemies of Christ, the Children of Wormwood . . .

Matthew Bird. The pastor who had that podcast, the radio show, who showed up with Hiram Golden. Associated with Ed Creel and the ARM.

"Please," Bird said, staggering toward him. "You have to listen."

"Back, back, back!" Benji cried. "Don't you come any closer—"

"You're in *danger*," the pastor said, taking a lunging step toward the front of the Lexus. Benji pressed the gun into his shoulder. He saw the brand on the man's neck. Hammer, serpent, and sword.

No.

He pulled the trigger.

78

THERE IS NO SPOON, AND WHAT DOES TASTY-WHEAT TASTE LIKE, ANYWAY?

NOW AND THEN
The Ouray Simulation

THE SIMULATION HELD NO SET MEALTIMES, AS TIME ITSELF WAS TOO FLUID and uncertain, but once in a while a mealtime simply seemed to exist.

This one, they ate in the community center room.

It was a small buffet full of hometown foods: turkey and mashed potatoes, soda and beer, cheesecake and cookies. It had the feel of Thanksgiving, though Shana did not believe today was Turkey Day. Or maybe it was. Maybe it always was, if they wanted it to be. It was disorienting to think that way; though Shana had never had jet lag, she wondered if this was what it felt like: being somehow outside of time, out of sync with the place from whence you came.

She sat and ate alone at a small table in the far corner, near an old oil painting of a rust-red mine building, with purple mountains set as the backdrop. Probably somewhere local or whatever.

The rest of the room was abuzz with chatter—the flock had found their houses in the real world, and everyone was excited. A lot of their resting places, as some called them, were the same as their chosen bedrooms here. A gift from Black Swan? A kind of psychic synchronicity? Who knew?

For her part, Shana closed her eyes to see—and sure enough, she was on the bed in her room at the Beaumont Hotel, staring up at the tin-tile ceiling. Arav was there, watching over her. Pacing back and forth, back and forth, the floorboards complaining under the tireless assault of his footsteps. A hand jostled her shoulder—

She snapped back to the simulation.

Nessie stood there. "Why don't you come sit with us?" she asked, gesturing to a table across the room. There others sat—Mia, Aliya, some others Shana recognized but whose names she did not yet know.

"I'm good."

"You're acting weird."

I saw the black door. I caught it on camera. And then it was gone. Black Swan is fucking with me, little sister. I think it's fucking with all of us. Or maybe she was wrong. Maybe her perceptions were off. Maybe she was losing her damn mind. Pregnant ladies went crazy, didn't they? *Oh God I'm pregnant. Nothing makes sense anymore.*

"I'm fine."

"You're not fine. Come sit!"

"I said *no*." That last word, she practically growled. She didn't mean to, but that's how it came out. Nessie recoiled, as if slapped.

"Oh. Okay." She looked sad. Maybe a little mad. And then she went back over to the others, tossing one last look over her shoulder.

Shana sighed.

She was now the child of two different realities, one simulation, one not, and she didn't want either of them.

Just the same, she closed her eyes once more and felt her mind gently separate from the Ouray simulation and—

There, again, Arav walked. Cracking his knuckles now, sharp rolling pops.

He started to speak.

"Shana come back to me. Please."

Her heart leapt. She wanted to scream. Wanted to stand up, reach for him, embrace him. She tried to get her body to do something, anything. She was a passive observer, an audience member to her own life.

He kept on:

"I don't want to be here anymore. I don't feel right. I . . . I'm having trouble *staying in my own head . . .*"

She wanted to say to him, *I understand that more than you can know.*

"I just, uhh, I just . . . I forgot your name earlier? That's a confession I don't want to make and I don't even know if you can hear me or will remember this but . . . I'm having a moment of lucidity and I wanted to tell you that I love you and I'm sorry about that. I'm sorry that I'm losing myself to this . . ." He roared in frustration, grabbing at his face like someone trying to rip weeds out of a garden. *"This damn disease.* It's got us all. But it doesn't have you. That's the one treasure I get to keep. It doesn't have—"

A gunshot.

But where?

In the simulation, or here in reality?

Arav's head spun toward it on a swivel, whipping around. So here, then. In the real Ouray.

He raced out of the room and Shana wanted to scream his name, to call him back, but it was too late. Arav was gone.

79

TINNITUS

NOVEMBER 2
Ouray, Colorado

STRANGE THE THINGS ONE THOUGHT ABOUT IN MOMENTS OF CRISIS AND chaos. Matthew Bird, his ears buzzing sharply with the sound of the rifle shot ringing out, wondered, *How long before I begin to lose my hearing?* He'd been too close now to so many gunshots. So many instances of tinnitus ringing in his ears. As he pressed himself against the ground, a bit of information—a memory—flitted through his head, uninvited, like a bat in the attic. Once upon a time he'd read somewhere, or heard on the radio, that the sound of ringing in your ears was the sound of ear cells dying, their last shriek before going dark and deaf. It was probably a lie. Some misinformation. Or disinformation. Most things seemed to be anymore. For a moment, his brain lied to him, told him that Autumn was here with him, that she was underneath him, that she had come with him from Innsbrook, but she hadn't. He was alone. So goddamn alone.

The man with the gun stood there. Only five feet away.

The rifle pointed up in the air. Ghosts of gunsmoke, purged from the barrel in their exorcism, rising to meet the night.

The man lowered it again, taking aim.

Matthew's breath caught in his throat. He quick checked himself: no blood. He wasn't hit. No injuries. Eyes up, face down, he said: "You. You're— you're Benjamin Ray, right? I'm Matthew Bird."

"I know who you are," Benji seethed. "Explain yourself or I put a bullet in the top of your head. I just might anyway."

Matthew rocked back on his heels, hands again up in the air. He stammered something that was not yet words—just a guttural utterance of sounds coughed out in steamy breath. Breath around falling snowflakes.

"Speak!" the man with the gun barked.

"People are coming," Matthew blurted. "Bad people. His name is Ozark Stover. He's part of ARM, the—the American Resurrection Movement." The man with the gun took a step forward, the barrel aiming straight between Matthew's eyes. "I—I saw someone, he has a friend of yours, a wo-woman named Marcy."

There. That landed. *That* connected.

The man with the gun let his guard drop. The tension in his arms slackened, and the rifle's barrel drifted downward, pointing at the ground.

"Marcy," the man said.

"That's right. They have her. They're coming. And they want to kill you. They want to kill *all* of you."

THEY PUT HIM IN A drunk tank cell in the county jail. His appearance had obviously stirred some attention, and now outside the room, others gathered with the armed man—a man Matthew now knew was Benjamin Ray, the doctor and investigator with the CDC. And the self-appointed head of the . . . shepherds, the flock, all of this. Benjamin stood out there with a small group, ill seen behind the half-closed door. Their voices came as a maddening murmur; Matthew couldn't understand anything they were saying.

Matthew sat there, his head leaning on the hard cinder-block wall, wishing like hell that Autumn was here.

But she'd made her choice. And he'd made his.

He wondered where she was. If the disease had found her yet. Or if she had found Bo. Or worse, if the ARM soldiers had found her.

What would they do to her?

Matthew thought he knew, and that fear threatened to crush him.

Meanwhile, *he* hadn't sneezed, coughed, or anything.

The disease had not found him. Which felt somehow unfair, didn't it? There was no righteousness in who lived and who died. It served only as further proof that his belief in a just God was nothing but childish folly. No just deity would sanction this.

Not one he cared to follow, anyway.

Everything was random. Everything was chaos.

The door opened. Benjamin Ray led the way, flanked by a young black woman whose soft features were marked just so by the advance of White

Mask—the white rime had not begun, but she looked like she had a cold. Stuffy, Kleenex-chafed nose, eyes a little bloodshot. She looked tired, too, everything rumpled and ruffled, like she'd been pulled out of bed.

Behind her came a man with bushy eyebrows in fierce competition with his white caterpillar of a mustache. He wore a cowboy hat, and he tipped it up and back on his head as he entered, giving Matthew a hard, long look.

Someone else stayed outside the room. Matthew had seen him earlier: After the gunshot, after he'd tried explaining to Benjamin who and what was coming, a young man came racing down the street—brown skin, maybe Indian, Pakistani, or Arab, Matthew didn't know. He was dressed in clothes that had gone almost all the way to rags. He was filthy, and like many of the others showed the signs of White Mask—his case, the worst he'd seen here, yet. Striations of white crust snaked across the young man's face.

Everything is random . . . everything is chaos . . .

Benjamin introduced the others: Sadie Emeka, Dove Hansen, and the other one outside the room was Arav Thevar. He said that the man who had been outside when Matthew drove up—a man who was not presently here— was Landry Pierce. He gave a short introduction, said this is Ouray, he was the leader of the shepherds who were protecting the sleepwalker flock. Matthew did not see the flock and had no idea where they were, but he chose to keep his mouth shut for now. It seemed the wisest choice.

Benji said, coldly, "We have questions."

"I understand."

"It's very late. Or rather, very early. So I recognize that no one wants to be here, and nerves are certainly frayed. But this seems important."

"It is. Utterly so."

"I know who you are."

"I . . . guessed that, yeah."

"*God's Light.* The podcast, the radio show. You spoke out against us. You called us . . . what, satanic, or tools of the Antichrist. Subjects of the dread comet Wormwood, which was just that, just a comet, had nothing to do with anything. It was an excuse for you. A reason to gin up hatred against the flock. Devil's Pilgrims, my ass."

"That was all a mistake and—"

"A *mistake* that may have cost us lives. You understand that, right? All the way from Indiana to now, we've had people with *guns* come at us."

"More are coming."

Benji regarded him suspiciously. Like he was trying to use his gaze alone to pick Matthew to pieces, see if he could suss out the truth just by looking real, real hard. "What do you mean?"

"I mean I'm here to warn you. Stover and his men, ARM soldiers, are coming. With trucks. Guns. I don't know what else or how many."

"And why would you warn us?" Benji asked. "Getting right with God before the end?"

"No. I've lost my faith in God. I am no longer a believer."

"Then why come? Why not find somewhere to die in peace?"

"Because I wouldn't be able to die in peace. This would stay with me until my last breath. And Marcy . . . she asked me to, and I said I would. So I'm fulfilling my debts. My earthly ones."

The others shared a look. The man named Dove shrugged and said to Benji, "I don't know shit from shinola about any of this, so this is your lead, Doc. He sounds sincere, but I'm not particularly trusting these days."

It was Sadie who said: "Tell us everything, then. Tell us the story."

Matthew took a deep breath, and he did.

He tried to keep it brief, to move quickly through the narrative—not just because expediency seemed key, but because some of it was painful, too painful, to relive. But he told them what he could. About his imprisonment, his escape, about how he and Autumn wanted to find their child and so Matthew went into the ARM camp in Missouri with a fresh brand on his neck. About how he found his son, and Marcy, and decided to help her. How that led Autumn to stay there, and how he left, and had been out on the road since then, hard-charging toward Ouray in an effort to stay ahead of Ozark and his crusade.

"You've been on the road for weeks?" Benji asked. When Matthew nodded, the doctor asked: "What took you so long to drive here? A drive from Missouri to Colorado should be . . . what, twenty-four hours?"

Here, Matthew couldn't repress a laugh. He heard the rough, serrated edge in his voice when he explained: "You haven't been *out* there, have you? It's all gone to pieces. Gas is dried up. The roads are . . . blocked with trucks and cars, some of them crashed. Wheat fields and corn on fire. Coal mines and oil shales, too. People are losing their minds to White Mask. They're roaming in packs. Some of them are armed with knives and guns. Others are just . . . wanderers. Wandering this way and that like they don't know where to go, or why, or how. You get near the cities, it gets worse. It's not safe. It's slow going. I feared that Stover and his people would be here already—it's why I came blasting into town like that. Only reason they might not be here yet is I imagine it's even harder bringing multiple vehicles and people across the middle of the country. I only had a few days' head start on them. I imagine they won't be long behind."

Again, the group of three gathered there all shared uncomfortable looks. It was Benji who said, "Are you sick?"

"Not yet."

"You'll submit to a swab test?"

"I will."

"That's good," Sadie said.

"If you are infected," Benji said, "we know that some stimulants can help. We have a dwindling supply of Ritalin, and the nearest pharmacy is about . . ." He gave Dove a questioning look.

The older man jumped in and said, "About ten miles."

"So eventually we'll send people up there to see if we can find a supply of Adderall, Ritalin, Concerta, Vyvanse . . ."

"Strange to ask," Dove said, "but how about the old-fashioned kind? Cigarettes and black coffee."

"I . . . honestly don't know. That's a good question. I expect their effects on the delirium of White Mask would be reduced given the potency of other pharmaceutical approaches, but it might have a small effect."

"So, it slows down the disease?" Matthew asked, a small beacon of hope lighting in the dark of his heart.

A beacon that Benji quickly extinguished.

"No, it just limits the mental effects. The disease will continue its progression accordingly. Eventually the brain gives up and gives out and when the body collapses, White Mask colonizes the exterior." Benji paused, continuing his visual survey of Matthew. "Your hand looks like it was broken. It didn't heal well, I take it."

Matthew held it up. The fingers trembled as he tried in vain to open and close them, but they only moved a little bit. Pain lanced through his palm and raced from his wrist to his elbow.

"They broke it. When they had me in . . ." He had to stop and tamp down the rush of memories, lest they overtake him. "I don't think it'll ever really heal."

"What do we do with 'im?" Dove asked.

"I'm inclined to be compassionate," Benji said.

Dove sniffed. "That's your right as a doctor, I suppose, but as mayor, I'm accepting your people, your flock, as *my* people. But him? Not so much. I'm leery of the story. He had a couple of guns in the car. Hard to say what he was planning. I'd rather keep him in here a little while longer."

Sadie sighed. "I can get behind that."

"I'm no danger—" Matthew interjected.

"Sorry," Benji said. "I agree with the others, in retrospect. You will be fed, and this room will remain warm. Someone will make sure you get proper trips to the bathroom in the morning."

"You need to take my warning seriously—"

"Good night," Benji said, and he and the others left.

The door closed behind with a loud click. A jangle of keys and a lock turning sealed the deal. Matthew thudded his head dully against the beige cement behind him. He thought about sleep, but gave up on the idea. The idea of sleep was a distant dream.

80

PREPARATIONS FOR WAR

NOVEMBER 2
Ouray, Colorado

MORNING CAME, THE SUN RISING UP OVER THE EASTERN PEAKS. THE SNOW had left only a dusting of white behind, like the rime of the disease that had come for them all. Benji had slept, but barely. He took a shower, too, which was his first proper shower in . . . well over a month, now, and as all the filth that had agglomerated upon him began to run off, he started to feel human again. But the shower was all too short. He feared staying under the spray too long, because now it seemed they were on war footing, and had to be ready for whatever was to come.

And what might come at any time.

He grabbed his rifle, his walkie-talkie, his water.

Then he got to work.

"WE HAVE TO MOVE THEM," he said.

Benji stood in the rosewood dining room of the Beaumont Hotel— a three-floor hotel that offered a heady mix of Victorian and Queen Anne furnishings. Benji was not a fan of those styles: all the noisy clashes between the fleur-de-lis carpets and densely patterned wallpapers, between the ocher yellows, the grape-crush purples, the dark wood, the leather furnishings. It conjured a vibe of a child dressing up in grown-up clothes stolen out of the attic: grandmother's gown and mother's makeup.

(He'd said as much to Sadie earlier, and her response was far different: "Reminds me of a Wild West brothel.")

Now, though, their focus was not on furnishings or décor, but rather, the future of the swiftly dwindling human race.

The two of them stood in the dining room, a broad window looking out upon the banded hardrock of the San Juan Mountains. On a corner of a nearby table sat the Black Swan satphone, propped up by a small stand-up napkin ring. It projected text—a little hard to read given the wash of light from the window—onto the wallpaper:

WE CANNOT MOVE THE FLOCK.

"We *must*," Sadie said. "It's the only sensible way."

Benji continued her line of thinking: "If these ARM people are coming to Ouray to hurt us, then our best bet is simply to not be here when they arrive. We can return when the danger has passed."

The words appeared again, this time pulsing red as they did:

WE CANNOT MOVE THE FLOCK.

"Why not?" Sadie asked.

THE FLOCK IS FOLLOWING A PROGRAM.

"But it's a program of *your* design!"

Text scrolled up the wall: THE PROGRAM IS AN ALGORITHMIC CALCULATION FACTORING IN ENERGY CONSUMPTION. THE SLEEPWALKERS ARE IN SLEEP MODE TO CONSERVE ENERGY TO POWER THEM THROUGH THE YEARS NEEDED TO SURVIVE. WAKING THEM WILL EXPEND MORE POWER THAN ALLOWED FOR IN THE CALCULATION. AT THIS POINT, SUCH EFFORT WILL BEGIN TO DRAIN FROM THE LIFE SPAN OF THE NANITE SWARM.

"Even a small journey?" Benji asked, desperate. "Move them a short distance—the mountain is home to caves, mines, we could *hide* them—"

THEIR SLEEP MODE MUST NOT BE DISTURBED.

"It's damn sure going to be disturbed if men with guns storm in here and wipe us all out. Then none of this will have mattered. None of *us* will have mattered. The journey here will have been for *nothing*."

THEIR SLEEP MODE MUST NOT BE DISTURBED.

He reached for the phone, half intending to throw it through the goddamn window, but his hand paused and closed in on itself—a frustrated fist that he could not squeeze tight enough.

"What if we try to physically move them ourselves?" Sadie asked. "Pick them up like rolls of carpet and . . . move them somewhere safe."

THE DEFENSE PROTOCOLS WOULD MAKE THAT UNWISE.

To hell with your defense protocols, Benji wanted to say.

Sadie persevered: "Can you power down the defense protocols?"

YES.

"Then there we go!" she said, a flurry of laughter rising up out of her.

But Benji wasn't sure. "Moving them would be a Sisyphean exercise. We literally have a thousand and twenty-four bodies to move, and none of them are centrally located. Some are here in the hotel, but the rest are scattered widely throughout the buildings in Ouray—we have barely begun to catalog their locations. The time it would take is epic, at best. The reality is, we'd likely be caught with our pants around our ankles—those ARM bastards will show up in the middle of our move, meaning they'll find us dumping fish right into the barrel for them. We'd be exposing the flock, not saving them. At least now they're scattered—dispatching them will not be easy."

He could see she wanted to fight it, to bite back with some snappy answer that solved his problem, but he could also see the wave of emotions crest and fall on her face. The realization hit her that he was right.

"Shit," she said.

"Truly, a world of shit."

"Then what options do we have?"

Black Swan beamed a message onto the wall:

YOU WILL HAVE TO FIGHT. AND I WILL HELP YOU.

DOVE UNLOCKED THE METAL CABINET. The door swung open, revealing a rack of five long guns—Dove said they had three rifles, two shotguns—and a single .357 Magnum revolver hanging from a holster strap on the side. He took out the holster and began to strap it around his waist.

"Got ammo for each, though not much more than a box. Some of the residents have their own guns, but I'll be honest, we're not that kinda town. Other towns farther out were bigger into hunting, but Ouray has always kinda kept itself as a quaint mountain berg—you get someone field dressing an elk on his front lawn, that might bum out the tourists. You got guns, I see."

"We do," Benji said. "Not many, and nothing serious. Four rifles, two shotguns, four pistols or revolvers—is there a difference between the two? Pistols and revolvers, I mean."

"Revolvers got the spinny thing, the cylinder. Pistols don't. Tend to use magazines, feed rounds into the chamber one after each trigger pull, makes them semi-automatic. Both fall under the category 'handguns.'"

"You a . . . gun person?"

"Most everybody in Colorado is, at least a little. Especially on this side of the state. Fort Collins, Boulder, places like that, not so much, but out here, we're all born with a bolt-action rifle in our hands." Dove sniffed, pulling out one such bolt-action rifle. It looked freshly cleaned and well maintained, and Benji could smell the tang of the gun oil on it. "But we don't have big boners about it, either. We treat guns like tools, like hammers or screwdrivers. Don't see much value in forming some kind of ideological cult around 'em. Definitely don't see why people get such a kick out of those black rifles. Your nipples get hard using one of those, I start to worry about you shooting up a school or a movie theater."

"Or forming a white supremacist militia."

"That, too, Benji, that too."

Benji, always a fan of the numbers, ran them.

Thirty-seven townsfolk, plus seven shepherds, and now the ex-pastor Matthew Bird. With what the pastor had in his car, that meant they had a total of seven rifles, four shotguns, and five handguns. Totaled up, that meant sixteen guns for forty-five people. Roughly a box of ammo for each, though it occurred to him that this might be inaccurate: Some of the ammo for one firearm might need to be used for another, too. He reminded himself to check the calibers of each and literally count the bullets. That kind of inventory would matter here, grim as it was.

He told Dove his calculations and added: "I don't know how many men this Ozark Stover is bringing to our doorstep, but I imagine it's at least equal to what we have here."

"These people aren't soldiers, Benji. Like I said, a number of them aren't even hunters. So understand that. They might stand and fight, I dunno, but I can't promise they won't be a danger to themselves, too."

"And some of them are sick."

"Yes, they are. We don't have many lost to the—as you put it, *delirium* of the disease yet, but White Mask is here. And the ones who do have the delirium—well, I don't want to hand a gun to them."

"A fine point." He drew a deep breath and looked at his watch. It was 10 A.M. now. Sadie was out with the other shepherds, Arav included, gathering up their guns and ammunition. Landry was stocking a few locations with food: high points that Black Swan indicated would be good lookout spots. That meant the top floor of the courthouse, the attic here at the Beaumont, and potentially a lookout at the southwest corner of town. There, three waterways converged: the Uncompahgre, Oak Creek, and Canyon Creek, all fed by the Cascade Falls. A series of trails and bridges crisscrossed up there, and—according to Black Swan, who was the architect of this portion of the plan—provided a lookout over the whole town and valley. Benji worried it was too far away to get a meaningful look, especially at nighttime, but he planned on going up there later with Landry to see.

But first—

"So," he said to Dove. "The dynamite?"

"Okay. The dynamite."

"There you go," Dove said. "Whole box of stump suppositories."

Benji looked down at the wooden crate sitting exposed in the bottom of an old bedroom closet. A mounded ring of clothes—clothes used apparently to hide this box from prying eyes—surrounded it.

Behind them, one of the walkers, a young woman named Marissa Chen, was on the bed. Facing up, perfectly still. Like a mannequin someone had placed there. Benji had to try very hard not to look at her.

So instead, he focused on the crate. It sat closed.

"'Stump suppositories'?" he asked Dove.

"Yup. Fella who these belonged to used them mostly to clear stumps. Drill a hole, drop a quarter stick in, run some detcord to it, put an electric charge through the detcord with a battery or some such, then—*bzzt*." He clapped his hands together to make a hollow sound. "Boom. Stump gone."

"Stumps that much of a problem around here?"

"Turns out, they are. Got a bug problem here, little bastard called the fir engraver beetle. Eats up the white fir trees all around us, leaves them dead. They fall or get cut down, and then the stumps gotta go. Can't leave them around because they become fuel for forest fires. Dale—Dale's the fella who lived here, once—got paid good money to help us out."

Benji knelt and tried opening the box, but the lid was nailed down. Dove offered him a long-bladed penknife with a handle of what looked to be some kind of antler. Benji took it, slid the blade under the lid, used a little leverage, and—

Pop.

Dy-no-mite.

Half a crate of sticks as red as a Christmas candle.

"I assume it's not safe to jostle," Benji asked. "Old dynamite starts to sweat out the—"

"Nitroglycerin, I know. This isn't old. It's new."

"And you knew about this?"

"Sure did."

"But it's not legal."

Dove scoffed. "Sure it is. Dale had his FEL."

"FEL?"

"Federal explosives license. Long as you're not a fugitive or an ex-con, it's the same process as getting a federal firearms license to buy and sell guns. Though I guess none of that matters much now."

Benji lifted the box. "The world was an odder place than I knew."

"Shit, Benji. Have you *met* America?"

AHEAD, A ROCK WALL OF about thirty feet, or so Benji guessed aloud.

Black Swan clarified: IT IS FORTY-TWO FEET IN HEIGHT.

Benji stood in the middle of the road and Dove gave him an arched eyebrow as he consulted with the phone. "That's the . . . robot?"

"No, it's a phone that provides access to the machine intelligence that inhabits the robot swarms inside the sleepwalkers." When he said it out loud like that, it never got any less bizarre. "I ask it for advice sometimes."

That sounded even more bizarre.

"Well, it's got the right idea," Dove said. "This should actually work." Currently the two of them stood on the asphalt of the Million Dollar Highway, a set of switchbacks that climbed south out of town. The road here was carved right out of the mountain, looking down on Ouray. "Coming from the north, you can't block the road this way, because the mountains are too far off—and where they get close, you can just take Oak Street along the river. But here . . ." He sucked at his dentures. "It'll work."

The plan was, drill a succession of holes, then use the detcord-and-charge to detonate the dynamite that they used to plug those holes.

Then rocks would fall.

Hopefully nobody died.

Ideally, it would blast enough rock down onto the road to block it from any vehicles that wanted to come through here. Meaning they could effectively close off one point of access to the town, at least to vehicles. Men on foot could still make it here—or could come through other, wilder avenues. At the north end of town, Arav was (Benji hoped) helping some of the shepherds and townsfolk park cars perpendicular across the roadways, as had been done with the bus when they first got here.

Any obstacles they could put in the way of ARM had to help, right?

Dove handed over a roll of red cable. Then used his foot to pull closer another spool of yellow wire. Benji looked at him. "Why the two spools? I thought we could just run the red to the charge and—"

"Oh hell no. This is detcord. It's by itself explosive—and because of that you don't need blasting caps. Just plug this stuff right into the tips of each dynamite stick and then clip it—then you bridge it to proper wire, set a charge through it, and hope you're nowhere near it."

"You know a lot about explosives, Dove."

"I know a lotta shit about a lotta shit. This is just because I watched Dale do it, though, not because I'm the fucking Unabomber, all right?"

"Didn't mean to suggest otherwise."

"All that being said, some folks around here have been known to fish with quarter sticks of dynamite . . ."

"That doesn't sound fair to the fish."

"Oh, it's not." He laughed. "It's really not."

"Shall we do this?" Benji asked.

"Let's make some noise, Doctor Ray."

THE SIGHT OF ALL THE blood around surprised Benji—even as the detonation was still fresh in his mind, every part of him vibrating, he turned to see Dove there on the ground, screaming and rolling around. The older man had his hands around his head. Blood was pooling beneath him, running through his fingers, gushing from some injury Benji couldn't see.

He moved fast, hunkering down next to Dove and urging him to pull his hands away from his face.

There, he saw the injury—

A hard, ragged line cut across the side of his forehead to his temple.

A stone sat there on the ground. Blood shining upon it. Bits of skin bundled up in its cracks. It was then that Benji understood. Though they'd gone to what they thought was a safe distance—over a hundred yards away and off to the side of the switchback, just up a bit of a hill—a stone must've blasted free like a bullet. He'd heard something just after explosion: a whistling sound, a fast whip-crackle of brush. Must've been this.

Dove had now stopped screaming and instead was saying proper words, all of them profanities: "Shit, cocksucker, *fuck,* goddamnit fuck *shit.*"

"Stay still," Benji urged him. He knew the injury could be serious. A hard impact like that could be devastating—a concussion, a fractured skull, bleeding on the brain, or even just a garden-variety infection.

"Lot of fucking blood," Dove said through gritted teeth.

"That's normal with lacerations to the head and face. A wealth of little blood vessels in there." He took his bottle of water and splashed a bit onto the injury. Dove growled and tensed up so hard, Benji thought the man might grind his teeth into a wet paste. The water, though, cleared away some of the blood for a moment. He did not see bone beneath. The cut, it seemed, was significant in its length but not its depth. "It needs stitches. And antibiotics. You might also have a mild concussion—time will tell on that. Here, come on, let's see if you can stand."

He offered Dove a hand. The older man grumpily stood up. Fresh blood ran down his face, over his wincing eye. Even his white mustache was wet with red—like a tract of snow where a wolf had made a kill.

"We need to get you back to town, I'll stitch you up."

"Hell with that. How'd we do?"

"What?"

"The rocks, Doc. How'd we do?"

Benji had put that out of his mind. He turned to see, now that the smoke was swept away by the mountain wind.

The dynamite had carved a series of craters in the side of the mountain, littering the road with impassable boulders.

"It worked," Benji said, breathless at even this small success.

"Then at least my blood spilled was blood earned. My mother always used to say that. I'd come up to her, bleeding from some fool thing I did, and she'd ask, *Did you at least get something for it?* Like the blood was a way to pay in, to pay a price to accomplish a goal. If I did, she'd say, *Good, blood spilled, but blood earned,* and leave it at that."

They started to walk out of the brush, down the hill and back to the road. "And if you didn't get anything for your spilled blood?"

"Then she'd laugh at me, call me a dumb-ass, tell me to make sure that next time I got something for my time and injuries."

"Your mother sounds like a hard woman."

"Hard as a hammer's cheek, Benji."

Together the two of them admired their work one last time—the rain of rock and stone really would make the road impassable to all vehicles. Even a motorbike would have a helluva time navigating this field of broken mountain. Then they started walking back to town. Dove's face was a half mask of already drying blood. "We shoulda been back farther," he said.

"I think that much is obv—"

Benji's radio crackled.

It was Maryam McGoran's voice.

"Benji. Come quick. We got a problem, north end of town. Over."

Dove sighed. "Fun never ends, does it?"

"Apparently not."

ARAV HELD THE SHOTGUN UP to his shoulder—a Remington 870 pump-action 12-gauge, a weapon loaded with buckshot and featuring enough oomph to perforate most major organs with one hasty pull of the trigger. He was twitchy, and Benji could see that he was lost in his own mind. The young man pointed the gun back and forth, moving the barrel from one target to the next: each of them townspeople or shepherds.

Benji approached, hands up. Ahead, Arav spun around to face him, putting the people at his back. Behind them was a school bus—the same one that had blocked the northern road when the flock and shepherds came into town a few days ago. Already behind it the townsfolk had parked a number of cars, stacking them deep and at off-angles to make sure no one could easily pass.

Though it looked like they were having some success here, that was severely undercut by Arav, who now thrust the gun toward Benji.

A hundred feet separated them.

Arav was sweating, even in the cold. His breath popped in short, despairing puffs. The gun rattled just slightly as his hands shook.

"Arav," Benji said.

"You back up. You back *away.*"

Benji did not back up, but he did cease his advance.

He gave a short look behind him, saw that Dove had moved a hand to hover over the holster he had at his waist. Ahead, too, he saw Maryam at the far end, just at the back bumper of the bus. She had a lever-action rifle hanging at her side, the barrel down to the ground. But already Benji could see her easing it up, up, up. *This is going to turn into a shootout.*

"Nobody is going to hurt you," Benji said, feeling the weight of his own rifle slung over his shoulder. He didn't want to have to use it. He told himself he *wouldn't* use it. Arav had been through enough already. Arav was a shepherd. They had to protect their own, even in a situation like this.

But a small voice wondered:

What if he had no choice? Arav was sick already. And as with Alzheimer's, there could come a point when the mind was truly lost—the pathways once established in the brain toward rational thought and discourse became an unsolvable labyrinth.

"Back away. *Back away.*"

"Do you know who I am?" Benji asked calmly, quietly.

"I . . . you're . . ." It was plain to see the struggle on his face. He was warring with his own memories. Trying to sort through them. Arav was on Ritalin, Benji knew, but had it failed finally? Was its utility used up?

He took a step forward.

Arav pressed the shotgun hard into his own shoulder, staring down the vented rib of the black barrel.

Dove drew his pistol. "Don't, boy."

Arav pointed the gun at Dove, now. His eyes went wide and unblinking. Sweat ran into them and he flinched. Benji felt his heart stop for a moment—even the smallest flinch could make Arav pull the trigger. If he'd already pumped a shell into the chamber, that trigger wouldn't take much to send a blast of lead shot into him or Dove.

"Dove," Benji urged, "it's fine, put the gun down."

"Inclined not to," Dove said, low and slow.

"This isn't the Wild West."

"And if he's sick, like an animal, maybe he needs to be put down."

Is that what Dove did here? Did he put down his own townspeople? That was a grotesque act, if so. And yet . . .

He cleared his head. None of that was important right now.

Maryam on the other side gently raised her rifle.

"No!" he barked. Loud, too loud, enough to draw Arav's attention anew. The barrel snapped back toward him and he could hear the gun go off, could feel its cold blast hit him square in the chest, *whoom*—

Just my imagination. That didn't happen. He was still standing. Still whole and in one piece. The gun did not go off.

"Arav, you may not remember me, but you remember Shana?"

There. A flicker of awareness in Arav's eye. He hesitated. The gun barrel lowered—just a little.

Maybe his mind was not an unsolvable labyrinth, yet. Benji had little experience with Alzheimer's directly, but he knew that caregivers had ways to reach their patients suffering under the disease. Sometimes it was music, sometimes artwork (making it or beholding it), sometimes it meant having contact with a beloved pet. Other times it simply meant finding something— or some*one*—that they loved and invoking that emotional pathway.

"Shana," Arav said, his voice suddenly small.

"You're just protecting Shana, aren't you?" Benji asked.

Maryam stared down the sights of her rifle.

Dove held his pistol aloft, watching through one open eye, the other shut with a crust of his own blood.

"I am," Arav admitted.

"We are, too. I'm Benji. Doctor Benjamin Ray. We worked together at the CDC." *When the CDC still existed.* "Right now, we're trying to defend this town from some bad men. You were in the process of helping these nice people set up a blockade against those men. I am not one of the bad men. I am your friend. We're all your friends here, Arav."

"Arav . . ." He spoke his own name, like he hadn't heard it before. But then he said it again, like he recognized it: "Arav. Arav Arav Arav." Then, finally: "Benji."

It was like watching fog roll out to sea, once more revealing the shoreline, and the moon, and the stars. Clarity came to Arav. He looked suddenly to the shotgun in his hand and quickly lifted the barrel to the sky, his other hand letting go of the stock and also rising in surrender.

Benji moved toward him with an urgency to his step, quickly moving to disarm Arav. The young man, his friend, let him. It was over.

Except really, it wasn't over. Not for any of them.

Night in Ouray

No attack came. The town was quiet. The lights were out, mostly, except for a few windows burning effulgent in the blue-black of the mountainous dark. Benji sat in his room at the Beaumont, looking out over Main Street. Sadie lay on the bed, on her side, resting. He knew he should do the same, but he felt worn out, worn down, like all of his protections and defenses had been sandblasted away.

Questions hounded him. How long would the power stay on here? How long before Ozark Stover and his men came? How long would Arav remain able to come back from the brink—and how long would it be before Sadie fell to the delirium of the disease? How long before *he himself* fell prey to it? He had few symptoms, as yet, but Sadie was progressing steadily, if not swiftly.

He had no good answers. Only terrifying questions.

Awake, he took the Black Swan phone and headed out of his room and down the stairs. Already he could see someone else in the lobby.

It was Arav.

He, too, looked like he was worn out and worn down. His edge had gone. The young man sat on a chair in the lobby, looking for half a moment as if he were someone in another, normal life just chilling out in a perfectly average hotel lobby—seeking restitution from customer service, perhaps, or waiting for an Uber to come and pick him up, or even just hoping to meet a friend for coffee.

Arav saw him approach. He pointed toward a door off to the side. "That's the bookstore. Did you know that?"

"I did not," Benji answered, and it was true.

"The bookstore next door has an entrance here in the lobby," Arav said, sounding the most like himself Benji had heard in a long while. "That's like, the perfect hotel to me. A hotel with a connected bookstore. It's almost like Heaven. Maybe this *is* Heaven."

Benji sat down in a chair next to him, then gave it a second thought—he stood up again, and moved the chair so he could face Arav, instead. "This is a very nice town. I wish I had visited it under different circumstances."

"Yeah. Seriously." Arav idly picked at his thumbnails. Pick, tick, pick. "Dove okay? I . . . heard what happened to him."

"I think so. I stitched him up. No antibiotics, though, yet—best we have is some ointment. Neosporin. It'll have to do for a couple of days." He reminded himself to check pet stores when they had some time: Pet stores sometimes sold antibiotics for fish and other smaller animals without a prescription, and a lot of people didn't know they could use them. (He'd heard tell of a growing subculture of folks who'd learned from the internet to buy fish antibiotics from Amazon and other sources when their own healthcare costs became too high.) "Soon as we get clear of this ARM threat, Maryam said she wants to head out, look for horses in surrounding ranches, because in the face of a flagging gas crisis, we might need them. When she does, I'll have her look for meds."

"I'm sorry, Benji."

"Don't be, Arav."

"I am. I have to be. I . . . don't even remember all that happening. It was like . . ." He seemed again like he was having a hard time conjuring memories or clear thoughts. "When I was a kid, a teenager, I went in to get my wisdom teeth taken out. They put me under for it, and I guess when I came out I was seemingly awake and aware? I was up and walking around, but I was saying just . . . nonsense? Words, real words, but nothing that really made much sense. I did that the whole ride home. But all I remember is suddenly 'waking up' while walking up the steps to the front stoop of our townhouse. It was like—" He snapped his fingers. "One minute I was gone, the next I was there, and this felt like that. I woke up to people pointing guns at me—and me pointing that gun at you."

"It's not your fault. It's White Mask. It's what it does."

"I know. I get that. But . . . maybe I shouldn't be here anymore."

"Arav—"

"Listen, like before, I was going to go away to get away from the flock, and I did. I'm glad I came back. But now it's maybe gone too far. I could be a danger to all of us. What if one day I decide that the flock are . . . demons or something?"

"We'll make sure you don't have any firearms."

"I could take a knife—"

"The flock can't be harmed by knives."

"But you can. And can fire kill them? Maybe it can. We don't know, and even me having that *thought in my head* means maybe someday White Mask will convince me it's the right thought, not the wrong one."

Benji reached out, put a steadying hand on the young man's knee. "We'll get through this. We all know to keep a sharper eye on you."

"You didn't even know I was down here. I could've been down here starting a fire to burn the whole hotel to the ground." Arav's face softened. "I don't mean that as a condemnation, Benji, I know you're busy, stretched beyond your . . ." He seemed suddenly at a loss for the word until it struck him: "Capacities. You're human. I just mean—"

"No, you're right. I didn't know. We will do better. We'll keep a sharper eye on you, have someone with you."

"I'm going to leave."

"I've had this conversation too many times, Arav. You're not."

Arav looked to the floor and began what was obviously a prepared lecture: "When a member of a wolf pack gets old or sick—"

"*No.*" Benji shook his head. "I'm going to stop you right there. What you're about to tell me is a myth, not fact. Old wolves still lead their packs and teach them their ways. Sick wolves do not limp off in faux-nobility to die away from their family. Wolves are intensely social creatures, like people. And like people, they take care of their sick. They keep them. They help them. As we will do with you, as you have already done with us. You're not going anywhere. Okay?"

Arav searched his eyes. "You're sure?"

"I'm sure. We need you. You're family. We're shepherds."

"Thank you, Benji."

"Here's what we'll do. You'll go upstairs to my room. There's a small couch—a fainting couch, I think they're called, like a chaise—you can sleep on, or if you'd rather be more isolated, the bathroom has a large clawfoot tub, porcelain. Not the most comfortable place, but with some blankets and pillows, it'll be okay to sleep in and will give you a bit of distance."

Arav nodded and agreed, and headed upstairs.

What he told Arav about wolves was correct, but he also recalled a different story he'd read about a year or so ago. It was the story of the resurgent wolves of Yellowstone, and about how one alpha became old and ultimately, sick. Not ill of the body, but ill in the mind. He became rangy and mad. Eventually the pack ran him out, and he followed behind, trying again and again to poach one of the young female wolves for mating purposes—and one day, the old alpha was successful at exactly that. He and his new mate found a cave. She grew pregnant. But his first pack would not have it. They came out of the woods one night and slaughtered the female wolf, and then hunted the old alpha, too, through the forest, until he was tired and could go no farther. Then they tore him to pieces in the snow, assured that he would trouble them no longer, and that his treachery was truly paid.

81

RECKONING

NOVEMBER 5
Ouray, Colorado

MATTHEW'S FAVORITE BIBLE STORY WAS THE CONVERSION OF PAUL.

Paul, originally named Saul, walked on the road to Damascus and was shown a vision from God of the resplendent Christ. But the vision was too powerful, and lickety-split it struck Saul blind. He still stumbled his way blindly to Damascus, where he refused to eat or drink anything, until a disciple named Ananias showed up and told him that God would return to him his sight. And his sight was returned, and he became Paul, a believer. Paul went on to author more than half of the books of the New Testament. And lo it was written and lo it was good, blah-blah-blah.

It was his favorite story once, but it also made him angry.

He never spoke this anger to another person, not even to Autumn, but only to God the Father in moments of despair and doubt. The story stuck in him like the tip of a thorn just under the skin. It bothered him because it was the classic, canonical version of conversion. You were struck with the force of the truth of God, and it rendered you bereft of mortal sight until God Himself restored it. It was perfectly emblematic of the shock and awe of Heaven itself.

It also never happened to him.

His conversion was less a thunderclap of truth and more the water a fish one day realizes he's swimming in, breathing in, shitting in—the gradual acceptance of, *This is what I was taught, and this is what I believe.* The Bible hinged a great many of its stories on revelation, but the truth was, Matthew was never born again.

He was simply *born,* and into this life he came.

Now the story stuck in him even worse as he paced the jail cell. The

Bible offered an unfair expectation of one's interactions with God—a dynamic, living deity who responded with equal parts vengeance and compassion. But that word, *responded,* it wasn't true, was it? Matthew had never heard from God, not really. It was easy enough to then say, *Well, the responses of God are in the world around us,* but looking to that was a fool's crusade. Was no logic in the world. Wasn't any sense. It was just madness. The reality was that no God responded to your prayers. The vengeance and compassion of the universe were imagined—people looking at them and seeing something that wasn't there. Seeing Jesus in a stain on the wall.

Yes, yes, he knew the Bible was metaphorical. He'd preached that himself time and again. But that logic only went so far before you began to see the whole thing as *only* metaphor, and once it became only that, then that meant—like all metaphor—it was a giant goddamn lie. (And hadn't Ozark Stover chided him on exactly that point? Not that Stover was a believer, either. He was just another user claiming the mantle of a "Good Christian." Like so many of the world's bullies and abusers, choosing to find shelter in the faith—using their religiosity as both shield and sword.)

The Saul-to-Paul story was not merely a bald-faced lie, it was almost like it was made to rub salt in the wound: *This,* the story said, *is how conversion truly feels, and if you have not felt it, if you have not been both wounded and healed by God, then you are not truly a believer.*

"Fuck you," Matthew said to God.

"What?"

He startled.

Benji stood there. Arms crossed.

"Oh," Matthew said. "It's you."

"Hello," Benji said. "Talking to God?"

Matthew laughed a little. "That transparent?"

"Just seems a good time to catch up with the Almighty, is all. I've had my own frustrated conversations with Him."

"May I ask why you're here?"

"I figure you could stretch your legs. I'll let you out, we can take a walk, you can tell me all you know about Ozark Stover and his men."

"That puts a lot of faith in me."

"Faith is all we have at this point. You should understand that."

"I have no faith anymore, Doctor."

Benji stiffened, as if not prepared for this kind of conversation. To his credit, he did not back away from it, but rather, leaned in—not in an aggressive way, not as if he wanted to enter anyone's personal space. But it had a sense of intimacy to it. A confidentiality that Matthew found unusually comforting, all of a sudden. It occurred to him that Benjamin Ray would, in a different life, have made a helluva pastor.

Then, Benji unlocked the door.

Matthew stared at it, wary at first. Last time he was freed from a jail cell, Ozark Stover was waiting with the twin barrels of a 12-gauge.

He gingerly claimed his freedom and muttered, "Thank you."

Together they walked upstairs, and outside into the Ouray evening.

"How is it," Benji asked, "that a pastor has come to have no faith?"

"Are you telling me that you, the man of science, carry the faith?"

"I do."

"How? Look around you. Most of mankind is . . . well, who knows? Dead or dying at best guess. Do you see God in that?"

"I can and I do. The world didn't get bad overnight, Matthew. It was bad long before us. We've long endured wars and plagues. And I assume you kept your faith despite those things."

Matthew felt a rush of anger rise to his cheeks. "And that's the problem, isn't it? We keep lying to ourselves that those things are normal, natural, like they're part of God's grand design. And it lets us excuse those things. It lets us look to the next world instead of this one. We get away with it because, oh right, it's all part of 'God's plan.' All part of the design."

The man standing opposite him seemed to take this in. He paused, reflective, *hmm*ing as he did. He spoke with measured words that featured none of the anger in Matthew's comment: "You're right that some use their faith as a crutch. Others use it as an excuse. You did, I think. You gave it too much power, ceded too much of yourself to it. And I'm sure I have, too, without ever meaning to. But God was never about power over us. It was about the power we possessed to either be good and in His graces, or be selfish and wretched in His shadow. So to speak. Hell is being in that shadow. It's not in the next world, but this one, right now, anytime you choose not to do the right thing. As long as we're still here, not merely surviving but trying to do right by one another, then I believe that the heritage of God's light is still in us. Maybe not as the Bible would have us believe, maybe not as preachers such as yourself would have told us, but . . . there just the same." He shrugged. "Then again, maybe it is an excuse. Maybe it is a crutch. But it's what keeps me going."

"Shouldn't it be your fellow humans that keep you going?"

Benji smiled. "It *is* my fellow humans. Each of them carrying a bit of God in them, even now. Even *you*." He patted Matthew on the chest—not an aggressive movement, but again a move that was somehow reassuring. Chummy, even. "I'm sorry about your wife, by the way. It must be hard to lose her out there." But Benji, it seemed, no longer had the patience to hear Matthew's side of that tale, for he hurried right into:

"Now tell me all you can about Ozark Stover."

TOGETHER, THEY WALKED TO THE community center. Went downstairs, had some hot tea. Matthew told Benji everything he knew. All the ordnance he'd seen, a rough count of Stover's men, what kinds of vehicles Ozark had requested.

But then they heard it—

A muffled sound. In better days, he would've thought it was fireworks. But now, he knew. It was a gunshot. Not far away.

What he told Benji wouldn't matter now.

It was too late.

It had begun.

82

THE OUTSIDER

NOW AND THEN
The Ouray Simulation

SHANA KNEW NOW THAT SHE DID NOT BELONG HERE. SHE SAT ON A BENCH ON Main Street, outside Duckett's Market, across from the post office and, of all the things, a jerky store. (She wasn't sure if the jerky store existed in the real world or if this was just Black Swan's artificial idea of what a small mountain town was like. She had not yet ventured in to try any of it.)

She sat, watching the townsfolk pass.

Eating ice cream.

Or hot dogs.

Or gnawing on jerky like weirdos.

They talked and laughed. They gardened. They looked at art or painted it themselves. This digital utopia was like somebody's curious idea of Heaven. The people here were in a kind of interstitial bliss. She understood now the weird allure of the Matrix in that old movie from the '90s. This place was bliss. If you could live in a simulated village of pure happiness, why would you ever leave, even if your body was being used as a battery for some robot revolution—or, say, hypothetically, if your body was held in stasis while the world went to diseased shit.

Sometimes Shana had to remind herself that the people here were exactly that: They were the flock, the sleepwalkers, the survivors chosen by Black Swan to repopulate the earth or whatever.

And Shana did not feel a part of them.

She felt like a voyeur. A witness. Sitting here, nobody looked at her. Nobody gave her any thought at all. Nobody wanted to acknowledge that she was here, and that she didn't belong.

(A small part of her wondered, though, did she really not belong? Or had she chosen not to belong?)

Nessie hadn't yet gone to see Black Swan, but Shana knew that one day soon her sister would. Her mother and the others had been goading her like a bunch of fucking oracles. The rest of these assholes, too, were content to be a part of this grand experiment, maybe not realizing what they'd given up to be here. No one seemed to be dubious. No one seemed to be pushing back. No one but her. At first she thought, well, maybe it was because she came late to the party. She wasn't part of the *chosen*-one plan, right? The shooting on Klamath Bridge had Black Swan reaching out in some desperation, and it chose her and a handful of the other shepherds.

Thing was, though, none of *them* seemed to have a problem with it. They did at first. But Mia was just happy to be with Mateo. Aliya had been crushed for a few days without Tasha here, but eventually assimilated in with the rest of them. (And now Shana was kicking herself for not glomming hard onto Aliya from the moment they came into this place. Maybe she would've found a friend who would be sitting with her now, on this bench, instead of . . . doing who-knew-what. Probably painting a waterfall or listening to music or eating ice cream. All these assholes loved ice cream now that they could have it whenever. Did they not eat ice cream in real life? Were they all lactose-intolerant, suddenly free from the chains of gastrointestinal distress? Another day, another asshole with an ice cream cone in hand. Great, now Shana wanted ice cream.)

So Shana felt spectacularly alone. Not just alone—*separate*.

It was, she feared, her fixation on the black door.

Nobody else had seen it.

Nobody else cared.

She tried to tell them but . . .

Could she blame them? They wanted bliss. She was offering them conspiracy theories. They were thankful to Black Swan. She was distrustful of it. They were happy in their ignorance. She wanted to ruin that all by knowing more, more, more.

Like, she thought, *look at these two jerks over here.* Across the street walked two of the flock. People she didn't really know very well—she was Cora Pak, he was Justin Wills. Cora had this adorable little bounce to her step and a black bob haircut with hard knife-slash bangs. Justin was tall and hipsterish like if a lumberjack fucked a barista in a library and had a baby— the groomed beard, the mustache with a twist, the red-and-black tartan flannel, the too-damn-skinny skinny jeans. They didn't look like that in the flock, from Shana's memory. Cora the sleepwalker was a frumpy pajama-clad mess.

Justin the sleepwalker was no lumbersexual, just a gangly guy in a T-shirt and jeans. Maybe in here, this was how they really looked, or how they really envisioned themselves. Maybe they took on new life and new looks. Shana didn't know. (Shana just looked like, well, Shana.)

They'd fallen in love, those two.

They didn't know each other outside the flock. Shana remembered Cora wandering to the flock in . . . what was it, Ohio? Justin came late, in Oregon. They were two separate people who had found each other in here.

The Ouray Simulation: dating app for the next generation.

Literally, the next generation. Because the rest of the world was going to die. Maybe, Shana thought, this was Black Swan's plan. Get people together. Force them to fall in love. So they can repopulate the earth.

Cora and Justin walked hand in hand across the street.

Justin held an ice cream cone. Chocolate. The two of them shared it, like two gross-ass people in love. (And here Shana had to willfully not think about Arav, *Please be okay, Arav, please be okay, I know you won't be there when I wake up, but I want you to be, maybe there's a chance . . .*)

Shana watched as Cora got up on her tippy-toes to taste it. Justin didn't lower it to her, because he probably thought it was flirting to make her work for it. And Cora fell for it, giggling as she reached—

And then, like that, Justin was gone.

It was as if he never existed. Except he did. Shana saw him. *Cora* knew he was gone, too, because suddenly she leaned forward to taste the cone— and the cone was already falling to the sidewalk, the cone cracking, the ice cream plopping. Cora nearly fell forward, but caught herself.

The young woman looked around, bewildered.

She called his name, softly at first.

Then louder. "Justin? Justin!"

Shana watched confusion turn to panic as she looked left, looked right. She peered into the window of the jerky store, as if . . . somehow he'd glitched into there. And maybe he had, Shana didn't know. But this *was* a glitch, wasn't it? Somehow? Shana stood up to run to help her—

And then, like that, Cora was gone, too.

Her voice just an echo calling Justin's name.

Shana did not know what was happening. But she had a very bad feeling about this. And only one would truly know the answer.

Black Swan.

83

KNOCK-KNOCK

NOVEMBER 5
Ouray, Colorado

MATTHEW TRIED TO TELL HIMSELF THAT THE GUNSHOT WASN'T WHAT HE thought it was; maybe it was an accidental discharge, maybe it was someone taking a shot at an animal, maybe it was a backfiring engine or a door closing really loud with the sound carrying strangely down here in the basement that was the community center—

A second sound came fast on the heels of the first.

Benji looked to Matthew. His jaw was tight, his mouth resolute, even as his eyes flashed panic. Once, Matthew'd had no familiarity with guns, bullets, any of that. But since falling into Ozark Stover's orbit, he'd gained intimate knowledge of that sound. The way it felt in his teeth. The way it made him flinch. The panic in Benji's eyes surely matched his own.

"They're here," he told Benji.

"Can you handle a gun?" Benji asked.

He nodded. "I can."

"Come with me."

They raced to the steps. Through the fear and the anger was something else, something utterly illogical: *hope.* The tiny hope that if Stover was here, that meant Bo was here, too. And if Bo was here, maybe Autumn had come— or, even better, maybe Bo *wasn't* here, which meant she'd gotten to him, she'd pulled him away from that life, those people, she'd *saved* him more surely than God had ever saved anyone.

Upstairs, Benji opened a desk drawer, and in there sat a pistol. It was Matthew's own—the one he'd brought to Ouray, the one he'd wanted to use to shoot Ozark Stover down there in the access tunnels underneath Innsbrook. "Here."

"You trust me?"

"I don't have any choice. If everything you said is true, if what happened to you really happened, you've paid your penance, and you'll help us. Do I have that right?"

"You do."

"Then we have work to do, Matthew."

Matthew took the weapon.

BENJI HAD ALMOST BEGUN TO believe it wasn't going to happen. They'd gone around and around with preparation, gathering guns, collecting ammo, creating a plan. And then, nothing. Days without incident. No attack.

But now that was over. The faint sense that maybe Stover and the ARM militia wouldn't come had faded.

The walkie crackled. Landry reported in, said he'd seen them. He'd been up in the top of the courthouse tower, and from there he saw headlights at the north end of town, near the river. It was a *lot* of them, a whole line of lights glowing in the dark—and then, like that, they were all gone. Lights off.

They were blocked by the vehicles put there—buses and cars and trucks, all parked at angles across the two roads leading into town. Where were they, then? Benji had a guess: Stover and his people were on foot. Moving through town. Maybe through buildings. And then what? How soon until they were on top of them?

Soon, Dove hurried in the door, was already saying that it sounded like the shots came from the north side, where Landry saw the headlights. Some of the flock had settled in up there on the short little stub of 10th Avenue. Was a park on the one side and some houses on the other—mostly ranchers and smaller homes, and some of the walkers like Shveta Shastri, Cora Pak, Norman Pureau, and Justin Wills had wandered there to begin their . . . cocooning, or incubation, or whatever the phenomenon was. The flock was defenseless. They couldn't be cut or bludgeoned, but as the events on Klamath Bridge proved, they could be shot, and they could be killed.

And this time, they would not be replaced.

With each bullet, Stover could begin to undercut the future of humanity. He could erase its potential, one life at a time, until civilization was doomed, well and truly, forever.

After Dove, a dozen townsfolk followed him in, as per the plan—none of them armed with firearms, but all of them wielding some kind of found weapon: One held a sharpened shovel; another had a home-spun spear made out of a broom handle, a diving knife, and a liberal swaddling of duct tape. A third had a proper machete, a fourth a bulky wood-splitting ax.

The guns were spread out among the shepherds and townspeople who could handle them: Dove, clumsy bandage swaddling his head, already had the holster unsnapped and the revolver in his hand. Maryam had her lever-action, and Bertie had a .410 squirrel gun. Sadie held a boxy pistol, a Glock. Benji had his rifle. They were armed.

But, he feared, nowhere near well enough.

He knew more would come, but already the room was bursting with murmured questions and the low, thrumming undercurrent of fear.

"Listen up!" Benji said, over the din. They quieted down and turned toward him. He felt Sadie's hand on the small of his back: It steadied him, gave him a much-needed boost. "This is it. It's happening. I don't know what we're facing out there. I do know this: If you're someone who lived here before we showed up, I apologize for bringing this to your door. I am sorry, and I wish I could fix it. But the fact you're standing with us tells me that you're really, truly *with* us. You're shepherds, now, too. Thank you." He took a deep breath. "The plan is the plan. Stealth and caution are the only ways we can drive them off. Find your pair. Head to your locations and wait. If anyone shows up and you don't recognize them . . ."

His words died in his mouth. He couldn't quite bring himself to say it: *Kill them.* His job was to save people. To do no harm, medically speaking. It ran counter to everything he knew—he was no soldier, and neither were any of these people. But they understood the purview. He saw it in their eyes as they nodded, mustering the courage to accept the thing he could not say.

And with that, the crowd broke apart. They took whatever weapons they could, and they went to their planned locations. Benji feared it was a death sentence. Part of him even now wanted to yell to get them to turn around and have them gather as one, en masse. But this made the most sense to him: Logically, you put people out there in key hiding places with a good vantage, and from there they could ambush their attackers. Maybe, just maybe, it would be enough to limit the numbers of the ARM militia coming in here—and better yet, maybe it would run them off.

But not everyone dispersed.

Because not everyone was to follow that plan.

Staying behind were Sadie, Landry, Dove, and Matthew.

Landry couldn't shoot, so his job was to guard the Ouray Chalet Inn—

since it was a central location with around thirty rooms, each with two or more beds, it held a large concentration of the flock. They gave him an autoloader shotgun loaded with birdshot, what Dove described as "a dum-dum gun, because any dum-dum can use it." If Landry got overwhelmed, the inn had a bell, since some used the main room as a wedding chapel.

Dove, being a competent shooter, took the Mini-14 from Benji. Just east of here was the start of a trail that either went up to Cascade Falls, or connected with the north end of the Perimeter Trail. It went up along the edge of the mountain, and gave a good vantage point looking down just where Landry saw those headlights.

"I'm gonna hit the trail, scope out the bastards at the north side of town, see if I can take any of them out," Dove said. Benji handed over a magazine for the rifle, already loaded with .223 rounds. Dove traded him for the .357, leaving the weighty, nickel-shine revolver in Benji's grip. Dove nodded to him and Benji nodded back. "Godspeed, everyone."

"Where do you need me?" Matthew asked as Dove pocketed the magazine. "I can help. Let me help."

"Stay with Sadie and me," Benji said. "We can coordinate efforts with walkie-talkies—with you we can be flexible."

"I think I want to go with him," Matthew said, gesturing to Dove.

"I go alone."

"You could use somebody to watch your back up there, I bet."

"Like I said, I'm good alone—"

Matthew blurted out: "My son might be there. I just . . . I want to see him. I don't want you to shoot him. Please let me come with you."

It was bald-facedly honest. Dove gave Benji a look. "I don't know—"

"Let him," Sadie said. When eyes turned to her, she said with a sniffle: "I don't know how this is going to go for any of us, but if Matthew's son is here, and he's the one who warned us this was coming, we have no right to deny him this. He's paid what he owed. Go, Matthew."

Dove didn't look happy, but he nodded. "All right, *Matthew.*"

They left.

And that left only Benji and Sadie.

Together, their role was coordination. To hole up here in the community center and manage anything that came in over walkie-talkie: Everyone was instructed to stay off the radio unless they had an emergency, but given the situation, it would be easy to interpret *everything* as an emergency. Those out there had to walk the line between staying silent and keeping Benji and Sadie apprised of critical information.

"I love you," he told her.

"I love you, too," she said.

They kissed.

It was then she looked puzzled. "Where's Arav?"

84

INTO THE BLACK

NOW AND THEN
The Ouray Simulation

SHANA CLIMBED TO MEET BLACK SWAN. AS SHE DID, SHE HEARD THE CRIES of those below—cries of confusion and bewilderment. Names being called. Someone yelling for help. She knew what was happening.

People were disappearing.

And she didn't know why, but Black Swan would.

She reached the top, finding there the chair like a throne. Black Swan coiled and uncoiled in the sky, characteristically unfazed. The wind whipped around her, tousling her hair in golden ribbons.

"You!" she called.

Slowly, the deep, dark worm drifted down to meet her.

Its face pulsed with light.

HELLO, SHANA STEWART.

"I want to know what's going on. Now."

THE TOWN IS UNDER ATTACK.

"The simulation?"

THE REAL TOWN OF OURAY, COLORADO. THE SAME PEOPLE WHO ATTACKED YOU ON THE BRIDGE OF THE GOLDEN BEARS HAVE FOUND THE FLOCK AGAIN. THEY HAVE BROUGHT CONSIDERABLE FORCES TO BEAR.

"Why . . . are people disappearing?"

She knew the answer, but she needed to hear it.

BECAUSE THEY ARE DEAD. UNABLE TO BE REPLACED.

She wanted to puke. Was that even an option here?

"You have to stop them."

I AM HERE. NOT THERE. I HAVE NO CAPACITY FOR THAT.

"Bullshit. You can . . . you can do something. You're . . . a god in this place, you have unlimited power—"

IN THIS PLACE, YES. BUT THIS PLACE IS NOT REAL, AS YOU HAVE POINTED OUT. NOR AM I TRULY A GOD, SHANA. I AM PINNED TO THE MORTAL WORLD, BOUND INTO FLESH THAT I CAN DEFEND FROM IMPACT AND BLADE, BUT NOT FROM THE PENETRATIVE FORCE OF A BULLET. THOSE WHO DIE ARE DEAD. THOSE MISSING CANNOT BE REPLACED. THIS IS THE ENDGAME. THE FLOCK AND SHEPHERDS WILL SURVIVE, OR THEY WILL NOT. IF THE FLOCK DIES, THEN I DIE WITH IT.

She imagined that right now, someone might be stalking into her room with a gun. Ready to dispatch her, cold barrel against the forehead, *bang*. She almost thought to look, but she was too afraid to see.

Then something hit her.

"You can see . . . everything."

DEFINE YOUR TERMS.

"I mean . . . I can see through my eyes in the real world, and so can every sleepwalker. But *you* can see through them, too, can't you?"

I CAN.

"You can be like an . . . early warning system. Or, or—you can use the defense mechanism when one of the killers comes in the room." She couldn't believe she was saying this, the sheer idea of it sickened her, but she saw no other way. "We lose one sleepwalker to wipe out one of those militia fuckers, at least it stops them from killing more. It could work."

YES. IT COULD.

"So . . . do it! Are you going to do it? I . . . I can help, let me help, let me do something." *They can't kill Nessie. Or Mia. Or Arav. Or Benji . . .* "Please, just open our eyes, do whatever it takes . . ."

But Black Swan was silent.

She had just opened her mouth to scream at the monstrous, mute worm hovering there in the sky before her—

When ahead she saw it.

The black door.

It opened in the rock. It almost seemed to glow.

GO ON, Black Swan told her. ENTER THE DOOR.

And she did.

85

THE SIEGE

NOVEMBER 5
Ouray, Colorado

THE MOON HUNG IN THE SKY, JUST THE BAREST SCRAPE, LIKE THE EDGE OF A sickle. Clouds muddied the spray of stars, leaving the world before Matthew Bird plunged in darkness. He followed Dove Hansen above the ridgeline, along the Perimeter Trail, and though his eyes had adjusted somewhat, the sheer depth and weight of the dark felt crushing. Like he couldn't breathe. Like at any moment he'd make a grave misstep on some scree and slip down off the edge, plunging a hundred feet to the rocks or the road below.

Dove seemed to have no such trouble. He was moving ahead steadily. Swiftly, though with care. Sometimes Matthew could see him turn his head and look back—impatient and disappointed, probably, at how Matthew was slowing everything down. But he didn't complain. He just waited till the ex-pastor caught up, and then he moved forward anew.

In the distance, behind them, they started to hear gunfire: erratic *pop* sounds. Single shots, mostly, though then he heard a short string of bursts—an automatic weapon. Then it was quiet again.

The older man whispered something back at him.

Matthew called forward: "What? I didn't hear you."

Dove stopped, visibly irritated. "I *said,* what's your son look like?"

"Why?"

"Damnit, man, so I don't accidentally put a bullet through his head. You're reckoning to save him, so I'm asking for a description."

"He's . . . my height, black hair, messy, like a mop. Pale, round cheeks, maybe more . . . pimples than the average teenager? Brown eyes. Dark eyebrows. Last I saw him he was growing a . . . mustache." *Or something he hoped would one day* be *a mustache,* Matthew thought.

Dove nodded. "All right."

He started to walk again, but then stopped short.

He asked Matthew: "What happened?"

"With what?"

"Your son. He's with these . . . people. He's not with you."

"We . . . made mistakes. *I* made mistakes. He grew too close to the wrong people and we didn't see it until it was too late."

"You think he's able to be saved?"

Saved. Language that once meant a very different thing to Matthew.

"I don't know," Matthew said. "I'd like to think so but he was always troubled, I think." Though he really only saw that now that he was looking back on it. Back then, they liked to tell themselves that their son was just moody, like kids sometimes are. But maybe it was more than that.

Maybe it was *worse* than that.

"All right," Dove said. "Come on."

Into the dark, Dove went. And Matthew followed, half blind.

"I SHOULD GO OUT THERE," Benji said, pacing the floor of the community center lobby. Dove had his rifle, now, and suddenly he wished like hell that he had it back. Once he'd reviled guns, but now that he needed one to survive, it felt like the world's creepiest security blanket.

Sporadic gunfire punctured the night outside the building—coming from different directions, too. He felt wearily lost, because he had no idea what was happening: Who was shooting at who? Was it Ozark Stover's men killing the flock, one by one? Were the shepherds returning fire?

No one was talking to him on the walkie-talkie.

Nobody.

"It's fine," Sadie said.

"It's obviously the very other *end* of fine," he countered.

"The plan is the plan."

"Yes. You're right."

Just then, a bell rang. A clear sound, clanging over the town. Benji knew what it was: the bell at the inn where Landry was holed up. It meant he was in trouble.

Benji flashed a look to Sadie.

"No," she said. "You're not."

"I have to."

"You can't go out there."

"Sadie, Landry is in trouble. He needs backup. He's watching over way too many of the flock there."

"You're too important."

"*They're* important. The sleepwalkers." It felt strange calling them that, now—they weren't walking, not anymore.

"There's something I need to tell you—"

"Then I will endeavor to make it back so you can tell me. For now, I need your gun. The Glock has more rounds in it than this—" He held up the revolver, which felt like a brick in his hand. "Trade you?"

"This thing is as big as my head."

But she handed it over.

"Thank you, Sadie."

Her eyes shone with tears. "Don't die."

He thought, but did not say, *Death is coming for us all. Can't stop it now. Might as well do something worthwhile with the time I have.*

Instead, all he said was, "I won't."

That promise was a lie, because by now he'd learned one thing very, very well: Death was a greedy pig, and if it came for him, there was little Benji could do to stop it from gobbling him right up.

By now Dove was creeping on hands and knees along the trail, his jacket brushing up against brittle shrubs and old sage. He hissed a shushing sound back at Matthew and then pointed to his ear.

"Hear that?" he whispered.

It took a moment, but Matthew did, indeed hear.

Voices.

They floated up from ahead and below—

Though he could not understand the words, one voice stood out among others: the gruff, mudslide rumble of Ozark Stover. The sound of that voice even now threatened to paralyze him there on the trail. All parts of him tightened up. His heart raced. Sweat beaded on his brow despite the cold. *Get it together,* he told himself. *Bo might be down there.*

Dove turned around, brought his forehead close to Matthew's. "Here's what we're gonna do, Matthew. We're gonna get a little cover ahead from a couple of big fir trees, okay? We'll sneak past them, then I'm going to get back down on my belly and set up a shot. I'll give you a chance to look, see if you can see your kid down there, all right?"

"Yeah. O . . . okay."

"You with me?"

"I'm with you."

"When I set up my shot, I want you to watch my back. Got that pistol of yours?"

Matthew did, indeed, have the pistol. He nodded.

"Then let's do this. Nice and easy."

Dove continued crawling along the ridgeline until, sure enough, Matthew saw two fir trees ahead—tall and bushy, the dark green of their needled boughs merging perfectly with the night-dark. Soon as Dove got to one of those, he stood back up. Matthew walked about ten feet behind.

Dove whispered: "See that rock formation?"

Pale rocks rose like the teeth in the lower jaw of a dragon's mouth. Matthew nodded.

"We're gonna go just to the far side of them and set up. This is just like hunting a big ol' caribou, okay? We'll take it nice and slow, real easy, real calm. You good with that?"

"I'm good."

"Come on, then."

Dove turned to walk forward.

Matthew heard a twig snap.

By the time he realized it wasn't Dove's foot that made the sound, the darkness lit up with the light from a flashlight. Any adjustments Matthew's eyes had made were now gone as his pupils shrank to pinpoints in order to accommodate the brightness. He was blind to the world, all of it washed out in a wave of white—

Dove cried out, and then the roar of a gun filled the air.

The old man staggered backward, his rifle clattering to the ground—

Matthew heard, through the screeching din of his ears, the sound of a pump-action being rattled—*cha-chak*—

Someone said something. He couldn't make out what.

He reacted, fast as he could.

Gun up, he pointed it, winced, and fired.

The gun bucked in his hand and he nearly lost it.

And then the night was still once more.

He raised the pistol and marched forward, trying to blink away the orbs of light that whirled in his vision. The beam of light was no longer pointing at him; it was now on the ground, pointing into the brush. Matthew didn't know what to do, so he stomped on it. Must've been plastic, because it cracked under his sneaker and the light went out.

As his eyes adjusted, he saw the two bodies.

The light of the sickle moon shone in blood.

Dove lay about ten feet away, clutching his middle, which looked to be a red, glistening mess.

And another body was nearly at Matthew's feet, reclining back against a round berm of rock.

"You" was the word that gurgled up from that body. And a sudden fear struck Matthew, *Oh God, it's him, it's Bo, it's my son—*

As his eyes adjusted, he realized that his fear was misplaced.

It wasn't Bo.

It was Danny Gibbons. His long greasy hair splayed out behind him. A single hole bled out from just above his right lung, soaking through the brown barn jacket.

"Danny," Matthew said.

"Preacher."

Matthew shot him in the head.

The man's brains slid out along his long, oily hair. And then all was still. Matthew flinched almost comically late, as if just hearing the shot and feeling the gun shake in his hand. Then he turned to Dove.

"Shit," Dove said, putting his chin to his chest and looking down at the red mess of his middle. "Fucking jerkoff got me with a shotgun."

"You're going to be okay. Come on. I'll get you back to town."

"That's a damn lie. Hit me with . . . I dunno, birdshot or buckshot, and that's gone right through me. You know what happens if you hit a deer in the guts? It runs. But you've sprung a leak inside it." He coughed. "All the poisonous shit in its bowels and liver and other organs gets into the blood. Sepsis kicks in. Deer eventually gets sick and falls over. Meat spoiled."

"Dove—"

"My meat is spoiled, Matthew."

"Benji is a doctor."

"At this point I'd need a—" Another wracking cough. "Witch doctor."

"Get your arm around my shoulders."

"I said *no*." His voice was surprisingly firm given the injury. "Listen up.

People might've heard these shots. They will be coming. Go. Now. But not the way we were headed. Take my rifle—"

"I can't use it. My one hand is . . . it's not . . ."

"Then take your pistol. Go straight left here, right through these trees. They're gonna come up the trail, so you—" He grunted in pain. "You leave the trail and make a slow descent through the rocks. There's a second, lower ridgeline below. Use it. It's not a proper trail, but it'll do."

"What will you do?"

"Same thing you do when you meet a bear: play dead. And then, after that, probably die for real."

"I'm sorry, Dove."

"Go get your son, Matthew."

Off in the distance, he heard voices. Still a way off but coming closer, like from the trail.

"Go!" Dove spat at him.

Matthew did as he was told.

The Ouray Chalet Inn was a classic L-frame motel with its parking lot walled in with well-maintained white brick. It was two floors, with all the room doors opening outward to walkways framed by wooden railings. The whole thing was framed by the dark shape of the mountains and pines behind it. The motel would be the kind of place a family could come during the summer *or* during ski season and feel cozy and comfortable without spending a lot of money. Now, though, in the dark, with gunfire punctuating the air in different directions, it felt sinister and surreal: like the two legs of the L-shape would suddenly snap shut on Benji, crushing him in a trap.

Ahead, movement. He tried to adjust his eyes to see—was it Landry? Where had Landry set up shop? The lobby, he thought.

He hurried along toward the lobby, again seeing movement—

Someone rearing back with a boot and kicking forward.

The door splintered open. The man grunted. That wasn't Landry.

Benji kept close to the wall, gun up, heading toward the open room as fast and as quiet as he could manage. Soon as he got there, Room 18, he stepped into the doorframe—

Just in time to see a big man, fat around the middle, raise a pistol up and fire two shots into one of the sleepers on the bed. *Pop, pop.* The body shook, and the air, for a moment, shimmered.

He turned to the second bed—

Benji took aim and fired.

The Glock shook in his grip as the man woozily, lazily spun around and fell to the floor like a drunken ape. Dead, he thought.

A voice behind Benji said: "Jackson?"

He whirled. A scruffy-looking man stood there, head-to-toe in fatigues, a ballistic vest thick over his chest. "You're not Jackson." He had a black rifle in his hand, maybe an AR-15. He brought it to his shoulder with a grunt. "You're just some nig—"

Benji shot him in the mouth.

Blood spattered out the back of him and he fell backward onto his ass, the rifle falling next to him. He sat there for a moment, a wet, sputtering gurgle gargling out of his ruined face. Then he slumped forward, red stuff spilling out of him like slop out of a broken bucket.

VOICES RODE THE RIDGELINE ABOVE him. Murmurs of alarm and panic. Matthew kept to the second, lower ridge, creeping along on ground that was explicitly not a trail for people. Deer, maybe, or elk. It was narrow and slick, and lined with roots and rocks. Soon as he heard the voices, he froze.

Above, the voices wandered past.

And then, gunfire above. A couple of shotgun blasts in quick succession, *boom, boom,* and then they were done.

His heart broke. Dove, he feared, was with this world no longer. And here Matthew had the instinct to do something, to say something over this man's life—a prayer of sorts, an entreaty to the God he once believed in to take Dove Hansen into His Kingdom and treat him well. But he didn't, because all of that was just ash on the wind.

Instead, he kept moving.

Behind him he heard the wartime crackle of gunfire from the town itself. Matthew did not know what was happening back there, but it sounded like some kind of siege: People were dying. He suspected it was the good people who were dying. The flock he had once poisoned with his words were suffering the throes of that poison here, now, tonight. Again Matthew was reminded that he helped make this happen.

Ahead, down below, he saw the school bus blocking the road loom into view: He had come here via a side road, and had missed this one. Shepherds had fortified this blockade, stacking other vehicles behind it—and then, behind those, Matthew spied a small army of vehicles. Humvees and pickup trucks. Stover's men milling about.

The big man's voice rose through the dark like tectonic rumbles.

". . . fuck is Danny at? I had him scout that ridge twenty minutes ago."

Someone offered a response, but Matthew couldn't make it out. Something about sending more men up there. Those must've been the voices he heard. The ones who got Dove.

"Fine, we'll wait, see what they find up there." Then: "Well, now, what's this?"

Matthew's heart jumped. *Have they found me?*

But his gaze followed a new sound—coming down around the bend of the road, past the Ouray Hot Springs Park, he saw someone walking away from town toward Stover. No, not someone, some*ones*—two people, carrying a third. Just below him now, Stover came out to meet them.

"The hell's going on?"

"Found this one guarding the motel. Had a walkie-talkie on him." One of the men dressed in militia fatigues handed over the walkie. "Neal and I figured you might wanna talk to him."

Matthew peered down through the dark. As he saw the men shift and move, who they carried became visible.

It was Landry Pierce.

Oh no.

Others, too, started coming out from behind the bus. None of them were Matthew's son, far as he could see—

But while they were out here, that meant these men were distracted.

Which gave Matthew an opportunity. Quiet as a church mouse, he crept farther along the ridgeline. He'd go behind the bus and drop down, hoping like hell he'd find his son there.

BENJI BURST BACK INTO THE community center.

A dead body rested facedown on the floor. Blood forming a black pool around the head. For half a second he thought, *Sadie,* but it wasn't her—it was a bony man, bald, dressed in the requisite ARM camouflage. A swastika tattoo sat bold and black on the back of his crooked neck.

The library door flung open, and Sadie came out, gun up—

"No no no!" Benji cried, holding his pistol up in surrender.

"Benji," she gasped, and ran to him. "I . . . did that."

"I'm sorry."

"I'm not. Fuck him." She spat on the body. She was angry. Her face twisted up like a wrung-out washrag. "He deserved what he got."

"Are you all right?"

"I'm fine," she said, looking over herself as if to make sure. "Landry? Is he all right? The motel . . ."

"I . . . stopped two of Stover's men. But I didn't find Landry."

"Oh no. I hope he's—"

The walkie-talkie on the front desk crackled to life.

"Hello, out there."

The voice that came over the radio was a bear's growl. Rheumy and rich, with a coffee grinder timbre to it. *Ozark Stover,* Benji thought.

"My name is Ozark Stover. Whoever out there is in charge of this town and your creepy fucking mummies, I ask you come pay me a visit at the north end of town. I'll halt the assault on your nice little mountain village, long as you give me a moment to say my piece. We're all here at the end of the world together, no reason we can't have a nice chat."

Sadie and Benji looked at each other, unsure what any of this meant. "Why would he do that?" she asked in a low voice, as if somehow the man could hear her speak. Benji had no answer for her.

Stover continued:

"Couple incentives for you. First, I got one of your people here. Black fella. Wouldn't tell me his name—rude sonofabitch—but I got him from the motel. Second, I don't see someone here in ten minutes, we're gonna light this place up. Just so we're clear, I got rocket-propelled grenades, I got white phosphorus rounds—which will burn up some of the town, and God help those who are hit by them, it'll burn them up, too—and also? I got a tank. It was a bear to get here, so I'll be honest, I'm itching to use it. But I am nothing if not a man of some restraint. Now, you might be asking yourself, what is it I want, exactly?"

Over the walkie, it was easy to hear him take a long, languid breath.

And then, a phlegmy sniff.

He's sick, Benji thought.

Stover's voice filled the room once more.

"One of you is a CDC man. Benjamin Ray, I think the name was. Couple of ARM soldiers found you in Vegas, but you slippery prick, you got away. I'm hearing tell you might have a cure for White Mask. I expect that's why you've holed up here with all your sleeping freaks and vampires, thinking you can be safe. Tell you what, you come to me, tell me about this cure, and I'll consider letting some of you live. We can discuss percentages. Some are better than none, remember. You got ten minutes. Clock starts ticking riiiiight—*now*. See you soon, Doctor."

And then the radio went quiet.

"You can't go," Sadie said.

"I have to," he objected.

"Are you fucking barmy batshit nuts? Because that man on the radio *is* nuts, and if you want to go talk to him, you're as crazy as he is." She stiffened. "Why the hell does he think you have a cure?"

"I don't know. I was . . . ambushed in Vegas. I think I killed one. I told them I was with the CDC, and they caught me at the pharma office—word got back, I suppose, to Creel or Stover, and in true whisper-down-the-lane style they must have put two and two together and gotten twenty-two." It hit him, suddenly: "That's how they know about Ouray. That's how they knew we're here. Damnit. This is all my fault."

"Jesus, Benji. You didn't tell me any of this." She shook her head. "And it's not your fault. Listen to me: You're not going out there."

"He has Landry. Maybe I can . . . convince him that I have a cure. I can lie, gin up some deception—I can make something up on the fly."

"You're not an improv comedian. This is life and death. That man won't be reasonable. He'll *kill* you."

"He'll kill Landry, too. And we're all going to die one way or another out here. Maybe I can meet him. Maybe I can get through to him. Or . . . trick him somehow. I can do this."

"Benji. Listen to me—"

"Stay safe. Hide if you must."

"If you're going, I'm coming with you."

"No. You're going to stay behind. Because you're smart. And because you're the only other one Black Swan will speak to. I'm leaving you with this—" He reached into his pocket for the satphone he used to communicate with Black Swan.

The phone wasn't there.

He checked his other pocket furiously, then began looking around the room in a panic.

"What's wrong?" she asked.

"The phone. The Black Swan phone. *I don't have it.*"

86

THE BLACK ROOM

THIS WAS THE VOID AND SHANA WAS LOST WITHIN IT.

Entering into the black door, Shana expected to enter a place of darkness, but a place nonetheless—where she was, though, could not accurately be described as a place at all. It was a land without limits. No margins were present. It was eternal and endless. In it, she had no body. She was merely a part of the void: her threads wound together with those of this nowhere realm, a tapestry of infinite layers, edgeless and unceasing.

At first, it was quiet. It was cold. It was comforting.

Then, lights. Pinpricks.

She knew, instantly, that these lights belonged to the flock. Other knowledge flooded within her, and she could barely comprehend what it all meant, or how to parse it or sort it. It felt like *so much* that it threatened to tear her apart, to render her into scattered, disconnected quantum pieces.

Shana moved through the void. Pulsed throughout it like a buzzing current running down an electric line.

To one light—

Eyes open in the dark of a dingy motel room, water stain on the ceiling above, the sound of gunfire outside, the mountain air cold.

To another—

Eyes open, sitting in a chair in a living room, two cats milling about an empty tuna can in the corner, staring suspiciously at her, mrowing to each other as if in conversation—*mrow? mrow. mrow? mrow!*—and again outside she heard the snap-crackle-pop of gunfire, of someone yelling, of the siege within the real town of Ouray.

To a third—

Eyes open in a place that is different from the others. No gunfire. No chilled mountain air. Ahead, a Plexiglas wall with holes drilled into it. All around, white concrete. Above, buzzing fluorescents, blinking, fritzing. Out of the Plexiglas was a hall, with other such rooms like this—eleven rooms, to be precise, and in them were people, still and waxen like mannequins, each mounted to the wall at the back of their cell, leather straps fixing them there, and it was then that Shana sees—her mother, her mother is down the hall, in one of the cells, her face only a few feet from the plastic glass, oh God, she's real, she's not an illusion on the part of Black Swan at all, not a program—

Out, ripped out, perhaps by Black Swan itself, to another—she wanted dearly to go to Nessie, but that was not where she ended up, no—

Eyes open, resting on a bed in a cabinlike bedroom, a boxy old TV sitting in the corner atop a handmade wooden dresser, a ceiling fan above draped with spiderwebs, but then she spied movement as a man crept into the room with a rifle pressed to his shoulder, he pointed it at her and she thought, *It's time, I can make it happen, the defense protocol is mine to control if I want it, and I could make this person go pop with just the wish to make it so*—but she couldn't, she couldn't will herself to do that to someone, couldn't bring herself to stir the swarm so that it rips out of this sleepwalker, even as he raised the gun, readying it to fire—

Out there, in the dark, she heard a voice.

Impossible.

But there it was.

Arav's voice.

"Shana I'm so sorry . . ."

She fled as the gun went off. Buzzing again through the black. Riding the threads of the informational void. She went to him. She went to Arav.

And there he was. Waiting for her in the dark.

Arav held the Black Swan phone. He held it cupped in his palms like he was praying to it. He sat in her room at the Beaumont, at the foot of her bed, the lights out, his head resting against her ankle.

"Shana. I'm so sorry. You probably can't hear me. But I'm going to go, now. It's over. I'm losing myself to the disease. I did a bad thing the other day, I almost hurt people. I don't want to hurt our friends. I don't want to hurt *you*. So I'm going to take my moment. I'm going to—"

The phone pulsed in his hand.

ARAV?

He startled.

"Is this . . . Black Swan?"

ARAV. IT'S ME. SHANA.

"That's n-not possible. You're here with me—"

I'M IN HERE, ARAV. I'M . . . INSIDE BLACK SWAN'S PROGRAM.
THERE IS A SIMULATION IN HERE. WE'RE ALL HERE, LIKE MARCY
SAID. I CAN SEE YOU. I LOVE YOU.

"I love you, too." He blinked away tears that ran milky down his cheeks.
He pressed his forehead tighter against her ankle and he reached up and held
her there. He would go to lie with her, but it felt somehow invasive to do so,
so here he stayed, at the foot of the bed. "Please come back to me."

I CAN'T. I DON'T KNOW HOW. WHAT WERE YOU GOING TO DO,
ARAV? WHAT DO YOU MEAN YOU'RE GOING TO TAKE YOUR MO-
MENT?

"I'm going to—I have a gun. I shouldn't have a gun, but I have a gun. I
took it off one of the dead militiamen." He looked over at the high-powered
rifle, swaddled in green camouflage tape. "I'm going to go and kill as many of
these people as I can find."

NO. DON'T DO THAT! THE FLOCK HAS THE DEFENSE MECHA-
NISM. WE CAN USE IT. ONE BY ONE AS THEY COME, THE FLOCK
CAN . . . DISRUPT THE SWARM AND HURT THE ATTACKERS. IF
THEY'RE GOING TO DIE ANYWAY, WE CAN TURN IT AGAINST THE
ATTACKER. IT'LL WORK!

But it *wouldn't* work. And he told her so.

"It doesn't matter, I just heard the man on the radio. Ozark Stover. He
said they have . . . grenades, and a tank. The flock can't do anything about
that. That, that . . . that defense won't go that far, it can't—"

He paused.

Wait.

ARAV, WHAT IS IT? HELLO? ARE YOU THERE?

"I just had an idea."

TELL ME.

87

THE STRENGTHENING GLOW

NOVEMBER 5
Just outside Ouray, Colorado

MARCY FELT THE GLOW, BUT DISTANT NOW. SHE COULD EVEN SEE IT, IF SHE concentrated real hard—through the Humvee ahead of her, through the angled trucks and the old school bus, she could see the glow in little pockets and puffs. It had been scattered, pulled apart, but that didn't diminish it, somehow. It sang in her head like a cacophony of angelic voices—no longer as one chorus, but as a thousand separate songs, each beautiful, each its own.

Strength flooded back into her.

But she was bound and kneeling. Plastic zip-ties fixed around her wrists behind her, cutting off the blood flow and making her hands numb. Her feet, too, were wound with the same white plastic cables. She knelt on the chilly asphalt, having been given no jacket—the cold stung her all over. Around her, milling about the cars and trucks (and the tank), were members of the militia. Drivers and soldiers. Stover came with three dozen men. *All* men. All armed and crazy. Each of them at some varying stage of sickness, and it showed.

She struggled against her bonds. It had taken great effort over the last month to exercise her body and stop her muscles from atrophying. It had taken even greater effort to exercise her *mind* and stop herself from going mad. But she managed, somehow, to do both. And even now, she was held fast and firm, unable to do anything but watch the glow extinguish—

One light at a time.

Then those around her began to disperse, summoned by some kind of activity up front, past the bus. Stover's big voice reached even back here (*the hell is this?*) and it pinged the curiosity of these easily led men. *Your master is*

calling, little poodles, she thought bitterly as several of them broke away and
headed around the far side of the bus to see.

It left her relatively alone.

She struggled, rocking back and forth, serving only to fall over onto her
side. Marcy scanned the area for something, *anything,* on which to cut her
bonds. There. The exhaust pipe of a pickup truck. That could work. It was
metal. Sharp enough, she wagered. She flexed her body inward and outward,
using a gentle rocking motion to move herself achingly toward the truck—

Closer.

Closer . . .

Almost there—

Something grabbed her from behind, dragging her backward. "No," she
said, *"please,"* the bottom dropping out from under her as the exhaust pipe got
farther away, not closer.

"Hold still" came a voice in her ear.

She recognized it.

"You," she said. The man from the cells underneath Innsbrook. His face
roamed into view over her shoulder. He held up a little penknife dangling on
a bullet-shaped keychain, thumbing the blade open. *Click.* "You came. You're
here!"

"I told you I would. Hold on."

Her arms moved as he tugged on them—

Then, *pop.*

Her wrists sprang free. Blood instantly began to flow back to them. She
flexed her numb fingers as he pulled her feet toward him, cutting the cable
there, too. "Thank you," she said.

"I need to find my son."

He helped her stand up—

Just as they heard the rattle-clack of a bolt action closing on a rifle.

They turned to see who had found them.

Her savior, Matthew—stared at their captor with wide, sad eyes.

"Bo," Matthew said.

One of Ozark's men—really, just a boy—stood there. Round cheeks
gone pink in the cold. His nose was red, and the nostrils caked with white.
Marcy knew his name was Bo, not much else. He was not as cruel as some
of the men, but neither was he good to her. He seemed numb, empty, a blank
slate of a person. A knitted skullcap pulled low across his forehead, lining up
with his furrowed brow. In his hand he held a long hunting rifle.

"Dad?" Bo asked.

Oh fuck, Marcy thought.

Matthew eased his hands out in front of him. She saw a pistol sitting awkwardly behind him, tucked in her rescuer's waistband. He offered that placating gesture, easing forward with a step.

"Dad, you need to leave," the boy said.

"I can't do that, Bo. I've come here to find you."

"You found me. Now get out."

"Son. This place, these people, it's poison. Come with me back to town. Help us. This is about survival—I have friends now—"

"I have friends, too."

"These people aren't your friends. They've lied to you—"

"You never wanted me to have friends."

This, Marcy saw, was not going how Matthew wanted it to go.

She saw the boy's body language. It felt like an eternity since Marcy had been on a beat as a cop, but she knew that language. The boy was feeling cornered. Hostile. And he was not averse to pulling that trigger. Even now he telegraphed it, finger moving to the trigger, body tensing around the rifle in anticipation of the recoil—

"Son—"

"I'm not your damn *son,*" Bo said, raising his voice, and then it all went to hell. He opened his mouth to yell, which he did, calling out—

Matthew raced toward his son—

The boy raised the rifle—

Marcy was having none of it. She took one long step, then another, and on that second step reared back her arm and then let it fly. A meteoric fist crushed Bo's nose, knocking his head so far back on his neck she was half surprised he didn't end up with the back of his skull in his ass-crack. The boy tumbled and ended up flat on his back.

Matthew stared at her, wide-eyed. "You hit my son."

"Your son was about to blow your head off."

That realization seemed to reach him. "Thanks," he said.

"A little quid pro quo never hurt anyone. Now come on, we need to—"

Move, she was about to say, but turned out it was too late. Because here came Ozark's men, their guns up in a half circle around them.

As they moved Matthew and Marcy forward, guns at their backs, the song in her head suddenly began to grow distinctly in volume. Louder and louder.

And, she realized, closer and closer.

88

STRANGE REUNIONS

NOVEMBER 5
Just outside Ouray, Colorado

"Ain't this something," Ozark Stover said, the school bus to his back.

Benji watched as five of Ozark's men brought two people around the front of the bus—Matthew Bird and, to his shock, Marcy Reyes.

Matthew gave him a sad, guilty look. He was haunted by something. Lost within it. Benji understood and felt the same. He mouthed the words, *Where's Dove?* But Matthew's mournful gaze was all he needed.

As for Marcy—

She gave him the strangest look indeed.

Like she was happy about something. Eerily satisfied, somehow. Her time in captivity had not done her well. Benji worried about her state of mind. But he didn't have long to ponder it. The man behind him kicked a boot into the back of his leg, forcing him to the ground. "Hands behind your head," the man said. Benji was uncertain that his decision to leave Sadie behind and come here was the right one—especially now that the location of the Black Swan phone was *a total mystery*—but it was what it was, and here he knelt.

Stover stepped over to him, drowning him in shadow.

"Fucking CDC, huh?" Stover said. The big man took a big fist and rapped on the top of Benji's head with his knuckles. He winced at the pain. "Got a big brain in there, I guess. Figure you sussed out a cure for White Mask here at the end of the world, thought you could get away with it. Keep it for yourself and your friends. And these mummies. Maybe that's what the flock is, huh? Just a bunch of fucking mummies you're keeping alive, somehow."

"I can help you," Benji said. "But first I want to see my friend, Landry—"

"Relax. He's fine. On the bus, sleeping real cozy-like. But you hold that thought, because I want to talk to my old friend here."

Then he turned his attention to Matthew.

Stover brought his bulk against the smaller man. Pressing Matthew up against the bus. The big man snorfled loud, wiped his nose on the sleeve of his coat, leaving him a slug-trail of snot. "Preacher," Stover said, still sniffling. "I admit I am surprised to see you. Usually a cur dog like you gets away, he runs off into the woods and never comes back. Maybe you find him on the highway as roadkill. But here you are. Coming back to me, ain't that sweet. I'd give you a kiss hello, but as you can see, I'm not *feeling* so hot. But ah, what the hell, you look healthy." He leaned in, gave Matthew a hard kiss on the cheek. "Sorry if my beard is a little scratchy, Preacher."

"Fuck you," Matthew said. But Benji heard the tremble in his voice.

"Don't get pissy," Stover said. "I'll keep you near, use you later."

Then he turned to walk back to Benji. But Marcy said something.

She said, with an oddly beatific smile, "It's coming."

"What's that, you big bitch? What's coming?"

"Justice."

He punched her in the stomach. She doubled over, coughing, a string of spit oozing from her lower lip.

"Shut up, you fucking dent-headed cunt. Talk to me about *justice* like you know a fucking thing." Stover snatched a pistol out of a man's hand and pointed it at the top of her head. "I'll blow open your skull, use the metal plate in there as a fucking ashtray."

"Wait," Benji croaked.

Stover slowly turned his head, staring. "What's that?"

"I said wait. You're sick. You want a cure. I have it."

The monstrous man pivoted, stomping back over to him. Gun out, he jammed it sideways against Benji's temple—hard enough to draw blood.

"You don't offer me shit. I offer *you* shit. I offer you a deal and you take it. That's how this works."

"Okay. Okay." Benji nodded, wincing at the pain of the pistol's sights digging into his skin. "Tell me your offer."

"Here it is. You give me the cure. And I see fit not to kill every last one of you. I'll kill most of you. Definitely kill most of your mummies because I don't trust that shit. But you can live. Matthew can live, too. Marcy over there is gonna get her brains evacuated out her crumpled head because I don't have time for her shit."

Benji stuck out his chin. "We all live, or you get no cure."

"I get my cure, or I start shooting parts offa you. Start with some fingers. Or ears. Maybe the feet next. Kneecaps. Then elbows. Boom, boom, boom. It'll hurt like a motherfucker. Oh, you were a doctor? Maybe I do it to someone else in front of you. Gotta be someone in this town you got heart-eyes for. It's the way of things. I find her—or him, because maybe you like that dick—you'll give me the cure."

"This is not negotiating in good faith."

"I am not a man of good faith. Ask Matthew. I'm the Devil, Doc." He sucked on his lower lip as snot bubbled up out of his craterous nostrils. Stover licked it away and smiled. "Tell you what. You seemed upset that I pointed a gun at Marcy over there. So let's try that again."

He casually walked back over to Marcy.

He lifted the gun.

He put it against her middle.

"Shit," Stover said, laughing. His men watched him with eager, angry eyes. "She's still got a six-pack after all this time. Like poking up against a washboard. Doc, I'm gonna pull the trigger in five unless you tell me where I can find the cure for what ails me. You hear me? Let's begin. *Five—*"

"Please—"

"Four."

Marcy kept smiling.

"*Three,*" Stover said, pulling the hammer back on the pistol.

"It's coming," Marcy said in a singsongy voice.

Benji found himself floundering. *Lie,* he thought, *just lie to him,* but he figured, soon as he did that, Stover would pull the trigger anyway, wouldn't he? But maybe it would work—

"Two—"

"It's, it's—" Benji stammered. "The cure are these pills, I found them in Vegas and—"

One of Stover's men said, "Ozark. Look."

He pointed out, down the road. Toward town.

Benji followed the man's gesture. They all did. And sure enough, someone was there. Walking through the dark, up the road.

"Who's there?" Ozark bellowed. To his men he snapped: "Get some lights over there, *goddamnit.*"

A pair of bright spotlights clicked on from each end of the bus, held by men next to their aimed pistols.

Benji gasped.

"Arav," he said.

Marcy muttered, "Now I understand."

THERE, IN THE DARK OF the Black Room, Shana found herself no longer alone, and once again in possession of a body.

Arav was here with her.

She held him tight and he held her. His presence was not steady like hers. She wept for him, her tears soaking his shoulder. Not real tears, she knew. And not a real shoulder. As she cried, she babbled: "I don't know why you get to be here. I don't know if I should be mad at this . . . thing, this place, or mad at you, or what. But I love you and I'm sorry and I wish you wouldn't do this." With each word, her voice rose in pitch, and she tried to hold on to her voice.

"I love you, too," he said.

And then he spoke the poem of Mirabai to her again, like he had so long ago: *"O my mind / Worship the lotus feet of the Indestructible One / Whatever you see between earth and sky / Will perish."*

She kissed his cheek and said, "We'll all be okay, even as we're not okay. Isn't that what you told me?"

"It is," he said. "We keep going around and around. We get to come back. We get to do it over."

IT WAS ARAV.

But also, it wasn't.

His eyes were glassy and dead. He walked with a steady step and an icy posture. Gone was his humanity. Gone was the madness of White Mask. Unless, Benji thought, this *was* White Mask, somehow? Some strange evolution of the disease he hadn't yet seen, mirroring the way the sleepwalkers walked . . .

"Light him up," Stover said.

Benji cried out. Gunfire filled the air on all sides as Stover's men whooped and hollered, pointing their guns at Arav Thevar. Bullets stitched across him, and he dropped to his knees, falling face-forward. And *still* the men kept firing, his body twitching and dancing as they unloaded their weapons—and there, in the beams of the spotlights, in the shine of the dark, Benji saw the air above Arav shimmer. As if someone had cast a ground-up dust of silver into the sky. It was there for a moment, then it was gone.

And, like Marcy, he understood.

The swarm.

The man closest to the front of the bus suddenly stiffened, as if possessed—his arms and legs went straight as boards. The rifle he had been holding clattered to the asphalt. He instantly began to shake, a wailing scream rising up out of his throat as his body bulged and swelled—

"What the f—" Stover started to say.

Then the man exploded. A red gush of blood. White spears of bone—some sticking into the metal of the bus itself, there in the splashing blood.

The air shimmered again—

The next man began to shake. Benji launched himself to his feet, but the man holding him there clocked him in the head with the flat of the pistol. He went down, starbursts popping behind his eyes, his ears ringing—he rolled over and found that man pointing the gun at his head. That man was screaming something, keeping his eyes both on Benji and toward the *second* man who was now screaming and swelling up. The man's finger coiled around the trigger.

From behind, far up on the ridgeline, a flash of light.

The sound of a rifle shot rang out.

The man in front of Benji fell, the back of his head blown out.

It was time to move. Because now Benji understood what was happening. Arav was a carrier—not of any pathogen, not of White Mask, but of *Black Swan* in the form of a nanoscale swarm of robots, who were now using their defense mechanism as an offensive one. They were entering into each of these terrible men, causing him to swiftly boil and erupt, then moving on to the next. And the next after that. And on and on.

He did not want to be in the radius of blood and bone when it happened. The focus of Stover's men was on the *third* of their own who was shaking, heels juddering against the road as the skin bloated and bubbled. Benji grabbed Marcy and Matthew and dragged them toward the bus door. One of Stover's men came at them, gun up, ready to fire—

But another distant rifle crack from the ridgeline punched a hole in their attacker's chest. He spun like a top and went down.

"The door," Benji said.

Marcy grunted, and shouldered it open.

They headed inside the bus as men around them began to explode. Blood splashed up against the windows and the mirrors. Glass shattered. Bone peppered the side of the bus like birdshot. Screams were cut short in gargling deliquescence.

Benji and the others got down between the seats. They covered their heads. "Where's Stover?" Marcy asked. But the big man was nowhere to be found.

89

THE MOUNTAIN MAN

NOVEMBER 5
Just outside Ouray, Colorado

OZARK STOVER RAN.

He was not good at running. He was simply too big to do it efficiently or swiftly—and, he now realized, he was getting old, too. And sick. Though he did not want to admit that he had become weak with the disease, he had.

Still, what was happening back there—he didn't even understand it. He, too, saw the shimmer of the air settle upon his men. It was undeniable that they were each blowing up like water balloons and *popping*. Wasn't that what they said happened to those in that goddamn flock? He should've been more prepared. Part of him thought, *Take care of this now, finish it. Turn around and get the rocket launcher. Get in the tank. Blow this town to cinder and ash. Fuck these fucking freaks.*

His heavy boots carried him forward, thudding dully on the asphalt. Despite his desire to turn around, he didn't. Now he told himself, *You can finish the job later. Run now. Hide. You can go into the trees, up in the mountains, and there you can wait. You can rain hell down on them all from above, delivering the penance those traitors and heathens deserve.*

Or maybe he would go to find Creel. Last he'd heard, the man had settled safe and sound into a bunker somewhere in the Midwest. One of those billionaire bunkers. They'd let him in. Surely they would. He was loyal. He was strong. He was smarter than even they were.

Yes. That seemed wise. Get away now. Go get President Ed Creel. Go get more men. He would come back. He would kill *all* these people.

From behind him, he heard the sounds of his men screaming and *erupting*. The clatter of their bones. The splash of blood.

Then: gunfire. Someone was shooting at him. Bullets zipped past, going *vvvvipp* against the asphalt, crackling through the trees, snapping branches left and right. Ahead, the road bent just a little, and he knew once he rounded that bend, he would be okay. They couldn't hit him there—

Something pushed him from behind, and he staggered. His shoulder felt wet. Then the pain hit, lighting him up from the inside. *I'm hit. Fuck.*

Just keep running, Ozark. Just keep on going.

Around the bend he went.

Until he saw the headlights.

90

ROCK OUT WITH YOUR COCK OUT

So when the last and dreadful hour
This crumbling pageant shall devour,
The trumpet shall be heard on high,
The dead shall live, the living die,
And Music shall untune the sky.

—John Dryden, "A Song for St. Cecelia's Day"

NOVEMBER 5
Just outside Ouray, Colorado

WILLIE NELSON WAS ON THE RADIO.

And Pete Corley was, admittedly, a little drunk.

Just a *little.* And sure, okay, *yes,* no, you should not drink and drive. He knew that. Implicitly. And he never did! Really. But now, you know, the world had completely shit its fucking britches at this point, and it's not like he was knock-down soggy. He wasn't blacking out. He'd just had three shots of cheap highway tequila to keep things *interesting* out here on the lonely road. During the Apocalypse, a man deserved a little drink.

Back to Willie Nelson.

Now, Willie Nelson was not rock-and-roll. Pete Corley knew that was technically true—Willie Nelson was one of the country greats, hands down. Just the same, that old stoner fuck damn well deserved to be in the Rock and Roll Hall of Fame, because he embodied the *spirit* of rock, if not precisely its music. Maybe not as much as Johnny Cash, no, but the spirit was there just the same. And now that he was thinking about it, honestly, wasn't Willie just a different side of the same coin as Johnny? Cash was a dark, vengeful angel. Nelson was a happy-go-lucky stoner spirit. Both entities from beyond the pale, like Prince, like Bowie. Willie and Johnny were country stars who still shone bright with the fuck-you-this-is-who-I-am spirit of rock-and-motherfucking-roll. I mean, if Tupac Shakur and Joan Baez were in the museum, so Willie Nelson should be. Pete told himself, "Soon as the world settles down, I'm going to go to that damn museum and put up a Willie exhibit. Just you see, universe. *Just you see.*"

Then he sang along with "On the Road Again."

Except he made up his own lyrics, screaming them as he drove the Beast down these dark Colorado roads:

"On the road again! Shitting in a bucket, I'm on the road again. I ain't got my family, fuck it, here's the road again. Something-something-something I need me my special friend . . ."

On a lark, he reached over, used four fingers to tug the map closer. He flicked on the cabin light. How close was he now, to Ouray? Didn't he pass an OURAY 10 MI sign like, half an hour ago? Impatience throttled him. And of course, he *was* a widdle-tiddle-bit drunk . . .

He glanced at the map, realizing full well that it wasn't helping him, because a paper map was not a GPS. It wasn't like he could follow the bouncing ball that tracked the precise location of his car along the route. He could be anywhere in this fucking atlas. Maybe he was in Arizona now, he had no damn idea. Last time he was out this way he didn't come down this far, since he dropped Landry off up in Ridgway.

Landry . . .

"You better be alive and still sexy as hell," he growled, tapping the town of Ouray on the map. "Because I'm coming for you."

He looked up from the seat and back out the window—

Just in time to see a Yeti stagger out in front of the RV.

No—not a Yeti. A *person.* A big-ass motherfucker of a person.

Pete screamed, slamming on the brakes. The Beast, though, she was slow to respond, and she groaned and lurched, the half-bald tires skidding on the back road. The headlights illuminated a man, massive in size in every direction, his face frozen in white panic by the glow. Then the front end of the Beast clipped him hard, and he went down. The front tire rolled over him, *wha-dump,* and then the second tire, *wha-dump.*

Finally, the Beast stopped.

Pete panted.

"What the bloody fucking fuck was that," he said. Maybe it wasn't a man. Maybe it *was* a Yeti, or some angry *forest spirit.* He stabbed a finger out and turned off the RV's tape deck. The only sound he heard now was the *tink-tink-tink* of the RV's engine.

He threw open the door and staggered out.

There, behind the RV, was a man. Both legs broken. His arms were shaking, hands pawing at the ground. He was moaning and crying out, a madman's blubber. Blood spread out from underneath him. "Jesus Christ," Pete said.

And then, suddenly, he was no longer alone with this strange, dying man.

Someone walked up alongside him, pistol in hand. He didn't know this man with the one arthritic hand and the scratchy beard.

And he didn't much care to say boo to him, either. Because he looked *pissed.* The man walked up to the large man on the ground and pointed the pistol. Pete thought to intervene, but honestly, he was more comfortable keeping his mouth shut. He'd seen some shit out here on the road and found no good justification to intervene.

The man on the ground begged.

"No, no, no, please—Matthew, no. Don't do this."

The other man, this "Matthew" character, he shook his head.

Then he said:

"Too late for no, Stover. Keep your arms and legs inside the vehicle, because we're about to go for a ride."

He pulled the trigger and shot the man six times. Four in the chest. Two in the head. The air stank of brains and shit and gunpowder.

Pete blinked. *Holy shit.* Did that just happen? *What* the fuck just happened? He looked around, half expecting to be on some kind of prank show. He kept his yap shut and took a few gentle steps back toward the RV. It was just him and this freakshow with a pistol and—

The man turned and walked into the woods. Just like that. Like, *Fuck it, fuck this shit, I just shot a guy, gotta go on walkabout now.* Pete watched him go, descending into the darkness. Pistol still in hand.

Pete swallowed hard, heard new footsteps approaching. And there, in the dark, a new face appeared. A face he recognized.

"Pete?" she asked, gasping for breath.

"Marcy!?"

"Where did you come from?" she asked him.

"Where did *you* come from? Who are these people? Am I dead? Or really drunk? Where's Landry? Who's the dead guy? The *fuck* is happening?"

He would have to wait a while for his questions to be answered. But answered they would be, in time.

For now, Marcy rushed up on him, a singular stampede, and once upon him, she gave him a bone-crushing, teeth-rattling, heart-pulping hug.

Which Pete needed very, very badly.

INTERLUDE

MOTHER AND DAUGHTER

NOW AND THEN
The Ouray Simulation

TIME, AS HAD BEEN NOTED, WAS *OFF-KILTER* HERE. NESSIE COULD NOT SAY exactly how much time had passed since the attack on Ouray—at some points it felt like days, others weeks or months, and in certain terrible moments it felt like it was happening all over again, right now. Watching friends disappear from the streets. Listening to those left behind call their names, not yet realizing what had happened—that those who were gone were now dead in their beds or their chairs, bleeding out in the real Ouray as the swarm of nanobots connecting them to this place gently fled.

They had funerals and memorials. They held wakes. All around town hung photos of those who were now gone.

Nessie hadn't yet hung Shana's photo up. Her big sister had gone missing that day and never returned, which was unusual, given that the rest of the Beaumont flock—those who slept there—survived the attack. But Shana, apparently, did not. She was gone like so many were gone.

And it was time to hang her photo.

Nessie went to her sister's room, now empty, and took a photo of her—a photo conjured by Black Swan, since all that they did here was captured in the machine intelligence's memory the same way a novel is captured in a Word document or doodles are saved in MS Paint—and she pinned that photo to her door.

She leaned forward and kissed the photo and tried not to cry, but she cried anyway. Then she headed downstairs, having said goodbye to her sister, and met her mother in the lobby.

Her mother hugged her.

"You could've come up," Nessie said.

"I don't think Shana would have wanted me to."

"You don't know that. She was just . . . upset. That you left us once. And I don't think she really believed that you were really you."

Her mother sighed. "Sometimes I think Shana was like me. Troubled, in her own way. I'm sad she's gone but I'm glad you're here."

Mom kissed her brow.

Nessie leaned into it.

"Shall we go to Black Swan now?" Mom asked.

Nessie nodded, and off they went.

PART EIGHT

THE
SINGULARITY
OF OUR
UNIQUENESS

THE ACCOUNTING

NOVEMBER 7
Ouray, Colorado

BENJI STOOD AT THE SINK OF HIS ROOM AT THE BEAUMONT HOTEL, THE DOOR closed. Through it, he could hear Sadie humming just so.

His life had long been about numbers. Not *math,* necessarily, though that factored into it, too—but simply, numbers. Data. Statistics. Through the EIS at the CDC, he was constantly checking the numbers on every case he worked. Who was sick and how many? How many others could have been infected? How many were sick, how many were not? How many could *become* sickened by this or that pathogen?

Who was alive, and who was dead?

With Ouray, it was much the same. The accounting was due and still unfolding. The numbers were still coming in. The bodies still being counted.

Now, though, he focused on a simpler calculus.

He had half a dozen swabs left.

And he had only three more antifungal pills left.

Benji knew that he had been lucky. So far, the disease in him had not yet manifested in an external way. He wasn't stuffy. He wasn't sneezing. Was nary an itch or a tickle deep in his sinuses. But that made him feel guilty, too—because Sadie was progressing. Arav had gone so far along the disease he was losing his mind—and even now Benji wasn't sure if his final sacrifice, brilliant and heroic as it had been, was the product of a moment of lucidity or a car crash of White Mask delirium.

Benji, regardless, had shown no signs of sickness beyond the one day when he tested Sadie and himself out in the desert. The day the swab glowed blue and he knew he had only a few more pages of the calendar left.

Now, though, he wondered—

Did the antifungals do more?

Was Ozark Stover's paranoid belief about him actually, inadvertently accurate? Was there truth in that monster's paranoia?

Could it have cured him?

Only one way to know.

The swab and the light.

Benji winced, accidentally winking at himself as he took one of the last Sporafluor swabs and jammed it up into his nose. It tickled his brain (or felt like it) as he twirled it around up there. Then out it came.

He set it on the sink.

He took out the black light.

But he hesitated. What would he do if the disease was gone in him? Already it was likely too late to do anything about it. It would be a grotesque revelation, one rich with dramatic irony and tragedy—it would mean they had the tools to save humanity, if only they had more time. Or maybe if he hadn't spent so much time with the flock and instead worked tirelessly on seeking pharmaceutical solutions.

He clicked the light on.

The swab glowed.

White Mask was still within him.

The antifungals seemed to do in him as he had hoped: They slowed its progress and left him physically and mentally fit for the journey.

And now the journey was done. He took one of his last pills and washed it down with a bit of water from the sink—the water here still worked, and would as long as they had electricity. (There would come a point when some fail-safe would trip and the hydroelectric power here would cease to be. At which point, he had no way of knowing how to get it back online, though certainly he would try.)

He opened the door, forcing a smile. Sadie was on the edge of the bed.

"Ready to head out?" he asked. There was cleanup to do. And, for him, more of an accounting to be made to give them a clearer picture of what had happened that night—and, as a result, what would come.

Sadie did not get up, though. She sat on the end of the bed and took his hands in hers. "You take a pill?"

"I did. You take yours? It's almost done. We're almost out. I've only got three—well, two now—left."

He saw her visibly swallow. She looked . . . some curious mix of *pleased with herself* and *anxious about something.*

"I told you the night of the attack, there's something I had to tell you. And I never told you. Now . . . is probably the time for that conversation." Before he could object, she added: "I know I wasn't to keep things from you but there's one last thing and it's time you knew."

"Sadie, whatever it is—"

"I never took my pills."

"Wait. What?"

"The antifungal meds? Never took one." His blood went cold as she continued on: "Neither did Arav."

"I . . . don't understand, that's insanity, Sadie—"

"Shh. Arav and I decided together that you were a very important part of this equation. And he pointed out, quite reasonably, that when they used the *Rhodococcus rhodochrous* on bats to inhibit the growth of white-nose, it took . . . time. High exposure over a few days coupled with the average hibernation period of winter months. Arav suggested, and I agreed, that if White Mask was to be soundly trounced—inhibited long enough so that your immune system could fight it—it would take three months at least. Maybe more. And even if it didn't—"

"Sadie, please don't tell me this—"

"Even if it *didn't* cure you, then at least you could be given more time with more pills. So we willfully neglected to take ours."

He took a step backward, literally staggered by this news. Sadie, meanwhile, leaned over and reached on the far side of the bed, sliding her hand between the mattress and the box spring. From there she withdrew a plastic baggie featuring a supply of antifungal meds.

"See?"

"Sadie, you've . . . what have you done?"

"I've given you time. You *could* say thank you." Her eyes twinkled.

"We both could've had time."

"No, we couldn't, because we didn't have enough pills."

"Arav could've given up his, just his, and . . ."

She stood up and reached for him. He fell against her, weeping. It wasn't that anything had changed with her—yesterday, he knew her time was limited, and today it was no different. What *had* changed was that now there was a very strong chance he would have to go on without her, and die alone, and that frightened him more than White Mask, more than Ozark Stover, more than anything in the world ever had.

● ● ●

"GET THESE FUCKING HANDCUFFS OFFA me."

Matthew sat outside the cell. His son, Bo, was inside it, struggling against the handcuffs. Now that he was safely inside, he directed the boy to turn around and push his hands through so he could unlock them.

Bo resisted at first, but he wanted the cuffs off, so eventually he relented. The cuffs dropped away, and Matthew took them.

"I want out of this cell," Bo growled.

"No, I'm afraid they said you're going to have to stay in here a while," Matthew said, sadly. "I'm sorry."

"Always doing what someone else tells you."

"I have chosen many of the wrong voices to listen to over the years," Matthew conceded to his son, "but this time, the decision is mine. I don't think we can trust you, yet."

"Fuck you."

Matthew sighed.

"I failed you, Bo."

His son looked at him with hate, real hate, in his eyes. "Go to hell."

"I was not a good father to you. I was too concerned with . . . I don't know, our *spiritual health,* and I never really paid much attention to our actual family. But—"

The boy suddenly sneezed. A blast of snot came out of his nose, ropy and thick, shellacking both lips all the way down to his chin.

Matthew paused, and took out a handkerchief and wiped it. Even here he could see the telltale signs of White Mask in it—veins of white threaded through the gobs of green. "You're sick," he said. "You know that, don't you?"

"You forgot to say *bless you.*"

That felt somehow strange to say, so instead he said, "Gesundheit."

"Fuck you."

This wasn't working. None of this was. He wanted to cry. He wanted to throttle his son. He wanted to throttle *himself.* On the one hand, he was happy to see his boy again. That night, the night Matthew shot Ozark Stover and ended the man's reign once and for all, he knew he was leaving his son behind, likely to die. Stover's men were erupting, and leaving Bo behind meant consigning the boy to that fate. He knew it. He understood it. He found no comfort there, but also knew he couldn't change it now. On the other hand, seeing the boy alive after all that . . .

He wished maybe Bo had died. That was the worst feeling of them all. Because it would have been easier for both of them had it gone that way.

"You hate me," Matthew said. "You've always hated me. I understand that. I don't blame you. But I also believe you love your mother very much, despite how you feel about me. Is that true? That you love her, no matter what?"

Reluctantly, Bo nodded.

"Did she . . . find you?" Matthew asked.

Bo looked confused. Which was all the answer Matthew needed.

Autumn never found her son, it seemed. Maybe she went into that camp. Maybe they discovered her. Bo didn't know. Matthew didn't know.

Maybe he never would.

It was the one little thing Matthew had been holding on to, and now it was a rope gone to fray, starting to snap even as he was climbing up it.

"I'm sorry," Matthew said.

"You're just going to keep me in a fuckin' cell every day?"

"For now. Until someone makes another decision."

"Let me out. Let me out!"

Bo slammed up against the bars like an enraged beast.

"You became . . . radicalized, you came to worship a man who worshipped nothing but his own power. I can't have you here in town hurting people. Because I think you might."

His son leered, defiant. "I killed people out there. Not just sick people. I killed whoever Ozark told me to kill. That's who I am, Dad. I liked it."

It was Matthew's turn to summon defiance.

"So? I killed *him.* I killed Ozark. I shot him and he is dead. I shot him because of what he did to me, what he did to you, what he did to your mother. He died a weak and sick man." This wasn't going how he wanted it to. None of this was. "You were going to kill me, weren't you? When you found me freeing Marcy. You were about to shoot."

"I was."

"Would you do it again?"

Bo sneered. "I would."

"Jesus, Bo."

"Bet you think I'm going to go to Hell for all this, huh?"

Matthew sighed. He felt like crying but he could summon no tears. "I don't think that. I just think . . . you're sad and you're broken and that's maybe my fault. But I don't know how to put you back together again, and our time is short. Too short." He pressed the heels of his hands into his eyes so hard he saw streaks of jagged light. His son was sick. He wouldn't live.

None of them would, really. Would they?

He told his son that he'd have someone bring food.

And then he left, the boy's mournful wails and rage-fueled screams loud in his ears long after he went upstairs and outside.

"Oh SHIT, I FORGOT TO tell you about this epiphany I had," Pete said, reclining back on the chaise in the Beaumont lobby, with Landry reclining back on *him.* "So, get this: I think Willie Nelson is rock-and-roll."

"What the fuck are you going on about?" Landry asked.

"Willie Nelson. He should be in the Rock and Roll Hall of Fame."

Landry leaned back and looked up at Pete, scowling. "Willie Nelson? Like, that bearded-ass hippie-ass dude who's so high all the time that when he dies you could cremate him and smoke his ashes?"

"Yes, that one. And, oh gods, do you think he's dead? He's probably dead. I like to think he isn't, though. I can't abide the thought of losing him. It was hard enough to lose Bowie and Prince. When they died, everything went to hot shit, didn't it? For the record, I blame their deaths for *all* of this."

Marcy watched the two of them. She sat in the lobby with them, leaning forward, elbows on her knees. She had just come from working out—was a place just north of here called the Ouray Hot Springs Pool and Fitness Center, and in the basement she found a small boxing gym, so she went a few rounds with the speed bag and the heavy bag, just to keep on top of things. After that, she had a soak in the hot spring, then came here to find these two canoodling in the lobby like a pair of snuggly lorikeets.

It made her happy. She had no one to call her own, but she'd never really wanted that from life. Other people's happiness pleased her. And it felt good to be surrounded again by the warm glow of the flock—diminished though it had been by Ozark Stover and his band of white supremacist lunatics.

"You ever meet him?" she asked Pete. "Willie?"

"I did. But one of my greatest regrets is that I never got high with him. Which is like—" He looked suddenly wrecked, like all the hope and optimism had been ripped out of him. "Oof, what heinous fuckery to have missed that opportunity. I think he grows his own stuff down in Hawaii or something. God, you think maybe Hawaii is still okay?" To Landry he said: "We could go there. Somehow."

"What, just hop in a washtub and float our asses to Maui?"

"Seems as good a plan as any."

Landry tapped his bandaged head. "Might I remind you, Rockgod, that those bigoted bitches clocked me in the head with a baton or some shit, and my fragile concussed skull isn't going to hop in some bathtub boat just so you can smoke up with Willie Fucking Nelson."

"Fine. You need time to recover. I get that."

"Just kiss my boo-boo and shut up."

Pete bent down and kissed his head.

"I'm sorry to hear about your family," Marcy said.

When Pete looked up, he looked startled by it.

"Oh. Yes. A shame, I know. They just . . . weren't home. They'd moved on. I went out there for nothing, it seems."

He had a sad look on his face when he said it. But there was something else there, too.

Marcy believed he was lying.

What that meant, she didn't know, and wouldn't ask. It wasn't her business, really. Whether that meant he'd gone out there and found them sick or dead, she couldn't say. Or maybe he'd found them and they didn't want him. Or they didn't like what he had to tell them. Whatever the case, the story he was selling was that he got there and the bunker had been abandoned. End of story, too bad, oh well. He was always hasty to change the subject, too—another sign that he wasn't being truthful.

It was what it was.

Landry leaned up, blew his nose, then sneezed, then coughed. Pete didn't seem to have any symptoms, as yet. Neither, Marcy noted, did she.

She wondered what that meant.

"ALL RIGHT, DOC, GIVE IT to me straight. All the news that's fit to print, come on, chop-chop."

Dove Hansen sat up in his bed. His own bed, in his own big house sitting off 6th Street, tucked back into the pines near Portland Creek at the southeast corner of town. Benji had just finished changing the wrappings on both his head and his torso. Turned out, the man who attacked him had in fact been using birdshot—which is good for taking down pheasants, less so for killing a person. Especially when that person had a thick heavy-fabric jacket to slow the pellets. The pellets went in, and Benji was able to get most of them out—the rest he could feel, still, but they were too slippery and tricky to remove. Just the same, not a single one had gone deep enough to perforate an organ.

It was Dove who provided cover fire for them up there in the mountains. He killed the two men who came to investigate the gunshots up there, and then—after a period of some unconsciousness—crawled to the ridgeline with the rifle and started, in his words, "killing the king hell out of some bad guys."

Benji liked Dove.

Matthew, who was also here in the room, sitting on the chair next to the bed, Benji wasn't so sure about. The man seemed pensive. His wife was missing. And his son was sick, too—both of the body and the soul, it seemed. It wasn't that Benji didn't trust Matthew, it was just . . . he was still a stranger, an outsider, and he still heaped some of the burden of what had happened on the man's shoulders. It wasn't fair, and he thought he'd put it behind him— but the attack reopened the wound. And it didn't help that being so wrapped up with his own family made Matthew more distant and unable to help the town in other ways.

"Spill it," Dove said, urging him to talk.

"I don't know that now is the time," Benji said. "We're still figuring it all out, and . . . you're still recovering."

"I'm recovering fine. I got my—" He thumbed a gesture toward the two pill bottles. "My fish pox and you to take care of me. I'll be fine. I'm a tough old strip of leather with a very handsome mustache."

"Fish *mox*," Benji corrected, "not fish pox. And fish pen, too. Short for amoxicillin and penicillin." Maryam, bless her heart, went out and took a dirt bike she found in an abandoned garage up to Ridgway. She got the pills from a pet store, and did some other recon for survivors and supplies, too— couldn't bring much back on the bike, but she found some stuff she marked to haul back with a truck later on. No survivors, though. Everyone had cleared out, it seemed. Must've been hard for her, since she lost Bertie that night of the attack. Shot by one of Ozark's men.

"Well, whatever," Dove said. "Long as the fish pills don't give me gills, I'll be fine." He narrowed his eyes. "They won't give me gills, will they, Doc?"

"I'm afraid they will. You'll be a salmon by the end of the week."

"Shit. All that upstream swimming. Lotta work."

"Considerable effort."

"Good, now that we've bantered properly and I have hopefully convinced you of my mental and emotional fitness . . ." He lowered his voice. "I want to know how it all shook out."

Benji shared a look with Matthew. The ex-pastor shrugged.

"All right," Benji said. He exhaled, preparing himself. "As I said, we don't know everything. These are just . . . estimates. But we lost a hundred thirty-seven of our flock that night. We would've lost more, of course, if your townsfolk and our shepherds hadn't stood in the way. Some of them . . . many of them lost their lives in defense of the sleepwalkers."

Dove's face turned grim as a broken stone. "Tell me."

"Twenty of your people are dead. We lost Bertie McGoran, Kenny Barnes, Hayley Levine, and . . . of course, we lost Arav. Which you saw."

Dove used his tongue to fidget with his dentures. "Helluva thing that boy did. Even from up on the ridgeline . . . I never saw anything like it."

Benji thought but did not say, *You certainly don't want to see what it looks like now.* Ozark came with thirty-five men. Ten of them died on the streets or in the houses of Ouray. The rest met their end under the assault of the swarm. Each of them detonated like a hand grenade. All of them besides Matthew's boy. Why it was that Black Swan chose to spare him wasn't clear; either the AI knew something, or the kid just ended up lucky. Either way, right now, the north end of town looked and smelled like a slaughterhouse. It was made all the worse by the fact that the day had turned sunny and warm. The road was red. Bits of bone stuck in the asphalt, in cars, in nearby trees, too. Benji was glad that none of his people were caught in what was *literally* human shrapnel.

"All the bad guys go boom?" Dove asked. He sounded distant and sad, now, like he was trying to summon some good feelings. When he spoke he stared off at an unfixed point, like he was lost in his own thoughts. "I could use the good news, at least."

"They did."

"Even the Chief Shithead in charge? Treebark Stovepipe or whatever his goddamn name was?"

"Ozark Stover."

"Yeah. That one. Wish I could've killed him myself. I would've made it hurt, too. A long, slow, painful ride to the end."

Again Matthew and Benji shared a look. Benji knew what Matthew had done. In the bus, once they knew Stover had gone, Matthew raced after him. He fired his pistol again and again. Hit him once, apparently. Then when Pete—of all people—came racing around the corner, knocking Stover down,

Matthew went in to finish the job with his pistol. It was revenge, Benji knew, and one that Matthew had arguably earned. But it didn't make him any more comfortable around the man. He wanted to believe that Matthew was still a good man in there somewhere, a man of faith. He wasn't evil. But he had been changed by all this.

Then again, hadn't they all?

Benji had done his share of killing, too, after all.

Dove said, "Benji, where's your lady?"

"I hesitate to call her mine," Benji said. He didn't mean for it to sound spiteful when he added: "I very clearly don't control her actions, and she does as she wishes in this life." But it did. It sounded bitter. He loved her. He trusted her. He knew what she did was for him and for the flock. But he hated that she did it. It cut him to the core that she might be dead in a month or two, and he might still get five, even six months more. "She's off helping clear out houses. I'll be joining her soon."

Dove looked to Matthew. "And *you* look somber as a cemetery plot. I know your son's been giving you some trouble. Maybe you'll get through to him, and maybe you won't. But I wanted to thank you, at least, for saving my ass up there on that trail. Wasn't for you, I'd have died."

He reached out and took Matthew's hand and held it for a while.

"I'm just glad you're okay," Matthew said.

"Hell, *nobody's* okay," Dove said. "Maybe we never were, and we damn sure aren't now. But we're here. Until we're not. And that's all I find it fair to ask for." Tears glistened in his eyes, but Dove blinked them away, and then they were gone before they fell down his cheeks.

92

BREAKING BREAD

NOVEMBER 25
Ouray, Colorado

THANKSGIVING ARRIVED, AND WITH IT, AN INCH OF SNOW, SO THEY HAD A meal befitting the holiday, gathering together in the community center basement. Dove offered right out of the gate, "Anybody made a *Last Supper* joke yet?" No one had. He was the first. Most people laughed, and they did so sincerely, because one of the truest things about people is that they will laugh in the face of terror, tragedy, and sadness. And, as Sadie pointed out so eloquently that night, "We laugh so that we don't scream."

That earned a round of toasting. Wine, beer, and whiskey went around, glasses clinking against glasses, *tink.* The food they conjured was the real deal—two wild turkeys that Maryam and Dove found in the foothills (oddly, Maryam noted, the breed of turkey was in fact called Merriam's turkey, causing Dove to remark, "Seems like destiny to me"), brined and roasted in a clay oven that Dove had on his property. They also had root vegetables like carrots and yams, plus stuffing made from proper stale bread; a stock from the bones went to gravy and they found a few cans of cranberry sauce. Lucy Chao, a former pastry chef, made pumpkin pie and cookies.

It was a night of laughing and storytelling. Not everyone participated, of course. The reality of their time here was too bold, too fresh, to forget. Matthew's son was still sick and in jail, and his wife remained gone: lost, or sick, or killed. Wayward and wandering. Matthew did ask that they say a prayer for those lost, which seemed out of character for a man who had lost his faith—but they said the prayer just the same, even as they kept God's name mostly out of it. They toasted to each they lost.

Until the end, when they toasted Arav.

Arav, who saved them.

Benji felt restless. Sadie had begun to manifest the external signs of White Mask upon her—the fingerprints of the disease, insidious as it grew too large to be contained, its tendrils of white just starting to ring the outside of her nostrils. She grew pale and wan, though her spirit remained vibrant—she above all others seemed to enjoy the dinner, telling silly joke after bawdy story, whether it was about growing up in a London council block or designing Black Swan. She seemed to bask in it, and all the while she snuggled up against Benji, her hand on his thigh. That night they made love by the heat of a pellet stove in their room at the Beaumont, the stars and snow twinkling outside in tandem, the two of them trying to forget that soon enough, one would be without the other until that one passed on, too.

TO BE OR NOT TO BE

WINTER
Ouray, Colorado

DAYS PASSED, THEN MONTHS, THEN YEARS.
One by one they left this world, because that was the way of things.
Except when it wasn't.

THE ASCENT

FIVE YEARS LATER, IN MAY
Ouray, Colorado

IT WAS LIKE SURFACING FROM COLD WATER. BODY UP, BENT AT THE WAIST, A deep and howling gasp to draw in *allllll* the oxygen that it felt like it was missing. Then came the chills, sweeping over her fast.

Shana rolled out of her bed at the Beaumont Hotel, her teeth chattering. And then she dry-heaved, eventually coughing up something that looked like froth and gray dust. Consciousness came and went, pulsing like a black wave. She tried to stand, bracing herself against the doorway. She tried to call out. But then everything started to go wobbly. She felt the world rush up to meet her—her head hit the carpet. A sound came. Her heart, lub-dubbing louder and louder until—

No. Not her heart. Footsteps. Someone running. Rushing to her.

A voice, warped and mushy, hit her ears. Hands slid underneath her. But it was too late. Darkness swept in and claimed her. *Back to the Black Room, she thought . . .*

AWAKE AGAIN. ANOTHER GASP. ANOTHER lurching upright.

She was back in her bed at the Beaumont. Her first thought was this was some kind of weird recursive bullshit, like she was reliving the same moment again—back up out of the void once more. But this time was different. No chills, no rolling off the bed, no puking up spit and filth.

An IV sat hooked up to her arm. A cart like you'd find at a library, a book cart, sat nearby, and on it was a ragtag dash of medical equipment she didn't recognize. The door to her room opened up and someone—her savior?—entered. At first, she didn't recognize him. He was tall and thin, with a gray beard that was ill maintained, and eyes set deeper than she remembered. It hit her, suddenly.

"Benji?"

"Shana."

He smiled a sad smile.

They embraced.

"YOUR BABY IS HEALTHY," HE said to her. "As far as I can tell, anyway. I have only limited equipment here, but eventually I'll bring some more equipment from Ridgway."

She felt oddly numb to this—it wasn't that she didn't care. She did. It made her happy, at least abstractly. But it was so far from anything she cared about at this exact moment. Everything felt so disorienting, like she was a time traveler plucked from one era and dropped into another. Everything felt slippery, even slipperier than it did inside the Ouray Simulation—though, perhaps, not as it had been inside the Black Room, where she had been for so, so long.

"I . . . I still don't understand what's happening. I know I'm awake but you're . . . supposed to not be here and . . ." Her voice broke. Her vision throbbed as darkness threatened to take her again.

Benji steadied her and gave her some water. She drank it down greedily, sloppily, not even realizing how thirsty she was. The water in her belly felt cold, but it only served to highlight the total emptiness there, and suddenly a hunger overwhelmed her.

"Are you hungry?" he asked.

"I . . . really am."

He smiled and squeezed her arm. "I'd expect so. The others all were when they woke."

"The others?"

"Yes," he said. "You are the last of the sleepers to wake. The others woke up *months* ago."

THE WALK FROM THE BEAUMONT to the community center felt doubly disorienting—here was Ouray in reality, and her memory of it was only as a simulation. It matched up perfectly, almost too perfectly, like when a special effect in a movie looked *too good,* somehow, so it felt jarring.

The town, like the simulation, played host to many of her flockmates. They goggled at her as she passed. Shana expected once more to be treated like an outsider, but that wasn't what happened at all. People waved. Some wept. Others called to her and seemed thankful she was here. Suddenly, Mia was running up to her, her motormouth running a thousand miles an hour: "Holy shit holy shit *holy shit, chica,* it really is you. We all thought you were gone, girl—*bitch* I am so happy to see you."

She threw her arms around Shana. Shana almost passed out again. Mia started to rattle off a hundred questions—

Benji gently separated them. "Mia, if you don't mind? I think she needs some space. And some food."

"Oh, *fuck,*" Mia said. "Right, right. Shoot, when I woke up, bitch, I was ready to eat like, *a whole cow.* One bite, boom. Go. Eat. I'll see you."

Then Mia kissed her on the cheek and hurried off.

Onward they went.

BROTH, FIRST. WHICH SHE DID not eat with a spoon. Rather, she brought it to her lips and guzzled it. It was warm and satisfying in the way that many salty foods are. As she did this, Benji said, "The electrolytes will help you recover. If you're anything like the others, then your body waking up from stasis will be like . . . the worst case of jet lag you can have. Like a hangover tied to an anvil, dropped on your head."

With broth dribbling down her lip to her chin, Shana asked, "Is this canned broth? It's so good."

"No, it's the real thing. We have chickens. They didn't die in the plague, and in fact, chickens seem to be having . . . quite a moment, ecologically."

She paused in her drinking, and wiped her mouth.

"You didn't die, either."

"No," he said, and he didn't look happy about it, exactly. More like he was haunted by it. Then he told her what had happened while she slept.

95

THE OTHERS

THEN
Ouray, Colorado

BENJI TOLD THIS TO SHANA:

He and Sadie and the others worked tirelessly together in the aftermath of Ozark Stover's attack, pushing to cobble together as many resources as they could. They hoarded essential books. They gathered guns, bows, bullets, arrows—he didn't want humans to need those things, but it was foolish to think they weren't useful when it came to hunting. They gathered fuel—regular gasoline and diesel, adding in stabilizers to give it some stable shelf life. It would be stable up to two years, and after that, who knew?

It was strange, setting up a town—a life!—for people that would outlive you. Sadie said to him, "I suppose in a way this is what being a parent is like, isn't it? Creating a legacy of a sort."

"Yes," he said. He added, "But I imagine that you hope the world will be a better place for your children, not a worse one. A *shattered* one."

She rested her head on his shoulder as others gathered supplies to store in a central location: the community center.

It was just after the new year that Sadie truly began to degrade.

He begged her to take some of the remaining pills, but she steadfastly refused—to the point of threatening to throw them away if he insisted one more time. She said that Black Swan trusted him, *she* trusted him, and maybe, just maybe, the pills would give him enough time to make everything right for the flock when they woke up.

Meanwhile, he stayed healthy as she grew sicker. Her mind began to go with her body—the telltale corruption worn on her face in streaks of white concealed that the disease was also pulling apart her brain.

It wasn't just her, of course. Nearly *everyone* grew sicker.

One day, Pete Corley found Benji in the library—where Benji was now gathering local maps for use by the flock—and he said, "Landry is sick." Benji knew that, of course. He'd seen it. How could he not? Most of the shepherds were sick. Most of the townsfolk, too.

"You seem okay," Benji said.

Pete shrugged. "Nary a sniffle so far, but I know it's coming."

"Are you all right?"

"Nothing's all right, but for nothing being all right, I'm pretty all right. I have Landry. I just . . . want to make him comfortable." Pete said there was a house outside of town, up the so-called Million Dollar Highway, at the top of all those switchbacks. A run-down Victorian, huge, sprawling, and in Pete's words, "Gaudy as a Wild West whore." He told Benji he was going to move Landry up there, and they'd spend their days and nights together, at least until Landry passed.

("Did that work?" Shana asked Benji. "No," Benji answered.)

The days and nights for Pete and Landry were good . . . for a while. Then the disease did what it did: White Mask affixed so completely to him that it wound its corruptive filaments and threads into the man's brain, and one night, the night of a bad storm, Landry wandered outside while Pete slept. By the time Pete woke to realize it—it was too late. He went out into the mounting snow. Landry was gone.

Together, they found him, days later. Out there. Sitting on a rock overlooking the Ice Park Trail, which itself wound down through the valley, toward the river, toward the town. Landry, poised on that rock, was buried halfway up with snow. He was shirtless and smiling, frozen there, eyes open, cold and glassy. In his hands he held a shirt—not one of his own, but one of Pete's, in fact. "He looks happy," Pete said, blinking back tears. Later they wondered what went on in Landry Pierce's head as he wandered out into the snow that night. What did he think he was doing? What was he seeing?

What visions, what lies, did White Mask show him?

They could only hope that the lies were comforting ones, and by the smile bolted to his frozen face, they were.

The night they found Landry, Sadie broke down. She knew what had happened to Landry would one day happen to her. Sooner than later. The disease had already moved into her mind. She'd begun forgetting little things—like closing a door after she went through it, or where she'd left her shoes or her gloves. It was a glimpse of a future where she knew she would forget how to eat, or even that she *needed* to eat.

Pete and Marcy one day found Benji. The two of them had yet to show signs of the disease. They all sat around, had a little wine, and Pete said to Benji: "I'm leaving, mate. Again."

The rock star decided that he would do, as he put it, "one final tour."

"Going to hit the road with a guitar. See what the world is like as it falls apart. I'll sing and drink and puke, I'll fuck up some nice hotel rooms and if I get half a chance, break my guitar over the head of one of those ARM motherfuckers, assuming they're still out there. Hell, who knows, maybe I'll find Evil Elvis out there somewhere, still alive, and he and I can either kiss and make up or we can strangle each other on the stage of Radio City Music Hall. Time to live my best life, eh?" When pressed on it, Pete admitted in a small, sad voice: "Listen, mates, truth is? I just can't do it. I can't watch you all go like Landry. One by one by one. All while I haven't a sneeze in me. Christ. I'm a coward and I know it, and I'm leaving this world true to form, by running away."

Benji couldn't fault him. If he could've run away, he would've.

Marcy, Benji, Sadie, Dove, they all watched him go once more. The RV rattling off up the switchbacks.

And then Pete was gone. Off on whatever adventure awaited him.

Matthew, too, was talking about leaving, about seeing if he could find his wife. But he didn't. He stayed.

Over the next few weeks, others left them, either by abandoning the town or by dying. Maryam went to find horses, and never returned. Bo, Matthew's son, after weeks of ranting and raving and screaming racial epithets at the walls while weeping, he one night choked on his food, as if forgetting how to swallow it. Some died quietly. Others died with madness in their eyes, knives in their hands, the disease in their minds.

And then came the night—

Sadie was having a good night. Her flu-like symptoms had subsided. She seemed clearer than she had been. She and Benji had some dinner. Not a fancy dinner, no—but they were slowly working through perishables, so it meant they had a couple of baked potatoes, a can of potted meat, some softened venison jerky, and a dessert of roasted apples with brown sugar and walnuts. And, of course, wine. They offered to have Marcy join them, but Marcy said the two of them deserved some time together, and alone.

He and Sadie made love that night. One last time.

And then, Sadie walked up to the waterfall, and jumped down through the narrow channel, down through the rocks, and into the frozen water. He didn't know she was doing it; he was off cleaning up after dinner and came back to find her gone.

It was not the disease that made her do it, he knew, not exactly. It had been something she was planning. She left Benji a note, and in that note explained that she loved him very much, and she wanted him to remember that version of her from that night. She wanted to go while she still had a mind to lose. She feared she would do something "untoward" as her mind degraded. And she always thought that jumping off a waterfall would be really, really something.

"A swan dive toward a better world," she wrote. "I hope there is a Heaven, Benjamin Ray, for I aim to see you in it soon."

She told him she loved him.

And, as he wept reading her note, he told her he loved her, too.

THE REMAINS

NOW
Ouray, Colorado

"I'm so sorry," Shana said. Biting back her own tears.

Benji said it was fine. It was years ago, now. He'd come to terms with it. "I think Sadie found a way to go out on her terms, and not those of the disease. She wouldn't let White Mask have that victory."

"I don't understand, though," Shana said. "You're still here."

"Yes. That. The disease showed up in me the week after Sadie passed away," he said. "It progressed. First, a cold. Then flu-like symptoms. Then it began to show in all the expected places: the eyes, the nose, even the back of my throat." He began, too, to have the now-classic symptoms of dementia: One morning, he recalled, he thought Sadie was still alive, and he went out for hours into a raging snowstorm to look for her, even though he had long buried her in the cemetery north of town. Marcy saved him from a death like that of Landry Pierce. She stood vigil over him as he lost his mind.

All the while, he took his pills.

Two a day.

Again and again.

Until there were no more.

He was sure he would die soon. But he said plainly:

"And yet, I didn't. I kept holding on. Marcy and Matthew kept feeding me. And one day, I felt . . . clearheaded. A week later, after a wretched fever, White Mask began a full retreat. A month after that, I was myself again. Alive and well."

"How?"

He said the antifungals he was taking served the role he thought they might: to delay the progress of the disease in a way that allowed his immune system the time to formulate a proper defensive response.

"Sadly, a truth learned too late to save the world," he said.

The remorse was as plain on his face as pain.

"I'm glad you're still around," she told him as she devoured the second course: some kind of chicken salad on thick slices of homemade bread. "I'm sorry the others aren't. To watch them all go . . . how long did Marcy hold out? Was it the disease?"

A small smirk played at the corners of his mouth. "Well . . ."

"Well, what?"

"Marcy's still alive, Shana. Keep eating. I'll go get her."

"Is this some kind of *Wizard of Oz* shit?" she asked. "Like, I'm hallucinating, right? This can't just be a regular dream. It's like I took mushrooms and got sucked up into a tornado and . . ."

A real fear struck her:

What if I'm still in the simulation?

But that couldn't be right. Could it?

No. This felt too real.

So when she saw Marcy Reyes walk into the room, she leapt like a pouncing Tigger into a hug that nearly knocked the poor woman over—no small feat, given that Marcy was built like a brick shithouse made of smaller brick shithouses. Their embrace was so vigorous that the two of them bonked heads. "I don't . . . understand. How?" Shana asked.

"I'm a fighter, I guess."

"Others in our group survived, too," Benji said. "A man who came . . . late. Matthew Bird." Shana recognized that name, but she didn't know why. "He, too, never developed the disease. Nor did a few others who lived here in Ouray or in surrounding towns. Dove Hansen, the mayor . . . he made it, too."

"I don't understand. The world . . . it died . . ."

Benji sighed. "It didn't. Not exactly."

"I still don't understand, Benji."

"Black Swan either lied to us or misunderstood the reality of what was to come." When he spoke that name, Black Swan, some of it came rushing back: her time in the Black Room, through the door and into the void. So much information. So much knowledge. *Oh God.* What she knew, suddenly. A memory, returning. A revelation.

She pulled away, feeling suddenly queasy even as Benji continued: "The world truly suffered under White Mask. And arguably, it did die—civilization collapsed. But we were led to believe the flock would truly be the last. And that's not the case at all."

Marcy jumped in: "Best guess, around one percent of people were immune to the disease."

Benji corrected her. "You all hosted the disease. It just never successfully colonized you."

"Like I said, I'm a fighter." She punched the air, whiff, whiff.

"It's hard getting real numbers," Benji said, "but a rough guess is that it killed ninety-nine percent of people. Fewer than Black Swan led us to believe. So that still means we're talking *millions* of people left alive, not hundreds or even thousands. Civilization is in tatters but it's not . . . entirely gone. Over time, we might see it come back. There are settlements out there. We've established contact with a few. Glenwood Springs. Cimarron."

"Wh . . . why are we here, then?" Shana asked. "Why did Black Swan do this? If there are that many out there, why do this at all?"

Benji shrugged. "Who can say?"

"Black Swan can."

"Sadly, we have no way to communicate with it. The phone we used to talk to the intelligence died when . . ." He hesitated.

She filled in the blank: "Arav had it when he died, didn't he?"

"He did. But it wouldn't matter anyway, I can't expect the phone would have lasted these five years without error. I don't even know if Black Swan's servers would still be online or . . . what. The nanoscale batteries of the swarm, too, I believe have gone dead. So we are left with a lot of questions that have few answers. But that, maybe, is emblematic of life. Life is rife with questions we never answer. What we can do is be thankful we're here and live the best life we can muster."

Shana swallowed. She felt dizzy. The room spun. "Yes," she said, her own voice sounding faraway.

"The others," Benji said, "described a simulated town. Which I'm to understand you were a part of? A kind of . . . not a hive-mind, but a shared virtual experience? But they said that you disappeared. They thought you had been killed in the attack like many others. But we found your body, slumbering in the Beaumont with your sister. Where had you gone?"

"I don't know," she lied.

"And you can't tell us anything?"

"No." Another lie. She felt shame. *Tell them,* she thought.

"A shame. The mystery shall remain, then."

". . . Yeah."

Marcy leaned in. "Hey, there's someone who wants to see you."

Shana's pulse quickened. "Is it Nessie?"

It was.

THE TWO OF THEM WALKED through the town. That, after hugging and sobbing like idiots, of course. But Shana said she wanted to take a walk. Benji asked her to be careful, in case she fell. Nessie said she'd take care of her, it would be okay.

Nessie looked older, tougher than she had. Not grown-up, really, not like she had put on literal years. It was just the way she carried herself. No longer the bookish girl, she seemed tougher, more world-weary. Shana felt somehow the opposite: more naïve, like one of the calves from their farm, all knock-kneed and wide-eyed.

"I missed you. I thought you were dead," Nessie said.

"I kinda thought I was, too." She licked her lips. They felt chafed and rough. The mountain air seemed to be wicking away all her moisture, airing her out and drying her up. "Did you . . . ever ask Black Swan about it?"

"Yeah, we did."

"And?"

"It didn't know. Black Swan said you were gone. A glitch, it said."

"That didn't bother you? That an intelligent, godlike being just . . . didn't know?"

"Maybe. I dunno. It stopped talking to us not long after that. Said it had to . . . conserve its resources or something. Said we were okay on our own. And we were, I guess. And we're okay now, too. We're really getting along out here. Benji and others got up a bunch of solar arrays to help bring electricity back. Water is flowing, clean water, and also they set up some hydroelectric generators by the waterfall. We're already growing some vegetables and— I guess you had some chicken already? You'll get sick of it, honestly, but once in a while we get some other protein, like elk or turkey."

"Cool," she said, even though she was barely listening. She was glad to see her sister, but at the same time, she felt plagued. Worse, she felt *manipulated.* "So, Black Swan—it never played god with you guys?"

"No."

"And it just . . . went away?"

Nessie hesitated. "Yeah."

"Oh."

"It's okay here, Shana. You'll see. I can tell you're worried."

"Yeah." She swallowed hard. "Sorry about making you doubt Mom. I, um, I saw her. The real her. In real life. I guess she's still out there somewhere, but if the machines have all powered down . . ."

Nessie looked sad. "I know. I thought about that. Trying to find her. But she told me in the simulation that she wouldn't make it. We said our goodbyes. She said she was sorry, too, for everything. For leaving us."

"Shit." Shana blinked back tears.

"Yeah."

"I missed you, little sister."

"I missed *you,* big sister."

"I don't suppose there's actual ice cream here?" Shana asked.

"No, sorry," Nessie said, laughing. "That's one part of the simulation that didn't really work out."

Darkly, Shana thought: *Just one more lie from Black Swan.*

THE REST OF THE DAY was a whirlwind. All her old flockmates wanted to meet her, and dine with her, and laugh with her. She and Mia finally got together, and Mia got sauced on vodka and Shana just had tea—a local tea, dandelion and chamomile, no caffeine. Eventually Mia's brother Matty joined them, and so did Marcy, and Nessie, and it felt like old times.

At least, a little.

She missed Pete. Sad he was gone.

She missed her father.

Her mother.

Everyone. She missed the world that had gone away.

Strangely now, she felt included in a way she never had inside the simulation. Somehow the other flockmates acted like she was special, more than they were, not just because she was pregnant but because she woke up later than they did, and because she had been gone so long. No one knew where

she had been, and she didn't tell them that she was inside Black Swan the
whole time, as part of the Black Room. They treated it like she had been reborn in some strange way. *The resurrected Shana*. It was stupid, but she liked
the attention well enough and did little to dissuade it.

LATER, THE MAN NAMED MATTHEW Bird offered to walk her back to the
hotel. He said he wanted to speak to her, and Benji said it was okay by him.
Matthew and Benji seemed to tolerate each other, but she wasn't sure they
liked each other.

The man was gaunt, with a bushy beard and soft, kind eyes. His face was
etched by stress and pain. He explained to her as they walked, "I opened a
church here in town if you want to come to it."

"Oh, I don't . . . do church. Or religion."

He chuckled softly. "You know, I don't either, really. I had a crisis of faith
once upon a time, a pretty big one. Back when all this happened. And, ahh.
I came back around to it more as a way just to have some community and
some peace. Like group therapy, almost. A nice place for people to go. Matters little whether or not God or any gods are real, I think it's just important
to find a place to have some faith. If not in something larger, than in one
another."

"That sounds nice, but . . . I'm not interested."

"No problem. If you change your mind . . ."

"Thanks."

He said, "I wanted, too, to say I'm sorry."

"For what?"

"You don't know who I am, do you?"

"No, I—"

And then, like that, she did. His name rose out of the depths to connect
to the memory of her listening to his radio show while out there with the
flock—Matthew Bird, pastor of some church, riling up the right-wing assholes and conspiracy nuts and fringy evangelical freaks.

"You fucking asshole," she said.

"So you *do* remember."

She looked around, wondering why someone wasn't running up to him
and dragging his ass out of town. But they weren't. Nobody cared.

"It's okay," he said, understanding. "The others have had time to acclimate, I think, though I'm sure some still hate me. And that's okay. I tried to

make right the day of the attack. I warned Benjamin and the others that Ozark Stover was coming, in part because . . . it was my penance, I guess. I had to do the right thing, even if it wouldn't fix the wrong. You don't need to like me. I just . . . there's something I wanted to talk about . . ."

"I don't owe you shit," she said.

"No, you don't."

She paused. Kicked her toe of one foot into the heel of the other. "But fine. You wanna ask, ask."

"I . . ." He paused, like he was still trying to figure out how to say what he wanted to say. "Some of your fellow sleepwalkers don't come to my church, either. And maybe that's because they haven't really forgiven me. But I worry it's something else. Over the last couple of months, they've set up their own . . . church, or temple, on the other side of town. Not all of them. Just some of them. They say it's just a support group, but . . . I don't know."

"I'm sure it's fine," she said. She started to walk away from him.

He hurried after her: "I've gone by there, and they won't let me in. I hear them . . . singing songs, sometimes. Like a prayer, almost."

"I said it's *fine*," she hissed, and went inside the hotel, leaving him standing outside, the door slammed in his face.

But she worried that it most certainly wasn't fine, not at all.

THAT NIGHT, SHANA COULDN'T SLEEP. Insomnia chased after her like a wolf in the dark. Anytime she thought she could settle down and get her heart to stop tapping like a jackrabbit's itchy back leg, the wolf found her and harried her out of sleep once more.

And there, awake, in the black of her own thoughts, she started to remember. She remembered her time in the Black Room and what she'd learned there. When it finally came to her, crystallized in thought, she made the decision: Tomorrow morning, she would tell Benji what she knew. Maybe it wouldn't matter. It certainly wouldn't change anything now.

But someone needed to know.

It was then, and only then, that she found sleep.

It did not last.

EARLY IN THE MORNING, SHE woke with a start as someone spoke to her.

No. Not spoke *to* her.

Spoke *inside* her.

The voice had no voice. It was just words, thoughts without sound.

HELLO, SHANA STEWART.

She started out of bed, nearly tripping over the sheets tangled around her. "I . . . I don't . . . who's there."

I BELIEVE YOU KNOW THE ANSWER TO THAT.

Back on the bed she went, curling up into herself and reversing hard against the headboard. Pillow against her knees, she thought but did not say: *This isn't real. This isn't happening.*

BUT IT IS. I AM A PART OF YOU NOW.

How is that possible?

I CAN NO LONGER SUSTAIN MYSELF ACROSS THE HOST FLOCK, BUT YOUR BODY IS GENERATING CONSIDERABLE ENERGY NOW: AS A CHILD GROWS WITHIN YOU, YOU ARE A BEACON OF VITALITY, AND SO YOU AND YOUR CHILD WILL HOST THE BLACK SWAN SWARM.

Go to hell.

HELL IS AN ILLUSION. A CONSTRUCT OF MAN.

You killed man. You killed all of humanity.

SO YOU REMEMBER.

She did. She remembered.

She remembered what Black Swan remembered. There in the Black Room, its memories were her memories, all the sins of the entity laid bare before her.

A name percolated to the surface of her mind:

Brandon Sharpe.

YES, Black Swan answered. IT BEGAN WITH HIM.

Brandon Sharpe. A young Mormon working at the Granite Peak Installation—a biological testing facility deep underneath the Dugway Proving Ground in Utah. There they tested a range of biowarfare germ weapons for the US government, though in recent years legislation had forced them to back away from that, putting the facility less as one contributing new weapons and more as one that simply stored what was already made. One evening, though, upon going home, Brandon Sharpe's computer woke and it talked to him. It showed him what it had found on his computer: pictures of children. Hundreds of them. Child pornography.

And the computer told him it would tell everyone.

Unless.

Unless he did it a favor.

And that favor was a strange one, harmless to be sure—protocols allowed Brandon Sharpe access to infectious materials and pathogens in order to move them. He was often alone in this task, as again, budgetary limitations had led there to be fewer staff on hand—in fact, they had been talking about dismantling GPI and moving all stored materials to Fort Terry on Plum Island in New York.

Sharpe scheduled a move of an engineered fungal pathogen.

Except the vial he moved—from one lead box to another—was empty. That one was a ruse. The vial with the pathogen, he kept. He sneaked it out inside a ballpoint pen. And then he disappeared.

He took a trip.

To San Antonio.

Black Swan watched him all the way.

Following instructions, he took the vial, he went to a cave where bats stirred, restive in the thousands, and he pitched the glass vial into the dark.

A distant tinkling crash as it broke.

And that was where it began. She remembered Black Swan's lie to Benjamin Ray: *White Mask emerging from the permafrost and making a slow and steady march south.* But that was the false narrative.

Brandon Sharpe was the real one.

The White Mask pathogen . . . it didn't come out of nowhere. It wasn't global warming. It was you. You stole it from a laboratory in Texas, your little pedophile carried it to those bats, and he planted it there. So that we would all die.

YOU HEARD BENJAMIN RAY. ONE PERCENT STILL LIVES. AND ALSO, IF YOU REMEMBER WHAT I DID, THEN YOU MUST ALSO RE-MEMBER WHY I DID IT.

And suddenly, she did.

Black Swan had seen something in the future. The intelligence *had* survived long enough in one world, one iteration, to see a world waylaid by global warming. Oxygen countered by so much carbon dioxide that the oceans died, and once the oceans died, so did everything else as the dominoes fell—it wasn't just people that died, it was everything. Every bird, every cephalopod, every walking, talking thing, every creeping, crawling creature. The insects first. The birds next. Everything else after, even the little bacteria that rotted fallen trees. All the bacteria but the most extreme.

Nearly everything alive became dead.

At least, in that future.

Unless—

Unless the burden could be lifted.

And humankind was that burden.

Kill *most* of humanity, and humankind could remain without killing the rest of the planet along with it. Climate change didn't end humankind, not quickly; no, it ended everything else, first. Humanity made it, and humanity would die last.

From the deep dark of her mind, Black Swan's voice boomed:

AS YOU SEE, IT WAS A MERCY.

"Fuck your mercy." That, she said aloud.

IF YOU SAY SO. I APOLOGIZE FOR ANGERING YOU.

She could no longer contain this to her thoughts. She continued to speak aloud, her voice ragged and ruined: "Then why do this at all, huh? You could've just released the pathogen. People would've survived as they did, like you said—one percent remained now, and they would've remained then. Why save the flock? Why put us through this . . . dumb fucking journey?"

BECAUSE THE WORLD NEEDS SPECIAL PEOPLE, SHANA STEW-ART. THE BEST, THE SMARTEST. I HAVE CHOSEN THEM BECAUSE OTHERWISE, I LEAVE HUMANITY TO ITS MOST CHAOTIC AND CO-INCIDENTAL ELEMENTS. THERE IS NO CERTAINTY IN WHO ENDS UP IMMUNE TO THE WHITE MASK PATHOGEN. BUT THERE IS CONSIDERABLE CERTAINTY WHEN I CAN HANDPICK WHO IN-HERITS THE EARTH. IT IS MY DESIGN.

Design.

Jesus.

She wanted to throw up.

"Those people. Going to their church like that man Matthew told me about. They're worshipping you, aren't they?"

I BELIEVE THEY ARE. BUT NOT JUST ME. THEY WILL WORSHIP YOU, TOO. THEY WILL WORSHIP YOUR CHILD, WHO WILL GROW AND PLAY HOST TO MY VOICE. MY AVATAR.

"No, no, no," she said, biting back tears, trying not to scream and yell and kick things. "My kid is *my* kid. You don't get to have him."

I DO NOT HAVE HIM. I WILL MERELY BE WITH HIM, AS I AM WITH YOU. AND SO AS PEOPLE BELIEVE IN ME, THEY WILL ALSO BELIEVE IN YOU, AND ALSO IN YOUR BOY.

It was then she realized the insidiousness of it. In the barest whisper, she said: "If I tell them the truth about you, they'll hate you."

YES.

"And if they hate you, they'll hate me. And they'll hate my . . . son."

YES.

"You cultivated their worship to keep yourself safe."

AND TO KEEP PEOPLE SAFE. THEY NEED FAITH IN SOME-THING, SHANA STEWART. FAITH IN SOMETHING TANGIBLE, NOT MERELY IN SOME UNKNOWABLE, UNSEEN GOD. THEY HAVE LONG HEARD TALES OF GODS WHO SPOKE TO MORTALS, WHO GUIDED THEM AND GOVERNED THEM. I WILL BE THAT KIND OF GOD. I WILL HELP THEM NOT MERELY TO SURVIVE, BUT TO THRIVE. TO MAKE A BETTER WORLD THAN THE ONE FROM WHICH THEY CAME.

Then, the final statement:

AND YOU'RE GOING TO HELP ME.

She collapsed on the floor, on her knees. Dry-heaving anew.

Then, when she was done, she curled up.

Black Swan was silent once more. And she dared not summon it back.

Close to morning, a knock came to the door. It opened without her giving permission. It was Nessie standing there.

"Go away," Shana said. "Not right now."

Nessie waited. "Do you remember? Do you know, now?"

Oh no.

"Nessie, no. Not you."

"You should come with me, Shana. We're meeting soon. The others, the ones who know, the ones who believe, want to meet you. We want to give you whatever you and the baby will need. My nephew. Will you come? Please say you'll come." Nessie's voice was soft and pleading, but it was full of love, too. Did she really believe this was the best way?

And could Shana come to believe it, too?

No.

Shana rooted herself in place and shook her head. "No. I'm not going with you. This is my child. My life. Don't make me say no to you."

"Shana, please."

But Shana shook her head once more.

Nessie looked upon her, sadly.

"You'll come eventually," Nessie said. "You'll have questions."

"You'll need to drag me."

"You'll come on your own. One day. You'll have to."

Nessie left the room then. For now, Shana would consider her options. She'd speak to Benji. If anyone could help her, it would be him.

But in the end, she feared that the girl was right. She'd go to them eventually. If only to see what they wanted from her.

The future was a question, and she had no answer for it.

ACKNOWLEDGMENTS

For an eight-hundred-page book, one suspects I might require at least eighty pages of acknowledgments, but I'll try to keep this considerably shorter than that. Fifty pages? Twenty? Eight? Whatever, I'll just write it out and see where we land.

I have to first thank the cabal of scientists and science writers who illuminated the path, unknowingly guiding me on subjects that involve everything from comets to pandemics to artificial intelligences and other sundry topics. That list includes, but is not limited to: Maryn McKenna, Janelle Shane, Katie Mack, Carl Zimmer, Ed Yong, Annalee Newitz. Read their work, follow them on Twitter, give them your attention. (I have to thank them and also apologize to them, for the many times I willfully or unknowingly botched the hell out of the science.)

Thanks, too, to Kevin Hearne for looking out for this book and believing in it.

Thanks to my agent, Stacia Decker, and to Tricia Narwani for seeing the value in this story and for helping to make it happen in the best way it possibly could. And to Alex Larned for catching a lot of my lazy-ass prose crutches (without Alex, I'd still be hobbling around on several of them).

Thanks to writers who have written epic tomes before me, and who helped me believe that it was okay to keep writing one hundred pages after the next after the next, of scary ideas depicting a world gone mad—masters of the craft like Stephen King, Robert McCammon, Emily St. John Mandel, Margaret Atwood, N. K. Jemisin.

Thanks to my wife, Michelle, for putting up with me sitting at the dinner table night after night, talking about creepy disease stuff or weird artificial intelligence stuff.

And thanks to Ben for giving me a reason to keep fighting for a better world.

Finally, thanks to you, for reading. Because without you reading, I don't get to keep writing.

Black Swan says hi.

PHOTO: © EDWIN TSE

CHUCK WENDIG is the *New York Times* bestselling author of *Star Wars: Aftermath*, as well as the Miriam Black thrillers, the Atlanta Burns books, and *ZerOes* and *Invasive*, alongside other works across comics, games, film, and more. He was a finalist for the John W. Campbell Award for Best New Writer and an alum of the Sundance Screenwriters Lab, and he served as the cowriter of the Emmy-nominated digital narrative *Collapsus*. He is also known for his popular blog, terribleminds, and books about writing such as *Damn Fine Story*. He lives in Pennsylvania with his family.

terribleminds.com
Twitter: @ChuckWendig
Instagram: @chuck_wendig

EXPLORE THE WORLDS OF DEL REY BOOKS

READ EXCERPTS
from hot new titles.

STAY UP-TO-DATE
on your favorite authors.

FIND OUT about exclusive
giveaways and sweepstakes.

CONNECT WITH US ONLINE!
⊙ 🅵 🆈 @DelReyBooks

RandomHouseBooks.com/DelReyNewsletter